# of love & life

Three novels selected and condensed
by Reader's Digest

The Reader's Digest Association Limited, London

CONTENTS

The
French Gardener
SANTA MONTEFIORE

Jean-Paul remembered how she had stood beside him on the little stone bridge, gazing across the languid river to the lovingly planted gardens beyond. Her arm had almost touched his, and the heady scent of orange blossom on her skin had captured his senses and enslaved his heart.

Now, years later, the gardens have grown wild and the passion they shared seems lost for ever. Yet love, like the snowdrop in winter, has the power to bloom again.

Prologue

SUMMER

HARTINGTON HOUSE, DORSET, 2005

IT WAS NEARLY DUSK when she reached the cottage, a cardboard box held tightly against her chest. The sun hung low in the sky, turning the clouds pink like tufts of candy floss. Long shadows fell across grass already damp with dew. The air smelt sweet, of fertile soil and flowers.

The cottage was quaint, symmetrical, with a tall roof that dwarfed the walls below it. The roof tiles were brown and covered in moss, the chimney leaning a little to the left. Roses tumbled over the front door. The place looked sadly neglected, forgotten at the bottom of the garden, by the river, hidden in a copse of chestnut trees.

She stood contemplating the gentle flow of the River Hart as it ran down the valley to the sea, and remembered fishing with nets and throwing sticks into the water from the little stone bridge. Nothing had changed. Cows still mooed in the field downriver and the distant sound of a tractor rattled up the track behind the hedge. She blinked through the mist of nostalgia and put the key in the lock.

The door opened with a whine and she entered the hall, noticing at once the lingering scent of orange blossom. When she saw the sitting room, cluttered with photographs and books, she assumed someone was living there. As far as she knew, the agent hadn't yet sold the estate, which included the cottage. It had been on the market now for over ten months. 'Hello,' she called out. 'Is anyone there?' No reply. She frowned and closed the front door behind her. She put the box down on the floor of the hall. The air was warm and musty, smelling of old memories and tears. Her eyes stung with tears of her own.

She went into the kitchen where the table was laid with china cups and a teapot, the chairs pulled out. The remains of a tea for two. She

put her hand on the back of a chair to steady herself. In all the years she had lived in the big house, she had never entered the cottage. It had always been locked and she had never been curious. Judging by the layer of dust that covered the table, no one else had been there either.

She heard a noise upstairs, like a footstep. 'Hello,' she called again, suddenly afraid. 'Is anyone here?'

Still no reply.

She returned to the hall and picked up the box. Her attention was once more drawn upstairs. She turned to face the light that flooded the landing and a silent call came from deep inside her heart.

Tentatively, she climbed the stairs. At the top, on the left, was an empty room. She put the box down in there. Inside it was something of enormous value. She found it almost impossible to part with it, but knew it was the right thing to do. Even if it was never found, she could rest in the certainty that she had done her very best. She didn't like to keep secrets from her own family, but this was one that she would take to her grave.

A bedroom across the landing drew her away from the box. It smelt familiar, of cut grass and the same sweet scent of orange blossom she had noticed in the hall. She sat on the bed, in the shaft of sunlight that streamed through the mildewed window, and closed her eyes, sensing the presence of someone close, and listened. Once again her eyes stung with tears. She knew if she opened them the moment would be lost.

'Don't go,' she said in the silence of her mind. 'Please don't leave me.' Then she leant back and waited for a response.

AUTUMN

I

HARTINGTON HOUSE, OCTOBER 2005

GUS CREPT UP to his mother's study door and put his ear to the crack. He knew she was talking to his teacher, Mr Marlow. He assumed, correctly, that she wasn't on his side. Gus was a problem no one wanted to take the trouble to solve. 'I don't believe it!' she exclaimed. 'I'm so sorry, Mr Marlow. It won't happen again. It really won't. His father will be down tonight from London. I'll make sure he talks to him . . . You're right, it's

absolutely not on to bite another child . . . I'll find him and send him straight back to school.' Then her tone softened and Gus heard her chair scrape across the wooden floorboards as she stood up. 'I know he can be a bit aggressive, but we only moved from London a couple of months ago. It's been difficult for him. He's left all his friends behind. He's only seven. He'll settle in. Just give him time, Mr Marlow? Please.'

Gus didn't hang around to hear more. He tiptoed back down the corridor and out of the garden door onto the terrace. The lawn was a rich, wet green, sparkling in the pale morning light. He took a deep breath and watched the mist rise into the air. He shoved his hands into his trouser pockets and shivered. He'd left his coat at school. Swallowing his resentment, he wandered across the terrace and up the thyme walk lined with shaggy round topiary balls. His shoulders hunched, his feet kicking out in front of him, his eyes searched for some small creature upon which to vent his anger.

At the end of the thyme walk was a field full of sheep belonging to their neighbour, Jeremy Fitzherbert. Among the sheep was a dishevelled old donkey called Charlie. Gus enjoyed nothing more than bullying the beast, chasing him round the field with a stick until his braying grew hoarse and desperate. He climbed the fence. Sensing danger, Charlie pricked up his ears. He spotted the little boy jumping down and his eyes widened with fear, nostrils flaring.

Gus felt a jolt of excitement. He forgot about biting Adam Hudson in the playground, about running out of the school gates and up the High Street, about his mother's angry voice and his own clawing sense of isolation. He forgot about everything except the sudden rush of blood as he set off in pursuit of the donkey.

'You a scaredy-cat?' he hissed as he approached the terrified animal. 'Whoooa!' He lunged at him, delighting in the clumsy way the donkey stumbled back before cantering stiffly off towards the woods at the top of the field, braying in panic. What a shame he hadn't brought the stick. It was more fun when he hit the animal.

Bored of that game, Gus continued into the woods. The sun shone weakly through the leaves, illuminating the spiders' webs that adorned the shrubbery with lace. Gus picked up a twig and began to swipe the webs, squashing the fleeing spiders underfoot.

Miranda Claybourne put down the telephone and went to the window, where she stared out over the orchard. The ground was littered with apples and the last of the plums. She had sensed her son's presence at

the door, but now he had gone. Of all the days Gus had to choose to play truant, he had chosen Deadline Day—she had her monthly column for *Red* to finish. She didn't have time to go looking for him and, anyway, she wouldn't know where to start, the grounds were so large and, she observed with a sinking feeling, desperately overgrown and wet. The thought of tramping about in gumboots was intolerable for a city girl used to Jimmy Choos and concrete.

So far, the only advantage of living in the country was not having to apply make-up for the school run. Gus and his five-year-old sister, Storm, cycled up the drive every morning, leaving their bikes by the gate to take the school bus that stopped for them at eight. In London she had had to get up early in order to make herself presentable to the other mums in four-by-fours, wearing Gucci and oversized sunglasses. In Hartington, she imagined that barely anyone would have heard of Gucci, which had seemed charmingly quaint on arrival, but was now simply quaint. She complained wittily in her column, which chronicled her struggle to adapt to country life and turned her resentment into hilarity. Along with the wet, dreary weather, the quaintness of Hartington was almost intolerable.

Unlike her husband, Miranda hadn't wanted to move out of London. The very thought of being farther than a whiff of perfume from Harvey Nichols made her break into a cold sweat. Eating at the local pub rather than at the Ivy or Le Caprice was almost enough to confine her permanently to her own kitchen table. How she missed her Pilates classes in Notting Hill and lunches at the Wolseley with her girlfriends. But Gus had been kicked out of his London school for being aggressive, and moving him to a quiet country school had seemed the sensible option. He had a year to go before they could pack him off to boarding school, but for Miranda and David Claybourne a year of Gus's bad behaviour was an incredibly long time.

'Oh God, what am I going to do? I really don't have time for this,' she muttered to herself. She wished she had hired another nanny instead of insisting she do it all single-handedly. David had suggested she employ a cook and a gardener. She didn't have time to plan meals, and living in the country wasn't like London, where one could order a home delivery of sushi or a Chinese takeaway. As for the garden, it was a proper garden with acres of land, not a patio with a few potted plants. But it wasn't so easy to find help in the country. London was full of foreigners begging for work; in Dorset there didn't seem to be any foreigners at all.

It was all so alien. She just didn't belong. David had fallen in love

with the house on sight because it appealed to his aspirations of grandeur. She had accepted it halfheartedly, yearning for Notting Hill and asphalt, guilty at not appreciating such a big house in so idyllic a setting. But what on earth was one to do in the countryside?

As a freelance journalist she was always under pressure. They didn't need the money—David worked for an investment bank in the City and earned more than most people could spend in a lifetime—but writing was in her blood and Miranda dreamt of one day writing a novel, a great big love story like *Anna Karenina*. However, she had yet to come up with a good plot. Until she did, she was stuck with writing articles for magazines and newspapers.

Miranda returned to her desk and busied herself so she didn't have to listen to the small voice of despair inside her head. She had hoped that David would admit it had all been a terrible mistake and take them back to where they belonged. After all, the countryside hadn't changed Gus. But David's enjoyment of the country rested on the fact that he could return to the city on Sunday and swank about having spent the weekend at his country estate. She was stuck down here indefinitely.

She considered her husband: handsome, debonair David Claybourne. Always in control, always strong and capable, cruising effortlessly through life. Now they had moved she rarely saw him. At first he had returned home on Thursday, staying until Sunday night. Now he arrived late on Friday and left after lunch on Sunday. He was tired, wanting to spend the weekend sitting in front of the television watching the golf. If she didn't know him so well, she would suspect he was having an affair . . . but David was much too concerned about what other people thought to stray.

She dialled her husband's number at Goldman Sachs. Apart from wanting to share her anxiety about Gus, she just wanted to hear his voice.

'Darling, it's me,' she said when he picked up the telephone.

'Now, what's going on down there, sweetheart? Everything all right?' He sounded buoyant. She was immediately reassured.

'It's Gus, he's run off.'

David heaved an impatient sigh. 'Not again!'

'You're going to have to give him a good talking-to tonight,' she said.

'A good hiding is what he deserves. Did you speak to Mr Marlow?'

'Yes. He's not very happy. God forbid Gus gets kicked out of this school too!' She began to toy with a pencil.

'He won't. They're more tolerant in the country. Besides, he'll grow out of it. He's just adjusting to his new surroundings.'

'I hope you're right.'

'You sound down, darling.'

'I'm just really up against it. I've got to finish my column and I've got so many domestic chores to see to. Now Gus has run off, I won't have time to write. I'm tearing my hair out!'

'And such pretty hair!' he quipped. 'Look, if you took the trouble to hire help you'd have time for the important things.' He was baffled by his wife's uncharacteristic ineptitude. 'You're the mistress of an estate now, Miranda. Get organised down there, for God's sake, before you drive us both mad. We were fools to let the nanny go. Jayne might have come with us to the country had we made her an offer she couldn't refuse. She was the only one Gus responded to.'

'He'll come back when he's hungry,' Miranda retorted casually, hurt that David was blaming her once again. 'Then I'll send him back to school.' She put down the telephone and glanced bleakly at the ironic title of her column: 'My Bucolic Dream'.

Gus sat under a tree and felt his stomach rumble. He wanted to go home and sit by the fire in the playroom and watch *The Lord of the Rings* on DVD. He longed for Jayne's cottage pie and apple crumble with custard. Slowly his anger ebbed away, cooled by the damp wind that now penetrated his bones. He rubbed his hands together and blew hot air into them. Even if he had had the vocabulary, he wouldn't have been able to explain his actions, even to himself. Suddenly a large bubble expanded in his belly, rose up his windpipe and escaped his throat in a large, uncontrollable sob.

'You all right, lad?' Gus swivelled round, swallowing his weeping with a gulp. He hadn't heard the man approach. Beside him panted two black sheepdogs. 'You're David Claybourne's boy, aren't you?' said the man. Gus nodded. The man introduced himself as Jeremy Fitzherbert, and his thin, weathered face creased into a smile. A tweed cap covered thinning brown hair and his eyes were bright and very blue. One of the dogs leant against his brown corduroy trousers, which were tucked into green Wellington boots. He patted the dog's head with one gloved hand, a long stick in the other. The very stick Gus had used to torment the donkey. 'Come on, let me take you home.'

Gus got to his feet reluctantly. One of the dogs made a rush for him and he recoiled.

'Oh, it's a wanting-to-jump-up dog!' said Jeremy with a chuckle. 'Don't worry, he doesn't bite. The thin one's Mr Ben, the fat one's

Wolfgang.' Jeremy patted Mr Ben fondly. Gus wiped his face with his sleeve and followed him down the path.

The sheep were gathered into a tight formation, ready to be shepherded. Charlie the donkey remained in the far corner of the field, watching them warily. 'Charlie!' Jeremy called, delving into his pocket for a carrot. 'Come on, old boy!' Charlie didn't move. 'What's up with him?' Jeremy muttered to himself. Gus shoved his hands into his pockets. 'Donkeys,' the farmer sighed, shaking his head. 'I'll go and take a look at him later. You know he's over ninety?'

'Really,' Gus replied, looking up from beneath his dark fringe. Jeremy noticed something hard in those pale blue eyes and frowned. He didn't know how to talk to someone Gus's age, so he strode on across the field and up the thyme walk. Gus trudged behind him, wondering how he was going to get that stick back. Once at the garden door, he slunk in, tossing Jeremy a hasty look, more of dismissal than of gratitude.

'Is your mother in? I'd like to see her,' said Jeremy.

Gus hesitated and bit his lip. He seemed to gather himself before he was able to contemplate facing his mother. 'Mu-um!' he shouted at last.

Miranda's hands froze over the keys of her laptop at the sound of her son's voice. She hurried into the hall to find Gus, face grubby with mud and tears. Her heart buckled. 'Darling, I've been so worried. Where have you been?' She knelt to pull him into her arms but he stiffened. 'You can't just run off like that.' Then she noticed Jeremy hovering at the door. 'Oh, I'm sorry, I didn't see you,' she said, getting up.

'I'm Jeremy Fitzherbert, your neighbour.' He took off his glove to shake her hand. 'We've waved at each other from a distance but never been properly introduced.'

'Oh, yes, and you've met my husband, David.' His hand was rough and warm. He noticed her manicured nails and the large sapphire-and-diamond ring on the third finger of her left hand. She smelt of lime. 'I'm Miranda. And this is Gus.' She ruffled her son's hair. 'Thank you for bringing him home. I've been doing my nut worrying about him.'

'He was in the woods,' said Jeremy. 'No harm can come to him there, I assure you. Unless he gets caught in a fox trap.'

'Fox trap?' Her eyes widened.

Jeremy shrugged. 'They eat my chickens. Even go for the odd sheep if they're feeling adventurous. I think Gus is far too astute to wind up in one of those.'

Miranda turned back to her son, but he had disappeared. 'I'm used to London parks, not the countryside,' she said, an edge to her voice.

Jeremy took in the long brown hair tied into a ponytail and the pale blue eyes, made of the same hard crystal as her son's. She was a beautiful woman with high, angular cheekbones, though rather too thin for his taste. 'Do you have a wife, Mr Fitzherbert?'

'Jeremy, please,' he insisted. 'No, I'm a poor bachelor. Every kind-hearted female I know is intent on finding me a bride, but who wants to be a farmer's wife these days?' He smiled, his eyes twinkling.

'Oh, I'm sure there's someone out there for you.' She didn't want to give him the impression that she was discontented. 'The reason I ask whether you have a wife is that I'm looking for a cook and a gardener. It's the sort of thing a woman might know. You don't happen to know anyone, do you? Or how I might go about it? You see, I'm extremely busy. I'm a writer. I can't just go scouring the countryside for help.'

Jeremy nodded. 'The best thing to do is post a notice in Cate's Cake Shop in the village. Cate's got a large clientele. Why don't you offer someone that cottage by the river? It's empty, isn't it?'

'That pile of rubble! I couldn't imagine anyone wanting to live there.'

Jeremy laughed. 'Oh, it has a certain charm. It wouldn't take too much to resurrect it. If you offer the cottage you're more likely to find someone to work on the estate. I'll ask around.'

'Thank you.' She looked at him standing outside in the cold and rashly offered him a cup of coffee, regretting it even as she spoke.

'I've got to take a look at Charlie,' he said, declining her offer.

'Charlie?'

'The donkey. He's cowering in the corner of the field. Not like him at all. Hope your lad's OK. Found him crying in the woods. I have a horse, Whisper, if he'd like a ride some time. Let me know. I'm in the book.'

'Thank you,' Miranda replied, closing the door behind him. She looked at her watch. What on earth was she going to give Gus for lunch?

She found her son sitting in the kitchen, playing with his Game Boy. When she entered he glared at her. 'Now, darling,' she said, endeavouring to sound stern. 'What's all this about biting another boy at school? How do you think you're going to make friends if you bite them?'

'Don't want any friends,' Gus replied, his eyes on the game.

'Why did you bite him?'

'He started it.'

'I don't care who started it. You can't go around bullying people. Do you want to be kicked out and go to boarding school early?'

'No,' he replied hastily, looking up. He didn't want to go to boarding

school at all. 'Are you going to make me go back to school today?'

'No,' she replied, reluctantly changing her mind. She didn't have the heart. 'I've got to go to the village to post a notice in the cake shop. You can hang out here, if you like. I'll put some fish cakes in the oven.'

'Can I watch *The Lord of the Rings*?' Gus had discarded his sulk like a coat that was no longer necessary.

'If you promise not to bully other children.'

'I promise,' he said lightly, climbing down from the bench.

Miranda gave him a hug. 'I love you,' she gushed, repeating the three words that always made up for the lack of time she gave her son. Gus didn't reply but hurried off to the playroom. Miranda went to telephone the school to inform them that Gus had been found but wouldn't be returning on account of a stomachache, and to arrange for an older child to look out for Storm on the school bus.

Miranda drove down the narrow, winding lane into Hartington. The small shops gave the impression of leaning in like trees along hedgerows, making the high street seem barely wide enough for a car. There was Troy's Hair Salon, Cate's Cake Shop, a gift shop, an antiques shop, a delicatessen and a bookshop. Then the street opened into a large green, which boasted a pond and a cricket pitch. Along one side stood the village hall and the Duck and Dapple Inn with its dark Tudor beams. On the other side was Hartington Primary School, where young Adam Hudson still smarted from his bite. The rectory and St Hilda's Church—where the Reverend Freda Beeley held services and prayer meetings, and old Colonel Pike complained that the vicar was a woman—dominated the green, dwarfing a small general store.

Since moving to Hartington House, Miranda had ventured into the village only on the odd occasion when she needed something. She hadn't bothered to speak to the locals, although it was plain that they all knew who she was. After all, she had moved into Hartington House, the big estate on the other side of the river. In London, people didn't stop to chat in the street, and neighbours who had lived in the same building for years were unacquainted. Miranda recoiled at the thought of everyone knowing things about her and judging her; of being invited to coffee mornings at the village hall or having to go to church and shake hands with people she had no desire to meet. It was bad enough that the children were at school and would start bringing their new friends home, though, judging by his recent attempts at striking up friendships, she doubted that Gus would find anyone to invite.

As she parked her jeep at the top of the street, in the car park behind the gift shop, she shuddered at the thought of having to butter up the lady who owned the cake shop. The last thing she needed was to get sucked into local life. Well, she resolved, I'll stick up my notice, smile sweetly and shoot off.

Cate Sharpe was perched at a table chatting to Henrietta Moon, who owned the gift shop. Cate's brown hair was cut into a bob, framing a thin, pale face with bitter chocolate eyes and a small mouth. 'You know, Henrietta,' she said. 'You shouldn't drink hot chocolate. If I had a weight battle like you, I'd drink coffee. It gets the metabolism going.'

Henrietta smiled, a defence mechanism she had adopted in childhood. She shook her head so that her long chestnut hair fell over her face. 'I've given up dieting,' she explained. It wasn't true, but it was easier to pretend she didn't care. 'Life is too short.'

Cate put her hand on Henrietta's in a motherly way, although Henrietta was thirty-eight, only seven years younger than Cate. 'Look, you're a pretty woman. If you lost the odd stone you'd have more chance of finding a man. I hate to say it,' she added smugly, 'but that amount of flesh just isn't attractive. I can say that to you, can't I, because I'm your friend and you know I have your best interests at heart?' Henrietta simply nodded and gulped down a mouthful of chocolate. 'Quiet today, isn't it?' Henrietta nodded again. 'Can't be easy, though, working opposite a cake shop!' Cate laughed. Cate, who never gained an ounce. Cate, whose white apron never carried a single stain. Cate, who no one liked, not even her own husband . . .

At that moment the door opened and in walked Miranda Claybourne. Both Cate and Henrietta recognised her immediately: the snooty Londoner who had moved into Hartington House.

'Good morning,' said Miranda, smiling graciously. She pushed her Chanel sunglasses to the top of her head and strode across the black and white tiled floor. Finding no one behind the counter, she turned to the two women. 'Do you know where she's gone?'

'You mean me,' said Cate, getting up. 'I'm Cate.'

'Miranda Claybourne,' Miranda replied, extending her hand. 'I've just moved down here and need to hire some help. Jeremy Fitzherbert, our neighbour, says you're the person to talk to. Apparently this is the heart of Hartington.' She chuckled at her own pun.

Cate was flattered. She proffered Miranda a limp hand. 'Well, I know everyone and this place is usually buzzing. I have a notice board over

there.' She pointed to the wall by the door. 'Can I offer you a coffee?' Cate was damned if she was going to let the new arrival get away. Miranda was reluctant, but there was something in Cate's demeanour that suggested she'd take offence if Miranda declined.

'I'd love to,' she said, thinking momentarily of Gus alone at home, before slipping out of her Prada coat and taking a seat at the table. Cate brought over a pink fairy cake and a cup of coffee and placed them in front of Miranda. Henrietta gazed at the cake longingly.

'What a gorgeous coat,' Cate said, sitting down. 'Oh, this is Henrietta,' she added as an afterthought. 'She owns the gift shop.'

'We have met,' said Henrietta, who would never expect a woman like Miranda Claybourne to remember her. 'You've been into my shop.'

'Oh, yes,' Miranda replied, recalling a hurried purchase of a scented candle and some notepaper. 'Of course we have.'

'So?' Cate persisted. 'What sort of help do you require?'

Miranda took a sip of coffee. It was delicious. 'Well, I need someone to cook and clean, and a gardener. The garden's a mess.'

'You know, that garden used to be a showpiece,' said Henrietta.

'Really?'

'Oh, yes,' agreed Cate. 'The Lightlys created the most beautiful gardens. I can't imagine that you're very into gardens, being a Londoner.'

'Ava Lightly was green-fingered,' Henrietta added hastily, worried Cate might have caused offence. 'But she left a couple of years ago. It doesn't take long for a garden to grow wild if it's not taken care of.'

'Well, I'm not at all green-fingered,' said Miranda, glancing at her polished nails, 'but it depresses me to look out onto a mess.' She bit into the cake. 'Do you make these yourself?'

Cate nodded. 'You won't find better coffee or cake anywhere in Dorset. Once you've bitten there's no going back.'

'I can see why,' said Miranda, wondering how such a scrawny woman could make such succulent cakes without eating them herself.

'I'll ask around for you,' Henrietta offered helpfully. 'I get a wide variety of people coming into my shop. Hartington attracts people from all around.' She smiled and Miranda warmed to her. She had the sweet, self-deprecating smile of a woman unaware of her prettiness.

The door opened again, letting in a cold gust of wind. 'Look at you!' cried a man with a wide grin and smooth, handsome face. 'Keeping her all to yourself? Etta, you're a shocker! Cate, your secrecy doesn't surprise me at all. From you I expect the worst.'

'This is Troy,' said Henrietta, her face opening into a beaming

smile. 'He's opposite if you need your hair done.'

Troy turned to Miranda, hands on the waist of his low-cut jeans. 'You've been here how long and you haven't even bothered to say hello? We're all terribly hurt, you know.' He pouted. Miranda's spirits rose at the sight of Troy's infectious grin. 'Cate, love of my life, I need a cake. I've got old Mrs Rattle-Bag coming in for her blue rinse at twelve.'

'You're so rude, Troy,' Henrietta gasped with a giggle. 'She's not called that at all, and Troy's really Peter,' she added to Miranda.

'May I join you?' said Troy, not waiting for a response. 'Make that a coffee, too.' He settled his hazel eyes on Miranda and appraised her shamelessly. 'You're the most glamorous thing to set foot in Hartington in years. The last time I saw such glamour was in the woods above Hartington, a vixen, if I recall, wearing a stunning coat all her own. I can see the Prada label on yours, by the way, and I'm loving your leather boots.' He sniffed with admiration, then added conspiratorially, 'You're beautiful as well. What's your husband like?' Miranda nearly spat her coffee all over his suede jacket. 'Is he gorgeous too?'

'God, I couldn't say. Beauty's in the eye of the beholder,' Miranda replied, laughing in astonishment. 'I think he's handsome.'

'You're posh too. I love posh. If you have a title I'll give you a free haircut!'

'I don't, I'm afraid. Simple Mrs Claybourne.'

'But Mrs Claybourne of Hartington House. That's terribly grand. Beautiful and grand, that's enough to turn a gay man straight.'

'She's looking for help,' Henrietta informed him. 'A cook—'

'I can cook,' he volunteered, without taking his eyes off her.

'And a gardener.'

He dropped his shoulders playfully. 'There I'm no help at all. Every green thing I touch dies. It would be a shame to kill off what were once the most beautiful gardens in Dorset.'

Henrietta noticed Cate had gone very quiet. She was making the coffee, her back turned. She threw an anxious glance at Troy, who turned his attention to the counter. 'How's my coffee, sweetheart?'

'Just coming,' Cate replied. The atmosphere had cooled, as it did according to Cate's moods. It had been careless of them to ignore her.

Miranda, sensing the shift, glanced at her watch. 'Goodness, I must get going. It's been very nice to meet you all.' She stood up and shrugged on her coat. The women watched her enviously. It was black and fitted, with wide fur-lined lapels and shoulders sharp enough to graze the air she walked through. 'Thank you for my coffee and cake,'

she said to Cate. 'I really haven't tasted better.' Cate perked up. 'May I stick this on your board?' She took a typed note out of her bag.

'I'll make sure they all read it,' said Cate.

'**W**ell,' gushed Troy when Miranda had disappeared into the street. 'She's quite a looker.'

'She was rather cool to start with but she warmed up. I don't think she knows what to make of you, Troy,' Henrietta teased.

'She's perfectly nice, but I think she's a little stuck-up, don't you? A typical Londoner, they always think they're better than the rest of us,' said Cate silkily, bringing over Troy's coffee and cake. 'She's clearly lost without a cleaner and a cook and a gardener and God knows what else. She bowled in here without any pleasantries as if this were the post office. It's taken her, what? Two months to come and introduce herself. Too grand for Hartington. She's pretty though,' she added with a little sniff. 'In a rather ordinary way.'

'You're being a bit harsh,' said Troy, aware that Cate rarely had anything nice to say about anyone. 'She wasn't too grand for your coffee.'

'That showed her, didn't it? She won't find a better coffee in London.'

'I should get back to the shop. I've left Clare there all on her own,' said Henrietta, referring to her sister.

'I shouldn't worry, it's not as if you're busy,' said Cate. 'Would you like a cake to take back with you?'

'Cake?' repeated Henrietta, confused. Hadn't Cate berated her for eating too much not five minutes ago?

'For Clare, silly,' said Cate, popping one into a bag. Henrietta took the bag and left, feeling thoroughly humiliated.

Miranda returned home to find Gus sitting in front of the fire watching *The Lord of the Rings*. 'Don't you have any homework to do?' she asked.

Gus shrugged. 'I left my bag at school.'

Miranda sighed. 'Well, you'd better bring it back on Monday or you'll be in trouble again. Your father's coming home tonight. He's not happy about what you did today.'

'I didn't mean it,' said Gus. 'I didn't start it.'

'I don't want to listen. Your sister will be home soon so you'll have to turn that off. She's frightened of those ghastly creatures.'

'Orcs,' Gus corrected.

'Whatever. Make sure you turn it off.'

'But, Mum—'

'Off!'

Miranda returned to her desk. She could still taste that delicious cake and her head buzzed from the coffee. The people she had just met would pepper her column rather nicely. Troy was marvellously fruity and Henrietta voluptuous and sweet and totally dominated by Cate, who was toxic. They'd make a nice little trio. The trick was to build characters that featured monthly, then she could write the book, sell the film rights . . . Her fingers began to tap swiftly over the keyboard.

After a while she heard the front door open and close and the soft footsteps of her five-year-old daughter, Storm. 'Darling,' she shouted, a little frustrated that Storm had come home just as she was getting into her characters. Storm appeared at the door looking glum. Her brown hair was swept off her face and her cheeks were pink from the cold. 'Did you have a good day at school?'

'No. Gus is a bully,' she said.

Miranda stopped typing and looked at her daughter. 'A bully?'

'Madeleine doesn't want to come for a play date because she's frightened of Gus.'

'I know. He bit a little boy today.'

'I saw the bite mark; it was bleeding.'

'I'm sure the child showed it off like a war wound,' said Miranda with irritation. No doubt the mother would complain.

'He pulls the legs off spiders.'

'Jolly good thing too; they're horrid.'

'They're God's creatures.' Storm's eyes sparkled with tears.

'Darling, who on earth have you been talking to?'

'Mrs Roberts says all creatures are special. Gus kills everything.'

'Come here, sweetie,' she said, pulling her daughter into her arms.

'I don't like Gus.'

'You're not alone,' said Miranda, with a sigh. 'Why don't you go and play in your bedroom? He's watching *The Lord of the Rings*.' Storm pulled away. 'Do you have any homework?'

'Yes.'

'I'll come up in a minute and help you with it.' But Storm knew that the minute would extend into an hour and she'd end up having to do it on her own. Her mother was always too busy.

Storm sat in her pink bedroom. The wallpaper matched the curtains, depicting little pink cherubs dancing among flowers. The bookshelves were laden with cuddly toys and books. She had pretty jewellery boxes

where she kept trinkets and hair-slides, glittery butterflies and bracelets. She had pink notebooks in which she pretended to write with pink pencils, and a playhouse made from embroidered pink cotton, full of the pink cushions she collected in every shade and size. It was there that she hid now with her reading book from school. She felt sad and alone. She pulled her favourite pink cushion to her chest and hugged it close, drying her tears on the corner. What was the point of a beautiful room if she had no friends to show it off to?

Miranda finished her column and emailed it off with a sigh of relief. She had forgotten about her daughter's homework. She wandered into the kitchen to pour herself a glass of wine. It was time for the children's tea and all she could think of was eggy bread. Gus had already had fish cakes for lunch. As she stared blankly into the fridge, the telephone rang. Sticking the handset between her cheek and shoulder, she pulled out a couple of eggs. 'Yes?' she said, expecting it to be her husband.

'Hi, it's Jeremy here.'

'Oh, hi.'

'You know you're looking for a gardener?'

'Yes,' she replied, brightening.

'I've found someone who might do. He's called Mr Underwood. He used to work on the farm and loves gardening. He's in his mid-sixties and semi-retired. He could do a few days a week for you.'

'Will he be up to it? There's a lot to be done over here.'

'Just give him a go. He's a good man.'

Storm padded in, dressed in a pink fairy outfit complete with glittering crown, wings and wand. 'Mummy, I'm hungry,' she whined, her large eyes red-rimmed from crying.

Miranda frowned. 'OK, I'll see him,' she agreed hastily. 'Can he come tomorrow morning? I know it's Saturday, but . . .'

'I'll send him over.'

'Good. Thanks, Jeremy.' She hung up and turned to her daughter. 'I'm making you eggy bread, darling. Are you all right?'

'Eggy bread?' exclaimed Gus from the doorway. 'I hate eggy bread.'

'Gus, you're in no position to complain about anything today. It's either that or spaghetti.'

'Spaghetti,' said Gus.

Storm screwed up her nose. 'I like eggy bread.'

'I'm not a restaurant. It's spaghetti for both of you.' Storm scowled. 'You can have as much ketchup as you like,' Miranda added to appease her. 'I really don't have the energy to fight with you today.'

She watched her children eat, taking pleasure from her glass of wine. David was coming home tonight. She'd bathe and change into something nice. Cook him calves' liver with a red wine sauce. She wanted to impress him, encourage him to spend more time at home. She craved his company. It was boring on her own in the country.

II

DAVID CLAYBOURNE ARRIVED at Hartington House at eight. Gus, in blue gingham pyjamas, was waiting in the kitchen with his mother. Storm was tucked up in bed with her toy rabbit and favourite pink cushion.

When she heard the front door open, Miranda told Gus to stay in the kitchen while she went to talk to his father. They lingered in the hall for what seemed like a long time, their voices low. Gus yawned and began to scratch lines into the pine table with a spoon.

Finally, his parents walked into the kitchen. His father didn't greet him, but pulled out a chair and sat down. His mother handed her husband a glass of wine, before pouring another one for herself. 'Your mother tells me that you bit a child and ran away from school today,' David said.

Gus stared at his father without blinking. He said nothing. He was determined not to show weakness. Aragorn never showed weakness.

'This has got to stop. Your behaviour is unacceptable. As a punishment you'll not watch television for a week.' Gus's mouth opened in silent protest. He was too stunned to complain. 'And I warn you, Gus, that if you continue to bully other children and disrupt classes we'll be left with no choice but to put you into boarding school early. Do you understand?' Gus fought a rebellious tear as it broke ranks and balanced on his eyelashes. 'What do you have to say for yourself?'

'I didn't start it,' Gus whispered. The tear fell onto his cheek and he brushed it off with his sleeve.

'I don't wish to hear the ins and outs of your playground antics. I've had enough. Now, off to bed.'

Gus slunk down from the bench and walked slowly past his parents. Neither made a move to kiss him good night. Once in his bedroom he

closed the door behind him, flung himself onto the bed and howled.

'I should go up and see him,' said Miranda anxiously.

'No, Miranda,' David replied firmly. 'This is the problem. You're too indulgent. You didn't send him back to school but let him watch DVDs all afternoon. No wonder he doesn't learn. What kind of message are you sending out? Let him cry himself to sleep. He's not going to learn if you go pandering to him all the time. It's not fair on Gus to let him grow into a monster. It's our responsibility to teach him how to behave.'

'But I don't know how to.' Miranda poured herself more wine and sank into a chair.

'Don't be ridiculous. It's not rocket science. Now, have you started looking for help?'

'Yes,' she replied, brightening. 'I've posted a notice in the cake shop in the village. According to our neighbour, Jeremy Fitzherbert, that's the nerve centre of Hartington. And Jeremy's sending someone to see me tomorrow. A gardener called Mr Underwood.'

'Appropriate name,' he replied, nodding his approval. 'Mmm. Something smells good.'

'Calves' liver,' she replied. 'Your favourite.'

David drained his glass and got up. 'Right, I'm going to have a bath.'

Miranda watched her husband leave the room. He hadn't even asked her about herself, nor had he noticed the cashmere dress she was wearing. She had gone to such trouble, washing her hair and applying make-up. She began to make the wine sauce. The onions made her eyes water and she suddenly felt exhausted.

The last year had been unrelenting, what with Gus being asked to leave school the previous Christmas and having to home-school him with a tutor. Meanwhile they had had to find a house, redecorate and move, all in time for the start of the September term. She could still hear Gus whimpering upstairs. 'Damn!' she swore as she cut her finger. 'Oh, I can't stay down here while Gus cries his eyes out in his room,' she hissed, opening one of the drawers and pulling out a Spiderman plaster. She wrapped it over the wound and set off up the stairs.

David finished his bath and changed into a pair of chinos and a blue Ralph Lauren shirt. He had shiny black hair, tanned skin and navy eyes framed by long eyelashes that would have looked too feminine on a less masculine face. He was also strong and muscular, working out every morning in the gym. He dressed well and wore expensive aftershave and was a man of self-confidence, having made a lot of money, married

a beautiful woman and become owner of a large country house, while also investing in a pied-à-terre in Kensington.

David reckoned he had it all: the perfect family in Dorset and the perfect mistress in London. Two separate lives. He loved his wife; he didn't love his mistress. But his wife could hardly expect him to remain celibate all week. She gets the house in the country, he gets laid in London; no one gets hurt.

Having settled Gus, Miranda was back in the kitchen and had finished cooking the liver. She laid the table for two and waited for her husband to appear. Lighting a candle now seemed too theatrical, so she blew it out and put it away. It was all very unfair, she thought to herself. She cooked, washed up, kept the house clean, did the laundry, drove to Sainsbury's once a week to do the shopping, looked after the children, on top of which she had her career. David just had the career. He didn't have to think of anyone but himself. 'Sod it,' she muttered and poured a fourth glass of wine. 'It's as if he doesn't see me any more.'

David was in a good mood when he appeared in the kitchen. Miranda was light-headed. He helped himself to dinner, then sat down.

'Darling, you've gone to so much trouble tonight.' He looked her over appreciatively. 'I have a very beautiful wife.'

Her spirits leapt like a rekindled flame. 'Thank you. Tell me about London. Who have you been hanging out with?'

'Usual crowd, when I have time. I've been in the office until ten every night this week. I'm shattered.'

'How's Blythe?' She had bumped into her old schoolfriend at Gus's judo class in Chelsea. After years of not seeing one another they had grown close again as Miranda supported her through an acrimonious divorce. 'I keep calling her but I just get her answering machine. That's what happens when you move to the country: your friends forget you.'

'She hasn't forgotten you. She's been busy with lawyers and accountants, as you can imagine. In fact, I've been giving her a little advice,' he replied pompously, holding his fork in midair. 'I told her she needs to manage her divorce like a business. She's her own biggest client. She's got to cut the best deal possible. It's no good expecting the lawyer to sort it all out for her. He might be the best in town, but she's still got to tell him what she wants. I told her to write a list. This is the Last Chance Saloon. Once she's closed the door, that's it.'

'Did she listen to you?'

'I think so. The trouble is she's overemotional, can't see the wood for the trees. At the moment she just wants out. I'm happy to help.'

'It's shocking how many of our friends are divorcing,' Miranda sighed. 'Once we get sorted we should invite Blythe and Rafael for the weekend. He's a dear little boy and might be a good influence on Gus.'

'So long as Gus doesn't bite him.'

'Let's give it some time. Gus will settle.' Her face darkened a moment. 'Do you think he should see someone?' she asked tentatively.

'A shrink?' David was appalled.

'Well, a child psychologist.'

'Over my dead body. There's nothing wrong with Gus. Nothing that boarding school won't put right.'

'But he doesn't want to go.'

'It's a stage. He'll grow out of it. You've just got to stay on top of it, Miranda. You're the one around all week. It's up to you.'

'I suppose you're going to tell me to run my family like a business. That Gus is my biggest client.' She let out a shallow laugh.

'No darling, *he's* the business,' David corrected, quite seriously. '*I'm* your biggest client.'

After watching the news they both went to bed. David sat up reading *The Economist* while Miranda, drunk and exhausted, curled into a ball with a pillow over her eyes to block out the light. They didn't make love. David made no advance and Miranda, while affronted that he didn't desire her after a week apart, was rather relieved.

The following morning, Storm entertained herself playing in her bedroom, while Gus, banned from television, wandered into the woods to set traps for unsuspecting animals.

David read the papers over a breakfast of eggs, bacon and toast, which Miranda cooked. She prepared to interview the gardener. 'Do you want to see him with me?' she asked David, who, without taking his eyes from the *Telegraph*, replied that it was her department.

'You're Minister for Domestic Policy,' he said.

'And who are you?' she asked, irritated by his lack of interest.

'I'm Prime Minister,' he replied. 'If you want a second opinion I'll gladly give it. Otherwise, darling, I trust your judgment implicitly.'

Miranda sent David off to sample Cate's coffee and waited in her study. She was tired of having to do everything herself. She recalled the army of builders and decorators she had marched down to Hartington to transform the house into her dream home. David had let her decorate it as she wished—her good taste was one of the reasons he had married her—and had paid the bills without resistance. As Minister for Domestic

Policy, she was expected to make a home for him and their children. It didn't occur to him to help. There was nothing they shared any more.

As she pondered the state of her marriage, the doorbell rang and she hurried across the hall. She took a deep breath and prayed that Mr Underwood would be the perfect gardener and added, while she was on the line to the Lord, that a cook and a cleaner might follow. She opened the door to find a gnome-like man dressed in a brown jacket and trousers with a tweed cap set on an abundant crown of grey hair. When he saw her he took off the cap and held it against his waistcoat.

'I'm Mr Underwood, come about the gardening job,' he said in a broad Dorset accent.

'Do come inside, Mr Underwood,' she replied, stepping aside to let him pass into the hall. A gust of damp wind blew in with him. 'Gosh, it is wet today!' she exclaimed, closing the door behind him.

'Global warming,' he said dolefully. 'One day it's as hot as summer, the next it's as cold as Siberia. You don't know what to expect now.'

'Please come into my study, Mr Underwood.'

He followed her, casting his eyes over the flagstone floor and freshly painted cream walls. There was a large, empty fireplace where logs should have been burning, and a pretty rug where one would expect a couple of sleeping dogs. When the Lightlys had owned Hartington there was always a fire in the grate and a cheery flower arrangement on the wide refectory table in the hall. The round table that now took its place looked lonely with only a lifeless sculpture positioned on top.

'Just moved in then?' he asked.

'Yes. Do you know the house?'

'Aye. This was once the most beautiful garden in Dorset.'

'Really,' she said, showing him to an armchair. He noticed she hadn't lit the fire in her study either.

'Mrs Lightly was a gifted lady.'

'So I'm told.'

'You should light the fires in this house. I could bring logs in for you.'

'Thank you, Mr Underwood. We need someone like you. Now tell me, I gather you worked for Jeremy Fitzherbert?'

'I worked on the farm for over forty years, ploughing and sowing, but what I enjoy most is gardens. Have you seen the toadstools in the woods?' His eyes shone. Miranda shook her head. 'Mrs Underwood cooks a good toadstool soup. She knows which ones to eat and which ones not to eat.'

Miranda noticed Mr Underwood's large belly. He was clearly well fed. She narrowed her eyes thoughtfully.

'This is a large property, Mr Underwood.'

'Mrs Lightly did it on her own,' he said, nodding slowly.

'Didn't she have anyone to help her?'

'Only Hector. It was her passion.'

'Well, it's been left to go wild for a year or two at least. There's a lot to be done. I'm not sure that you're strong enough to do it on your own.'

He looked affronted. 'Not strong enough!' he gasped, insulted. He jumped up, took off his jacket and stood, flexing his muscles in his shirtsleeves. 'Look at this. Hard as rock it is. Hard as solid rock.'

'Thank you, Mr Underwood.'

'You're as old as you feel, M'Lady. Inside here I'm a strapping lad.'

'I'm sure you are, Mr Underwood. Mrs Underwood is very lucky to have you. Tell me, how well does she cook?'

He rubbed his belly. 'The little wife? She's a good woman. No one can cook like Mrs Underwood.'

Miranda decided to take a gamble. Desperation compelled her to be impulsive. 'We're looking for a cook,' she said.

Mr Underwood's face widened into a smile and his cheeks shone pink. 'Look no further, M'Lady. Mrs Underwood will feed you all up good and proper. Used to cook for Mrs Lightly when she had visitors.'

'Would she have the time?'

He nodded eagerly. 'Aye, she's got time all right. Little nippers are grown up now with nippers of their own.'

Miranda's mind was racing. 'I'd like to meet Mrs Underwood,' she said. 'Perhaps she could come tomorrow and cook Sunday lunch for the four of us. As for you, Mr Underwood, let me speak plainly. This place is a mess and you clearly know a thing or two about gardens. Perhaps you could start sweeping leaves and chopping logs so we can light our fires and I'll keep looking for someone'—she hesitated, anxious to find the right word so as not to offend him—'to work with you on the landscaping side. I think this place requires two pairs of hands.'

Mr Underwood nodded slowly. He didn't quite understand what she meant by landscaping. However, he loved chopping logs and lighting fires, and was already envisaging vast mountains of leaves.

'I'll pay you eight pounds an hour and you do as much as you're able.'

'That's as good to me as plum pudding, M'Lady,' he replied, pleased.

'Call me Mrs Claybourne,' she added.

'Mrs Claybourne, M'Lady.'

She sighed and let it go. 'You can start on Monday, and don't forget to ask Mrs Underwood to come tomorrow, if she can.'

David returned from Cate's Cake Shop in a good mood. He strode into the kitchen, where Miranda was roasting a chicken, and grabbed her round the waist, kissing her neck behind her ponytail. 'You were right about that coffee. It's given me a real buzz. Charming people too. I can't think why we've never explored before. It's a quaint place. I chatted to Cate, who's definitely hot for me. And a Colonel Pike—asked him a bit about the war. The locals I met in the village all knew who I was and were suitably deferential. I think I'm going to enjoy being lord of the manor. I should spend a little more time down here.'

'That Cate's a snake in the grass. Watch out for her.'

'Saw your notice up on the board. Sweet!'

'It's not sweet. It's practical. You'll see, it'll do the trick.'

'Let's hope so. The lady of the manor shouldn't be getting her fingers dirty in the garden and cleaning the house. I want my wife to have the smooth hands of a duchess.'

'Lucky my work is all at the computer then, isn't it?'

David smiled. 'How did your meeting with Mr Underwood go?'

'He can do odd jobs, raking leaves, mowing, logs, that sort of thing. We still need a proper gardener, though. Mrs Underwood is coming to cook lunch tomorrow. She used to cook for the previous owners.'

'I'm impressed, darling.' He lifted her chin. 'I never thought you'd pull it all together.'

'I've been so busy—' He silenced her with a kiss.

'Shhh. Don't forget your biggest client!'

Miranda woke in the middle of the night. David lay on his stomach, fast asleep. She watched him for a moment, his back rising and falling in the silvery light of the moon that entered through the gap in the curtains. She could almost feel the heat of his body and yet she felt an ache of loneliness. They seemed not to connect any more.

She climbed out of bed, slipped on her dressing gown and padded into her walk-in cupboard. She closed the door and turned on the light. Decorated like a boutique with shelves and drawers in mahogany, it was the room she had particularly looked forward to: an entire room dedicated to her clothes. Now the dresses and suits that hung neatly on wooden hangers, divided by season and occasion, seemed redundant. She had nothing to go to down here. She had no friends. Even her friends in London were beginning to forget she existed.

She was only thirty-three and yet she felt life was over. Glancing at her reflection in the mirror she was struck by how stringy she looked.

She didn't have the youthful bloom she was once envied for; there were blue-grey shadows under her eyes and her skin was pale and sallow. She had to get a grip. She couldn't allow herself to wallow in self-pity. The thought of hitting Ralph Lauren for a stylish country wardrobe made her spirits rise before she remembered she had no one to leave the children with. If only she could get away for a day, Bond Street would surely resuscitate her. She turned off the light and returned to bed, where David slept on, oblivious to his wife's unhappiness.

The following morning Gus wandered round to the front of the house and saw an old Fiat parked on the gravel. He looked at it curiously. In the back seat sat a springer spaniel breathing fog onto the windows. He tapped against the glass and the dog wagged his tail. When he walked away the animal began to bark. 'Shut up, you silly mutt!' he shouted.

'Who are you calling a silly mutt? Not my Ranger, I hope.' Gus was stunned to see a strange woman standing at the front door of his home, her hands on wide hips. She fixed him with narrowed eyes. 'You'll be young Gus, then,' she said, nodding thoughtfully. 'I hear you have quite a bite on you.'

Gus knew instinctively that this was a woman he wouldn't confront. He wondered how she knew.

She looked at his bewildered face and softened. 'Let's give Ranger a run around. He'll be misting up the windows of my car.' She strode towards the vehicle. 'Open it then, lad, it's not locked.'

Gus did as he was told and Ranger jumped out, wagging his tail excitedly and springing up to greet his mistress.

'Who are you?' said Gus, watching her pat the animal fondly.

'I'm Mrs Underwood. I'll be cooking your lunch today, young Master Gus. Roast leg of lamb, potatoes from my own garden, beans, peas and carrots. Growing lads like you need vegetables. Off you go, Ranger, and have a run round!' The dog did as he was told and galloped off into the field that led down to the river. 'That used to be a beautiful meadow of wild flowers.' She sighed and shook her head. 'Mrs Lightly would have a seizure if she saw what has become of it.'

Gus followed her into the house, where the aroma of cooking meat filled the hall. His stomach rumbled.

'I'd have thought a family like yours would be at church,' Mrs Underwood said, walking down the corridor towards the kitchen. 'I'd be there if I weren't here. Can't say I'm a great fan of the Reverend Beeley. I like a man to represent God. A man I can look up to.'

Miranda was perched on a stool in the kitchen, reading the papers. The smell of cooking had drawn her there too. 'Smells good, doesn't it, Gus?' said Miranda. 'Mrs Underwood is cooking for us today. And Mr Underwood is going to help in the garden.'

'He might be old but he's as strong as an ox, Miranda,' said Mrs Underwood. Miranda noticed that she had been called by her Christian name right from the first, while Miranda called her Mrs. It didn't seem right but Mrs Underwood was clearly a woman used to doing things her own way.

'Where's Dad?' asked Gus.

'In the sitting room. Don't go and bother him, he's reading the paper.'

'Can I watch *The Lord of the Rings*?'

'No, darling. You know Daddy said you can't watch it for a week. Why don't you go outside? It's not raining.'

Outside, Gus found a stick. It wasn't large enough to torment the donkey, but it was the perfect size to throw for a dog. He headed across the field towards the river, scanning the countryside for Ranger. He hadn't explored that side of the garden, but Ranger had gone this way.

After a while he came to the river. It was about twenty feet wide and straddled by a grey stone bridge. Close by, a little cottage nestled among a cluster of chestnut trees. Gus could tell no one lived there, for the windows were dark and dusty. Distracted by a noise in the water, he turned his attention to the river. His spirits rose when he saw Ranger climbing up the bank and shaking his black and white coat until it stuck up in pointy tufts. 'Ranger!' he shouted. The dog bounded up and he let him sniff the stick before throwing it as far as he could. Ranger was used to the game and galloped after it. Gus patted him when he returned with the stick, dropping it at the boy's feet. He threw it again and again.

What finally brought the game to an end was Gus's curiosity about the little abandoned cottage. There was something compelling about those blind windows and neglected walls where ivy was slowly creeping over the bricks. He left the stick on the ground and approached it. The door was locked, the pale blue paint chipped and peeling. He rubbed a window with his sleeve and peered inside. To his surprise the room was full of furniture. A sofa and two armchairs sat in front of a fireplace. Pictures hung on walls that were decorated with stripy yellow paper. He walked round trying all the windows until he came to one that was swinging on its hinges.

His heart pounding with excitement as he climbed inside, he forgot the injustice of being punished for a fight he didn't start and began to

explore. There were papers on the desk in the sitting room, books on the shelves against the wall, logs in the basket by the fire. Everything was as if the occupier had gone out one day and never returned.

There was a kitchen with a rough table on which two teacups were placed alongside a teapot, milk jug and an empty plate. Although Gus was only a boy, he sensed he was walking over someone else's sadness. It was as if the air was damp with tears.

After a while his rumbling stomach reminded him of Mrs Underwood's roast lamb. He climbed back out the way he had come and called Ranger, then set off over the bridge and through the field. It wasn't until he was back at the house that the dog appeared, galloping over the long grass towards him.

'Where have you been?' Miranda asked when she saw her son's sweaty red face and sparkling eyes.

'Nowhere,' he replied. He wasn't going to share the cottage with anyone. 'Just mucking around outside.'

'Good. It's lunch time. Go and call your sister.'

Storm was watching *Fifi and the Flowertots* on television. Reluctantly she turned off the set and followed Gus through to the dining room.

David had spent the morning reading the papers and watching the golf on television in the sitting room. After a busy working week, he needed time on his own to unwind. It hadn't occurred to him that his wife might welcome his company.

The smell of roast lamb wafted through the house and mingled with the wood smoke from the fire that Mrs Underwood had insisted on lighting in the hall. The day before, Mr Underwood had filled the basket with logs from the barn beside the walled vegetable garden.

David walked across the hall to the dining room. 'Something smells good,' he exclaimed, finding his family already seated at the table. He peered over at the sideboard, where the roast leg of lamb was placed, ready to be carved.

'I think we've found our cook,' said Miranda.

'I'll reserve judgment until I've tasted it,' said David, pulling out his chair and sitting down. 'I think we should use this room more often,' he added, casting his eyes over his wife's tasteful decoration.

Mrs Underwood entered, carrying a tray of vegetable dishes, and David made a move to help her.

'Oh no you don't, Mr Claybourne, I can manage it. God didn't make me big and strong to let others do my work for me.' Miranda was slightly put out at hearing her husband referred to as Mr. Mrs

Underwood balanced the tray on the corner of the sideboard and unloaded the vegetables, saying, 'These potatoes are from my own garden.' Gus had never seen so many. There were also beans, peas and carrots, sprinkled with parsley and butter. She began to carve. The meat was tender and rose-pink in the middle. David's mouth watered.

The first bite confirmed what Miranda already knew: Mrs Underwood would be a fine addition to the family. 'I don't think I've tasted better,' said David, as the lamb melted on his tongue.

'It's organic Dorset lamb,' said Mrs Underwood proudly. 'There's a farmers' market in Hartington every Saturday morning.'

'Really?' said Miranda.

'I'm surprised you don't know about it.' Mrs Underwood placed the gravy on the table. 'But once you've settled in you'll get to know Hartington and its people. The best way to become part of the community is to go to church. The Lightlys always sat in the front pew.'

Miranda cringed at the idea of playing lady of the manor, but it added another piece to David's picture-perfect country life. 'I think it's a terrific idea,' he said. 'It's about time we got to know the locals.'

'Do you?' said Miranda. She envisaged ghastly coffee mornings and meetings in the church hall to discuss the flower rota. 'Darling, we never went to church in London.'

'More reason why we should start now. Gus and Storm should have a religious education. It'll do them good to become part of the fabric of the place. Help them settle in.' Miranda looked at Gus, who was tucking into his vegetables. He usually hated vegetables.

'I'll leave you to it, then,' said Mrs Underwood, making for the door. 'There's steamed pudding for dessert. Let me know when you're ready.'

'You're hired,' David called after her.

'I know,' she replied with a chuckle. 'It's good to be back.'

After lunch David's satisfied gaze rested on his wife. There was nothing like a belly full of good food to make him feel horny. 'How would you children like to watch a video for a while?' Miranda frowned. Hadn't he forbidden Gus to watch television? 'Mummy and I would like a siesta.' Her frown melted into a smile. Gus jumped down from his chair.

'Make sure you watch something that Storm will enjoy,' Miranda shouted as they bolted for the playroom. David took his wife's hand.

'How about it, Mrs Claybourne?'

'How about it indeed,' she replied, squeezing his hand. She felt the warm sensation of their reconnection.

'Well done, darling. You've found a cook and a gardener. There's a fire blazing in the hall and the children are happy. Now, before I have to catch that train for London, you can make me happy.' He stood up and led her out of the room.

Gus and Storm sat in front of the television watching *Nanny McPhee*. They had already seen it before, loads of times, but it was the only DVD that they both enjoyed. Storm noticed Gus had been rather quiet over lunch, as if he was keeping a secret. After a while he announced that he was bored of the telly and was going outside. 'Can I come too?' Storm asked, not because she wanted to play with him, but because he reeked of something mysterious.

'No,' he replied. 'I want to play on my own.'

'That's not very nice,' she complained. 'You're a poo!'

'You're a baby.' He stood up and marched out of the room.

Storm gave him a minute, then followed him.

Gus noticed Mrs Underwood's car had gone, taking Ranger with it. He was disappointed. The dog had been good company. He wasn't stupid like Charlie. He ran off through the field to the little bridge. The clouds had cleared and the sun shone, catching the ripples in the river and making them sparkle. The air was sweet with the smell of wet earth and foliage, and the breeze had turned unexpectedly warm. He hurried across to his secret cottage and climbed inside.

Storm watched from a distance. She had never been to that side of the garden. She saw Gus disappear inside the cottage and stood for a while looking about. The stone bridge reminded her of the bridge in *Winnie the Pooh*. She walked onto it and peered down into the pebbles and rocks hidden among the weeds and wondered whether there were fish.

Storm turned her attention back to the cottage. Gus had been in there ages. She knew he'd be cross if he discovered she had followed him. She bit her nails, half-hoping that he would appear. But he didn't.

Slowly, she began to walk towards the cottage. She peered through the window to the left of the front door. It had already been rubbed clean by Gus's sleeve, so she could see inside. She gasped as she took in the room. Someone obviously lived there. With an accelerating heart she tiptoed round to the window at the other side of the front door.

Suddenly, Gus appeared round the corner. 'What are you doing here?' he demanded. 'I told you I want to play on my own.'

'But I've got no one to play with.' Storm pulled away from the window, her eyes glittering with tears.

'Tough!'

'I want to go inside.'

'You can't,' Gus shouted. 'Only boys can climb in and, besides, this is my house.'

Storm began to sob. 'You're not my brother!' she said. 'I hate you!' She turned and ran along the river bank, ignoring the little stone bridge that would lead her home.

Gus watched her go, then returned to the cottage. He was furious that she had discovered his secret, though he also felt a niggling worry that she hadn't returned over the bridge but had continued up the river into unknown territory. He felt guilty. If anything happened it would be his fault. The worry didn't niggle for long. He began to explore upstairs where two bedrooms and a bathroom nestled beneath the eaves.

Storm hurried along the river bank, sobbing loudly. She hated Gus, she hated the countryside, she hated her new school and she hated the new house. She wanted to go back to London, to her old bedroom, to her school where she had lots of friends, to all that was familiar. After a while she came to a fence. On the other side was a field full of cows. She leant on the gate and rested her head on her arms.

Suddenly she heard the squelch of hoofs and a gentle snorting as the shiny black cows approached her. She raised her eyes. If she were Gus she would have tried to frighten them, but Storm was frightened herself. She dared not move. The cows formed a semicircle on the other side of the gate, jostling each other, their large eyes bright and curious.

'Put out your hand,' came a voice beside her. She was surprised to see a stranger lean on the fence and extend his hand towards the cows. He smiled at her and his weathered brown face creased about the eyes where the crow's-feet were already long and deep. He had the kind of smile that warmed a person from the inside and Storm immediately felt better. She remembered her mother telling her not to talk to strangers. But this man was nice, not at all like the men she'd been warned about.

Storm copied the man and stuck out her hand. At first the cows didn't move any closer, just observed the extended hands, snorting their hot steamy breath into the damp October air. Storm waited, excited now that she was no longer alone. At last the cows began to edge their way towards them. Storm began to tremble as one of them stretched its neck and brought its wet nose closer. 'Don't be afraid,' said the man. He had a funny accent. 'They're Aberdeen Angus cows, very gentle creatures. They are afraid of *you*.' He put his hand closer to hers

and the cow blew onto their skin. 'You see. She likes you.' With the back of his fingers he stroked the cow's nose. The cow put out her tongue and licked Storm's hand.

'Her tongue is all rough,' she said, giggling with pleasure.

'That's because it's got to grab hold of the grass. If it were smooth the grass would slip through.'

The rest of the herd now saw that the two humans were friendly and surged forward, each wanting a turn. 'We have some new friends,' he said and laughed. He was surprised that the child had suddenly made him happy. A while ago he had been sitting on the river bank, head in his hands, the unhappiest he had been in nearly twenty-six years. 'What is your name?' he asked.

'Storm.'

'Storm is an unusual name. My name is Jean-Paul.' He studied her flushed face, grubby where her tears had fallen, and felt a wave of compassion. A child her age shouldn't be wandering the fields on her own. 'Do you live near here?'

'Hartington House,' she replied, repeating the name her mother had taught her. Jean-Paul blanched and for a moment he was lost for words. 'It's the other side of the river,' Storm continued. But Jean-Paul knew that. He raised his eyes as if he could see over the trees to where the house nestled in the neglected gardens.

'I think I should take you home,' he suggested quietly. Storm nodded, disappointed. She didn't want to go home. She wanted to stay with the cows. Jean-Paul sensed her disappointment. 'You can come back another time. The cows will always be pleased to see you. They know you now.'

'My brother doesn't want to play with me,' she said. 'He's mean.'

'Do you have any other brothers or sisters?'

Storm shook her head sadly. 'Just Gus.'

'How long have you lived here?'

'Not long,' she replied. 'We used to live in London.'

'I bet you did not have such a big garden in London.'

'We didn't have a garden at all, but we had the park.'

Jean-Paul shrugged. 'But a garden is more magical than a park. Gardens are full of secret places.'

'Gus's house is secret.'

'You need to ask your father to build you a playhouse of your own.'

'He's busy,' she said, lowering her eyes.

'Then you should make a house in the hollow tree in the wild

garden.' The child had clearly never heard of the tree or the wild garden. 'Come, I'll show you.'

They approached the little stone bridge and Jean-Paul cast his eyes at the cottage. 'That's Gus's secret house,' said Storm, pointing at it. Jean-Paul said nothing. His heart had broken all over again. She had gone. Why had he bothered coming back? What had he expected to find? He should have let ivy grow over his memories as it was growing over the cottage. He should have moved on. But he loved with all his heart.

'Come, Storm. I'll show you the hollow tree.' He walked over the bridge without glancing back. The wild garden, once full of purply-blue camassias and buttercups, cowslips and fluffy dandelions, had been neglected. Instead of being cut down for winter, the grasses were long. How he had loved to walk through them on those balmy spring evenings on his way to the cottage. Now it had been starved of love.

'You see that tree over there.' He pointed to a large oak that dominated the garden. 'It's hollow, like a shell. You can climb into it and make it into a camp.' He took a deep breath. 'It's been done before.' Storm's curiosity was aroused, but Jean-Paul began to walk towards the house. 'Shouldn't we let your mother know that you are back?'

'She's busy,' said Storm.

Jean-Paul frowned. He ran his hand through his dark hair, now greying at the temples, and looked at the little girl. 'I doubt she is too busy to notice that you have been gone. How old are you, Storm?'

'Nearly six,' she replied proudly.

'You are very grown up. But even grown-ups look out for each other. Let's go and tell her you are back, just in case, eh?' His natural instinct was to hold her hand. How often he had walked those gardens holding the hands of small children, teaching them the magic and mystery of nature. But he knew it wouldn't be appropriate with this little girl. Instead, he put his hands in his jacket pockets and continued to walk towards the front of the house.

It was just as he remembered it: the soft grey stone walls and tiled slate roof; the tall, elegant chimneys where doves used to settle and coo; the three dormer windows with their little square panes of glass where the children had peered out and waved.

Jean-Paul rang the bell. Storm stood beside him, waiting for her mother to appear. She didn't imagine she would have been worried; Mummy had been asleep. After a while, the door opened to reveal Miranda in a brown velour track suit, hair pulled back into a ponytail, cheeks glowing. She looked at the strange man and then at Storm. 'Are

you all right, darling?' she said, crouching down to look at her daughter. She could see from Storm's grubby face that she had been crying. 'What happened?' She directed her question at the stranger.

'I found her down by the river. She was alone.' Miranda noticed the man's French accent. She couldn't fail to notice, too, how attractive he was. 'My name is Jean-Paul.'

'Please come in,' she said. 'Thank you so much for bringing her home.'

'I don't want to trouble you,' he said, his face solemn.

'You're not troubling me at all. Please, I'd like to thank you.' Miranda wished she wasn't so scruffy. 'I can't imagine what she was doing down by the river. Goodness, my children are running wild. Our neighbour brought Gus back from the woods only a couple of days ago.'

Jean-Paul followed Miranda down the corridor to the kitchen. He noticed at once how different the house was on the inside and felt the dramatic change in vibration, as if a cold draught ran through the hall, lowering the temperature in spite of the fire in the grate.

Storm skipped beside Jean-Paul. He was her new friend.

'I thought you were watching a video,' said Miranda to Storm, taking two cups from the painted cream dresser and placing them on the black granite worktop. 'Would you like tea or coffee, Jean-Paul?'

'Coffee, please,' Jean-Paul replied, perching on a stool.

'We saw some cows,' said Storm. 'One licked my hand.' She held it up, grinning proudly.

'God! How horrible. You'd better wash it at once. I hope you haven't put your fingers in your mouth.' She shuffled Storm to the sink, turned on the tap and lifted her up. Storm grabbed the soap and put her hands under the water.

'Her tongue is rough so she can eat the grass,' the child continued.

'That's right, give them a good wash,' Miranda encouraged, more concerned about germs than the nature of the cow's tongue. When she had finished, Miranda put Storm down and began to make the coffee. She noticed Jean-Paul looking at her with a bemused expression on his face. His mouth was sensual, uneven and twisted into a small smile. His eyes were warm, toffee-brown and deep-set, surrounded by long dark lashes. What struck her most was not the colour, though it was rich and velvety, but their expression. They were filled with compassion as if he had a deep understanding of the world.

'We've just moved here,' she said, pouring ground coffee into the machine. 'We're still adjusting.'

'Change takes time. But this is a beautiful place. You will be very

happy here.' The way he spoke sounded almost prophetic.

'What brings a Frenchman to Hartington? You don't look like a tourist.'

'I am not.'

Storm pulled a stool over to where Jean-Paul was perched and climbed up. 'Jean-Paul is going to build me a little house in a tree,' she said, smiling up at him.

'She was sad she didn't have a secret house, like her brother,' said Jean-Paul.

'Gus won't play with her, that's the trouble. He's nearly eight. Storm's too young for him. Do you have children?'

'No, I never married,' he said.

What a waste of an attractive man, she thought.

'Gus will be going to boarding school next year,' she continued.

'Boarding school? He is very little.'

'Believe me, if anyone needs boarding school, it's Gus.' She chuckled. 'Besides, I work. The sooner they're both packed off to boarding school the better.' She opened the fridge and took out a carton of milk.

'What do you do?'

'I'm a journalist. A frustrated novelist, actually. When the children go to boarding school I hope I'll have the time to write a book.'

He looked down at Storm. 'Little Storm will go too?'

'When she's eight and a half. I've got you for a while longer, haven't I, darling?' said Miranda, smiling at her daughter. But Storm only had eyes for the handsome Frenchman.

'What do you do, Jean-Paul?' She poured coffee into a cup and handed it to him.

He hesitated, then he looked at her steadily and replied, 'I garden.'

Miranda was astonished at the coincidence. 'You're a gardener?'

He gave a wry smile. 'Yes, why not?' He shrugged in the way Frenchmen do, lifting his shoulders and raising the palms of his hands to the sky. 'I garden.'

'I'm sorry, it's just that I've been frantically looking for someone to do our garden. Everyone keeps telling me that the previous owners were brilliant gardeners and that this was the most beautiful garden in the country. I'm now feeling guilty that I'm letting it go.'

He lifted his cup and took a sip of coffee. 'Did you know the people who lived here before you?'

Miranda shook her head. 'No. Old people, I think. Lightly or something. They moved away.'

'I see.'

'You're not . . . I mean . . . you wouldn't consider . . .?'

'I will bring this garden back to life,' he said.

Miranda looked pleased. 'My husband will think I'm mad. I don't even know you.'

She couldn't have known why he offered himself. That it wasn't a wondrous coincidence but a promise made over two decades before.

'Trust me, I am more than qualified. This is no ordinary garden.'

'We have a cottage just over the river. It's in need of repair but it wouldn't take long. We'd be happy for you to live there rent-free.'

He turned to Storm. 'Gus's secret house, no?'

'It's very dirty,' Storm piped up. 'It's all dusty. I've looked inside.'

'We'd clean it out, of course. It's a charming place. I bet it's an idyll in the summertime.'

'It will do,' he replied. He stood up and walked over to the window. 'It would be a shame to let it go,' he said gravely. 'After all the work that has gone into it.' *After all the love that has gone into it.*

He drained his cup. 'I must go,' he said. 'I have some things to sort out in France. I will return at the end of the month and I will give you a year.'

'That gives us enough time to prepare your cottage.'

'You never told me your name,' he said, walking into the corridor.

'Miranda Claybourne.'

'I ask of you one thing, Mrs Claybourne.' His gaze was so intense she felt her stomach lurch.

'Yes, what is it?'

'That you take my advice without question. I promise, you will be more than satisfied.'

'Of course,' she replied, blushing again. His charisma was alarming.

'You don't trust me now, but you will.' He turned to Storm, who was following them into the hall. 'There is magic in the garden,' he said, crouching to her level.

'Magic?' she gasped, eyes wide with excitement.

His voice was a whisper. 'Magic, and I am the only one who knows how to use it.'

'Can I help you?' she whispered back.

'I cannot do it without you.' He grinned at her. Miranda caught her breath at the sight of his smile. It transformed his entire face, giving it an air of mischief. 'You will see what happens to the garden when we look after it. The more love we put into it, the more love it gives back.'

'Mummy, Mummy, I want to help find the magic!'

Miranda laughed. 'I'd like to find the magic too,' she said, shaking his hand. He took hers and raised it to his lips. Her stomach flipped over like a pancake.

She watched him disappear into the darkness. That was the oddest job interview she had ever conducted. They hadn't even discussed his wages. She bit her lip, feeling excited but uneasy; she hadn't found him, he had found her.

With a light step she returned to the kitchen to make the children's tea.

'He's nice,' said Storm, jumping after her with excitement.

'Yes, he is,' Miranda replied, picking up his empty coffee cup. 'He's very nice. Although I know nothing about him. I have no references.' She shook her head. 'No, I've got good gut instinct. He's honest. After all, he brought you home, didn't he?'

'I was frightened of the cows,' said Storm.

'Were you, darling? Is that why you had been crying?'

'He taught me how to put my hand out.'

'Where did you find him?'

'By the river.'

'What was he doing there?' Miranda loaded cups into the dishwasher.

'I don't know.'

'What were *you* doing there?'

'Gus wouldn't play with me. When will I see Jean-Paul again?'

'Well, he's going to be our gardener. We have to clean out the little cottage.' Miranda frowned at her daughter. 'Why did he say it was Gus's secret house?'

'Because Gus says it's his.'

'Ah, so that's where he's been running off to.'

'He won't play with me.'

'That's because you're smaller than him and you're a girl. Little boys don't like playing with girls.'

'He doesn't play with boys either. No one likes him.'

Miranda pulled out a loaf of bread. 'You can have sandwiches for tea,' she said, ignoring Storm's comment. Miranda didn't like to think of Gus being unpopular. It highlighted the fact that her son had a problem. A problem she was too frightened to deal with.

At that moment Gus burst in. He was relieved to see his sister alive.

'Mummy's going to clean out the cottage,' said Storm triumphantly.

'What cottage?' said Gus, making furious eyes at his sister.

'*Your* cottage,' Storm replied.

'The little cottage by the river,' his mother added. 'We have to clean it out for the new gardener.'

'He's my friend,' said Storm.

'What gardener?' Gus asked, feeling cornered. Everyone knew but him.

'A nice Frenchman is going to do the garden for us and he's going to live in the cottage,' said Miranda.

'But it's my secret place!' Gus protested.

'You'll have to find another,' said Miranda.

Storm smirked at her brother, thinking of the hollow tree. That was *her* secret place and she wasn't going to share it with Gus.

That evening Miranda called David on his mobile phone to explain about Jean-Paul. To her surprise he accepted the news without question. He was short with her and distracted, which was just as well; had she told him at any other time, he might have taken more interest.

David turned to his mistress with a sigh. 'That was Miranda,' he said, tossing his mobile onto the bed. 'She's found a gardener.'

Blythe ran her fingers across his chest. 'Lady Chatterley,' she giggled. 'Beware!'

'I don't think my wife has it in her.'

'Oh, I think there's a little of Lady Chatterley in all of us.'

'She's too much of a snob,' he said.

'Have you seen him?'

'I doubt he's competition. He's a gardener, for Christ's sake!'

'She might like a bit of rough.'

'Miranda?'

'I'm joking.' She kissed him. 'Oh Romeo, I've really got you going, haven't I?'

'And now I will punish you!'

Aroused by the thought of the two women in his life, both beautiful, both his, David climbed on top of his mistress.

Cate's Cake Shop was busy for a Monday morning. Colonel Pike sat in the corner by the window reading *The Times*, a cup of coffee steaming on the table beside a hot buttered crumpet. Every now and then his moustache would twitch and he'd mutter under his breath. The Reverend Freda Beeley was enjoying tea with a couple of her choir members, Jack Tinton and Malcolm Shawditch, and discussing plans for a Christmas carol concert to raise money to repair the church spire. Two elderly ladies sat gossiping nearby, and William van den Bos, who

owned the bookshop, was at the table nearest the cakes, tucking into a large slice of lemon drizzle.

Henrietta hadn't yet opened her gift shop and was sitting with Troy, whose first appointment of the day had been cancelled. Cate had come from behind the counter to join them. What interested them was the attractive Frenchman who had sat alone in the shop the day before.

'He barely uttered a word,' said Cate, perching tidily at Henrietta and Troy's table. 'But what he did say was delivered in such a sexy French accent I almost forgot I was married and declared myself available.'

'What was he like?' Henrietta asked.

'Gorgeous,' said Cate.

'Gay?' asked Troy hopefully.

'Single?' laughed Henrietta.

'Frenchmen like skinny women,' said Cate, screwing up her freckled nose in mock sympathy. Henrietta took another bite of brioche. 'Definitely not gay. Sorry, you two.'

'Did he have that smug married look?' Troy interjected icily. Cate ignored the jibe. Troy always stuck up for Henrietta.

'No. He looked single, actually,' she replied, lifting her chin. 'But he looked serious and sad. I treated him to coffee. His face brightened a little after that. He was clearly a tourist. He asked about Hartington House. I think he thought the gardens were open to the public. He seemed very disappointed when I told him the place was all overgrown and a posh new family from London had moved in.'

'Did you tell him to go and see the castle?' Troy lowered his voice and leant into the table conspiratorially. 'Seeing Jack and Mary Tinton in fancy dress would have cheered him up. They're a hoot!'

'What do you mean, fancy dress?' Henrietta glanced over at Jack Tinton. He looked like any other fifty-year-old in jeans.

'They've just taken it upon themselves to dress up as Elizabethan characters and walk about the place for tourists. They charge a pound to have their photograph taken. If you want a laugh, go up there at a weekend and watch them prance around in long skirts and breeches.'

'Bah!' exclaimed the colonel from the corner. He folded his paper and stood up crossly. 'Nothing good about the world these days.' The vicar and her two companions stopped talking and looked up at him in surprise. 'Bloody lucky my number's nearly up.' He moved stiffly across the room, threw some change onto the counter and shuffled out.

Cate put the change in the till and returned to her chair.

'I wonder if the Frenchman'll come back,' sighed Henrietta. There

were precious few attractive single men in Hartington.

'Who can say? Just passing through, I should imagine,' Cate said. 'He was delicious, though. His eyes were the softest brown I've ever seen.'

'How old was he?'

'Early fifties. He gave me quite a look when he left.' Cate always had to bring the conversation around to herself. 'You know, that lazy, bed-room look.' She nodded knowingly. 'He might come back. A man like that appreciates good coffee.'

They all turned as the door opened, letting in a gust of cold air. 'Told you,' said Cate triumphantly. 'They always come back.' She stood up and greeted Miranda as if she were an old friend. 'What can I get you?'

'A coffee with hot milk on the side, please,' said Miranda. She turned to the notice board and ripped off the piece of paper advertising the two job vacancies.

'Found someone, have you?' said Cate.

'Yes,' replied Miranda cagily. 'As a matter of fact, I have.'

'A cook *and* a gardener? That's quick,' said Troy.

'Not in this village. Everyone passes through my cake shop.'

Miranda didn't have the heart to tell Cate that neither Mrs Underwood nor Jean-Paul had seen her notice board. She greeted Troy and Henrietta with a polite smile—she didn't want to encourage them—and went to sit by the window. No sooner had her bottom touched the wood than the Reverend Beeley leant over, heaving her large bosom across the gap between their chairs. 'Hello,' she said in a fruity voice. 'I'm Rev Beeley, your vicar. I gather you're new in town.'

'Yes.' Miranda realised that she had been stupid to think there was such a thing as a quiet coffee in Cate's Cake Shop.

'As the vicar of Hartington I'd like to welcome you. I'd be delighted to welcome you to church, too, if you feel the desire to attend our ser-vices. I hope you have received the parish magazine.'

'Yes, thank you,' Miranda replied, pulling a tight smile.

'It is a pleasure. The Lightlys were very devout. They attended every Sunday. The church really came to life when Mrs Lightly arranged the flowers. She had a magic touch. Her gardens were the most beautiful—'

'So I've been told,' Miranda interjected briskly. 'If they had the most beautiful gardens in England, why did they move?'

'I suppose they didn't want to rattle about in a big house. The chil-dren had grown up and moved away, except the youngest, who inherited her mother's green fingers. Then, what with Phillip's illness . . .' The vicar broke off with a sigh and shook her head mournfully.

'Phillip?'

'Mr Lightly. He's much older than Ava, his wife. He suffered a stroke.' She hissed the sentence as if it were a heavily guarded secret. 'Ava looks after him herself. She's a good woman.'

'Where did they move to?'

'I don't know. They left quietly.' The vicar inhaled, lowering her lids. 'A most respectable couple. An example to us all.'

Cate brought Miranda her coffee. 'I met your husband on Saturday,' she said, watching Miranda pour hot milk into the cup.

'He enjoyed your coffee.'

'Of course. He was very friendly, talking to everyone in here, making lots of new friends. He's charming.' Miranda half-expected Cate to finish with the words, 'not like you'. The woman hovered, waiting for Miranda to continue the conversation, then moved away with a sniff.

Miranda didn't mind if Cate was offended. She turned her thoughts to her children, hoping Gus was behaving himself at school. Storm had been in a bright mood that morning, chattering away about the magic that Jean-Paul was going to show her in the garden. Miranda had found her in her playhouse talking to her cushions, telling them all about a special friend she had found by the river, some sort of tree, and going back to see the cows.

'They know me now,' she had told her mother. 'They'll recognise me when I go back. Jean-Paul said so.' Miranda recalled the kind expression in the Frenchman's eyes. The way his smile had illuminated his tanned face like a beautiful dawn. He didn't look like a gardener, he looked more like a film star.

Miranda paid for her coffee and left the cake shop. She pulled her Chanel sunglasses out of her handbag and walked up the road towards the car park. It was sunny and the air was crisp, the shadows inky blue. She felt a spring in her step. Was it the coffee, or the knowledge that Jean-Paul was returning at the end of the month?

'She didn't even say thank you!' Cate exclaimed when Miranda had gone. Troy looked at Henrietta and frowned.

'For her coffee?' he said.

'No, for finding her a gardener and a cook!'

'You don't know that you did,' said Troy.

Henrietta watched him in awe; she would never have dared talk to Cate like that. Cate who was always right. Cate who knew everything.

'Of course I did. Thanks to the notice on *my* board. How very rude.' She cleared away the cup and milk jug from Miranda's table. 'I told you

she was snooty. Can't think what that delightful husband is doing married to her.' She walked past Troy and gave Henrietta a look. 'Forget the Frenchman, darling. Miranda's husband is gorgeous and if she continues to walk around with a face like a boot, he'll soon be free. Lose a stone and you can have him too!'

Troy put a hand on his friend's and waited for Cate to disappear into the small kitchen behind the counter. 'Don't listen to her, Etta. I love you just the way you are. If I were straight, I'd marry you in an instant.'

'Thank you,' said Henrietta, her eyes glistening with gratitude.

'Imagine the bruises poor Nigel suffers from having to lie on her night after night. You'd be delicious to lie on. Soft and warm. Some man is going to be very lucky indeed to find you.'

'I don't think I'll ever find anyone,' Henrietta sniffed. 'I'm fat and dull.'

'Fat and dull!' Troy exclaimed. 'Listen to yourself! You're neither fat nor dull. You're lovely and sweet, with no side. You shouldn't let Cate treat you like that.' He patted her hand again. 'Come on, let's get out of here before she comes back. Why don't you come in at five and I'll give you a blow-dry. Nothing like a hairdo to lift the spirits.'

'But I've got nowhere to go.'

'Yes, you have. You're having dinner with me.'

'Thank you, Troy. You're a good friend,' she said, kissing his cheek.

Miranda walked down the path towards the river. The sun shone enthusiastically upon the wild grasses and weeds, catching the droplets of rain that had fallen during the night, turning them into diamonds. The wind had blown wildly in the early hours of the morning and yet orange and brown leaves clung to the branches, not yet ready to relinquish the last remains of summer. She had walked down to the river once or twice, but it hadn't held the enchantment it did today.

She stood a moment on the stone bridge, gazing down into the clear water below. She could see weeds and stones and the occasional fish that floated lazily across the sunbeams. She imagined her children playing there, throwing sticks into the water. Then she glanced over to Gus's secret house. She hadn't looked at it properly before. The estate agent had simply mentioned a cottage in need of repair, and, as she'd had no immediate use for it, she had thought nothing more about it. There was no driveway, and there was something wonderfully romantic about its isolation. It was a secret hideaway that time had left behind.

Miranda walked to the front door and turned the key in the lock. It was a rusty old thing, but the door opened with a low squeak. Inside,

the hall was tiled with dark stone slabs, the staircase narrow with a little landing where it turned the corner. She went into the sitting room. The room was full of furniture and the bookshelves were heavy with books stacked in tidy rows. She ran her hand along the top of one. There was only a light coating of dust. The books were a mixture of old and contemporary and to her surprise there was a shelf of French novels.

She moved on to the kitchen. She noticed the table laid for two and thought how odd it was that the cups and plates were still there, as if the inhabitants had been spirited away in the middle of tea. She resisted the temptation to clear them away. She'd get her rubber gloves on, hire some help and do it all at once.

The floorboards creaked beneath her feet as she climbed the stairs. There were two bedrooms and a bathroom. The bathroom was very old-fashioned. The iron bath was stained, its enamel worn away, and the taps were tarnished. One of the bedrooms was completely empty except for a box that sat in the middle of the floor, as if it had been forgotten. Before she had a moment to look inside, a rattle from the bedroom next door distracted her. Her heart jumped. Surely she was the only person in the cottage?

For a second she thought it might be Gus. Her irritation mounted as she stepped across the landing to the other bedroom. A mischievous squirrel startled her as it shot back out of the window, carelessly left ajar by her son, no doubt. She put her hand on her chest and took a deep breath, relieved that it wasn't an intruder.

She looked around. There was a large iron bed, made up with sheets and a quilted bedspread in a pale green flowered material. On top of two bedside tables were tall pillar lamps, the shades stained with yellow patches. A faded trunk sat at the end of the bed, a cherrywood chest of drawers with a Queen Anne mirror on top, and a prettily painted pine wardrobe stood against the wall. She wondered why the Lightlys hadn't taken this furniture with them. Perhaps they had downsized and hadn't the room. She opened the window wider and looked out over the field. She could see down the river to the field of cows—Storm's cows. Her spirits soared, stirred by the strange magic of the room and the glorious view.

Her thoughts returned to the box in the spare room. She closed the window, then went in search of it. There was only one thing inside: a large, faded green scrapbook. It was thick with flowers and leaves pressed between its many pages. On the front the title was written in looped handwriting: *Rainbows and Roses*. Miranda knelt on the floor and flicked through it. It was a diary of poems, recollections and essays,

clearly something that was not meant to have been left behind, nor seen by the eyes of a stranger. The mystery intrigued her. The writing was feminine. The paper smelt sweet, like cut grass in early spring. She sat back against the wall and turned to the first page where four sentences stood alone, heavy with sorrow: *It has now been 24 years. I grow old loving you and one day I shall die loving you. For now I live on the memory of you here in our cottage. It is all I have left.*

AUTUMN

III

Hartington House, October 1979

Ava Lightly's voice could be heard from deep within the herbaceous border. Although she was obscured by dead lupins and the large viburnum she was busily cutting back, her enthusiastic singing stirred the crisp morning air and sent the dogs into an excited frolic on the grass. Ava was dressed in purple dungarees and a short-sleeved T-shirt, her streaky blonde hair roughly secured on the top of her head with a pencil. Her hands were rough from gardening, her nails short and ragged, yet her cheeks glowed with health and her pale green eyes sparkled. She was happiest outside, whatever the weather, and rarely felt the cold although she was a slender woman. She was often seen with bare arms in midwinter. At thirty-seven she retained the bloom of youth, born of an inner contentment that shone through her skin. Her face was handsome rather than pretty: her nose a little too long and very straight, her mouth large and sensual. Yet, if the features weren't beautiful in isolation, they were made so by the sensitive, cheerful expression that held them together. Her eccentric nature made her compelling. No one loved her more than her husband, Phillip Lightly, and their three small children, Archie, Angus and Poppy.

'Hey, Shrub!' called Phillip, striding across the lawn. Bernie, the fluffy Saint Bernard, and Tarquin, the young labrador, stopped rolling about on the grass and galloped up to him. He was fifteen years older than his wife, six foot four with a straight back and wide shoulders. With round glasses perched on an aristocratic nose, fine bones and a high forehead, Phillip Lightly cut a distinguished figure. He spent most of the time in

his study writing the definitive history of wine, or abroad, visiting vineyards. However, he wasn't inclined to solitude. He enjoyed shooting parties and long dinners, discussing history and politics over glasses of port. And he took pleasure from socialising with the people of Hartington after church on Sundays, and invited the village to an annual wine and cheese party at the house every summer.

When he reached the border, he waited a while, enjoying his wife's tuneful singing, then he called her again by the nickname he had given her in the early days of their courtship. 'Shrub, darling!'

'Oh, hello there, you!' she replied, scrambling out. There were leaves caught in her hair and a smear of mud down one cheek. She wiped her nose with the back of her hand.

'Jean-Paul will be at the station in half an hour. You haven't forgotten about him, have you?'

The surprise on her face confirmed that she had. Ava was famously vague, her mind absorbed by the trees and flowers of her garden.

'I'd completely forgotten. I've done nothing about the cottage.'

'Well.' Phillip sighed, smiling indulgently. 'He's young, he'll be happy in a sleeping-bag.' He folded his arms against the cold. 'Look, I'll pick him up but then it's over to you, Shrub.'

'Thank you.' She wrapped her arms round his neck. He stepped back, aware that she was covered in mud and dead leaves, but her affection won him over and he wound his arms round her, lifting her off the ground, breathing in the scent of damp grass that clung to her hair. 'You're a darling,' she laughed into his neck.

'You're freezing,' he replied. 'I'd like to wrap you in a blanket and give you a cup of hot chocolate.'

'Is that all?'

'For now, yes. Got to go and collect your apprentice.'

'Is this really a good idea?' she asked, pulling away. 'You know I like to do the gardens on my own, and Hector helps with the weeding and mowing when I need him. We really don't need anyone else.'

'Shrub, we've been through this before. We're doing Jean-Paul's father a favour. After all Henri has done for me, I'm glad to have an opportunity to pay him back. Thanks to him, doors have opened for me the length and breadth of France. You're very gifted, Shrub. Jean-Paul will learn a lot from you. If he's going to inherit Château les Lucioles, he's got to know about running an estate.'

'Can't he just hire people to do it for him?'

'That's not the point. Henri wants him in the English countryside,

away from Paris. He's been allowed to do as he pleases there. Henri wants Jean-Paul to be inspired. Wants him to take responsibility. The château and vineyard are magnificent. Any man worth his salt would do all he could to keep Les Lucioles in the family.'

'I see.' She felt very unenthusiastic about it all.

'Besides, it will be good for the boys to have a young man about the place to rag around with. I'm an old father.'

'I keep you young,' Ava protested.

'That's true.' He chuckled. 'But I don't speak French.'

Ava smiled at him sheepishly. She spoke fluent French, having been sent to finishing school in Switzerland at sixteen. 'Now you make me feel guilty for not having spoken French to them,' she said.

'I'd never expect that of you, Shrub. I expect you to get up in the morning—the rest is a surprise!'

She smacked him playfully. 'You beast!'

'You haven't called me that for a while.' He kissed her forehead.

'I don't know what you're talking about.' She kissed him back, letting him go with a wide, loving smile.

She watched Phillip stride back across the lawn towards the house. How lucky she was to have everything she could possibly want: a husband who loved her, three happy children, the most beautiful house in England and her beloved gardens.

She was still working in the border when Phillip returned an hour later with Jean-Paul. Bernie and Tarquin shot round to the front of the house, barking loudly. She climbed out and wiped the sweat from her forehead as the scrunching of wheels on gravel came to an abrupt stop. She heard the opening and closing of doors, then her husband's voice greeting the dogs as if they were people. She hastened through the gate nestled in the yew hedge that hid the gardens from the front of the house. Phillip was opening the boot of his old Mercedes estate car. No sooner had he opened it than the two dogs jumped in. Jean-Paul looked on in amazement as they planted muddy paws all over his leather case. Phillip made no move to extract them. He just chuckled at the familiar sight, paying no heed to the young man's discomfort.

Ava watched Jean-Paul turn away from the car as she walked towards it. He was the most handsome young man she had ever seen.

'Hello, I'm Ava,' she said, wiping her hand on her dungarees before offering it to Jean-Paul. To her surprise he brought it to his mouth with a formal bow.

'It is a pleasure to meet you,' he said, looking her straight in the eye. His eyes were soft like brown suede, his gaze intense. She would have replied to him in French, but his English was perfect, although strongly accented, containing within it all that was romantic and sensual about his country. She felt something flutter inside her stomach.

'Did you have a pleasant flight?' she asked.

'I arrived in London a few days ago. I wanted to experience a little culture before I came down here,' he replied.

Phillip carried Jean-Paul's case towards the house, and Ava and Jean-Paul followed him in through the porch.

Jean-Paul was not at all what Ava had expected. First, he didn't look like a gardener. He was beautifully dressed in a soft tweed jacket, blue shirt and pressed jeans. His hair was thick, the colour of chestnuts, his nose aquiline, his mouth asymmetrical and sensitive. His hands were clean, nails tidy, not the hands of a man used to digging. On his feet were Gucci loafers. She hoped he had gardening boots.

They sat on stools in the kitchen while Ava prepared lunch. She had gathered leeks and sprouts from her kitchen garden and bought trout from the fishmonger. She grew herbs against the garden wall in an old water trough and had made basil butter and broad-bean hummous to eat with homemade rosemary bread. She adored the smell of healthy cooking and gained great satisfaction from watching her children grow strong on her own produce.

On first meeting Ava, one would never imagine she was shy. Phillip knew she entertained in order to hide her shyness and he loved her for it. She always rose to the occasion, telling witty stories and making people laugh, only to disappear afterwards into blissful solitude in her garden, depleted after having given so much of herself. Now she began to chatter away to Jean-Paul, who looked at her with an arrogant expression, as if she were an eccentric relative to be tolerated. He listened and smiled politely, but not with his eyes, until they all moved to the table for lunch.

'So, Jean-Paul,' she said, passing him a dish of steaming vegetables. 'I hear your family has a beautiful garden in France?'

'Yes,' he replied, picking up the spoon and helping himself. 'We have a château near Bordeaux. My mother loves gardens and I admire what she has done there. One day I will create a beautiful garden of my own.'

'So what do you hope to learn here?'

He shrugged. 'Papa says that yours is the best he has ever seen.'

'I wish I had met him. He popped in once, about eight years ago when I was away visiting my mother. I'm surprised Phillip showed him the estate beyond his wine cellar.'

'Darling, there is nothing nicer than walking round your gardens with a glass of wine,' responded Phillip with a chuckle.

'He says you have a great talent,' Jean-Paul continued. Ava was flattered in spite of an uneasy twist in her gut. As attractive as he was, she simply couldn't see them working together.

'Have you left a girl behind in Paris?' Phillip asked with a grin.

Jean-Paul smirked and raised one eyebrow. 'A few,' he replied.

'Oh dear,' said Ava, bristling at his arrogance. 'I hope you don't suffer from a broken heart.'

'I have never suffered in love,' he said. 'My heart will break when my mother dies. That is inevitable.' She looked at him quizzically. It was a strange comment for a man of his age to make.

'You are obviously close.'

'Of course. I am her only child. I am spoilt and indulged. My mother is an incredible woman. I admire her.'

'I hope our sons feel that way when they are your age,' she said, though she wasn't sure whether she really did.

'You have three children, yes?'

'Two boys and a girl. You'll meet them later today when they come home from school.'

'It must be nice to have siblings.'

'They fight a fair bit. None of them really likes to share. Jean-Paul, your English is perfect. Where did you learn to speak it so well?'

'I grew up with an English nanny.'

'An English nanny?' Ava repeated. 'What was she called?'

Jean-Paul gave the most enchanting smile. 'Nanny,' he replied and laughed heartily. 'I never knew her real name.' He looked bashful. 'She left when I was twenty-one.'

Later, while Jean-Paul was unpacking in his attic bedroom, Ava confronted her husband in his study. 'It's never going to work,' she protested. 'You can tell he's never done a day's labour in his life. What on earth is his father thinking, sending him here? If he was eighteen, and fresh out of school, I would understand. But he must be in his late twenties. What am I going to do with him for a year? He's going to be bored stiff in Hartington. I can't imagine him picking up girls in the Duck and Dapple. It's hardly buzzing. He should be in London with

other young people, not with me and the children. God, it's a disaster!'

Phillip put his hand on her shoulder and smiled. 'Don't worry, Shrub, it'll work out. A bit of hard labour will do him good. You'll have an extra pair of hands and you can create all those wonderful gardens you've been longing to make but couldn't do on your own.'

'He's more suited to a yacht in St Tropez than to a lawn mower here in Hartington. He's just not what I expected.'

'What did you expect?'

She turned away and walked over to the window. Grey clouds were gathering. 'I don't know.' She sighed. 'Someone less smooth. With rough hands and dirty fingernails like mine. In boots and grubby trousers. Not a dapper city swinger in cashmere and Gucci loafers, for God's sake.' She shook her head at the absurdity of it. 'He'll last a week!'

Phillip chuckled. 'I think you'll inject him with enthusiasm and he'll stay for ever.'

'I hope to God he doesn't. I don't think *I'll* last more than a week.'

Ava picked the children up at 3.30. She parked her yellow car on the green and stepped out of it just as it was beginning to drizzle. Toddy Finton was there with her ferret, Mr Frisby, sitting obediently on her shoulder. She had twin boys in the same class as Angus.

'Hi, Ava,' Toddy said, her cheeks pink from having spent the morning hacking across the countryside on her chestnut mare.

'Hi, Toddy. How's Mr Frisby?' She stroked him under the chin.

'A bit dozy. It's the weather.'

'It makes Tarquin snuggle up in front of the Aga. Bernie just lies outside, enjoying the cold. Like me, I suppose.'

'Can I send the twins over to you this weekend, Ava? They tell me they've built a camp in a hollow tree.'

Ava smiled. 'The oak, the perfect place for a camp. I'm going to grow a wild-flower meadow there. Cowslips, violets, dandelions, red and white campion. I've got someone to help me. A young Frenchman.'

Toddy raised her eyebrows. 'Is he gorgeous?'

'Yes, but much too young and arrogant for my taste. Actually, I think he'll be bored and go home. Still, I'll use him while he's here.'

'I love the idea of a wild-flower meadow. It'll be pretty in spring and lovely to look out over from your bedroom window.'

'That's the idea. And why don't you bring the twins over tomorrow?' Ava suggested, then narrowed her eyes, scheming. 'In fact, you could do me a favour.'

'What's that then?'

'Take Jean-Paul out for a ride. Then I can get into the cottage. I'd for-gotten he was coming and it's a total mess. Why don't you all come to lunch? I'd be rather relieved to have your company, actually. I don't know what to talk to Jean-Paul about and Phillip isn't much help.'

'Fine. I'd love to come and check him out,' Toddy said. 'He might do for one of my cousins. They're in their early twenties and very pretty.'

'Good. That'll be a diversion. He considers himself something of a stud, I think.'

'That's the French for you.'

Ava recalled the way he had bent over to kiss her hand, looking up as he bowed, fixing her with those soft brown eyes. 'Yes, they can be quite charming, can't they,' she added drily. 'Charming but arrogant.'

Archie, Angus and Poppy stared at the stranger, mute with shyness. Archie was eight, tall like his father with his mother's green eyes. Angus was six, with the build of a little rugby player. He had dark hair and pale blue eyes, a wide, infectious smile and creamy, freckled skin. Poppy was only four, but strong in both personality and opinion. She always said exactly what she thought. With long dark hair, blue eyes, fine features and her father's classical face, she was the beauty her mother was not. Yet she was very much her mother's little girl, adoring fauna and flora and never feeling the cold. It could be said that she had inherited the best of both parents.

'Jean-Paul is going to be living with us for a while. He's going to help me design the most beautiful gardens in England,' Ava explained, feel-ing a fraud. She didn't believe him capable of designing so much as a cabbage patch.

Archie stared at his feet. Angus stifled a giggle. Finally Poppy spoke. 'You speak funny,' she said, screwing up her nose.

'I'm from France,' he replied.

'Are you going to play with us?' she asked.

Jean-Paul shrugged. 'I don't know. What do you like to play?' The boys looked at their sister in alarm. The last thing they wanted was a grown-up crashing in on their games.

'I like planting vegetables.'

'I like planting vegetables too,' he agreed.

'I have a marrow this big!' she exclaimed, holding her hands apart. 'He's called Monty and he's in bed with a cold.' Jean-Paul looked quizzi-cally at Ava.

'I'm afraid he's avoided the saucepan by becoming a friend,' Ava explained. 'He gets taken out in the pram and to Show and Tell on Fridays, if he's good.'

Jean-Paul's face melted into a wide smile that won over the children. Poppy ran out to fetch Monty and the boys grinned up at him, their shyness evaporating in the warmth of the Frenchman's charm. Ava was intrigued by how easily he was able to switch it on and off.

Poppy returned with a very large, dark green marrow. Jean-Paul took Monty and weighed him in his hands.

'He's very heavy for a baby,' he said to Poppy.

'He's not a baby,' she replied stridently. 'He's a marrow.'

'But of course. A baby marrow.' Jean-Paul looked a little alarmed.

Poppy took the marrow back and cuddled it. 'He's shy. You frightened him,' she accused.

'Shall we show Jean-Paul round the garden?' Ava suggested hastily. 'You boys can show him your hollow tree.'

Angus looked delighted, Archie less so. He wasn't sure he wanted a strange grown-up coming to their secret camp. 'Come on, Angus,' he said to his brother, tearing off before the adults had a chance to follow.

'They have much spirit,' said Jean-Paul, folding his arms.

'Why don't you put on some boots and a coat? It's rather wet.'

Jean-Paul left the room and returned a short while later with a pair of leather boots and a sheepskin coat.

'You don't expect to garden in those, do you?' she asked.

'Of course.'

'But they'll be ruined.'

He shrugged. 'Then I can buy a new pair.'

'Gracious! No point wasting good boots when you don't have to. As for the sheepskin, don't you have a scruffier coat?'

'No.'

Ava took a deep breath, gathered her patience and told him that they would go into the village and buy him boots at least. 'Tell me one thing, Jean-Paul,' she began, knowing that now probably wasn't the best time to ask him, but unable to wait. 'How much gardening have you done?'

He shook his head and grinned. She felt her annoyance fizzle away, disarmed once again by his smile. 'None. I have watched my mother in the garden all my life. But I have little practical experience.'

'Do you *want* to learn?'

'Of course. The gardens at Les Lucioles are my inheritance. I will leave at the end of the summer, taking away all that you have taught me.'

'And I get a spare pair of hands,' she said, wondering who would gain more from this unlikely partnership.

'I hope so,' he replied, his face breaking into a smile again. 'I hope to leave you with something special too.'

They walked out onto the terrace. Made of York stone and cobbles, and surrounded by vast urns of plants and clumps of *alchemilla mollis*, it extended into a stone path planted with thyme and lined with topiary balls of ragged yew. The stones were dark and damp from dew, the grass glistening in the orange-pink light of late afternoon. At the end of the thyme walk, beyond the old, neglected dovecote, they could see a field of cows and the woods beyond, where beech and hazel trees were beginning to turn yellow and scatter the ground with leaves. Jean-Paul gazed around him. 'It's very beautiful,' he said in a quiet voice.

'Thank you,' Ava replied. 'I like it.'

Poppy followed them down the thyme walk to the dovecote, chattering away to Monty. She skipped through the hedges, her ponytail flying out behind her as she weaved in and out. Bernie and Tarquin had heard the children's voices from Phillip's study and galloped out to join them. Ava was surprised to see Jean-Paul transfixed by the dovecote. It was a round stone building painted white, with a pretty wooden roof sweeping up into a point like a Chinese hat. 'Pigeons live there now,' she said. 'We've never done anything to it.'

'And you mustn't,' he said, placing his hand against the wall in a caress. 'It's enchanting just the way it is.'

'These surrounding maples will turn the most astonishing red in November. Can you see they're just beginning?' She plucked a leaf and handed it to him and he twirled it between his fingers. They turned left and strolled past a copse of towering larches, their leaves the colour of butter. There was a long wall lining the lawn where Ava had planted the herbaceous border. 'I've been busily cutting it back,' she told him. 'Putting it to bed for the winter.'

'There is much to do, eh?' he mused.

'Much to do.'

Poppy was keen to show him the vegetable garden, hidden behind an old stone wall where roses grew in summer among honeysuckle and jasmine. The door was stiff. Poppy pushed as hard as she could, but it wouldn't budge. Jean-Paul leant against it with his shoulder. 'Is this your favourite part of the garden?' he asked her.

'Monty's favourite, because all his friends live here.'

'I cannot wait to meet them.'

'They might have gone away. Mummy says we have to wait until next year. They come back in spring.'

'Then I will have to wait for spring. I hope Monty doesn't get sad.'

'Oh, no,' she whispered secretively. 'He's only a marrow.'

The door swung open, leading into a large square garden, divided by gravel paths and box-lined borders, where an abundance of vegetables grew. The walls were heavy with the remains of dying clematis, roses, wisteria and honeysuckle. The dogs rushed in, squeezing between their legs and the door post.

'We harvest quite a crop in here,' Ava said, watching her daughter skipping ahead up the gravel path towards the patch where marrows had grown all summer. She led him under the tunnel of apple trees, where ripe red fruit was strewn all over the ground. Jean-Paul bent down and picked one up, taking a bite. 'It's sweet,' he said.

'The best are those already nibbled by insects,' said Ava. 'They have the nose for the tastiest fruit.'

'I hope I don't bite into a wasp!'

'You'll know all about it if you do! But I don't think there are many wasps left now. Hector is good at finding the nests and destroying them.'

They left the vegetable garden and wandered through the archway in the hedge. In the centre of the field an old oak tree stood like a galleon in the middle of a sea of grass. 'This is where I want to plant a wild garden,' she said, imagining it full of colour in spring. 'Beyond is the River Hart and your cottage.'

'May I see it?'

'I'd rather not show it to you until I have cleaned it. I'm ashamed.'

He looked at her, his eyes twinkling with amusement. 'Why would you be ashamed? I am only a gardener.'

She couldn't help but smile back at him. 'You're not a gardener yet,' she replied drily. 'I've never seen a gardener in cashmere.'

'Don't judge people by how they look.' He gazed over to the tree, where two pink faces peeped out of a hole in the trunk. 'There is the hollow tree,' he said, striding across the grass. 'It's magical!' Ava watched him with a frown. There was something very curious about him.

Archie and Angus disappeared inside the tree when they saw the grown-ups approaching. Poppy ran in front, shouting at the boys to let her in. 'They're coming, they're coming!' she cried, her voice sending a couple of partridges into the sky. She climbed in through the opening cut into the bark. Jean-Paul patted the tree as if it were an animal. 'This is a beautiful old oak,' he said.

'I love it!' Ava exclaimed. 'An old friend. Imagine what this tree has seen in its lifetime.'

'What would human beings have done without trees, eh?' He stood back to take in its glorious height. 'No trees, no fuel. No fuel, no smelting. So, no Bronze or Iron Age. No wood, no ships, no travel overseas. No empires. Perhaps no civilisation at all.'

'We'd still be living in caves,' said Ava with a smile.

'I think your children would be all right,' he chuckled, bending down to look in on them. They sat in the dark like three little pirates. 'Is there room for me?'

'No, go away!' they shouted, squealing with pleasure. 'Help! Help! It's Captain Hook!'

Ava left the children in the tree and took Jean-Paul to the orchard. There were plum trees, apple trees, pear trees and peach trees; it was a banqueting hall for wasps and bees. The sun hung low in the sky, glinting through the trees and casting long shadows over the grass, which was already glittering with dew. They wandered through the trees in silence, listening to the whispering sounds of nature.

'I love evening and morning the best,' said Jean-Paul, his expression settled once again into solemnity. 'I love the transience of it. The moment you appreciate it, it is gone.' He snapped his fingers.

'Come. Let me show you where I want to create the new garden. A cottage garden full of roses and campanula and daisies. I want tulips and daffodils in spring. I want a magical garden full of colour and scent. Somewhere I can sit in peace and quiet. An abundance of flowers.'

They arrived at an area of lawn enclosed on two sides by yew hedge. In the middle stood a solitary mountain ash. They stood at one end, watching the sun blinking through the branches of the yellow larches beyond. It was a large space, big enough to create something dramatic. 'It has a good feeling in here,' said Jean-Paul.

'Doesn't it,' Ava agreed. 'I've been wanting to do something with this for so long. The children play on the other side of the house or on the lawn by the herbaceous border. This is hidden away, like a secret.'

'It will be a secret garden.'

'I hope so. A surprise garden. Come on,' she said with a smile. 'Time for tea, I think, don't you? The children will be getting hungry now.'

That night Ava sat in bed with her book, *An Enchanted April*, but while her eyes scanned the pages, her mind was not on the words. Phillip sat beside her, his reading glasses perched on the bridge of his nose. He

always had at least four books on the go, placed in different parts of the house, so he never found himself with nothing to read.

'Darling,' Ava began, allowing her book to rest against her knees. 'I can't make Jean-Paul out. This afternoon I showed him round the gardens. On the one hand he's not really interested in plants, but on the other he's moved by the beauty of the gardens. He really loved the old dovecote and the oak tree.'

'What's wrong with that?' Phillip sighed, endeavouring to be patient.

'I don't know what makes him tick.'

'You've only known him for a day,' Phillip pointed out.

'You just don't see it, do you?'

'I don't think there is anything *to* see. He's not interested in plants but appreciates the beauty of the garden.'

She lifted her book off her knee. 'Don't worry, darling. Go back to your book.' Phillip smiled and began to read again. 'After all, I'm the one who's got to work with him and find him things to do. It's all very well your paying Henri back for helping you, but I'm the one with the responsibility.' She looked at him but his face was impassive. 'Oh, I'll shut up. Just remember my reservations when it all goes up in smoke and Henri closes all those doors the length and breadth of France.'

The following morning, Toddy kept her word and took Jean-Paul riding, leaving the twins with Archie, Angus and Poppy, playing around the hollow tree. Mr Frisby slept in the porch, curled up in an old jersey. Phillip had gone shooting for the weekend in Gloucestershire, taking Tarquin with him. Ava was left alone with Bernie and the children.

She took the opportunity to tidy the cottage. The last resident had been Phillip's bachelor brother, who had used it as a weekend home. He had finally married and bought a house near Sherborne, and Phillip had tried to rent the cottage out. He had put in a new kitchen and given everything a fresh coat of paint, but it had proved unpopular as there was no driveway. A tenant would have to park up at the house and walk across the field, which was a big inconvenience for both parties.

Despite that, Ava had always liked the pretty, isolated cottage, nestling beneath leafy chestnut trees, with pink and white roses that scaled the walls and tumbled over the front door in summer. Outside, the river flowed slowly beneath the stone bridge.

She made the iron bed with clean sheets and threw the bedspread into a corner to take back to the house to wash. She hoovered the carpets and polished the furniture, scrubbed the floor in the kitchen and

hall. She threw open the windows to let autumn imbue the rooms with the sweet scent of damp grass. Satisfied with a job well done, she stood a while to admire it. A few logs in the grate, a boisterous fire, a good book and some classical music and it would feel just like home. She smiled with pleasure, then left with the bedspread.

Toddy returned with Jean-Paul in time for lunch. The children had played all morning in the tree, finally running into the hall with muddy boots and red cheeks. Jean-Paul disappeared upstairs to change. Toddy rummaged about in the boot of her Land Rover for a pair of slippers. Mr Frisby woke up and scampered over the gravel to take up position round her neck. She let out a bellow of laughter as he nibbled her ear lobe. 'Did you miss me?' she asked, nuzzling him fondly.

Ava had roasted a couple of chickens. She stood by the Aga making gravy, while the children jostled each other over the sink, fighting to wash their hands. Toddy came in and helped herself to a glass of apple juice from the fridge. Her black hair was short and spiky from having been trapped under her riding hat, her face flushed from the wind. She sidled up to Ava. 'Jean-Paul's rather dishy,' she whispered, her eyes shining. 'Fine figure of a man on a horse. He reminds me of a polo player I had in the Argentine before I married.'

'Curb your excitement. The last thing his ego needs is someone like you fancying him. Though I dare say he's probably worked it out already.'

'There's no harm in a little window-shopping. I'm not intending to buy.' She leant back against the Aga to warm her bottom. 'He doesn't look like your average gardener, does he?'

'Do you see what I mean? He's too neat and tidy.'

At that moment Jean-Paul appeared in the doorway. He had changed into jeans, a pale blue shirt tucked in to reveal a leather cowboy belt. Toddy gave Ava a look, which she chose to ignore. 'Right, children, to the table, please.' The children clambered onto the banquette. 'Jean-Paul, please help yourself to a drink. They are in the fridge or in the larder out there,' she instructed, pointing to a door leading off the kitchen. 'Glasses in the cupboard. Did you have a good morning?'

'Fantastic!' he exclaimed. 'We rode up on the hill, so high we could see the sea.'

'We galloped over Planchett's plateau,' Toddy added, putting down her glass so she could help dish up. 'Big Red went like the clappers, but I knew Jean-Paul would handle him. I wasn't worried.'

'I was, a little,' Jean-Paul admitted with a grin. 'He's a strong horse.'

Both women wavered, spoons in the air, disarmed by the allure of his smile. Hastily, Ava dug her spoon into a dish of steaming peas.

Jean-Paul handed out the plates, helped the children to ketchup and gravy, then made himself busy carving chicken for the three adults. The children were sitting quietly, already eating their food.

'Jean-Paul, you're a natural!' gushed Toddy, taking a plate and helping herself to some slices of chicken. 'If you get bored over here you can always come and help out at Bucksley Farm.'

'This household is very English,' he replied, smiling at Ava. 'If it continues like this, I think boredom will be the least of my problems.'

'I've finished tidying the cottage,' Ava said, sitting down with her lunch. 'I'll take you there this afternoon. Then you can come and go as you wish. It'll be your home for as long as you are here.'

'You are very generous.'

'And you can come out riding with me whenever you want,' Toddy interjected. Then, responding to a look from Ava, she added, 'I have some pretty cousins, about your age, who live nearby. They'd be good company for you. If you prefer, you can ride out with them.'

'I have a lot of choice,' he replied, taking a mouthful of chicken. 'Ava is a marvellous cook!' He nodded appreciatively. 'Everything you prepare is delicious. I don't think I want to live in the cottage after all!'

Ava was flattered. 'You can have lunch and dinner with us whenever you like.' She doubted he'd want either once he had settled in the cottage.

After lunch they all walked through the field to the river to show Jean-Paul his new home. The children played on the bridge, throwing twigs into the water. The air was damp, the sky grey on the horizon. It would rain later.

'I haven't done anything about firewood,' Ava told Jean-Paul. 'But the barn is full of logs. Take as many as you need. There's a cart you can fill and pull down here. If you wait until Monday, Hector will help you.'

'Don't worry, I can do it myself.'

'It's going to pour,' said Toddy, thinking of her horses out in the field. 'I suggest you stay at the house tonight, Jean-Paul, and move into the cottage tomorrow. You can take my car into the village on Monday and buy everything you need. Fred the milkman comes daily and Ned the bread man comes three days a week. I have an account with both. Please feel free to order whatever you require.'

At the sight of the cottage Jean-Paul's face widened into a broad smile. 'I will be happy here, for sure,' he said, striding towards it.

Toddy nudged Ava. 'Won't be going home then,' she chuckled.

'Or to live with you,' Ava replied. 'Bad luck!'

They joined him as the first drops of rain began to fall. Ava fished in her trouser pocket for the key. The door opened with a whine and they walked inside. The children remained outside on the bridge, watching the rain create patterns on the water.

Inside it was warmer. The air was perfumed with wood polish and pine-scented floor cleaner. Upstairs, the windows were still open. A draught hurtled down the staircase. They took off their boots and Ava ran upstairs to shut out the rain, while Jean-Paul and Toddy went into the sitting room.

As Ava closed the window, the sky suddenly opened, throwing out buckets of rain. The children all squealed like startled mice and she watched them scampering off in the direction of the hollow tree.

Then, in the midst of the rain, the clouds parted and the sun unexpectedly shone through, setting the sky alight with the most beautiful rainbow. The sunshine flooded her spirit with joy and she was at once gripped with the need to share it. She ran downstairs.

'Hurry, outside!' she yelled, her voice quivering with excitement.

Toddy and Jean-Paul appeared in the hall. 'What's going on?' Toddy demanded, her thoughts turning immediately to her children. She had a vision of them drowning in the river.

'A rainbow!' Ava replied, opening the door. 'You've got to see it.' She struggled into her boots and dashed outside. She could feel the rain dripping down her neck but she didn't mind. It was worth it. She had never seen a rainbow so clear that she could pick out every colour, even the elusive pink that sits between green and turquoise and is usually so blurred as to be hidden altogether.

She looked at Jean-Paul and caught him looking at her. She smiled, masking the unease she felt beneath the intensity of his stare.

'Wow! That's impressive!' Toddy exclaimed, wrapping her coat tightly about her. 'Can we go back inside now?'

'You go. Take Jean-Paul with you. I want to stay here until it goes,' Ava replied.

Toddy hurried back to the cottage and Jean-Paul was left with no option but to follow.

Ava walked over to the bridge where she stood in the rain, glad to be alone. Here on the bridge, alone with the elements, she felt better.

Finally, the rain became a light drizzle and the rainbow faded. Toddy and Jean-Paul emerged from the cottage and she turned towards them.

'I think a cup of tea would warm us all up, don't you, Ava?' said Toddy, setting off towards the house.

'I bet the children hid in the hollow tree,' Ava said. 'They're probably as dry as little moles.'

She was right. They saw the grown-ups approaching and Poppy spilt out. 'Did you see the rainbow?' she cried. 'It was enormous!'

Ava took her hand. 'Did you see pink?'

'Yes!' Poppy listed the colours one by one. 'Pink and green go together, don't they, Mummy?'

'You're right, darling. Pink and green go together. They are my favourite colours.' She turned to Jean-Paul. 'Next time, look out for pink. It's there, but you really have to look for it.'

'Like beauty,' he said. 'Beauty is in everything if you really look for it.'

'That's open to debate,' interjected Toddy. 'I look for it every morning in the mirror but it still eludes me.'

'I think your children see it every time they look at you,' said Jean-Paul. Toddy looked embarrassed. 'Your own beauty is not yours to find,' he continued.

Ava walked on, still holding her daughter's hand. She was certain that Jean-Paul had found his own beauty in the mirror a long time ago.

That night Ava laid two places for dinner at the kitchen table. She busied herself cooking a lasagne so that she didn't have to look at them. Those two place settings made her feel anxious, as if she were on a first date. It was years since she had eaten alone with a strange man. It didn't feel right. Had Jean-Paul been plain or gauche, it wouldn't have mattered. The fact was, he was handsome. Worse, he was *predatory*. Her stomach twisted with nerves. What on earth was she going to talk about? She decided not to have pudding. That way dinner would be short and she could leave him in the sitting room watching *Dallas* and go to bed. She contemplated keeping Archie up, but that might look odd. She didn't want to behave like an inexperienced twenty-something. Finally, she put the place settings on trays and decided they could both eat in front of the telly.

To her surprise, Jean-Paul left straight after he had eaten. He said he was tired and thanked her for a magical day. 'I have already learned a lot,' he told her. Then, with a smile that made Ava regret her churlishness, he added, 'I have learned to look out for pink. Next time I see a rainbow I will look harder.' With that, he took her hand and brought it to his lips in the same formal way with which he had first greeted her.

The following day, Jean-Paul moved into the cottage. Ava took the children to church in the morning and she didn't see him all day. Hidden away on the other side of the river, he kept himself to himself, though he did borrow her Morris Minor. He said he wanted to explore the neighbourhood. Ava didn't think he'd be too impressed.

After lunch, wearing an old pair of jeans and shirt, her hair piled on top of her head and held in place with a pencil, Ava pottered about the garden while the children played on the lawn. It was an unusually warm October day, the temperature rising to twenty degrees. Poppy discarded her clothes and ran about in her pants. The boys dragged all the terrace cushions out of the shed and made a castle on the grass.

Bernie lay under an apple tree, sleeping through the whoops of laughter echoing across the lawn. He woke a few minutes before Phillip's car could be heard coming up the drive. Ears pricked, he sat up, then galloped down the lawn to the archway cut into the hedge and bounded to the front of the house. The children followed excitedly.

By the time Ava reached him, Phillip was holding Poppy in his arms, patting Bernie and listening to his sons' breathless chatter.

'Hello, Shrub!'

'Hello there, you!' she replied, looking at him coquettishly.

'I've brought back a brace of pheasants.'

'Wonderful! And Jean-Paul has moved into the cottage.'

'Ask him to join us for dinner, then. More the merrier.' Ava was disappointed. She had hoped they could enjoy a quiet meal together.

'I haven't seen him all day. I think we should leave him in peace,' she replied. No sooner had she uttered those words than Jean-Paul came striding up the field in a pair of new Wellington boots.

'Jean-Paul!' Phillip greeted him warmly. 'I hear you have moved into the château!'

Jean Paul grinned. 'And I had to buy these boots to get there. Luckily, that little shop by the church was open. It has everything.'

Ava's heart sank. She knew Phillip was going to ask him for dinner and that he would accept.

'Would you like to join us for dinner?' Phillip asked. 'I've brought back a brace of pheasants. Ava's a splendid cook.' Poppy wriggled down and followed her brothers back onto the lawn.

'I would love to, thank you,' Jean-Paul replied.

Infuriated by her husband's lack of sensitivity, Ava turned on her heel and followed the children, leaving the two men talking like old friends.

On Monday morning, Ava introduced Jean-Paul to Hector. She was relieved to see that the Frenchman was wearing his boots and was dressed appropriately in jeans and a country shirt in muted colours.

Hector was in his sixties, dressed in the same tweed cap and waistcoat he had worn for as long as Ava had known him. His face was gnarled like an old tree, his eyes bright as new conkers. He spoke with a strong Dorset drawl, curling his Rs as tight as pigs' tails. If Jean-Paul managed to understand half of what Hector said it would be a miracle.

'Could do with a little help in the garden,' he said, unsmiling. Hector rarely smiled. 'Especially as them leaves are coming down quicker than I can rake them up.'

Jean-Paul spent all day raking leaves, mowing grass, cutting down a dead pear tree and clearing away the debris of a plentiful summer. By midafternoon, he looked done in.

'I think it would be a good idea for you to work with Hector all this week. Get to know the place a bit,' Ava suggested.

Jean-Paul was not amused. His face clouded but he made no complaint. '*Bon,*' he said briskly. 'If that is what you want.'

'I do,' she replied. 'And you'll get very fit.'

'I'm already fit.' He spat the words, flashing his eyes at her angrily. 'I'm going to light the bonfire. I was wondering whether the children are home. They might like to help me.'

'I'm going to pick them up from school now. I'm sure they'd love to help. Have a cup of tea in the kitchen.'

He shook his head.

'No. I have a few more loads to take to the fire.'

'I'll send the children up with marshmallows.'

'Marshmallows?'

'You don't know what they are?' He shook his head. 'Then it will be a surprise. They'll love showing you.' She smiled at him, but he did not return the smile.

She drove to school, justifying the jobs she had made Jean-Paul do. If he was sulky in sunshine, what was he going to be like in rain and snow? She consoled herself that he wouldn't last until winter.

The children were thrilled at the prospect of showing Jean-Paul how to roast marshmallows. Back at home they ran to the vegetable garden where Hector and Jean-Paul were standing in front of an enormous mountain of leaves and cardboard boxes. The sky had clouded over and it was getting cold. Ava followed with the bag of marshmallows.

'I want to show him!' cried Poppy, skipping up to her mother. 'Please, can I!'

Ava opened the packet and handed her daughter a pink marshmallow and stick. 'All right, but let me help you,' she said, taking her hand.

Jean-Paul watched the boys take a handful of marshmallows each and accepted the one they gave him.

'You have to put it on a stick,' said Archie importantly. 'Otherwise you'll burn your fingers.'

'Thank you,' said Jean-Paul. 'I would not want to burn my fingers.'

'Watch!' Poppy shouted, holding her marshmallow in a bright yellow flame until it caught a little flame of its own. 'See!' she hissed excitedly.

'Right, you can take it out now,' said Ava.

'Blow, Mummy!'

Ava brought it to her mouth and blew. It had melted into a sticky, sugary ball. She blew again, then handed it to her daughter.

Poppy smiled in delight. 'Yummy!' she exclaimed.

'Have a go,' Ava said to Jean-Paul. 'Consider this your initiation into the garden. If you pass this test, you can be a member of our club.'

Jean-Paul held his marshmallow over the fire while the boys shouted instructions at him. The Frenchman indulged them, doing as he was told, asking questions to make them feel important. Ava noticed how much the children enjoyed having him around, especially the boys.

They ate all the marshmallows and then Jean-Paul suggested they play a game. 'If this is my initiation into *your* club, then you have to be initiated into mine,' he said seriously.

Ava watched in astonishment as he began to dance round the fire making whooping noises with his hand over his mouth. His unbuttoned shirt blew about his body illuminating his skin in the firelight. He lifted his feet and jumped about, pretending to be a Red Indian. The children joined in, following Jean-Paul closely, copying his erratic movements, their small figures casting eerie shadows on the garden wall. Ava roared with laughter and clapped her hands.

That evening, she was sorry Jean-Paul didn't come for supper. She had seen a different side of him. She thought of him in the cottage and wondered whether he was lonely. She resolved to remind Toddy to introduce him to her cousins. He'd appreciate the company of girls his age.

The next few days Jean-Paul continued to work with Hector while Ava busied herself in the borders. She tried to work out how she was going to plant her cottage garden, tried to imagine it, but nothing came.

On Wednesday, after Jean-Paul had declined her third invitation for dinner, and she had eaten alone, she decided she was being unfair. He had come to help her, but she couldn't send him off to work with Hector all day. That wasn't keeping her side of the bargain.

She walked across the field towards the river. She wasn't going to apologise, but she was going to ask his advice on the cottage garden. Perhaps he would have ideas. She hadn't given him a chance.

The bridge looked silver in the moonlight, straddling the river that trickled gently in the silence. She loved the night, and her spirits rose as she approached the cottage. The lights were on, the smell of smoke scenting the damp air with nostalgia. She stood a moment, enjoying the romance of it. Then she knocked on the door.

Jean-Paul's face blanched with surprise when he saw her. She wore only a T-shirt under her purple dungarees and seemed not to feel the cold. He shivered as the wind swept into the hall. 'Come in,' he said, standing aside. She took off her boots and walked into the sitting room. There was a fire in the grate, and a box of paints and glass of murky water on the coffee table. She hadn't imagined he could paint.

He didn't offer her a drink, but stood in the doorway, waiting for her to speak. She crossed to the fire. 'I've come to ask your advice,' she said.

'Advice?' He looked unconvinced. 'Why would you want to do that? You clearly don't think I have anything to offer.' He flopped onto the sofa. He had bathed and his hair was still wet. His blue shirt, the sleeves rolled up, hung over his Levi's. He put his hands behind his head and stretched out his legs. 'You've sent me off with Hector. How do you know what I can do and what I can't do?'

'I don't,' she conceded. 'Let's be honest, shall we? You coming here was not my idea. It was Phillip's. I didn't want you. I didn't need any help. I'm more than capable of doing the garden on my own.'

'Then why are you here asking my advice?'

'Because I am at a loss and perhaps you can help me. You said yourself not to judge people. I judged you. I'm hoping I was wrong.'

'How can I help you?'

'The cottage garden.'

'Ah.' He sat forward and rubbed his chin. Ava felt a surge of relief. Her white flag had been accepted. 'The cottage garden,' he repeated.

'Yes,' she said. 'I've tried, but I can't picture it.'

'As it happens, I have had some thoughts. I have painted something for you,' he said. He reached over the arm of the sofa and picked up a large ring-bound block of artist's paper. He placed it on her knee.

Ava gazed at it, speechless. There, in vibrant colours, was a picture of her cottage garden. A grassy path snaked across it, bordered on both sides by flowers and shrubs. In the middle was the mountain ash, encircled by a pretty round bench in French grey. It was perfect. She could not have dreamt of a more beautiful garden.

IV

HARTINGTON HOUSE, 2005

It was then that I realised MF wasn't so very different from me. We were two artistic people, yearning to create something beautiful . . .

MIRANDA'S EYES STUNG with tears. Folded in half and stuck to the page was a picture of the cottage garden. She ran her fingers across the paper and imagined the dawning of love. For a moment she felt a wave of melancholy at the emptiness in her own heart and focused all her attention on the picture. That bench was still circling the mountain ash. She wondered whether they had sat there, creating the gardens together, their affection growing with each plant they sowed. Perhaps Jean-Paul could resurrect that garden and breathe life back into it.

Although there were no names in the scrapbook she assumed the book belonged to the previous owner, Mrs Lightly. Little was written about the physical aspects of 'MF'. Much was written about his nature: a creative young man, one moment smiling and joyous, the next sullen and petulant. She wondered why Mrs Lightly had left the book in the cottage. Perhaps she had felt the affair was best left in the past.

Miranda flicked through the pages, pausing occasionally to dwell on pressed leaves and flowers, and the sentences written beside them in Mrs Lightly's pretty looped writing. The love story held such allure, but Mrs Underwood was coming at midday and she didn't have time to linger over it. She closed the book reluctantly and left the cottage with it tucked under her arm.

As she made her way up the field towards the house, she saw Mrs Underwood's car parked on the gravel. Ranger was cocking his leg on one of the tyres while Mrs Underwood waited on the step, arms crossed

over the buttress of her expansive bosom, her face sagging in repose.

'Hello!' Miranda shouted, quickening her pace. 'I'm so sorry, I've been delayed. Got to sort out that cottage for the gardener.' She checked herself, remembering the woman's husband. 'The *landscape* gardener.' Mrs Underwood nodded. 'I haven't seen Mr Underwood yet, I assume he's in the garden.'

'Oh, aye, keeping himself busy, I should imagine. Hard to keep that man down.' Miranda unlocked the door and Mrs Underwood sighed. 'Sign of the times. In my day, no one locked their doors. We were in and out of each other's houses all day long. It's not like it was.'

'Well, you didn't have microwaves and email, mobile phones and satellite telly, did you? So, it's not all bad.'

Mrs Underwood looked appalled. 'What do you need all that rubbish for? They don't save time, just give you more time to fill up. In my day we all had time for a chat.'

Miranda thought it best not to argue. People like Mrs Underwood were content to sit in the past. She put the scrapbook in her study, then took Mrs Underwood into the kitchen to discuss wages and hours. She noticed Mr Underwood had filled the log baskets and lit the fires.

Mrs Underwood commented on it proudly. 'Mrs Lightly always had the fires lit. Not that she ever felt the cold. Oh no, Mrs Lightly wore short sleeves even in snow.'

Now Miranda's curiosity had been aroused, she wanted to know more about the woman in the scrapbook. 'Let's have a cup of tea, Mrs Underwood,' she suggested, pulling out a stool. 'What will you have? Earl Grey?'

'Allow me, Miranda. I can't sit like a pudding being waited on by my employer. It's not right.' She took the kettle from Miranda and held it under the tap. 'Besides, I've got to get to know the kitchen. It's changed since Mrs Lightly was here.'

Miranda sat on the stool. 'What was Mrs Lightly like?' she asked. 'I've heard all about her beautiful gardens but nothing about her.'

Mrs Underwood paused a moment. 'She was an original. God broke the mould when He made her. Mr Lightly was tall as a tree, with a big friendly smile. He was the sort of man who always had time to talk. Mrs Lightly, she was an eccentric. She'd come alive like a fire, telling funny stories and entertaining everyone, then she'd suddenly run out of fuel, make her excuses and leave. You always knew when she'd had enough. She'd be out in her garden, enjoying the silence. That's not to say she didn't love her children and Mr Lightly, but she wasn't a sociable person

like him. Mr Lightly liked having guests in the house, but she was happier when she had the house to herself.'

'What did she look like?'

Mrs Underwood plugged the kettle in and took two cups down from the dresser. 'She wasn't beautiful like you, Miranda. She was handsome, I'd say. Her features were so alive, her expression so kind and sensitive that she became beautiful the better you got to know her. Some people are like that, aren't they? Her hair was long and curly. She'd twist it up on the top of her head and stick a pencil through it, then spend all afternoon looking for her pencil.' She chuckled again. 'She was scatty. The house was full of clutter because she never put anything away. She had a wonderful sense of humour. Everything had a funny side, even the bad times. Though I don't imagine her finding a funny side to Mr Lightly's sickness. After that I didn't see much of them. She looked after him herself.' She shook her head, popping two tea bags into the pot. 'That's love, isn't it? If my old man got sick I'd do the same for him.'

Miranda knew instinctively not to mention the scrapbook. 'The cottage,' she began carefully. 'Who lived there?'

'Oh, I don't know.' Mrs Underwood looked puzzled. 'Mr Lightly's brother used it as a weekend cottage, but that was before I knew them. I think Mr Lightly tried to rent it out after his brother moved away. But it's very impractical being in the middle of a field.'

'Did you always cook for the Lightlys?'

'Not in the early days. They had an old cook called Mrs Marley. When she retired, I came to do the odd weekend. They had a lot of literary types down here from London. Mr Lightly was a famous writer, you know. I once read his name in the papers. He won all sorts of prizes. He was a very modest man, though.'

'What did he write about?'

'Wine. He spent a lot of time in France. He'd leave his wife alone in the house for weeks on end while he travelled to vineyards.'

'Ah, that would account for all those French books in the cottage.'

'Mr Lightly loved books. His study was full of them. I've only ever read one book: *The Secret Garden*. Mrs Lightly gave it to me. It took me weeks to finish. I'm ever such a slow reader. I prefer to sew. If I'm not cooking and growing my own vegetables, I'm doing my needlepoint.'

They drank their tea, agreed the terms of Mrs Underwood's employment and Miranda handed her a key.

'That'll suit me perfectly,' said Mrs Underwood. 'If you're looking for a cleaner, I know a lady who could do it. Fatima, mother of Jemal who

owns the convenience shop in the village. She's a good woman and hard-working.'

'How do I get in touch with her?'

'I'll be seeing her this afternoon. I'll give her your number.'

'Thank you. She sounds ideal. By the way, who's the local builder?'

'That'll be Derek Heath and his boys, Nick and Steve. You'd better give him a call right away if you want to get them before Christmas.'

'Are they reliable?'

'Reliable? Gold dust, that's what they are, gold dust! They're honest, hard-working lads and they get the job done.' She jotted the number down for Miranda. 'They used to do the odd thing for Mrs Lightly.'

Once Mrs Underwood had gone, Miranda telephoned Derek Heath on his mobile. To her surprise he said he could start in a week—the job he had booked had been cancelled. 'You're lucky,' he said in his country drawl. 'Or perhaps it's fate. I'm not a believer myself, but my wife is and she'd say it was definitely meant to be.' Miranda put down the receiver and thought of Jean-Paul. Was he fate too?

At five o'clock, Henrietta left Clare in charge of the shop to nip across the street to Troy's for her cut and blow-dry. She had felt low all day. Little by little, Cate's bitchiness had worn her down.

'It makes her feel better to put you down,' said Troy, settling her into the chair. 'I'm going to give you long layers, darling. It'll lift you. That Cate's a miserable old cow. She might make the best coffee in Dorset but she's as bitter as a bar of Green & Black's.'

'I'm not happy in my skin, Troy. I'd feel better if I had less of it!' She gave a weak laugh.

'There's too much pressure on women these days to be thin. Thin doesn't mean happy.'

'But it means married.'

'Not necessarily. There are plenty of men out there who like fulsome women. You're a nice height and have a gorgeous, voluptuous shape. You should celebrate your size. I'm going to give you a killer hairdo.'

'What's the point? There aren't any single men in Hartington.'

'I bet there's somebody here, right under your nose.'

'You?' She gazed at him longingly.

'If only,' he sighed. 'But you need a man to make love to you, not to put you on a pedestal and worship you while he makes eyes at the postman.'

'Not our Tony?'

'Not specifically, no. There has to be someone in Hartington. Isn't

that what happens in romantic novels? The heroine always ends up with the local man she'd never noticed before.'

'I'd make a good wife. I'd cook him delicious dinners, run him hot baths and massage his feet after a busy day. I'd give him roly-poly children and a bit of roly-poly myself. I'd make him happy. But if I don't find someone soon I'll ferment into vinegar.'

'You talk a lot of nonsense, Etta. You've got plenty of time. It'll happen and when it does I'll be more than a little jealous.' He watched her smile. 'God made me gay to torment me.'

'He made you handsome to torment me,' she giggled.

'At least we can laugh about it. That makes it bearable.' He bent down and planted a kiss on her exposed neck. 'I do love you, though.'

'I know. And I love you. Hell would be a place without you.'

Derek Heath began on the cottage the following week, with the help of his two sons and his older brother, Arthur, who came out of retirement to help. Miranda watched them tear out Mrs Lightly's memories and felt a moment's regret. This was 'their' cottage. It was where she had left the scrapbook. She couldn't help but feel ashamed of her callous disregard for the woman's past.

Fatima came for an interview. She was a big-featured woman with brown skin and small brown eyes, her head covered in a scarf. Before Miranda could explain what she wanted, Fatima silenced her with a sweep of her hand. 'I know how rich people like their houses cleaned,' she declared in a thick Moroccan accent. 'Fatima clean your house until it shine.' She flashed Miranda a wide smile. 'Fatima know.'

Miranda was left with no option but to hire her, then she returned to her desk to write an article on the joys of self-employment, wondering how other self-employed mothers managed to get anything done.

On Friday night, David arrived exhausted and in an ill temper. However, the fish pie Mrs Underwood had left for dinner transformed his mood and by the apple crumble he was almost jolly.

'Darling,' he said. 'Things are looking up! The fires are lit, dinner is delicious. Gus hasn't played truant all week.' He sat back in his chair. 'This is the life.' He patted his stomach. 'I'm going to have a bath and then I'll turn on the telly. See if there's anything worth watching.'

He left Miranda feeling a mixture of pride and resentment. The house was perfect but he hadn't asked about her, or about the children. She drained her wineglass and looked at the dishes David had left

on the table. Before she indulged in self-pity she remembered the scrapbook smouldering in her study. She wouldn't tell David. It would be her secret. She'd watch television with him and share his bed but, on Sunday night, when he left, she would have the scrapbook to curl up with and someone else's love to feast upon.

At the end of October, the cottage was finished and, late one afternoon, Jean-Paul returned to Hartington. Gus and Storm were on half term, hanging around the bridge, waiting for the enigmatic Frenchman to appear. Gus pretended he wasn't interested, throwing sticks into the water, but in reality he was curious and put out that Storm had met Jean-Paul.

When Miranda opened the front door her heart stalled a moment; he was even more handsome than she remembered. He stepped into the hall and took off his hat. His greying hair was tousled and he ran a hand through it, casting his eyes about the place.

'The children are waiting for you at the cottage,' she said. 'I've filled your fridge so I can offer you a cup of tea down there.'

'Good, then let's go.'

The sky was a deep navy, turning to pink and gold just above the tree line. The air was damp, the ground wet from a heavy shower that morning. Brown and red leaves gathered on the grass, blown about by the wind, and a couple of grey squirrels chased each other up the oak tree. Jean-Paul watched them and, for an instant, was sure he saw three little faces peering out like Red Indians in a tepee. But it was just the evening light filtering old memories; the oak tree was empty and silent.

They continued down the path to the bridge where Storm and Gus waited. When she saw him, Storm broke into a run, eager to show off to Gus. 'Mummy! Mummy!' she cried. 'I'm going to make magic in the garden!' Jean-Paul's face relaxed into an affectionate smile, the sight of the children putting right all that was wrong. 'We've tidied the cottage for you,' she said proudly, springing beside him like a kangaroo.

Gus remained on the bridge, watching Jean-Paul warily. The Frenchman sensed the boy's suspicion but nodded affably. He knew not to force his friendship. Gus would come when he was ready.

He watched as Miranda opened the door to the cottage with the same rusty key that Ava had used a lifetime ago. They had both been young then, neither knowing that they would forge a love so strong that in all the years that followed she would remain at the very centre of his heart like a thorny rose—beautiful but inflicting pain. The house

and the gardens remained, yet Ava had been the breath that had brought it all to life. Without her, the place was dead.

He stepped inside the cottage. There was a smell of fresh paint and polish—and the unexpected scent of orange blossom. He was aware that Miranda was expecting a reaction, but he wanted to be alone to retrace their every moment together. The afternoons they had made love on the sofa in front of the fire, the mornings they had crept beneath the sheets to hold each other for a few stolen moments, the terrible day they had sat staring at each other across the kitchen table, knowing it had come to an end.

He took off his coat and almost stumbled into the kitchen behind Miranda, where she put the kettle on to make tea. He saw that everything had changed. There were new units, a smart black Aga, grey floor tiles where there had been wood. Miranda looked at him anxiously. 'Do you like it?' Storm brought him a biscuit and the little girl's bashful smile soothed the cracks in his heart.

'I like it,' he replied.

Miranda's shoulders dropped with relief. 'I'm so pleased,' she said, taking cups down from the cupboard. 'I did a big shop for you. I didn't know what you'd want so I bought a bit of everything. Sainsbury's is a few miles out the other side of the village, past the castle. You can borrow my car to shop, if you like. I must take the children to the castle. I haven't had time yet.'

Jean-Paul remembered her using that excuse before. *Time.* He glanced at Gus standing shiftily in the corner and felt his loneliness; it leaked out of every pore. 'Will you show me where I will sleep?' he asked the boy. Gus shrugged and left the room.

'I'll show you!' Storm squeaked, hurrying out after her brother.

'But you gave him a biscuit,' retorted Gus angrily, grabbing her shirt.

'Let me tell you a secret,' Jean-Paul said calmly. Both children turned to stare at him. 'Come upstairs,' he added, striding past them. Once in the bedroom he opened the window. 'I think you will find there is a family of squirrels who think that this is their house.'

'I know,' said Gus, sitting on the bed. 'I've seen them.'

'You have?'

'This was my secret camp,' he said grumpily.

'I think you can do better than this,' said Jean-Paul. 'How about a camp in a tree?'

'A tree house?' said Gus, unconvinced.

'A tree house built in the branches so that in summer no one knows

you are there. A tree house that has an upstairs and a downstairs.'

'There isn't one of those here,' Gus scoffed.

'Not yet, but we will build it.'

'Can you do that?'

'Not on my own. But you and Storm will help me.'

'Mummy says you're the gardener,' said Gus.

'Isn't a tree part of the garden too?'

'The hollow tree!' Storm cried. 'But that's going to be *my* secret camp.'

Jean-Paul shook his head. 'Come here, Storm,' he said, beckoning her over. She stood before him, her bottom lip sticking out sulkily. 'Do you remember I told you about the magic in the garden?'

'Yes.'

'The magic works only when we all act together. Do you understand?' Storm frowned, Gus looked sceptical. 'Imagine what incredible things we can create together.'

'Can we build the tree house tomorrow?' Storm asked.

'I don't see why not,' said Jean-Paul. *We will breathe life back into the garden and the sound of children's laughter will once again ring out from the old oak tree. I cannot bring the love back but I can create new love. That is how I will remember her.*

Downstairs, Miranda had made the tea. She took it into the sitting room on a tray and lit the fire. She was pleased with the cottage. She had kept all the books and ornaments; Jean-Paul wouldn't know that they had belonged to Phillip Lightly. She hoped the children weren't bothering him. For a man who had no children of his own, he was very patient with Gus and Storm. She wondered again why such a handsome man had never married. Perhaps he had suffered a loss or tragedy.

After a while all three came downstairs. Jean-Paul sat beside the fire in the armchair that Miranda had had recovered in green ticking. She gave him a cup of tea and sat opposite him.

'The children are on half term this week. I hope they won't get in your way,' she said.

'Jean-Paul is going to build us a tree house,' said Gus, trying not to sound too excited in case it didn't happen. He was used to his father making promises he didn't keep. 'If he's not too busy,' he added.

Jean-Paul looked at him intently. 'Your tree house is at the very top of my list of priorities,' he said seriously. 'What is a garden without a tree house? What is a garden without magic? We have to build a tree house for the magic to work.' Storm giggled and Gus stared at Jean-Paul, who turned his attention to Miranda. 'I will walk round the garden

tomorrow and see what we can salvage, what needs to be cut back, what needs to be replanted. Already I can see the wild garden needs to be replanted so that it flowers in the spring.'

'Whatever you suggest.' Miranda didn't want to know the details. She just wanted it done.

'Is there a vegetable garden?' he asked, blinking away the sudden vision of Archie, Angus and Poppy dancing round the bonfire that autumn evening after roasting marshmallows in the flames.

'Yes, it's a mess.'

He turned to the children. 'Who would like to help me plant the vegetable garden in the spring?'

'Me, me!' Storm volunteered immediately. 'What shall we plant?'

Jean-Paul rubbed his chin in thought. 'Marrows, pumpkins, rhubarb, raspberries, strawberries, potatoes, carrots . . .'

'You're going to plant all those?' said Gus.

'Of course. With your help. After all, you're going to eat them.'

'I think that's a wonderful idea,' enthused Miranda. 'You'll meet Mrs Underwood. She cooks for us. There's nothing she likes more than fresh vegetables. There's a farmers' market in the village on a Saturday, though I'm ashamed to say I haven't been yet.'

'Then, what we don't eat we will sell.' Gus's eyes lit up. 'And you, Gus, can take a cut of the money.' Jean-Paul looked at Miranda for approval. She nodded. She could tell Gus was warming to Jean-Paul, in spite of himself. There was something compelling about the man, like the Pied Piper of Hamelin with his magic flute.

They finished tea and Miranda felt it wasn't fair to linger. 'I'm sure you want to settle in,' she said, standing up. 'We'll see you tomorrow.'

'I will assess the garden and let you know what is needed. Then we have work to do, no?' He spoke to the children.

'Our tree house,' said Storm happily. Gus said nothing. His head was buzzing with conflicting thoughts.

Jean-Paul stood in the doorway, watching them go, remembering the sight of Ava on the bridge gazing at a rainbow. Alone, in France, he'd searched for the pink in every rainbow, but it had always eluded him. He wondered whether it really did exist, or whether it was a figment of Ava's lively imagination.

Where is she now? He was too afraid to enquire. He didn't think he would have the will to go on if she had stopped loving him. He had come back for her, but she had gone. Perhaps that was a sign. If she still loved him she would have waited. She would have kept their garden

alive, not let it shrivel and die. There was no use searching for her, she obviously didn't want to be found.

He returned to the sitting room and began to move about, picking up ornaments, turning them over in his hands. To the uninitiated those objects meant nothing; to Jean-Paul they were tokens of love that Ava had given to him over the year he had lived there. A little enamel box in the shape of a bouquet of flowers, a china frog, a heart box containing a dried rosebud, a set of eight wooden apples, a crystal tree. He was heartened to find them there, along with all his books neatly arranged in the bookshelves. He hoped Ava might have kept them to remember him by but, with a sinking heart, he realised that she had left them behind with her memories, to die like the flowers in her gardens.

When Jean-Paul woke the next morning, it took him a moment to orientate himself. He opened his eyes to the familiar sight of the bedroom ceiling and heard the twittering birds in the chestnut trees outside, heralding the dawn. He lay there with nothing but a memory. It was a memory so strong he could smell the scent of damp grass in her hair, feel the softness of her skin, run his fingers down the smoothness of her face, hold her slim body against his and kiss her lips. Then the memory faded. Their cottage remained but her love no longer warmed it.

What did he hope to achieve? Surely it would be better to return to his château? He sat up and rubbed his eyes. How could he return now, without her? His whole life had been gradually moving towards this point. He had dreamt it, planned it, fantasised about it. He hadn't considered what came after. He got up and walked into the bathroom, where his reflection in the mirror stared back at him unhappily, his eyes raw, the shadows dark beneath them. He looked old. *Oh God, if nothing comes after, I can't go on. I can't live in nothing.*

He dressed, made himself a cup of strong coffee and left the cottage. It was a crisp morning and his breath rose on the air like smoke. The scent of damp earth was sweet on the breeze. Those squirrels, intrepid and mischievous, watched him walk over the bridge then made a dash for his bedroom window, only to find he had outwitted them and closed it.

He stood for a moment in the middle of the field that had once been Ava's wild garden. The oak tree dominated it like a small fortress. He would build the children their house and they would play in it, as Archie, Angus and Poppy had done. He crouched down and ran his hands through the wet weeds that grew in abundance. He'd have to

replant it so that in March it would dazzle with crocuses, cowslips, daffodils and buttercups. Ava had loved to see the flowers when she opened her bedroom curtains. He looked towards the house. It was bewildering to witness it belonging to another family, strangers using the rooms that had once been Ava's and Phillip's. It was far more splendid now than when it had belonged to them, and yet it had no soul.

He strode across the gravel to the archway in the hedge. There was now a smart black gate, its hinges oiled to perfection. The walled vegetable garden was, as he expected, neglected and overrun with weeds. The old brick wall was intact, but the borders were heaped high with dead flowers and bushes, the climbing roses falling away from the wall and drooping sadly. The box hedge that lined the vegetable patches was in need of a dramatic haircut. It wouldn't take long to tidy it all up and replant. They'd have vegetables in spring.

He wandered along the stone pathways that led through the vegetable patches. He was uplifted to see the arched frame that straddled the path still in one piece, though no sweet peas had flourished there that summer. He found Hector's old toolbox in one of the greenhouses, and Ava's gardening gloves and instruments beneath a table strewn with empty pots. It would be a challenge to sort the place out, but he'd do it for her.

The herbaceous border was as overgrown and ignored as the rest of the grounds, but he found a wheelbarrow full of dead branches at the far end, indicating that someone had already started work. He didn't imagine that was Miranda. She had the hands of a woman who had never done a day's digging—as clean and manicured as his had once been. Finally, he came to the dovecote. How often he had used it in his paintings, in the pink light of dusk, the pale liquid light of morning and the silvery light of a full moon.

Ava had been surprised to see that he painted. She had written him off as a shallow, spoilt young man, who drifted aimlessly through life. But he had been far from aimless; his longings were bullied into hiding by his controlling father. At Hartington he had been able to set them free: to paint without guilt, to create and be admired for it.

It wasn't long before the children found him. Jean-Paul greeted them with a smile, their presence in the garden banishing his sorrow like sunshine breaking through cloud.

'I am glad you are up,' he said, putting his hands on his hips. 'I thought I would have to start without you. We have lots of work to do.' He led them to the greenhouse, where they picked up tools Jean-Paul selected from Hector's box, then proceeded towards the hollow tree.

'It's completely hollow,' Storm cried, poking her head out at Gus. Her brother forgot his resentment and climbed in, as enthralled as she was.

'It's a real den,' he said, gazing round at the husk of bark that formed a perfect playhouse. 'We should find something to put on the ground. Something soft like hay. Jean-Paul!' Gus shouted, sticking his head out. 'Where can we find hay to put on the floor?'

'You won't find hay at this time of year. But wood shavings will do and I know just the place. We need wood for the tree house and a ladder. Come with me!'

They pulled their supplies in a cart across the field to the tree. Jean-Paul left the children in their den while he went in search of the ladder, kept in one of the greenhouses. When he got back, Miranda had emerged from the house and was watching the children. She had never seen them so animated. Not even *The Lord of the Rings* had put so wide a smile on her son's face.

When she saw Jean-Paul, she thrust her hands into her coat pockets and grinned. 'I see you've been busy,' she said, hugging her sheepskin around her. His eyes were drawn to her feet and she followed his gaze and grinned. 'You can take the girl out of London but not London out of the girl!' she laughed, knowing her open-toed heels looked ridiculous in the countryside.

'If they are going to help me in the garden, I have to bribe them with a house. I've looked round the garden and there is much to do. Who has been weeding in the border?'

'Oh, that's Mr Underwood. I've just hired him. He's helping out. You know, clearing up the leaves.' She didn't quite know what he did.

'He can help me then. I need more than one pair of hands. It is a big job. We need to get things cut back and replanted.'

He leant the ladder against the tree and scaled it, a plank of wood and bailer twine under his arm. He worked in shirtsleeves and jeans, moving from branch to branch as if trees were his natural habitat.

'Gus, pass me the hammer,' he instructed, pulling a nail out of his breast pocket and placing it between his lips. Gus scrambled out of the tree, then climbed the ladder with the hammer and passed it to Jean-Paul. 'Right, come up here and hold this plank still.' Gus glanced at his mother. She was looking up at him, her face suddenly serious.

Fuelled by his mother's attention and Jean-Paul's confidence in him, Gus did everything he was told with eagerness. Jean-Paul didn't treat him like a little boy, but as an equal, as capable of assisting as any man. He ran up and down the ladder with tools and passed him small planks

of wood. He watched as the Frenchman built a platform round the branches. Once that was secure, he built the walls, leaving gaps for two windows and a door. He made a proper roof using two boards of ply-wood he had found in the barn, and a sturdy beam. For the door he used part of an old cupboard that he knew had been Poppy's. Phillip had hated throwing things away, keeping the oddest assortment of objects in a shed attached to the back of the barn. Miranda was sur-prised Jean-Paul had found it. She didn't even know it existed.

She looked at her watch, aware that she should have been writing, but she was enjoying watching Jean-Paul entertaining her children.

'We will leave the ladder here for the moment,' Jean-Paul told Gus. 'Until we build our steps. For that we need the right size of wood. You can come with me and choose it. There must be a timber yard somewhere.'

'Mr Fitzherbert will know,' said Gus. 'He's our neighbour.'

'Then we will ask him,' said Jean-Paul, climbing down the ladder.

Gus remained on a branch, gazing over the treetops to where the spire of St Hilda's soared into the sky. 'Look! It's Mr Underwood!' he exclaimed, waving. 'Mr Underwood! I'm in a tree!'

Mr Underwood gazed up at the tree house. 'It's a palace!' he gasped, taking off his cap in homage.

'This is Jean-Paul, the landscape gardener,' said Miranda.

'Pleased to meet you,' said Mr Underwood. 'I've been doing a bit of clearing up,' he informed him importantly. 'There's a lot of work to be done in the garden. I'm glad there'll be the two of us.' Jean-Paul looked at the elderly man and recognised his need to feel useful.

'I'm glad to be of help,' he said. 'And we have two more helpers: Gus and Storm,' he added with a wink.

Miranda entered the silence of her study with reluctance, sat at her desk and switched on her computer. After a while she was absorbed by her emails and finally by her article, her fingers tapping over the keys.

That afternoon, Jean-Paul took Gus and Storm to buy seeds and on the way back they stopped at Jeremy Fitzherbert's farm. Jean-Paul doubted he would remember him. They had never been introduced. Jeremy's father, Ian, had run the farm back then.

Jeremy was in the workshop with his manager, discussing the need to replace the old Massey Ferguson tractor. When he saw the children standing in the doorway, he broke off his conversation and approached. Mr Ben trotted up to Gus and sniffed his boots, his thick tail wagging with excitement. They smelt of Ranger. 'Hi there,' Jeremy exclaimed.

'My name is Jean-Paul. I'm working for Miranda Claybourne up at the house.'

'Ah.' Jeremy nodded. 'These two helping you, are they?'

'They are. I couldn't do without them,' he replied, smiling.

Jeremy warmed to the Frenchman's grin. 'What can I do for you?'

'I need timber to make a ladder for the children's tree house. I thought you might know where I could buy some.'

'Buy some? Good Lord. You don't need to buy it. I have a barn full of timber. Come, I'll show you.' The two men walked through the farm, followed by the children and Mr Ben. It was exactly as Jean-Paul remembered it.

Jeremy's barn was full of timber, logs and hay bales. 'As you see, we've got more than we need. You'd be doing me a favour.' He looked at Jean-Paul. 'How are you finding it down there?'

'I only arrived yesterday.'

'Oh,' Jeremy replied, wondering what Miranda had hired him to do. 'They're nice people, the Claybournes.'

'Yes.' Jean-Paul rubbed his chin. 'I am the new gardener.'

'Ah,' said Jeremy sympathetically. 'You're taking on quite a legacy. Ava Lightly was a wonderful gardener.'

'I know.' He pulled a face. 'Do you know why the Lightlys moved?'

'Phillip had a stroke. I think the house became too much for them.'

'Do you know where they moved to?'

'No idea, I'm afraid. They went very quiet for a few years and then were gone without any fuss or fanfare. The village would have liked to say goodbye. They were very popular around here.' He hesitated a moment then added, 'And devoted to each other.'

Jean-Paul turned away, pretending to be looking for the children. He did not want Jeremy to see the pain those words had caused him. He gritted his teeth and tried to pull himself together, but a lump of grief had lodged itself in his throat. In an effort to dissemble he bent down to pat the dog. Mr Ben buried his wet nose in his hand and Jean-Paul rested his forehead against Mr Ben's. 'Beautiful animal,' he said.

'Mr Ben's rather special,' Jeremy replied with a chuckle. 'Wolfgang's a little long in the tooth these days. Spends most of the day asleep.'

Jean-Paul called the children and arranged to return later with a suitable vehicle to transport the timber. 'It's good to meet you,' said Jeremy. 'If you need help, I would be happy to lend you a few men.'

'Are those your cows down by the river?' Jean-Paul asked.

'Yes. Aberdeen Angus.'

'Storm's new friends.' He looked down at the little girl.

'I have horses. I've told Miranda, but if you and the children want to ride, let me know. Whisper's very docile.'

'That would be fun,' Jean-Paul replied.

'Good.' Jeremy watched them climb into Miranda's jeep. 'I hope to see more of you, then.'

WINTER

V

Hartington House, 1979

So began our project together. Darling Phillip was as thrilled as I; Henri would be pleased his son was getting involved and doors would continue to open the length and breadth of France. He returned to his study and buried himself in research. We were left to create our cottage garden. I didn't show Phillip the painting. It was so personal, so intimate, coming from the very core of MF, that I didn't feel it was right to share it with anyone. He had painted it for me and I was surprised and touched that he had taken the trouble to understand what moved me. It was the first secret I had ever kept from my husband. It would be the first of many . . .

AVA AND JEAN-PAUL set about digging the borders in the cottage garden according to Jean-Paul's painting. They marked out the path with sticks so that it meandered like a stream, wide enough for two people to walk together comfortably. The borders were to be edged with stones to allow the plants to spill over. Hector helped in his quiet, solemn way, and Ian Fitzherbert let them use his small tractor and trailer to carry away unwanted earth.

They ate sandwiches for lunch, sitting on a rug while Hector went to fetch his lunch box from the greenhouse.

'How can your father disapprove of your painting?' she asked Jean-Paul, biting into a turkey sandwich.

He shrugged. 'He wants me to be a reflection of himself. I am his only son. His only child. And I am realistic, Ava. I know I am not good enough to be an artist. Papa knows that too.'

'So, what does your father expect of you?'

'To run the vineyard. To uphold the family name. To inherit the

château and produce a son to pass it all on as he has done.'

'Couldn't you just tell him to bugger off? You're not a child.'

Jean-Paul looked troubled. 'I don't want to hurt my mother. I am all she has.' He held her a moment with his eyes. 'My father has a mistress in Paris. *Maman* lives in Bordeaux. The château means everything to her. The love she should be investing in my father she invests in me and Les Lucioles. It would break her heart if Papa disinherited me.'

'You are doing what he wants because of a château?'

'It's not just any château. It is as magical to me as Hartington House is to you. I agreed to come here because *Maman* asked me to.'

'Some people make their lives so complicated. I'm grateful for my simple life. It might not be spicy but it's tranquil.'

'You and Phillip are lucky. You have a good marriage.'

'I know.'

That afternoon, when the children returned from school, they came to watch their mother in the garden.

Phillip strode out, in a green Barbour and Wellies, to take the dogs for a walk. Bernie and Tarquin rolled about on the grass in excitement, their barking biting into the damp air. 'Don't forget your parents are coming for the weekend, Shrub,' he reminded her, as he set off.

'Phillip thinks I have no memory for things other than plants,' she told Jean-Paul with a chuckle. 'He thinks I inhabit another world. "Planet Ava!"'

'I'd like to live on Planet Ava,' he said.

'I don't think you would. It's a lonely planet really.'

'I like to be alone too.'

'Good. I won't worry about you in the cottage then. I was about to invite all Toddy's cousins over to meet you.'

'There's alone and lonely,' he said with a grin. 'I like to be alone, but I don't like to be lonely. If they are pretty, I would be happy to meet them.'

'All right, Mr Frenchman!' she said. 'I'll call Toddy. But if they're pigs don't blame me.'

Archie, Angus and Poppy helped load the cart with the turf that Ava and Jean-Paul cut with their spades, rolling it up like long carpets. When they grew bored of that game they searched for insects in the newly exposed soil, squeaking in delight when they found a fat worm or centipede. Ava had taught them to love all creatures, explaining their purpose in the garden and how they lived, so that the children respected them as living beings. 'Look Mummy! Here's a really juicy

worm,' cried Archie, placing it on a leaf and carrying it to his mother.

'He's delicious,' she agreed, stopping to look. 'Now, darling, find a nice place for him.' Archie did as he was told and settled the worm in the mud. Angus climbed onto the tractor and made purring noises, turning the steering wheel left and right, while Poppy pretended the rolls of turf were Swiss rolls on their way to the bakery. The garden rang with their laughter. For Jean-Paul it was a new and exciting world. He had no experience of a united and loving family.

That evening Ava invited Jean-Paul to stay for dinner. They sat in the drawing room, by the fire, having bathed and changed. The children were in bed. Phillip came downstairs in a smoking jacket and slippers, having read them *The Velveteen Rabbit*, and opened a bottle of wine.

'Your garden's beginning to take shape, darling,' he said, bringing in a tray of glasses. Ava sat on the sofa, her hair tied in a loose ponytail. She wore wide trousers under a long Moroccan housecoat and a pair of crimson sequinned slippers. Her cheeks glowed from having worked in the cold all day and her eyes sparkled with happiness.

'We'll plant it up next,' she said, grinning at Jean-Paul. 'Our reward will come in spring. It's going to look marvellous!'

'I never thought digging a garden would be fun,' Jean-Paul admitted.

'This is only the beginning. The planting is the fun part,' said Ava.

'What are you going to plant?' Phillip asked, handing them each a glass of wine, then taking a seat himself.

'I've drawn a sketch,' she said, pulling a folded piece of paper from her coat pocket. 'I want an explosion of colour.' She looked at Jean-Paul, knowing that he knew she was thinking of his painting. 'I thought buddleia, geraniums, roses, polyanthus, campanula, lavender, lupins, daisies, delphiniums. Goodness, I haven't held back.'

'It sounds marvellously chaotic. Rather like you, Shrub.' Phillip chuckled in his good-natured way.

'Mummy.' Poppy was standing in the doorway in her nightie, holding her marrow in a blanket. 'He can't sleep,' she said, hugging it close.

'Oh dear,' said Phillip, playing along. 'Have you tried rocking him?'

'Yes,' she said. 'But he keeps waking up. He keeps waking *me* up.'

'Come here,' said Ava, opening her arms. 'I think you need a cuddle, darling. It's not fun being kept awake by that naughty Monty, is it?'

Poppy shook her head. 'I'm very tired,' she said, shuffling over to her mother. Ava pulled the little girl onto her lap and wrapped her arms round her, kissing her temple. 'Daddy, if I love Monty like the little boy loved the velveteen rabbit, will he become real?'

'Ah,' said Phillip with a frown. 'I'm not sure the nursery magic extends to vegetables. That's a question for the vegetable fairy.'

'I so want him to be real,' she sighed.

'If you want him to be real, darling, he will be. He'll be whatever you want him to be. You just have to use your imagination,' said Ava.

'But I want everyone else to see that he's real.'

'We do,' Jean-Paul interjected, leaning forward and resting his elbows on his knees. 'To me, he's been real since I was introduced to him.' Poppy hid her smile behind the blanket.

'You see,' said Ava, kissing her again.

'I think you should take him back to bed,' said Phillip. 'He'll only be grumpy in the morning if he doesn't get his sleep.' Ava lifted Poppy off her lap and led her out of the drawing room. The child caught Jean-Paul's eye and smiled shyly.

Ava's parents, Donald and Verity, arrived on Friday night with their dog, Heinz, a red sausage dog with short scurrying legs. Verity was similar to her daughter, but her strident nature had been mercifully diluted in Ava. 'Did you know that Daisy Hopeton has left her husband and four children to run off with a South African who owns a vineyard?' she asked over dinner. Ava's appalled reaction was very gratifying. 'I know,' continued Verity, shaking her head. 'It's ghastly. Poor Michael doesn't know whether he's coming or going. Oliver's only Archie's age.'

'That's terrible,' gasped Ava, who had been a childhood friend of Daisy's. 'How can a woman leave four children?'

'Quite,' Phillip agreed. 'It's disgraceful.'

'Disgraceful,' Donald repeated. He'd listened to nothing else all the way from Hampshire and was tired of the subject. Verity had also been on the phone, spreading the news round her friends.

'She must have been dreadfully unhappy,' said Ava, trying to find something nice to say.

'Well, one can't expect to be happy all the time,' Verity said. 'That's the trouble with your generation, Ava: you expect to be happy, as if it's a right. It's not. It's a bonus. Daisy's children are going to have to live with the knowledge that they were abandoned and my heart bleeds for them. *Bleeds* for them,' she repeated with emphasis. 'Darling, this soup is frightfully good. What is it?'

'Parsnip and ginger,' said Ava, still reeling from the scandal.

'Perhaps if you'd remained friends with Daisy, she wouldn't have got into this mess,' continued Verity. 'You'd have been a good example to her.'

The following day, Ava showed her mother round the garden. Jean-Paul appeared for work even though it was Saturday. 'I want to water those plants,' he explained. 'And the children want to build a bonfire.'

'I'm Ava's mother,' said Verity. It didn't occur to her to shake his hand; after all, he was just the gardener. So when Jean-Paul took hers and raised it to his lips, murmuring, '*Enchanté*', Verity didn't know whether to be shocked or flattered.

'Where are you from?' she asked.

'Bordeaux,' he replied.

'They produce gardeners there, do they?'

'Indeed,' Jean-Paul replied.

She frowned at him. 'What do your parents do?'

The corners of Jean-Paul's mouth twitched. 'They work in the iron and steel industry,' he replied. Ava looked on in bewilderment.

'Really?' Verity exclaimed, shocked.

'Yes, my mother irons and my father steals.' And with that he sauntered off.

'Goodness, he's rude,' commented Verity, watching him go. 'Did you hear what he said? His father steals! Don't tell me he's your gardener?'

'Mummy, he's teasing! Remember I told you about Phillip's French friend, Henri de la Grandière? Jean-Paul is his son. He's come to work for a year to gain experience.'

'I remember you said something about it. Still, he's jolly rude. If he wasn't so easy on the eye, I'd be offended.'

'I've asked Toddy for lunch tomorrow with some of her cousins. I thought I should introduce him to girls his own age.'

'That's very good of you, darling. I'm sure that's beyond the call of duty. Mind you, one never really knows how to treat someone in his position. He's neither staff nor guest.'

'Friend,' interjected Ava.

'If you say so, but I like things to be clearly defined. Trouble brews when the lines are blurred. When people don't know where they stand.'

'Mother, you're very out of date.'

'Well, yes, I suppose I am. But I am right, you know.'

On Sunday, Toddy arrived for lunch with Mr Frisby, the twins, and the two pretty young cousins, Lizzie and Samantha. The boys ran off to the bonfire, which they could see smoking over the wall of the vegetable garden. Ava welcomed the two girls warmly, showing them into

the drawing room, where Verity was holding court on the sofa with Phillip and Donald. They were certainly pretty. Blondes, with blue eyes accentuated by blue eyeliner. Lizzie was the slimmer of the two, Samantha was rounder with rosy cheeks. Ava watched them shake hands with her mother. They were polite, though a little too gushing.

'Where is he?' Toddy hissed, taking Mr Frisby off her shoulder to cradle him and scratch his tummy.

'He's out with the children,' Ava replied.

'Let's take the girls outside,' Toddy suggested. 'Much less awkward than meeting in here.'

'Good idea,' said Ava. 'Come on Lizzie, Samantha. Let's go and see the bonfire.'

Jean-Paul was leaning on a pitchfork, his shirt roughly tucked into jeans that emphasised his slim hips and long legs. He had rolled up his sleeves, baring brown forearms and hands now rough from labouring in the garden. Ava watched the two girls flirt and giggle with the young Frenchman. He gazed at them arrogantly, his mouth curling in amusement, clearly enjoying their attention. In the company of these two young creatures Ava felt old and dowdy.

'Are you thinking what I'm thinking?' said Toddy, letting Mr Frisby jump off her shoulder to run about the vegetable patches. 'Lizzie and Samantha make me feel uncomfortably grown up.'

'Yes, I know what you mean,' Ava agreed with a sigh.

'It makes me sad to think I'll never flirt like that again.'

'We have new things to look forward to,' said Ava.

'What, like extramarital affairs and divorce?'

'Don't be so cynical, Toddy.'

'People shouldn't stay married for so long. In the old days we died at thirty. Now we live so long, I think one should be able to call it quits halfway through and enjoy another marriage when it starts to grow humdrum. Do you know what I mean?'

'Sort of.' Ava laughed affectionately.

'I won't leave him, you know that. Just enjoy thinking about it sometimes. My marriage is a bit too comfortable, like a trusty old slipper I can't be bothered to wear any more. The desire's gone. If I was honest, I wouldn't mind an affair . . . Do you and Phillip roll about a lot?'

'Toddy, you can't ask me that!' Ava was embarrassed.

'Come on. Is it the same for all of us?'

Ava crossed her arms. 'Phillip and I have a very healthy marriage.'

'Oh.' Toddy sounded disappointed. 'No affair for you, then?'

'No. I'm pleased to say that I'm happy with the man I've got.'

Ava went inside to check on Mrs Marley, the cook. A scrawny little woman with grey hair and a kindly smile, she was at the sink straining the summer peas and broad beans that Ava had picked and frozen.

'Can I carry something in for you?' Ava asked.

Mrs Marley smiled at her gratefully through the cloud of steam. 'That would be good, Mrs L, if you wouldn't mind.'

As Ava was leaving the kitchen, a dish of crisp roast potatoes in her hands, she was met by Jean-Paul. 'Can I help?' he asked.

'Thank you,' she replied. 'But it's in hand. You go and entertain those girls.' She grinned at him mischievously.

'You don't think I'm interested, do you? They are too young and inexperienced for my taste. I like a woman who has lived. Those girls are nice but they are as unripe as a pair of green apples on a tree.'

'Really, Jean-Paul,' she protested, feeling her cheeks turn hot.

'I prefer the apple to have fallen off the tree.'

'Those bruised and browning fruit ravaged by bees?' She walked past him down the corridor towards the dining room. But the way he had looked at her remained in the crimson hue of her cheeks.

'Yes. Those are the best. They taste sweeter.'

Ava walked into the dining room with a bounce in her step. She felt attractive, something she hadn't considered in a long time. Of course, Jean-Paul was teasing. She was married and there was no chemistry between them anyway. But a little flattery never did any harm.

After tea Verity announced that it was time to leave. 'The A303 is a nightmare on a Sunday afternoon if you don't leave early.'

When Ava's parents had driven away, Toddy gathered the girls and her children from the hollow tree and said her own goodbyes. The twins were sparkly-eyed from having played outside all afternoon. Once in the back of the Land Rover they grew quiet, not bothering to stifle their yawns.

Ava bathed her children and put them to bed, reading them a shorter story than usual because it was late and they were all tired. Poppy insisted on a long hug, wrapping her arms round her mother's neck.

That night Ava lay in bed with Phillip, enjoying their usual post-mortem of the day. 'Toddy asked me if we still rolled about a bit,' she said.

Her husband looked suitably horrified. 'What did you say?'

'That it's something I never discuss.'

'I'm happy to hear it.'

'But I did say that we have a very healthy marriage.'

'Well done.' He grinned boyishly. 'We do, don't we, Shrub?'

'Yes, darling, very healthy.'

He leant forward and kissed her neck. 'You smell of damp grass.'

'I can't. I've had a bath.'

'It's in your blood. You know it's not like normal blood, it's green.'

'You're silly.' She considered telling him what Jean-Paul had said. But it sounded so arrogant, assuming a young man was flirting with her. She was so much older and she wasn't pretty. She was probably as far from Jean-Paul's tastes as it was possible to get. 'I think those girls hit it off with Jean-Paul,' she said instead.

'Oh, yes,' he replied, nodding. 'They'll give Jean-Paul a run for his money!' He turned to embrace his wife. 'So, we roll about a bit, do we?' he breathed into her neck and the bristles on his face tickled her skin. She wrapped her arms round him and returned his kiss. He was warm and soft and familiar. How could Toddy refer to her marriage as an old slipper? If she tired of making love to Phillip she'd be tired of life.

'Mummy,' came a small voice from the doorway. Both parents sprang apart as if scalded. 'I can't sleep.' It was Angus, in his blue aeroplane pyjamas, hugging his toy rabbit. Phillip sighed resignedly, kissed his wife and left the bed to sleep in his dressing room. Ava watched him go with regret, then patted the bed.

'Come on, darling. Mummy will look after you.' Angus crawled beneath the blankets, closed his eyes and fell asleep immediately. Ava lay on her side, stroking the soft skin of her child's hand. Her heart flooded with tenderness before she closed her eyes and fell asleep.

November brought shorter days and cold winds and Jean-Paul and Ava busied themselves planting the wild garden. As the days moved towards Christmas they began to anticipate each other's actions, to understand without having to explain. Having thought that they had nothing in common, they realised that they had a great deal.

When the children returned from school, Ava didn't like to work unless she was doing something that included them. She knew they liked to have Jean-Paul around, too. They'd watch birds, drawing them in notebooks and writing about their habits in large, childish scrawl. Poppy collected feathers and stuck them onto the pages along with leaves of interest, and she carried round a shoe box in which she collected worms and slugs to look at before setting them back in the earth.

Jean-Paul taught the children how to observe and put down on paper what they saw. Angus, although only six, had a natural talent, taking his sketches back to the house to colour in at the kitchen table.

One afternoon in early December they went on an expedition to the woods, carrying baskets to fill with 'treasure' from the woodland floor. As the three children busied themselves among the trees and bushes, Jean-Paul and Ava walked together up the path that cut through the middle of the wood. The sun hung low in the western sky, hitting the tops of the trees and turning them golden. Finally they reached the edge of the wood and Jean-Paul stopped.

'There is great beauty in the tragedy of sunset,' he said.

'It's because it's transient,' Ava replied, gazing across the field. 'You can enjoy it for a moment only and then it's gone.'

'I suppose it is human nature to want what we cannot have.'

Ava pretended not to notice the significance of his words.

'I love this time of year,' she said brightly, walking on. 'The weather is crisp yet there are still leaves on the trees. Midwinter makes me sad. Nothing grows, everything is dead.'

'I admire you,' Jean-Paul said suddenly. 'You have a loving family. Your children are happy. Your home has a magical warmth. And you, Ava, have an inner beauty. You are a good woman.'

'Thank you,' she said briskly. 'I'll tell Phillip. He'll be pleased someone admires me.'

'I don't think he would be pleased to know another man is falling in love with his wife.'

Ava was silenced.

'You don't have to answer. I know that you are married and that you love your husband.'

'Then why tell me?' she asked crossly. This declaration would spoil what had been an enjoyable friendship.

'Because one day you might tell me that you feel the same way.'

'I'm far too old for you,' Ava said, trying to make light of it. 'You're French, you fall in love with everyone.'

'I have never lost my heart to anyone before. And I enjoy every line on your face, Ava, every expression, because it is always changing.'

They walked on, the silence now awkward between them.

'I'm sorry if I have made you sad,' he said at last. 'That was never my intention.'

She looked at him and felt a wave of compassion. 'I'm sorry too,' she replied, realising that he deserved to have his feelings treated with

respect. 'I'm sorry that I can't love you back,' she added softly.

'Do you want me to leave?'

'Not if you want to stay.'

'I want to stay. I wish I hadn't said it now. I wish I hadn't destroyed our friendship.'

'Oh, Jean-Paul, how could you?' Impulsively, she hugged him. He wrapped his arms round her and hugged her back. She caught her breath. It felt so natural to be there.

She pulled away, unbalanced. 'We still have so much to do in the garden. I need you.'

They continued to walk along the side of the wood, as the sun sank lower until it was a mere orange glow on the horizon. The children ran out of the woods, their baskets full. Archie held a spider in cupped hands and Poppy had tucked feathers into her hairband. Angus had collected snails and a giant mushroom.

'We'll show it to Mrs Marley,' Ava said, taking his basket from him. 'She'll know if we can eat it. In the meantime, don't lick your fingers.' For the rest of the way home the children remained close, and Ava chatted about the garden, trying to put Jean-Paul's words out of her mind.

'Do you want to come in for a cup of tea?' she asked, when they arrived back at the house.

'No. Thank you. I'll get back to the cottage. I feel like painting.'

Ava understood. When she felt melancholy she liked to sit alone in the garden. 'I'll see you tomorrow then.'

'Good night,' he said, resting his eyes on her for a moment longer than was natural.

That night she sat in the sitting room with Phillip, trying to read. Her eyes scanned the words, but her mind was playing over and over her conversation with Jean-Paul. She knew he had fallen in love with her. She glanced at Phillip, sitting in the armchair. He sensed her gaze and raised his eyes above his glasses. 'What are you looking at, Shrub?'

'You,' she replied with a smile.

'Do you see anything you like?'

'I see someone I love,' she said truthfully.

'I'm so pleased. Anything less and I'd be very disappointed.' He returned to his book.

She shook Jean-Paul from her mind and returned to hers. However, Jean-Paul's confession had made a small chink in her heart. A chink that, though tiny, weakened the whole.

VI

HARTINGTON HOUSE, 2005

*I admit that I was flattered by his confession and more than a little excited.
A man as handsome as MF finding me attractive . . . I had never entertained
even the smallest idea of love. As alarming as I found our conversation in
the woods, I kept it to myself. I didn't share it with Phillip. Perhaps, in the
darkest corners of my heart, I was falling for MF too . . . I should have sent
him back to France and avoided the pain that was to follow. But how could
I have known? I didn't anticipate the danger I was sailing into.*

ALONE IN HER STUDY, curled up in the armchair beside the fire, Miranda
ran her fingers over the page and began to cry. She had been married
for eight years but she had never felt a love as intense as Ava's.

David Claybourne wasn't the least bit curious about Jean-Paul. The
garden was Miranda's department, like decoration and general maintenance; he trusted her judgment. The first weekend after the gardener
had moved into the cottage David didn't notice much difference, except
for the tree house, which kept the children occupied right up until
bathtime. Gus had shown it off, proudly demanding that he climb the
ladder and take a look inside. He wondered what sort of gardener
would go to the trouble of building such an exquisite playhouse, but as
Jean-Paul never came up to the house, David felt no compulsion to
introduce himself and find out.

By the end of November he began to notice a marked change in the
gardens. The borders looked groomed, the rich soil was free of weeds,
the dead clematis that had scaled the front of the house had been
pulled down and carted away. Great heaps of rotten foliage were piled
high in the vegetable garden ready to be burned. The stones along the
thyme walk had been weeded, the balls of topiary trimmed into perfect
spheres. David didn't usually bother to walk round his estate, but now
he was drawn away from the golf to enjoy the marvels of his property.

The more he saw, the more his admiration grew. Miranda showed her
husband round enthusiastically, pointing to the things Jean-Paul had

done, deriving pleasure from these rare moments together. She watched his astonishment with a real sense of achievement.

'The children help. They rush home from school to dig up all the weeds and fill the wheelbarrow. They even showed Jean-Paul how to roast marshmallows on a bonfire.'

David started to feel uneasy. 'I'd better meet this Jean-Paul. He sounds like Mary Poppins,' he said grudgingly.

'That's exactly what he is! The children can't get enough of him.'

'Well, let's go down to the cottage and see if he's there.'

'I don't think we should disturb him on a Saturday.'

'I'm the boss. I can disturb him whenever I like.' He sounded more severe than he meant to. Miranda followed him across the field. The children waved from their tree then disappeared inside.

'That tree house is a godsend. It keeps them busy for hours.'

'I suppose it's better than television,' he grunted. Miranda frowned. A moment ago he had been so happy. She mentally replayed their conversation, wondering if it was something she had said.

At the cottage, smoke billowed from the chimney, suggesting that Jean-Paul was at home. David knocked on the door and shoved his hands into his pockets. It was bitter out of the sun.

Jean-Paul was painting in the spare room. When he heard the knock on the door, he put down his brush and went downstairs to open it. David extended his hand and introduced himself formally. He did not smile. He was relieved to see how old the Frenchman was.

'Please come in,' said Jean-Paul, standing back to allow them into the hall. 'It's cold outside.'

'But beautiful,' Miranda added, shrugging off her sheepskin coat. 'The children are in your tree. We can't get them out!'

David noticed the excitement in her voice and felt his irritation mount. 'I see you've been busy in the garden,' he said, wandering into the sitting room. The fire glowed, and Crystal Gale sang from the CD player. 'Do you really like this music?' he asked.

'Of course,' Jean-Paul replied with an affable shrug.

'I suppose you are a different generation,' David went on. Miranda began to feel uncomfortable. She so wanted him to like Jean-Paul.

'Please, sit down. Can I make you coffee or tea?'

'No, thanks, we're not staying. I just wanted to meet you. I trust my wife's judgment but I like to know those I employ.'

'Naturally.' Jean-Paul understood the younger man's disquiet. 'You have a beautiful home. I hope you are satisfied with my work so far.'

David straightened up, flattered by the Frenchman's words. 'I'm impressed with the tree house,' he said, returning the compliment. He found the ease with which Jean-Paul had mollified him almost as irritating as his jealousy. 'It's good to see Gus and Storm enjoying themselves.'

'You were right to leave the city. Children need to be in the countryside where they have space to run around. They are full of energy. You must be very proud.'

'I am,' he replied. 'We both are.' He turned to Miranda and took her hand. The sensation of his skin against hers made her flinch. 'You're doing a wonderful job.'

'Thank you.' Jean-Paul smiled.

Miranda's heart flipped and, as he stood to leave, even David felt moved to smile in return. 'If there's anything you need, let me know. Before you arrived I hadn't turned my thoughts to the garden so we're probably in need of tools and things.'

'I have enough. The previous owners left everything behind.' Jean-Paul's face grew suddenly serious.

'Good. Well, we'll leave you in peace. Maybe take the children for a walk.' Miranda, picking up her coat, looked at her husband in astonishment. He had never taken the children for a walk.

Once outside, he dropped her hand. 'He's perfectly nice,' he said, striding towards the bridge. 'I see he's taken a shine to the children.'

'They've taken a shine to him too,' she replied, shrugging on her coat.

'He's not what I expected.'

'Really? What did you expect?'

'Another Mr Underwood.'

'Oh no.' Miranda laughed. 'He's well educated.'

'What's he doing gardening then, if he's so well educated?'

'Perhaps he loves it.'

'Has he left a wife back in France?'

'Not that I'm aware of.'

He chuckled cynically. 'He'll soon make his way through all the women in Hartington. I wouldn't trust him as far as I could throw him. He's much too good-looking.'

'Oh, really, darling! He's not like that at all.'

'Just because he doesn't flirt with you.'

Miranda dropped her eyes to the ground and shoved her hands into her pockets. There was a sharp edge to his words. 'No, he doesn't.'

'I should hope not. He knows his place.'

When they reached the hollow tree, David announced that they were

all going for a walk. 'I want you to show me your cows, Storm,' he said, watching her crawl excitedly out through the hole in the bark. Her hair was strewn with twigs and pieces of moss and her cheeks glowed. Gus jumped down from halfway up the ladder, wishing he had something to show his father.

With Storm leading the way, they returned over the bridge and along the river bank towards the field of cows. Jean-Paul heard their voices and went to watch them at the window. He stood a while, enjoying the sight of the little girl skipping through the long grasses. Poppy used to walk with a dance in her step, her dark hair flying about her shoulders in the wind. Storm was beginning to learn the magic of the garden, magic that Poppy had known instinctively. It was an enchanted world, ready for her to explore. He looked forward to showing her the spring, when the ground would come to life and all the work they had put in would reward them with flowers. Then the magic would really begin.

Gus walked behind his father, whacking the grass with a stick, as if he carried the weight of the world on his small shoulders. There was something angry about him, simmering at his core like lava. Now Jean-Paul had met both parents, it was easy to understand the boy's frustration. He knew that children needed to be listened to, needed love and time. He didn't doubt Miranda and David loved their children, but they had little time to give. He recalled the little gestures that daily demonstrated Ava's love for her children. That sort of foundation was a priceless gift for a child; a solid base camp from which to embark upon life.

He returned to his painting. With each brush stroke on the canvas he felt connected to her again.

After lunch, David didn't retreat as normal but suggested they light the bonfire in the vegetable garden. Gus informed him that it was Jean-Paul's pile of rubbish to be burned the following week.

'It's my house and therefore my pile of rubbish,' said David, striding off to put on his boots. Miranda suddenly realised that he was jealous of Jean-Paul. That was why he had taken her hand and why he had gone for a walk with the children. She felt ashamed that her husband had to compete with the gardener to prove himself a worthy father.

That night they made love. After weeks of no contact, Miranda knew she should have felt grateful, but she felt only resentment. She knew his actions were motivated by the presence of Jean-Paul. He was marking his territory like a dog pissing on a tree. She closed her eyes and tried to put Jean-Paul out of her mind. But suddenly it was Jean-Paul's mouth

kissing her and his hands caressing her and, in that delicious moment, she realised that the Frenchman excited her. With unexpected ferocity, she held her husband close, wrapped her arms and legs around him and tried to focus on the familiar feel of his skin, as if afraid those disloyal thoughts would drive him further away.

The following morning the Claybournes went to church. It was their first visit, and they were viewed with excited curiosity.

As they walked down the aisle, Miranda caught the eyes of Troy and Henrietta and smiled. David made for the front pew, fully expecting it to be on permanent hold for them, the first family of Hartington, but it was occupied by old Colonel Pike, studying the prayer book. Grudgingly, he led the family into the pew behind.

Storm and Gus would have been bored by the service had it not been for the organist, Dorothy Dipwood, speeding up and slowing down during the hymns without any regard for the congregation. Only the last line was sung in time with the organ. The Reverend Freda Beeley bounced about the nave, gesticulating wildly and speaking with emphasis as if she were talking to children. David thought it amusing, while Miranda, who had never liked church, since being made to go so often as a child, was more entertained watching her children.

After the service, the Reverend Beeley clasped David's hand enthusiastically between her own doughy ones. 'It is such a pleasure to see you. I knew you would come eventually.'

On the green outside, Colonel Pike invited David to his home to show off the medals he had won in the war, and Miranda chatted to Henrietta and Troy.

'Why don't you come and have a trim, darling?' suggested Troy. 'Your hair's lovely and shiny, but a few layers would give it more body.'

'Oh, I've never had layers,' she replied, doubtful that anyone other than Robert at Richard Ward in Chelsea could do a proper job.

'Well, come for a cup of tea in the salon then. Just the three of us.'

'I'd love to. Tomorrow morning?'

'Come as soon as the kids are at school; I haven't got an appointment until ten.'

'And I don't open until ten,' Henrietta added. 'I'll bring some hot croissants from Cate's, but we'll have to hide in the back. If she sees us she'll go mad.'

'Wouldn't it be simpler to meet in her shop?' said Miranda.

'No!' they replied in unison.

With the clear skies and the lunch Mrs Underwood had cooked, Miranda was sure an idyllic afternoon would follow. David had been in high spirits after their sociable morning, promising the children he'd take them to Jeremy's farm after lunch to play on the tractors. Storm had found a few friends from school and Gus had managed to join in without frightening them. Miranda had had to drag the children away from the church, promising play dates after school. She was uplifted.

Then David appeared in the hall with his bag, announcing that he was going to catch the early afternoon train to London. Everything had been going so well. What was the hurry? Weren't the important things in his life here in Hartington? Miranda kissed him goodbye, but his kiss was hasty and he didn't hold her. A nugget of doubt had started to worry her, like a stone in her shoe. Could he be seeing someone else?

Gus watched his father disappear up the drive in a taxi and felt a sharp stab of disappointment. He had been looking forward to playing on Mr Fitzherbert's tractors. He picked up a stone and threw it at an unsuspecting blackbird, then headed for the woods. When he came to the dovecote he stopped. There, nestling in the long grasses, was a hedgehog. He crouched down and prodded its face. The hedgehog rolled into a ball and Gus grinned. It would make a good football.

'What have you found there?' came Jean-Paul's voice behind him.

Gus stood up guiltily, the blood rushing to his cheeks. 'A hedgehog.'

Jean-Paul knelt down. 'Do you know why he has rolled into a ball?'

'Because he's frightened.'

'That's right. Come, let's take a closer look,' said Jean-Paul, sensing an opportunity to teach the child a valuable lesson. 'Can you see he's trembling?' Gus nodded. 'You know, the funny thing about animals is that they know who to trust and who to be afraid of.'

'They do?' said Gus, thankful that the hedgehog couldn't tell tales.

'Watch.' Jean-Paul placed his hands under the hedgehog and scooped him up. He held him close to his shirt. It wasn't long before the animal uncurled and began sniffing Jean-Paul's skin. 'I think he's hungry. Let's take him back to the cottage and make him a bed.'

Once they reached the cottage, Jean-Paul wrapped the hedgehog in a cloth and gave him to Gus. At first the boy was alarmed, afraid that the hedgehog would bite him for having prodded his face. But Jean-Paul reassured him and, sure enough, the hedgehog soon stopped trembling and began to sniff the palms of his hands.

Gus giggled. 'He wants to eat me.'

'No, he doesn't, he's just exploring. We'll put him in a box and give

him some milk, then put him back in the wild tomorrow.' Jean-Paul poured some milk into a bowl. 'What's your sister up to this afternoon?'

'With Mummy. Daddy went up to London.' The boy's face clouded.

'Are you disappointed?'

'He said he was going to take us to Mr Fitzherbert's farm to play on the tractors.'

'He's very busy, isn't he?'

'He's always busy. He never has time to play with us.' Quite unexpectedly, Gus opened his heart to Jean-Paul. Feelings he had never put into words poured out in a jumble. 'They want to send me away to boarding school—but it's not my fault—I never started it—I only bit him because he called me names—Daddy always promises to play with me—but he never does—he's always too busy—other daddies play with their children—why can't he play with me?' The little boy began to sob. Jean-Paul put an arm round him, listening to the barely comprehensible soliloquy of injustices. Finally, Gus grew quiet, his body jerking with the odd sharp intake of breath he was unable to control.

'Grown-ups are very hard to understand sometimes. It's not fair that your father promises to play with you then lets you down. But the intention was there. He wanted to play with you. Perhaps he was called away urgently and he's as disappointed as you are.' Gus sniffed, incredulous. 'You must tell them you don't want to go to boarding school.'

'They won't listen. They never listen.'

'Then you must ask them to listen and be strong about it. But don't get cross. You have to set them a good example. They will do as you do.' Gus looked unconvinced. 'Do you still want to play on the tractors?' The boy's eyes lit up. 'Come on then, we have time before tea.'

Miranda wasn't the sort of person to snoop. There were no secrets between herself and her husband. But after the children had gone to bed, she began to go through his desk. There were files for letters, household maintenance, invoices and insurance, but nothing incriminating. She ran a bath and soaked in lavender oil, closing her eyes and inhaling the steam, and cursed herself for having a suspicious mind.

Afterwards, she curled up in bed and opened the scrapbook. There was a strange magic to it, like opening the door into a world infinitely more beautiful than the one she lived in. It absorbed her, the memories wrapping their silver threads about her heart and pulling her in. As she read, she escaped from the increasing coldness of her marriage into the warmth of someone else's secret.

Ours was a love doomed from the very beginning. It was as transient as
sunset. You once said that the setting of the sun was a tragedy, filling you with
melancholy as you tried unsuccessfully to hold onto it. Perhaps its transience
is its beauty. Perhaps our love is made sweeter by its hopelessness. If one
could halt the sunset and live in a perpetual dusk, would it retain such magic?
Would our love be as tender without the expectation of loss? We will never
know, because all we have is loss and the memory of the crimson and gold.

Jean-Paul stood on the stone bridge. It was dark and cold, the sky a
deep navy studded with stars. The moon was high, not quite full, and
he put his hands on the stone balustrade and leant over to look at the
river. The light bounced off the ripples. He stared for so long that his
eyes stung, but before he blinked he was sure he could see her face,
reflected with the moon, gazing back at him with the same yearning.

It was hard to find peace in the cottage that used to be theirs. Every
room echoed with her presence, every sound triggered a memory, the
smell of orange blossom tormented him with longing. He could leave
tonight, but the thought of the empty château caused him more discomfort than the cottage. If he couldn't spend his future with her, then
he'd have to be satisfied in the past, still warm with her memory.

Miranda was due at Troy's at nine, so she decided to take the children
to school by car, leaving their bikes at the end of the drive for them to
cycle home on after the school bus dropped them off later. She was on
the point of setting off when the telephone rang.

To her surprise, the caller was a shop assistant from Theo Fennell, a
jeweller in London where Miranda had been a good customer for years.

'I'm sorry to call you so early in the morning, Mrs Claybourne,' said
the girl, her voice breathy and upper class. 'But I've mislaid your husband's office number and he's keen to get an engraving done before
Christmas. I'm really embarrassed to have been so silly. Theo would kill
me!' Miranda's curiosity was aroused. Perhaps David was buying her
something expensive for Christmas.

'What's he been buying there?' she said, angling for more information.

'I don't think I should say,' replied the girl nervously.

'No, perhaps you shouldn't. I'll give you the number, but don't tell
him you spoke to me. If it's a surprise I don't want to ruin it.'

'Thank you, Mrs Claybourne.' The girl sounded relieved.

Miranda dictated the number and hung up. A beautiful piece of jewellery from Theo Fennell would certainly go towards making up for his
long absences. How could she have doubted him?

When she arrived at Troy's, Henrietta was already there, biting into a hot croissant. Troy hissed at her to hurry to the back before Cate looked out of her window. The three of them sat huddled together, the air charged with excitement. It wasn't often that they defied Cate. 'If she finds out, we're in shit,' said Troy, handing Miranda a mug of tea.

'Then she'll never tell us when that gorgeous Frenchman comes in again,' added Henrietta.

'We're all in love.' Troy sighed dramatically.

'Who with?' Miranda asked.

'He's a mystery Frenchman,' said Henrietta breathlessly. 'He first came in October. We thought he was a tourist. Now he's back. We've spotted him across the road. He has black coffee and a croissant for breakfast. But as much as Cate asks him about himself, he won't reveal anything!'

'You're not talking about *my* Frenchman, are you?' They both stared. 'In his fifties, very good-looking, deep-set brown eyes, longish greying hair, devastating smile?'

Troy gasped. 'He *is* your Frenchman! What does he do for you?'

'He gardens.'

'Gardens?' they repeated in unison.

'Don't be silly,' said Henrietta. 'He's a film producer or a writer. He can't be a gardener!'

'Well, he is,' Miranda replied simply.

'How on earth did you find him?' asked Troy.

'He found me, actually.' Miranda recounted the story, during which time neither Troy nor Henrietta said a word. 'So,' she concluded, 'he brought Storm home and we got talking. I asked him what he did and he said he gardened. I asked him if he'd do ours and he accepted without hesitation. It was very bizarre.'

'Is he married?' Henrietta asked.

'No,' Miranda replied.

'Oh good!' she exclaimed, determined to start a new diet as soon as she'd finished her croissant.

'Is he gay?' asked Troy.

'That I don't know,' said Miranda. 'But I doubt it. Just a hunch.'

'How do you control yourself during the week when your husband's in London?' Troy asked.

'I don't fancy him,' she lied, giving a little shrug.

'That just goes to show what a happy marriage you have,' said Henrietta, sighing with envy.

'Your husband must be mad with jealousy,' said Troy.

'Miranda's husband is very attractive, Troy.'

'But not as attractive as the Frenchman. What's his name?'

'Jean-Paul,' said Miranda.

'Oh, how sexy! Jean-Paul. Isn't it irritating that Cate was right?'

'What do you mean?' asked Miranda, sipping her tea.

'She insisted you found your gardener thanks to her notice board.'

'We saw him in Cate's in October,' said Henrietta. 'He asked her about the house and who lived there. We assumed he was a tourist.'

Miranda put down her mug and frowned. 'Did he see my notice?'

'He couldn't miss it, darling,' said Troy. 'Everyone saw your notice.'

Miranda felt uncomfortable. 'He never said anything when I met him.'

'You probably jumped in before he had a chance,' suggested Henrietta.

'Yes, you're right. I think I did. I get like that when I'm nervous.'

Troy grinned. 'So you did fancy him?'

Miranda grinned back. 'A little, but not any more,' she added hastily.

'What a relief!' he exclaimed. 'She's human after all!'

Miranda drove home, dispelling her doubts about Jean-Paul. There was no reason for him to mention her advert. Perhaps he hadn't considered the job until she spoke to him about it. After all, it was Storm who brought him to the house. He might not have come otherwise.

When she got home, Fatima was in the kitchen clearing up breakfast. 'Good morning, Mrs Claybourne,' she exclaimed when she saw Miranda. 'Leave it all to me,' she added in her sing-song voice. 'You go and work, I will make your house shine, shine, shine!'

Miranda sat in her office trying to write an article for the *Telegraph* magazine, reining in her mind every time it wandered off. It would soon be Christmas and they had invited Miranda's parents and Constance, her spinster aunt. She was dreading the whole event.

Just as she was typing the end of the first paragraph, Mr Underwood entered with an armful of logs, which he dropped into the basket beside the fireplace. He stood for a moment watching her.

'Don't let me bother you, M'Lady. But I spoke to J-P this morning. We're going to rip out the cottage garden. Rip it all out and start again.'

Miranda thought of Ava and the garden she had created with MF. She couldn't allow them to rip it out. 'What, all of it?' she asked.

'Aye, Mrs C, M'Lady. It's all dead or rotting. Then we'll build a big fire and burn the lot.' His eyes blazed at the prospect.

Miranda got to her feet. 'I must go and talk to Jean-Paul.'

She found him sitting on the bench in the middle of the cottage garden,

leaning forward, deep in thought. 'Good morning,' she said, not wanting to startle him. He looked up at her, his brown eyes so intense she blushed.

'I was miles away,' he said, sitting up with a heavy sigh.

'Anywhere nice?' she asked brightly.

'Oh, yes,' he replied. 'The past is sweet.'

She sat down beside him. 'Mr Underwood tells me that you want to rip out this garden.'

'No. Not everything. Some things we can save, some things need to be replanted. We are late, it is already December. But the weather is unusually mild, and with a little magic . . .'

Miranda bit her lip. 'I know you asked me to leave you to it. That I could trust you,' she began. 'But the thing is, Mrs Lightly really loved this garden and I don't think it would be right to change it.'

Jean-Paul looked at her. 'How do you know about Mrs Lightly?'

'Oh, I've been told. She was very popular here. Everyone knows about her gardens. Apparently, the cottage garden was very dear to her.' She longed to share the scrapbook with him, but she was too deeply involved now to betray the woman who had made it.

'Listen, Miranda. I understand that you do not want to ruin what your predecessor created. I don't want to ruin it either. In spite of the weeds, I can see what was there. I will endeavour to re-create it as it once was.'

Miranda was relieved. 'Oh, thank you so much. I couldn't bear her to come back one day and see that we had spoilt it.'

'You think she will come back?'

'You never know, do you?'

'No.' He shook his head wistfully. 'You never do.'

VII

THE CHILDREN BROKE UP from school. Miranda had taken to driving them there in the mornings, then meeting Troy and Henrietta either in the salon or at Cate's Cake Shop after drop-off. Slowly she began to be integrated into the community. She hadn't intended to, but it had happened without her noticing.

In order for Miranda to go to London to do her Christmas shopping, Henrietta offered to look after Gus and Storm. Clare was perfectly capable of manning the shop in her absence, and, secretly, she longed to meet the elusive Jean-Paul, who drank his black coffee in silence every morning in Cate's Cake Shop. Miranda departed on the early train, leaving Henrietta at the breakfast table with the children.

Troy had layered Henrietta's hair and given her spirits a lift. Knowing that she was likely to bump into Jean-Paul, she had applied mascara. She didn't feel at ease wearing make-up, but today she had felt her confidence needed a little boosting. However, she hadn't been brave enough to show her fulsome figure, hiding it beneath a large jumper.

Henrietta adored children. Gus and Storm sensed it immediately and began to show off. She listened to them, laughed at their jokes and let them show her their bedrooms and toys. She admired Storm's pink playhouse, cuddled her cushions and gushed about the fairy dresses hanging in her cupboard. Gus showed her the tree house. 'Jean-Paul made it for us,' he told her. 'I can see for miles. J-P!' he shouted.

'J-P?' repeated Henrietta with a laugh.

'That's his nickname. He's J-P, I'm Gus-the-Strong and Storm is Bright-Sky.'

'I like it,' she enthused.

He shouted again. 'He's probably in the cottage garden. He's always in there.' Henrietta longed for Jean-Paul to appear, but he didn't.

At eleven she took them hot chocolate and digestive biscuits in their tree house. She chased them round the tree, pretending to be Captain Hook, then she thrust her head into the aperture and shouted, 'Ooh aah, me hearties!', her large behind sticking out like a mushroom. That is how Jeremy Fitzherbert's dogs found her, sniffing her with excitement as she struggled to extract herself.

When she emerged, her hair was a mess, her face flushed and her blue eyes glittering like dewy cornflowers. 'I hope I'm not interrupting anything,' said Jeremy, grinning at the sight of her.

'Oh God, I'm so sorry,' she gushed, pushing herself up. 'I'm a pirate.'

'You make a very good pirate,' he replied.

She tried to smooth her hair. 'More like Pooh Bear stuck in Rabbit's front door, I think. You got the wrong end, I'm afraid.'

'Nothing wrong with that end. It looked perfect to me.'

'Have we met?' she asked, puzzled.

'Indeed. You're Henrietta Moon, aren't you?'

'Yes,' she said, frowning.

'I'm Jeremy Fitzherbert. I own the neighbouring farm.'

'Of course we've met,' she replied as everything clicked into place.

'I've been into your shop. You sell those large jars of candy sticks. They're my favourites.'

'Mine too,' she exclaimed, feeling bad at not having remembered him. 'The butterscotch ones especially.'

'Exactly. Once I start I can't stop.'

'Unfortunately, that's my problem too.'

'You look very well on it.'

She stared at him, not knowing what to say. She wasn't used to compliments. She didn't imagine for a minute that he meant it. There passed a moment of awkwardness while Henrietta struggled to move her tongue and Jeremy found himself swallowed into her eyes. He wanted to tell her how beautiful they were, but felt embarrassed.

'*Bonjour*, Jeremy,' came a voice, the jovial greeting breaking the silence. They both turned to see Jean-Paul striding up the path. Henrietta caught her breath at the sight of his smile. '*Bonjour, madame*,' he said, as he reached her. He took her hand and raised it to his lips. Henrietta didn't know where to look. No one had ever kissed her hand before. It must be a French thing, she thought, struggling to recover.

'I've brought you the small tractor and trailer you wanted,' said Jeremy. Storm and Gus wriggled out of the hole in the tree to run about with the dogs.

'Thank you,' said Jean-Paul. 'That will be a big help.' He turned to Henrietta. 'I gather you are looking after Gus-the-Strong and Bright-Sky today,' he said, his eyes deep and twinkling.

'Yes,' she croaked.

'How do you like my house?'

'It's terrific, it really is.'

'I see you completed the ladder,' said Jeremy, patting the wood. 'Good solid oak, that. Have you been up?' he asked Henrietta.

'No,' she replied. 'As you saw, I had difficulty getting out. I'm sure I'd suffer worse coming down.'

'Not at all. Come on!' Jeremy stood on the first rung of the ladder.

'I made it to take the weight of an elephant,' said Jean-Paul.

'Then it should hold me.' Henrietta laughed nervously, praying that it wouldn't collapse beneath her weight. Jeremy climbed up first, then he encouraged Henrietta to follow. When she reached the top she took Jeremy's hand and stepped onto the platform on which the house was built. Gus was right, the view was stunning.

'If it weren't for the trees we'd see my farm,' said Jeremy.

'I'd like to see your farm,' Henrietta replied, remembering childhood picnics while watching the combines.

'You can come over any time,' he said softly, wondering why he had never noticed her before. She was delicious, like a toffee-apple. He glanced down at her left hand and saw she didn't wear a ring.

Henrietta noticed Jean-Paul didn't join them. He stood on the grass below, talking to the children. They clearly adored him.

Jeremy watched her watching Jean-Paul and felt a jolt of disappointment. Not that it surprised him; how could a man like him compete with Jean-Paul, with his thick accent and deep-set brown eyes?

He left them at the tree and returned to his farm, Mr Ben and Wolfgang trotting along beside him. Henrietta managed to overcome her shyness in the company of Jean-Paul, and the children took her off to the cottage garden to help with the planting.

Miranda had arrived in London early, hitting Peter Jones in Sloane Square when it opened at nine thirty. She felt a shiver of happiness. She was back where she belonged. The traffic rumbled, horns hooted, sirens screamed, people shouted, the pavements were crowded, everyone went about their own business anonymously.

She spent all morning buying presents and by lunch time she had ticked almost everything off her list. She made her way to the fifth floor restaurant at Harvey Nichols, where she had arranged to meet Blythe. Catching sight of herself in a mirror, she was satisfied that, although she lived in the countryside, she still retained her urban glamour.

'Darling, you look gorgeous,' said Blythe, who was already seated in the restaurant. Her green eyes slid silkily up and down Miranda's body.

'Thank you,' Miranda replied, sitting down.

'So, how's it all going down there?'

'It's taken a while, but I'm beginning to settle in now. You'll have to come and stay after Christmas.'

'I'd love to, when I'm back. I'm off to Mauritius for ten days. The bastard has made me so miserable I have no qualms about spending his money. I bet he won't give me a divorce for the full two years.'

'I'm so sorry. David tells me he's been giving you advice.'

'David,' she repeated, smiling tenderly. 'I don't know what I'd have done without him. He's so patient and thoughtful.'

'Oh good,' Miranda replied, wishing he was as patient and thoughtful with her.

'He's given me invaluable advice. Thanks to him I'm going to fleece the bastard. I deserve his money for having put up with his infidelities for the past ten years. I might embark on some infidelity myself.'

'Have you found someone?'

'Maybe.' She looked coy.

'You have!' Miranda exclaimed. 'Do I know him?'

'No,' said Blythe quickly. 'No one knows him. It's not big love, but it is big sex. He's delicious in the sack.'

'Is he married?'

Blythe pulled a face.

'Oh, Blythe!' Miranda exclaimed. 'Be careful. Remember how it feels. Don't put some poor wife through the hell you went through.'

'It won't last,' she said dismissively. 'It's only a bit of fun. I promise.'

When she reached home, Miranda was a little surprised to see that Henrietta had put the children to bed and was sitting in the kitchen having supper with Jean-Paul. 'I hope you don't mind,' said Henrietta. 'The children are done in; they fell asleep the moment Jean-Paul finished telling them the story of the velveteen rabbit. We thought we'd celebrate the end of a hard day's planting.'

'I'm delighted,' Miranda replied, drawing up a chair. 'I can't thank you enough for looking after them for me.'

'You look exhausted,' said Jean-Paul. 'Let me pour you a glass of wine. There was a time when I thought the city was the only place to live. Then I discovered how shallow and empty it was.'

'That's just how I feel. I was so excited to get up there, but by the end of the day all I wanted was to come home.'

'I've never liked the city,' said Henrietta. 'Much too unfriendly.'

'So, have you finished my little garden?' Miranda asked, already feeling better for their company.

Jean-Paul smiled. 'We have completed the planting. With a little magic, it will flower in spring.'

'Why do you always say "magic", Jean-Paul?' Miranda asked.

'Magic is love, Miranda. If you love someone they grow in beauty and confidence. They flower before your eyes. The garden is the same. With love it will grow brighter and more abundant. There's no secret to love or magic, just the limitations of our own courage and self-belief. True love begins with loving ourselves. Love is not purely a feeling but an act of will. A very exceptional woman taught me that long ago.'

Henrietta and Miranda sat in silence. Henrietta dreamt of being loved by him; Miranda knew loving him was only a dream. Her heart reached out to the man who would only ever love one woman. The woman he was bringing to life in the tender planting of their garden.

Jean-Paul returned to the Château les Lucioles for Christmas. He drove through the large iron gates, up the drive that swept in a magnificent curve around an ancient cedar tree and parked the car on the gravel in front of the impressive façade.

Françoise unlocked the door with much rattling of keys. '*Monsieur*, come inside quickly before you catch your death. Gerard has lit fires in the hall and drawing room and Armandine has left a *daube* in the oven. Come, come, it is cold.' The housekeeper beckoned him inside, closing the door behind him with a loud clank.

'Is Hubert here?' he asked, thinking of the garden.

'Yes. Why don't you eat first, see him later? He is outside.'

He glanced about the hall, at the blazing fire in the grate, the flag-stone floor and faded Persian rugs, and sighed with pleasure. It was good to be home. He took off his coat and handed it to Françoise. 'You can bring the *daube* to the drawing room on a tray. I'll eat in there.'

'Shall I let the dogs in?' she asked. 'They have been restless all morning. They knew you were coming home.'

'Yes. I've missed them.'

'Why do you stay away? The animals miss you.' She lowered her eyes. 'So do we.'

He looked at her tenderly. 'Ah, Françoise, you are a sentimental woman underneath that efficient exterior. Now, please, bring me my food, I'm ravenous. And tell Hubert I want to see him.'

Two Great Danes bounded into the drawing room, rushing up to him excitedly. He fell to his knees and embraced them both, allowing them to lick his face. There had always been Great Danes at Les Lucioles. A house of that size needed big animals to fill it.

He stood up and went to sit on the club fender. The fire warmed his back as he looked out through the French doors that led into the garden, now hidden beneath frost. He had hoped to return with Ava. To show her the gardens he had created for her. To live out the rest of their lives together. She had promised. He had promised, too. Promises sealed with love. He had kept his side of the bargain, but what of hers?

Françoise entered with his *daube* on a tray. 'Are you going to spend Christmas on your own?' she asked.

'I have no choice.'

'What a shame. If any man is worthy of love it is you, *monsieur*. I have known you since you were a boy. It causes me pain to see you live alone. I want a good, honest girl and a brood of healthy children for you.'

'I'm past that now.'

'Not if you marry a fertile young woman.'

'Françoise, you are dreaming.' He chuckled cynically.

Hubert entered, cap in hand. '*Bonjour, monsieur*. I am glad you have returned safely.' He bowed formally.

'I am being cross-examined, Hubert. Françoise, bring Hubert a glass of brandy. Now tell me. How are the gardens?'

Back at Hartington, Miranda's parents, with her father's sister, Constance, arrived in a silver Rover packed with presents and luggage. This was their first visit. Diana Stanley-Kline had much to comment on, wafting about from room to room in ivory slacks, matching cashmere sweater, suede shoes and pearls the size of grapes.

.'Oh dear,' she sniffed at her daughter's kitchen stools. 'The distressed look might be very fashionable, but you wouldn't want to sit on one of these in your best tights.' She raised her eyebrows at the sculpture on the hall table. 'What an odd thing to have in a house with small children!' And when Miranda told her how the gardens had once been the most beautiful in Dorset, she scrunched her nose and remarked, 'Well, everything's relative.' As usual, nothing could please her mother. Miranda longed for Christmas to be over and for everyone to go home.

On Christmas Eve, Gus and Storm put their stockings out for Father Christmas and went to bed without any fuss. Gus declared that he was going to lie in wait for him, while Storm argued that if he did, Father Christmas wouldn't come and neither of them would get any presents.

Miranda tucked them up and returned to the drawing room to add a log or two to the fire. She closed the curtains, put on a CD and had just sat down on the fender when David entered, dressed in a burgundy smoking jacket and matching velvet slippers. He saw his wife on the fender and smiled. 'Are the stockings ready? I'm looking forward to playing Santa!'

'I do hope Gus doesn't stay awake.'

'He's been out all day. I don't imagine he'll manage to keep his eyes open for more than five minutes.'

'Mummy's being very awkward,' she said, changing the subject.

'Only because you let her.' He popped open a bottle of champagne. 'You're a grown woman. Just tell her to shut up.'

'Easier said than done.'

'Darling, people treat you according to how you let them. All you have to do is say "no".'

She frowned at him. 'I can see why Blythe raves about you.'

'Does she?'

'Yes, she says you give good advice. Now I know she's right.'

David poured her a glass of champagne. 'Here's to you, darling,' he said, kissing her cheek.

'What's that for?' she asked.

'Just to tell you how much I appreciate you. I've bought you a splendid present.'

Miranda smiled, thinking of Theo Fennell.

'Have you?' she asked coyly. 'When are you going to give it to me?'

'I could give it to you now,' he said, kissing her again. 'You smell delicious. Why don't we sneak upstairs for ten minutes? I heard your mother running a bath, they're going to be a while.'

He took her hand and led her upstairs, both giggling like a couple of children afraid of being caught. Once in the bedroom he pushed her playfully onto the bed and she forgot about the present as he pulled her shirt out of her jeans and ran his hand over her stomach. Aware that they could be disturbed at any moment they made love quickly. When it was over they lay together, bound by their lovemaking.

'You were a feast, darling!' he exclaimed. 'Now I shall give you your reward.' He got up and wandered into his dressing room.

Miranda covered herself with the duvet and prepared herself for her gift. 'I hope you haven't gone mad,' she said.

'Don't you think you deserve it, darling? This is to tell you how much I appreciate and love you.' He returned holding a red box. Miranda knew immediately that it couldn't be from Theo Fennell, whose boxes were pink and black. She felt a wave of disappointment but made an effort to dissemble. 'Happy Christmas, darling.'

'Thank you.' She hesitated a moment before opening it.

'Go on,' he encouraged, smiling in anticipation.

Inside the box was a diamond heart pendant. If she hadn't had the call from Theo Fennell she would have been thrilled with it. But all she could think of was the piece of jewellery David had had engraved. If it wasn't for her, who was it for?

SPRING

VIII

HARTINGTON HOUSE, 1980

The change of season brought on a change in me, a blossoming, like an unexpected flower bursting through snow. Outwardly, I continued as if nothing had been said, but inwardly I could not forget MF's declaration of love. I should have sent him home, but how could I have predicted what was to come when at the time I truly felt nothing but affection? As winter thawed I found myself thinking more and more about him. The days became charged with electricity that continued to build between us. Perhaps if Phillip had been at home more, it might not have happened. But he continued in his merry way, disappearing to France and Spain for weeks on end, even travelling as far as Argentina and Chile in search of new wine. He was oblivious of the growing kernel in my heart.

AVA WAS PLAGUED with confusion. How could she love two men at the same time? Her love for Phillip had not diminished, not even an inch, yet she found herself growing more and more attracted to Jean-Paul. At first she tried to distance herself from him, then she dismissed her feelings as sisterly fondness. But as the snowdrops and daffodils began to raise their heads, she could deny it no longer. Her feelings were sexual and they weren't going away.

One day in March, Jean-Paul suggested they drive to a beach. 'We can have lunch in a pub. I'd like to see a little more of Dorset.' He put his hands out and shrugged. 'It's drizzling. There is little we can do in this drizzle.' His grin of entreaty made it impossible for her to refuse.

'That's a good idea,' she replied, trying to mask her anxiety. Somehow the idea of spending the day together on the beach felt improper. 'Perhaps Phillip'd like to come. He's probably too busy, but I know he'd appreciate being asked,' she said, making for the house.

Phillip sat in his study in a worn leather armchair. The dogs were lying on the rug beside the fire, and classical music resounded from a tape recorder. He was so deeply engrossed in a book that he did not hear his wife enter. 'Darling,' she said, drawing near. He raised his eyes, startled a moment, then smiled at the sight of her. 'Sorry to interrupt.'

'You never interrupt, Shrub,' he replied, putting the book on his knee.

'It's a miserable day, so Jean-Paul suggests we go for a walk on the beach. He wants to see more of Dorset. Why don't you join us?'

'As much as the thought of strolling in drizzle with my wife appeals to me, I will decline,' he replied and Ava was horrified that she felt such relief. In an effort to assuage her guilt she managed to look suitably disappointed, planting a lingering kiss on his cheek.

'You're very transparent, Shrub,' he said with a chuckle.

'Transparent?' she repeated, blushing.

'Yes.' He scrutinised her face. 'You think you'll be bored with Jean-Paul on your own, don't you?'

'No.'

'I know you, Shrub. I can read you like a book.' He laughed. 'I'm afraid you'll have to go alone. I'm sure you'll survive.'

'You're a beast!' she exclaimed. 'You leave him to me all the time. You owe me for this. You know that, don't you?'

'Whatever you want is yours,' he replied.

'I'll hold you to that.'

He pulled her down and kissed her on her forehead. 'I hope you do.'

Ava drove down the narrow winding lanes towards the coast. She felt unusually nervous, like a teenager on her first date. Jean-Paul, sitting beside her, looked relaxed, clearly enjoying her company and the sight of the newly budding countryside. The windscreen wipers swept the rain off the glass with the regularity of a ticking clock. Ava sensed more keenly than ever the swift passing of time. At the end of the summer he would return to France and they would both recover from their infatuation. She would reflect on what might have been, certain that as a married woman she had had no choice but to refuse him.

She parked the car in a lay-by and led him down a snaking path to a secluded beach. 'No one comes here,' she told him. 'It's stony. But I love the roughness of it and the sound of pebbles under my feet.'

On the beach, Jean-Paul walked beside her. He wasn't towering like Phillip, but next to Ava, who was a little over five foot six, he walked tall. The wind tasted of salt, blustering one moment, dropping the next, reflecting the awkward exchanges between Ava and Jean-Paul. He wanted so much to hold her in his arms, to release the words locked inside his heart and tell her how deeply he loved her. She in turn burned with the desire to be held by him, if only for a moment, a forbidden second on which she could feed during those nights when she

longed for him. She was reminded of the tragedy of sunset and, without warning, she began to cry.

Jean-Paul stopped and held her shoulders, searching her face.

'I'm sorry,' she whispered.

'For what?' he asked and his voice was so soft that it made her cry all the more. 'I don't understand.'

She shook her head. 'It's like a sunset. Something so beautiful I want to hold on to it. But then it's gone.'

'Ava . . .'

'Or a rainbow,' she sobbed. 'Loved from a distance, but impossible . . .'

He didn't wait for her to finish, but pulled her into his arms and kissed her ardently. She didn't have the strength to resist. She let him hold her and closed her eyes, relinquishing control. His kiss was urgent yet gentle and she wound her arms round his neck, willing the moment to last. But like all beautiful things, the end was but a breath away and the high was followed by a terrible low. She thought of her children and Phillip and was flooded with guilt.

She pulled away. 'I can't,' she gasped, touching her lips, still warm from his kiss. He stared at her in mortification. 'Don't look at me like that. I can't bear it.' She placed her fingers on his cheek, cold from the wind and wet from the drizzle. 'We shouldn't have come. Out here, there are no boundaries to keep us apart.'

'But we can't go back now,' he said. 'We have come too far for that.'

'Then what can we do?'

'I don't know, Ava. All I know is what is in my heart. The more time I spend with you the more of my heart you take.' She rested her head against his chest and listened to the sound of the waves and the plaintive cry of a gull, and felt her spirit flood with sadness.

'It is not meant to be, Jean-Paul,' she said at last. 'I can't betray Phillip. I love him too. And the children . . .' Her voice cracked, for he suddenly grew tense with anguish. 'There is nothing in the world that would make me leave them.'

'Then I will go back to France.'

'No!' she exclaimed fiercely, pulling away again.

'I have no choice, Ava.'

'But I want to share spring with you, and summer. I want to enjoy the gardens with you. No one understands them like you do.' She swallowed hard and gazed at him, debilitated by his stricken face. 'No one understands me like you do.'

'No one loves you like I do,' he retorted, holding her arms so tightly

she winced. 'But you are right,' he said, letting go. 'I cannot live without you, so I have only one choice—and hope.'

'Hope?'

'Hope that the rain will last and the sun will break through and there will shine the most exquisite rainbow.'

They tried to continue as if the kiss had never happened but although they spoke of other things, the memory of it remained. Jean-Paul had been given a taste of paradise and was left wanting more, while Ava had been singed by her rashness.

They drove home in silence. Jean-Paul returned to his cottage and Ava returned to her husband. She crept up to where he was standing in front of his bookcase and wrapped her arms round his waist.

'So you're back,' he said jovially. He turned round. 'You've caught the wind,' he remarked, noticing her red eyes and cheeks.

'It was blowing a gale down there.'

'So I see.' She sank into his arms. 'Are you all right, Shrub?'

'I'm fine. Just a bit of a headache.'

'Do you want me to pick up the children?'

'Would you?'

'Of course. Why don't you have a lie-down?'

'I will.' She shut her eyes. How close she had come to putting in danger the things she cherished. Phillip held her close. 'That feels good,' she murmured. But Phillip couldn't know just how good it felt.

Ava woke early. She hadn't slept well since that kiss on the beach. She lay listening to the cheerful clamour of birds in the trees and thought of the garden stirring to life with the warmer weather and longer days.

Phillip lay on his back, his hand by his ear in carefree abandon. Ava turned onto her side and watched the rise and fall of his chest as he breathed with the slow regularity of a man contented with his lot. He had done nothing to deserve her betrayal. He left her in no doubt that he loved her greatly. So, why did she risk it all by loving a man she couldn't have? Was it worth losing everything?

She thought of her three trusting children, whose lives depended on the solidity of the foundations she had built for them with Phillip. If she were to shake those foundations, what future did they have? But even while she held their futures in her hands, she was still distracted by the irresistible draw of Jean-Paul.

There was only one thing to do. She didn't wait for Phillip to wake up but manoeuvred herself on top of him, nuzzling into his neck. He

stirred as he felt her warm body on his and wrapped his arms round her dreamily. 'I want another baby,' she whispered into his ear.

Phillip awoke with a jolt. 'What?' he mumbled.

'I want another baby,' she repeated.

'Shrub, darling. Another baby? Right now?'

She held him tightly, frightened of losing him. 'Yes.'

'I think we should think this through sensibly.'

'I've thought it through. I can think of nothing else.' *To tie me to home so I don't run away . . . I can't trust myself any more.*

'I don't think I could give you a baby right now even if I wanted to,' he said, pushing her gently off him. 'That's not the sexiest way to wake a man.'

'I'm sorry,' she said, rolling onto her back and throwing an arm over her face. 'You know how I am. If I have an idea I have to act upon it.'

'Usually one of your most endearing qualities,' he said drily, stumbling into the bathroom.

'If I don't have another one soon, I'll miss my chance.'

'Aren't three children enough?'

Her reply was drowned by the sound of gushing water as Phillip brushed his teeth and splashed his face.

'Then why don't we go away for a few days,' she suggested when he emerged. 'Just the two of us. It's been so long. I never see you. You're either in your study working, or abroad. I need to see more of you. I want you to look on me as a woman and not just a mother.'

Phillip sat down on the bed. 'You're all woman to me, Shrub.' He tried to smile, but her sudden, uncharacteristic outburst worried him.

'Let's go abroad. Somewhere warm. We can lie in the sun and walk hand in hand on a beach. Do you remember before Archie was born?'

'Tuscany. Of course I remember.'

'We made love all afternoon after big glasses of rosé and big plates of pasta. I remember the smell of eucalyptus that scented the air. At night we wandered the streets of Sienna and Florence without a care in the world. Let's do it again.' Her eyes blazed with enthusiasm.

'I remember you in that black and white polka-dot sundress. You were the most lovely creature I had ever seen.' Phillip kissed her forehead. 'You still are, you know.'

'We can make a baby in Tuscany. A celebration of our marriage and our love. Oh, Phillip, it'll be so romantic.'

'I'm not sure sleepless nights and nappies are very romantic. Think about it, Shrub. You're talking about another human being. Another

member of our family. A child too small to play with his siblings. And I'm not going to get any younger. If you really yearn for another child I won't deny you. But I want you to think about it very carefully.'

With those thoughts she prepared to face Jean-Paul. Having suffered guilt that morning in the arms of her husband, she now suffered it all over again as she stepped into the garden in search of Jean-Paul. She was considering bringing another child into the world solely to prevent herself from yielding to him. Suddenly that felt like a betrayal too.

She wandered into the wild garden and stood in the sea of daffodils. All around her the trees vibrated with nesting birds, but instead of uplifting her, the sound made her sad. My life does not belong only to me, she concluded. I'm bound to my family by love and nothing will ever change that. I must be content with his friendship.

She lifted her eyes to see Jean-Paul striding purposefully up the meadow towards her just as Phillip's car disappeared down the drive. As he approached, she saw that his face was drawn. Before she could speak he took her hand and pulled her behind the hollow tree, wound his fingers through her hair and kissed her on the mouth.

'I can't go on like this,' he said at last. 'Every day I love you more. What began as a pleasure simply to be with you is now a curse. I am permitted to look but not touch and that, my beautiful Ava, is slowly killing me. So, I have decided to go back to France.'

His words winded her as violently as if he had struck her. 'I don't want you to leave. I can't live without you, Jean-Paul. Please don't make me live without you.'

'I can't live with you if I'm not able to hold you,' he replied gruffly. 'I'm a man, Ava. *Un homme qui t'aime.*'

'*Et je suis une femme qui t'aime.*'

He stared at her. 'You speak French? My God, I thought I knew everything about you.' He traced a finger down her cheek as if willing himself to remember every contour.

'Will I never see you again?'

He wiped her tears with his thumbs. 'I don't know.'

'Jean-Paul, you can't leave me like this. Just when the garden is bursting into flower. All that we've created together . . .'

'Will remind you of me.' He laughed cynically. 'Maybe it will convince you to come and join me.' He drew her close. She heard the beating of his heart and inhaled the spicy scent of him she hoped she'd never forget. She closed her eyes but the tears escaped, soaking his shirt.

'You won't see your cottage garden in full bloom,' she whispered.

'I don't care about the cottage garden. I care only about you. I will never see you in full bloom and for that I am heartbroken.' He lowered his head and kissed her again.

This time she shut her eyes and parted her lips and let him kiss her deeply. She didn't think about her children or Phillip. Jean-Paul was walking out of her life for ever.

Ava didn't know how she was going to tell her family that Jean-Paul had gone. She decided to tell them that he had gone home to see his mother. That way, if he changed his mind, he could always come back. How she hoped that he would change his mind.

She told the children at tea time. They gave it a moment's attention before returning to more important things like building a camp under the hall table. They would never know the sacrifice she had made for them.

When Phillip returned for dinner, the children were in bed. Ava had made a cheese soufflé and roasted a pheasant in order to take her mind off Jean-Paul's departure. Now she handed Phillip a glass of red wine, warmed by the Aga, and kissed him. Seeing his smiling face confirmed that her sacrifice had been worth it. What sort of woman would she be if she left him and the children and ran off to France?

But the fact that she had made the right decision didn't make it any easier to bear. She had to pick the right moment to tell her husband of Jean-Paul's departure: it was vital that she showed no emotion. She decided to toss the news to him while she was bent over the dishwasher, stacking the soufflé plates.

'Darling, Jean-Paul has gone home for a break, to see his mother.' She stood up and faced the window where her miserable reflection stared back at her from the glass.

'Good,' was Phillip's reply. 'I've been thinking about your holiday idea. Do you suppose your mother would look after the children?'

Finally, it was safe to turn round. She took the pheasant out of the oven. 'I'm sure Mummy would love it, and I can ask Toddy to keep an eye. Maybe she could have the boys for a couple of afternoons.'

'Splendid.'

'When were you thinking we should go?' She served them both, then sat down.

'For a week at the end of May.'

Ava pulled a face. 'You don't think that's too long?'

'Seven days? No, you need a proper rest, and the children will still be at school.'

'Make it five, darling. I'll get twitchy after that and they'll miss us. Where shall we go?'

'Leave it to me. Tuscany perhaps, or somewhere in Spain.'

'Thank you,' she said, sighing heavily.

'Are you all right, Shrub?' He took her hand across the table and studied her face. 'You're still thinking about having another baby, aren't you?'

'It's on my mind, yes.'

'Don't let it make you miserable, Shrub. If you really want another child, I'll do my best to comply. You know I can't deny you anything.'

'I know. I'm just not sure I'm doing it for the right reasons.'

'Think about it on holiday. The sunshine and rest will do you the power of good and put life into perspective. Now, give me a smile, darling.' He brought her hand to his lips and kissed it. Ava was stunned. That was a gesture unique to Jean-Paul. She felt her cheeks burn and the overwhelming desire to cry.

'You're so good to me,' she said, unable to hold back any more.

Phillip chuckled, assuming her tears were inspired by his loving reassurance. 'You deserve nothing less. I'm the luckiest man in the world to have you. Cry all you like, Shrub darling,' he said gently.

Just when Ava was beginning to tolerate life without Jean-Paul, Phillip announced he'd had a telephone call from Jean-Paul's father, Henri. Ava was in the vegetable garden planting seeds with Hector. She stood up, trowel in hand, her face and hands grubby with mud. 'You've heard from Henri?' she repeated. 'What did he say?'

'He's asked us to stay at the beginning of May.'

'To stay?' she repeated, incredulous.

'Yes. I thought you'd be pleased. You'll love Henri, he's a real character, and Antoinette, his wife, is a keen gardener like you.'

'What about Jean-Paul?'

'What about him?'

'Didn't Henri think it odd that his son had returned home?'

'Clearly not. Why? Is it odd?'

'He's been away three weeks.'

'You're not missing him, are you, Shrub? The woman who said she wouldn't last more than a week with him?'

She turned away, pretending to be keeping an eye on Hector. 'Well, we could do with his help. There's an awful lot to do around here.' She wiped her forehead with the back of her hand. 'So he'll be there?'

'I'm sure he will, if he hasn't returned to us by then. I told Henri that

we're very pleased with Jean-Paul's work. That he's learning a great deal.' He paused. 'I know you and he haven't exactly gelled. Is it going to ruin your holiday if he's at Les Lucioles?'

'No. Not at all.'

'Good. I want you to have a good rest, Shrub. We don't have to hang around with Henri and Antoinette all day. We can venture off on our own and explore. I know you want us to spend time together.'

'That's OK. I'm sure they're charming.'

'So, what should I tell Henri?'

Ava lost her focus among the greenhouses, aware that she was standing at a crossroads and that her fate and perhaps the fate of her whole family depended on the choice she made now. Then something pulled at her. An invisible cord attached to her heart, pulling her across an unseen threshold.

'Tell him yes,' she said slowly, knowing that she should have taken the other path. 'Tell him we'd love to stay at the château.'

'Good. I knew you'd be pleased. Don't I always come up with the goods?' He chuckled and wandered through the gate back to the house.

Ava knelt down and continued to plant the seeds. Inside, her stomach was filled with bubbles. She told herself that her desire to see Jean-Paul again was innocent. They would be dear friends. That was all.

That night Phillip made love to her. She was so overwhelmed with happiness that she received him enthusiastically, pulling him into her arms, kissing him passionately, savouring his attention, telling him how much she loved him. Masking the secret feelings she had for Jean-Paul.

IX

CHÂTEAU LES LUCIOLES, 1980

THEY WERE MET AT BORDEAUX airport by Henri's driver, who was holding up a sign saying: *Phillip Lightly, welcome!* He spoke no English and Ava was thrilled to speak French to him. Phillip listened with pride as she chatted easily. He had never seen her look more beautiful. Her hair was loose and falling down her back in shiny curls. Her cheeks were pink, which accentuated the sparkling green of her eyes, and her face had

tanned the colour of warm honey. She wore glittery pink velvet slippers on her feet, a rather old-fashioned black dress printed with small pink flowers, and a short olive-green cardigan. He noticed that she walked with a bounce in her step and he was pleased that he had organised this break away from home. It was just what she needed.

Ava was as taut as a tightly strung violin. Outwardly she put on a good show of being excited by the holiday, but inside she was quivering with nerves. What would Jean-Paul think of her appearing at his home?

France was in the full throes of spring. The trees were all in leaf, tall white candles adorned the horse chestnuts, and undulating fields of vines shimmered with their first leaves. Roses grew in abundance. The driver told Ava that they were planted at the ends of the rows to stop the ploughing oxen from nibbling the vines.

Finally, the car swept up a long, curved drive, beneath an ancient avenue of towering trees that plunged them into shadow. At the end, the house stood bathed in sunshine. It was a majestic Neo-classical building on a grand scale. Built in pale, sand-coloured stone, symmetrical, with tall windows framed by blue shutters and ornate black balconies, its beauty filled Ava with wonder. As they approached, she could see the steep roof of slate tiles with dormer windows, each one capped by a curving pediment like a graceful eyebrow. Narrow stone chimneys reached into the sky with fanciful, cone-topped towers, and Virginia creeper scaled the walls, alongside honeysuckle and wisteria.

The car drew up on the gravel outside the house and a pair of Great Danes charged out of the open door, their deep barks biting into the still air and echoing off the walls of the château. Ava climbed out of the car, her heart beating with anticipation. She raised her eyes to see an elegant, olive-skinned woman standing at the door.

'Welcome,' she said, stepping towards Ava. Her black hair was pulled into a chignon, showing off beautiful bone structure and deep-set brown eyes. 'I am Antoinette de la Grandière. I hope you had a pleasant journey.'

'Splendid,' said Phillip, striding over to her. She gave him her hand and he leant forward to kiss her. 'This is my wife, Ava,' he added, introducing her.

'I have heard so much about you,' Antoinette said warmly. 'Jean-Paul is so fond of you.' Ava shook her hand, thin and surprisingly cold to touch, and wondered how much he had told her. 'Please come inside.'

They walked across a hall dominated by a sweeping stone staircase and a giant fireplace full of neatly cut logs piled one on top of the other.

On the mantelpiece were ancient bottles of wine lined up on display.

Antoinette took them through to the drawing room, a grand red *salon* with high ceilings and long curtains framing French doors that opened onto a wide terrace, surrounded by a stone balustrade. Faded tapestries of hunting scenes hung on the walls, flanked by gilded portraits of the family ancestors.

A maid entered the room and Antoinette asked her to bring a tray of drinks to the terrace. 'And, Françoise, where is my son?' she added.

'He is out, *madame*,' the maid replied.

Antoinette sighed. 'Well, please go and find my husband and tell him our guests have arrived.'

'Yes, *madame*,' said Françoise obediently.

'Come, let us sit on the terrace. It is warm there in the sun. Françoise will bring us some wine.' She opened the French doors wide and stepped outside. The dogs followed her, trotting off to sniff the borders. Below, the gardens stretched out to an old wall covered in climbing roses and pink bougainvillea, where ancient trees watched over the grounds and, beyond, the domed roof of a dovecote was silhouetted against the sky. Ava could see why the château was so special to Jean-Paul and why he did what his father asked of him in order not to lose it.

'Ah, my friends, you have arrived!' exclaimed Henri, approaching the terrace from round the side of the house. His voice was loud and booming. 'You should have sent Françoise to find me,' he added to his wife.

'I did,' she replied coolly.

He embraced Phillip with the warmth of an old friend and kissed Ava's hand, smiling broadly, dark eyes appraising her beneath a thick head of brown curls. Ava remembered Jean-Paul telling her that he had a mistress in Paris. It didn't surprise her. He was devilishly handsome. 'Where's the wine? Françoise!' he bellowed.

Françoise appeared almost at once, struggling beneath the weight of a large tray heavy with bottles and glasses as well as a jug of iced water. Henri made no move to help her.

'Good! We were in danger of dying of thirst,' he said. He sat down and pulled out a cigar. 'So, Phillip, my friend, how is the book?'

Antoinette turned to Ava. 'Would you like to see the dovecote? Jean-Paul tells me you have one in your garden.'

'I would love to. Is that its dome over there?'

'Yes.'

'It's far more magnificent than ours.'

'Jean-Paul says you have the most beautiful estate.'

'I wish he were there now. Everything is bursting into flower—and the smells; it's never smelt more delicious.'

'Come, I need to talk to you, Ava.'

They left the men talking and drinking on the terrace, and Ava followed Antoinette down the wide steps to the garden. Once again she felt the blood rushing through her veins with panic. Had Jean-Paul told his mother that he was in love with her? Was she going to warn her off? Say he needed to marry a young woman from his own country and have a son to inherit the château, just as he would do? She began to feel nauseous and rubbed her forehead in agitation. The sun was very hot, in spite of the cool breeze, and her own pulse thumped in her ears.

'May I speak with you plainly?' Antoinette asked, as they walked across the lawn towards an iron gate built into the wall.

'Of course,' Ava replied.

'It's about Jean-Paul.' Antoinette glanced across at her. 'He is my only child, you know, and I love him deeply. The trouble is his father is insensitive to his needs. Jean-Paul is a talented artist, but Henri does not like him to paint. He writes beautiful poetry, but Henri thinks nothing of poetry. Henri wants him to help run the vineyard here, but Jean-Paul was never interested, until now.'

'Now?' Ava wondered where the conversation was leading.

'He wants to stay here and learn about the vineyard, but, Ava, he needs to go back with you.' Ava was unable to reply, her throat was so tight with emotion. 'I think he wants to stay for me. You see, I'm alone here most of the time. Henri lives in Paris. I'm sure Jean-Paul told you. He speaks about you with such affection, Ava. It makes me so happy to know that he is understood. He told me he painted a garden for you.'

'It is the most beautiful painting, Antoinette. We have planted the garden just as he painted it. He has such imagination and flair.'

'I know.' She smiled. 'I understand him, of course.' She opened the iron gate, which whined on its hinges like an old dog, and led her into a wild meadow in the midst of which stood the round stone dovecote. 'I can tell he is unhappy, Ava. With you he is able to enjoy freedom to be himself. I couldn't bear it if he sacrificed that for me. This is the opportunity of a lifetime and I want him to enjoy it. Tell him, for me, that he has to return with you.'

'I'll try,' Ava replied huskily.

Suddenly, from round the back of the dovecote, Jean-Paul appeared.

He stood with his hands in his pockets, looking at them warily. 'Jean-Paul, show Ava the dovecote. I must check on lunch.' She looked at her watch. 'Goodness, it is nearly time. Don't be long.' She turned and slipped through the gate, leaving them alone.

'Why have you come?' Jean-Paul demanded, his tone aggressive. He stared at her, awaiting her response, expecting rejection.

'I'm sorry,' Ava whispered, approaching him. 'I'm miserable too.'

His face softened. 'You look radiant,' he replied, a small smile curling the corners of his lips.

'That is because I knew I was going to see you.'

'Then you have missed me too?'

'Yes.'

He slipped his hand round the back of her neck, beneath her hair, and pulled her to him, pressing his lips to hers. She parted her lips and let him in, winding her arms round his waist, feeling the muscles tense beneath his shirt as she touched him. His breathing grew heavy, his body hot and taut. He pulled her behind the building so they could not be seen from the gate.

Ava felt reckless. Intoxicated by the feel of his body in her arms, combined with the scents of France, she forgot that her husband sat on the terrace with Henri. She dwelt in a fantasy world where only she and Jean-Paul resided.

He took her hand and led her to the door of the dovecote. Inside it was warm and sweet-smelling. He closed it behind him and lay down with her on the straw. She caught her breath as he moved on top of her, and her stomach swam with pleasure as he ran his tongue over her skin. Then he was kissing her and unfastening the buttons on the front of her dress. He slipped his hand inside and felt the warm softness of her breast, caressing it with his thumb. Her head fell back as he took it in his mouth. She could feel his bristles against the tender flesh and her body shivered with the guilty pleasure of enjoying what she had dreamt of in the secret recesses of her imagination.

As they made love he took her hand and entwined his fingers through hers. She didn't regret her adultery, not for a moment.

When she opened her eyes she saw that he was looking at her as if she were the most beautiful woman in the world. 'Will you come back to Hartington?' she asked.

'Yes,' he said. 'You know I would move mountains for you.'

'You don't have to, my darling,' she replied, lovingly caressing his face. 'I'm here now.'

Hastily, they tidied themselves in preparation for lunch. Ava fastened the front of her dress and smoothed it down, brushing off any telltale wisps of straw. Jean-Paul made for the door, then turned and kissed her again. 'You look beautiful,' he said, stroking her face with his eyes. 'I don't think I've ever seen you in a dress.'

'I wore it for you.'

'It suits you. And your hair is down. I like it down. What happened to the pencil?'

She laughed at his teasing. 'Seriously now, how do I look?' She wiped her mouth with the back of her hand.

'Flushed.' He took her hand. 'Come, we'll walk back the long way round. That way any evidence will be blown away by the wind.'

When they reached the terrace, Antoinette, Henri and Phillip were just getting up to go in for lunch.

'Perhaps you'd like to freshen up in your room,' said Antoinette to Ava. 'I'm sorry, I should have offered when you arrived. Françoise will show you.'

Ava followed the older woman up the stone staircase and along a corridor to a door at the end. Françoise opened it to reveal a large bed-room with a four-poster iron bed draped in white linen. A window was wide open, giving onto the dovecote and the fields of vines beyond, and a pair of white curtains billowed in the breeze.

Françoise was surprised that Ava spoke French. 'Is there anything I can do for you?' she asked, grateful to be understood.

'No, thank you, Françoise. I'll be down in a minute.' She noticed that her suitcase was on a stand, open and ready to be unpacked. She delved inside for her sponge bag and hurried into the bathroom to wash away the evidence of adultery. Catching herself in the mirror she paused to see if there was anything in her appearance that might give her away. Her cheeks were rosy, her eyes shining, her hair tousled and tumbling over her shoulders. She pulled out a piece of straw that had gone unnoticed. Instead of throwing it in the bin she put it in the pocket of her sponge bag. Something to treasure. It would always remind her of the first time they made love.

Ava sat through lunch exuding a radiance that affected them all. Phillip delighted in his wife's happiness and silently congratulated himself on arranging this break away from home. It was obviously what she needed; she was back on sparkling form, looking lovelier than ever.

After lunch, Henri insisted on showing them round the vineyard. Antoinette declined gracefully, floating off for a siesta.

Ava walked behind Phillip and Henri with a bounce in her step, her shoulder almost touching Jean-Paul's arm. She was unable to hide her exhilaration, taking pleasure from every moment. Henri led them down the garden to the dovecote. 'Thank goodness doves can't talk,' Jean-Paul commented under his breath, as they slipped through the gate.

'Les Lucioles has been in my family for five hundred years,' said Henri, puffing his chest out with pride. 'This dovecote was built in the time of Louis the Thirteenth.' He patted Jean-Paul on the back, feigning fatherly affection. 'One day my son will inherit all that is mine. It has lasted five hundred years; there is no reason why it won't last another five hundred. Eh?'

Ava winced as he flung open the door so that it crashed against the wall, sending the doves shooting into the air like bullets. 'It's beautiful,' she commented, stepping inside.

'It is very special to me,' said Jean-Paul, without looking at her.

Phillip glanced at his wife. 'Slightly more charming than ours, don't you think, Shrub?'

'Oh, I think ours has a lot to recommend it.'

'No doves,' he added.

'We should buy some. We can't have a dovecote without doves.'

'And give it a lick of paint,' Phillip continued.

'No, no. Don't paint it. You will ruin it if you paint it,' said Jean-Paul.

'So, when are you planning on returning to Hartington?' Phillip asked him.

'Next week,' he replied. 'I needed to spend some time—'

'Can't you find him a suitable English girl?' Henri interrupted. 'Don't they make them like you any more?' he added to Ava with a wink.

'You flatter me,' Ava replied, shrugging off his comment with a laugh.

'Come, let me show you Antoinette's garden.' He put his hand in the small of her back and escorted her out of the dovecote. 'We need to find him a girl,' he said, lowering his voice. 'Between you and me, I had to get him out of Paris. He was living the life of a playboy, dating the most unsuitable girls.'

'Don't you find him changed?' she asked. 'When he arrived in England, I'll be honest, I didn't think he'd last a week. He was completely ill-equipped to work in a garden, and arrogant with it. But he's worked so hard to create something beautiful. When he returns he'll enjoy the fruits of his labour.'

'I am pleased,' Henri shrugged. 'I wouldn't believe it had anyone told me but you.'

'I think he worries about Antoinette,' she added carefully. 'He's a dutiful son.'

'He's her only son. That makes her very anxious. You understand, you're a mother. She's overprotective and overindulgent.'

'And you're tougher, to compensate?'

'Perhaps. I can see the bigger picture. Life is not a fairy-tale. I need my son to be as solid as me, with a good head for business. He must find a decent girl and start a family. A girl who knows her place, not a flighty girl with ambitions of her own. Jean-Paul needs to return to England in order to stay away from his mother. Sometimes love can be suffocating. There is nothing wrong with love, but we all need a little space. Relationships work better when the air is able to circulate between two people. Antoinette would have liked to have had more children. It would have been easier for Jean-Paul if she had.'

'He will make a wonderful *vigneron*,' she said diplomatically.

'He had watched the machinations of the business since he was a little boy and then, bam! All of a sudden he lost interest and I lost him. I had such high expectations of him.'

'Don't be too hard, Henri. On yourself or on him. If you give a horse a long rein he won't run away; if you pull it in tight, he'll bolt.'

He looked at her with narrowed eyes. 'You're very perceptive, Ava Lightly.'

'It's easier to see if one's not involved.'

Antoinette's garden was bursting into flower. Pink roses were budding against a wall where great stone urns of white tulips sprang up with yellow senecio and violas. The box hedges were frothy and pale green, and wild yellow narcissi grew in abundance among rampaging honeysuckle and daisies. The air was sweet with the scent of spring, stirred by the merry twittering of birds as they flirted in the cedar and sycamore trees. In the middle of her carefully designed garden was an ornamental pond, a statue of a little boy, his hand outstretched, touching the wing of a bird in flight. Ava was drawn to it. She stood beneath the sculpture, admiring the way the boy's fingers barely touched the bird so that it appeared to be unsupported. Jean-Paul came up behind her.

'Isn't it incredible?' he said. 'This was commissioned for me, by my mother. I am the little boy, the bird symbolises freedom. As you can see, I can almost touch it.'

'You can be free at Hartington.'

'I know,' he replied, so softly she could barely hear him. She felt the breeze ruffle her hair. 'I want to kiss your neck,' he added.

'Be careful. We are being watched.'

'They are not interested, *ma pêche*. Look, they are busy discussing the history of the *cave* and the great freeze of ninety-one. Papa will not cease to worry about frost until *la lune Russe*.' He sighed heavily. 'But I couldn't care less about frost. I want to kiss you all over, slowly, carefully, savouring the taste of you inch by inch.'

'Stop,' she pleaded. 'Phillip . . .'

'Your Phillip is enraptured by my father. Listen, they are discussing the quality of the grape.'

'There's nothing that interests him more than that.'

'Then leave them to it. He is happy. Come. I want to show you the greenhouses. They are spectacular.'

'It's too obvious!'

'Only to you. They suspect nothing. Isn't it natural that I should want to show you my home?' He began to walk towards the yew hedge.

Ava turned. Phillip raised his eyes, she waved, he waved back, then she was gone through the hedge and Jean-Paul had taken her hand.

Once inside one of the greenhouses, he closed the door and kissed her. It was hot and humid, smelling of damp earth and freesias. She felt his excitement as he pulled her hips towards him. 'We can't . . .' But it was useless to protest. His mouth silenced her and his arms wound round her in a passionate embrace.

'I wish we were alone. You drive me crazy,' he gasped. 'I want to lie naked with you so nothing separates us.'

'Darling Jean-Paul, it's not possible here. Phillip and your father could come in at any time.'

'Curse them both!' He scowled. 'I will engineer it so that we can be alone. You will see.'

Ava pulled away to inspect the greenhouse. There were pots of highly scented tuberose, rows of orchids in a myriad colours, and pretty nerine lilies, just opening. Jean-Paul followed her, holding her hand, turning her round every few minutes to steal another kiss. It was fortunate that when Henri entered with Phillip they were on either side of a table of rare purple orchids.

'Phillip, do come and look at these,' she called to her husband. 'They're almost checked.'

Phillip strode over, admiring the plants as he passed them.

'This is quite something,' he agreed.

'I think you should take Phillip and Ava round the vineyard in the truck,' Jean-Paul suggested to his father, who enjoyed nothing more than showing off to his guests.

'We have just started spraying the crop,' Henri said. 'Would you like to see?'

'That would be splendid,' said Phillip.

Jean-Paul waited for Ava to back out so that they could be together.

'I think I'll leave you boys to it,' she said, on cue. Jean-Paul threw her a secret smile.

Phillip frowned. 'Why don't we go for a walk?' he asked his wife.

'A walk?' Ava repeated.

'How far is it into town?' he asked Henri.

'A fifteen-minute walk. There are some pretty shops you might like, Ava. Women's shops, soaps and things.'

'I'd love to,' she replied. She wanted to explain her actions to Jean-Paul. They had to behave with caution. Her desire to be alone with her lover would have to wait.

'I can show you the vines tomorrow,' said Henri. 'Now, let me show you how to get to town.'

Reluctantly, Ava left Jean-Paul in the garden by the fountain and accompanied her husband to the front of the house. 'Isn't this a beautiful place?' she said as they walked down the drive.

'Beautiful,' he agreed. 'Now you can see why it matters so much to Henri that his son should gain experience of running an estate.'

'Completely. And it's good for him to get away from his parents . . . do you think someone will say that some day about Archie and Angus?'

'Of course not, Shrub,' he reassured her. 'You and I are pretty solid parents.'

'I hope so. I'd hate to think of them escaping to another country to avoid us.'

'Children go through stages. They have to spread their wings and fly. Jean-Paul will come back in the end and run this place as his father did.' He took her hand. 'So, you're happy I brought you here?'

'Very happy.'

'You're not missing the children?'

'Not yet.'

'And your thoughts on motherhood?'

'I've moved on,' she said simply. 'I've decided I don't need another child. I don't want to be chained to the nursery again.'

'Quite.'

'I'm just beginning to enjoy my freedom.'

They wandered round the town, a pretty cluster of reddish-brown buildings that surrounded a square dominated by an ancient church and a town hall. In the middle was a fountain, where a couple of old men in caps sat smoking pipes on a bench, and a grandmother and child threw crumbs to a flock of pigeons. There was a small market where wizened country folk sold fruit and vegetables and tall bottles of olive oil. They stopped at a little pavement café, where they drank coffee served by waiters in black and white.

A few tourist shops sold patterned tablecloths and soaps and, in one of them, Ava bought some lavender bath oil for her mother and sprayed herself with orange blossom perfume. Then she bought the scent. 'This will always remind me of France,' she said, walking lightly out into the street, where Phillip was looking into the window of a bookshop.

'Shame they're all in French,' he said.

'Come on, don't you have enough books?'

'Oh no, there's always room for more.'

They returned exhilarated from the walk. Antoinette appeared in the hall from the drawing room. 'You must need some refreshment,' she said. 'Tea or lemonade?'

'Tea would be lovely,' Ava replied.

'Same for me,' said Phillip, following Antoinette into the drawing room, where the two Great Danes lay in front of the fireplace.

'I'm going to go upstairs to put my shopping away,' Ava called after him.

'All right, darling,' he replied.

Ava ascended the stairs, clutching her parcel. As she was walking along the corridor towards her room, a door opened and a hand grabbed her, pulling her inside where it was dark and cool.

'Don't say a word,' Jean-Paul hissed. Ava was stunned. He had closed the shutters; thin beams of light filtered through the cracks.

'You're crazy!' she hissed back.

'Crazy for you!' he replied, pulling her onto the bed.

'What if someone . . .?'

'They won't. Relax, *ma pêche*.'

'How long have you been waiting?'

He laughed, then looked at her with an expression so serious and so tender that her stomach lurched. 'For you, I would wait for ever.'

X

HARTINGTON HOUSE, 2006

MIRANDA SAT AT HER DESK. She had been asked by the *Daily Mail* Femail section to write about her experiences of moving out of London to the countryside; how the reality had turned out to be less blissful than the vision. She could have written it on autopilot a couple of months ago, but now she felt different. She could hear the children's voices behind the wall of the vegetable garden and yearned to be with them. Country life was an adventure with Jean-Paul when they were home. He took them out at night to watch badgers, to the river to catch fish, up to the woods to build camps and light fires. Her children, who at first had found nothing to do in the countryside except miss the city, were as much a part of nature now as the animals they watched.

As for her, she had grown accustomed to leaving her hair unbrushed and wearing little make-up. She didn't mind wearing gumboots and, although she still retained a muted longing to wear the beautiful clothes that languished in her wardrobe, she had no desire to return to the frenetic social life that had driven her to exhaustion in London.

Miranda wrote a swift email to the editor on her laptop, suggesting the article be a positive one. The editor replied that it had to be negative; they already had another journalist writing the positive version. To hell with it! They'd have to find someone else. 'Right,' she sighed, standing up. 'That's the last time she'll ask me to write for her.'

She went out to the vegetable garden where Jean-Paul was planting seeds with Storm and Gus. The children were on their knees, their small hands delving into the earth. Mr Underwood leant on his fork, having done very little all morning except stand about making obvious comments like, 'I'll be damned, there's a caterpillar, Storm.'

Miranda didn't mind. She was in good spirits. Jean-Paul was more uplifting than sunshine. In fact, just being near him was a bolt of excitement. He made her feel good about herself. Not that he asked her much about her life—they talked mainly about the garden—but he took an interest in what she said. He encouraged her to learn about plants and to take pleasure from the bulbs emerging from the soil. She had begun

to enjoy being with her children to the exclusion of everything else. They shared an enjoyment of the garden and that was thanks to Jean-Paul.

The grounds looked magnificent. The blossom was out and birdsong filled the honey-scented air. Fat bees buzzed about the borders where bulbs were now flowering. The wild garden was peppered with buttercups, purple camassias, cowslips and feathery dandelions. In the cottage garden a luxuriant bed of green shrubs grew up with tulips, narcissi and primulas. In the middle of it stood the mountain ash, covered in a canopy of white flowers, beneath which was the circular bench where Jean-Paul sat from time to time, his brow furrowed in thought.

'Mummy, look at this one!' Gus beckoned his mother to observe the worm he was waving in the air. 'It's enormous.'

'I want to keep one as a friend,' said Storm. 'Can I, J-P?'

'Of course. We can put it in a jar and give it a name.'

'Why not call him Worzel the Worm,' suggested Miranda. Then, inspired by the idea, she announced that she would go to get a jar.

'Clever Mummy,' said Storm, spotting another worm hiding in the soil and bending down to pull it out.

'That's a fat one,' said Mr Underwood, chuckling happily. 'You've got quite a few there.'

'Bring something to drink,' Jean-Paul shouted after Miranda. 'This is thirsty work, eh!'

'*Je suis faim*,' said Storm.

'*J'ai faim*,' Jean-Paul corrected. '*J'ai soif aussi*,' he added.

'That means thirsty,' said Gus.

'Gus-the-Strong and Bright-Sky, you are learning fast!'

'That'll be French,' said Mr Underwood, nodding admiringly.

'Correct,' said Jean-Paul, grinning at him.

While Miranda was in the kitchen, the telephone rang.

'Hi there, stranger.' It was Blythe.

Miranda was pleasantly surprised. She hadn't heard from her friend since their lunch before Christmas. 'How are you?' she asked.

'Fine. I have to go to court next Monday for the settlement.'

'Don't let him get off lightly. Remember what David advised.'

'How is he? I haven't seen him for a while.' She sounded down.

'Truth is, Blythe, I don't see much of him either. He's working really hard. Comes down on Friday night and leaves early Sunday afternoon.'

'You should take a lover,' said Blythe brightly. 'That's what I'd do if I were stuck in the middle of the countryside.'

'Don't tempt me,' Miranda replied, thinking of Jean-Paul. 'Why don't you come down for the weekend? David would love to see you. The gardens look beautiful and I'd like to show off the house.'

'You're settling in then?'

'Yes. Right now, there's no place I'd rather be. I wake up every morning to the sound of a hundred birds in the trees and the scent of flowers wafting in through my window. It's heaven. Do come.'

'I thought you were a city girl.'

'I was, I've just got out of step with the rhythm of London. I prefer the slower pace down here.'

'It sounds blissful. This weekend I'm tied up but the one after . . .?'

'Great. I'll tell David. If you're not careful he'll give you some more of his advice. Great big pearls of wisdom.' She laughed. 'And my garden will make you feel wonderful. I feel utterly transformed.'

'You *sound* utterly transformed. Though I wonder how long it will take before you scamper back to the city?' asked Blythe cynically. 'All those autumn designer collections. You can't have changed that much.'

'We'll see,' Miranda replied.

She made up a jug of elderflower cordial and found an empty jar in the store room. As she walked back into the hall she glanced into her study at her laptop and didn't feel any guilt. She almost skipped through the French doors onto the terrace. The sun was out, the air was warm, Jean-Paul was in the garden, transforming the place with his own, unique brand of magic. Magic she was beginning to understand.

The children had gathered a merry collection of worms and beetles, which they poured into the jar along with a few leaves and blades of grass. 'Will they die?' Storm asked Jean-Paul.

'Not if you put them back at the end of the day. They belong in the garden.' The children set off in search of more. Mr Underwood finished his cup of juice and returned to where he had left off before the children's laughter had lured him into the vegetable garden.

Miranda sat on the grass with her own cup of juice as Jean-Paul set about putting up the sweet-pea frame with pig wire. She watched him work, his fingers rough, his nails short. 'Have you always been a gardener?' she asked.

'For as long as I can remember.' His hands paused a moment. 'My life before meant nothing. I tossed it away on frivolities.'

'What inspired you?'

'My mother. I grew up in a vineyard in Bordeaux. She was a passionate gardener.'

'Is she still alive?'

'No. She died last summer.'

'I'm sorry. You were close?' She slowly prised him open like a rare shell. She knew there was something beautiful inside if she could get in.

'I was her only son. We were very close. She was dignified and quietly spoken. She had an air of serenity. She was very strong.'

'Was she beautiful?' she asked, knowing the answer.

'She had black hair that she tied into a chignon. I rarely saw it down, except at night. She would kiss me good night when I was a boy and I would see her with her hair down, and I thought she must be an angel, she was so beautiful. It would fall down her back shining like silk. As she got older it went grey. Then I never saw it loose.'

'If you don't mind me asking, how did she die?'

'She died in her sleep, peacefully. She was seventy-three. There was nothing wrong with her. She simply didn't wake up.' He shrugged and shook his head. 'Like a clock, her heart ceased to tick.'

'Is your father alive?'

'Yes. He lives in Paris. They were not close.'

Boldly she asked the question she had been longing to ask since she first met him. 'Jean-Paul, have you ever been in love?'

For a moment she feared she had gone too far. His face closed into that of a stranger's, pulled down and grey with sorrow. 'Once,' he replied evenly. 'And once only. I will never love again.'

Miranda felt a wave of disappointment, as if his answer had crushed her heart. 'So you pour all your love into the gardens,' she said hoarsely. He didn't reply, but his face softened. 'You have a gift, Jean-Paul,' she continued, emboldened. 'Your love not only makes the garden grow but my children too. Thanks to you they don't fight. They've stopped watching television. You've taught them the wonders of nature and the fun there is to be had among the trees and flowers. I'm so grateful.'

'It's not all me,' he said, taking a pot of sweet peas to plant beneath the frame. 'Your children want to be with you and David.'

'I didn't know what to do with them before,' she admitted. 'In London they had a nanny. I realise now that I never really saw them. And Gus was such a problem, fighting with the other children at school, disrupting the classes. Moving out here has been the best thing we ever did for him. He's really settled down. It's thanks to you, Jean-Paul. You and the garden.'

'Gus just wants to feel important and valued, Miranda. Children are very easy to please; they just want your attention and your love.'

'I *do* love them.'

'It is not enough to tell them you love them. You have to show them.'

'How come you're so wise when you don't have children of your own?'

'Because I learned from a very special woman many years ago. She put her children above everything, even above her heart's desire.'

'Is it wrong to be a working mother?'

'No. You have to satisfy yourself as well. If you are unhappy they sense it. Children need their mothers and fathers. Gus needs his father.'

'I know.' *But he has you. You include him, inspire him, play with him, make him feel special and important. David thinks only of himself. You're the one Gus looks up to. You're the one he loves.* Suddenly, a cloud of resentment cast her in shadow. 'I need a husband too,' she confessed huskily.

'Tell him,' he said simply.

She got to her feet, then collected up the empty cups and jug. 'Life is so complicated.' She sighed. 'Love is complicated.'

'But life is unbearable without it.'

'Then how do you bear it?' she asked before she could stop herself. She realised that David had shifted away from the centre of her world. Jean-Paul had taken his place in her affections. She loved him. She couldn't help herself.

'Because I have no choice,' he replied. She walked away, turning as she reached the gate, hoping that he might still be watching her. But he was bent over the sweet peas, lost in thought.

It occurred to Miranda that her life was beginning to mirror Ava's. Both women had fallen in love with their gardeners. David appeared in her mind like a small boat drifting away on the current.

Suddenly she was inspired to write. With a pounding heart she realised she had found her story. A great love story in the grand style of *Anna Karenina* and *Gone with the Wind*. It was right here beneath her nose. She was living it. If she couldn't have Jean-Paul she would satisfy her desire in a work of fiction.

While the children played in the gardens, she opened the windows in her study, filling the room with the honey-scented blossom from the orchard. She chose a CD of light classical music and sat at her desk, in front of her computer screen. The music carried her deep into her imagination where her longings lay like dormant seeds in a bed of rich and fertile soil. Her fingers tapped over the keys, faster and faster as she watered those seeds with expression and felt them grow. She inhaled, sure that she could smell the tangy scent of orange blossom.

That night, as she read the children a bedtime story, Gus snuggled up against her, resting his head on her shoulder. She could tell by his frown that something was troubling him.

'Mummy, why doesn't Daddy ever play with us?'

'Because he's very busy, darling. He has to work in London.'

'But at weekends?'

'He's tired.'

'I wish J-P was my daddy.'

Miranda felt a cold fist squeeze her heart. 'You don't mean that, Gus,' she replied. 'Daddy would love to spend all day with you like Jean-Paul does. But he has to work in the City to earn money so we can live in this beautiful house and so you and Storm can go to school—'

'But he's going to send me away to boarding school.'

Miranda took a deep breath, She couldn't deny that boarding school was on the cards for both children. 'You'll love boarding school, Gus. You'll play sport and make loads of friends.' He looked away. 'And you'll come home at weekends. Only big boys go to boarding school.'

'I don't want to be a big boy,' he whispered.

Miranda was in high spirits. Having acknowledged her love for Jean-Paul, she had put the children to bed after reading them *The Three Little Wolves* in a very theatrical voice, and returned to her computer to write until four in the morning. The words had spilt out from deep inside her. Inspired by love, and Ava's secret scrapbook, she had written prose so lyrical it was as if someone else were writing through her.

When David came home on Friday night, he was tired and irritable. He strode into the hall enveloped in a cloud of fury. Miranda was impervious to his mood. She kissed him cheerfully, and announced that she had tried a new recipe for dinner. 'Salmon pancakes. Why don't you have a glass of wine, darling? You look exhausted.'

David was startled by the change in his wife. She seemed in her own happy world, unaffected by him. He followed her into the kitchen. She looked good, too. Her eyes sparkled, her skin glowed and she walked with a spring in her step. Her exuberance made him feel all the more bad-tempered.

'How are the children?' he asked, taking the glass of wine she offered him.

'They're on very good form. Gus has some schoolfriends coming to tea tomorrow. It's a big step for him. Storm has invited Madeleine. They're all going fishing with Jean-Paul. He's made them all nets. I'm

sure they won't catch anything, but I'm going to make them a picnic. You can join us if you like.'

'I might,' he replied noncommittally.

'Good wine, isn't it?' she said, taking a sip. 'Fatima's son, who owns the convenience store, recommended it to me. He says it's as good as Château Latour.'

'I hope it's not as expensive as Château Latour.'

'Twelve pounds a bottle.'

He took a sip and raised his eyebrows. 'Not bad.'

'Dinner will be at eight thirty. I've got one or two things to do in my study. Why don't you have a nice bath? Oh, by the way, I've asked Blythe down next weekend.'

He looked even more furious. 'Why?'

'Because I haven't seen her since Christmas and I've been meaning to ask her for ages. Do you have a problem with it?'

'No,' he replied hastily.

'Good.' She disappeared up the corridor. David was left in the kitchen, wondering why everything felt wrong.

Miranda printed out the novel so far. It began the day Jean-Paul had turned up with Storm, although she had changed the names of all the characters and added a little invention to detach it as best she could from her own life. She was particularly pleased with Angelica, the central character. She could see her clearly in her mind's eye: small, slight, with tousled hair the colour of sun-dried hay, twisted up on the top of her head and secured casually with a pencil. Her eyes were pale green, the colour of early leaves, and her smile was wide and infectious.

Miranda was overcome by the need to put the story down on paper and her fingers seemed to move automatically, the story writing itself. She reread the first couple of chapters and was impressed. She never knew she had the ability to write like this.

That night, while David made love to her, her mind was in the gardens with Angelica and Jean-Paul, with Ava and the enigmatic young man who dominated her secret scrapbook. She closed her eyes and imagined David was Jean-Paul. Swept away in her imagination, she enjoyed his attentions. Afterwards he rolled over and went to sleep, but Miranda lay awake, staring at the ceiling through the darkness.

In the morning she got up early, leaving David asleep in bed. Gus and Storm were in a state of high excitement, anticipating the afternoon with their friends. Miranda slipped into a pair of jeans and a shirt. She

tied her hair into a ponytail and skipped about the kitchen humming to herself while she made breakfast for her children.

She had just poured herself a cup of coffee when Jean-Paul appeared at the window. The children waved excitedly. 'Do you want to come in for a coffee?' she asked, holding up her cup in case he couldn't hear her through the glass. He grinned and nodded. A few moments later he appeared in the kitchen in his socks, having left his boots at the door.

'*Bonjour*,' he said. The children replied in French, their faces beaming.

'Fred and Joe are coming to play today,' Gus reminded him.

'And Madeleine,' added Storm.

'And we are going fishing, no?' said Jean-Paul. He took his coffee and perched on a stool. 'Then we will make a fire and cook what we catch.'

'Do you think you'll catch anything?' Miranda asked.

Jean-Paul shrugged. 'If we don't, I have a fresh salmon in my fridge.'

'Ah,' she replied, grinning at him conspiratorially. Jean-Paul stared at her. She was all fired up as if her heart were a burning coal. Things must have improved between her and David. He was pleased.

David woke and stretched, finding the space beside him empty and cold. He got up and showered. He felt disgruntled, remembering Miranda had asked Blythe down the following weekend. David was trying to distance himself from Blythe. She had grown needy, telephoning him in the day, insisting on seeing him. He had tried to let her down gently, but then she had turned up at his office in a fur coat, opening it a little so that he could see she was wearing nothing but a pair of lace stockings and a little shirt that barely reached her belly. Unable to resist, he had made love to her in the women's lavatory, which he now regretted. It had given her the wrong message. Now Miranda had asked her down for a weekend. He resolved to organise a business trip and avoid her altogether.

The kitchen was empty; used cups sat in the sink and a pan of hot milk was keeping warm on the Aga. He sighed resentfully. There was a time when Miranda had made him breakfast every morning, fussing over him like a geisha. Now she didn't even bother to stick around. He poured himself a cup of coffee, made a couple of pieces of toast and marmalade, and sat down at the head of the table to read the papers.

After breakfast he went into the garden. The sound of birds was loud and cheery, a background to the excited squeals of his children behind the wall of the vegetable garden. Curious to see what they were doing, he walked up the path and opened the gate to find Storm and Gus

chasing each other up and down the gravel pathways that separated the vegetable patches, holding long worms between their fingers. Jean-Paul was on his hands and knees planting. More surprisingly, Miranda was on her knees too, her face flushed. David felt excluded. They looked like any happy family on a Saturday morning, enjoying the sunshine.

He had to admit it was beautiful, though: the white apple blossom, the neat borders of box that enclosed each vegetable patch, the arched frames that Jean-Paul had constructed for the sweet peas and beans. The old wall was covered in white wisteria tangling through blue ceanothus.

Miranda beckoned him over. 'Come and join us!' He raised a hand and forced a smile. But he didn't feel like helping; he felt jealous, an outcast in his own home. The usurper was there with his knees in the mud, slipping into his place while he was in London. He was turning to leave, his heart heavy, when a high-pitched voice shouted after him.

'Daddy!' Storm ran up to him. 'Daddy, come and see what we've done in the garden.' He looked down at her enthusiastic face and was left no option but to follow her. Gus stood watching warily from under his dark fringe. David looked at his son, suddenly tall and handsome, and wondered how he had grown so much without him noticing.

'What have you been doing, Gus?' he asked.

Gus proudly held out the jar of creepy-crawlies. 'Say hello to our friends,' he said, and Jean-Paul paused his planting to watch.

XI

BLYTHE ARRIVED WITH RAFAEL on Friday afternoon. She stepped out of the taxi and swept her eyes over David and Miranda's beautiful house with an uncomfortable mixture of admiration and envy. It was a warm afternoon, the sky a rich blue. Birds twittered noisily in the trees and a pair of fat pigeons sat on the roof of the house lazily watching the hours pass. A gentle breeze raked through the long grasses and flowers in the wild-flower meadow like fingers through hair, and in the middle of it all stood an old oak tree, where a group of giggling children played,

their cries ringing out in joyful abandon. It was an idyllic scene, not at all what Blythe had envisaged. When she thought of the country she imagined rain, mud, gumboots, cold houses and boredom.

Gus shouted at Rafael excitedly from his tree house. Blythe held her son's hand. Gus was a menace. The last time they had played together Gus had hit him over the head with a heavy wooden train track. She had warned Rafael never to be left alone with him. 'He's a horrid little boy,' she had told him. Now, Rafael gazed longingly at the tree house.

Gus was Captain Hook in the crow's nest of his ship, scanning the sea for enemies. Inside the hollow, Joe and Madeleine were imprisoned Lost Boys, while outside, Tinkerbell, played by Storm, and Peter, played by Fred, were sneaking through the grass to rescue them. The game was halted while Storm and Gus shouted for Rafael to join them. Rafael hovered by his mother's side until, finally, his curiosity got the better of him and he dragged her over to the tree.

'Do you want to play?' Gus asked, jumping to the ground, a broad grin eating up the freckles on his face. Blythe was surprised. He didn't look like the surly child she knew. 'He can be another Lost Boy if he likes.' His politeness grated. She almost preferred him sullen and uncommunicative. It seemed as if Miranda had everything. Then she thought of David. *Almost* everything.

As Rafael was bundled into the hollow with Joe and Madeleine, Miranda stepped out of the front door. She waved at Blythe. 'I didn't hear your taxi,' she said as she approached. Blythe studied her carefully. In a pair of jeans and shirt she looked radiant. I never knew she had quite such long legs, Blythe thought grudgingly, even in trainers!

'You look so good, Miranda, I'm feeling sick!' she gushed.

'Don't be silly!'

'You do. Your house is divine, by the way. Stunning. It's paradise down here. You're so lucky. I want it all and I want it now.' She laughed huskily and delved in her handbag for a cigarette. 'Do you want one?'

'I've given up.'

'Hence the glow.' Blythe sighed before popping a Marlboro Lite into her mouth and flicking her lighter. 'I'll give up once this bloody divorce is done with.'

'How's it all going?'

'Dreadful. I feel like I've been through a mangle.'

'You look well on it.'

'That's because I have a lover,' she whispered smugly. She couldn't resist. Miranda's perfect life was too much to bear.

'Same one?'

'Same one.'

'Come inside and have a cup of tea,' Miranda suggested. Blythe glanced at her son. 'Rafael's fine here,' Miranda added. 'Gus will take care of him.'

'It's Gus I'm afraid of,' said Blythe drily. 'He's Captain Hook!'

Miranda laughed. 'Don't worry. His battle cry is worse than his hook.'

'It's an amazing tree house. Did David make it?'

'No, Jean-Paul, the gardener.'

'Wow. Some gardener!'

'He's wonderful. I'll show you round. The garden is really beautiful. It used to belong to this fascinating old woman called Ava Lightly. When I arrived no one could talk of anything but her amazing garden. When we bought the house it had been unoccupied for two years and the garden had been left to rot. Then Jean-Paul took over and agreed to bring it back to its former glory. He's done the most incredible job. I'd like to invite Ava Lightly over to see it. I think she'd be really pleased.'

'Or appalled. Old people can be so ungrateful.'

'I don't know. She sounds such a nice person.'

'Do you have friends down here?'

'Yes. The people range from charming to eccentric. A mixed bag. You'd love Troy; he's gay and has a hair salon on the high street. Henrietta Moon, who owns the gift shop, has become a good friend. We've just started doing Pilates together, which is hilarious. It's hard work, but great fun. Some of the other girls are really nice. We all have coffee together after the class.' As they walked into the hall Miranda added, 'The vicar is having a drinks party in the village hall tomorrow night in order to raise money. It's ten pounds a ticket. If you'd like to check out the local flavour, we could go. Might be a laugh.'

'Or hell!'

'David will go. He loves lording it over everyone. He's dragged me to church once or twice just so he can stride up the aisle and sit in the front pew, which I was amused to find already taken by some oldies who weren't going to budge for him. You can imagine his disappointment. He chatted to everyone afterwards, dispensing pearls of wisdom, no doubt. The generous-spirited person that he is!'

'He's incorrigible,' said Blythe, smiling as she thought of him. 'What time does he come home?'

'In time for dinner.'

Blythe gazed round the oval hall. At the end, large French doors gave

out onto a leafy terrace where she could see vast urns of tulips and a stone walkway that extended into the distance, lined by big fat topiary balls. In the middle of the hall stood a round table on which sat a luxurious display of pink lilies beside a sculpture. The walls had been painted a warm ivory on which Miranda had hung a collage of large black and white photographs in silver frames.

'You've done it beautifully,' Blythe said. 'I want to repaint my house. What is that paint?' She pressed her nose up against the wall to take a closer look.

'Sanderson.'

'Of course. Very subtle. What happens outside?'

'Let's get a cup of tea, then I'll show you everything.'

'I think it's time for a glass of wine,' said Blythe, needing fortification.

Blythe took her glass of chardonnay around the entire house, taking her time to poke her nose into each room. Once she'd seen inside, the two women wandered up the thyme walk, stepping across long shadows cast by the topiary balls, watching the setting sun bleed into the sky. The children's voices could be heard on the other side of the house, rising into the air like the loud chirping of birds.

Miranda showed her the vegetable garden, telling her proudly about sowing the vegetable seeds.

'I thought you were miserable down here.' Blythe had preferred it when Miranda had been unhappy.

'I was. Now I love it. I have Jean-Paul to thank for that.' They walked up the meandering path of the cottage garden. Miranda pointed out the shrubs and plants beginning to flower. Blythe was surprised how she knew them all by name. Her friend had changed and she wasn't sure she liked it. They walked on until they came to the dovecote, watched over by towering larches. 'I want to buy some doves,' said Miranda. 'There's something very lonely about this place. It's like a neglected corner of the garden. Doves will put the life back, don't you think?'

At that moment, Jean-Paul strode out of the trees, pushing a wheelbarrow full of dead branches. Blythe caught her breath. 'Hello, Miranda,' he said, knocking Blythe off-balance with a wide smile.

'Wasn't Mr Underwood supposed to clear away that tree?'

'Yes, but he's old.' Jean-Paul shrugged and settled his eyes on her friend.

'This is Blythe,' Miranda said. 'She's come to stay for the weekend.'

'I've heard so much about you,' said Blythe in French, gazing back at him coyly. 'You've done wonderful things in this garden.'

'Thank you,' he replied, smiling. 'I commend your French.' He turned to Miranda. 'I think I'll go and be a crocodile for a while,' he said.

'The children'll love that,' she replied, spotting the knowing twinkle in his eye as he departed.

Blythe watched him walk away, her gaze lingering appreciatively on his slim hips and faded jeans. 'Christ, Miranda!' she exclaimed once he had gone. 'No wonder you like it down here. He's delicious!'

'I know. Everyone fancies him.' Miranda turned away.

'Are you sleeping with him?'

Miranda was appalled. 'Of course not! I'm married.'

'So? You said yourself, David's never here.'

'What difference does that make? I love David. Why would I want to be unfaithful? There's more to life than sex.'

'Is there? Life would be very dull without it.' They continued their walk towards the field where Charlie the donkey stood chewing grass. 'You'd want Jean-Paul if you weren't married,' she added with a smirk. 'How did you find him?'

'He just turned up here one day with Storm. He found her in a field and brought her back.'

'What was he doing in the field?'

'I don't know.' On reflection it was all very bizarre. 'He was on his way here. I think he'd seen my advert in town. Anyway, what does it matter? He's a good gardener and that's what counts.'

'He's obviously not married. Divorced?'

'I don't think so.'

'You don't know? Haven't you asked him? Has he any children?'

'No.'

'What were his references like? Who was he working for before he came here? A grand English family, no doubt.'

'I have no idea.'

'You didn't check him out?'

'I didn't need to. I sensed he was right.'

Blythe raised her eyebrows. 'You hired him because he's handsome. He could be a criminal on the run, for all you know.'

'I doubt it.' Miranda grew irritated. 'Look, Blythe, I don't care if he's a criminal on the run or has three wives across different continents. He does a wonderful job here and he's good company. I enjoy being around him. I don't ask him about himself out of respect. I don't want to pry.'

'You mean you don't want to look too interested.'

'I don't fancy him, Blythe!'

'Of course you don't.' She gave a little snort. 'But I do.'

'You're unavailable.'

'I don't know. Once my lover showered me with gifts, now he rarely has time for me. But I turned up at his office the other day in nothing but a fur coat and suspenders. He couldn't resist me then.'

'You've got a nerve. Do you think he'll leave his wife for you?'

'I don't know.' She surveyed the estate and fantasised about living there. It was an appealing thought. 'I don't think I'm wife material any more.'

'Have you met the wife?'

'Yes.' Blythe cast a sidelong glance at Miranda, relishing her secret.

'What's she like?'

Blythe chewed the inside of her cheek as she pondered the best way to answer without giving the game away. She knew she was taking a risk even discussing it with Miranda, but there was something about Miranda's perfect life—and perfect Frenchman—that made her want to burst one or two of her bubbles. 'Nice,' she replied carefully. 'I'm a bitch!' She gave a throaty laugh, then pushed her wrist out of her sleeve. 'Look, this is what he gave me for Christmas.' Miranda looked at the Theo Fennell diamond watch and recalled the strange telephone call in December. Her stomach twisted with anxiety.

'It's from Theo's,' she observed.

'Yes. Isn't it gorgeous? I'm loving the pink strap. And it's engraved. It says "Big Pussycat" on the back. Private joke. But that was Christmas. He hasn't given me anything since,' she pouted.

No, it can't be. It's just a coincidence, Miranda thought, suddenly feeling nauseous. Anyone could have bought Blythe that watch.

But her mind began whirring with possibilities. Was David Blythe's lover? Did Blythe, the friend she had known since school, have the malice to steal her husband?

As they walked back to the house, she tried to hide her anxiety by asking Blythe about herself and letting her rattle on, but she could not dispel the feeling that David was seeing someone else. And the more she thought about it, the more her suspicions were aroused.

David had originally planned to be away on business for Blythe's weekend, but his desire to spend more time with Miranda and the children overrode his wish to distance himself from his mistress. When he arrived, the children were watching a video in their pyjamas. Madeleine, Joe and Fred had been collected and taken home.

David met Miranda warmly, sliding a hand round her waist and

kissing her affectionately on her cheek. She flushed with pleasure and surprise, then watched him greet Blythe with the scrutiny of a scientist observing an organism beneath a microscope.

Despite having been irritated when Miranda had mentioned she had invited Blythe for the weekend, David seemed pleased enough to see her. He looked tired after a week in the office and the journey from London. Miranda poured him a glass of wine and, after saying hello to the children in the playroom, he disappeared upstairs to have a bath.

Blythe sat at the kitchen table, watching Miranda prepare the roast chicken for dinner. She sipped her wine and nibbled on a carrot. 'David's looking very tired,' she said.

'Every weekend it's the same. By the time he's recovered he's back on that train to start the whole process again. A banker's life isn't a life. It's just money. Frankly, I'd rather have a husband.'

'I didn't know things weren't good between you.' Blythe looked genuinely concerned. Her sympathy was reassuring and Miranda hastily dismissed her suspicions as irrational. After basting the chicken she picked up her wineglass and joined Blythe at the table.

'I just don't see much of him, that's all. It's hard to have a marriage when you spend so little time together.'

'Perhaps this move out to the country wasn't such a good idea. I mean, for Gus and Storm it's been fantastic, anyone can see that. Gus especially. He was once so angry. Now he's charming.'

'He has more of a relationship with Jean-Paul than he does with his own father,' Miranda confided.

'Doesn't that sadden David?'

'I don't think he's noticed.' Miranda laughed bitterly. 'I have more of a marriage with Jean-Paul than I do with him. And no, I'm not sleeping with him. But I spend more time with him. I've changed, too. You know something, Blythe, I don't think David knows me any more.'

'Darling, this is so sad. You and David are two of my dearest friends. I thought you had the best marriage in London.'

Blythe's reaction to her troubled marriage dispelled any fears of duplicity.

'What should I do?' Miranda asked.

'Talk to him. Work it out. I would hate you two to have to go through what I'm going through. It's hell.'

Miranda and Blythe put the children to bed. Gus was sharing his room with Rafael, but they fell asleep immediately. David came out of his bedroom, dressed in a pair of slacks and a clean, open-necked shirt.

He saw the women hovering outside Gus's room and went to join them. 'Are they asleep?' he asked.

'Why don't you go and kiss them good night,' said Miranda. 'Even if they're half-asleep, they'll like it.'

David nodded and disappeared into Gus's room.

Gus felt his father's prickly face as he kissed him on his cheek. He opened his eyes. 'I wasn't really asleep,' he hissed.

'Just pretending?' said his father.

'Yes.'

'What did you do today?'

'We played pirates. Jean-Paul was the crocodile,' he said with a giggle.

'Was he?' David bristled with jealousy. 'Didn't Captain Hook kill the crocodile?'

'No! I was Captain Hook and the crocodile ate me.'

'You look in pretty good shape for someone who's been in the belly of a crocodile.'

'I escaped. Will you play with us tomorrow?'

'What, be a crocodile?'

'You can be Smee.'

David considered his proposal. 'I'll think of a more exciting game.'

'OK,' Gus replied. But he knew his father would forget and find something better to do. He rolled over and closed his eyes. It didn't matter if his father didn't play with him: he had Jean-Paul.

Miranda was carving the chicken when David came in. He had a strange look on his face, as if someone had put their hand in his stomach and twisted his gut. 'Are you all right?' Miranda asked.

'I'm fine. Just need another glass of wine. It's been a bad week.'

Miranda refilled his glass. 'Was Gus asleep?'

David grinned and took a swig. 'No, the little monkey was just pretending. Clever boy.'

'Like his father,' said Blythe. 'Clever, I mean.'

David didn't react. 'Here, let me help you with that,' he said to Miranda. She handed over the knife and fork in surprise. 'This chicken looks delicious!' he exclaimed.

'It's from the farmers' market. Should taste good.'

'Let's have a try.' He carved a piece and popped it in his mouth. The colour returned to his cheeks. 'It'll do,' he quipped, feeling better. 'Right, Blythe, come and help yourself,' said David. He handed her a plate, then put his arm round Miranda's waist and planted a kiss on her cheek.

Miranda looked at him. Perhaps their marriage wasn't on the rocks after all, she thought, noticing a warmth in his eyes she hadn't seen in a long time. The mystery engraving at Theo Fennell was probably a misunderstanding and not David at all. He worked hard to give them the life they enjoyed and she had been unfair to doubt him.

'And how have you been, darling?' he asked her.

'Well, we've planted loads of vegetables and the children have had some friends home for tea. We wouldn't have imagined that happening six months ago, would we?' In her enthusiasm she was about to tell him she had started writing a novel, but something made her hold back. 'Everything's good,' she concluded.

David tucked into his chicken, drank half a bottle of wine and finally began to relax. Last weekend, the sight of his wife and children in the vegetable garden with Jean-Paul had given him a painful jolt. They had looked like a happy family, laughing and playing in the sunshine. Miranda didn't smile at him the way she smiled at Jean-Paul. He had noticed the way they seemed to communicate silently like two people who shared secrets. And now he felt Gus and Storm drifting away from him like bright helium balloons in a big blue sky, too far away to reach. They had settled into Hartington with their mother, but there didn't seem to be a place there for him.

It had been reckless of Blythe to accept Miranda's invitation. Now he chatted to her as any friend would, hoping to give nothing away. He regretted his affair with her. It had meant nothing. Just a bit of fun. He'd get through the weekend without raising suspicion, then he'd tell her clearly it was over. Recently, he had tried to let her down gently, seeing less of her, not taking her calls. But she was persistent and he had made the error of weakening at the sight of her in suspenders and fur coat. She had to be told straight. Their affair had to stop.

After dinner they remained at the table discussing Blythe's divorce. There was nothing more gratifying for her than talking about herself, sweeping everyone into her drama. The more she drank, the less attractive she became. By contrast, Miranda looked serene, if a little detached.

Later, in bed, Miranda turned over onto her side, facing away from him. Her breathing was so quiet he could barely hear her. 'Miranda,' David whispered. 'Are you still awake?'

'Yes,' she whispered back.

'Come here.'

'I'm tired,' she replied, without moving. She didn't feel like making love. He put an arm round her waist and edged close behind her.

'I want to spend time with the children tomorrow,' he said. 'What would they like to do?'

'Why don't you take them up to the castle?'

'Would they like that?'

'I'm sure they would if you make it fun.'

David thought about it. He wanted to confess that he had forgotten how to make things fun. 'I'll do my best,' he said.

'You're making me hot,' she said, not unkindly.

He moved back to his side of the bed. The sheets were cold. 'What's happening to us?' he said suddenly. 'We used to laugh all the time. We used to share everything. Now we exist in the same world but apart. I want to make it right between us. I want to go back to the way we were.' He reached out his hand and placed it on her hip. 'I love you, Miranda. The trouble is I get so caught up in work that I forget to tell you. I feel you drifting away, and I don't want to lose you.'

She turned over to face him and ran her fingers down his face. 'You're not going to lose me, darling. But we have to work at this.'

'Then let's work at it. My family is more important to me than work. I'd quit my job in a heartbeat if I felt it was driving a wedge between us.'

'You don't have to go that far. Just watch less golf at weekends. Gus and Storm are such fun. They just want you to spend time with them.'

'You're so right. I wish Blythe wasn't here, then we could be alone together.' He drew Miranda into his arms and kissed her forehead.

I wish I had never fooled around with Blythe, he thought to himself. I'll tell her it's over and put the whole stupid mess behind me.

Blythe lay in bed unable to sleep. The room spun. She stuck her foot out and planted it firmly on the floor to steady herself. It wasn't much help. She seethed in fury. David hadn't paid her any attention. He had kissed his wife in front of her—what an insult!—and not even given her a secret smile or knowing look. He had acted as if she were like any other guest. So much for Miranda's floundering marriage. They looked as smugly content as any happily married couple could look.

As the room slowed down she resolved to get him on his own the following day. She'd drag him into a bush if she had to.

Henrietta sat in Troy's sitting room curled up on the sofa with a digestive biscuit and a mug of hot milk. 'You know, Miranda's going to take me up to London for a make-over,' she informed him. 'We're going to the personal shopping place at Selfridges.'

'Lucky you!' he breathed enviously. 'You might even get Pandora. She's gorgeous, blonde, as bubbly as a magnum of Moët & Chandon.'

'How on earth do you know that?'

'I make it my business to know important things.' He laughed. '*Grazia* magazine or *InStyle*, I can't remember which one, but they gave her a whole feature. She takes care of the rich and famous. She'll turn Cinderetta into a real princess at the ball.'

'You're silly!' She grinned at him fondly. 'I'm rather excited. It's so generous of Miranda.'

'She's got a heart as big as her wallet and we love her for it!'

'She's given me Trinny & Susannah's book,' she said, pulling *What Not to Wear* out of her bag.

'Great! Let's read it now.'

'Now? But it's after midnight?'

'Well, you're not a pumpkin, are you? You can stay the night here.'

'But I haven't brought my toothbrush.'

'I have enough of everything for both of us.' He snorted. 'If you're going to meet the glorious Pandora, you must know what suits you. Go on, open the book!'

Five miles away, Jeremy Fitzherbert lay in his large wooden bed. He slept with the curtains open and a window ajar. He liked the smell of the countryside and the sound of birds in the early morning, and he relished the pale, liquid light of dawn. It was a clear night. Small twinkling stars shone through the darkness and a crescent moon hung low in the sky.

He sighed, thinking of Henrietta and replaying the moment they had met. He smiled at the recollection of her extricating herself from the hollow tree. Her face had flushed with embarrassment, but her eyes had sparkled and her smile was so endearing he had wanted to kiss her right there. He liked full-bodied women. To Jeremy a full-bodied woman was a woman who ate enthusiastically from the tree of life.

He hadn't intended to go to the village hall party the following night. The older he got the more solitary he became. But there was a chance Henrietta might be there and he didn't want to miss her. In Henrietta he saw a woman with simple tastes like his own, a voluptuous body like a delicious fruit, and a smile that revealed a gentle nature and tender disposition. She was perfect, but out of reach. As he drifted to sleep he considered his life. He was forty-five years old. It was time he shared it with someone.

XII

DAVID WAS UP with Miranda and the children at 7.30 a.m. He heard the sound of footsteps on the gravel and bristled at the thought of Jean-Paul striding into the core of his family and taking it over.

He peered through the window. Outside, the garden was bathed in the fresh, sparkling light of morning. The place looked this beautiful because of Jean-Paul; David was wise enough to know that if his children preferred to spend time with the gardener it was his own fault.

'We're going to have a picnic at the castle,' he announced over breakfast. Storm and Rafael wriggled on the bench excitedly.

Gus looked at his father mistrustfully. 'What's there to do at the castle?' he asked.

'Explore,' said David, pouring coffee into his cup. 'It's a ruin. There might even be ghosts.'

'Really!' gasped Storm.

'Don't be silly. Ghosts don't exist,' said Gus.

'We'll see,' added their father. 'Mummy, put a chilled bottle of wine in the bag, will you?'

'Good idea,' she replied, trying not to show her surprise. This is what family life is supposed to be like, she thought contentedly, laying rashers of bacon on the grill.

'Did I hear someone say "chilled bottle of wine"?'

Blythe entered the room in a red cashmere sweater and tight black jeans tucked into leather boots. Her face was immaculately made up and her hair washed and shiny, falling in thick waves down her back. Miranda looked at her enviously. She had barely had time to moisturise her face.

Blythe pulled out the chair beside David and sat down. 'Morning, my love,' she said to her son. She didn't look at David, but she could feel his eyes on her. 'The country air is doing you good,' she said. 'Your cheeks are pink.'

'Those boots are more suited to Knightsbridge than castle-creeping,' said David, running his eyes over her appreciatively.

'Are we castle-creeping?'

'We are. We're taking a picnic.'

'That's so quaint. I shall sit on the rug drinking white wine while you do the creeping!'

Hartington Castle was built on a natural hill overlooking the town. The central structure, now a ruin, dated back to the thirteenth century. Sadly, the castle had burnt down in the late eighteenth century and had never been rebuilt. However, as a ruin it held great allure. There were walls and towers still standing, and a grand stone staircase leading up to a landing where the great queen, Elizabeth I, would surely have set foot.

They parked the car at the bottom of the hill and walked the well-trodden path up to the castle. The children ran about excitedly, chasing each other up the grassy slope. A few families were already settling their rugs on the grass, nestled against the walls out of the wind. David found a sheltered spot beside a gnarled tree, which some claimed had once given Elizabeth I shelter. Blythe, who had carried the rugs, threw them onto the grass, then sat down, wrapping her coat round her to keep warm. Miranda poured them all a glass of wine and gave the children each a carton of apple juice. Gus took his father's hand. Miranda noticed, but said nothing, not wanting to draw attention to this rare moment, in case she jinxed it. 'Daddy, will you come and look round with us?' he asked. To Gus's surprise, his father agreed.

By midday, the castle was busy. It had become a hot May day, an optimistic prelude to summer. Blythe took off her coat and sweated in her cashmere. Miranda sat in her T-shirt, feeling the sun hot on her skin. She opened the second bottle of wine and the children ate their sandwiches hungrily, having run about all morning. Rafael had long forgotten his fear of Gus and followed him devotedly. David lay back and let the rays warm his face. He closed his eyes and drifted off to sleep.

Blythe watched him while he slept. She wondered when they were going to find a moment to be alone. She shuffled uncomfortably in her cashmere and felt her face burning in the sunshine. By contrast, Miranda looked serene and cool in her white T-shirt. Blythe envied her. She herself might look glamorous but her jeans were too tight, her boots too hot and her foundation was melting like wax.

Miranda saw a couple in Elizabethan fancy dress and remembered Troy pointing to Jack and Mary Tinton in Cate's Cake Shop and mentioning that they dressed up at weekends to parade about the castle. The

sight was hilarious. 'I've got to get the children,' she told Blythe, standing up. 'They have to see that couple dressed up. Do you want to come?'

Blythe declined. 'I'm already too hot,' she said. 'And, sadly, I've got nothing on beneath my sweater except my bra.'

She waited until Miranda was out of sight, then reached across and stroked David's cheek. He stirred a little, but slept on. She ran her finger across his lips then, in an act of extreme rashness, bent down and kissed him. He opened his eyes, saw it was Blythe and sat up. 'Are you insane?' he snapped, wiping off her lipstick with his hand.

'I couldn't resist,' she replied smoothly. 'You looked so adorable. I want to be alone with you.'

'Not here.'

'OK, so not here. Can I see you in London? We've had fun, haven't we?' She shook her head so that her hair fell across her cheeks like shiny curtains, and fixed him with her steady green eyes.

'Yes,' he conceded grudgingly. 'But, Blythe . . .' He looked at her, and was suddenly gripped with fear. If he finished the affair now she could be dangerous in her fury. He had to be careful.

Miranda was no longer suspicious that David was having an affair, least of all with Blythe. She felt ashamed for having imagined it.

That night they decided to skip the party at the village hall and have dinner at home. The children ragged around until late, then David read them *Peter and the Wolf*, putting on voices that made them laugh.

Miranda left him to it, enjoying a glass of wine with Blythe at the kitchen table. At dinner, her mood was buoyant and optimistic, until Blythe did something that caught her attention. It was a minor gesture; if she hadn't already harboured a grain of doubt she would not have dwelt on it. As it was, it caused her throat to constrict and her happiness to evaporate.

When she was at the Aga, pulling out the fish pie, something made her turn her eyes to the table. She saw Blythe reach out and take David's wineglass, then put it to her lips and take a sip. Miranda froze in horror, reeling from the intimacy of the gesture. David continued to listen to Blythe, as if it was the most normal thing in the world for her to drink from his glass, then picked it up and took a sip himself. When Miranda returned to the table she noticed that Blythe's own glass was full.

This time she did not dismiss it. Had Blythe's gesture been an isolated one, she wouldn't have given it so much weight. But it was one of many small things that, added together, made a heavy package.

Jeremy arrived late at the village hall. The party was well underway by the time he entered, wearing a pair of brown trousers and blue open-necked shirt. He had bathed and shaved, shut the dogs in the kitchen, then driven into town with the intention of arriving on time. However, half a mile out of town the car began to wobble, then limp, and finally grind to a halt on the side of the road. He swore and hit the steering wheel in fury, but there was nothing he could do. The tyre was flat. Instead of dropping to his knees and changing it, he left the car there and proceeded to walk instead. He was damned if he was going to ruin his chances with Henrietta by turning up covered in mud and sweat.

Henrietta arrived clad in a pair of wide black trousers and a long ivory jacket with sharp shoulders and nipped-in waist. She had read *What not to Wear* and gone shopping in Blandford with Troy. They had chosen the outfit together. 'Monochrome is very in, darling,' Troy had said, helping her slip into the jacket.

She gazed round the crowded room and spotted the vicar talking to Colonel Pike, and Mrs Underwood in her best floral dress, talking to Derek Heath, the builder, and his wife Lesley. His blond and handsome sons, Nick and Steve, were surrounded by a group of excitable girls, all vying for their attention. Even Henrietta's sister, Clare, was busy talking to William van den Bos from the bookshop.

Then a voice came from behind. She turned to see Jeremy's long, handsome face smiling diffidently at her. His pink cheeks accentuated the blue of his eyes and the indecent length of his feathery blond eyelashes. She wondered why she hadn't noticed them before.

'Jeremy.' She greeted him as if he were her oldest, dearest friend. 'It's so nice to see you.'

She was more beautiful than he remembered. 'You look well,' he said, wincing at the inadequate words.

She blushed. 'Thank you.'

'It's the heat,' cut in Cate. 'You look like you need some fresh air.'

'Actually, you're absolutely right,' Henrietta replied, gaining strength from Jeremy's presence beside her. 'Jeremy, would you come with me? You never know who might be lurking on the green.'

Jeremy was thrilled by her forwardness. 'It would be my pleasure. My car broke down a mile outside town so I had to walk. It's a lovely evening,' he said, descending the steps to the pavement.

'It's been very warm, hasn't it? Do you think it means we'll have a good summer?'

'We usually have a hot week in May. June might be warm, but I think July will be a scorcher.'

'Are you saying that on authority because you're a farmer?'

'No, because I'm an optimist.'

She giggled and Jeremy's spirits soared. 'I'm an optimist too,' she said. 'It suits you.'

'Do you mind walking a little, after you've walked so far already?'

'I can't think of anyone I'd rather walk with.'

Henrietta felt her belly fill with bubbles. From the sincerity in his voice, she knew he meant it.

That night Miranda couldn't sleep. She was convinced that David was indeed having an affair with Blythe, but had no concrete proof of her suspicions. She wondered how he could make love to her and play so naturally with the children, if all the time he was betraying them.

David slept the peaceful sleep of a man without conscience. Miranda debated silently in the dark. Should she confront him? Should she confront Blythe? She envisaged the scene. The row. The irreparable damage that would shatter their family life for ever.

After breakfast the following morning the children ran outside to the hollow tree, leaving Miranda washing up in the kitchen. Blythe linked her arm through David's. 'Right, M'Lord, show me around your estate.'

'Darling, I'm going to take Blythe round the garden. We'll go and watch the children for a while. Do you want to come?'

'No, thanks. I'll finish the dishes then I'd like to wash my hair.' She winced at the underhand way they had manipulated her to spend time alone together. Her instincts told her to go with them, but she remained by the sink. This might be her only opportunity to catch them at it.

Blythe and David walked to the hollow tree, where the children had resumed the game they had been playing two days before. Jean-Paul was nowhere to be seen. They'd have to make do without the crocodile. Blythe and David stood watching them scamper around like squirrels, and then headed off towards the vegetable garden.

'I love greenhouses.' Blythe inhaled huskily. 'They're hot and humid. They make me feel horny.'

'This isn't a good idea,' said David weakly.

'Of course it is. We're quite alone. I've missed you.'

'It's got to stop,' he added, thinking of his children and longing to be with them. 'This affair must end. It's been fun, but you deserve better,' he said tactfully.

'There is no better than you, David. Every time we part I think it's going to be the last time. But then I see you again and my resolve weakens. I love Miranda, I love your children. I don't want you to jeopardise your marriage, David. Miranda's my oldest friend, I didn't come here to betray her. If you hadn't turned up, I really wouldn't have minded. I don't *want* to seduce you in your own home, I just can't help myself.'

'We haven't done anything wrong this weekend.'

'And we won't,' Blythe agreed. 'It's just a bit of harmless flirting.'

'So you agree that it has to come to an end?'

'Most definitely.'

'It's not because I don't desire you, but because I respect my wife.'

'That's OK. I respect her too.'

They reached the greenhouse and slipped inside. 'Wow!' Blythe exclaimed at the neat rows of orchids and tuberoses. The smell was intoxicating. 'This is incredible. Your gardener is a wonder!'

'He's pretty good, isn't he?'

'Handsome too,' she said, hoping to make him jealous. 'But you're better looking. You're younger for a start.' She placed her hand on his flies. 'Well, this is a little disappointing. Shall I wake him up?'

'Absolutely not!' David replied, backing away. She dropped to her knees and unzipped him. He pulled her up. 'Blythe! I said no.' Then as her face melted with desire he added. 'Not here.'

A sudden movement in the greenhouse distracted Jean-Paul on his way to the vegetable garden. It didn't take him long to work out what was happening. He had been there before, many years ago. He stood rooted to the spot. Instinct told him it was Blythe with David. His heart faltered, thinking of Miranda and those children. The parallels were impossible to ignore. He was allied to Miranda and therefore found himself in Phillip's shoes. It was not a comfortable position.

The sound of the gate alerted him to Miranda's arrival. She could tell from Jean-Paul's ashen face that something was wrong. He strode towards her. 'Come with me,' he said, taking her hand. His tone was firm and masterful as he tried to lead her from the greenhouse.

'What's going on?'

'Just come.'

'No. If it's Blythe and David I need to know.'

He stopped and looked at her intently. 'You already know?'

She began to cry. 'I suspected . . . but I couldn't believe . . .' She fell against him.

He held her close and let her cry. 'Let's get out of here.'

Miranda shook her head. 'No.' Her face had turned red with fury. 'I want to catch them. Then I want to throw them out.'

'It is not a good idea to talk to your husband while you're angry. You will only say things you regret.'

'This is no time to be wise, Jean-Paul.' She pulled away, strode up the path to the greenhouse and banged on the door. 'Come out!' she shouted. 'Come out!'

There was a short pause while Blythe ran her hands through her hair and David felt his orderly world fall about his head like the shattered pieces of a beautiful mosaic. He was the first to emerge.

'It's not what you think . . .' he began.

Miranda looked at him scornfully. 'Oh really! Admiring the flowers were you? Then why are your flies undone?' He looked down, rolled his eyes at his stupidity and zipped them up.

'Let me explain.'

'Please do.'

Blythe stepped out. At least she had the decency to look ashamed.

'You bought her the Theo Fennell watch! You know, the shop called me for your office telephone number? I thought you'd bought me something and taken the trouble to have it engraved. Big Pussycat has never been my nickname, though, has it?'

'Darling—'

'Oh, save it. Doesn't your tart have anything to say or did you swallow her tongue?'

'You can't leave a husband alone all week and expect him not to look for it elsewhere,' said Blythe.

'Clearly not *my* husband. I thought better of you than that, David. Now I know you're just the same as every other cheating husband. Do you love her?'

'Of course not!' he exclaimed. Blythe's face flushed.

'Then I pity you—losing your family for a shag. I want you both out of the house in ten minutes. If you think you've had it bad, Blythe, David's going to have it much worse. I hope you'll stick by him!'

Jean-Paul followed her to the gate, where she collapsed in tears. 'Come,' he said. 'Go to my cottage until they leave. I will look after the children. They mustn't know what has happened.'

He watched her go, her shoulders hunched, her arms crossed in front of her chest. For a moment she reminded him of Ava and his heart reached out to her.

David ran through the gardens and house calling Miranda's name, but she didn't appear. Blythe packed her bag, called Rafael away from the tree house and waited impatiently for the taxi to arrive. David kissed the children goodbye, his head swimming with the realisation that he had risked everything and lost. Only now, as he hugged them, did he fully appreciate what they meant to him.

'Why are you in a hurry?' Gus asked.

'Because I've been called away urgently. Daddy's work.'

'You haven't had lunch,' said Storm.

'I know. I'll have a sandwich on the train.'

'Did you make Mummy cry?' asked Gus, frowning. He had seen her hurrying down the path towards the river.

'She's fine.'

Both children looked at him in bewilderment.

Jean-Paul stood some distance away while Blythe and Rafael piled into the taxi, then David strode across the grass to talk to Jean-Paul. 'Look, I know she likes you. Talk to her, please. I don't love Blythe. I love my wife and my children. I just thought I could have it all.' He rubbed his forehead in agitation. 'I don't want to lose them.'

Jean-Paul shrugged in that expressive French way of his. 'Of course you don't.'

'I'm a fool. I'm a damn, stupid fool.'

'So, you can stop being a fool and be a man.'

'It wasn't what you think! I had an affair with her, but it was over. I was telling her it was over!' Jean-Paul didn't know what to say. David turned on his heel and returned to the taxi. In a moment it was gone.

Jean-Paul stepped into the breach of Miranda and David's falling out. 'I have seen a warren full of baby rabbits in the wood,' he told the children. 'Shall we go and take them some carrots?'

Storm slipped her hand into Jean-Paul's. 'Mummy has some lettuce in the fridge. Do they like lettuce?' she asked.

'They love lettuce, but Mummy might need it for you.'

'Daddy made Mummy cry,' said Gus quietly.

'Let me tell you about grown-ups, Gus,' Jean-Paul began. He didn't modify his tone but talked as he would to an adult. 'They argue and fight just like children. But that doesn't mean they don't love each other. Your mother and father have had a fight, like you and Storm arguing over what game to play. But they will make up and be friends again. I promise you. Do you know why?' The children shook their

heads. 'Because they are united by one very important thing.'

'The garden?' said Gus innocently.

'No,' Jean-Paul replied with a smile. 'Their love for you and Storm.'

Gus took Jean-Paul's other hand and the three of them walked off towards the wood.

Down in the cottage, Miranda sat on the sofa and cried. Her instincts had been right. She wondered how long David and Blythe had been seeing each other. She wished Jean-Paul were there. He always had the right words. She stayed there until she became aware that the children would be wanting lunch. It was midday. The morning had disappeared, swallowed into betrayal and rage.

She dried her eyes, got up and wandered round the cottage. She had not been alone there since Jean-Paul had moved in and was suddenly drawn by the curiosity that had inflamed her since meeting him. How lucky for him the bookshelves are full of French books, she thought as she ran a finger across the bindings.

She went into the kitchen and opened the fridge. It was full of vegetables and some fish. She stole a carrot and glanced round the room. The kitchen was clean, but cluttered with books, newspapers, box files, unopened parcels. A jacket hung over the back of a chair, a sweater lay across another. It was a lived-in room. However, there was something about the files that gave her the feeling that he had another life besides her garden. She peered outside to check he wasn't about to burst in, and lifted the lid of the first box. Inside were official-looking papers. All written in French. Her French wasn't very good, but it was adequate to understand the frequently repeated words 'Château les Lucioles'.

With a racing heart, she flicked through letters addressed to Monsieur de la Grandière of Château les Lucioles. Could Jean-Paul live in a château? She recalled him saying he had grown up in a vineyard. She hadn't imagined he might *own* it. Her curiosity aroused, she went on looking through the papers. There were balance sheets of figures she didn't understand, but she could understand vintages and years and the French word for wine. It didn't take long to convince herself that Jean-Paul de la Grandière owned a vineyard in Bordeaux. That while he was her gardener, he was also a businessman. There was nothing wrong with that, she thought. He had never pretended to live in England. The fact that he hadn't told her meant nothing. She had never asked. She had hired him as her gardener and he had done his job beautifully.

As she left the cottage she suddenly got a whiff of orange blossom

again. How strange, she thought. As far as I know there are no orange trees in the garden. She walked over the bridge, her curiosity in no way abated. If Jean-Paul owned a vineyard and lived in a château that would account for his lack of interest in money. He clearly had more than enough. She couldn't help but ask herself why, with a successful business in France, he would want to be a simple gardener in Hartington? What had drawn him to her corner of Dorset, and why did he remain?

SUMMER

XIII

HARTINGTON HOUSE, 1980

JEAN-PAUL RETURNED to England and into Ava's welcome embrace. She smelt of France. Of orange blossom and grapes, freshly cut grass and hay. They lay entwined beneath the eaves of the cottage as the midday sun fell over the bed, turning her skin a golden brown. He ran his fingers over her shoulder, down the gentle descent of ribs to the soft curve of her waist and hips. Her body was slight, but feminine, with undulations in all the right places. He had pulled out the pencil on top of her head and scrunched her hair in his hands so that it tumbled round her face, framing it like Botticelli's *Venus*.

He had come to know her face better than his own. Her sensitive green eyes, her long, intelligent nose, her short upper lip and her large, sensual mouth that smiled so easily and with such charm. When they made love she looked like a girl of twenty. Her cheeks flushed pink, her eyes sparkled, her lips swelled with desire and her skin shimmered with a dewy translucence.

He pushed her gently onto her back and kissed her stomach where the skin was scarred by the marks of pregnancy. 'Your stomach is very sexy,' he said, pressing his face to it.

Ava laughed. 'You can't find scars attractive!'

'You don't understand. You should wear them like badges of honour. They're marks of womanhood, motherhood, femininity. The miracle of childbirth. They make you even more beautiful.'

'Now I know why I love you,' she said, stroking his hair.

He rested his head on her belly. 'I would like you to carry *my* child,'

he said. 'I would like to see your belly swell with love. A part of you and a part of me.' He closed his eyes. 'A son to work with me at the vineyard. A daughter to spoil and indulge as I would like to spoil and indulge you, if only I could take you back to France. I want more of you, Ava. More than you can ever give me.' He laid his head beside hers on the pillow. With his hand against her cheek, he turned her face and kissed her. 'I curse the God that let you meet Phillip before me.'

'Don't curse, Jean-Paul. We should thank the God that brought us together, even if—'

He put his finger across her lips. 'Don't say it. Please don't say it. *Un arc-en-ciel*,' he said softly, smiling in resignation. 'Even if He has given us nothing more than a beautiful rainbow.'

Ava could not curse the God that gave her Phillip. She couldn't explain to Jean-Paul that she loved her husband. That she loved them both, at the same time, in different ways. He would not understand and she hoped he would never ask her. She thanked God for giving her Archie, Angus and Poppy, even though they were obstacles to her happiness with Jean-Paul. If she had a wish, it would be for another life where she was free to love him without restraint. She was aware that her affair jeopardised her marriage but she never imagined that Phillip would find out. He was away so much of the time. Besides, it felt so natural working with Jean-Paul in the garden and making love to him there. The two were intertwined; her love for him and her love for the garden.

May became June, and the vegetables they had planted with the children were grown and ready to pick. The square patches were neatly planted with rows of lettuces, carrots, leeks, onions, cabbages, marrows and rhubarb. Sweet peas had begun to climb the arched frames Jean-Paul had erected for them, intertwined with peas. The ancient walls that enclosed the garden were adorned with roses, white wisteria, clematis and honeysuckle, and bright yellow senecio billowed out from under the wall, spilling over the gravel path that divided the garden by way of a large cross.

The long summer days, when the children were at school, and Phillip was working on his book, either locked away in his study or travelling abroad, belonged to Ava and Jean-Paul. They weeded with Hector, stealing kisses in the borders, sneaking off to make love under the eaves of the cottage, where only the squirrels were likely to invade their privacy. They shared jokes, and a growing love for each other and the natural world that surrounded them.

In July the children broke up from school and Ava and Jean-Paul had

to take more care not to be caught. As long as they were together, they were content. The smiles they shared said more than words ever could, and the thousand times a day they brushed against each other were as electrifying as those indulgent afternoons in June when they had lain naked together and made love.

When he came home, Phillip recognised the glow of love in his wife's cheeks and wanted her more than ever. She looked like the girl he had taken to Tuscany before Archie was born. She welcomed his advances at night, ashamed of her duplicity, knowing that her marriage was something she would never discuss with Jean-Paul.

One afternoon, while the children played with Toddy's children at Bucksley Farm, Jean-Paul and Ava rode out onto the hills. Purple clouds gathered above them, setting the countryside below in a dusky light. The wind swept in off the sea, causing the horses to spring about excitedly. They galloped over the grass, their laughter rising into the air with the distant cry of gulls. At times like this they could imagine they were alone in the world, just the two of them. Up here they could see for miles, the rolling fields, the silver river snaking down to the sea, the misty horizon where it was already raining.

Jean-Paul stopped first. His cheeks were flushed, his brown eyes sparkling. 'We're going to get very wet,' he said, holding out his hand for Ava to take.

'Let's tie the horses up under a tree. We'll never get back before it rains,' she suggested.

He squeezed her hand before letting it go. 'I love you,' he said, smiling. 'I don't think I've ever loved you more.'

'*Et moi aussi, je t'aime,*' she replied, smiling back.

They rode over to a small copse where they dismounted and tied up the horses. No sooner were they under the umbrella of leaves than it started to rain. Jean-Paul held her close, leaning back against the thick trunk. 'I'm grateful to the rain,' he said with a chuckle. 'Today we have the perfect excuse to remain up here all afternoon.'

'Toddy can give the children tea.'

'And we can steal an hour or two. But I'm selfish, Ava. I want you for myself. Exclusively. I want to marry you, have armfuls of children to run up and down the vines at Les Lucioles as I did. Just think what we could do to the gardens there. With our magic we could make it the most beautiful château in France.'

'Yes. But I am married and I already have children to run around the

gardens here. We cannot change what is past; we can only live in the moment. It's all we have.'

'Do you still sleep with Phillip?' His question caught her off guard.

She stiffened. She didn't want to lie to him, but neither did she want to hurt him. 'Please don't ask me.'

'Don't I have a right to know?'

'What difference would it make?'

'Peace of mind.'

'It changes nothing between us.'

'I want you to belong to me.'

'I never will, my darling. I will always be married to Phillip.'

'I could bear it if you were his wife in name only.'

'Isn't love more important than ownership? Isn't it enough to know that I love you body and soul?'

He kissed her forehead. 'It should be.'

'It must be. It is all I can give you.'

At that moment the clouds parted and the sun beamed through. They walked into the rain to watch as a vibrant rainbow straddled the valley. The colours were glorious, from deep red to pale purple.

'That is what we have,' said Jean-Paul.

'And look how beautiful it is.'

He swung her into his arms and kissed her. 'I don't want to lose you. I'm so frightened I will lose you.'

'Don't . . .'

'Promise me that you will come to me when your children are grown up and no longer need you?'

'I can't promise.'

'Yes, you can. If you love me you will be here when I come back to get you. Your children will be grown up. Phillip will be an old man. You will be free.'

'But you will marry and have children of your own.'

'I will never love another.'

'You can't put your life on hold for me. I love you, but I'm realistic enough to know that life will part us. Like that rainbow, the rain will take us.'

'It will not take our love. I will love you for ever.'

She took his face in her hands and gazed at him lovingly. 'You won't want me when I'm old. You will still be young and handsome.'

'My heart will always belong to you. Just promise me.'

'OK. I promise you. When the children no longer need me. When

Phillip is an old man. When I'm free, you can come back to get me.'

He hugged her fiercely. 'Now I can breathe again, because whatever happens I have something to look forward to.'

Ava leant against him, certain that one day he'd give his heart to another woman, raise his own children at Les Lucioles and forget the promise they had made. She gazed at the rainbow, willing it to last. 'Can you see pink between the green and the blue?'

'You tease me. There is no pink there. I don't believe it exists.'

'Of course it does. I can see it. My eyes don't lie.'

'Then you have a sense that I lack.'

'Look, the rain has stopped.'

'We will lose the rainbow.'

'But we have one of our own, right here, inside us.' She pressed her hand to her heart. 'It will last as long as we want it to.'

At the end of August, Jean-Paul received a telephone call from his mother. It was time to come home. 'Your father wants you to take over the vineyard,' she said. 'He is getting older and his health is not good.'

'Is he ill?'

'No, but he's tired and wants to hand it over to you. The truth is, Jean-Paul, he spends so much time in Paris . . .' Her voice trailed off. 'He wants you home by early September. He insists.'

Jean-Paul was winded with panic. He couldn't bear to face the end of their affair. A giant crack was splitting his heart in two. He had to tell someone. '*Maman*, I am in love,' he confessed. The tone of his voice told her that the situation wasn't a happy one. 'You know her. She came to Les Lucioles. It is Ava.'

There was a long pause while Antoinette struggled with the terrible revelation. 'Not Ava Lightly, surely?'

'Yes, *Maman*. We are in love.'

'But she is married, Jean-Paul.'

'I know.' His voice wavered, but Antoinette's gained an edge of steel. 'Does Phillip know?'

'No.'

'It must end,' she instructed firmly. 'It must end at once! She is not available to you, Jean-Paul. She has a husband and children. Not to mention the fact that Phillip is a close friend of your father. You have no idea what you're getting yourself into. It can only bring unhappiness to everyone, including you. You must come home immediately.'

'I thought you'd understand.'

'Understand? Yes, I understand. I have suffered for years as a conse-
quence of your father's continuing adultery. Let's speak no more about
it. I don't want to hear her name mentioned ever again.' Her voice softened. 'You are my only son, Jean-Paul. I love you and I have high hopes
for you: a good marriage, children, a life here at Les Lucioles. Ava
Lightly is a dead end.'

'Ava Lightly is my life.'

'You are young enough to start a new one. You will recover. She is
irresponsible to have led you astray.'

'I will not hear a word against her. It was I who was irresponsible.
She would not have yielded had I not pushed and pushed. Be certain of
this, *Maman*, if I have to leave her, I will never recover.'

His mother tut-tutted down the line. 'This is nonsense. You will
come home the first week of September. Let's speak no more about it.'

Jean-Paul fumed alone in the cottage. Of course, his mother was
right. Ava Lightly was not his to have. He couldn't convince her to leave
her children; love and loyalty were two of the qualities he most
admired in her. Would she be the Ava he adored if she were capable of
leaving her young family for him?

He couldn't remember the last time he had cried, yet the thought of
leaving Ava reduced him to sobs. He buried his face in a pillow. He had
ridden the rainbow knowing that in the end he'd pay for it with his
own blood. For all the pain, he was certain of one thing: it had been
worth it—a lifetime of suffering for a summer of joy.

As if to reflect their misery, the skies were grey, the rain heavy and
unrelenting on the roof of the cottage. Ava made tea in the small
kitchen in the cottage, trying to retain a sense of normality while her
world was collapsing about her. She laid the table. Two teacups, two
saucers, a coffee cake on a plate and a jug of milk.

They held hands across the table like prisoners through bars and
gazed at each other in despair. They both felt the same pain in their
hearts, the same tearing of nerves and flesh, the same irreparable
damage to their souls. Ava poured tea and sliced two pieces of cake, but
its delicious taste was of little consolation.

'It is September. I have to return to France. Even though I would sacrifice the vineyard and my inheritance for you, living here in secret is
no life.'

'Darling Jean-Paul, I would never ask that of you. We always knew
the summer would come to an end.'

'Please don't cry,' he said when her eyes filled with tears. 'If you cry I will never be able to leave.'

'Loving you has been my greatest joy and my most dreadful sorrow. You will always be here in my heart. Every day I walk round our garden I will think of you, and with every year that passes my love will grow stronger and deeper.'

'I will wait for you, *ma pêche*. I wish you could leave with me now, but you're not that sort of woman and I love you for it. We have got away without hurting anyone. Only ourselves.'

She wiped her cheek with the back of her hand. 'Everything will be so empty once you're gone. So pointless. There will be no more magic.'

He looked at her with fire in his eyes. 'The magic is deep in the earth, Ava. It will always be there because we sowed it. Don't ever forget that.'

They made love one last time as the rain rattled against the windows. 'One day I'll come back to this cottage and reclaim you,' he said, kissing her temple. 'I'll find you here, waiting for me, and nothing will have changed. This is our special place. Leave it as it is. As a shrine to us, so that one day, when I come back, I will walk in as though I have only been away for an hour and we will pick up where we left off. I will take you to France and we will sow our magic in the gardens of Les Lucioles and live out the rest of our days together.'

'What a beautiful dream,' she sighed, burying her face in his neck.

'If we dream hard enough it might come true. Like your silly pink in the rainbow. If we look hard enough we may see it.'

'We'll create a rainbow to last,' she whispered.

She stood in the doorway and watched him walk away. It was as he wanted, a small bag in his hand, as if he were only going for an hour. She watched until he was out of sight, walking down the river towards the village where he would take a taxi to the station. He hadn't wanted to say goodbye to the children or Phillip; he didn't think he could bear it. Instead, he had kissed the woman he loved and taken her love with him.

No one else seemed in the least surprised that Jean-Paul had gone, though Phillip was a little put out that he hadn't bothered to say goodbye. It was the end of the summer and he had always said he would stay a year. Hector and Ava continued in the gardens as they always had. Ava wondered whether Hector had known of their affair; he looked at her with such sympathy in his eyes, as if he understood her pain.

The children went back to school and Phillip finished his book. Toddy took Ava riding on the hills and noticed that the bounce had

gone from her and that she had lost her glow. When Ava had told her that Jean-Paul had left, Toddy had seen the pain behind her eyes, but she had kept her questions to herself. She knew if she pressed Ava on the subject she would cause her friend terrible suffering. Ava would tell her when she was ready. In the meantime, Toddy stayed close, as an old and trusted friend, giving comfort with her familiar presence.

Ava wandered round the gardens at Hartington House like a spectre. Alone at night she sat on the bench beneath the mountain ash, recalling her relationship with Jean-Paul in painstaking detail, from the day they met to the day they had parted, until, finally, she withdrew to the cottage where she began her scrapbook, sticking in petals from the flowers they had planted together and leaves from the trees and shrubs that held a special significance for them. She wrote poems, descriptions of the gardens, lists of the things she loved the most—from the morning light on the lawn to snowdrops peeping through frost. She wrote because it was cathartic and because her memories relieved the pain.

Jean-Paul returned to France, his heart bleeding from a wound that would never heal. He felt that his life stretched out before him like an eternal sea upon which he would drift, abandoned and alone, like the Flying Dutchman.

He had no desire to discuss his feelings, but when his father picked him up at the airport and drove him home, he found himself confiding in him. To Jean-Paul's surprise, Henri didn't berate him as his mother had done, but smiled indulgently. 'Look,' he began when they were on the open road. 'Let's talk man to man. I make it no secret that I have lived half my life in Paris with Yvette. There is nothing wrong with a man taking a mistress. There's a great deal wrong with a man wanting to *marry* his mistress. Especially if the woman in question is Ava Lightly.'

'I didn't plan to fall in love with her, Papa.'

'I don't question your taste, Jean-Paul. In fact, I admire it. She's a rather fascinating woman. But you have a responsibility at Les Lucioles. You are my only son and I need you to produce an heir to continue after you are gone. Ava has her own family. Nothing will come from a relationship with her. You need a fertile young filly—'

'I don't want anyone else,' Jean-Paul interrupted.

'I'm not asking you to fall in love with another woman. I didn't fall in love with your mother. I admired her, respected her. I knew she would be good for me and Les Lucioles and I was right. Look what she has done to the gardens! She created them out of nothing and now they are

the envy of France. She is the perfect hostess to my clients. A good wife
and mother. It is a shame she did not bear me more children . . .

'Marry a lady like I did, Jean-Paul. Take a mistress. But Ava is the
wife of my friend and therefore she is out of bounds. Cut your losses
and thank the stars that Phillip never found out.'

'I don't want to marry a woman I don't love,' Jean-Paul began, but he
knew his father wouldn't understand.

'Love,' he said dismissively. 'Love with your head not with your
heart. That is the advice I give to you.' He patted his son's knee and his
voice softened. 'I admire you for walking away, though. For leaving
without causing ripples. Had Ava not been married, she would have
made the perfect wife for Les Lucioles. Find another Ava.'

'There is only one.'

Henri shook his head and chuckled. 'You will learn that no woman is
unique. But if you marry your mistress, you create a vacancy.'

As the car swept up the drive to the château, Jean-Paul felt more isolated than ever. Without Ava by his side its beauty was an affront. He
wished the sky were grey and the vines less luxuriant. It was indecent
that the place should vibrate with such magnificence when his heart
was so full of unhappiness. As the car came to a halt, the dogs trotted
out to greet them. Jean-Paul opened the door, then patted their heads
and rubbed his face into their necks.

'Go and see your mother,' said Henri. 'She is beside herself. She
thinks this is all her fault.'

Jean-Paul found his mother on her knees beside the dovecote,
pulling out weeds. When she turned to greet him, he could see that she
had been crying. '*Maman*?' he enquired anxiously, hurrying to her side
to embrace her. 'I'm so sorry that I've caused you pain.'

'It is all my fault,' she whispered, taking his hand. 'I encouraged her
to persuade you to return to England. She must have thought I con-
doned the affair. But I didn't know. I was only thinking of you. I didn't
consider her, not for a moment.'

'It's not your fault. I was already in love with her. If she hadn't come
I would have returned to her in the end.'

Antoinette's voice hardened. She looked at him steadily. 'But you
won't ever go back, will you, Jean-Paul?' When he hesitated, she
pressed him further. 'Your father has made my life a misery because of
Yvette. Don't ruin Phillip's life. Think of the children.'

'We have both thought of nothing but the children. That is why
I am here.'

Her shoulders dropped. 'Thank God.' She pushed herself up. Jean-Paul followed her back through the gate to the château. 'You are young. You will love again. You can't see it now, but you will. The heart has a miraculous way of mending. It survives to love again.

'Find a girl who can make you happy and give you children. Fill Les Lucioles with love and laughter. Make her happy by remaining faithful to her as your father should have remained loyal to me. Look at this beautiful corner of Bordeaux. It is ripe for a new family and a new beginning. You will promise me, Jean-Paul?'

'I will try.'

She stopped on the lawn and turned to him, determined to bring the matter to a close. 'No, you will promise me. Don't contact Ava again. Leave her in peace with her family. Please, Jean-Paul. If you want to be happy, consign her to the past and let her go.'

'I will wait for her children to grow up. When they no longer need her she will come to me.'

'*Eh bien*, let us leave it at that,' she conceded, certain that he would forget about Ava in time and marry someone else. 'Come, now, I want to show you what I have planted in the orchard.' He let her slip her hand through his arm and walk him back up the garden.

Jean-Paul felt a small spark ignite in the stone chambers of his heart. He would nurture the gardens and tend the vineyard, plant more trees and shrubs. He would channel his love into Les Lucioles so that when Ava finally came here, she would see what a paradise he had built for her. She would know that he had never stopped loving her.

It was in the cottage that Ava began to feel sick, a continuous nausea that she put down to misery. She didn't want to eat and only Coca-Cola calmed her stomach. She drank it by the can, lying on the bed beneath the eaves, writing her scrapbook in her pretty looped handwriting.

If it wasn't for the approach of autumn, which she noticed in the cooler wind and the gradual fading of colour in her garden, all the days would have merged into one long, miserable day. She wanted to write to Jean-Paul, or to telephone him just to hear his voice, but she knew that she couldn't. Only time would dull the pain of their parting and she had to give herself that. So she wrote the scrapbook with the intention of one day giving it to him so that he would know how much she had missed him. That she had never given up.

'You're looking rather pale, Shrub,' said Phillip one evening during dinner. 'You're not eating. Are you unwell?'

'I don't think so. I just feel tired and deflated. Must be the weather.'

'Nonsense. I think you're pregnant.'

Ava was astonished. 'Pregnant? Do you think?'

'Absolutely. You're feeling sick. You're tired all the time. You're not eating. Why don't you get one of those pregnancy kits and check?'

'I hope you're wrong.'

'Why? It wasn't so long ago that you yearned for another child.' He took her hand. 'Perhaps your wish has been granted. Why not, eh?' Ava paled at the thought of another baby. Then a small spark of optimism ignited in her heart. If she was pregnant, it could be Jean-Paul's baby. She put her hand across her lips to hide her smile. Jean-Paul's baby. She barely dared cast the wish.

The following day she drove to the chemist and bought a kit. With trembling fingers she dipped the stick into her urine, then waited. She closed her eyes and wished. *If there is a God, please give me the blessing of Jean-Paul's child so that I may keep a part of him to love. I haven't hurt anyone. I've sacrificed my love for my husband and children. A baby shall be my reward, were I to deserve it.* She opened her eyes to see the clear blue stripe of a positive result. She was indeed pregnant.

She rushed to the telephone to tell Jean-Paul that the child he had longed for was growing in her belly. A part of him and a part of her, created with love.

She opened the address book to find the number of Les Lucioles, but she didn't dial. She stood staring at the page, her enthusiasm shrivelling in the harsh glare of reality. What would it achieve? It would only make their situation even more impossible. He'd have every right to claim their child. He had nothing to lose. She, on the other hand, had everything to lose. If she confessed to Phillip, she would risk her own children and hurt the very people she had sacrificed everything for. She closed the book. It would have to be her secret. Phillip would think it was his child and the children would accept their new brother or sister without question. She would take the truth to her grave.

The following spring, when daffodils raised their pretty heads and blossom floated on the breeze like confetti, Ava gave birth to a little girl. She insisted on calling her Peach after Jean-Paul's nickname for her, and Phillip indulged her choice. He gazed upon his new daughter with pride. According to him, Peach looked just like her mother. Ava was relieved at the baby's blonde hair and fair skin, but she saw Jean-Paul in the beauty of her smile. To Ava, every smile was a gift.

XIV

London and Hartington House, 2006

David had never felt lonelier. He had lost everything. Miranda refused to answer his calls. He had written to her, hoping she'd take the time to read his lengthy apology and confessions of stupidity and arrogance. Most of all he missed his children. He tried to keep focused at work, yet Gus and Storm's enquiring little faces surfaced to flood his heart with shame. He hadn't spoken to Blythe since they had parted at Waterloo Station. He had watched her walk through the crowds, holding Rafael by the hand and had suffered a pang of self-loathing. The people who lost the most were the children. Rafael would never again enjoy a weekend in the hollow tree, and Gus and Storm would never again run around the old ruined castle with their father. Just when he was beginning to enjoy them. He'd do anything to put back the clock. Anything.

David had many acquaintances, but there was only one friend he could really talk to. Somerled Macdonald, nicknamed Mac, was someone he had known for a very long time. The kind of man he could trust to keep the most shameful of secrets and not think any less of him for it. Mac was reliable and consistent, with a sense of humour that always made the best out of the very worst.

Mac's wife, Lottie, had grown close to Miranda over the years they had been married. They had enjoyed weekends at Mac's family estate in Yorkshire, and David shared Mac's obsession with rugby and cricket, staying up late in Mac's Fulham sitting room to watch the Ashes on TV. Mac was Gus's godfather and David was godfather to Mac and Lottie's son, Alexander. Now it was he who needed a godfather's wise counsel.

While Lottie was upstairs putting Alexander to bed, David broke down in front of his old friend. 'I've been a total bastard,' he said, sitting on the sofa and rubbing his face in his hands. 'I've lost everything for what? A meaningless affair!' Mac listened patiently while he recounted his foolishness. 'Miranda's only ever been the perfect wife and look how I've treated her! My mother would say what goes around comes around and I fully deserve to be kicked out.' He raised red-rimmed eyes in supplication. 'Tell me, Mac. How do I get her back?'

Mac sat with his legs crossed, a glass of lager in his hand. 'You'll get her back, David. But she'll make you crawl through the mud first. The first thing to do is write to her.'

'I've done that. I bet she threw my letter in the bin.' He took a gulp of whisky.

'I doubt it. If she still loves you, as I bet she does, she'll want to hear your apology. She'll want to hear that you wish it had never happened, that you love her and want her back. She's hurt and humiliated now, but you're the father of her children and she's not going to want to lose you.' Mac took a swig of lager. 'It's only when you lose someone that you realise how much they mean to you. Send her flowers with a note telling her that she's the only woman in your life. I don't mean a small bunch. Fill her kitchen with roses. If you really want her back you're going to have to fight hard. She'll want you to suffer as much as she's suffering. Prepare to spend the next ten years of marriage eating humble pie.'

'I don't want my kids to see me as a monster. I couldn't bear them to think that . . .' He put his head in his hands again.

'She's a sensible woman. She's not going to poison her children against you.'

'People do stupid things when they're in a corner.' He heaved a sigh and sat back against the cushions. 'You know, I've been a terrible father. I spent weekends watching sport on TV rather than take my kids off to build camps and catch fish. Then I saw the gardener, Jean-Paul, worming his way into my shoes.' He laughed bitterly. 'I saw him in the vegetable garden with Miranda and the children. The sun was out, the birds chirping in the trees, all picture perfect. I realised I was being pushed out of my own family and you know what? It was all my fault. Not Jean-Paul's. God, he was just doing his job brilliantly. After that I resolved to finish it with Blythe and spend more time with my family. I was just beginning to enjoy them when Miranda went and asked Blythe down for the weekend. I tried to finish the affair, but Miranda thought I was fucking Blythe in the greenhouse. That's what it looked like, but it simply wasn't true. God, I'm stupid.'

'Oh, there were plenty of stupid men before you and there'll be plenty of stupid men after you. You're not unique.'

'Look at you, Mac,' said David admiringly, draining his glass. 'You and Lottie are so strong. I envy you. You'd never be so foolish.'

Mac shrugged. 'Everyone makes mistakes. She'll forgive you. Look, here comes my lovely wife.'

Lottie descended the stairs with the contented smile of a mother whose child is asleep at last. 'Would you like another whisky?' she asked David, looking at him sympathetically. She had heard the whole conversation from Alexander's room above.

'You're close to Miranda, Lottie. Can you talk to her? Persuade her to see me at least.' Lottie didn't know whether to play ignorant, or admit that she had listened. She looked to Mac, who nodded encouragement.

'I couldn't help hearing,' she said, taking his glass to refill. 'I'll call her.'

David looked relieved. 'Thank you, Lottie. You're an angel.'

'I can't promise anything. What do you want me to say?'

'That I love her. I'm sorry. I want her back.' He rubbed his eyes. 'I miss her and I miss the kids. I'm in Hell.'

Mac smiled confidently. Lottie would know exactly what to say.

Down at Hartington House, Miranda sat at her desk typing furiously on her laptop. Absorbed by her novel, she was able to block out the horror of her own relationship. Drawing heavily on Ava Lightly's scrapbook, Jean-Paul, and her own misery, she found the words spilt out so fast her fingers were barely able to keep up. In spite of the collapse of her marriage, she felt optimistic that at least something good would come out of her unhappiness.

Miranda took consolation in Jean-Paul. He listened as she cried in his sitting room. He encouraged her to dwell on the things she loved about David. The good times they had enjoyed. The reasons they had married in the first place. She longed to tell Jean-Paul that she had fallen in love with him, but she was ashamed. He was so dignified, she did not want to embarrass him.

Miranda wrote obsessively. She wrote at night, once the children were in bed, until the early hours of the morning, when the sound of waking birds and the watery light of dawn tumbled into her study to remind her of the time. She wrote until her eyes stung and her eyelids grew heavy. During the day she was able to work because the children were out with Jean-Paul. To them, nothing had changed. They seemed to accept that their father was busy at work and so unable to come down at weekends. Gus had looked up at her with dark, suspicious eyes, but she had been able to convince him that, in spite of their argument, Mummy and Daddy were friends again. Jean-Paul took them riding on Jeremy's horses, up onto the hill from where they could see the sea. He gazed at the horizon, remembering that day when it had rained and he and Ava had sought shelter beneath the trees.

He was proud of the gardens. With the help of Mr Underwood and Miranda, he had indeed brought them back to their former glory. There were still spaces to plant things and some shrubs would take a few seasons to grow to their full promise, but the place no longer felt soulless.

Sometimes, when he sat on the bench that surrounded the mountain ash, he thought he could smell the sweet scent of orange blossom. He would close his eyes and feel her sitting beside him, congratulating him on the garden. Those times were bittersweet. He would blink back tears and wonder whether he had wasted his life waiting for her. He would watch Gus and Storm playing in the garden just as Archie, Angus and Poppy had done twenty-six years before, and yearn for what he had never had.

David's letter was five pages long, full of apologies and of how much he missed her and the children. A week later she received a vanload of red roses with a note that said: *It is only through losing you that I realise how much I love you. I was an idiot to take someone so special and so precious for granted.*

Then she received a telephone call from Lottie Macdonald. 'David was over the other night talking to Mac,' she told her. 'He's devastated. I've never seen him look so tragic.'

'He deserves everything he gets. He slept with a friend of mine. He even shagged her in our greenhouse!'

'He said he didn't.'

'Well, why were his flies undone?'

'That I can't answer,' Lottie conceded. 'Look, he's made a terrible mistake and he's very aware of it. He wishes that it had never happened.'

'I know. I got a five-page letter.'

'He asked Mac for advice. He's desperate to get you back. He misses the children . . .'

'Jean-Paul is a better father than he's ever been.'

'Yes, he mentioned Jean-Paul.'

'I bet he did. He puts David to shame.'

'David's put himself to shame,' said Lottie wisely. 'Why don't you at least talk to him?'

'It's too soon. I've got to clear my head. I'm just getting by, you know.'

'Let him see the children, then,' Lottie suggested. She was determined to come away with something to give David.

Miranda thought for a moment. 'You're right,' she conceded. 'The fight's between me and David. It's got nothing to do with the children.'

'That's very big of you, Miranda,' Lottie said, relieved. It was a start.

'Tell him he can come down this weekend. I'll come up to London and stay in a hotel. I've promised a friend a day's shopping and I don't want to let her down. I'll book into the Berkeley on Friday night and return Sunday afternoon.'

'You're more than welcome to stay with us,' Lottie suggested.

'You're sweet, Lottie, thank you. I'll be with my friend, Etta. Anyway, the least David can do is pay for a major suite. I'd stay in Kensington if it wasn't for the fact that he's probably shagged Blythe there.'

'Good idea. I'll pass all that on, except the last bit, and call you back.'

'Thanks, Lottie.'

'It's a pleasure. I hope you can work through this.'

'So do I.' But Miranda's thoughts turned to Jean-Paul. Until she confronted him, she wasn't sure what she wanted.

Jean-Paul was sitting on the bench beneath the mountain ash and the children were digging a hole among the larches by the dovecote. 'Do you mind if I join you?' she asked.

'Please. How are you feeling?' he asked.

She sat down beside him and sighed, not knowing where to start. 'David's written a long love letter. He apologised, said he regrets everything and wants me back. He's filled my kitchen with red roses.'

'That is a good start.'

'I've decided to let him see the children this weekend. I'll go up to London with Henrietta and stay in a nice hotel. After all, it's not their fight. Why should they suffer?'

'You are very wise.'

'I wish I was. You're wise, Jean-Paul. You're a better father than he is. I guess Gus just needed a dad who took trouble with him. David wasn't that dad. You were.' She lowered her eyes. 'Thanks to you, Jean-Paul, I've learned to enjoy their company and get my hands dirty. I've grown to love these gardens. I never thought I would. I was such a Londoner. The idea of gumboots made me recoil in horror, now I rarely wear my heels and I don't mind. I've changed. You've changed me.'

'It is not me,' Jean-Paul said softly. 'I wish I could take credit, but I can't. It is the magic in the garden.'

'The magic didn't come all by itself. You put it there.' She felt herself blush.

'The magic was always there, Miranda, I just brought it back to life.'

She took a deep breath. 'You're an incredible man, Jean-Paul. You're

wise, you're kind, you're adorable with the children. You're there for me, too. I've come to rely on you. In fact, I'm falling in love with you.'

He didn't reply, but put his arm round her shoulders and held her close. 'Miranda, you're not in love with me. You're confused.'

'I'm not. I think I fell in love with you the day Storm brought you home.'

He took a moment to find the right words to avoid hurting her. 'I cannot love you back. Not in the way you want me to,' he said at last.

Miranda felt the sudden rise of tears and tried to blink them away. 'You can't?'

'I love you as a dear friend. But I will always love another. No one can ever take her place in my heart. She has it for always.'

'Who is she?'

'Someone I knew a long time ago. She was married with children. We suffered an impossible love.'

'She stayed with her husband?'

'She wouldn't leave her children for me. Her love for them was deeper. It was the right thing to do. It was a long time ago. I was young. Now I am old.' He chuckled at his own foolishness. 'I have given her every year of my life since the day we parted almost thirty years ago.'

'You never tried to move on?' Miranda was astonished by such devotion. 'I didn't think people loved like that in this day and age.'

'When you love like that, you cannot move on. I had lived a great love affair, nothing less would do.'

'What was she like?'

'She was unique, eccentric, funny and sweet. A talented gardener. Someone who appreciated nature. She taught me all I know.'

Miranda felt she had heard this story somewhere before. Suddenly she grew dizzy with the realisation that the secret scrapbook that had so captured her imagination had possibly been meant for him. Had Ava Lightly loved Jean-Paul? 'How long did your affair last?' she asked.

'A year,' he replied. Now she was certain. But what did MF stand for? She would have to read through the book again to find the answer.

Miranda hurried into the house. The scrapbook was so fat, with so many pages. If Jean-Paul was indeed MF then it was no coincidence that he had come to work in her gardens. It was no coincidence that he had resurrected the gardens the way Ava Lightly had planted them. He had known every inch of the estate because he had worked on it with her. He had painted the picture of the cottage garden. He had

come back to find Ava, but found Miranda and her family instead. That's why he looked so sad. Ava hadn't waited for him as she had promised. Then why had she left the scrapbook in the cottage? Why hadn't she simply sent it to him in France?

She flicked through the pages searching for descriptions of MF. Now she had made the connection it all began to fit into place. At last she found the sentence that gave him away:

Oh, Mr Frenchman, you took a large slice of my heart with you when you left. The wound will never heal but will bleed and bleed until there is nothing left of me. My children are my consolation; without them my heart would be devoid of love.

That night Miranda refrained from writing her own novel and settled into bed with a cup of soup. She wanted to finish the scrapbook. She turned the pages until she reached the place where she had left off and resumed impatiently.

In the cottage, Jean-Paul sat in his sitting room contemplating the empty château with a sinking heart. He couldn't stay at Hartington for ever. He had done what he had set out to do: revive the gardens as Ava would have wanted. He had no idea where she was and a part of him was too afraid to find out. She had left without a word, that was all there was to it. Almost three decades had passed without a murmur of reassurance from her. She had moved on with her life.

He had gone home to the château to lick his wounds and throw himself into his new life. His mother had dedicated herself to introducing him to all the respectable, beautiful French women she could find, but his heart was numb and there was no one who could rouse it. He did not remain celibate, but the soulless encounters that came and went like shadows in the night meant nothing.

It was his mother's death that propelled him to return to Hartington. He had looked after her as a devoted son, but once free he did what he had waited twenty-six years to do: find Ava and bring her back. But life is not a storybook with a happy ending. If he expected her to be waiting for him in the cottage, he was disappointed. What good would it do to search the country for her? That chapter was closed.

Miranda began to cry. The end of the book was more tragic than she could have imagined. Ava had kept the cottage as a shrine. That was why Miranda had found the table there still laid for two; the only way Ava could prove her loyalty to Jean-Paul was to leave the place exactly

as it was. She remained married, raised her children and continued as before, yet the cottage stood as testament of her love for him.

Miranda was surprised to read that Ava had had another child, and assumed it was another tie to keep herself from leaving.

Peach is my consolation and my joy. I am blessed. Every day she fills me with wonder and appreciation. Out of the ashes this little soul rises to dry my tears and stroke my wounded heart with her gentle gaze and enchanting smile. I thought that part of me had died the day he left, but I was wrong. It was growing inside me as bright and beautiful as the man himself. Peach came with enough love to bind together the broken pieces of my spirit and mend my shattered world. If it hadn't been for her I would surely have shrivelled like an early flower killed by frost. Peach is my everything and she doesn't even know it. One day I'll tell her. God give me that courage . . . God, give me the time . . .

Miranda was stunned. She reread the last paragraph through her tears and realised that Peach was Jean-Paul's child. The child he had longed for. The child he didn't know he had. She was overwhelmed by the gravity of the secret she now held in the palm of her hand. *What am I to do?* She shuddered at the prospect of telling him that she had had the scrapbook all this time. Would he curse her for removing it from the cottage? How would he react when she told him of the table laid for two, frozen for twenty-six years, exactly as he had left it? Would he ever forgive her?

The following day, Miranda telephoned Henrietta to explain the plans for the weekend. Henrietta was beside herself with excitement. She hadn't told Miranda about Jeremy. They had spent the evening together that Saturday at the fundraising party in the village hall and since then he had called in at her shop frequently. Sometimes she had been with Troy, and Clare would report his visit. 'It's him again,' her sister would say with a wry smile. 'Why doesn't he just ask you out?'

Henrietta didn't know why he didn't ask her for dinner. Perhaps he was shy? Perhaps he just wanted her friendship? She couldn't imagine someone like Jeremy falling in love with her.

After Miranda had booked the Berkeley Hotel, she set about finding out where Phillip and Ava Lightly had moved to. She decided to call at the post office under the pretext of having received a package for Mrs Lightly. Surely when they moved they had left a forwarding address.

The excitement of unravelling the mystery of Jean-Paul's and Ava

Lightly's secret world distracted her from the ghastliness of her own marriage breakdown. Far from feeling rejected by Jean-Paul, she felt compassion. Her love for him paled beside the blaze of Ava's. Her heart bled for them both. If she could bring them together again, after all this time, Jean-Paul would forgive her for having kept the scrapbook.

She marched into the post office, which was housed in the shop owned by Fatima's son, Jamal.

'How are you, Jamal?' she asked breezily.

'Very well, thank you.'

'I have a favour to ask you.' Miranda tried not to look nervous. She wasn't used to being underhand. 'I have received a package for Mrs Lightly. It has no return address on it and I don't want to open it.'

'Of course. Would you like me to send it to her?'

'I thought I'd telephone her, actually, and ask whether she'd like to see what I've done to her gardens. She could pick up the package at the same time. It's rather too large to post.'

'I see. Not a problem. Let me have a look for you.'

He turned and searched among a shelf of old grey files all neatly labelled alphabetically. When he found the right one, he pulled it down and opened it. Miranda's heart thudded at the anticipation of getting closer to the woman whose love story had so fascinated her. At last he found it. 'She lives in Cornwall, somewhere called Pendrift. Shall I write it down for you?'

'Yes, please.'

'There's a telephone number too. They were a very charming couple. We didn't see much of Mr Lightly after he fell ill, but Mrs Lightly came in regularly to send letters and buy the occasional item.'

'I look forward to meeting her,' said Miranda, taking the piece of paper. She couldn't wait to get home and telephone Ava.

When she arrived back at Hartington House, Fatima was in the hall cleaning the floor and Mr Underwood stood in the doorway enjoying a long coffee break. The sunshine lit up the terrace and the thyme walk like a beautiful stage and Miranda stopped for a moment to admire it, before walking across the hall to her study.

Once inside, she listened to her phone messages. There was one from Lottie confirming that David was coming down for the weekend to see Gus and Storm. Miranda wondered what he was going to do with them for two days and decided to book Mrs Underwood to cook, and to put Jean-Paul on standby.

She closed the door and sat down at her desk, deliberating over what

she was going to say. She decided to introduce herself and then invite Ava to come and see the gardens. The plan was to get her to Hartington, where she would find Jean-Paul. Afterwards, Miranda would give Jean-Paul the scrapbook and explain that she had taken it without knowing why it had been put in the cottage.

Confidently she dialled the number. It rang for a while. Just before she hung up in disappointment, a woman's voice came on the line.

'Hello?'

Miranda plunged in. 'Hello, am I speaking to Mrs Lightly?'

There was a long pause. Miranda looked down at the piece of paper and wondered whether, in her excitement, she had dialled the wrong number.

'Who's speaking?'

'My name is Miranda Claybourne, I live at Hartington House . . .'

The woman's voice softened. 'I'm afraid my mother died a year ago.'

Miranda was shocked. 'Ava Lightly is dead?'

'Yes.'

'And Mr Lightly?'

'My father's getting on a bit, but he's well, thank you.'

'Am I speaking to Poppy?'

'No, I'm her sister, Peach.'

Miranda's mouth went dry and she frantically tried to think of something to say. 'I'm so sorry about your mother, Peach. I've heard so much about her. She was very popular in Hartington. When we moved here, all anyone could talk about were her incredible gardens.'

'They were her passion. It was very hard for her to leave.'

'Forgive me for asking, but I've been so curious. Why did she go?'

'Dad had a stroke and couldn't cope with the stairs. She looked after him single-handedly. She had no choice. I think it broke her heart.'

'I'm sure it did. When we moved in the gardens had gone to seed. They needed a lot of work. Well, I've brought them back to life. I felt it was my duty to restore them to their former glory, for your mother.'

'That's so sweet of you. She'd have loved that.'

'I didn't do it on my own. I enlisted the help of this wonderful Frenchman called Jean-Paul de la Grandière.' As Miranda expected, there was long pause. 'He seemed to know what I wanted, so I left it to him. Anyway, if you're able, I'd love you to see the gardens. You can always come and stay. After all, it was your home.'

'It was my home for twenty-three years,' she said hesitantly. 'I loved it.'

'Please come.'

'I don't know . . .' Miranda heard a man's voice in the background. 'That's my father. I'll tell him you called. We all loved Hartington.'

Miranda put down the receiver and sat back in her chair. So, Ava Lightly was dead. She felt as sad as if she had really known her. The disappointment was overwhelming. For almost a year she had lived Ava's story while her own had unravelled around her. Ava had kept her going. Now, there was nothing left.

Surely Jean-Paul didn't know that Ava had died. Why had he returned to Hartington if not to find her, as he had promised he would? Perhaps Ava had wanted Jean-Paul to know that she had kept her side of the bargain and had left the scrapbook in the cottage because she knew she was dying?

Miranda sighed. It didn't add up. Why didn't she just send the book to him? Why didn't she telephone and tell him she was ill? Why didn't she make an effort to see him before she died, rather than leave the scrapbook in the cottage at the mercy of the new people who would come to live at Hartington House?

She got up and went out to the cottage garden to sit beneath the mountain ash and think. There was no reason why she had to tell Jean-Paul immediately. While there was life there was hope. She'd pick her moment carefully.

XV

DAVID ARRIVED AT HARTINGTON HOUSE a few hours after Miranda had left for the station with Henrietta, who had parked her Fiat in their drive to pick up on her return. Mrs Underwood was supervising the children in the kitchen, while cooking dinner. There was no point putting them to bed the moment their father walked through the door. Besides, it was the weekend; they could all sleep in the following morning.

Mrs Underwood heard the front door open. Gus and Storm jumped down from the bench where they had been podding broad beans, and rushed up the corridor. She heard squeals of 'Daddy!' from Storm and David's laughter as he must have picked her up and swung her in the

air. It was a happy reunion. She had heard rumours about an affair, and Miranda discovering them in the greenhouse, but she wasn't one to pry.

'How's my boy?' David said to Gus, bending down to ruffle his hair. 'You've grown!'

'No I haven't,' said Gus. 'You need glasses.'

'You're right about that. But I've acquired some, metaphorically speaking, and I've never seen you better than I do now.' Gus scrunched up his nose. His father sounded different. 'Let's go and find out when dinner is.' The three of them went back down the corridor to the kitchen, where Mrs Underwood was drying her hands on her apron.

'Good evening, Mr Claybourne,' she said, smiling at the sight of him. He had lost weight, she noticed. Could do with a little feeding up. 'I've done roast chicken with potatoes,' she informed him, wishing she'd added a few more potatoes to the roasting tin.

'Smells delicious! When do you want us to eat?'

She looked at her watch. 'An hour? Eight thirty-ish?'

'Good. Come on children, let's go outside before dinner. It's a shame to waste such a glorious evening.'

They set off down the thyme walk, towards the woods. 'What are we going to do, Daddy?' asked Storm.

'I don't know. Let's see what comes up.'

'We made a camp in the dovecote with Jean-Paul,' said Gus, running ahead to show it off.

David winced at the mention of that man's name. 'I bet you did,' he said drily, watching Storm follow her brother. He gazed round the gardens, fragrant in the soft evening light, and noticed how there was little colour now, just different shades of green and white. There was something soothing about the lack of vibrant hues and he felt the tension that had built up ever since he had been discovered with Blythe ebb slowly away like a gentle tide carrying away debris with every wave.

The children lingered by the dovecote, showing their father the fire they had built to cook on and the hole in the ground where they were going to bury their treasure. David noticed the purple shadows thrown across it, the way the white was turned to pink, and to his surprise he saw a pair of doves fly in through one of the little windows below the roof. His spirit was suddenly filled with optimism.

'Come on! Let's keep going,' he said. The children ran after him. David felt a hand slip into his and expected to see Storm, skipping along beside him. To his surprise it was Gus. He smiled down at his son and Gus grinned up at him bashfully.

They reached the field where Jeremy Fitzherbert kept his cows and climbed over the fence. Charlie the donkey lifted his head and stopped chewing grass.

'Come on, Charlie,' Storm called, but the donkey didn't move. He watched them warily. 'Don't be frightened,' she continued. 'Daddy, why won't he come? He normally does.'

'He's not used to me,' said David. 'Come on, Charlie.' David put out his hand and smiled encouragingly. Gus withdrew his hand from his father's and delved inside his trouser pocket for a mint. He had started a packet that afternoon. He placed one on the palm of his hand and stretched his hand out towards Charlie.

'Here, Charlie. I'm not going to hurt you.' He fixed the donkey with his eyes, hoping to communicate kindness and honesty. He knew the animal was afraid of him and he didn't blame him. He had been unkind and he was ashamed. Now he was more grown up he knew all living creatures deserved respect. Jean-Paul had taught him that. 'Don't be frightened, Charlie. I'm not going to hurt you, *ever again*,' he added under his breath, hoping his father had not overheard.

Tentatively, the donkey stretched his neck and sniffed Gus's hand with large, velvet nostrils. The scent was too much to resist. He extended his lips and sucked up the mint. Storm wriggled in delight. David put his hands on his hips and watched as Gus pulled out a couple more mints, giving one to his sister so she could feed him too.

Storm patted his neck. 'He needs a good brush,' she said. 'I'm going to ask Jeremy if we can take him out and groom him.'

'Good idea,' Gus agreed. 'We can take him for walks on a rope.'

'Yes, and feed him. He can be our pet.'

'I think he'll like that,' said David. 'He certainly liked those mints.'

Gus pressed his forehead to Charlie's and whispered that he was sorry. Charlie seemed to understand him. He puffed and snorted and pricked up his long ears.

When they continued up the field to the woods, Charlie followed them right to the gate. Gus felt elated. Now his past mistakes were erased. With renewed energy he ran off up the path that cut through the trees, hurdling fallen branches and brambles.

Storm walked with her father, keeping an eye out for the fairies who lived among the leaves. David wondered why he had always been too busy for these simple pleasures. He gazed around as the light faded, and realised that here was where he belonged. Here with his family. Whatever happened, he'd fight to save it.

Miranda and Henrietta settled into their light and spacious suite at the Berkeley Hotel in London. Harvey Nichols was just a block away and Harrods a little farther on from that. Miranda should have felt euphoric, yet she felt subdued. All she could think about was Ava Lightly and Jean-Paul and the hopelessness of their love story.

Henrietta was awed by the grandeur of the hotel. She rushed about the suite, marvelling at the marble bathroom. She held a fluffy white dressing-gown against her and did a twirl as if it were an exquisite ball dress. 'They've even provided slippers!' she squealed.

'There's a swimming pool upstairs if you fancy a swim, and a spa. You have to have a massage.'

'I've never had a massage,' Henrietta confessed, blushing. 'I don't think I'd be happy to take my clothes off in front of a stranger.'

'Don't be silly, Etta. Go on, I insist. Tomorrow at six when we've exhausted ourselves, I'll certainly be having one.'

Henrietta watched her friend. Although she was smiling, she could not hide her unhappiness. She longed for Miranda to confide in her so that she could be a proper friend, like Troy, who was always there for her during the bad times as well as the good.

That night they had dinner in their suite, in their dressing gowns. The waiter brought it in on a trolley, the dishes kept warm beneath large silver domes.

'I'm sorry I've been a terrible friend,' said Miranda, fortifying herself with a glass of wine. 'I'm sure you've heard the rumours that David and I have separated for the time being. I caught him sleeping with an old friend of mine. He'd been having an affair with her for months.'

'I had heard something along those lines. I didn't want to ask . . .'

'I hadn't seen her for years then bumped into her in London. Her son's the same age as Gus.'

'You don't expect to be betrayed by a friend like that. I'm so sorry.'

'Thanks. I would have told you, but I needed to get it all sorted in my head first. Anyway, David's apologised.'

'Do you still love him?'

Miranda took a swig of wine and narrowed her eyes. 'I think I do.'

'You *think* you do?'

'I've been rather distracted lately.' Miranda had to tell someone, the secret was burning a hole in her heart.

'What could possibly distract you from worrying about your marriage?'

Miranda laughed. 'I know. I don't really understand it myself. To be honest, I'm glad something's hotter than David. It's Jean-Paul.'

'You're not in love with him, are you?'

'No, and that would make two of us,' said Miranda, grinning knowingly at her friend. 'You're not in love with Jean-Paul either, are you?'

Henrietta shook her head.

'Who then? There's someone, I can tell by the look on your face.'

'I want to hear your story first,' said Henrietta.

'I'll only tell you if you tell me who you're in love with.'

'Jeremy Fitzherbert. There, now I've said it.'

Miranda sat back in her chair and stared at Henrietta. 'Jeremy Fitzherbert. I'd never have put you two together. But now you mention it, I can't believe I never did. How far has it gone?'

'Oh, not very far,' she mumbled, lowering her eyes. 'We haven't even kissed. Maybe he doesn't want to.'

'If you're not kissing, what *are* you doing?'

'Well, since the fundraising party in the village hall, he often comes into my shop to buy cards, or bath oil and soap. He says they're for his mother.'

'My guess is he must almost have enough of your stock to set up a shop of his own by now,' said Miranda softly.

'He's sweet.'

'And he's handsome,' said Miranda. 'I remember the first time I met him, I noticed his eyes. They're very blue.'

'Yes, they are, aren't they?'

'Well, why don't you make the first move, Etta?'

'Oh, I couldn't.'

'Then you have to give him more encouragement.'

'Perhaps he just wants to be my friend.'

Miranda nearly choked on her wine. 'No man is going to go to all that trouble for friendship—unless he's gay.'

'Like Troy,' said Henrietta. 'So, what's *your* secret?'

Miranda drained her glass and poured another. 'I'll begin at the very beginning . . .'

'That's always a good place,' giggled Henrietta.

' . . . with a scrapbook I found in the little cottage on the estate . . .'

Henrietta listened while Miranda told her of Ava Lightly, her affair with a mystery man she called MF and the gardens they had planted together. 'The man Ava referred to as MF is Jean-Paul.'

'Oh my God!' Henrietta gasped. 'Are you sure?'

'Mr Frenchman—he owns a château and a vineyard in France. He's a rich man. Only love could make a man of his means and status work as

a gardener and live in a little cottage. He said he'd bring the gardens back to life and he has. But he can't bring Ava back to life. She's dead.'

Henrietta paled. 'Dead?'

'I rang her up and spoke to her daughter instead.'

'Have you told Jean-Paul?'

'Not yet. I'm too frightened.'

'You have to tell him! And you have to give him the scrapbook! It's his by right.'

'At least he'll know how much she loved him.'

'You have to tell him that you found the cottage as a shrine to their love. The table laid for two, the teapot and cups. The house kept as if they had just gone out for a walk and never returned. It's the most romantic story I've ever heard.'

'But there's more, Etta. Peach, the daughter I spoke to, is his.'

'You're sure?'

'I'm certain. Ava writes it clearly in the book. After Jean-Paul returned to France, she realised she was pregnant. She writes that Phillip thought the baby looked just like her, but she saw Jean-Paul's smile. She called the baby Peach, which is what Jean-Paul called her— *ma pêche.*' Miranda began to cry. 'Do you know what she said? She said that every smile her daughter gave her was a gift.'

The two women sat at the table, tears streaming down their cheeks. The waiter came to take the trolley away, took one look at them, apologised and withdrew like a scalded penguin.

'What must we look like?' said Henrietta, laughing through her tears.

'There's only one thing that doesn't add up. If Ava knew she was dying and wanted him to have the scrapbook, why didn't she just send it?'

Henrietta looked as perplexed as Miranda. 'Maybe she wanted him to have it only if he kept his side of the bargain. She couldn't send it out of the blue, just in case he had married and forgotten about her. It had been over twenty years. But if he came back for her, as he promised he would, then he'd find it. He'd deserve it. Do you see?'

'You know, that's possible. I'm amazed you can think clearly with the amount of wine you've drunk.'

'It's made me more lucid.' Henrietta laughed. 'Do you think he'll be hurt that Ava never told him about Peach?'

'Yes, but the MF of the book would understand. She couldn't tell him. The only way she could protect her family was to keep it secret.'

'Do you think Phillip ever wondered?'

'I don't know. I doubt it. She never thought that he suspected.'

'It's the stuff of a novel. You could write it.'

'I could . . .' said Miranda. She didn't dare tell Henrietta that she'd already written it. It suddenly felt wrong, like walking over Ava's grave.

The following day Miranda and Henrietta hit the shops. They went to Harvey Nichols and wandered up Sloane Street, where Miranda had arranged for Henrietta to have her highlights done at Richard Ward. Afterwards, they had lunch at Le Caprice and then headed for Selfridges, where the celebrated Pandora awaited them with flutes of champagne and her own confident sense of style.

'Miranda said she wanted you to have a complete make-over—a Trinny & Susannah make-over,' Pandora told Henrietta. She held up a selection of bras and smiled. 'The secret of their success is the bra! Now it's going to be the secret of *your* success.' Miranda sat in a comfortable chair while Henrietta tried on dresses and coats, trousers and jackets from the rail Pandora had prepared.

The bags were too big and too numerous for Henrietta and Miranda to carry back to the hotel themselves, so Pandora arranged for them to be delivered. Henrietta was overwhelmed by Miranda's generosity.

'This is giving me more pleasure than it's giving you,' said Miranda. 'I used to live for shopping, now I don't care for it as much. I'm looking forward to my massage though.'

'I'm feeling confident today,' said Henrietta, taking a breath, feeling renewed. 'I'll have one too.'

When Miranda and Henrietta returned to Hartington, David had already left. Miranda felt a twinge of disappointment. She had enjoyed her weekend away with Henrietta and it had been good to put some distance between herself and her home, but in spite of his wickedness, she missed David. Before she could dwell on his departure, she was distracted by Jeremy and the children walking up the thyme walk with Charlie on a lead. Henrietta swept her hand through her new highlights and waved. Jeremy lifted his hat and waved back. The children ran ahead, into their mother's arms.

'Did you buy me a present?' asked Storm.

'Charlie's our pet!' said Gus. 'He eats out of our hands!'

Miranda turned to see Mrs Underwood standing in the doorway. 'Henrietta, I'd better go and catch up with Mrs Underwood. I've so enjoyed myself. Thank you for making it such fun.'

'No, thank *you* for everything. I'm a changed woman.' Henrietta

laughed, swinging her car keys on her finger. 'I certainly look like one!'

'You look great! Now, go get him!'

Henrietta flushed with excitement. 'And you do what's right.'

'I will. I'll do it now, while Mrs Underwood is still here to look after the children.'

She watched as Henrietta walked away with Jeremy and Charlie, then went to talk to Mrs Underwood. 'How's it all been?' she asked.

Mrs Underwood folded her arms. 'They've had a lovely time together. Mr Claybourne's had more fun, I think, than he's had in years. He loves those children. They'll tell you about it, I'm sure. I know it's none of my business, Miranda, but the Christian thing to do is forgive. Men do silly things. He needs his wrist slapped, but he's a good man and a good father. Right, now I've said it.' She pursed her lips.

'Thank you, Mrs Underwood. I appreciate your thoughts,' Miranda replied humbly. 'I've got a favour to ask you. I need to see Jean-Paul this evening. It's important. Would you mind staying with the children?'

Mrs Underwood raised her eyebrows. 'If it's important, I can't decline. Tell you what, I need to get Mr Underwood his tea. I'll nip home now, while you give the children their bath, then come back to babysit. Is that all right?'

'Thank you, Mrs Underwood. That would be brilliant.'

Jeremy looked at Henrietta appreciatively. 'You're radiant,' he said.

'Thank you,' she replied, blushing. 'I've had a wonderful time.'

His eyes lingered on her face longer than normal. She looked away. They walked up the lawn towards the field. The sun was setting, flooding the sky with golden syrup, and dew was already forming on the grass. The breeze was warm and sweet. She cast her eyes round the gardens, sensing the magic that Ava and Jean-Paul had created there.

'Jeremy,' Henrietta said suddenly, as she realised the strength of her feelings for him. 'There's something I want to say to you.'

'Yes?' His expression grew serious.

'Well, I've been wanting to ask you for some time . . .' She swallowed hard. 'Do you have a shop in your home to rival mine?' she stammered, feeling foolish. He grinned. She felt her confidence return. 'You see, if you have then I have no choice but to join the two together and make one big shop because I can't take the competition.'

Jeremy took off his hat and put his hand on her shoulder. 'I've been worrying about it too,' he said. 'You're so clever to come up with a solution.' Jeremy leant down and kissed her.

Astonished, she let him draw her to him. 'I think you should move in with me as quickly as possible in order to capitalise on our union,' he said. 'There are, however, legal matters to consider.'

She frowned at him, uncomprehending. 'Legal matters?'

'Marriage, Henrietta. If you knew how long I've waited to find you, you'd understand why I don't want to waste any time. I love you and I want to share my life with you. I can offer you a couple of soppy dogs and a rambling farmhouse, a herd of milking cows and a big red tractor. Please say yes, or I don't know what I'm going to do with all that soap!'

Miranda found Jean-Paul in the kitchen. 'That looks good,' she said, watching him prepare a poussin with onions and tomatoes.

'Next time I will make it for two.' He looked at her curiously. Then his eyes fell on the scrapbook.

'We need to talk,' she said, unsure how to begin. 'May I sit down?'

'Of course.'

He watched as she placed the book on the table.

'What is this?' he asked. But he knew. He had recognised the writing.

'I think this was intended for you,' she explained. 'It was here when we bought the house. This cottage had been kept as a shrine. This table was still laid for two, as if the people taking tea had just got up and walked out. I confess I have read the book. It broke my heart. I now realise that you are the man Ava Lightly loved but couldn't have. You are her impossible love, the man she called MF.'

'Mr Frenchman,' he said, his voice barely audible.

'I've only just worked it out. Now I'm ashamed that I took it and read it and that I erased her memory in renovating this cottage. I think she meant you to see it as it was, as if you had never left. I think she wanted you to see that she had never forgotten you or given up.'

Jean-Paul picked up the book and ran his hand over the cover, as if the paper was the soft skin of Ava's face.

Miranda couldn't bear to look. She gazed out of the window instead. It was getting dark. 'I telephoned her house, but she wasn't there.' She fought through the lump in her throat. 'She died last year.' The words came out in a whisper. She watched him sink into a chair. Miranda got up. She needed to leave the cottage. It wasn't right that she was there. 'I'm so sorry,' she gasped. 'I'm sorry I am the one to tell you.' With tears running down her face, she hurried through the door, closing it behind her.

She stood on the stone bridge, her heart pounding against her rib

cage. She had wanted to tell him about Peach. But it wasn't her place. He would read the scrapbook and find out for himself. It was bad enough that she had been the person to tell him Ava had died. Nothing in the world was as important as love. She rushed up the path towards the house, desperate to hold her children against her and breathe in a love that was warm and living.

The telephone was ringing as she stumbled through the door. She ran into her study to answer it, but it rang off just before she could reach it. 'Damn!' she swore.

Mrs Underwood appeared at the door. 'I've left your supper on the Aga,' she said.

'Did you get the phone?' Miranda asked.

'No. I don't like to answer your private line. There's an answer machine, isn't there?' Miranda nodded and pressed 1571. There was no message. 'Are you all right, Miranda?' Mrs Underwood was concerned.

'I'm fine. I hoped it would be David.'

Mrs Underwood nodded knowingly. 'You can always telephone him.'

'Yes.' Miranda felt drained. She could barely muster the energy to talk to Mrs Underwood. 'I think I'll eat and go straight to bed,' she said.

'I'll be going then,' said Mrs Underwood, untying her apron.

'Thanks again, Mrs Underwood. I don't know what I'd do without you.'

'Better than you think, I'm sure.' She smiled sympathetically.

After Mrs Underwood had left, Miranda ran upstairs to kiss the children. They slept contentedly in their cosy rooms, and she inhaled the sleepy scent of them, nuzzling her nose into their hair, and silently thanked God for the gift of children and the blessing of love.

She ate in her bedroom after wallowing in a hot, pine-scented bath. Mrs Underwood had made her a delicious vegetable soup with butternut squash and sweet potato. She lay in bed watching television. She needed to forget the scrapbook and Jean-Paul and turn her mind to neutral. She finished her soup, then switched off the light.

The telephone rang.

'I love you, Miranda.' It was David. Miranda felt a surge of relief.

'I love you, too,' she replied huskily.

David was taken aback. 'You do? I don't deserve it.'

'Let's start again,' she said. 'Forget what's done and begin again.'

'I'll never forgive myself for hurting you.'

'But I can forgive you and I will. I want to move on.'

'I realise now that only you and the children matter. Nothing

should put our family at risk. It's all that we have.'

'We have to spend more time together, David.'

'Well, I've been thinking . . . I'm going to quit the City.'

'You are?' Miranda was astonished. 'What are you going to do?'

'I don't know. Write the life cycle of the flea? The City is a money-spinner, but it's no life. I've worked hard and it's time to reap my reward. By that I mean you, Gus and Storm. We should take a long family holiday. I don't want to send the children to boarding school. I want them at home where I can enjoy them. What's the point of having them if all we do is send them away?'

'You *have* done a lot of thinking.' Miranda was impressed. 'Gus'll be pleased.'

'He was. I told him. We had a man-to-man, you know. We understand each other now.'

Miranda felt her stomach fizz. David sounded like the old David she had fallen in love with. 'Come home, darling. I've missed you.'

He sighed heavily. There was a long pause as he gathered himself together. 'Those are the sweetest words I've ever heard.'

The following morning, Miranda awoke with a strange knot in her stomach. She looked out of the window. The sky was grey, the clouds thick and heavy, a melancholy light hanging over the gardens. There was no breeze. Something was missing. Something was wrong. Hurriedly, she dressed, pulling on a pair of jeans and a cotton sweater. The children were in the kitchen helping themselves to cereal, cheerily making plans for the day. 'I'll be back in a minute,' she shouted, as she ran through the hall. Gus frowned at his sister, who shrugged.

Miranda sprinted across the gravel and through the wild-flower meadow. It was just beginning to drizzle, light feathery drops that fell softly on her face. To her relief Jean-Paul hadn't left, but was standing on the bridge, gazing into the water. When he saw her, he didn't smile, but looked at her with weary red eyes, his skin grey.

'Are you all right?' she asked, standing beside him, catching her breath.

'I have read the book,' he told her.

'The whole book?' Miranda was amazed. It had taken her months.

'I haven't slept.' He shook his head and ran a rough hand through his hair. 'I had to finish it. I think I always knew in my heart that she was dead. That is why I didn't look for her. I was afraid.'

'What are you going to do?' She dreaded his answer, but she knew it before he spoke.

'Return to France.'

'What about Peach?' she asked softly.

He shrugged. 'I don't know.' He seemed confused. 'Ava always put her children first. I must do the same.'

'You mean, you won't contact her?'

'I cannot. She may not know.'

'But you're her father. You said yourself, *a part of you and a part of me.*' For the first time since she had met Jean-Paul, he seemed unsure of himself.

They both became aware of someone standing on the river bank. She approached, dressed in pale blue dungarees, white T-shirt, her long curly hair the colour of summer hay.

Jean-Paul caught his breath. 'Ava,' he gasped. 'It can't be.'

The young woman smiled and waved tentatively.

'Jean-Paul,' muttered Miranda, marvelling at how beautifully his smile translated into a woman's face. 'That's Peach.'

She reached them and her smile dissolved into diffidence. 'Jean-Paul,' she said. 'You don't know me but . . .'

'I know you,' he said. 'I recognise your mother in you.'

'And you in me too,' she said with an embarrassed laugh.

'You have your mother's directness,' he observed, running his eyes over her features, impatient to take her all in.

'I've had a while to get used to the idea.' She turned to Miranda. 'You must be Miranda.'

'Yes. You don't know how good it is to see you.' They embraced as if they were old friends.

'I tried to telephone you over the weekend, but no one answered. I hope it's OK that I just turned up.' She gazed around. 'Nothing's changed. It looks wonderful.'

'Come inside,' Jean-Paul suggested. 'It's about to pour.'

'I'd better get back to my children,' said Miranda, backing away.

'You're welcome to join us,' Jean-Paul said. Miranda noticed the colour had returned to his face. He looked handsome again, the irresistible twinkle in his eyes restored.

'I'd love to, but I think it's right that I leave you together. You've got a lot to catch up on. Maybe, when you're done, I can show you the gardens. It's all credit to Jean-Paul, but they're stunning.'

'Yes, please,' said Peach. 'I'd love that. My mother would be so happy to see them restored. I want to thank you, Miranda.'

'Whatever for?'

'For making this possible.'

Miranda felt her spirits leap. 'Did I?'

'Of course. I never thought I'd find Mr Frenchman. Thanks to you, I have.' She looked at Jean-Paul and grinned. It was as if she had known him all her life. 'Don't be alarmed,' she said, sensing his astonishment. 'I've had a year to get used to this.'

Miranda walked up the garden to the house. Around her the gardens radiated their magic and inside she felt complete. She belonged.

Storm and Gus tumbled out onto the porch as a taxi drew up on the gravel. Miranda turned to see David stepping out with a suitcase. He wasn't in his suit, but in jeans and a green shirt. Miranda smiled, but she had to wait her turn for he opened his arms and the children flew into them. They belonged there too, she thought contentedly; at last.

Inside the cottage, Jean-Paul put the kettle on. The two of them sat at the kitchen table as Ava and Jean-Paul had done twenty-six years before. But this time it was not to say goodbye but to begin a whole new life together. 'There is so much I have to tell you,' said Peach, her green eyes glittering with emotion. 'I don't know where to begin.'

'Tell me about your mother. How did she die?'

'Let's go back a bit further, or I'll lose track. Darling Daddy— Phillip—had a stroke about four years ago and for a while we all continued to live here in spite of his slow recovery. Mummy looked after him like a nurse. She refused to seek help. You know what she's like. The stairs became a big problem and everyone told her we had to move. Of course, she was torn between what she knew was right for Phillip and what was right for her. She loved this place and the gardens, and I know now that the reason for her determination to hold on to them was you. She must have hoped that one day you'd come back and get her. We were all grown up. Poppy lives in London, is married with children of her own, Archie married a Chilean and lives in Valparaíso. Angus is a historian. He hasn't married.'

'And you?'

'I've never flown the nest. I'm a gardener.' She grinned proudly.

'I am not surprised,' he mused, shaking his head at the miracle of her. 'Go on with your story,' he said, anxious to hear more.

'Well, she stayed on here long after she should have gone. Finally, she was left no choice. She discovered a lump in her stomach. It turned out to be malignant. We moved to Cornwall because Mummy had always loved the sea. She put the house on the market at an exorbitant

price. Maybe she hoped it wouldn't sell and she could one day move back. It caused her such pain to let it go.

'While Daddy recovered, Mummy got worse. It all happened very quickly. Now I've read the scrapbook, I think the tumour was a manifestation of the heartbreak she suffered after you left. Her grief was so deep and she kept it secret all those years. She never told me and I was closer to her than the others, being the youngest.' She hesitated, then added shyly, 'And being yours.' They looked at each other as the rain rattled against the windowpanes, and realised that in spite of the fact that they were strangers, the reality of their shared blood and their mutual love for Ava gave them an immediate sense of unity.

'When did she die?' he asked.

'In spring last year. May the fifth. We buried her in a little churchyard overlooking the sea. She left me the scrapbook, not in her will, but in a letter of wishes. She had hidden it in the house.'

'So it was you who put the book in the cottage?'

'Yes. I read it all. I understood why she had never told me about you. What good would have come of it? I love Phillip as my father, and he will always be my father. Think how lucky I am to have two.'

'She never told you?'

'No. Maybe she felt guilty for not telling us both. But dying people always want to tie up loose ends and I suppose it is my right to know who made me. I decided to put the scrapbook in here so that if you returned you would find it and know that she had never stopped loving you. I didn't know where to find you and I didn't want to ask my father. At that stage I didn't even know whether I wanted to find you. It's not an easy thing to learn that the man you believe is your father is not.'

'Does Phillip know?'

'Goodness no. And he never will. It would be wrong of me to tell him. Besides, my mother gave her life to him. Maybe she would have left had he not fallen ill. Who knows?'

'Why did you come today?'

'Because it's what Mummy would have wanted. You both longed for a child so badly, it's only right that you should know.' She smiled again and Jean-Paul saw his own face mirrored in hers. He felt his stomach lurch at the sight of it. She blushed. 'I was also captivated by the scrapbook and the romance of my mother's secret love affair. She never stopped loving you, or hoping that you would one day be reunited. When Miranda telephoned, I knew it was my chance.'

'Why didn't she let me know that she was dying?'

'I've wondered about that too. I think she wouldn't have wanted you to see her like that. Her hair fell out. She aged terribly. She was very sick. I would imagine she wanted you to remember her the way she was.'

'But she knew I loved her.'

Peach's eyes filled with tears. Once again she could smell the scent of orange blossom. It crept round her like a familiar blanket and invaded her senses, demanding to be noticed. She looked at Jean-Paul. He lifted his chin, aware of it too.

'Yes, she did,' she said, her voice barely a whisper. 'You can smell her too?' Jean-Paul closed his eyes. How often he had dismissed her perfume as wishful dreaming.

The room filled with sunshine. It was bright and twinkling as it caught the little specks of dust and lit them up like fireflies. Father and daughter opened their eyes to see that the clouds had parted to let the sun shine through. Jean-Paul stood up hastily. 'Come,' he said, taking her hand. Peach followed him outside, into the rain. There, in a dazzling arc above them, stood a magnificent rainbow.

'It's beautiful,' she said in wonder. '*Un arc-en-ciel.*'

'*Un arc-en-ciel,*' he repeated, knowing that Ava was up there somewhere in the midst of all those colours. Then he laughed, for there, between green and blue, was the most splendid colour of all.

'Can you see pink?' He pointed to the vibrating light, the colour of a perfect summer rose.

'I see it!' she said, her face wet with tears. 'I see it! The elusive pink.'

'She's there,' said Jean-Paul, squeezing her hand. 'She's there. I know she is.'

XVI

HARTINGTON, 2006

THE DAY OF HENRIETTA and Jeremy's wedding could not have been more beautiful. The sky dazzled with sunshine, a cold breeze whipped in off the sea, swirling through the red and gold leaves, breathing autumn on the final remains of summer, and yet the sun was warm.

Troy sat in the front pew with Henrietta's mother and sister. He had

put the bride's hair up in a glossy bun encircled with purple roses and wiped her tears away himself when she had seen how beautiful she looked. On the other side of the aisle, Jeremy waited nervously, his large hands trembling as he fidgeted with the service sheet, exchanging looks with David, whom he had asked to be best man.

Miranda sat behind David. She thought of Jean-Paul and Peach: he had lost his lover but gained a daughter. Ava had said that love was all she had to give him, but that was no longer true; she had given him Peach. Miranda thought of them both in France, at Les Lucioles, where he would show her the gardens he had cultivated for her mother. Together they would share memories, building a bridge to span the years that had separated them.

David caught her eye and smiled. She gave him her hand over the pew and he squeezed it. That squeeze said so much. Her eyes began to well. 'Don't cry now, darling. She hasn't come in yet!' he whispered and she nodded, dabbing her face with a hanky.

At that moment the large wooden doors creaked open and Dorothy Dipwood began to play the organ. The congregation stood. Miranda leant into the aisle to see Henrietta in the elegant ivory dress embroidered with pearls that Miranda had helped her choose. Her face was veiled, but her grin was visible beneath it. She walked on the arm of her father, his face pink with pride. Miranda's eyes were so filled with tears that she was barely able to distinguish Gus and Storm, who stepped behind her as page and bridesmaid. Storm held a ball of purple roses hung from a ribbon and Gus held her hand, his face serious with concentration, taking care not to step on Henrietta's train.

Henrietta watched Jeremy, who stepped into the aisle to receive her, beaming as he watched his bride walk slowly towards him. He was relieved he wasn't expected to speak because a knot of emotion had lodged itself in his throat. Henrietta's father placed his daughter's hand in Jeremy's and they gazed at each other for a long moment.

At the end of the service, they all spilt out of the church into the sunshine. Jeremy and Henrietta climbed onto Jeremy's red tractor and waved as they set off to Hartington House, where Miranda had organised the reception.

David slipped his arm round her waist and pulled her against him. 'Henrietta looks beautiful,' he said. 'Clever you.'

'Not at all,' Miranda replied. 'Her beauty is entirely her own.'

'Now you've shared Jean-Paul and Ava's story with me, will you let me read your novel?'

Miranda looked at him. 'How did you know I'd written one?'

'Gus told me.'

'How did he know?'

'Children know everything.'

'I might.'

'Might?'

'OK, I will. But I won't ever publish it.'

'What if it's brilliant?'

'It is brilliant, but it wouldn't be right and besides, I don't think I did it all by myself.' David frowned at her quizzically. 'I had help,' she said, enigmatically. There was no point explaining.

She raised her eyes to the sky, remembering the scent of orange blossom that had filled the room whenever she had sat down to write. Since finishing the book she hadn't smelt it. Ava's ghost had gone.

'So what are you going to do with it?' he asked.

'Give it to Peach,' she said.

'To Peach? Why?'

'Because I know now that I wrote it for her.' She took David's hand. 'Come on, darling. We'd better gather up the page and bridesmaid, we've a reception to get to.'

'Gus! Storm!' David shouted. The children bounded up, their cheeks red with exertion. 'Time to go home,' he said, ruffling Gus's hair. Miranda sighed with pleasure. Home. How good that sounded.

Santa Montefiore

You wrote your first published novel after taking a gap year in Argentina. Why was that country your source of inspiration?

I actually started to write *Meet Me Under the Ombu Tree* six years after I'd spent what was, I think, the most important year of my life in Argentina. I loved the place so much and it changed me completely. But when I returned a year later and tried to recapture the magic, it was no longer there. I felt I'd lost something very precious. And I can't think why it never occurred to me then that it was the thing I should be writing about. I'd been casting around for ideas for a novel, but it was only when I met my husband [Simon Sebag Montefiore] and he said, 'Write about something that means something to you—something that hurts when you think about it' that I I realised it had to be the time I'd spent in Argentina. Writing the novel was cathartic really.

Did you enjoy writing *The French Gardener*?

Very much. It's the first contemporary novel I've written and I wasn't sure I'd be able to pull it off, having been used to writing about the past when old-fashioned values existed. But the secret is to fall in love with your characters, and I did.

Have you ever met a man like the French gardener, Jean-Paul?

No, but I channelled my father into the older Jean-Paul: that craggy face . . .

My father is very wise, very deep, very spiritual. For him, family is important, love is important, silence is important, God is important. He's not materialistic.

What about the heroine, Ava? Is she based on someone you know?

I loved Ava. Yes, I know someone who was married, with two young children, and then met her soulmate. It was just bad timing. She was ready to leave her husband but, when it came to it, she couldn't leave her children. She's in her early seventies now and her husband has never known about her affair. Another influence was a wonderful, eccentric garden designer in Dorset. When I met her she was dressed in purple dungarees with a white T-shirt and her hair was held back with a pencil. Ava's beauty is very like hers.

When you first set eyes on your husband, did you know that he was 'the one'?

No. I met him at a party and he asked for my telephone number. He rang the next day and he had a very sexy voice, but I couldn't remember what he looked like and I was a bit nervous that he might turn out to be really ugly. He asked me to tea at his parents' flat, which I thought was very odd. Thankfully he was very handsome, but I wasn't actually offered a cup of tea—not even a piece of toast! Instead, we sang the whole score of *Evita* to his parents' gramophone! Sebag was dressed in a Russian officer's coat (he loves uniforms) and sang Ché and Perón and I sang the Eva songs. I fell passionately in love with him.

What matters most to you both now?

Our children, without any question. Sebag and I both have offices at our home in London. I'm at the top of the house and he works in a kind of conservatory. We often go out for lunch together and it's so lovely when Sacha and Lily, now seven and five, come back from school because we're both in the hall when they arrive home. My husband is very good about nurturing the children, reading them stories and encouraging them to read.

Do you have a bolthole in the country?

I had an idyllic childhood, growing up in a beautiful Jacobean house on a farm in Hampshire wth my parents, who still live there, and we now have a cottage just an orchard away from them. We go there at weekends and in the holidays.

What do you want most for your children?

Health. That's all I ask. If you have good health you can achieve anything.

Has being a mother changed your view on life?

When you're a parent you realise that you love your children far more than you love yourself and it makes you feel quite vulnerable. I never gave a thought for my own safety when I was single, but now I do everything more carefully.

Favourite way to spend a sunny day?

In the bluebell woods at home in Hampshire, with my husband and children, with nothing to do but sit, play and eat. And I'd take my dad along, too!

Anne Jenkins

Star Gazing
Linda Gillard

Marianne Fraser, because of her situation, has to be a very careful woman. Every step she takes is counted; every piece of clothing she wears is either black or cream, the two colours never mixing. Her life has to be exact, with everything in its rightful place, otherwise she will falter. But from the moment she meets Keir Harvey, Marianne's narrow world begins to open up.

Winter—2006

CHAPTER ONE

Marianne

This is not a ghost story. Not really. But it was Christmas and I did feel as if I'd seen a ghost. Or rather heard a ghost. Except that you don't hear ghosts, do you? Clanking chains, hideous moans perhaps, but on the whole people see ghosts, or so I understand. It's an experience I've been spared.

But I thought I'd heard one.

The woman takes care getting out of the taxi, reaches inside and removes a briefcase and a carrier bag. She sets them carefully on the kerb and fumbles in a capacious handbag for her purse.

As the taxi pulls away, she turns to face the grey Georgian terrace, elegantly anonymous, typical of many in Edinburgh. Dressed in a full-length woollen coat and dashing velvet hat, the woman extends a booted toe and places it, deliberately, on a manhole cover. She bends and picks up her bags, straightens, pauses for a moment, then without looking to left or right, she strides across the pavement towards the steps leading up to a front door. A keen-eared observer might hear her counting under her breath.

Before she has taken four paces, there is a hiss of braking wheels and the sound of a bicycle skidding on pavement, followed by an angry adolescent shout.

'Jesus! Didn't you see me coming? Are you blind or what?'

Shaken, the woman turns to face the cyclist. As she adjusts her hat, knocked askew, her hands are unsteady but her voice is firm. 'Yes. As a matter of fact, I am.'

Marianne

That's right, I'm blind.

I'll just give you a moment or two to adjust your prejudices.

But, I hear you ask, shouldn't I have been escorted by a Labrador? Or waving a white stick? At the very least, shouldn't I have been wearing enormous dark glasses, as favoured by Roy Orbison and Ray Charles?

I know, I know—it really was my own stupid fault for wandering about looking *normal*. (Well, I'm told I do. How would I know?)

'**I** *am* blind and *you* have no right to be cycling on the pavement. If you have a bell, might I suggest you try using it in future?'

But the cyclist has already gone. She bends to pick up the bag she dropped, feels the shifting of broken glass, hears the steady drip of liquid onto the pavement. With sinking heart she mounts the steps and delves into her handbag again for her door key. The loss of the Burgundy is a disaster—how will they cook boeuf bourguignon without it? Encountering the cold metal of her phone, she wonders whether to ring her sister with a last-minute shopping list.

The door key falls from her chilled fingers. She gasps, straining her ears to locate the direction of the small sound it makes as it hits the ground. She bends, sweeps the stone with bare hands, cursing the cyclist, Christmas and most particularly her blindness. Something wet and weightless lands on the back of her hand. Snow . . .

She feels the prickle of tears, blinks rapidly and sweeps the doorstep again, then plunges her hand into the evergreen foliage of a potted plant, shaking it, listening for the clink of a falling key. Silence.

She is considering what comfort might be derived from sitting on the steps and bursting into tears when she hears footsteps approach, then come to a halt. She registers a habitual flutter of apprehension. The footsteps are male.

'Can I help?' A man's voice, not local, nor one that she knows. Or . . .?

'I've dropped my door key and I can't find it. I'm blind.'

She hears the sound of change jingling in pockets as he mounts the steps. After a moment he says, 'It's fallen onto the basement step . . . Here you are.' He takes her chilled hand, places the key in her palm and murmurs, '*Che gelida manina . . .*'

'Yes, I've lost my gloves too. Must have dropped them somewhere.'

'No, they're dangling from your coat pocket.'

'Are they?' She feels for the gloves. 'Thank you. And thank you for finding my key.'

'No bother. I hate to tell you this, but your shopping seems to be bleeding.'

'It's red wine. I dropped it. It's been one of those days.' She opens her handbag and pushes the gloves inside. 'Do you like opera? Or do you just break out in Italian every so often?'

'I'm a sucker for Puccini.'

She considers. 'Musically very appealing, but ideologically unsound, I always think. Women as passive victims of glamorous men. Rather repellent in the twenty-first century.'

'I hadn't really thought about it like that.'

'You wouldn't. You're a man.'

'A chromosomal accident. I'm sorry.'

She laughs. 'No, *I'm* sorry. For being so rude. Forgive me—I was rather shaken, losing my key. Cross with myself and taking it out on you. I keep my key on a chain that I put round my wrist so I *can't* drop it, but I was in a hurry and I didn't bother . . . Are you from Skye?'

'Aye. Well, I was brought up there. I was born on Harris. But my parents hankered after bright lights and the big city. So they moved to Portree.'

She laughs again.

'I take it you know Portree?'

'Only by reputation. I knew a Skye man . . . A *Sgiathanach*.'

'*Sgiathanaich* are loyal. We tend to go back when we can. It's a great place. As long as you don't crave excitement.'

'Your parents were disappointed, then?'

'Och, no, they died happy in their beds.' She senses a smile. 'Of culture shock.'

'Well, there are worse ways to die.'

'Aye. A lot worse. Will you manage with the broken glass?'

'My sister will deal with it. I'll just leave the bag on the doorstep.'

'Well, if you're sure there's nothing more I can do?'

'Thanks, I'll be fine now.'

She hears his feet on the steps again. He calls up, his voice more distant now, 'I'll run into you at the opera, maybe? I presume *Turandot* meets your stringent feminist criteria?'

'Ah, now *she's* a girl after my own heart. Puccini's misogyny always triumphs in the end.'

'You're getting cold. Away indoors. And wipe your feet—you're standing in a pool of red wine. I'll see you around, maybe.'

'Well, you might see *me*, but I definitely won't see you. Goodbye.'

Marianne

Has it ever struck you how language favours the sighted? (Of course not, because you can see.) I don't just have a problem seeing, I have a problem talking, trying to find words and phrases appropriate to my experience. Just listen to how people go on: *Oh, I see what you mean . . . Now look here . . . The way I see it . . . Reading between the lines . . . I didn't see that coming!*

You get the picture?

I, of course, don't.

People often ask me why I go to the opera when I can't see the singers act, I can't see the set or costumes, and I can't see any lighting effects. Why don't I just stay home and listen to a CD—surely it's the same? I ask them if they think it's the same looking at a reproduction of Van Gogh's *Starry Night* as standing in front of the actual painting.

I tell sceptics and doubters that I go to the opera because opera pours a vision of a wider world into my ears in a way that no other art form that I can access does. Sculpture and textiles, on the rare occasion I'm permitted to touch them, excite me. Plays, novels and poems move, entertain and educate me, but they don't rock me to my foundations and make me *see*. I can read Tolstoy's account of the French retreat from Moscow, either in Braille or as an audio-book, but I have never seen a city. Or snow. I've never seen a man, let alone an army. Tolstoy uses a visual language that I can read, haltingly. It's not my mother tongue.

But music I can 'read' much more easily. In fact, I don't need to read it at all. When I hear music, it goes directly to my heart. It pierces my soul and stirs me with nameless emotions, countless ideas and aural pictures. Nowhere am I more conscious of this than at the opera. At times I am so shaken by what I hear, by what I feel, that I wonder if my constitution could actually cope with the addition of a visual component.

I lied to the man on my doorstep about my dislike of Puccini's victim-heroines, or rather I told him a half-truth. What I cannot bear is their *pain*, and when their suffering seems random, pointless—as Tosca's, Mimi's and Butterfly's does—I think what I feel, at some deep level, is angry. And I don't want to feel angry, especially not in the opera house.

I have far too much to be angry about.

Anger is a place I don't go, a colour I never wear.

I have two wardrobes in my large bedroom. One of them contains black clothes, and the other contains cream and ivory. (These adjectives are labels that my elder sister, Louisa, has allocated for me. For all I know she could be dressing me in sky-blue pink, as our mother used to say, a colour

no more difficult for me to imagine than black or ivory.)

Wearing coloured clothes would be too complicated for me. If I wish to be independent, I have to have clothes that will match or blend. Louisa and I thought this through carefully. Louisa said black and cream would co-ordinate even if I got confused and put an item of clothing away in the wrong wardrobe. I don't ever have to stand in front of a mirror agonising over what to wear. It's either a cream day or a black day. Occasionally Lou prevails upon me to wear a brightly coloured scarf or pashmina to ring the changes. She says my eyes are an attractive opal blue and certain colours bring it out.

I hope the colour is more attractive than the word. 'Opal' is an ugly-sounding word. When you cannot see what words describe, you tend to focus on the words themselves. Words are a form of music and I suppose I hear them differently from the sighted. Louisa describes my opal eyes in breathless tones, as if she is paying me a huge compliment based, I gather, on a comparison with the precious stone, which she tells me is quite spectacular. I just hear an ugly, faintly ridiculous word.

I don't wear colours. I don't do anger. Nor, I'm afraid, love. Not any more.

A monochrome existence, the sighted might say, but even that implies the presence of one colour. *You* might use the word 'colourless', but what colour do you then see? People seem to describe dull things as 'colourless' when—apparently—they are grey or brown.

When we were young, I asked Louisa if anything was *literally* colourless. She thought for a while and said 'glass'. Then she said 'rain'. I asked her if all water was colourless and she said, no, not from a distance. The sea or a lake is coloured because it reflects the sky, but she said individual drops of water were colourless; rain, as it fell through the air, was colourless.

It's a paradox. Things that look colourless to you are my artist's palette. Rain is the only thing apart from my sense of touch that gives me any sense of three dimensions. Water falling from the sky defines shape, size and quality by the sounds it makes when it lands.

Water colourless? Not for me.

Harvey was dead. Long dead. I hardly thought about him any more, per-haps because I'd never had any visual memories of him—no photographs, no wedding video to watch to keep the memories alive, no children to remind me of him. To me, Harvey was just a body and a voice. A very faint one now, but then he was always soft-spoken, perhaps to compensate for the fact that some people believe blindness affects the ears as well as

the eyes, so they raise their voice when speaking to you. Harvey didn't do that. He knew how sensitive my hearing was, how I saw with my ears.

But Harvey died. I didn't see *that* coming either.

I ran into him again. Not Harvey, the man from Skye. At the theatre. The opera, in fact. During the interval of Wagner's *Die Walküre*, Louisa bought us both drinks, settled me at a table and then went off to join the queue in the Ladies. She left me stewing in a soup of sound: the clatter of teaspoons and the chink of sturdy cups; English women sounding like neighing horses; Scotsmen scouring the ear with aural Brillo pads. I was thinking of abandoning the two G&Ts and joining Louisa in the Ladies, when a male voice asked me if a chair was taken. I recognised him immediately. I was about to reply but by then he'd recognised me and was sitting down, asking me what I thought of the singing.

His voice was so similar. Like toffee. Smooth and pitched low. But this voice didn't have the drop of vanilla, the hint of a drawl that Harvey had inherited from his Canadian mother. This voice hit its Highland consonants with the same satisfying 'click' that good chocolate makes when you snap it.

When I'd met him on my doorstep, I'd known immediately that it wasn't Harvey's voice. In any case, Harvey was dead. When I heard that voice for the second time, I knew at once who it was, but again I remembered . . . So I was already thinking about Harvey when he told me his name.

'Harvey.'

'I beg your pardon?'

'My name's Harvey. Keir Harvey.'

'Did you say Hardy?'

'*Harvey*. Keir Hardie was a founder of the Labour Party.'

'I'm aware of that. He's also dead.'

'Aye, but his spirit lives on.'

'In you? Do you have socialist leanings?'

'Practically toppling over.'

'Well, that might account for it. If you were possessed, I mean. Perhaps you should change your name.'

'It's *Harvey*. Like the rabbit.'

'What rabbit?'

'In the film. With James Stewart. *Harvey*.'

'I've never seen it.'

'Have you ever seen any film?'

'No. I've been blind since birth.'

'Aye, well, you missed a good one there. Harvey is a six-foot rabbit that only James Stewart can see, which could have something to do with him being always out on the bevvy. But the rabbit is remarkably good company, for all he's invisible.'

'You didn't apologise.'

'What for?'

'When I told you I've been blind since birth, you didn't say, "I'm sorry" in a tragic voice. People usually do.'

'Well, it wasn't my fault, so I don't really see why I should apologise. Is it obligatory?'

'I think it's said more as an expression of compassion. Fellow feeling.'

'Embarassment, more like.'

'Yes, very probably. And you're not embarrassed?'

'Not by your inability to see. I'm deeply embarrassed that you mistook me for a dead socialist.'

'It could have been worse. I might have taken you for a six-foot rabbit.'

'How d'you know I'm not?'

The small, plump, middle-aged woman bustles through the crowded bar to a low table where a woman sits nursing a gin and tonic, staring into space. The family resemblance is striking. Both women are fair, even-featured, blue-eyed. The extravagant blondeness of the woman on her feet owes much to the skills of her hairdresser. The fair hair of her seated sister, Marianne, is ashen, in places grey, drawn back into a simple chignon suggesting the pale, poised severity of a ballerina. Despite her greying hair she is evidently younger than her sister.

'Sorry I was so long, darling. There was an interminable queue in the Ladies and then I was accosted by a fan. She wanted to know when *Eldest Night and Chaos* was coming out.'

Marianne doesn't look up but sighs. 'Really, Lou, the imbecility of your titles beggars belief.'

'That's Milton, I'll have you know.'

'I'm aware it's Milton. You, my dear, are not. Now let me introduce you to Mr Harvey.' She indicates a chair on her right with her hand. 'This is the kind man who retrieved my door key for me—when I lost it at Christmas, do you remember? Mr Harvey, this is my sister, Louisa Potter, who, in another guise, is a famous author. Of very silly books.'

Louisa laughs nervously. 'Marianne, darling, there's nobody there! The chair's empty.'

'Is it?' Marianne's large eyes register no emotion but her head inclines slightly towards the adjacent chair as if she is listening. 'Well, he was here a moment ago. He was talking to me. How very odd!'

Louisa sinks into the empty chair beside her sister. 'Did you have a nice chat? With your mystery man?'

'Yes, thanks.'

'I wonder why he slipped off like that. Very bad-mannered.' Louisa swirls her ice cubes round in her glass. 'Maybe he was paged. A medical emergency. He might have been a surgeon.'

'For goodness' sake, Lou, do you have to turn everything into a melodrama? He wasn't a surgeon anyway.'

'Oh? What does he do?'

'I've no idea, but he's not a surgeon. We shook hands. His was rough and decidedly workmanlike. I'd say he works outdoors.'

'Now who's inventing mysteries?'

'I'm not inventing, I'm *deducing*. From the evidence of my senses.'

'Damn, that's the bell for Act Two.' Louisa takes a final mouthful of watery gin. 'Listen out for his voice. He might be sitting near us.'

'He won't be talking. He's here on his own.'

'Well, now I *am* intrigued . . . I presume he's not elderly?'

'The handshake wasn't.'

'Young, then?'

'No, not young. Well, he didn't *sound* young.'

'Was he chatting you up?'

'No, of course not! Lou, you really are impossible.'

As Marianne rises from her chair, Louisa turns the pages of her programme. 'I know Wagner was supposed to be an orchestral genius—you've told me often enough—but I just feel sorry for the poor singers, rambling on and on in search of a tune. Give me Puccini any day.'

'You and Mr Harvey both.' Marianne extends her arm in the direction of her sister's voice. Louisa takes her arm and links it affectionately with her own as they join the throng moving slowly towards the auditorium.

'I'd really like to meet this man. A solitary male opera-goer with labourer's hands who loves Puccini. Fascinating! If you put him in a book, no one would believe you.'

'I wasn't aware that credibility was a criterion in fiction these days. Especially not yours.'

'I write fantasy, darling,' Louisa replies amiably, patting her sister's hand. 'Anything goes. You don't have to believe it. You just *consume* it. Like chocolate.'

Louisa

I feel I should explain. About my sister. Marianne.

What you need to understand about Marianne is that, despite the fact that she's blind—perhaps *because* she's blind—she's always had a very vivid imagination. So certain allowances have to be made, were always made: by our parents, doctors, teachers and so on. It was always understood that Marianne lived life in her head—well, what else could she do, poor thing? She was blind—and the boundaries between fantasy and reality were a little hazy for her at times.

She developed a philosophical bent at university. She used to say that, as sisters, we had more in common than genes. We *both* lived in imaginary worlds of our own creating. The only difference was, mine made me a lot of money. (That was a dig, of course. I didn't mind. As I said, you have to make allowances and I do.)

It occurs to me, you don't know who I am, do you? Let me introduce myself! My name is Louisa Potter, but you'll know me as Waverley Ross. My publishers didn't think Louisa Potter sounded either Scottish or sexy, and I had to agree. As an English pupil in a Scottish school I was known as 'Potty Lou' and dreamt of marriage so I could change my prosaic surname to something glamorous like Traquair or Urquhart. A husband never materialised, so I settled for a nom de plume. 'Waverley Ross' sounds Scottish, doesn't it? I gather my hordes of American fans conjure up swirling mists and Sir Walter Scott.

I'm an author—a very successful one—of vampire romance. *Upmarket* vampire romance, I hasten to add. There's an awful lot of tat out there. Sick tat too. I don't write that. I write Scottish Gothic vampire romance. I did a history degree in Edinburgh, fell in love with the city and nineteenth-century Scottish literature, and my writing career grew out of my passions. All my books are set in Edinburgh. They're pretty formulaic, I admit, but that's what people like. You know where you are with a Waverley Ross. In Edinburgh, doing battle with the powers of darkness, righting wrongs, fending off over-sexed vampires of both genders and all sexual proclivities.

I do quite a lot of sex but nothing distasteful. (In my books, I mean.) No rape and *definitely* no S&M. My books are very traditional love stories really, but the men have to be supernatural because, frankly, a good hero is hard to come by these days. It's difficult finding an excuse to create a tall, dark and handsome hero who dresses in flamboyant clothes and behaves in an unpredictable but masterful way. (And, believe me, that *is* what women want in fiction.)

I began my literary career writing Regency romances (don't knock it—so

did Joanna Trollope) but they didn't sell and I wasn't getting anywhere. Then it occurred to me what we actually wanted was bad boys. But not *real* bad boys. Vampires. Sexy vampires who were—to a man—tall, dark and handsome. (I do throw in the occasional blond, just to ring the changes. I don't think you can do anything with redheads but my assistant, Garth, says I should be more open-minded.)

Being supernatural, my vampires have extraordinary powers and physical attributes, plus an uncanny facility for shedding their clothes at key dramatic moments. To be honest, this last trait is a bit difficult to make convincing because, as any Scot will tell you, it's extremely cold and damp in Auld Reekie.

Anyway, I digress. My books have enabled me to live with my sister in a certain degree of luxury in a desirable part of Edinburgh. Marianne may scoff at my work—she refers to my characters as my 'imaginary friends'— but she's happy enough to enjoy what my labours buy. I don't begrudge her a penny. She's all the family I have, she's excellent company (if you have a thick skin), and she keeps the flat ticking over when I'm away on promotional tours. She works part-time answering the phone for a blind charity, but she doesn't need to. She does it to assert her independence.

So we rub along together quite nicely; a couple of old spinsters becoming increasingly eccentric with the passing of the years. I said to Marianne the other day, 'I'm over fifty—I need to slow down,' and she said, 'I'm nearly fifty—I need to *speed up.*' She was exaggerating, of course. At forty-five Marianne is six years younger than me. I'd already started school when she was born, so Marianne was always something of a solitary child, isolated by her age and her handicap. That's probably why she developed such a vivid imagination. She had imaginary friends too! I'm sure they were a great comfort to her. Heaven knows, there have been times when poor Marianne has needed comfort.

Marianne

One of my favourite walks in all seasons is Edinburgh's Royal Botanic Garden. I can find my way there on my own. I've memorised the route as a sequence of numbers—the paces I take before turning a corner or crossing a road. There are landmarks that I navigate by—a manhole cover, a postbox. I usually take my cane because people leave things on the pavement that I don't expect to be there: rubbish bins, bicycles and the like. But these unexpected obstacles aside, I can walk confidently to the Botanics, enjoying the scents and sounds.

I love the garden in all seasons, especially when it rains. I like to shelter

under the trees when they're in full leaf and listen to the patter of rain as it forms a kind of sound-sculpture for me, defining the size and shape of a tree, giving me an aural sense of scale, of distance.

Music gives me some inkling of landscape. The sheer scale of orchestral music, the volume and the detail, can put me in touch with something much bigger than myself, take me beyond my personal boundaries, the world that I experience with my fingertips or my cane. Music tells me there is a wider world and what it might be like.

For me, the Earth is a conceit, something I'm told exists but cannot see—like Pluto or Neptune for you. Astronomers deduced that Neptune must exist long before they devised telescopes powerful enough to view it. There was a gap in the galaxy where a planet ought to be and they trusted that there was. It was an act of faith: faith in mathematics and physics. There is a gap in my life where the Earth ought to be. I have to take its existence on trust. I cannot see or feel the Earth, I am merely informed by my senses of the minutiae of its being, but when I listen to an orchestra play a symphony, I have a sense of what it might be like to contemplate a mountain range, a fast-flowing river, the skyline of a city. Music helps me see. So does rain. Rain helps me see things that my fingers can't encompass, like a tree or a glasshouse. That's where you'll find me when it rains. In the Botanics. In one of the glasshouses, or sheltering under one of my favourite trees.

But I dislike winter. Not for all the usual reasons—dreary weather, short days. What are those to me? I don't like winter because there are no leaves left on the trees, no leaves to make music with the rain. My trees fall silent. Once a blanket of snow has fallen, my whole world becomes muffled, indistinct. (You would say blurred.) There are no dead leaves crackling underfoot, few birds sing, and I'm deprived of many of my markers, like manhole covers, sometimes even the kerb. My walk to the Botanics becomes a perilous undertaking.

I hate the silent world of winter because it makes me feel blind. I can experience the cold and wetness of snow, but I can never have a sense of a wintry landscape except as an almost silent world. In the depths of winter I suffer from depression, brought on by a kind of aural blankness. Every single winter this comes as a dreadful shock.

I knew I was being watched. To begin with I sensed it, but dismissed the feeling, then I became certain.

One of the reasons I don't use my cane much is because I don't like to advertise to the world that I'm blind. I'm vulnerable enough as a woman

without letting criminals and perverts know that I'm easy prey. I try to look and behave as if I'm sighted. What I actually look, I suspect, is drunk. I stumble, touch railings and walls, as if I'm unsteady on my feet, but it probably draws the attention less than a white stick.

But despite my precautions, my attempts at invisibility, my dressing in black, my intention of blending in with the leafless skeletons of trees, someone had noticed me. And was watching.

Seated on a wooden bench, Marianne turns her head in the direction of the approaching footsteps. She thinks of getting to her feet and walking briskly in the opposite direction, but she finds it difficult to walk quickly. Instead she reaches into her bag for her personal alarm.

A cold gust of wind lifts a wisp of hair and blows it across her face. *Hamamelis.* Witch hazel . . . And something else, another scent. But it's wrong. Out of season. A memory surfaces and seconds later she places it. 'Is that you, Mr Harvey?'

Silence and stillness. Then, 'I thought you were supposed to be *blind*? Are you working some kind of benefit fraud?'

'I *am* blind.'

'And a seer? Or just a mind-reader?'

'What, might I ask, are *you*? A stalker? You've been watching me.'

'Only because I was trying to work out if it *was* you, then whether you'd mind being disturbed. You seemed deep in thought.'

'I was listening.'

'To the birds?'

'To the trees.'

He sits beside her. 'How did you know it was me?'

'Smell. I was downwind of you.'

'*Smell?* I showered this morning. Very thoroughly.'

'I didn't mean a bad smell. It's probably your shampoo. Or maybe it's just your natural smell. My nose is very sensitive. I recognise people by voice and smell. I'm pretty good at it, but it's not a lot of help with judging character. It's harder for the blind, meeting new people. You have to be . . . cautious.'

'It's always a blind date.'

'Exactly. You *aren't* a six-foot rabbit, are you?'

'No. I'm six foot two.'

'And furry?'

'Only in the usual places.'

'I could hear you were tall.'

'*How?*'

'Where your voice comes from. You must get bored looking at the tops of people's heads.'

'Not as bored as they must get looking up my nostrils. What did you smell? I'm fascinated.'

'Oh, hawthorn blossom, I think.' She lifts her head and he watches her profile as her delicate nostrils flare, like an animal scenting danger. 'I think it's you, not the shampoo. I can smell a soapy, chemical scent on top of the hawthorn. What were you photographing? Not me, I hope.'

'How—? Och, you heard the shutter! I was photographing trees.'

'Why?'

'I compare what I see this year with what I saw this time last year. I make notes, keep a record. I'm tracking climate change.'

'Is that your job?'

'No, just an interest of mine.'

'Do you live in Edinburgh?'

'No. But I sometimes work here. And Aberdeen. Sometimes abroad.'

'Where's home?'

'Wherever I happen to be.'

'I get the impression you don't like personal questions.'

'Do you?'

'Not particularly.'

'Another thing we have in common.'

'Apart from a love of opera, you mean?'

'Aye, and a love of trees.'

'How do you know I love trees?'

'Folk who sit here on a cold winter's day must love trees. There's little else to look—' He pauses. 'Ah.'

'You fell into the trap. Don't worry. You lasted longer than most before making your faux pas.'

'So was I wrong? About you and trees?'

'No. I do love trees.'

'Even though you can't see them?'

'I can *hear* them. You can hear the bare branches tapping against each other in the breeze. Listen! . . . It sounds like me, feeling my way along the pavement with my cane. I listen to trees. And I lie my hands on them. Feel the texture of their bark. Primitive, isn't it? But satisfying. Are you superstitious, Mr Harvey?'

'Keir. Aye, I suppose so. I'm from the islands. A healthy respect for the supernatural goes with the territory.'

'Do you believe in an afterlife?'

'No.'

'Neither do I. I sometimes wish I did, but I don't. I think this is it, don't you? We get one crack at life and have to make the best of it.'

After a moment he says, 'You lost someone.'

It's not a question and she is thrown. 'What makes you say that?'

'Folk talk like that when they've been through the fire. Death concentrates the mind.'

'Yes, it certainly does. That's about all that can be said for it.'

He looks down at her ungloved hands. 'You're not married?'

'I was. Many years ago.'

'Divorced?'

'Widowed.'

'I'm sorry. You must have been quite young.'

'Twenty-seven. My husband was only thirty-three.'

'What happened?'

'I don't talk about it.'

They are silent for a long time; then she hears him clear his throat.

'Would you prefer to be on your own? I was gate-crashing anyway and I seem to have effectively killed the conversation.'

'Oh, you're still there, are you? I thought you might have vanished again, like you did at the opera. You know, I blithely introduced you to my sister, then felt a complete fool.'

'I'm sorry. I saw someone. Someone who shouldn't have been there. Someone I really didn't want to see . . . But that's no excuse. My behaviour was very rude. Would you like me to vanish now?'

'No. I mean, if you *want* to leave—'

'I don't.'

'Then stay. I'm enjoying your company—though you might think I have a funny way of showing it. I sit here for hours on my own while my sister writes. If you can call what she does writing. What do you do?'

'I'm a geophysicist. I work in oil and gas exploration.'

Standing abruptly, she says, 'You know, it's too cold to sit here. We'll catch our deaths. I need a coffee. Better still, a hot chocolate.' She puts a hand up to her eyes, masking them, but not before he has seen tears.

'Are you OK? What did I say? I've upset you.'

'No, it wasn't you. I just wasn't expecting . . .' She turns away.

He knows she would run if she could. Extending an arm, he gently lifts the chilled fingers of one of her hands. He places them between his palms and she feels warmth radiating from his rough skin, restoring the

circulation. 'Come on, let's get some coffee. Will you take my arm?'

She looks up. 'My husband was an oil man too . . . He died. In 1988. July the 6th.'

She hears the faint whistle of breath between his teeth. 'Piper Alpha?'

'Yes.'

'Marianne, I'm sorry.'

'That's why I don't talk about being widowed. What, in God's name, is there to say? I'm still angry. Incandescently angry.'

Marianne

It was—still is—the world's worst-ever offshore disaster. The flames could be seen for sixty miles. One hundred and sixty-five oil workers died in an inferno when the Piper Alpha oil rig exploded. The sixty-one men who survived did so by leaping hundreds of feet into the sea, despite serious injuries. Two heroic crewmen died attempting to rescue workers from the sea by boat. The bodies of thirty men—including my husband—were never recovered.

It was, apparently, an accident waiting to happen. The Cullen inquiry concluded that the management had been grossly deficient. It was a corporate massacre, but no one was ever prosecuted.

There's a memorial in Hazlehead Park in Aberdeen. It's surrounded by a rose garden. The names of the 167 victims are engraved on a granite plinth. I can read Harvey's name with my fingers, but I can't see it, of course. I can't see the rest of the memorial, can't even feel it. The three bronze figures of oilmen in working gear and survival suits are mounted above head height. To give visitors a good view, I suppose.

I spend some time every July sitting in the re-named, specially dedicated North Sea Rose Garden, facing a memorial I cannot see. (The roses smell nice.) Then I take a taxi to the seafront and sit on a bench facing out to sea in the direction of the marker buoy, 120 miles northeast of Aberdeen, which marks my husband's grave.

They tell me there's a light so the marker buoy is visible day and night. I can't see the marker. I can't see the sea. But I face them both every summer, believing they are there, believing that it matters I am there, trying to believe that somehow Harvey knows I'm there.

'I think outside Scotland people have practically forgotten. Well, it's not the sort of thing you want to remember, is it?' In the café Marianne sips hot chocolate, warming her hands on the mug. 'I didn't just lose my husband . . . I was pregnant.'

'Are you sure you want—'

'Oh, yes. The only people I ever talk to about it are people I don't know. You're performing a sort of service—if you can bear to listen.'

'Aye.' He touches her hand briefly, as if to reassure her of his physical presence. 'If you can bear to talk, I can bear to listen.'

'I was three months pregnant when Harvey died.'

'*Harvey?* Oh Christ, I'm really sorry—'

'Don't worry about it. I like rabbits. The idea of them, anyway. And I think I like you . . . First of all people told me the pregnancy was a blessing—I'd have something to remember him by. Then, when I lost the baby, people said that was a blessing too. I could marry again, unencumbered. I used to wonder if I was on the receiving end of more than the usual amount of crass insensitivity, simply because I was blind.' She sighs and takes a mouthful of chocolate. 'Oh, let's change the subject. Keir, are you still there? I'd hate to think I've been unburdening myself to thin air.'

'I'm still here. Would you like me to describe myself to you?'

'Would you tell the truth?'

'I'd try.' She hears him shift in his chair. 'I'm forty-two. A big guy, I suppose. Big bones and a fair bit of muscle. My hair's dark. Very short.'

'Eyes?'

'Two. One's blue and one's green.'

'*Really?*'

'Aye. They're different colours. Most folk don't notice. Or they notice there's something odd about my eyes, but can't work out what it is.'

'How extraordinary. Go on.'

'What more is there to say?'

'Well, would you say you're attractive?'

'How would I know?'

'Oh, come on! Men always know if women find them attractive.'

'I'm not sure that I do. Do *you* find me attractive?'

'I can't see you.'

'You can't see anyone. It's a level playing field. Voice and smell, I believe you said.'

'And touch. But that comes later.'

'It needn't. You could read me with your hands.'

She turns towards him. Raising her hand towards his face, she finds it, then spreads her fingers, tracing the lines and planes of his brow, cheeks, nose and—lingering a moment—his mouth. She places both hands at the sides of his head and smiles as she feels short, spiky hair,

sleek like an animal's coat. She extends a palm until it meets his chest, registering a soft woollen jumper. She moves her hand across, feeling the muscle, until she finds his upper arm, which she follows downwards, arriving at a large hand resting on his thigh. She sketches his hand with her fingertips, then moves them to his thigh, where she lets them rest for a moment. Withdrawing her hand, she leans back.

'Thank you. I think you sold yourself a bit short in the physique department. Not so much a rabbit—more of a bear. If the colour of your hair were a smell, what would it be?'

'That's a tough one. It's a rich brown. Goes a bit red in the summer.'

'Useless. I need smells.'

'Walnuts. Walnuts when you crack them open at Christmas.'

'And your eyes?'

'Which one? The blue or the green?'

'The blue.'

He is silent for a moment, then says, 'Juniper.'

'And the green?'

'The smell of . . . autumn leaves. Decaying. Smoky.'

'Lovely! You're good at this game—I can *see* you now. You aren't a rabbit at all. Or even a bear.' She extends a hand again and places her palm on his chest, leaving it there. 'You're a tree.'

CHAPTER TWO

Louisa

I have to confess I didn't really notice any change in Marianne. I was very busy with the final stages of one book and the birth pangs of another. It had struck me, though, that she seemed more cheerful. She took more care with her appearance, even asking me to advise her about accessories. I should have twigged, I suppose, but she never mentioned anyone and I never saw her with anyone.

Marianne had been single for so long that, frankly, I didn't ever think of her in relation to men. Not that she's unattractive, more *uninterested*. Her eyes are a little disconcerting of course, but they're large and an unusual

blue. Her blonde hair is going grey now, but she has a reasonable figure, I suppose because she eats very little and walks a lot. I tend to sit at the PC, nibbling, so the less said about my figure, the better. Marianne eats sensibly, walks for miles, and never misses an opportunity to tell me I'm a heart attack waiting to happen. I take no notice. I know it's just her rather warped way of saying she worries about me.

Perhaps I should have worried more about *her*. If I'd been less preoccupied with my own affairs, I might have realised. But the irony was (I say irony because Marianne is, of course, blind), it appeared she was being courted by the Invisible Man.

Marianne

He said he supposed we'd run into each other again. I said I hoped so. It was one of those awkward conversations where no one actually issues an invitation. Well, what sort of invitation would seem appropriate? I'd told him half my life story; he'd told me nothing of his. I didn't know where he lived and clearly he didn't want me to know.

I asked for his mobile number but he said he was about to go away. I said, 'Anywhere nice?' He said, 'The Arctic Circle.' He didn't ask for my number. Eventually I said, 'Well, you know where I live,' and he said, 'Aye, I do.' I assumed I'd never see him again.

Two weeks later, when I'd almost forgotten about the conversation in the café (almost, but not quite), I received a padded envelope containing a cassette. Louisa sorts the post and she'd left mine on the hall table, as usual. Lou had gone out to the hairdresser's so I couldn't ask her to read the label on the tape. I took it into my bedroom, dropped it into the cassette player and pressed PLAY.

After a few seconds I heard a wind howling. It was eerie: a constant whine. Suddenly a man's voice was raised above it, almost shouting: 'Hello, Marianne. This is a postcard from Keir. I'm in Hammerfest, Norway, seven hundred miles inside the Arctic Circle, and it's bloody cold. They used to hunt polar bear but now the ice is receding, everyone's looking for black gold—including me. It's another Klondyke up here. Plenty of fights and not enough women to go round. Lots of reindeer, though . . . Guess what? I'm the tallest tree.'

There was a click, followed by the sound of raucous singing and inebriated male laughter. There was another click, followed by Keir's voice once again, sounding stern. 'PS. Do *not* attempt to get that rousing little ditty translated from the original Norwegian. Believe me, you're better off not

knowing.' He paused, then added, 'Och, it was kind of catchy, though, wasn't it? . . . Cheers, Marianne.'

I don't know when I've been more touched or thrilled by a gift.

Not since Harvey used to send me taped love letters.

I carried Keir's tape around in my handbag for a week. I liked the thought of a piece of the Arctic living in my handbag, like Narnia inside the wardrobe. But then I had my bag snatched outside Jenners. (Needless to say, I was using my cane.) I think I was possibly more upset about losing the cassette than the contents of my handbag. I hadn't made a copy or even played it to Louisa. If I'm honest, I have to admit I enjoyed the extraordinary luxury of a secret, something I didn't have to share with Lou, something I didn't have to experience *through* her.

At least, I think that's why I didn't tell her. Of course, it might have been because I feared I'd blush.

I received a second postcard-cassette. It purported to be the sound of a glacier calving, dropping icebergs into the sea: creaks and groans, then a noise like a rifle shot, followed by a tremendous roar. Keir appeared to be on board ship. I could hear waves and a ship's hooter. At the end of the message he said, 'I'll be back in Edinburgh on the 30th. If you want to hear any travellers' tales, I'll be in the Botanics café at twelve on the 31st. Fortunately you'll be spared the holiday snaps.'

If I'd known what flight he was on, I might have gone to meet it, but there was no way of letting him know I'd be there. In any case, it would have been ridiculous. I chastised myself for thinking like a lovesick teenager and dropped the tape into the wastepaper bin.

Later that day I went to retrieve it, but our cleaning lady had been and she'd emptied the bins. I was livid—livid that I'd thrown the tape away, livid that I'd tried to retrieve it, but mostly livid that I was livid.

I recited the date and time of the proposed assignation, like a mantra, until I felt calm again.

Louisa

Marianne came home one day, all smiles, and said she'd invited someone to dinner: a Mr Harvey. She was irritated when I didn't know who she meant. She explained and I had to point out that I hadn't actually met Mr Harvey at the opera—he'd disappeared before I arrived.

She said it didn't matter, she was sure we'd get on and that I should invite a friend to make it a foursome. So I invited Garth.

Garth is a Goth. (In case you don't know about Goths, they dress in

black satin with silver chains, wear black eyeliner and white foundation. And that's just the boys.) When Marianne first met Garth, she enquired where the noise of rattling chains was coming from. Apart from that, she seemed to have no problem with him, which might not have been the case if she'd been able to *see* him.

Garth is a sweet boy, one of my most devoted fans, and he maintains my website. He looks like one of the living dead but actually he has a very practical side. He's extremely thorough and pays scrupulous attention to detail. He's doing a PhD on the history of witchcraft in Scotland, but he also helps me with research. Despite what my critics say—foremost among them, Marianne—I don't just churn out books. A good deal of historical research goes into them.

We took a lot of trouble over the menu for Mr Harvey, so I wasn't best pleased when he was late. When he was thirty minutes overdue, Marianne went to the kitchen and turned the oven down very low. (There are blobs of nail polish on the controls, in case you were wondering.) The mood wasn't very convivial. I was hungry, Marianne was tense, and Garth's small talk was limited. Marianne suddenly got to her feet and said, 'Sod it. Let's eat.' And so we did. Garth and I tucked in, but Marianne just picked at salad. She looked worn out, poor thing.

I could have *killed* that man. There was no excuse for not ringing unless he was lying in casualty. I don't know why, but I started to wonder . . . Perhaps because she seemed so upset but, at the same time, she didn't seem surprised. It was almost as if she'd known he wouldn't show.

As soon as Garth left, Marianne started loading the dishwasher. I could tell from the clatter in the kitchen that she was angry. She was scraping plates noisily into the bin when I said, 'Marianne, do you think it's possible you could have been overdoing things lately?'

She said, rather sharply, 'What are you getting at, Lou?'

'Nothing! I just wondered if you might have been . . . mistaken.'

She turned abruptly. 'Mistaken? About what?'

'About this man. Mr Harvey. It must be very difficult having only your hearing to go by. And everybody knows ears can play tricks on you.'

'Are you suggesting I *imagined* him?'

'Of course not! It just seems odd. Not turning up. Not even phoning.'

'It's not odd, it's bloody rude.' She bent over the dishwasher and rammed a handful of dirty cutlery into the basket.

'There could be all sorts of reasons why he isn't here,' I said, trying to be conciliatory. 'Why don't you give him a ring?'

'I don't have his number. I don't even know where he lives.'

'Marianne, forgive me for speaking so bluntly, but what evidence is there that this man actually exists?'

'You think I've made him up?'

'Not *deliberately*, no. But I think it's possible that your mind is playing tricks on you. It's probably all my fault for leaving you so much to your own devices, but with the deadline for *Blood Will Have Blood* looming, things have been just insane.'

'Is that what you think I am? Insane?'

'No, of course not, my dear.'

'Don't you "my dear" me!'

'Marianne, calm down! Naturally you're upset. Nobody likes being stood up.'

'Oh, so you admit he exists, then? Or do you think I've been stood up by a figment of my own imagination?'

'I don't know what to think! All I'm saying is, it doesn't add up.'

'He sent me a postcard!'

'Did he? Oh, that was nice . . . How did you know it was from him?'

'It was a tape. A message on a cassette.'

'Where from?'

'The Arctic.'

'*The Arctic?* Oh, for goodness' sake! Show me!'

'I can't. It was in my handbag when it was snatched.'

'Well, it's hardly evidence, then, is it?'

'Who's on trial here—him or me?'

'I'm just trying to establish beyond a shadow of doubt that Keith exists.'

'*Keir!* His name's Keir Harvey, he's nothing to do with the Labour Party, and before you ask, no, he is *not* a rabbit!' Marianne was shaking.

I laid my hand on her arm. 'I really think you should take one of my tablets, Marianne; they'll make you feel much calmer—'

She yanked her arm away and yelled, 'I'm perfectly calm!' then stalked out of the kitchen, colliding with a chair. I heard her bedroom door slam, then the sound of crying.

Marianne

There had been men. A few. I was widowed at twenty-seven and, for a blind woman, I was not unattractive, or so I was told. In my thirties I went through an interesting period of trying to find a life partner in an abortive attempt to escape from the smothering symbiotic relationship I'd developed living with my sister. I'd gone to stay with Louisa when Harvey died and so she was around for the miscarriage. By the time we'd got over

that, we thought it would be a good idea to pool our financial resources and buy somewhere in Edinburgh.

My period of modest promiscuity probably had more to do with finding a father for a child than finding myself another husband. I failed, and entered my forties childless and celibate. And, it has to be said, slightly relieved. Blind motherhood would always have been a tough option. Blind sexual relationships are even more fraught with difficulty than the sighted variety, especially for women.

Perhaps I should explain. The sort of men you attract if you're blind fall into one of three categories:

A. *The Romantics*. These are men who think there's something spiritual, beautiful, quintessentially *feminine* about being blind (for which read helpless). Blindness brings out the Galahad in this type. They charge about being helpful on a heroic scale. Woe betide you if you don't wish to be set upon a pedestal.

B. *The Sexually Insecure*. These men believe that if you're blind (i.e. defective), you'll be grateful for any interest shown in you, even if it comes from a short, fat, malodorous clod so unappealing a sighted woman would cross the road to avoid him.

C. *The Perverts*. There are, unfortunately, a number of men who are turned on by the idea of a blind woman.

What all these men have in common is, they expect a blind woman to be *grateful* for their attentions. That's what renders me a second-class citizen. Not being blind. Blindness is just a series of practical problems. I don't consider myself handicapped, except by others' views of me. What constrains me, angers me, demeans me, are other people's expectations that I should be grateful for their help, for inclusion in their sighted world, to which I don't really belong.

Keir hadn't treated me like that. He didn't seem to be Type A, B or C. He was offhand, almost rude. He made no concessions to my blindness. It was almost as if 'sight, lack of' wasn't an issue, simply a distinguishing characteristic, like his height. The only person who'd ever treated me like that was Harvey and he learned how to do it over a period of years.

So I was caught off-guard. I was vulnerable. (When is one not, when one is blind?) I was almost forty-six. I'd assumed my sexual organs and appetite had long atrophied through lack of use and was surprised to find that this wasn't so, although to say I felt a sexual attraction to Keir would have been overstating the case.

All right, it wouldn't. Who am I kidding? I have only voice, touch and

smell to go on and he'd passed with flying colours in all those depart-
ments. In addition, he seemed not only an interesting person, but a nice
one. I liked his rudeness. It was stimulating. Refreshing. And his off-the-wall
take on things seemed to be the result of his seeing fairly clearly (for a
sighted person) what life was actually like for me. So add empathy to his
list of virtues.

I suppose it's no wonder my sister thought I'd made him up. So did I at
times. Like when he didn't show up for dinner. I couldn't forgive Keir for not
turning up, for not ringing me the day after. I couldn't forgive him for disappointing me, for creating his own category of dilettante, a combination of
A, B and C, without the staying power of any of them.

No doubt I'd had a lucky escape, for which I should be grateful. (You
see? Gratitude is unavoidable, however hard you try.) But I wasn't grateful. I was hurt. Humiliated. I was angry.

I was still angry a week later when I decided to go for a walk in the
Botanics. I slammed the door of the flat and set off down the wide staircase, rehearsing exactly what I'd say to Mr Keir Harvey if he had the misfortune to bump into me. But of course he wouldn't. He'd see me coming
and walk the other way.

My anger flared again as I opened the heavy front door. I stepped over
the threshold, turning, and walked into a wall of flesh and bone. I shrieked
and stepped back, tripping over the doorsill. Hands caught me by the
elbows. A voice, his voice, was saying, 'It's me. Sorry, Marianne. It's Keir.'

A wave of relief overwhelmed me: I wasn't about to be mugged or murdered. But I didn't want to feel relieved. Not grateful. Lord, *anything* but
that. I opened and closed my mouth, trying to find words to express the
cocktail of emotions provoked by the sudden shock of Keir's presence. I'd
intended, if I ever met him again, to be frigidly polite, dismissive. But what
came out was anger.

You've got a bloody nerve—just turning up on my doorstep! Why
didn't you ring?'

'I didn't have your number.'

'Rubbish! I heard you put it on your mobile.'

'My phone got smashed. So did I.'

'You were *drunk*?'

'No. There was an accident. On the rig. I fell.' He lifts her hand and
carries it to his forehead, where she feels scabbed flesh quilted with
stitches. She recoils.

'Good grief! I'm sorry. Are you all right?'

'I am now. I *was* concussed, otherwise you'd have had flowers and a grovelling apology.'

'Oh, don't worry about that. As long as you're all right.'

'Oh, aye. Limping a bit. One of the other guys is not so good, though.'

'Come upstairs and I'll make us some coffee. You can tell me about the accident.'

'There's nothing to tell. Accidents happen all the time. I'll live.'

'I sincerely hope so,' Marianne replies as she closes the door.

She calms herself with the ritual of making coffee. Carrying a loaded tray into the sitting room, she asks, 'Where are you sitting?'

'I'm not. I'm standing, so you don't trip over my big feet. Here, let me take the tray.'

She sits in an armchair opposite the sofa and hears the asthmatic wheeze of cushions as he sits down facing her. Reaching for a mug of coffee, she says, 'Help yourself to milk and sugar.'

'Thanks.'

'Why didn't they send you home?'

'They wanted to keep me in. For observation.'

'No, I mean when you were discharged, why didn't you go home? I presume you do have one?'

'I owed you an apology. I don't make a habit of standing women up. Besides, I wanted to see you again.'

'Why?'

She hears him sigh. 'You don't make things easy, do you? Look, I know I'm supposed to suggest we have dinner, then go through the waiting-for-phone-calls routine, meet the family and pets—'

'Did I ever tell you about Garth? My sister's pet Goth?'

'Is that a breed of dog?'

'Never mind. You were saying?'

'I was saying, I wondered if we could just cut all the crap and skip to the part where you say "No".'

'Keir, what on earth are you talking about?'

'I've got sick leave, so I'm going home for a wee while.'

'And where exactly *is* home?'

'Skye. I was wondering . . . Would you like to come?'

'To Skye? You mean come and stay with you?'

'Aye.' She makes no reply and he continues, 'There'd be separate sleeping accommodation—you need have no worries on that score. I'm not importing you for lewd purposes.'

'Well, you needn't say it as if that was the last thing on your mind. You make me feel like the antidote to desire.'

He sighs again. 'I'm sorry, that did sound pretty crass, didn't it? I thought you might be . . . concerned.'

'For my virtue, you mean? What use is virtue to me? Anyway, I'm a widow, if you remember. Not somebody's maiden aunt.'

'Now who's talking about herself as if she's the antidote to desire?'

'Oh, I'm scarcely a woman in the eyes of the world. I don't see, so I don't shop. I don't have a man. In the eyes of the world, I'm just *blind*.'

'In the eyes of the world, maybe. Not mine.'

She hears him swallow coffee, then place his mug on the table.

'So you're inviting me for a sort of holiday?'

'Aye.'

'I'm not much of a one for scenery.'

'I realise that.'

'And I get awfully crabby when I'm off my home turf.'

'You can be pretty crabby *on* it.'

'So why are you asking me?'

'I want to show you Skye. And I use the word advisedly.'

'I get the guest room?'

'No, you get my bed. There's only two rooms.'

'But you're optional?'

'Entirely. As is the full Scottish breakfast. There's no electricity but the house is warm and dry. From an aesthetic point of view, it's a bit primitive, but you'll not be into interior design in a big way, I imagine.'

She is silent, her head bowed, apparently deep in thought.

He clears his throat and says wearily, 'This is the point where you say, "No, I couldn't possibly."'

She lifts her head. 'Why would I say that?'

'I don't know. You can't get leave from work, maybe?'

'But I can.'

'You don't actually *know* me?'

'That's very true. There have been times when I've even doubted your existence.'

'Don't apologise. God has the same problem.'

'And works in equally mysterious ways, His wonders to perform.'

'I'm not promising wonders. The weather will be terrible. You'll be holed up, listening to the wind and rain. But if it ever stops, you'll be climbing hills and watching stars.'

'I can't watch stars.'

'Maybe not, but I can tell you about them.'

'You're going to teach me about the stars?'

'Aye.'

She puts her coffee mug down. 'How did you *know*?'

'Know what?'

'That I've always wanted to know—since I was a tiny child—what twinkling looks like? I mean, what twinkling is *like*.'

Keir thinks for a moment, then says, 'It's a kind of pulse. A gentle throbbing of light. A beautiful, magical throbbing . . . I had a girlfriend once who tried to explain the mysteries of female sexual arousal to me and she said, "You know he's the one for you if the sight of him makes your genitals twinkle."'

Marianne is silent, then asks, 'Were you the one for her?'

'I think so.'

'But she wasn't the one for you.'

'Afraid not, for all she was a poet. Will you come with me, Marianne?'

'To listen to the stars? Try stopping me.'

Louisa

Well, he wasn't what I expected. But then I'd been expecting nothing, so anything at all would have been a pleasant surprise. And what I got was a very pleasant surprise.

He came to the flat to collect Marianne and her luggage before they set off for Skye. He was tall, well over six feet. He looked younger than Marianne. I don't know why I'd thought he'd be older, or indeed any age at all, since I'd assumed he didn't exist. He was dark, with short, conker-brown hair cropped close to the head, giving him something of an ascetic look, like a monk, but his eyes were lively and humorous. Crinkly. Otherwise his face was unlined. There was something disquieting about those eyes. I got the impression they didn't miss much.

He had stitches in his forehead and some technicolour bruising, but it was nevertheless a handsome face with a straight nose and a generous, slightly crooked mouth, which seemed to go with his ironic turns of phrase.

He was broad in the shoulder and very tall. Oh, I think I already said that, didn't I? It's just that it really *struck* you, the size of him, as he stood there looking so solid and masculine in our fussy sitting room, so much so that I caught myself thinking, Gosh, I hope Marianne doesn't fall in a big way and get hurt. Then he did something that made me think again.

Marianne was buttoning up her coat, her back turned towards Keir.

Over her shoulder I saw him look at her, then hesitate. He lifted his great big hands and—so gently—he slipped his fingers under her long, loose hair where it was caught inside her coat collar. He gently pulled it free, then watched it cascade over her shoulders and, as he did so, he smiled. Not at me, or at Marianne. He just smiled.

That was when I had second thoughts. I looked at the pair of them and thought, Oh Lord—I hope *he* doesn't fall in a big way and get hurt.

I kissed Marianne goodbye. I was a bit tearful, I don't know why. She was only going away for a week. Keir handed me a small carrier bag and grinned, saying it was a gift for me. I looked inside and there were two gift-wrapped boxes. Probably chocolates, I thought.

After they'd gone, I felt quite flat. I couldn't settle to work. Far from feeling apprehensive about her eccentric holiday, with her even more eccentric companion, what I actually felt was jealous. That realisation made me feel quite disgruntled, so at lunchtime I switched off the PC and settled down to watch daytime TV. I was about to tune in to a re-run of *Buffy the Vampire Slayer* when I remembered Keir's presents. Sure enough, one box contained Belgian chocolates. The other turned out to be a DVD.

I don't suppose I need to tell you what it was. *Harvey*. It was awfully good. (So were the chocs.)

CHAPTER THREE

Marianne

I hardly ever think about sex and I don't particularly miss it. I can barely remember what it feels like to have sex, and you can't really fantasise about something you've almost forgotten. And when you try to remember, you know the only thing that could remind you what it was like would be making love with a man.

But that wasn't going to happen. I was quite clear about that. I was quite clear because there was absolutely no question of my asking Louisa to shop for condoms. Whether the lack of sexual opportunity was a disappointment, I didn't bother to ask myself (though I suppose the fact that the shopping difficulty had occurred to me tells its own story). I confess I might

have envisaged—briefly—some romantic scenario worthy of Louisa at her worst. I was, after all, about to be whisked away to an island in the far north by a man I hardly knew and who was (Louisa assured me) quite attractive. Nevertheless, there would be no sex. Unless, of course, Keir, in true Boy Scout fashion, came prepared.

He struck me as the sort of man who might be ready for anything.

Keir installs Marianne in a waiting black cab, loads their luggage and announces 'Waverley' to the driver. As he eases his bulky frame between Marianne and their cases, she says, 'We're going by *train*?'

'Aye.'

'It's an awfully long way.'

'That's why we're going by train. My Land Rover's parked at Inverness anyway. D'you not like trains?'

'I've hardly ever used them. They're pretty awkward if you're blind. Do we have to change?'

'No, we go all the way to Inverness, have lunch, then pick up the Land Rover, head west to Kyle, then drive over the bridge to Skye.'

'You know, I'm not sure I approve of islands being connected to the mainland by bridges. Seems perverse to me.'

'You might think differently if you lived there. Isolation can be a mixed blessing. And the bridge has brought us many benefits.'

'Such as?'

'Pine martens.'

'*Pine martens?* They walked across the bridge?'

'Aye . . . Carrying their wee suitcases.'

At Waverley, Keir escorts her across the concourse to the platform.

'You walk very confidently without your cane.'

'I fall over very confidently too. I've got one in my bag but I don't use it if I can help it. But then I don't often venture out of familiar territory.'

'So I'm taking you outside your comfort zone?'

'Oh, yes. In more ways than one . . . Are you laughing at me?'

'No, I'm not.'

'But you were grinning?'

'Aye, as it happens, I was. How did you know?'

'An educated guess.'

'Based on what evidence?'

'The silence . . . And your arm relaxed suddenly.'

'I feel like Dr Watson tagging along with Sherlock Holmes. I can see I'm going to have trouble keeping up with you.'

'**D**o you want the window seat?'

'So I can admire the view?'

'No, so you don't have folk thumping you with their luggage.'

'Oh . . . Sorry. Forgive the sarcasm. I'm feeling rather nervous. The unfamiliarity.'

'No problem. Will I take your coat? I'll put it in the rack overhead.'

'Thanks.' Marianne hands him her coat and settles into her seat. He sits down beside her and Marianne is thrown momentarily by the unexpected body contact. 'When do we get to Inverness?'

'Midday or thereabouts. Then we'll have lunch and drive to Skye.'

'You're really excited about showing me your island, aren't you?'

'It's not mine, I'm merely a custodian. A caretaker.'

'You're not there much of the time.'

'No, but when I am, I take care of things.'

'What sort of things?'

'All creatures great and small . . . Och, that's not strictly true. They take care of themselves. I just make sure the right conditions prevail. I'm not really a caretaker. More a maintenance man. Part-time,' he adds.

'What sort of things do you do?'

Keir is thoughtful, then says, 'Keep the twenty-first century at bay.'

'**A**re you waiting for a call?'

'How did you *know*?'

'You keep checking your phone. I hear you pick it up off the table; then you put it down again.'

'I'm not exactly waiting. It's a call I hope I don't get.'

Marianne waits for him to say more. When he doesn't, she asks, 'Do you have many visitors? On Skye?'

'No. You're the first.'

'*Really?* Are you taking me because I'm blind? As some kind of good deed? I have a suspicion you suffer from a Boy Scout complex.'

'I'm taking you because you're the first person I've met who I think might appreciate my world the way I do.'

'Which is?'

'With your whole mind and body, not just your eyes.'

She frowns. 'I'm not sure I understand.'

'Well, *seeing* seems to me a pretty narrow way of appreciating the world. Superficial.' Keir turns his head and looks at her profile outlined against the window. Not for the first time he's thrown by the lack of eye contact. Instead he focuses on her ear, small, neat and convoluted.

'Sound penetrates your body. So does smell. Touch affects your body too, obviously. These seats are too narrow for a guy like me. You can feel the pressure of my body against yours, can't you?'

'Yes, I can.'

'If you didn't know me, that would feel like an invasion of your personal space. Och, maybe it does anyway.'

'No, it doesn't. It's rather reassuring, actually. I know you're there.'

'But sight leaves the body untouched. When you see something—I mean when sighted folk see—it's out there, *beyond* the self. It isn't in your eye the way a sound is in your ear, or a smell is in your nose. It's detached from the self.'

'Fascinating! Of course, I'll have to take your word for it.'

'It's not you with limited perception, Marianne. Folk who can see just don't seem to *look*. If you could see them, would you still touch trees?'

'I don't know. I like to think I would.'

'Aye, it's natural human behaviour! Think of the way we clamber on rocks and climb trees when we're kids. We want to feel our bodies in touch with the earth, with other living things. Then we forget. We . . . disconnect.' Leaning back in his seat, he murmurs, 'That's when the trouble starts.'

'Trouble?'

'Some people think conservation is about saving animal species. They don't realise we're also trying to prevent the human race from committing suicide.' He pauses for a moment. 'We're links in a chain. The chain only works when we're all linked together.'

'People and animals, you mean?'

'*Everything.*'

Marianne

Keir's voice was his own now. I'd heard it often enough and for long enough to become acquainted with its distinct timbre. The pitch and accent were Harvey's but the vocal mannerisms weren't. The vocabulary wasn't. The silences weren't.

Keir had become his own man but my enjoyment of his company was coloured by memories I was reluctant to revisit. To my utter dismay, the pleasure that I felt in his presence was marred—already—by fear of loss. But how could I fear to lose what I didn't even possess?

Perhaps it was just habit. It's hard to describe the loneliness of being an oil wife, the hatefulness of it. When your husband's offshore, you wish your life away waiting for him to come home. That's on good days. On bad

days, you are *consumed* by worry, haunted by premonitions of danger, injury, even death.

Because of my blindness there were special hardships. I could never comfort myself with photographs. When Harvey was abroad, I couldn't anticipate long love letters. I had to content myself with phone calls until a friend, finding me in tears one day after speaking to him, suggested I tape our calls to play back at leisure. It was a short step from there to Harvey sending me taped letters and journals, self-conscious at first, but eventually entertaining and briefly romantic as he signed off. (Try getting a male Highlander to talk about his feelings. You'll need the conversational equivalent of the culinary device that removes snails from their shell.)

I dated and labelled all the tapes in Braille as I received them. When Harvey died, I put them away with his clothes, his books and his CDs. After a year I was able to get rid of the clothes, with Louisa's help. She was very good, very practical. I was anaesthetised by exhaustion after months of grief—first for Harvey, then for the baby. Selling up in Aberdeen, getting rid of Harvey's stuff, telling people about the miscarriage, Louisa saw me through all of it. She was tactful but brisk. It was necessary. I was only twenty-seven. I needed to begin again.

The tapes now live in a beautiful oblong mahogany box. I know it's beautiful. I can feel. The box is Indian and ornately carved. After Harvey's death the box became the repository for his tapes and the photos of us he used to have on display. After I'd shut it and put it away, I felt as if I'd buried Harvey's voice. Perhaps this too was necessary. There had been no funeral. His body had never been recovered, had never been laid to rest in a coffin.

I can't listen to the tapes. I tried once or twice many years ago and it all but destroyed me. Now I don't dare. To listen to those tapes is to summon up Harvey's ghost. But he was a ghost even while he was alive. Each time he went away, it was a kind of death. My husband existed for me only when I could hear him, touch him, hold him in my arms, and the joy of his homecomings was intensified by a sense that he'd come back to life. Each time he came home safely, it felt like a miracle. A *big* miracle.

After Harvey died, I used to jump whenever the phone rang and my heart would pound with hope. It was months before I stopped praying it would be Harvey resurrected, his voice telling me he was on his way home, there'd been a terrible mistake . . . When Keir first spoke to me, I thought for a moment the miracle had occurred again.

Now Keir had begun to sound like himself. I knew his voice and delighted in it. But when he wasn't there, when I had only the memory of his

voice, when I couldn't feel (as I did then, on the train,) the pressure of his body adjacent to mine, a small, fearful and familiar voice asked if he existed. If Keir didn't speak, didn't touch me, he became a ghost, like Harvey.

His shoulder was at the level of my ear now. I sensed the slight rise and fall as he breathed. If I angled my head slightly, I knew my hair must fall onto his shoulder. My scalp sensed the contact. It seemed the most comfortable and natural thing in the world to incline my head further, to rest it on his shoulder and close my eyes. He said nothing but became very still. I enjoyed what was for me a rare luxury: Keir was silent but I knew he was there. I didn't have to believe it. I *knew*.

After lunch in Inverness, Keir escorts Marianne from the restaurant to the car park. Cold gusts of wind scythe the air and she turns up the collar of her coat as she waits for him to load their luggage.

He opens the Land Rover's passenger door. 'There's a step up. Quite high. Then there's a handle . . . here.' He takes one of her hands and places it on the inside of the door. 'But the really useful one is here. Lean in.' He places her other hand above the dashboard. 'You can haul yourself in using that bar.'

She lifts her foot and pedals in mid-air, searching for the step.

'May I?' Keir lifts her foot up to the step. 'There you go. It's higher than is convenient for a woman, even one as fit as yourself.' He closes the door behind her and reappears at the other.

'All right, Sherlock—how do you know I'm fit?'

'Muscle tone. And you don't get out of breath keeping up with me.' He climbs in and fastens his safety belt. 'You must walk a lot.'

'I do. And I swim. Sometimes Louisa and I go to the gym together. It's part of her eternal and entirely unsuccessful weight-loss plan.'

'That's where I've seen you before. I thought when we first met I knew you from somewhere.'

'Me too.'

'My voice?' He sounds surprised.

'Yes. You sounded—you sound a bit like my husband. Like Harvey.'

The name hangs in the air between them for a moment. Then Keir says softly, 'The accent, I suppose.'

'Yes. When we met, for a minute I thought—' She breaks off. Tactfully, Keir turns the ignition key.

Two hours later, they stretch their legs at Kyle of Lochalsh on the northwest coast, in sight of Skye. Marianne's spirits lift at the smell of the sea and the sound of squabbling gulls. As they set off again, Keir

says, 'In a minute or two, when we start to climb, we'll be going over the bridge. Welcome to the Misty Isle, Marianne. Welcome to Skye.'

They have been driving for a few minutes and Keir is describing a view of the islands of Scalpay, Raasay and the mainland beyond when his phone rings. He looks down at the display briefly. Swinging the wheel, he pulls over to the side of the road and answers the phone.

'Annie? Any news?' He listens while a woman talks. Marianne hears his breathing change, then the sound of a woman sobbing at the other end of the phone. Keir utters a single despairing word: 'When?'

Marianne starts to get out of the car. Keir's hand shoots out to restrain her. 'It's OK,' he whispers. He speaks into the phone again. 'Annie? Are you there? The signal's not so good . . . Is your mother with you? . . . You'll let me know, then? About the funeral? . . . No, I'm on Skye just now. But I'll be there . . . Look, Annie, if there's anything, anything at all . . . Aye, you too, pet . . .'

Keir tosses his phone onto the shelf above the dashboard, startling Marianne. He opens his door, jumps down and stands staring out to sea. It begins to rain and he turns his already wet face to the sky.

'Keir?'

He looks back and sees Marianne standing beside the Land Rover. He jogs to her side.

'Was it the man who was in the accident with you?'

'Aye. Did I tell you about that?'

'Yes. Well, you mentioned another man had been injured. I guessed things didn't look too hopeful.'

'No. He died this morning. That was his wife.'

'Poor woman. He was a friend of yours?'

'Aye. An old pal. We go way back.'

Marianne waits for Keir to elaborate, then realises his silence speaks of the inarticulate depths of male friendship. 'If you want to turn round and go back,' she says gently, 'that's fine by me.'

'Och, no, what I need to do now is get home, light the stove, crack open a good bottle and brood—at length—on the transience of life and the whims of the Grim Reaper. Do you drink whisky, Marianne?'

'Yes.'

'Then we'll raise a glass to Mac tonight. Ach . . .' Keir bows his head and says, his voice suddenly harsh with anger, 'He was full of life, that guy! And one hell of a shinty player. You should have seen him!'

Marianne lifts her hand up to his face. She lays her fingers on his

cold, damp cheek. 'You mustn't feel guilty, you know. For surviving. There's nothing you could have done.'

'I'm not so sure. But thanks anyway.' He opens the passenger door. 'Hop in. We'll be on our way.' He takes her arm but she doesn't move.

'You know, I sometimes wish we would all treat each other as if we were about to die. Say all the things that should be said. And *not* say the things that shouldn't.'

'If you *could* see death coming, what would you do differently?'

They stand facing each other, buffeted by the wind. Marianne shivers violently, then says, 'I wouldn't have told Harvey I was pregnant.'

'Why not?'

'It was just one more thing for him to worry about. The pregnancy wasn't planned and he didn't think I would cope. If he had time to think before he was incinerated, his last thoughts might have been, "I'm leaving a wife behind. And she's pregnant. And blind."'

'Maybe it was a comfort to him to know life would go on.'

'Maybe. Did Mac have kids?'

'Three. They'll be taken care of. Annie's family will see her through it. So will Mac's. It will be very hard, but she'll cope.'

Marianne leans into the Land Rover and grips the bar ready to heave herself in, then says, 'You think you won't cope. But you do.'

'Aye. You look death in the eye and renegotiate terms . . . Come on, into the wagon with you. We've a way to go yet.'

Marianne
I remember the last conversation I had with my husband. I remember his very last words. It wasn't a conversation, it was a row. We parted in anger. We didn't even kiss each other goodbye. But you cope.

'This is as far as the wheels take us.'

Keir switches off the ignition and peers through the windscreen at the torrent of rain hammering the bonnet of the Land Rover. 'The rest of our journey's on foot and we've two choices. There's a narrow winding path that leads down to the house. You'd manage that, but it will take a while and you'll get soaked. Or . . .' He pauses. 'Or I can carry you down the steps—I've set a series of flat rocks into the hillside at intervals.'

'*Carry* me? Don't be ridiculous! I can walk down. I'll just be slow.'

As they get out of the Land Rover, the wind whips the door out of Marianne's hand. She climbs down, then cries out, '*Sod* it!'

Keir calls from the back of the vehicle where he is opening the door for their luggage, 'What's wrong?'

'I just stepped into a hole full of water and flooded my shoes.' She feels her way to the back of the car. She hears him haul her suitcase out and says hurriedly, 'I can carry my case. It's really not that heavy.'

'I suggest you just concentrate on coping with new and uneven terrain and leave the luggage to me.'

'Keir, I wish you'd stop behaving like something out of Jane Austen.'

'Why?'

'Because it makes me *feel* like something out of Jane Austen.'

'And that's bad?'

'Yes.'

'Because you've spent your whole life trying not to feel helpless.'

'Yes,' she replies, lifting her chin. 'I have.'

He is silent for a moment and regards her tired, wet face, framed by hair hanging in sodden rats' tails. 'And just supposing I've spent my whole life wanting to be a hero?'

She puts her head on one side like a bird, as if listening more intently. 'Have you?'

'Aye . . . Some.'

Marianne says nothing. As the rain drums more heavily, she kicks her feet together in an attempt to stir her circulation. She groans and says, 'I'm probably heavier than I look.'

'And I'm probably stronger than I look.' He takes her arm and says, 'Come over here. There's a rock in front of you. Step up onto it.' She climbs onto the slippery, uneven stone. 'OK, I'm standing in front of you now with my back towards you.'

She extends her hands and finds his shoulders level with her chest. 'Oh Lord—I'm frightened of strangling you.'

'You won't. Hop on.' With a whoop, Marianne flings herself at his back and he hooks his arms behind her knees. 'Hold tight now.'

She wraps her arms more firmly round his neck and Keir descends crab-like, stepping sideways. Marianne giggles. 'This is rather fun, actually.' Her mouth close to his ear, she says, 'I think we should come to some arrangement. Schedule the heroics, I mean.'

'Yours or mine?'

'Both, so it's your shift until we get indoors, then I'll wow you with my sightless cooking. Juggling with Sabatier knives, plate-spinning, turning water into wine. It's quite a performance.'

'Och, well, that's good. With no electricity, we'll have to make our

own entertainment.' He stands still, breathing heavily.

'Am I getting heavy? Do you want a rest?'

'No, I was stopping to admire the view in the last of the light. Can you hear running water? That's the burn.'

'Yes. And what sounds like . . . a waterfall?'

'Aye, the water falls; then the burn circles the house and carries on down to meet the sea about a quarter of a mile away.'

The noise of the stream recedes. The ground begins to level out and Keir walks more quickly, then stops. He releases her legs and Marianne slides down his back to the ground. Opening a door, he leads her into a structure that she can tell straight away has a corrugated-iron roof.

'Oh, listen to the rain! It sounds like the Edinburgh Tattoo.'

'This is what Americans would call the mudroom.' Taking her arm, Keir leads her inside the house. 'Stand there and drip while I light the stove.'

As she unlaces her shoes, Marianne hears him move away, then the clank of a metal door, a scrabble for matches and the sound of wood and paper catching light. 'That was quick!'

'I always lay the fire before I leave. Come and sit down.' He leads her to an armchair by the stove. 'I'll go back up and get the luggage. You'll be OK for a few minutes?'

'Yes, of course. I shall sit and inhale wood smoke. Glorious.'

'If carcinogenic.'

'Oh, who cares? Life is terminal.'

'Aye, right enough.'

Her face falls and her fingers fly to her mouth. 'Oh, that was really tactless of me considering the news you had today. I was forgetting in all the excitement. I'm so sorry, Keir.'

'Don't be. I never thought Mac would make it. I've had more than a week to grieve already . . . *Are* you excited, Marianne?'

'About this trip? You bet I am. This is a real adventure for me. Pure Enid Blyton—a much maligned author, in my opinion. I hope you've got in a good supply of cocoa,' she says, rubbing her hands together to warm them. 'I feel a midnight feast coming on . . . Keir, you've gone quiet again. Are you laughing at me?'

'No, I'm just tired. And relieved.'

'What about?'

'That you're pleased to be here. That you haven't complained about the rain. Or the cold. Or the undignified mode of transport.'

'I wouldn't have missed that for the world. You can't afford to stand

on your dignity if you're blind, you know. It doesn't do. I can just about cope with feeling beholden, but I warn you now, I don't really do grateful. You'll just have to take that as read.'

'I think you'll find I'm pretty good at reading between the lines.'

'Then you'll know how relieved I am.'

'Relieved?'

'That it was poor Mac and not you.' He doesn't reply and she adds brightly, extending her hands towards the stove, 'It's definitely warming up now. Wood-burners are marvellous, aren't they?'

He opens the front door. 'I'm away up the hill now to get the luggage. Speak kindly to the stove—it needs encouragement.'

Keir places a glass of whisky in her hand and says, 'Now you get the tour. It won't take long. This place is tiny but it's as well to point out some hazards. Which, as it happens, is what I do for a living.'

'What is?'

'Hazard prediction. Identifying conditions that could be hazardous to drilling operations.'

'How on earth do you do that?'

'Well, 3D seismic technology is how. And I have a wee crystal ball that comes in handy . . . We're in the kitchen now and it has an old Rayburn. When it's alight you'll be aware of the heat, so that's not a hazard. The table and chairs are over here against the wall, out of the way, and everything is stored on shelves or cupboards, so there's nothing to trip you, apart from the rug. I'll maybe roll that up.'

'Really, there's no need. I have a very good memory. Once I've moved around a bit, I'll remember the layout. Mobility isn't a problem for me except when people *move* things.'

'OK, there's a back door on the far wall. Outside there's a rough sort of garden and a pond, so mind your footing if you go out there. There are paths—I'll show you round tomorrow. So, if we retrace our steps to the entrance to the kitchen, on your left you have the front door where we came in. On your right, a door leading to the bathroom, which is very small, just a loo and a shower. If you step across the hall now—Marianne, are you *counting*?'

'Yes. And memorising. I navigate by a sequence of numbers, you see. The number of paces between things. Where are we now?'

'In the sitting room. To your right is the open-tread staircase that leads up to the sleeping area. That's a platform over the sitting room and it's partly open, but there's a safety rail, about waist height. In here

we have my desk by the window and the armchair beside the stove. On the far wall is the sofa where I'll sleep. Shall we try negotiating the stair now? Will you follow me up? There's a handrail on your left. There's ten steps and they're open-tread, mind.'

Marianne follows him up the staircase. He draws her into the middle of the room, then positions himself at the head of the stairs. 'I'm standing in front of the stair now so you can't fall. You'll only be able to stand upright in the centre of the room: put your hands up and you'll feel the sloping ceiling. There's a double bed—not made up yet—and a small table and a chair under the window. There's a chest of drawers beside the bed. On the wall facing the bed there's shelves and baskets containing clothes and assorted junk. One other thing I should mention—there's no electricity so the lighting is oil lamps.'

'Keir, I don't need any light!'

'I know, but the oil lamps will be another hazard. You'll need to know where they are and if they're alight.'

'I imagine I'll feel the heat and I'll smell them.'

'Aye, that's what I thought. How's your glass?'

'Empty.'

'A shocking dereliction of duty on the part of the host. Will you come down and have another, or will I bring it up to you while you unpack? Do you need a hand with anything?'

'No, just find me a space to put my clothes.'

She hears him pull open a drawer and scrape the contents out and dump them elsewhere. 'Top drawer beside the bed is now empty. Do you want some hangers?'

'No, but if there was a hook for my dressing gown, it would make it easier to find.'

'No problem. There's a picture hanging on a cup-hook here, at the side of the bed. If I remove the picture . . .' He presses her fingers to the wall. 'There. Can you feel? Hang your dressing gown on that.'

'What is it a picture of?'

'Why d'you ask?'

'Well, you've given me a tour of your home without telling me anything about it. Nothing about the pictures, the books, the mementos. You've shown me the skeleton. Tell me about your books. What's your *favourite*? If you were about to be thrown into a prison cell—solitary confinement, say—what would you grab?'

'*Walden*. Henry David Thoreau. Or—no, perhaps a volume of poetry by Norman MacCaig.'

'Which one?'

'The *Collected Poems*. That would get me through a long stretch.'

'Thank you! Now I know something about you. What was the picture you took down, by the way?'

'My family. An old photo of us visiting this house. In the 1970s. My granny. My parents. My brother and sister. And my dog.'

'But this wasn't your home, surely? It's too small.'

'It was my grandparents'. We often came to visit. My grandparents gave the house to my mother, who wanted to sell it as a building plot. But I wanted to keep the house as it was, so I bought it from my parents.'

'Is it the house or the land that means so much to you?'

'The land.'

'What are you doing with it?'

'I'll tell you tomorrow when I show you round. Let's go and eat.'

'In a minute. I just want to unpack a few things. Take my glass and go on down and I'll see if I can find my way around on my own.'

'Supper in half an hour, then?'

'Sounds good to me.'

Marianne hears his feet descending the wooden stairs. She unpacks and paces the room a couple of times, counting, and decides the safest way to locate the stairs is to count from the window.

She extracts a heavy object from her case: a bottle swathed in tissue. Cradling it in one arm, she reaches out, searching for the window. She turns about-face and counts five paces to the head of the stairs and feels for the rail. Descending carefully, counting, she finds herself on level ground and breathes more easily. 'Keir? Are you in the kitchen?'

'Sitting room. I'm behind the stair.'

She extends her arm in the direction of his voice. 'A contribution.'

He takes the bottle from her hand and unwraps it. 'Champagne? Och, we must drink this before you go.'

'Well, that *was* the general idea. You never know—cocoa might begin to pall after a while. I'm off in search of the kitchen.'

As she turns away, Keir shouts, 'Mind the stair!' and pulls her to one side. Marianne loses her footing but he keeps her upright with an arm round her waist. 'You were going to walk into the staircase. You're underneath it and you'd have cracked your head. Sorry if I startled you.'

'No, I'm all right, thanks.' Righting herself, she lays a hand against his chest and encounters crisp, curling hair, then bare skin. Pulling away quickly, she stutters, 'God, Keir—you aren't naked, are you?'

Laughing, he replies, 'No, but I was getting changed.'

'Oh. I'm sorry, I didn't mean to barge in. I should have knocked.'

'There's no door.'

Still flustered, she says, 'We're going to need some sort of system, aren't we? There's no door upstairs either.'

'I've already thought of that. Come to the foot of the stair.' He takes her elbow and leads her. 'Over here, just before you go into the kitchen, I've hung a wind chime.' A random but not unpleasant series of notes sounds. 'We'll use it like a doorbell. I'll jangle it if I'm coming up, and you can do the same if you want to let me know you're around.'

'A brilliant idea. I shall enjoy using it.'

'It will also let you know when I'm coming in and out of the house. As soon as the front door opens, it will ring and let you know.'

'Really, there is no end to your thoughtfulness. Thank you. The kitchen's just here, isn't it?'

'Aye, straight ahead. Marianne . . .' He touches her elbow. 'I'm sorry if I alarmed you. When I caught hold of you. But it would have been an almighty crack on the head.'

'Oh, take no notice of me—I was just a bit thrown, that's all. And feeling vulnerable, I suppose. Men try some funny things on once they know you're blind.'

'Bastards!'

'Oh, I've had some unpleasant experiences in my time. But don't worry—that wasn't one of them.'

Marianne

On the contrary. But I withdrew in confusion, like something out of Jane Austen. I suppose I might have handled it better if it hadn't been so long since I'd touched a man. It's at times like these that I miss having eyes, which I gather can signal your feelings, regardless of the words one utters for form's sake. How, without expressive eyes, could I have kept a door open, signalled to Keir that he could enter if he wished?

By touching him again. Which is what I wanted to do, but didn't. (So much for treating people as if we were about to die. What a load of sentimental codswallop I talk.)

I felt my way back upstairs, counting, and sat on the bed. Below me I could hear Keir moving around. I felt for my toilet bag and took out my hairbrush. I brushed my hair vigorously, showing no mercy to tangles. I vented my irritation with myself and my blindness, with the game I wanted to play but couldn't, because I hadn't been dealt a full hand.

Penance observed, I sat composed on the edge of the bed, hands

folded demurely in my lap, mentally undressing Keir. I comforted myself
with the thought that, although difficulties and confusion might arise with
the two of us confined in such a small space, my thoughts at least were my
own. Which, given the direction they were running in, was just as well.

After supper Keir writes a letter of condolence to Mac's mother while
Marianne—at her insistence—makes up her bed above the sitting
room. She retires early, exhausted with the effort of negotiating and
memorising new territory. In bed she lies on her back trying to catch
sounds from beyond the interior of the house. The wind has dropped
now. Beyond the hiss of the stove and the grumble of falling logs she
hears a chuckling noise which she realises is the burn running beside
the house, tumbling over rocks and stones as it hurtles down to the sea.
The sound is constant and constantly changing. Marianne lies in bed,
enthralled. She longs to share her excitement with the man who had
the vision to bring her here, but suspects he's already asleep.

Re-tuning her ears to the room below, she identifies the rustle of
pages turning. Too noisy for a book. A magazine, presumably. A professional journal? Or a wildlife magazine? That seems more likely. Keir
appears to compartmentalise his highly organised life and Marianne
thinks his life as an oil man will not be allowed to impinge on his alternative life here on Skye. 'Keir? Are you awake?'

'Aye. What's the matter?'

'Nothing. I'm just wondering what you are reading.'

'The RSPB magazine.'

'Thought so.'

'That would be the way I whistle as I turn the pages?'

'If it had been *Playboy*, you'd have been turning them more quickly.
Less text. What are we doing tomorrow?'

'I'll give you the tour in the morning. Then I thought we'd take a
picnic and maybe have lunch in the tree-house.'

'Tree-house?' She sits up. 'Is there really a tree-house?'

'Aye. My grandfather built it. I've modified it. Have you been in one?'

'Of course I haven't! How do you get up there?'

'A rope ladder.'

'Oh . . . Will I be able to get up there, do you think? A rope ladder
will be tricky.'

'We'll get you up there if I have to give you a fireman's lift.'

'Permission granted to employ whatever undignified mode of transport deemed necessary. This is *so* exciting!' Marianne lies down again,

curls up in her duvet and murmurs, 'All this . . . and cocoa too.' The last thing she remembers hearing is the sound of Keir chuckling. Or perhaps it was the burn.

He is woken by a dream. Mac on the rig, laughing, not seeing, not hearing the badly welded steel upright behind him as it comes adrift, then falls. Keir dives full length, aiming his body at Mac. As the two men hit the ground, Keir wakes. Putting a hand to his stitches, he remembers hitting the ground and splitting his forehead, watching his blood pool, then hearing Mac fall, but not being able to move . . .

In the end it had been a glancing blow, but still fatal. Keir's dive made sure Mac wasn't killed outright, but that was all. His heroics simply prolonged the agony for the family.

Keir sits up and looks out of the window at the night sky. No stars. A moon almost obscured by cloud. He shivers and rubs bare arms. It's cold, very cold. Snow tomorrow, probably.

Marianne stirs again and murmurs, a sound that catches Keir by surprise. 'Keir?'

'Aye?'

'You can put the light on if you want to read—it won't bother me.'

'No, I'm just lying here, thinking.'

'About Mac?'

He hesitates, then says, 'Aye.'

'Do you want to talk about it?'

He thinks what a relief it might be, just to unburden himself to an understanding female. Instead he says, 'I'd rather talk about the stars.'

'Oh, yes, please do! What can you see? Are the stars twinkling? You said there are no curtains. Is the room full of moonlight? What is moonlight like? People do go *on* about it.'

'Moonlight? It's eerie. Like cold, still water . . . And mysterious . . . It can look very beautiful. Or sinister.'

'Tell me about the stars.'

'Are you cold up there? The stove's out now. It's always a bit temperamental on the first night. Wait and I'll light it again.' He unzips his sleeping-bag and kneels in front of the wood-burner, feeling on the hearth for a box of matches and a candle. He lights it, opens the stove door, then rakes over the ashes and a few glowing embers. He pushes in screws of paper, kindling, then, as the wood catches light, a log.

'Mmm, wonderful smells!' Marianne calls down from upstairs. 'A candle? I can smell beeswax. You haven't lit the lamp?'

'No. Too bright. You need darkness to see stars,' he says, blowing out the candle. 'I used to hate the summer when I was a kid. Being eaten alive by midges and it never getting dark . . . You don't see stars unless it's dark and I used to miss them. Can you hear me?'

'Perfectly. The wooden floor reverberates with your voice.'

'In summer I used to stand at my bedroom window staring up at the sky, knowing that the stars were there, I just couldn't see them. So I used to work out where they'd be if I could see them.'

'Like the astronomers who predicted Neptune.'

'Aye! You know about that?'

'Oh, yes. I collect stories about the redundancy of sight. Tell me what you can see now. And don't worry whether or not I understand. I'll just listen to it as story. No, as *music*. The music of the spheres.' She laughs.

Keir gets into his sleeping-bag again and looks out of the window. As the moon appears from behind a cloud, he sees that snow has started to fall in big, slow flakes. He lies down on his back and speaks in a soft, steady monotone, as much incantation as description.

'If you look east, one of the brightest stars you'll see is Arcturus. It has a yellow-orange glow. Most stars look cold. Icy. They'd sound like . . . flutes. No, piccolos. *Shrill*. Arcturus looks warmer. A cello maybe . . . Arcturus glows, but it doesn't burn or blaze like the sun. It's like the feeling you might have for an old friend . . . Steady. Passionless. On second thoughts, make that a viola. How am I doing?'

'Utter *bliss*. I want you to make me a tape of this. Tell me more.'

Keir rolls onto his side. 'If you look west, you'll see Orion, the hunter. He's easy to spot. He's massive. His right arm's raised up in the air, wielding his club. His left arm is extended and holds a shield. His shoulders are wide and a big, bright star called Betelgeuse sits on his shoulder. What I really like about Orion—och, this guy is so cool!—is, he has a fancy belt. He's big in the shoulder but kind of narrow in the waist and he has a belt made up of three bright stars. And hanging from this superb belt is another cluster of stars, quite close together, that dangle and form his sword. Now if you look to the left of Orion, snapping at his heels you'll find the brightest star in the sky: Sirius, the Dog Star, Orion's hunting dog. Sirius is quite close, only eight light years away and it's forty times more luminous than the sun, so that's why it looks so bright. Think of . . . a clarinet, the way it dominates the other instruments of the orchestra. Sirius outshines all the other stars and draws your eye. My grandfather had a sheepdog like that, Star. No good as a working dog—unreliable. So he gave him to me. Star was always at

my heels. I loved him. I gave him a secret name. Sirius. And I used to pretend to be Orion, the hunter, with a stick for a sword . . . Once Sirius caught a hare and brought it to me, like an offering. I was choked.'

'Why?'

'At the foot of Orion there's another constellation. Lepus. The Hare. I thought this was proof that Sirius *knew*, knew what his secret name meant, knew who I was pretending to be.' Keir watches snowflakes swarming outside, then says, 'Are you still awake? You're very quiet.'

'I'm completely entranced, that's why.' He hears the rustle of bedclothes as she turns over. 'Thank you, Keir. That was wonderful.'

He doesn't reply, then after a moment begins to recite:

> *'Thou being of marvels,*
> *Shield me with might,*
> *Thou being of statutes*
> *And of stars . . .'*

'What's that?'

'A Gaelic prayer for sleep. More of a charm, half-pagan as it is.

> *'Compass me this night,*
> *Both soul and body,*
> *Compass me aright*
> *Between earth and sky,*
> *Between the mystery of Thy laws*
> *And mine eye of blindness . . .'*

He hears her sudden intake of breath. 'Good night, Marianne.'

Louisa

When she'd been gone for several days, I received a postcard from Marianne. I presumed she must have dictated the message.

Dear Lou, Sightseeing is not an option but I'm nevertheless experiencing Skye. Everywhere we go I hear a beautiful, soothing texture of sounds. I feel as if I've been given spectacles for my ears— my world of the senses is suddenly in sharp focus. I'm drunk on a cocktail of peat smoke, damp vegetation and the sea, washed down with the odd dram of very good whisky. Love, M. x

Keir also sent me a card. The message was brief: *Hi, Louisa. Marianne appears to be enjoying herself. No mishaps and she's coping very well off*

home territory. She even seems to like our terrible weather. Best wishes, Keir.
It was sweet of them both to think of me, but of course neither of them had told me what I really wanted to know.

I showed both cards to Garth when he called round to fix a problem with my laptop. Despite (or perhaps because of) his public school education, Garth likes to affect the speech patterns of a cockney costermonger. He read both cards, handed them back to me and said with a grin, 'You reckon they're shaggin', then?'

CHAPTER FOUR

Louisa

Life took an interesting turn while Marianne was away. Garth and I had been to an evening lecture on Mary Shelley and we walked home, deep in discussion. As the February sleet turned to snow, we took a short cut up a side street, then through an alley. We were debating whether *Frankenstein* constituted a study of bad parenting as well as motherlessness when a man suddenly sprang up from behind a pile of rubbish bags, like Magwitch among the tombstones, and lurched towards us.

Clutching Garth's arm, I was aware he was shaking. He must have seen the knife before I did. Magwitch said, 'Don't move!', a quite unnecessary instruction since Garth and I were rooted to the spot with terror. He lifted the knife, brandishing it in my face, but kept his eyes on Garth. 'Wallet and phone, pal. One at a time.'

Garth reached inside his long black overcoat and slowly handed over his mobile, then his wallet. Magwitch pocketed them both, turned to me and snarled, 'Bag.' I proffered it without hesitation. It was a large leather bag. I could see Magwitch thinking how conspicuous it would be. He gestured with the knife, then barked, 'Open it. Gie's your purse.'

Now, there was a flaw in the design of that bag. If you held it by one handle and released the catch, it tended to gape open and, if you weren't careful, the contents of the bag fell out.

I wasn't careful.

I released the catch and the contents of my handbag fell at Magwitch's

feet. Phone, purse, spectacles, powder compact and key ring clattered to the ground. If looks could kill, I'd have been a goner. He muttered, 'Stupid fucking bitch,' then did a little dance of indecision. I prayed for him to turn and run. Instead he growled, 'Pick them up! Purse, then phone.'

I clutched at Garth's arm as I kneeled down among my belongings. Garth must have bent to help me because Magwitch grunted, then said, 'Don't move, laddie, or Ma's had it.'

Well, that was the last straw. I was frightened and tearful, but now I was *angry*. Grasping my phone in one hand and my purse in the other, I got up from my knees into a crouching position, took a deep breath and launched myself upwards, head-butting him in the groin.

He fell over backwards, screaming. I yelled, 'Run!' and, without waiting to see if Garth followed, ran as fast as I could towards light, noise and traffic, shedding my high-heeled shoes at the earliest opportunity. Only when I hit the busy thoroughfare of Lothian Road did I pause for breath. I was overjoyed to find Garth beside me, laughing and weeping, black eyeliner coursing down his whitened cheeks. We stood on a street corner, hugging and congratulating each other until Garth had the wit to hail a taxi. I gave the driver my address; then Garth pointed out that my keys were still lying in the alley. I explained that, since the time Marianne had lost her key, I'd left a spare with a neighbour.

When we arrived home, I told Garth that under no circumstances was I spending the night alone in the flat since Magwitch now had my keys, my address book and a motive for murder. Garth lived alone in a seedy area populated by Magwitches, so I wasn't the least surprised when he agreed to stay. And *that's* how it all started.

Marianne

When I woke, something was different. *Everything* was different. The sounds, the scents, the smell and feel of the duvet cover, the chill in the air, all of this was unfamiliar. I tried to work out where I was.

There was a smell of frying bacon (Louisa never cooked breakfast) and there were other smells: coffee, wood smoke, something herbal and soapy. Gradually my senses assembled the jigsaw: I was upstairs in Keir's house. He was below, in the kitchen, freshly showered, brewing coffee, cooking breakfast, tending the stove.

I lay still on my pillows. There was something else different, something I couldn't put my finger on . . . The burn. I couldn't hear the burn.

At the foot of the stairs the wind chime rang, then rang again, a little louder. I heard Keir's footsteps on the stairs, slow, deliberate.

'**M**arianne? Are you awake?'

She sits up in bed. 'Yes. Are you in the room yet?'

'No, on the stair. I've made you some breakfast.' Keir ducks his head as he enters with a tray. 'I've a tray here and I'm putting it in front of you. There's coffee on your right and a bacon sandwich on your left.'

He stands at the end of the bed and watches her bite into the sandwich; thinks how different she looks with her smooth, ash-blonde hair disordered. 'It's nice and warm in the kitchen when you want to come down. I'll teach you how the shower works.'

'Thanks.' She waves the sandwich in the direction of his voice. 'This is delicious, by the way.' Swallowing, she says, 'Keir, there's something odd about the sounds outside. What is it? It seems quieter.'

He smiles. 'Can you sense that? Even with me banging around in the kitchen? Aye. It's snowed. Inches of the stuff. Are you up for a snowball fight? You can blindfold me to make it fair. We'll do it like Jedi Knights in training. *Feel the force, Luke . . .*'

Choking, she exclaims, 'Your jokes are in appalling taste!'

'Aye, but they make you laugh.' Keir sits at the end of the bed and says, 'It must be bad enough being blind, but not being able to laugh about it—that would be terrible. Wouldn't it?' he adds, a note of uncertainty in his voice.

'You're right, it would. *I* don't mind, but Louisa would have forty thousand fits. Her illusions would be completely shattered.'

'Louisa's illusions? What might they be?'

'Oh, I don't know exactly. I don't ask.' Marianne takes another bite of her sandwich. 'I think she perceives you as a tall, dark stranger, whisking me off for an adventure. Who knows what Louisa thinks? She scarcely lives in the real world.'

'And you do?'

She stops chewing and says, '*That* was a bit cutting.'

'No, I meant, d'you feel as if you're living in the *same* world? As me? As Louisa? Your world must extend only as far as you can reach with your stick. As far as you can hear, smell. Am I wrong?'

'No. It is a much smaller world.'

'But deeper. More intensely felt, I'd imagine. Or do you worry that you imagine too much? Or inaccurately?'

'Six-foot rabbits, you mean?'

'Well, the feedback must be very limited where you can't touch.'

'Not as limited as you might think. I'm aware of your every movement. The mattress transmits it to the muscles of my legs. Even if I

hadn't already read you with my hands, I'd know you were a big man because of the way the mattress is responding.'

'Does Louisa's world include a man?'

'No.' Marianne leans back on her pillows, licking her fingers. 'I don't know why. I'm sure she'd like one. She's kind. And rich. And not nearly as stupid as she makes out. She cultivates the daffy blonde bit.'

'Why?'

'To redress the balance, I suppose. She probably thinks it reduces my sense of being handicapped, makes me feel more competent. I suspect no man has taken her on because he thinks he'd have to take me on as well. Which isn't the case. I could live independently. I'm curious. How does Louisa strike you? Speaking as a man, I mean?'

'Well, she's not my type, but she's attractive if you like your women ample. And fluffy. And plenty of men do. And you can tell she's interested; that's attractive to a man. The old antennae are still waving. Has Louisa never married?'

'No. Nor has she lived the life of a nun. But nothing's lasted.'

'What about Garth the Goth?'

'*Garth?* He can't be more than twenty-five! What would a man Garth's age see in *Louisa?*'

'You'd be surprised. Kindness. Humour. An accommodating and sensual woman, one who isn't obsessed with cellulite and liposuction. And then there's always gratitude.'

'*Gratitude?*'

'Don't underestimate it. Men are just as insecure as women, maybe more so. We've far more to prove, to women and to ourselves. Young women can be pretty damn scary. Someone like Louisa might seem a more relaxing proposition to young Garth.'

Marianne considers her sister in this new light and says, 'Were *you* interested, then?'

'In Louisa? No, I was speaking hypothetically.'

'Have you had relationships with older women?'

'Aye, when I was younger. I was young enough to feel flattered by the attention and callow enough not to mind being treated as a sex object. It was fun while it lasted.'

'You never married?'

'I've never looked for anything permanent.'

'Oil marriages don't tend to last, anyway.'

'It's a lousy deal for both partners. For the wife especially. Have there been many men since Harvey?'

She pauses before answering, then says carefully, 'A few.'

'Ah! We entered a conversational no-go zone. I didn't see the sign.'

'I'm sorry, Keir, but I suddenly feel very odd sitting here in my pyjamas talking about my sex life—and yours—with you sitting on the end of the bed. I don't know what's going on.'

'Nothing's going on. We're just talking. You told me Louisa saw me as some sort of . . . *hero*. I wondered how you saw me. Don't worry, I'm not going to try anything on. I find you too fascinating to risk frightening you away. And I'm too much of a hero—in my *own* eyes—to take advantage of you. But I thought it might be good to deal honestly with each other. Not least because I don't know how to read you. You don't give out the usual signs, so I'm having to make it up as I go along.'

'So am I.'

'My, aren't we the spontaneous ones! Would you like more coffee?'

She laughs. 'You don't have to back off, you know.'

'I wasn't. I was offering you more coffee before asking my killer question.' He shifts his weight on the bed, then says, 'When you heard about Mac's death, you said you wished we treated folk as if we knew we were about to die. Say all we wanted to say. I've been wondering . . . What would you say to me if you knew you were going to die? Or *I* was?'

'Oh, that's not fair!'

He shrugs. 'You don't have to answer.'

'But you know I will.' She sighs. 'If we didn't have long, I'd . . . I *think* I'd ask you to hold me . . . I'd probably ask you to make love to me as well.' She covers her mouth with a hand. 'Oh God, I can't believe I just said that! What on earth did you put in the coffee?'

He is silent for a moment, then says, 'But you're not asking now?'

She places her fingertips together in front of her lips, as if about to pray. 'No. I'm not asking now.'

'Then I'll get you that coffee.'

As his footsteps retreat towards the staircase, she calls out, 'Keir?'

'Aye?'

'What would *you* say?'

He pauses at the top of the stairs, his head and shoulders bowed to accommodate the sloping ceiling. 'Much the same.'

Marianne

I negotiated the stairs, the shower, then the stairs again. I got dressed and presented myself in the kitchen where Keir was washing up. After a moment he said, 'D'you always wear black?'

'No. Sometimes I wear cream. It makes life simpler. What are you wearing?'

'Jeans and a polo neck. And a zip-up fleece. The polo neck's dark brown. Think . . . double bass. And the fleece is greeny-blue . . . Harp.'

'Greeny-blue? Like your eyes?'

'No, they're green *and* blue.'

'Now, that I would like to see.'

'Twinkling stars . . . My eyes . . . Anything else?'

'Snow.'

I hear the washing-up water splash, then drain away. Keir takes my arm. 'Come with me . . .'

Keir leads her across to the back door. As he opens it, Marianne feels a wave of cold, damp air envelop her. He shuts the door behind her and she shivers at the sudden change in temperature. Folding her arms across her chest for warmth, she says, 'Tell me what you see.'

'Snow. And sunlight shining on the snow.'

'What does it look like?'

'Dazzling. It hurts your eyes almost.'

'And if it were a sound?'

'If it were a sound . . .' He gazes at the snow-covered landscape. 'Aye, you know those strings at the beginning of *The Flying Dutchman* overture? The very opening chords?'

'Oh, yes. They're *piercing*!'

'That's what it looks like.'

'*Thank* you!' She turns away, smiling, and faces the white landscape, as if equipped now to assess the view.

Marianne

Keir cleared snow from a garden bench, spread something waterproof and we sat in the weak February sun. I turned my face up towards the warmth. Behind us there was the constant drip of melting snow falling from the roof; to one side, a furious flurry of bird activity in a hedge. We stopped talking to listen to a wren that was sheltering, Keir said, in a pile of dead and damaged wood he'd cut back after a gale.

'Are you getting cold?' he asked after a while.

'A bit.'

'We'll go inside, get togged up, then go for a walk. There'll be more snow, but not yet awhile.'

As I got to my feet I felt the touch of his hand on my elbow, guiding me

discreetly between obstacles. 'Keir, why *did* you bring me here?'

'Three reasons. I wanted to show you Skye. And I wanted to show you my home and what I'm doing here.'

'Keeping the twenty-first century at bay.'

'It's a tough job, but someone's got to do it. A third of all plants and a quarter of all mammals face extinction in the century ahead.'

'Good God!'

'Well, no, not particularly. As deities go, rather a negligent God. Mind the step as you go indoors.'

We stepped back into the fuggy warmth of the kitchen.

'And the third reason?'

'Pure self-indulgence. You're a treat, Marianne. Like a box of chocolates without the card that tells you what they are. I never know what I'm going to get with you: a soft, creamy centre or an explosion of alcohol.'

'I thought you didn't like living dangerously?'

'Unidentified chocolates I can handle.'

A few minutes later they are dressed for outdoor walking. As he shoulders a rucksack, Keir says, 'The terrain is uneven but we'll take it slow. I'll make sure you don't fall. Have you ever used trekking poles?'

'No. I've rarely walked on anything but pavements and footpaths.'

'Try one . . .' He slips the loop of one pole over her wrist and arranges her fingers round the handle. 'Now stand still while I adjust it for length. You have to have the handles quite high. You could use one pole and take my arm, or hand, or you could try going it alone using both poles. If you use two, it will be impossible to fall over but you won't be attached to me in any way. It's up to you.'

'They feel really comfy. I think I might like them. If I walk along right behind you, it will be like following a path. I'll feel your footprints. Like King Wenceslas and the page. You'll have to remember to tell me if you stop or we'll collide. Where are you taking me?'

'We'll follow the burn, maybe as far as the waterfall, if the weather holds. We'll see how you get on with the poles. I hope we'll be able to move fast enough to keep you warm.'

'I'll be fine. Stop fretting.'

They set off, slowly to begin with, then, as Marianne gains confidence, they achieve a normal walking speed. This despite the fact that most of the time, unbeknown to Marianne, Keir is walking backwards to monitor her progress.

Marianne calls out, 'Does the waterfall ever freeze?'

'It has. But it won't be frozen today. It's not cold enough.'

'Ice is silent, isn't it?'

'You've lost me.'

'I was thinking of the burn and the waterfall, stopping in their tracks, transformed into ice. The water music stops. When it does, the silence must be uncanny. Frozen music.' Marianne plods through the snow, seeking the indentations of Keir's footprints. He is complimenting her on the ease with which she walks when he trips backwards over an unseen tree root. Snow falls around them in a sudden shower.

Marianne turns her face upwards, laughing, and licks the snow that lands on her lips. 'Are you walking backwards, Keir?'

'How did you know?'

'Your voice has been facing me. And then you tripped. Someone like you wouldn't trip. Not on home territory.'

'It's a fair cop, Officer. Tell me more about this frozen music.'

'Face the way you're walking and I will.' As they set off again, Marianne resumes, 'It's how someone once described architecture to me. I found that quite helpful. Buildings are things I can never grasp, especially big ones. I can feel the texture of stone in a cathedral, but I can't get much of a sense of light passing through stained-glass windows, flying buttresses, the sheer scale of the thing.'

He doesn't reply for a moment, then stops walking and stands still. As she approaches he reaches for her arm. 'I've stopped.'

'Is something wrong? I don't need a rest yet.'

'OK, this is a long shot. D'you know Poulenc's organ concerto?'

'Yes, I do. Not very well. I find it an intimidating piece—a bit overwhelming, to be honest. Oh . . .' Her voice fades. 'Is *that*—'

'Aye, it's pretty close, I reckon. It'll do for now anyway. I'll give it more thought. What's the matter? Marianne? Have I upset you?'

She turns up her eyes and he sees they are brimming with tears. 'No, I was just . . . so *touched*. That you always try to translate things for me. And you do it so *well*. I'm really grateful, you know.'

'Aye, well . . . As I said, when you get to my age, you dream of grateful women.'

'There're steppingstones here, where the burn gets wider. We need to cross to the other side. Will I carry you over?'

Marianne pauses beside the stream. 'Are they flat stones?'

'Aye. But wet. Possibly icy.'

'I'll let you carry me over.'

As Keir lifts her, Marianne hooks her free arm round his neck. She pats the rucksack. 'What have you got in here?'

'Waterproofs. Camera. Picnic.'

'A picnic in the snow?'

'At the tree-house. Setting you down now.' He straightens up and tugs gently at her arm. 'This way. Take it slowly.'

Marianne plods on for a moment, then says, 'You wanted to show me what you were doing here. What exactly *are* you doing?'

'Planting trees, mainly. Looking after them. Trying to educate folk about trees. Trying to make them love trees, I suppose. *Know* them.'

'Why trees? Why not animals or birds?'

'Trees encourage wildlife and increase the space available for it. Bark provides a habitat for insects, also for lichens and mosses and all the animals that live in and on those plants. Dead or dying wood provides food and nesting sites for insects like bees and beetles . . . and you've stopped listening, but you're far too polite to tell me I'm being boring.'

'No, carry on! Educate me.'

'I'll pretend I detect a note of genuine interest . . . Deciduous trees provide shade and decaying plant material, which in turn provides homes for slugs, snails, earthworms, woodlice, spiders, millipedes, centipedes, and those invertebrates feed animals higher up the food chain, like birds, frogs and hedgehogs. It's an amazing symbiotic system. If you want to deal a body blow to local wildlife, just fell a tree.' Keir stops suddenly and says, 'We're here.' He removes the pole from Marianne's hand, and places her gloved fingers on a piece of hanging rope. 'This is the ladder. There are wooden rungs between two thick ropes. It's strong and it's safe, but you need to go up first because the ladder will swing unless I hold it steady at the bottom.'

'What will I find at the top?'

'A platform. There's a safety rail. You'll be fine if you stand still.'

'How many steps are there on the ladder?'

There is a pause while Keir counts. 'Sixteen. When you get to ten, your head should be level with the platform. Climb on and wait for me.'

'And if I fall out of the tree?'

'I'll endeavour to catch you.'

Marianne

The wooden rungs were slimy with damp, and treacherous. My gloved hands slipped but my boots gripped. At first I was frightened; then I began to feel a creeping exhilaration.

'Oh, I've lost count now. Am I nearly there?'

'Your feet are on the tenth rung. It should get easier now. The ladder will feel more secure where it's attached to the platform.'

Reaching above me, my hand found wooden staging with a rough surface. Keir called up, 'There's a handle to your right, on the platform itself. Have you found it? You can use that to pull yourself on.'

I clambered onto the platform, trying not to think about how far it was to the ground. Keir called out, 'That's right! You're on! You can stand up if you want. There's headroom.'

'No, thanks. I think I'll just wait for you to join me.'

'I'm coming up.'

I heard him arrive; then he helped me to my feet. Cowering, I said, 'Are we standing with our heads in the branches? I'm worried about my eyes. They may be useless but I'm still quite attached to them.'

'We're under a sort of wooden porch here. Part of the tree-house. There are no branches near your eyes. But if you come over here . . .' He put an arm round my shoulders and propelled me forwards. 'You're out from under the porch.' He placed my hand on a branch the thickness of my arm. 'Up in the tree's canopy.'

I grasped the branch and bounced it up and down. There was a shuffling noise and a slap as snow fell from upper branches and landed on the platform. 'Did I get you that time?'

'No, you missed.'

'I always was a rotten shot. God, it's cold up here, isn't it?'

'Hot chocolate, madam? Brandy?'

'Is that what you've got in the rucksack?'

'Aye. Though it's the St Bernard that's so damn heavy.'

There was the sound of a latch being lifted, then an agonised creak as a door swung open on its hinges. I felt Kier's hand on my arm. 'Step this way, madam. Refreshments will be served shortly.'

'The space is probably small enough for you to navigate with your hands. But you've got plenty of head clearance.'

'Have you?'

'Enough. My grandfather was a big man.'

Marianne removes her gloves and extends her hands, exploring. In the middle of the room she encounters a rough, curved surface. She reels back, astonished, then extends her hands again, eagerly. 'This is the tree-trunk! The tree is growing *inside* the house!'

'Aye. There's a branch as well. It travels across the room.' Keir places

Marianne's hand where trunk and branch fork. 'It forms a sort of room-divider. This side's the living room; the other's the sleeping quarters.'

'There's a *bed*?'

'Oh, aye. Grandfather didn't do anything by halves. There's two beds and hooks to sling hammocks. There's a collection of old blankets and eiderdowns in a wooden kist to the right of your feet.'

'What else is there? Oh, this is *so* exciting!'

Keir looks at her and grins. 'We've a small round table and some shelves with big lips on them to stop things falling off in a gale.'

'Have you been up here in a gale?'

'I've slept up here in a gale.'

Marianne exhales, her fingertips placed to her lips in a childlike gesture of wonder. Something catches at the back of Keir's throat and he swallows before continuing, 'There's plates, mugs, cutlery, plastic glasses—everything you might need for a picnic or a midnight feast.' He hands Marianne a sturdy, rectangular wooden stool and she sits. He places another in front of her, sets two enamel mugs on it and pours chocolate from a Thermos.

'That smells wonderful.'

'It's right in front of you. Are you hungry? Tree-houses bring on the munchies.' He reaches down a tin from a shelf and rattles it.

'You keep food up here?'

'Bird food. And a little for humans. Tablet. It's not that old. Hold out your hand.' Marianne obeys and he places a cube in her palm.

She pops the fudge-like sweet into her mouth. 'It's practically frozen! But it tastes really good. Describe the tree-house to me. How on earth did your grandfather build it to accommodate live branches?'

'Basically the house sits on a framework built around bits of the tree and there are sliding bolts that shift to accommodate movement.'

Marianne stands and places her hands on the tree. 'But what about the girth of the trunk? That must have increased over the years. And the branch inside? I assume it passes out again through the roof or wall?'

'The holes he cut in the floor, roof and wall were all bigger than was necessary at the time. They're smaller now, and sealed with rope.'

'How clever! Will the tree outgrow the holes?'

'Not in my lifetime.'

'In your children's?'

'I don't have any.'

'I was speaking figuratively. Any nieces or nephews?'

'Not so far.'

'That's a shame.' Marianne sighs. 'A place as special as this should have children to love it.'

'I don't think I love it any less now than I did when I was a boy. And there was a time in my teens when I abandoned it to my wee sister and her dolls. She commandeered it as a sort of sanatorium for broken toys. Some of them are still lying around.'

'Describe them for me.'

'There's a wooden horse on wheels, and the remains of a collection of wooden animals. The Lonely Hearts Club.'

'Why do you call them that?'

'They were pairs originally and they lived in an ark. But over the years we lost some of them, so their partners ended up as singletons. Poor old Noah was accidentally used for kindling a campfire, so Mrs Noah became a harassed single parent and zoo-keeper.'

'A widow, in fact.'

He pauses, then continues softly, 'Aye, I suppose so.'

Marianne sets down her cup of chocolate. 'I'm sorry. I've reminded you of Annie, haven't I?'

'And I reminded you of Harvey.'

After a moment she says brightly, 'May I hold one?'

Keir hands her an animal and says, 'Can you guess what it is?'

As Marianne runs her fingers over the wooden shape, Keir studies her wide, expressionless eyes, a cloudy blue, like a sky threatening rain. He notes a flicker of an eyelid, a quiver at the corner of her mouth as she runs her fingers lightly over the wood, her head lifted, her throat exposed, like an animal scenting the air.

'Easy. A giraffe. I can feel the spots as well as the long neck.'

'Aye, it does have something of the look of a Dalmatian about it.' As Keir reaches for the giraffe, his eye is caught by the veins at her wrist, blue against her pale skin. He lays his fingers on the veins.

'Are you taking my pulse?'

'No. But I can feel the blood in your veins. Just. Your wrist is so small, the bones so fine . . . I wanted to touch. Sorry, I should have asked first.' He takes the wooden animal from her palm. '*Should* I? I feel like I'm stalking an animal here. I'm always downwind of you and you never know what I'm going to do. It doesn't seem fair.'

'No, but that's how it always is for me. I'm used to men taking advantage of it.'

'I'm sorry.'

'Oh, I didn't mean *you*. I meant other men. Ages ago . . . I spend my

life touching things, but very little touches *me* now. People, I mean.'

'Do you mean people don't touch you?' He takes her hand and runs his thumb over her inner wrist again, smoothing the protruding veins. 'Or did you mean what you said? "Very little touches me now."'

Marianne stands quite still. Eventually she says, 'There's music, I suppose. And my walks in the Botanics. And . . . there's you.'

He lets go of her wrist. 'Do you want to touch me?'

He watches her lashes flicker with indecision, then the tip of her tongue as she moistens dry lips. 'All the time. I want you to be more than just a *voice* to me . . . Like my trees. I know a lot about them from the noises they make—or don't make—but I want to know about their physical being. And the only way I can do that is by holding them. So I do. Sometimes I press my face to the bark and I . . . breathe them in.'

His voice, barely a whisper, says, 'Show me. Show me what you do.'

They stand facing one another and she extends her palm in the direction of his voice. She undoes his jacket and, pushing it aside, lays both her palms on the ribbed woollen jersey beneath, placing them, with fingers spread, above his diaphragm. 'You're warm. And softer than the trees. I can feel the ribs of your jumper . . . and they run in the opposite direction to *your* ribs . . . There's a crisscross pattern. And it's all moving, very slowly, as you breathe . . . in and out.'

She moves her hands under the fleece jacket, round to his back, then turns her head to one side and lays her cheek against his chest. She inhales deeply but says nothing as her head rises and falls.

'May I put my arms round you?'

'Yes.' She feels the contraction of muscle as he encloses her in fleece-clad arms. She's aware of a gentle pressure on the crown of her head and guesses its significance. Curbing an impulse to lift her head, she says, 'You prefer trees and animals to people, don't you?'

'I feel more at home with trees. And I find animals easier to be with.'

'Why is that, do you think?'

He releases her. 'I'm just not good with folk. For a start I don't do a lot of eye contact—something you wouldn't be aware of. That's one of the reasons I find you easy to talk to. I don't have to look at you. Though I *do*, so I suppose I mean I don't have to be looked *at*.'

'Why does it bother you? It's not as if you're ugly or disfigured.'

'I suppose it's mostly the eye-contact thing. Folk are unsettled by my eyes but they don't know why. And sometimes . . . sometimes I see more than I want to.'

'What do you mean?'

Marianne hears him move away. 'It's some sort of over-developed crap-detector. It must be the result of a lifetime spent watching animals and birds, registering tiny changes in behaviour. I can stand very still for a long time and just . . . take something in. When I look at folk, they must feel as if they're being X-rayed.'

'I think I know what you're referring to. After she'd met you, Louisa said, "That man's eyes don't miss much."'

'Did she now? Well, I bet Louisa doesn't miss much either.'

'You picked up on her sexual availability, didn't you? And you knew I'd lost someone close. You just stated it as a fact, as if you knew.'

'Seemed pretty obvious to me.'

'But most people can't read blind faces. We don't do expressions. Our voices sound normal, but most people just see the dead eyes, feel very uncomfortable, then back off as fast as they can. The more socially skilled raise their voices and address us as if we're mentally defective.' She pauses, her head on one side. 'You've gone quiet. Am I ranting?'

'No, I'm just observing you. It's fast becoming one of my favourite occupations. Your expressiveness is concentrated around your mouth. You touch it a lot. With your fingertips. And your tongue. It's very alluring. You want to watch that when you're with those predatory types you mentioned. It maybe gives out a message you don't intend.'

Marianne's fingers fly to her lips. 'Oh dear. Do you think so?'

Keir laughs. 'See? You did it then. I think you react with your mouth the way other folk react with their eyes.'

'But this morning . . . when you asked me if I wanted you to make love to me, you didn't know what I wanted?'

'Did *you*?' She is silent and after a moment he resumes, 'I thought I knew what you wanted but I wasn't sure if I'd been given permission. And I hadn't. That's what I mean about not being skilled with folk.'

Marianne purses her lips. 'Let's change the subject. I'm getting out of my depth. Is there more chocolate?'

Keir refills her cup. After a pause in which they both drink in silence, he says, 'Marianne, if it's OK with you, I'd like to go and ring Annie.'

'There's no reception here, surely?'

'No. None at the house either. I'll have to drive up to the main road. I could do with going into Broadford for supplies anyway. Would you like to come along for the very bumpy ride?'

'I think I'd rather stay at home. I feel quite tired after all that trekking through the snow.'

'I can imagine. Let's head back to the house.'

Keir tucks the stools under the table and puts the empty mugs into a plastic bag inside the rucksack. He zips up his fleece, guides Marianne towards the door and opens it. 'Are you ready for the descent now?'

'As ready as I'll ever be. This has been such an adventure! Lou is never going to believe what I've been up to. She wouldn't approve.'

Keir's voice travels up from below. 'Does that bother you?'

'Not in the slightest,' Marianne replies.

CHAPTER FIVE

Louisa

Marianne would *not* approve. That was my first thought when I woke up, the day after the mugging. Actually, my *very* first thought was my stomach was going to evacuate its contents before I managed to get to the bathroom. As my eyes swivelled round the room in search of a suitable receptacle, I spied—with a shudder—a bottle of brandy and two empty glasses. Then, as I completed a visual circuit of the bedroom, Garth came into view, horizontal, naked and fast asleep beside me.

That was when it occurred to me that Marianne would not approve. Not only would Marianne not approve, she wouldn't understand, since I don't even *like* brandy, but Garth had said brandy was what we needed after our ordeal, so I drank the large measure he'd poured and I did feel slightly better for it. He asked if I wanted to ring the police but we decided not to bother.

I was halfway through the second brandy when, unaccountably, I started to cry. Garth put his arm round me and said it was just shock, that I'd been 'a total star' and that he'd been very proud of me.

I stopped crying then and started laughing, not at Garth's words, which were so sweet, but at the sight of his face. He looked like a panda, with eyeliner smudged round his eyes. His pale foundation was wearing off and beneath the make-up I could see what I thought at first was a virulent rash, then realised was a mass of freckles. His black, spiky hair had wilted and now hung low over his forehead. The damp night air had produced the suspicion of a curl. Looking at the wreckage of his face, I wondered,

possibly for the first time, what Garth really looked like and why he took such trouble to disguise his appearance.

He stared back at me. 'What *you* lookin' at, then?'

'You. You look *ghastly*.'

'Well, you don't look a million dollars yourself, love. D'you mind if I use your cleanser an' stuff?'

'Of course not. Help yourself to anything you need in the bathroom. My things are in the cupboard, Marianne's are on the shelf. Don't move anything of hers—it all has to be kept in the same position so she can find it.' I heaved myself off the sofa. 'I'll change the sheets on her bed.'

'Nah, don't bother,' Garth replied. 'The sofa'll do me.'

'I won't hear of it—not after what we've been through! You need a good night's sleep. We both do.'

But that wasn't, in the event, what either of us got.

When Garth emerged from the bathroom with a naked face and wearing my red silk kimono, I didn't recognise him. His skin *au naturel* was as pale as ever, but he was covered in freckles. Completely covered, I assumed, as the casually belted kimono revealed constellations of them scattered across his narrow, almost hairless chest.

I know it wasn't the most tactful thing to say, but I'd had two large brandies. 'Garth, surely your hair must be *red*?'

He stood still and eyed me suspiciously. 'Yeah. It is. What of it?'

'You *dye* it? Why?'

''Cos I 'ate it. Kids at school used to make fun of it. That's why I became a Goth. It meant I could dye me 'air and cover meself up with make-up.' He shrugged and helped himself to another brandy. 'It was that or be gay. An' I'm *not*, so becomin' a Goth was easier.'

I stared open-mouthed. 'What colour is your hair really? Carrotty?'

'Nah, sort of red-setter colour. Me mum said the colour's called *titian*. Like *that* helped,' he added, staring morosely into his glass. 'An' it's curly an' all. If I'm not careful, I look like a bleedin' King Charles spaniel.' He tugged self-consciously at long black locks that were beginning to coil like springs. 'I've been mistaken for a woman from behind. 'Ad me arse pinched by drunks needin' glasses. Pretty embarrassin'. So I straightened it an' dyed it black. But with all me freckles I looked like I'd got some sort of plague or somethin'. But I 'ad this girlfriend, see, an' she was a Goth. She did me face one day, just for a laugh, like. An' I loved it! So I stuck with it.' He grinned. 'Aven't 'ad me arse pinched since.'

As I struggled to assimilate a new Garth, I noticed his lovely even teeth and large green eyes. His appearance was really quite arresting.

'Garth, I realise I've never really *looked* at you before. I just saw the daunting Goth exterior, not the man beneath. I wish I could see your hair in its natural state. It sounds gorgeous! Oh, I could *murder* the brats who teased you! Why do children have to be so cruel?'

'You know what kids are like.' Garth took a step towards me, his head bent. 'You can see the real colour at the roots.' He stood in front of me and raised his arms, parting his thick black hair. As he did so, the kimono belt slipped undone and the scarlet silk gaped open. Garth looked down. So did I. 'Ah—there you go!' he said and pointed. 'It's *that* colour!'

After a simple lunch of cheese and oatcakes, Keir makes a shopping list, tends the stove and brews a pot of coffee for Marianne.

'I'm away to Broadford now. What will you do?'

'Fall asleep in a chair, probably. Or I might sit outside and listen to the sounds of Mother Nature at work. What's the weather doing now?'

'The sun's shining but there could be more snow on the way. You'll find a dish by the back door with bacon scraps. On the windowsill on the right. If you throw those down around your feet, you'll not be short of company. There's a robin feeds from my hand but I doubt he'll do you the same honour. You might get the weasels, though. There's a nosey pair that come to the back door.'

Marianne

I took a mug of coffee and the dish of bacon rinds out into the garden. Sitting on the bench, I tossed the scraps down and waited for visitors. I turned my face upwards, shutting my eyes, absorbing the sounds and smells around me. Basking in the sun, surprised I felt no need for a coat or hat, I considered the information Keir had given me over lunch. The house had been built in a clearing among the remnants of old, decaying woodland, sheltered but still with a view of the sea and the Cuillin mountain range beyond. (I asked Keir if he could suggest a musical equivalent for the Cuillin, mountains being even more beyond my grasp than cathedrals. He was silent for some time, then said, 'The Third Movement of the *Hammerklavier*.' He'd named the longest and most beautiful *adagio* Beethoven had ever written for the piano. I hoped I wasn't falling in love with this man. I was resigned, however, to falling for his mind.)

Keir said water was supplied to the house from a tank filled by a spring that never dried up. Dead and dying trees provided a constant supply of fuel, as did the sea, turning up all manner of combustible material and even furniture. He was now regenerating the woodland, systematically

planting trees—fast-growing birch alongside slow-growing oak. I knew Keir wouldn't live to see many of his trees reach maturity, so I'd asked him about his motives.

'I want to give something back to the Earth. In recompense for what I've taken out. I work in the oil industry. I've spent my whole working life screwing the planet for resources so that oil-greedy Westerners can live in mindless comfort. By the time I woke up to the mess we were making of the world, I could see the oil industry itself was an endangered species. It's not a career path young folk pursue any more. It's an industry full of guys in their forties, like me.'

'If there's no future in oil, what will you do?'

'Good question. There's still work in my field—one of the effects of global warming is that hazard prediction has become something of a growth area. But it means spending even more time abroad.'

'And you don't want to?'

'Och, no. If I had my way, I'd live here year-round, but I don't know what I'd do to pay the bills. There's very little work on Skye apart from the tourist industry, and that's not year-round anyway.'

'What about ecological tourism? Teaching people about wildlife, woodland management, living a greener life? Wouldn't it be marvellous if children could come here—school parties, I mean—and learn about wildlife. And the stars . . . And wouldn't they just *adore* the tree-house!'

'Aye, I've had similar thoughts myself. This place would be an excellent teaching resource because of the variety of habitats. It's tempting. But this house would be no good as a base. It's inaccessible and it's not big enough . . . Och, I have my dreams, but not the resources or the will to live them. But I've made a start.'

'Regenerating the woodland, you mean?'

'No, bringing you here. It's enabled me to see what I could do . . .'

Marianne

A fluttering at my feet told me some birds had braved my unfamiliar presence. I sat completely still. Behind me I could hear a constant drip from the gutter as the sun melted the snow on the roof. With a noisy flapping of wings, the birds suddenly took flight, even though I hadn't moved a muscle. Had a weasel appeared?

There was a change in the quality of the silence. Without knowing why, I reached for my cane, then remembered I'd left it indoors. I'll never know if I actually heard something before the grating noise above my head or

whether I just sensed movement. Did the dripping accelerate? I don't know, but when I heard the strange noise above and behind me, I was already anxious. I stood up, ready to go back indoors. As I turned towards the back door, there was an almighty rushing sound and I sensed a current of cold air on my face. Terrified, I turned and ran, my arms extended in front of me.

I hadn't moved far when the noise resolved itself into a long hiss, a thump and a wet splashing sound: an avalanche of snow falling from the roof above the bench where I'd been sitting. The bench was probably covered in snow now. I laughed at myself and walked back the way I'd run.

Except that I didn't, for my hands met a tree I hadn't encountered when I'd fled from the bench. I stood still and took stock for a moment. I must have lost my sense of direction after running. I'd panicked and stupidly lost my bearings. Now I didn't know if I was facing the house, so I would just have to find my footprints in the snow and trace them back to the bench.

I bent and felt the ground with my bare hands, tracing the depressions. I followed these carefully but, after a minute or two, it dawned on me that they were too large, too deep. These were Keir's footprints, not mine, and I had no idea where they'd led me. Feeling in the snow, I could detect only one set of footprints. An outward journey, no return. So these would probably lead to the steps down which Keir had carried me when we arrived, or they might lead to the winding path that he'd said led down to the house—not back the way I'd come.

The sun went in and I felt the temperature drop several degrees. I was beginning to feel a little concerned, but not frightened. How could I lose a *house*? I turned round and retraced my steps to the tree. I told myself I couldn't be far from the house, I just didn't know in what direction. I bent down and felt in the snow for something to throw. My frozen fingers found a stone. I clasped it and, aiming low, hurled it, hoping that the sound of it hitting something would tell me if it was a wall, a door or just a tree.

Nothing. I heard the stone land with a distant sigh in the snow. I found another stone and threw that in a different direction. There was a dull thud. Not the crack of the stone hitting a wall. Perhaps the bench? I set off in the direction of the sound, striding purposefully to get my circulation moving. My foot slipped on something smooth. Arms flailing, I skidded and lost my balance. There was a hideous crack as the ground gave way beneath me, plunging me to my knees into icy water.

I'd walked into a frozen pond. The cold was so intense I screamed. I stepped back out of the pond and stood still, shivering convulsively, furious with myself, but now frightened as well. My feet and legs were soaked up

to my knees. My hands were numb. I had no hat, no coat. And I was lost. I might be a matter of metres from the house and a wood-burning stove but, to all intents and purposes, I was lost.

I'd no idea how long Keir had been gone, or when he would be back. But he *would* be back. Eventually. As long as the weather held, I told myself I couldn't come to much harm. I turned my face upwards, hoping to feel once again the blessing of the weak February sun. Instead I felt flakes of snow as they drifted down and settled on my cheeks.

I knew about hypothermia. Harvey, a Skye man, and a keen hill-walker and climber, had taught me. It's a killer and it can kill quite quickly. Without a hat I was losing one-fifth of my body heat via my head. I needed to find the house or some shelter. In a hurry.

I stood, stamping my feet, trying to think, becoming colder by the minute. It was then that I conceded a kind of defeat and stopped trying to be brave. Something snapped and I yelled at the top of my voice, 'Keir!' It was a futile and quite hopeless gesture.

There was a flapping sound as a couple of birds took off above me. If I was among trees I probably wasn't very near the house, so I decided to walk, to set off in a random direction. I told myself walking would not only keep me warm, it would help me think.

I walked with my arms extended, my hands freezing in the cold air. Perhaps if I kept going, I would hit the road and come across a vehicle. As I listened out for distant sounds of a car, I caught instead a cheerful, gurgling sound—literally music to my ears. The burn. At last something to navigate by. The burn flowed downhill, towards the sea, Keir had said. It also flowed round the house. Surely with all this information I could find my way back?

The snow was heavier now. Large flakes had settled on my head and shoulders. I brushed them off, alarmed to feel how much there was. As I did so, I walked smack into a tree. Stunned, I sank down to its base. I was tired and just wanted to curl up in a ball. Harvey had said something about that . . . Conserving core body heat . . . You should hug your knees, curl up in a foetal position and wait for rescue. That's what he'd said. I hugged my wet knees and waited for Harvey to come and find me.

Not Harvey. *Keir.* Harvey was dead, long dead . . . I pressed my back against the tree trunk, trying to derive some comfort from its solidity. I thought of Keir, the warmth of his big body, the strength. How he'd lifted me and carried me across icy steppingstones to the other side of the burn, on the way to the tree-house.

The tree-house . . .

Shelter. Blankets, Keir had said. And tablet in the tin. I struggled to my feet. If I could find the burn . . . If I could find the steppingstones . . . It wasn't far from the stones to the tree-house. We'd walked for only a minute or two and I remembered the route as a straight line.

But even if I could locate it, how could I follow the burn without falling into it? Supposing there was more than one set of steppingstones? He'd taken maybe three or four steps, but the last one would have been onto the opposite bank. So I was trying to find three flat steppingstones. *Maybe*.

But how do you find steppingstones in the middle of a burn when you're blind? I started to laugh at my own idiocy, lost my balance and reeled into a low-hanging branch. I seized hold of it angrily; to my surprise it came away from the trunk. I staggered, but regained my balance at the last moment, using the branch like a walking stick.

Now I had a cane. I could trail my branch through the burn and it would tell me when it encountered obstacles. Like large, flat stones that would take me across the burn to the tree-house, where I could curl up in an old eiderdown, with the spotty giraffe and Mrs Noah. Poor, lonely Mrs Noah, waiting patiently for a husband who isn't ever coming home because he burned in the fire . . .

My face felt hot suddenly and I touched it with my fingertips. Warm water was running down my cheeks, cheeks that felt as cold and dead as stone. I rubbed my useless eyes with my sleeve and set off. Trailing my branch through the snow, I walked towards the sound of the burn. I found it—as I'd feared—by walking into it. I heard a loud splashing noise but my feet felt nothing, nothing at all. I stood dripping on the bank, struggling to order my thoughts. The tree-house was on the other side. But *where* on the other side? Should I walk up- or downstream?

Sod it, sod it, *sod* it!

My shivering seemed to have got much worse. I wrapped my arms round my shaking body and realised I was crying, my body racked with sobs. I heard it then: a shriek, a terrible animal cry. A name. Harvey? Keir? I don't know. It didn't matter any more. I lifted my branch and plunged it into the burn. Dragging it along beside me, I trudged upstream.

After some time, I don't know how long, there was a jarring sensation in my arms and I knew the branch had struck an obstacle. My coordination was poor now. I bent over, then, stumbling, fell to my knees. Stretching my hands out over the water, I tried to find the obstruction. One flattish stone. Were there more? I stepped cautiously onto the first stone and used the branch to find the next. Stepping carefully again, my spirits lifted a little. Maybe this *was* where Keir and I had crossed. There was a third flat stone

and that was the last. I could feel the expanse of ground on the other side of the burn. When I reached the other side, I dropped the branch, got down on my hands and knees, and felt for depressions in the fresh snow. I found a hollow, then another, then lots of them. These must be our footprints. I turned back to retrieve my branch and swept it in front of me. The line of footprints was straight and easy to follow.

The footprints stopped. I extended my makeshift cane, sweeping the air in front of me. It hit something. Not something solid, something that yielded. Oh dear God, *please* . . . I walked forwards, a hand stretched out in front of me. It collided with a piece of slimy wood at chest height. The rope ladder.

I clung to the ladder as if I'd found a friend, weeping with relief and pride that I'd found it. I grasped the rungs and then climbed slowly, finally hauling myself onto the platform. Crawling around, I soon located the door. But I found I couldn't get to my feet. My legs had given out completely with the effort of climbing the ladder. I reached up with my hand, searching for the latch, then raising it. As the door opened with its familiar creak, I fell into the room.

'*There's a collection of old blankets and eiderdowns in a wooden kist,*' Keir had said. I crawled across the floor in search of something that felt like a wooden box. I found one. I plunged my hand in but instead of the softness of textiles, I met a jumble of wood and metal. The toys. *The Lonely Hearts Club.* I grasped one of the wooden figures as if it were some sort of talisman, then sat back on my haunches, no longer feeling any sense of urgency. A vague calm had settled on me. All that seemed to matter was whether my frozen fingers could identify the wooden figure in my palm. It had curves. An elephant? No, a small head. And a face. It was Mrs Noah. Mrs Noah, waiting for her husband.

Still clutching the figure, I found another box. Lifting the lid, I smelt a mixture of camphor, lavender and old sweat. I dragged the blankets and quilts out onto the floor and lay down. With the last of my strength, I rolled myself up in them and curled into a ball.

So we lay together, Mrs Noah and I. Waiting.

Waiting for our men-folk to come.

When Keir arrives in Broadford, he pulls into the car park, performs a neat, fast three-point turn, pulls out again and sets off, back the way he has come. Murdo MacDonald, walking slowly on the arm of his wife, Katie, follows the speeding car with his eyes, then resumes his gentle pace. 'That was Keir Harvey. Back home again.'

'Oh, aye? He was in a mighty hurry.'

'Aye, he was. Looked as if he'd seen a ghost.'

'Och, well,' says Katie placidly. 'If it was Keir Harvey, maybe he *had*.'

The Land Rover slews to a halt and Keir jumps out. He heads for the steps leading to the house and scrambles down. Arriving at the bottom of the steep slope, he runs to the door, opens it, leans in and calls, 'Marianne?' Barely waiting for an answer, he slams the door and runs round to the other side of the house. Despite the fresh fall of snow he can see a great pile has slid from the roof, narrowly missing the bench. Footprints crisscross the garden. One line of prints leads to a black hole in the ground. Seeing it, Keir swears and calls Marianne's name again, louder this time.

He scans the garden looking for a trail of prints. He follows a track away from the house, one that leads straight into a tree. At its base the snow is alternately churned and compressed where Marianne has reeled backwards, fallen and tried to get her bearings again. Reading the eloquent patterns in the snow, something tightens in Keir's stomach and he smashes a gloved fist against the trunk of the offending tree.

He picks up a trail leading in another direction. Alongside this set of footprints is another track, of something being dragged. Keir looks back at the tree and notes the jagged edge of a broken branch. He murmurs, 'That's my girl . . .'

Keir follows the trail but he already knows where Marianne was trying to go. Did she get there? He stops for a moment and lifts his head, as if he's surveying the woodland, searching, but his eyes are closed. He breathes, 'Hang on, Marianne . . .' and runs upstream, following the course of the burn.

When he enters the tree-house, all Keir can see at first is a pile of blankets heaped on the floor. As his eyes adjust to the low level of light, he sees a projecting foot and registers a pool of muddy water that has leaked out of Marianne's shoe on to the wooden floor. Spotting a long coil of wet hair, he removes his fleece hat, uncovers Marianne's head and puts the hat on her. She stirs. Flipping open the blade of a Swiss Army knife, Keir slices through the sodden laces of her shoes, pulls them off, then peels off her wet socks. He pushes each of her icy feet into one of his gloves and then covers them again.

He tries to rouse her. 'Marianne, wake up. Can you hear me?'

She groans. 'Go away . . . I need to sleep.'

'Marianne, I need to find out how cold you are. I'm going to put my hand under your jumper and feel your tummy, OK?'

As he delves under the blankets, she wriggles away from his exploring hands. 'What are you doing?' A wooden figure falls from her hand.

'I'm sorry, but I need to know your body temperature. Listen, I'm going to ask you a question. Who's the Prime Minister?'

'Get your hands *off* me, Keir!'

'The name of the Prime Minister, Marianne. Tell me. Please.'

'Tony bloody Blair! Now will you just bugger off and let me sleep?' She shrugs her way under the blankets again.

'Marianne, you're suffering from hypothermia and we have to get you back to the house and get you warm. So listen to me—Marianne? Are you listening?' He shakes her gently. 'I'm going to lower you down. There's a pulley system. I'm going to put you into a kind of sling and I'll lower you down to the ground. You'll be quite safe. Then I'll climb down the ladder and carry you back to the house.'

'But I'm *tired*, Keir. I just want to sleep.'

'When we get back to the house, you can sleep, I promise. Now I'm going to pick you up, take you outside and lower you. Try not to move. I want you to stay wrapped in the blankets. When you get to the ground, just sit still and wait for me. D'you understand? That's important. Just sit still. You've no shoes on, so don't try to walk away.'

'Where *are* my shoes?'

'Never mind. Can you count backwards from one hundred?'

'Of course I can. What a stupid question!'

'Do it. If you can, it's a good sign; then I'll stop worrying. Go on.' Keir opens the door, turns back and lifts Marianne.

'This is ridiculous, Keir!'

'Just do it. Ninety-nine . . . *Please*, Marianne.'

She feels a wave of cold air on her face. 'Oh, for goodness' sake . . . Ninety-eight . . . ninety-seven . . . ninety-six . . .'

Keir sets her down on a bench beside a hanging tarpaulin. He lowers it onto the platform and pulls the rope till the tarpaulin gathers. He lifts Marianne again and sets her down inside the canvas bag. 'I'm going to hoist you up, then swing you out. Don't be frightened—keep counting.'

Marianne's voice is muffled. 'I've lost count.'

'Ninety-six.' Keir swings the load round so Marianne dangles.

'Ninety-seven . . . ninety-eight . . .'

'No. Backwards. Ninety-five . . .'

'Ninety-four . . . ninety-three . . . ninety-two . . .'

Her voice fades as Keir passes the rope slowly through his hands. He feels her touch the ground, lets go of the rope and scrambles onto the ladder, descending quickly, jumping the last few feet. Disentangling Marianne from the tarpaulin, he pulls her hat down firmly and wraps her more tightly in the blankets, ignoring her protests.

'I'm quite capable of walking!'

'Not without shoes. Anyway, this'll be quicker. What happened to the counting? Come on, eighty-nine . . . '

'I passed that ages ago. On the way down. I'm into the seventies.'

'Good. Carry on. Seventy-nine . . . '

'Seventy-eight . . . Seventy-seven . . . It's still snowing, isn't it?' Her head flops suddenly onto his shoulder. 'I'm so *tired*, Keir.'

'Aye, I know. You've had a hell of a time and I was a stupid bastard to leave you behind. But you're going to be OK. Seventy-six.'

'Seventy-five . . . I wasn't scared. Not very. I knew you'd come. I knew you'd find me somehow. How did you know where I was?'

'It's a long story. I'll tell you later. Seventy-four . . . '

The house feels warm as Keir carries Marianne up to the bedroom. He sets her down on the bed, still swaddled in blankets. 'Listen to me, Marianne. We have to get you warm, and quickly. I want you to take off your wet things—your jeans and jumper. I'm not going to look at you, I promise.' Keir turns away and unzips his jacket. 'I'm taking off my fleece and jumper now and I want you to put them on because they're warm and dry. Or . . . if you'll let me, there's a better way.'

'What?'

'I can warm you up much quicker with my skin. I can get into bed with you and get you warm. I'm the warmest thing we've got. And after carrying you, I'm very warm. And,' he adds, 'there's a lot of me.'

She frowns; then her face crumples. 'Keir, what's happening? I don't remember where I am!'

'Don't cry! You're going to be OK. Just take off your wet clothes now.'

She struggles with her jumper for a moment, then gives up and whimpers, 'My head's stuck. My hands are *useless*!'

'Here, let me.' He helps her out of the wet wool, retrieves the hat and replaces it on her head. 'Under the duvet with you now.'

She sniffs. 'I must look a complete idiot.'

'Wouldn't know, I'm not looking.'

Marianne climbs under the duvet and lies on her back, shivering violently. 'What are you doing now?'

'Taking off my jumper. But not my jeans. I'm going to get under the duvet with you and use my skin to warm you. Believe me, it's standard procedure.' She feels the mattress subside as he gets into bed beside her. 'Lie on your side, facing me. Now . . . I want you to press yourself up against me.' Marianne hesitates, then edges across the mattress. She feels him flinch. 'Christ Almighty, you're cold! Try and get as much of your skin in contact with mine as you can . . . That's good.'

'The hair on your chest is tickling my nose.'

'You can feel your nose? Och, that's a good sign. Turn your face to one side. Lay your cheek against my chest. Better?'

'Mmm . . . Shouldn't I be moving about, though?' she asks drowsily. 'To get the circulation going?'

'No, it's not safe to do that. The warm-up has to be gentle. You're very, very cold. Your body is struggling to keep your core warm. We mustn't take blood away from your organs.'

'How do you *know* all this?'

'I've friends in the Mountain Rescue team. Turn over; we'll try a different position. Draw up your knees.' He curves his body round hers, enfolding her with his arms. 'Press your back up against me. Aye, like that!'

They lie still, breathing in unison, until Marianne says, 'I walked into the pond. Fell straight through the ice.'

'I know, I saw. You must have given the frogs a hell of a fright. But the pond's not close to the house. Why did you move so far away?'

'I was frightened. Snow fell off the roof. I just heard a strange noise and I ran. Ran away from the house. Then I couldn't find it again.'

'But you managed to find the tree-house.'

'Eventually. I followed the burn. It was just luck.'

'Don't you believe it! That was excellent navigation and hill-craft. You're a wonder, Marianne.' He squeezes her gently. 'A bloody wonder.'

'Thank you.' He feels her body relax against him and wonders if she's falling asleep when she announces, 'I'm *starving*. I hope you bought us something nice for supper.'

He hesitates before saying, 'I didn't do any shopping. I got to Broadford, then turned round and came back.'

'Why?' She is aware of his chest rising and falling behind her, but he doesn't reply. 'I suppose you heard me . . . calling out.'

'Aye. In a manner of speaking.'

After a moment, she turns her head and says over her shoulder, 'You can't have! You must have been miles away by then.'

'Lie still now . . . It's hard to explain. I picked up a kind of . . . distress signal. I thought you might be in trouble, so I turned back.'

Marianne struggles to grasp the meaning of his words. 'Are you saying you can read *minds*?'

'No. It's not like that; I just . . . pick things up. Hear things other folk don't hear. It's like when you get a hunch about something. I get hunches. Lots of them. Really strong ones. And they're always right.'

'*Always?*'

'Aye. It's a kind of . . . radar, I suppose.'

'Does it only work with people you know?'

'No. I knew you were in trouble when we first met. *Before* we met, in fact. That's why I stopped. I sensed it walking along the street. Some folk give off really clear signals. You're one of them. I suspect it's something to do with being blind. You transmit as well as receive. Like bats.'

'But you can't actually read my thoughts?' she asks anxiously.

She feels his chest move again and senses silent laughter. 'No, it's not that specific. It's more . . . moods. Emotions. Like music. It's like picking up music on long-wave radio. Faint. Crackly. Then it comes over loud and clear for a wee while.'

Marianne is silent for a moment, then says solemnly, 'That must be terrible. I can't imagine feeling that . . . vulnerable.'

Keir struggles with relief and something he can't quite place, which he thinks might be gratitude. 'Och, I think *you* probably can.'

'Do you pick up big things? Earthquakes? Tsunamis?'

'I do in my job. I look and listen for geological hazards. And I predict when and where they might happen.'

'But you do that using state-of-the-art equipment, don't you?'

'Aye. And by following some very unscientific hunches. So, yes, I do sometimes pick up big things.' She is silent again and he feels the question form as her body tenses. 'Aye . . . I saw Piper coming.'

Marianne exclaims, 'But if you *saw*—'

'I saw it coming, but I'd no idea what it was! So what could I do?'

'I don't understand!'

'No, neither do I. Look, this is all going to sound crazy, but you're alive because of it. I don't talk about it, except sometimes to local folk who . . . *accept* it. If you came from these parts, you'd know what I'm talking about.'

She clutches at his broad hand. 'You have *second sight*?'

'Aye.'

'Oh my God . . . How *awful*.'

'Well, I'm glad I don't have to explain that part! As you seem to realise, the sight's not a gift, it's a burden. You know something's going to happen and whom it's going to affect, but you don't know when and how. And you see it, you *receive* it until . . . until it's over.'

He is aware of Marianne's fingers moving gently on the back of his hand, as if reading the complex data of skin, tendon and bone.

'Keir, did you know about Mac? Before it happened?'

'Aye . . . You remember when we met at the opera? We were talking and I disappeared.'

'You said you'd seen someone . . . who shouldn't have been there—'

'I saw Mac. Standing in the middle of the bar in his working gear, with his helmet smashed in and his face covered in blood. So I went to make a call. In a hurry. I phoned Annie. Mac wasn't even offshore. So I knew it wasn't something that had happened, but something that was *going* to happen. But I didn't know when.' She lifts his hand and, in a gesture that almost unmans him, lays the palm against her mouth. He feels her lips move; then she replaces his hand on her waist. Swallowing, he continues, 'I always pray I'm going to be wrong. I used to hope I was just . . . *mad*. Hearing voices, seeing things. But I knew. It's not uncommon in the islands. My grandfather had the sight too.'

'Did Mac know you'd seen—'

'Och, no, I never *tell* folk! Nobody knows about it except my family and a few folk on Skye. I told a woman once . . . Someone I felt a lot for. She was completely spooked. We lived together for a while but it didn't work out. She couldn't handle it. Said it was like living with an undertaker, only worse. At least an undertaker would know when the funeral was and who was to be buried. I could see her point. You'd be for ever asking yourself, What has he seen? Who's next? Och, it's no way to live! So I never talk about it. And I don't get involved with women, except on a pretty casual basis.'

The room is dark now. Keir sits up. The stove needs attention but he's loath to move. He feels the flutter of Marianne's fingers on his naked back—a touch that, for the first time that afternoon, travels straight to his groin. He swings his legs out of bed. 'I'll see to the stove.'

'Keir, you said you saw Piper Alpha . . . before it happened.'

He sits hunched on the edge of the bed. 'Aye. But I didn't know that's what it was. I'd seen it for years. My parents told me it was a recurring nightmare, but I knew it wasn't. I only ever saw it when I was awake.'

'How old were you?'

'When I first saw it? About eight or nine, I suppose. It didn't make

any sense to me. The picture I saw. It was just . . . an impression. I never knew what it meant, just that it was bad. Very bad.'

'What did you see?'

'I saw the sea . . . and it was on fire.'

Marianne sits up, searches with her hands for his face, for his eyes, finds the eyelids tight shut, the lashes wet. She takes him in her arms and he lies down beside her, not moving, not speaking, for in the end there is no need for words.

Spring—2007

CHAPTER SIX

Louisa

Keir delivered Marianne to the door late at night. She looked even paler than usual, apart from a bruise on her forehead where I suppose she must have collided with something. Keir looked hollow-eyed with tiredness, the lines in his face much deeper than I remembered. Marianne didn't kiss him goodbye and Keir didn't kiss her, but I noticed her hand reach for his arm and rest there a moment as they said their brief farewells. After I'd shut the door, my sister announced that she needed a long hot bath and then sleep. Clearly, girlie chats over a nightcap were not on the agenda.

Marianne seemed very odd once she was home. Quiet or, rather, preoccupied. She also seemed more bad-tempered than usual, but perhaps I was being more irritating than usual. I too was preoccupied with a man and hadn't yet found either the opportunity or the courage to tell Marianne what had happened with Garth.

On the subject of Keir, Marianne simply wouldn't be drawn. She told me about his home, the tree-house, the clever ways he found to share his world with her. As to her relationship with him, whether it was on a new and better footing, or whether everything had gone pear-shaped, I didn't know. Nor, it would seem, did Marianne *want* me to know.

When I helped her unpack, I found a pair of muddy shoes in a polythene bag. I said, 'What happened to your shoes?' She replied, 'They got very wet.' Since I was holding them, this was hardly news to me, but I said

nothing more. Then I came across a cashmere scarf I didn't recognise—bottle-green, a colour Marianne never wears. I presumed it must have been a gift from Keir, but I thought it best not to enquire.

I left her putting things away and went to make some tea. When I passed her door a few minutes later, I happened to glance in and saw Marianne sitting on the bed with her face buried in the scarf. I thought she must be crying and was about to go in when she raised her head. I saw that she was, in fact, quite composed. She stroked her cheek with the scarf, then buried her face in it once again, inhaling audibly.

Then it dawned on me. The scarf wasn't a gift. It was Keir's.

Marianne had never been the weepy type. Nor had she ever been prone to self-pity, not even when she lost her husband and baby in quick succession. So I was surprised to find her so unsettled after she came back from Skye. The slightest thing seemed to upset her. I braced myself for what looked like the onset of an early menopause and resolved to broach the subject of HRT the next time she dissolved.

I didn't have to wait long.

Keir was back in Norway. This much she'd volunteered. When she'd been back in Edinburgh a couple of weeks, she received another of his audio-postcards. I confirmed for her that it was a cassette from Keir and she retreated into her bedroom to listen to it. She was gone a long time and I wondered if she was having trouble with her ancient cassette player.

I knocked on her door and received an indistinct reply. I went in and found her sitting on the bed beside the machine, tears running down her face. The tape was still playing but it just sounded like radio interference. I could hear no words, only whistling sounds and hissing. There was the odd weird hoot and a sinister *whooshing* noise that for some reason made me think of a fire-breathing dragon. Marianne pressed the STOP button and wiped her eyes.

I sat down and put my arm round her. 'Is the tape faulty? Oh, darling, how disappointing!' Marianne still didn't speak, but felt for the cassette player and pressed REWIND, then when the tape stopped, she pressed PLAY. After a few seconds we heard Keir's voice: 'Hi, Marianne. This is a postcard of the Northern Lights, which I've been watching for the last couple of nights and I'm telling you, it's a grand sight. Did you know some folk say they can hear the lights? Technically, this is impossible because where they're coming from—about a hundred kilometres above the Earth—it's almost a vacuum, so sound can't travel. Nevertheless some folk claim to have heard sounds while observing the lights. I haven't been able to

record an Aurora Borealis symphony for you, but what I can offer is a recording made by a magnetometer hooked up to an audio recorder. Try to contain your excitement now, while I explain . . . A magnetometer measures variations in the strength and direction of the geomagnetic field—variations due to electric currents in the upper atmosphere. The electrons and ions that produce the Aurora also cause these currents, so a magnetometer measures a quantity that is directly related to the Northern Lights. The variation in sound you're about to hear is the variation in the magnetic field caused by incoming solar particles. The stronger the magnetic variations, the greater the auroral activity . . .

'Och, well, that's the best I can do for now. Give it a whirl. After a few plays you might find it grows on you. Like Pink Floyd. You might get a wee feel of the night sky full of random coloured lights . . .'

Keir's voice changed then, as if to say something more personal. Marianne's hand shot out and pressed the STOP button. I sat not knowing what to say. I still had no idea why she was so upset. She sighed, then said, 'I'm sorry, but I just can't cope with the kindness of the bloody man. Nor,' she added faintly, 'the onslaught of his imagination.'

Still at a loss for something to say, I decided to tell her about Garth. I thought it might provide us with a little light relief. In a way, it did. Marianne laughed until she cried.

Marianne deposits a mug of coffee on the table where Garth is working. 'Louisa tells me you've given up the Goth glad rags.'

He slits open an envelope, scans a letter and places it on top of a pile of correspondence. 'Yeah. You wouldn't recognise me now. Well, *you* would, 'cos me voice is still the same. She didn't, though.'

'Really? She didn't tell me *that*.'

'I turned up on 'er doorstep with some flowers an' she thought I was a delivery man. You should've seen 'er face! Oh—sorry, Marianne.'

'Don't be silly—I'm not that sensitive. You must look quite different.'

'I do. I got me 'air cut, really short, so what's left is me natural colour. An' I leave me face natural now . . . An' I bought meself a suit.'

'Good gracious! What made you do that?'

'Well, Lou's been sayin' she wants me to go to business meetin's. 'Er agent's been talkin' about film deals, merchandisin' an' stuff, an' Lou says she'd feel 'appier if I was there, for moral support, though as it 'appens, I do know a bit about the film biz. Me brother's a cameraman. But I knew she wouldn't want me there lookin' like somethin' out of one of 'er books, minus the muscles. So I decided it was time I cleaned up me act.'

'Well, good for you! Does Lou approve of the new you?'

'Seems to.' A faint flush tinges Garth's pale cheeks and, forgetting his embarrassment is unobserved, he bows his head over the pile of mail. 'She says I look a lot older now. Which is probably a good thing . . . under the circumstances. She won't get quite so much stick about me.'

'Oh, Lou wouldn't care. She doesn't give a damn what people think, never has. But I'm sure from a career point of view—*yours*, I mean—the transformation will prove to be a good move. People do seem to jump to conclusions about appearances. Sighted people, anyway. But I have to say, I miss the jingling.'

'Me chains? Yeah, so do I! They used to keep me company.'

'Yes, it was a cheerful sort of noise. Friendly. It was *you*, that sound.'

'Yeah.' Garth shuffles a pile of letters. 'You know, when me dad died I thought I'd miss 'is laugh or 'im grumblin' at me to cut me 'air, but what I miss, what's missin' when I go and see me mum, is Dad's *wheeze*. 'E was asthmatic, you see, all 'is life. Bet if I was to 'ear someone wheezin' now, it'd crack me right up. Memories of poor ol' Dad would come floodin' back . . . Funny thing, memory, innit?'

'Yes,' Marianne replies, sipping her coffee thoughtfully. 'Very funny.'

Marianne

I don't know why I didn't confide in Louisa about Keir, but I couldn't. I didn't want to explain about getting lost in the snow. There seemed no point in worrying her and I still felt a complete idiot about it.

Some memories of my time on Skye were vague, elusive; others so vivid they seemed almost tangible: the scents on the cold, damp air, Keir's body lying beside me, massive, inert, like a felled tree. These details I could remember, but what had actually *happened* between Keir and me, why, or what any of it meant, I didn't know.

Perhaps I didn't want to know. It was bad enough knowing that on the last day, when I'd come across his scarf hanging on the back door, I'd taken it without asking and stashed it in my suitcase. When I got home, I'd hidden it in my bedside drawer.

I tried not to take it out more than once a day. Mostly I failed.

I received another packet a few days later, which made me wonder if Keir was seriously under-employed in the Arctic. It was a CD this time and Louisa said it was labelled 'Rautavaara's *Cantus Arcticus*'. She read me the short note from Keir, which said: *You'll either love this or think it a musical abomination. I'm hoping that blindness will incline you towards the former, a position I occupy.*

Garth kindly read the descriptive notes Keir had written for me. *Cantus Arcticus* is a concerto 'for Birds and Orchestra'. Rautavaara is Finnish and the bird sounds were apparently taped in the Arctic Circle. The first movement is called *The Marsh* and represents bog birds in spring. The second movement is called *Melancholy* and the featured bird is the shore lark. The third movement is called *Swans Migrating*.

Those are the facts. I barely know how to describe the music or its effect on me. It was, as far as I could tell, like *being* there, surrounded by wheeling flocks of birds in a cold, northern wasteland. I felt a sense of vastness; I had an inkling of what people mean when they talk about sky. The bleak beauty of it all was inexplicably moving.

I've never held a live bird. I've never seen one fly and have no concept of the movement of birds in the sky. *Cantus Arcticus* revealed to me the movement of the flock, the emptiness of their natural habitat, its scale. Birdsong alone could not have done this for me. Nor could music. I'm familiar with pieces such as *The Firebird* and *The Carnival of the Animals*, but they assume prior knowledge of what birds and animals look like. Their composers aren't trying to depict animals for someone who has never seen them. Nor, I am sure, was Rautavaara, but that is what he managed to do for me. I listened to the concerto crying tears of joy. And gratitude.

Louisa

Marianne seemed a little more settled after receiving her two parcels but she still looked peaky. Choosing my moment carefully, I suggested she go and talk to Dr Greig, our female GP, about coping with the onset of the menopause. I expected resistance but, to my surprise, met none. Marianne said she'd been wondering whether that was what was wrong with her, especially as her periods seemed to have become erratic. Before she could change her mind about going, I rang the surgery and made an appointment for her the next day. We strolled round to the surgery together and I sat in the waiting room, happily leafing through back numbers of *OK!* and *Hello!*

Marianne thinks she must have misheard. 'I'm sorry, could you repeat that? I didn't quite catch . . .'

Dr Greig enunciates clearly, but not unkindly, 'I said, the commonest cause for the cessation of periods in a woman your age, in good health, is pregnancy. It would also account for the mood swings. Is it possible, Mrs Fraser, that you could be pregnant?'

Marianne blinks several times. 'Yes . . . yes, it's possible.'

'Then I suggest a pregnancy test. I think you'll probably find you get a positive.' Dr Greig notes her patient's pallor. 'I take it this would come as something of a shock to you and your husband?'

'It comes as a shock to me. My husband died eighteen years ago.'

Dr Greig searches Marianne's impassive face. 'I see . . . And the baby's father?'

'He's somewhere in the Arctic Circle. But it doesn't really matter where he is, he's just the biological father.'

'This would be . . . a *casual* relationship, then, I take it?'

'Yes, it is. I mean, it was.'

'So . . . you've no partner currently?'

'No. I live with my sister.'

Dr Greig glances at Marianne's notes. 'And you're . . . let me see now—forty-five? Do you have any children?'

'No.'

'Does your sister?'

'No. Not unless you count her lover. He's not long reached years of majority.'

'I *see*,' says Dr Greig, only just managing to keep the surprise out of her voice. 'Well, Mrs Fraser, assuming you *are* pregnant, you have various options. You'll no doubt want to give them some thought. Single parenthood is a challenge at any age, but given your added *difficulties* . . . As I expect you're aware'—Dr Greig lowers her voice tactfully—'at your age, there is a greater risk of miscarriage. There's also a higher risk of abnormality. But we're jumping the gun. We can do a pregnancy test now if you could provide us with a urine sample?'

'Thank you.' Marianne stands and gathers her handbag and cane. 'I can probably manage that if you'd care to direct me towards the loo.'

'No bother at all.' Dr Greig rifles in a drawer, then places a plastic container in Marianne's hand. Taking her arm, she walks her to the door. 'You have someone waiting for you, I take it?'

'Yes. My sister. Oh, but please don't mention this to her. I'd rather she didn't know. For now. She'll only make a fuss.'

'And there's no chance that the baby's father—'

'No,' Marianne says firmly. 'No chance at all.'

Spotting a nurse, Dr Greig calls out, 'Peggy, could I have a word? I'd like you to assist Mrs Fraser here.' Turning back to Marianne, she says, 'I'm handing you over to Nurse Peggy now. She'll do the necessary. Now come back and see me if there's anything you'd like to discuss. *Anything* at all. Good luck, Mrs Fraser.'

Marianne

At some level I suppose I must have known. Known it was a possibility. But if I'd admitted pregnancy was a possibility, I would have had to admit how little I actually remembered about the encounter that had led to my interesting condition. I remembered waking up and finding Keir lying beside me, asleep. I could remember taking him in my arms the night before, but not what had made me do it. I thought I remembered tears. But were they mine or his? As I moved slightly in bed, I became aware of my own tender flesh and a moistness that left me in no doubt as to what had happened, but I had no memory of anything said, least of all about a condom. If you'd asked me, if Keir had asked me—and perhaps he *did*— I'd have said that, at nearly forty-six, my chances of conceiving were so remote as to be not worth considering.

Life always has the last laugh, doesn't it?

The harder I tried to remember what had happened, the less I could recall, but a conviction was forming in my mind that Keir had probably saved my life. I knew, though, that gratitude wasn't the reason I'd taken him into my arms, into my body. I *did* remember just how much I'd wanted him, and how suddenly, how fiercely.

I'd woken early the following morning, got out of bed without disturbing Keir and gone downstairs to shower. By the time he had woken, I was dressed and drinking coffee. I heard him walk slowly downstairs into the kitchen. He stood still for several moments, trying, I suppose, to gauge how things were between us. My nerve broke and I said, 'It's not fair. If you don't speak or move, there's nothing for me to *read*.'

Eventually he said softly, tentatively, 'Marianne . . . I have to go back to Norway. Next week, for a couple of months.'

'Oh . . . I hope you'll send me one of your postcards.'

After another long silence he said, 'Yesterday . . . was . . . was it not what you wanted?'

'Yes, it was. It was what I wanted. *Then*. I thought I'd nearly died.'

'But now?'

'You mean, what do I want if I'm not going to die? I don't know. I think it probably best to act as if it didn't happen. For now.'

He was silent again; then I heard a great intake of breath and he spoke in a rush. 'If I misread the signs, I'm very sorry. I thought—I mean, you made it pretty clear—'

'Yes, I'm sure I did. Please don't feel badly, Keir. I don't remember the details but I do remember how much I wanted you. I'm not saying it shouldn't have happened, all I'm saying is, now that it has, I haven't the

slightest idea where it leaves us. Especially if you're off to Norway.' He didn't reply. I knew he must be staring at me, uncomprehending. 'Keir, I wonder if you'll understand if I say my body got way ahead of my mind?'

'Oh, aye. Men live like that all the time.'

'My mind needs time to . . . catch up. Assimilate.' A memory tugged at my brain and I shivered, but not with cold. 'Keir, I didn't dream it, did I?'

'Making love?'

'No. What you said about . . . the things you see.'

I heard him exhale. When he finally answered, he sounded tired. 'No. You didn't dream it.'

There was, of course, no question of my keeping the baby, even if I did manage to carry it to term. My age, my blindness and my circumstances were such that I couldn't entertain the idea for a moment. My dilemma wasn't so much what to do, but how best to do what undoubtedly had to be done. I didn't see myself coping with an abortion unaided. The obvious course of action was to confide in Louisa (who was in fact my closest friend), but this I was reluctant to do and I wasn't sure why.

I thought she probably had a shrewd idea of the nature of my entanglement with Keir, so my present difficulties wouldn't come as a complete shock to her, nor did I fear her censure. Louisa is and always has been tolerant by nature. Even if she *had* had the slightest inclination to disapprove of my carelessness, she scarcely had a leg to stand on since she herself was engaged in an unaccountable relationship with a man half her age. I couldn't really grasp how and why the relationship was ongoing, yet Garth appeared to be making her seriously happy. I think that was why I couldn't talk to Louisa about an abortion. I didn't want to spoil things by burdening her with my problems.

On the other hand, it's possible I couldn't face confiding in Lou simply because she seemed so very happy and I was so very miserable.

Garth lies on his back in bed. 'She's cryin' again.'

Louisa stirs, groans and opens her eyes. 'Oh God, it *must* be her hormones. Either that or she's fallen in love with that wretched man.'

'I thought you liked 'im? What's 'e done?'

'*Nothing.* That's the point. He doesn't ring, he doesn't write, he's stuck out in Norway somewhere and she's here—pining.'

'Well, not much point writin' to Marianne, is there?'

'He could ring her!'

'P'r'aps she told 'im not to.'

'Why would she do that?'

'Dunno. 'Cos she doesn't want to be over'eard by us? She's a very private person, is our Marianne.' Garth sits up in bed. 'Can you 'ear what I 'ear? She's throwin' up in the bathroom.'

'Oh, poor thing! I'd better go and see if she's all right. Put the kettle on, would you? Be a love and make us some tea.'

As Louisa hurries out of the room, fastening her dressing gown, he throws back the duvet and mutters, 'But I think you might be needin' somethin' stronger than tea, ladies . . .'

Louisa

Marianne was pregnant. My little sister was pregnant. 'Pole-axed' doesn't begin to describe my consternation. Marianne emerged from the bathroom, white-faced and haggard. I said, 'Marianne, is there something you aren't telling me?' She didn't bother to deny her condition, she just burst into tears and wailed, 'Oh, Lou—I'm so sorry!' I threw my arms round her and we stood in the hallway—Marianne crying her eyes out—until Garth appeared and said, with ineffable tact, 'Tea's up, girls.'

I don't know when I last saw her so unhappy. Certainly not since she lost Harvey's baby. Although I wanted to sympathise, I couldn't disguise the fact that my feelings about this pregnancy were quite unequivocal.

I was completely and utterly *thrilled*.

The breakfast table is a curious but comforting sight. Garth has placed on it a large pot of tea, two bowls of porridge and a bottle of brandy. He disappears to the kitchen to wash up. Louisa pours them both a brandy and insists her sister drink it. To her surprise, Marianne finds the brandy settles her rebellious stomach.

Louisa spoons porridge into her mouth. 'How many weeks are you?'

'Six. No—nearly seven now. Time flies when you're having fun. Dr Greig's been very helpful. She's given me all the information I need about a termination. Now I just need to stop crying—and vomiting— long enough to get it done. You don't need to worry, Lou, everything's in hand. I had hoped you'd never know.'

'Well, I'm very glad I found out! I *hate* to think of you going through all this on your own.' Louisa looks at her sister for a long moment, then says, 'You have to tell him, Marianne.'

'No, I do not. What would be the point?'

'It's Keir's responsibility as much as yours.'

'No, it isn't. It's my body that's been hijacked, not his.'

'All the more reason why he should share the responsibility.'

'For what? Getting rid of it? Do you seriously think he's going to fly back from the Arctic to hold my hand? For heaven's sake, Lou, be realistic. He's a man! He's an *oil* man.' Marianne reaches for her brandy. 'And he's a bloody Highlander. They don't do feelings.'

'But Keir isn't like that!'

'How would *you* know? You've only met him twice.'

'If he were as you describe, he wouldn't have sent you a CD of Arctic birdsong or a tape explaining the Northern Lights. If he were the clod you make out, you surely wouldn't have slept with him!'

Marianne feels for her cup, warming chilly fingers on the bone china. 'There's absolutely nothing to be gained from telling him. I certainly don't need his support to go through a termination.'

'I realise that, darling, I just thought that if you met him again and explained . . .' Louisa's voice tails off.

'What, Lou?'

'I thought if you had his support you might not *want* a termination.'

Marianne sits quite still and says nothing. Louisa remembers a time when, as a girl, she'd hidden under the dining table to avoid her little sister's wrath and randomly flung missiles. She is considering this option again when Marianne speaks, her tone and bearing imperious.

'Do I understand you correctly? Are you suggesting there is the faintest possibility that I could *keep* this baby?'

Louisa says in a small voice, 'Yes, I am.'

'You must be out of your mind.'

'Well, perhaps I am. I write books about vampires and sleep with a man half my age, who until recently *looked* like a vampire.' Louisa reaches for the teapot and refills her cup. 'Wanting to become an aunt, or a sort of surrogate mother, at fifty-one is no doubt further proof that I'm losing my marbles. But that doesn't necessarily mean I'd be an unfit mother. Does it?' she adds doubtfully, stirring her tea.

'Let me get this straight—you're saying you want me to have this baby so *you* can raise it?'

'No, I want *you* to raise it! But if you don't want to, or feel that you can't, then I'm saying *I* would raise it. With your help,' she adds. 'Let's face it, darling—it's the Last Chance Saloon for both of us.'

'Lou, we are both middle-aged women. And one of us is blind!'

'So what? Some women my age are still giving birth.'

'Not naturally. Their reproductive lives have been extended with IVF and hormones. They're biological freaks.'

'No, they aren't, they're just desperate women.'

'And is that what you are? Desperate?'

'No, not at all! I have a fulfilling career, pots of money, a man I'm very fond of and all the sex I can use, thank you very much. But I would *love* an addition to our family. I would love you to have a child!'

Marianne doesn't move. 'It would be totally insane. And I would be the world's worst mother. And blind.'

'It wouldn't be easy, I do admit. But you'd have me. And maybe Garth if he sticks around. He knows an awful lot about babies and children. He's the eldest of six, did you know?'

'What about when you're away? How would I manage then?'

'We'd employ a nanny. We'd have to move. The child would need a garden to play in . . . fresh air . . . trees to climb.'

'Stop it! Stop this *fantasy*! For God's sake, Lou, stop scheming! This isn't the plot of one of your books. This is real life! *Mine!*'

'Yes. It's also the baby's.'

'That's emotional blackmail. I do not feel guilty about being pregnant, nor do I feel guilty about getting rid of it.' Marianne swallows some more tea. 'I'll probably miscarry anyway.'

'Ah! I see why you're so dead-set on getting rid of it. You think you'll lose it anyway. So you're getting your retaliation in first.'

'Well, I probably *will* lose it. I'm forty-five!'

'But you're fit. And what about Cherie Blair?'

'Dr Greig said the chances are high that the baby would suffer from some abnormality.'

'Well, the chances of the baby being normal are much higher. And there are all sorts of tests they can do these days. Anyway, who are we to play God and decide who's fit to be born? You were born "handicapped", as they used to say in the bad old days. Has anyone ever loved you the less for it, or wished your life away?'

'If Keir happens to be a carrier for my condition, this baby could be born blind. There's no prenatal screening for LCA.'

'You know perfectly well that it's a one in two hundred chance of that happening. You're more likely to be knocked down by a car on the way to the antenatal clinic. Tell me,' says Louisa, scraping the last of the porridge from her bowl, 'Did you go through all this soul-searching when you found you were expecting Harvey's baby?'

'That was different. I was married to Harvey. There were two of us.'

'There are two of *us*! If you gave Keir a chance, perhaps there would be three.'

'*No! I don't want this baby!*'

'I don't believe you, Marianne. I don't believe you've even asked yourself if you want it. Or, for that matter, if you want Keir.' Louisa leans across the table. 'Tell him. Give him a chance. *Please.*'

'No, Lou. And that's final.'

Marianne

I had several reasons for not wanting to tell Keir I was pregnant.

The very last conversation I had with my late husband was a row. A terrible row. A row so bad we hadn't even telephoned each other to kiss and make up before he died in the Piper Alpha conflagration.

When my period was a week late, I'd bought a pregnancy test. Harvey was away so I'd asked a friend, Yvonne, another oil wife, to come round and read the test result for me. It was positive.

We'd never discussed having a family except in vague terms. Harvey had asked if any children I had would be blind. I'd said they wouldn't be, not unless I'd had the misfortune to fall in love with an unwitting carrier of Leber's congenital amaurosis, and the chances of that were about one in two hundred. Harvey never asked if I wanted children and I never said that I did. I didn't think I *did*, but I realised I just hadn't asked myself the question. Harvey—so I discovered when he came home—didn't think we could afford a child. He had a point. We couldn't afford a child without making big changes to our lifestyle. All this I knew before Harvey said it, but I hoped he would say something different. I hoped he would *feel* differently, just as I had done once fate had taken a hand.

I was on the pill and took it conscientiously. There was no element of deceit—something Harvey accused me of in the heat of the moment. I'd had a gastric bug and spent a day vomiting. That must have been enough. I found myself unintentionally pregnant, simultaneously thrilled and appalled.

Harvey was just appalled. He didn't realise at first—because of the impassivity of my face, I suppose—that I was pleased, that I actually wanted the baby. That was when he got angry. He dug in his heels. He wouldn't even listen. My feelings weren't taken into consideration. They were subsidiary to the two irrefutable arguments against having a baby: we couldn't afford one and Harvey hadn't been consulted.

I got very upset and then I got angry. I don't remember exactly what was said but I do remember his last words, the last words he ever spoke to me. He said, 'I'm sorry, Marianne. You're going to have to get rid of it. And that's final.'

And it was.

Garth stands at Marianne's bedside holding a tray of coffee, with a newspaper tucked under his arm. After breakfast Louisa had insisted that Marianne go back to bed and rest. As she stirs, he registers the plainness of her room, the interior of which he has rarely seen. There are no table lamps, no pictures, no photographs. There is no dressing table, just a desk with toiletries arrayed in regimental order, like a shop window display. Built-in shelves house books, CDs and tapes labelled in Braille and various objects chosen for shape and texture: shells, stones, driftwood, glass ornaments, small sculptures.

Surfacing, Marianne props herself up on an elbow. 'Lou?'

'Nah, it's me. I did knock but you were out for the count. I've brought you a nice cup of coffee and some biccies—gingernuts. Me mum says, eat little an' often. That's the way to keep the nausea at bay—an' believe me, she should know.'

Marianne hears pillows being plumped and rearranged behind her. 'Lou tells me you have a lot of siblings. What are they all called?'

Garth sits beside the bed. 'After me there's Rhodri, Hywell and Aled, and the little ones are Rhiannon and Angharad. They're twins.'

'All those names are Welsh, aren't they?'

'Blimey, Marianne, you don't miss a thing.'

'Enough of your cheek. You're not to take advantage of my debilitated state. Garth sounds Scandinavian to me. Why have your brothers and sisters got Welsh names and you haven't?'

'Ah, well, that's me dark secret. Mum 'ad me christened—wait for it—*Geraint*. Well, no way was I goin' to step outside Wales with a name like that, so when I was packed off to school—posh English boardin' school it was—I lost me accent an' changed me name to Garth. I thought that was dead cool. Garth Vaughan. Unfortunately, I still got it in the neck, but at least they never knew me name was Geraint.' Garth shakes his shorn auburn head. 'Jeez, I'd've been dead meat.'

'Oh dear, it sounds really grim. Poor you.'

'Nah, it made me the mature, well-adjusted individual I am now!'

'You know you really are a tonic, Garth. You're such a positive person to have around.'

'Thank you. That's what 'er ladyship says an' all. Now, 'ow's about I read to you from the paper? That'll take your mind off things.'

'That would be a treat. Not depressing news, though.'

Garth offers to read an article claiming the greatest threat to the ozone layer is flatulence in cows.

Marianne chokes on her gingernut. 'Oh, now you're pulling my leg!'

'Nah, it's true! Listen . . . "Bovine flatulence is responsible for a quarter of the UK's methane emissions. In Scotland, where there is a greater concentration of agriculture, sheep and cows produce forty-six per cent of all emissions. A single dairy cow produces about four hundred litres of methane each day." Stone the crows . . . I dunno why you're laughin', Marianne,' Garth says sternly, trying to suppress a grin. 'This is dead serious. The 'eadline says, "Farting Furore," in great big letters.'

'It doesn't!'

'You're right, it doesn't. My mistake.'

Helpless with laughter, Marianne pleads, 'Oh, move on to something else, before I wet the bed.'

'Right . . . 'Ow about this, then? "The discovery of a parrot with unparalleled powers to communicate with humans—both verbally and telepathically—has brought scientists up short. The bird, a captive African grey called N'kisi, has a vocabulary of nine hundred and fifty words. N'kisi also appears to be able to read his owner's mind. In an experiment, the parrot and his owner, Aimée Morgana, were put in separate rooms and filmed as she opened random envelopes containing picture cards. When Aimée opened a picture of a man with a telephone and looked at it, N'kisi called out, "What ya doing on the phone?" When Aimée looked at a picture of a couple embracing, the parrot said, "Can I give you a hug?"' Garth lays the newspaper aside. 'Amazin'!'

'Keir had a dog he thought could read his mind. He was called Star. But he also had another name, a secret name. Sirius . . . Keir told me about the stars, you know. When I was on Skye. I was so moved.'

Marianne's voice is unsteady and Garth watches her anxiously. 'I'd like to meet this Keir. What's 'e like? I mean, what kind of bloke listens to a bird concerto? A bird-lover or a music-lover?'

'Keir's both. He's a polymath. A geologist who's interested in zoology, astronomy and music, an acutely sensitive man working in a world populated by stoical tough guys. He views the world holistically, as an entity. He doesn't really make divisions. That's why he can describe colour in terms of smell; why he sees landscape in terms of music. But he splits himself into his component parts and lives divided.'

'Why? Sounds tricky.'

'A survival mechanism, I suppose. Self-protection. You'd know all about that. He never exposes all of himself, just the bits he's prepared to show you. He offered someone the whole show once and she didn't want to know. I suspect he clammed up after that. When I first met

him, I actually thought he was a figment of my imagination. He didn't seem real somehow, he was so strange. Then, as I got to know him, I couldn't understand what he would see in someone like me.'

'Well, there you go. "As a man is, so he sees." That's William Blake, another visionary. This Keir obviously sees beyond the surface of things.'

'Oh, yes, he does. Way, *way* beyond the surface . . .'

Marianne

Although I sounded as if my mind was made up, my feelings about the termination were mixed, because I seemed unable to separate my feelings about the pregnancy from my feelings for Keir. At times I was certain I wanted the man, but not the baby; at others I was convinced I didn't want the man, but possibly wanted the baby. Under the circumstances, a clean slate seemed to be the only sensible plan.

Louisa had insisted on booking me into a private clinic. I packed my case, leaving the CD of *Cantus Arcticus* on the bed. I was trying not to pack it—a symbolic act of severance. I put it in, then hurriedly took it out again, rearranging a packet of sturdy sanitary towels. Tears came to my eyes as I thought about why I was going to need them.

Overwhelmed with grief and shame, I sank down onto the bed, on top of *Cantus Arcticus*, cracking the CD case. I swore aloud, glad of a reason to be furious with myself. As I worked myself up into a lather of self-loathing, the phone rang. And I knew it would be him.

CHAPTER SEVEN

'MARIANNE? IT'S KEIR.'

'Yes. I recognised your voice. Where are you?'

'Oslo. The airport. I'm on my way back to Edinburgh. How are you?'

'I'm . . . I'm very well, thanks. Thank you for the parcels. I did enjoy them. It was kind of you to think of me.'

'No bother. Thinking of you is one of my preferred recreational activities—there's no hangover . . . You're sure you're OK? You sound a wee bit fragile, is all. Are *you* hung-over?'

'No, I was just surprised. Hearing your voice after so many weeks.'

'We agreed we wouldn't ring. That was what you wanted.'

'Yes, I know. Why are you ringing now?'

'I just wanted to know if you were OK. You *are* OK?'

'Yes, I'm *fine*! Keir? I've been wanting to ask you . . . Why *do* you take so much trouble? I mean, why do you take the trouble to share so many things with me? What's in it for you?'

When Keir answers, Marianne hears a different note in his voice: something raw and unprepared. 'There's no one else I can share these things with.' She hears an intake of breath, then his voice, louder now, resumes its customary bantering tone. 'You're a captive audience and I exploit you mercilessly. Who else wants to know about Rautavaara's *Cantus Arcticus*—apart from Mrs Rautavaara?'

'I have to say, Louisa was unimpressed with the bird concerto, but Garth and I are completely hooked. I play it almost every day. You were right about Garth and Louisa, by the way.'

'You're kidding me?'

'No. Love's young dream. I was sceptical to begin with, but actually they're very sweet together. Garth's not a Goth any more, I'm afraid.'

'Is it love, d'you think?'

'Far too early to say. But they seem to be having fun.'

'Good for them. Though that must leave you feeling like a spare part.' She doesn't answer and, after a moment, he says, 'I'm flying back to Edinburgh this afternoon. I won't be there for long: I'm on my way to Skye. I was ringing to say . . . you're very welcome to come with me. To Skye. No strings. And no snow either.' She says nothing and he continues, 'No pressure, I just thought . . . Och, hell—how d'you say to a blind person, "Do you want to see me again?" when see doesn't mean *see*, but "resume our tentative and decidedly weird relationship"?'

'I think you say, "Do you want to see me again?" and hope the blind person can read minds.'

'Do you?'

'Not as well as you.'

'I meant, do you want to resume where we left off?'

Marianne breathes deeply and says, 'Keir, can I think about it? I'm not sure . . . I've been a little unwell lately.'

'I'm sorry to hear that. When I asked earlier, you said you were fine. Your illness—it's nothing serious?'

'Oh, no, I'm not *ill*, just a little run down. I'm not sure if I'm up to the rigours of Skye. Can I let you know? When are you setting off?'

'Soon. Day after tomorrow, probably. I was going to spend a day catching up with sleep. And my family.'

'You have family in Edinburgh?'

'Aye, I've a wee sister. I'm taking her and my brother-in-law out to dinner tomorrow night. We're celebrating.'

'What's the occasion?'

'She's pregnant. I'm going to become an uncle.'

'Oh . . . Congratulations. Are you pleased?'

'Aye, I'm fair bursting with excitement!'

Marianne fights down a wave of nausea. 'Keir, I'm sorry, I have to go. The doorbell just rang. I'll ring you tomorrow. Bye.'

Marianne puts the phone down and covers her face with her hands. Eventually she raises her head and says softly, but with feeling, 'That bloody man . . .that bloody, *bloody* man.'

Marianne

My case was already packed. It seemed easier to go to Skye with Keir than check in to a clinic and abort his baby. *Much* easier. I was aware of a drastic element of procrastination but knew if I turned him down, Keir probably wouldn't invite me again. I may not have known what I wanted, but I knew I didn't want *that*.

I extracted my cotton nightdress and replaced it with fleece pyjamas, added a pair of jeans, some jumpers, thick socks and gloves. I also packed Keir's scarf in the hope that I'd be able to return it without his noticing or, depending on how things went, tell him why I'd taken it.

My hand fell once again on the sanitary towels. I'd heard that love-making could cause a miscarriage or start labour if you were due. Was sex likely to be an option? The decision would probably be mine. Would Keir notice I was pregnant? Unlikely. In any case, the problem was easily avoided. I simply had to refrain from going to bed with the man.

Which was possibly easier said than done.

Keir arrived to collect me and, since Garth was in the flat, introductions had to be made. Keir didn't kiss me in greeting, but I felt his rough, warm fingers enclose both my hands for a moment. He fell oddly silent but the room was still full of him: his hawthorn scent; the movement of air displaced as his large body moved around the flat, greeting Louisa, reaching past me to shake Garth's hand.

Louisa, in cheerful hostess-mode, was offering us coffee. She went off to clatter about in the kitchen and I said, in the direction of Keir, who I thought was still standing beside me, 'Is the sofa empty?'

'Aye. Garth's gone to help Louisa in the kitchen.'

'How very tactful. We get to have a tête-à-tête.' I sat down on the sofa and Keir seated himself beside me. 'How was your sister? Well, I hope?'

'Aye, she looked bonny! It was grand to see her looking so healthy and happy. They've been trying for a while and she's miscarried twice.'

'When is she due?'

'September.'

'Will you be around then?'

'I don't know. I never really know. I take the work when and where I can get it.'

There was a lull in the conversation during which I could hear Louisa humming. Lou never hums.

Blimey, 'e's a big feller.'

She looks at her watch. 'How long do you think we can string this out for? I want to give them time to chat. You know, I'm really worried she's going to change her mind.'

'About the abortion?'

'Sshh! No, about going to Skye.'

'Well, unless you want them to be 'ere all day, it might be a good idea to switch the kettle on.'

'Oh God, yes.' Louisa flicks a switch. 'Thank you.' She grabs a cloth and, humming, begins to wipe down an already clean worktop. With Zen-like calm and precision, Garth arranges biscuits on a plate.

Marianne

Coffee finally. It seemed Garth knew Skye from childhood holidays and he and Keir struck up a conversation about the advent of wind farms and their impact on bird life. Despite the subject being close to his heart, Keir sounded ill at ease and I remembered what he'd said about not feeling comfortable with people.

Finding myself tongue-tied by the awkwardness of my situation, I was happy to leave social niceties to Garth and Louisa. My befuddled brain was busy coping with the fact that I was pregnant with Keir's child and he was the only person in the room who didn't know.

They say their goodbyes and Keir carries Marianne's case downstairs. As they reach the massive front door, he turns to Marianne and says, 'You're sure now? You do want to come?'

'Of course! Why do you ask?'

He shrugs. 'The Ice Maiden performance, I suppose.'

'*Ice Maiden?* What do you mean?'

'Your behaviour. And you're dressed head to foot in white.'

'*Am* I? Damn! It was meant to be black.'

'It's not just your clothes. You seem . . . unreachable somehow.'

'*You're* the one who's unreachable.' Marianne raises her hand in the direction of his voice. Her fingers falter when she encounters stubble. She cranes to press her lips against his rough cheek, then, navigating her way across his face with her fingertips, she kisses his mouth.

When he speaks, she can hear his smile. 'If I'd thought you'd do that, I'd have shaved. Your double messages are coming over loud and clear.'

'I'm sorry. I am pretty confused. Can we just take it one step at a time, Keir? Make no assumptions?'

'I'm not thinking about the future. I try not to. You know why.'

Marianne

I was a fool. A complete fool. A fool to go back to Skye, a fool to think I could control the situation, control my body, keep that man out of my bed. Did I think I'd be able to hide my feelings? From *Keir* of all people?

I was a fool to think I would be able to resist the island: the scent of daffodils and primroses; the pitiful bleating of day-old lambs; the symphonic dawn chorus. Everywhere we walked, there was teeming life, scents and sounds to make one swoon. We walked in wind, rain and surprisingly strong sun, till my muscles screamed for mercy. But the only mercy Keir showed was to carry me, laughing, up the stairs to bed.

'This *is* what you want?'

'Oh, yes. You can have it in writing, if you like. Give me a pin and I'll punch it out in Braille.'

'That won't be necessary.'

She hears sounds of clothing being removed, falling to the floor. Unbuttoning her shirt with clumsy fingers, she asks, 'Is it still light? I feel a bit nervous . . . about you looking at me.'

'It's dusk. But I can see you. Just. You look beautiful.'

She reaches a hand out towards his voice and meets his naked chest. She lets her fingers trail down through curling, springy hairs, over his chest, his belly and into his lap. He leans forward and kisses her.

'So . . . I have your permission to do this?'

'Yes.'

'And . . . *this?*'

Marianne's reply is indistinct. Keir assumes something in the affirmative. His lovemaking is gentle at first, considered, as if compensating for the excess of exhausted, despairing passion that fuelled their previous encounter. He is surprised, then excited by the eagerness of her responses. He feels every part of his body touched by her seeing hands, feels her mind reaching out towards his, but he senses something, somebody between them, some barrier. Used to seeing death in the midst of life, Keir assumes it must be Harvey.

Marianne lies in the crook of Keir's arm, her head pillowed on his shoulder. She turns, kisses his chest, then murmurs, 'Where exactly do you see your visions? Are they inside your head? Like memories? Or are they outside, in front of you, "before your very eyes"?'

He doesn't reply at once. She feels his lungs inflate and then, with a jerk of his diaphragm, he speaks abruptly, his voice too loud for the intimacy of the bed. 'What I see seems real enough. I mean, it appears the same as reality. Mac appeared to be in the theatre bar. He didn't look like a ghost. Not that I know what ghosts look like. But my visions are layered, as if one kind of reality is being superimposed on another.'

'That's a bit hard for me to understand.'

His arm tightens round her and his voice softens. 'It's hard for *anyone* to understand, and that includes me. Think of an orchestra playing. When a new theme is introduced, the sound becomes layered. The instruments blend but they also have their own music that exists independently. You hear them both separately and together. How I see is something like that. The vision is both inside my head and outside it.' He sighs. 'Did that make any sense at all?'

'Yes, it did. I think I'm beginning to get an idea . . . But are you all right talking about it?'

'Aye, I suppose so. To be honest, I preferred our previous activity.'

She checks his roving hand and says, 'How long did you know about Mac? Before it happened, I mean.'

'I saw him when I was talking to you at the opera. That was the beginning of January. The accident happened on February the 3rd.'

'So you had about a month of knowing.'

'*Thinking*. I never *know*.' He removes his arm from behind her and sits up in bed. 'I always hope I'm going to be wrong.'

'Have you ever been wrong?'

His laugh is short and humourless. 'How can I be? If they're still alive, they just haven't died yet. I'm not given a timetable.'

Behind him, Marianne stirs and says, 'So . . . you had about a month of treating Mac—how? Differently?'

'Aye, I suppose so. I laughed at his jokes. Mac tells—*told*—jokes. Badly. But in that last month, I laughed.'

She says, tentatively, 'You know, it *is* a kind of gift. A gift of time. Time to put things right if need be.' She sits up and slips her arms round his waist, resting her cheek against the curve of his back. 'Have you ever foreseen the death of a family member?'

'No.' The sound is low, a growl from deep inside his body.

'Do you know of anyone who's foreseen the death of a family member?'

'No.'

'That's interesting. Maybe something blocks it, such as love?'

'Why would love block the visions?'

'I don't know. Because love is blind?'

'Coming from you, that's very funny.'

'So you've never foreseen the death of anyone you loved . . . but that's your greatest fear?'

After a pause he says, 'Aye.'

'You're a scientist, Keir. Look at the lack of evidence. Your hypothesis is that it's possible you'll foresee the death of a loved one and feel utterly helpless. My hypothesis is that such visions are blocked by feelings of love. Or fear. My evidence for this? You've never foreseen the death of a loved one and you don't know of anyone who has. What's the evidence for *your* hypothesis?'

'I don't have any.'

'It's just a fear that it could happen?'

'I suppose so.'

'So you're prepared to allow primitive superstition to outweigh a complete absence of verifiable evidence. Call yourself a scientist?'

He turns and lies down again beside her. 'I'm also a visionary. A seer. Science tells me what I am doesn't exist. *Can't* exist.'

'But just because we fear something—fear it *terribly*—doesn't mean it's likely to happen! There's no correlation between fear and likelihood. It just feels as if there should be.'

'Marianne Fraser, you're a woman of profound good sense.'

'There you go again, making me sound like something out of Jane Austen.'

'I don't think Austen heroines do what *you* were doing about twenty minutes ago.'

Marianne

I was a fool. A fool to indulge, however briefly, in the fantasy of Happy Families; to think my future held more possibilities than I had imagined. Then, when the fantasy came crashing down around my ears, I didn't even handle it with a good grace. I was a complete, bloody fool, brain addled by hormones and what even a blind man could see was love.

After breakfast Keir looks out of the kitchen window and announces that the rain has stopped. They don boots and fleeces.

'Where to today?'

'The beach, I think. It's not too wild now.'

Keir leads her through the garden, over springy rough grass, down to the seashore. Marianne enjoys clambering over the rocks on all fours, removing her gloves so she can feel the rough textures. Keir eyes her anxiously, ready to spring towards her if she falls. Pausing for a moment, Marianne lifts her head.

'What's that bird called? The piping sound, a bit like a piccolo.'

He doesn't need to look. 'An oystercatcher by the shoreline.'

Marianne turns her face up to the emerging sun. 'Shall we just sit for a bit? I'd like to listen to the sea. Describe the view for me.'

He sits down on her windward side to provide some shelter. 'We're at the top of the beach, which becomes pebbles, then eventually sand. The tide's going out. We're looking northwest, facing a stupendous view of the Cuillin. The ridge looks serrated, something like holly leaves. Have you ever felt those?'

'Oh, yes. At Christmas. Can you translate the view into music for me?'

Keir is silent for a moment, then says, 'I think you've finally stumped me. It's just too big for any music I know. Possibly too beautiful.'

'You once said the Cuillin were like the *Hammerklavier*.'

'Aye, I did. But the Cuillin covered in snow, viewed across the sea, on an April day in bright sunshine . . . Ach, it moves me so deeply, makes me feel so proud. Yet at the same time so . . . *insignificant*. I'm sorry to disappoint you, but I don't know how to translate it.'

'Thanks for trying. I know I ask a lot.'

He puts an arm around her and pulls her towards him. 'Hell, I *do* know what it's like.'

'What? Your wonderful view?'

'Aye. It's like making love. Don't laugh, I'm serious! How this view makes me feel, it's . . . like an orgasm. Well, mine, anyway. You feel the

biggest and strongest you've ever felt. *And* the smallest and weakest. Vulnerable. And full of wonder.'

'Was it like that for you with me?' she asks shyly.

'Aye, it was. That's what made me think of it . . . You OK? You've gone very quiet.'

'Struck dumb by the view.' She gets to her feet unsteadily and says, 'Come on. Let's walk.'

Keir takes her hand. 'If we go closer to the water's edge, we can walk on wet sand, which will be easier for you.' He leads her out of the shelter of the bay, down towards the sea. 'I'll walk by the sea so if a rogue wave comes in, I'll see it coming. It's not yet the weather for paddling.' He studies her profile as the wind whips her hair back from her pale, exhilarated face. He notes how the cold has turned her ears a glowing pink. He feels a tenderness mixed with an urge to protect, emotions he rarely feels for people, only birds and animals, sometimes trees. As a strong gust of wind buffets them, she lifts up her head and laughs.

He stops walking and tugs at her hand, drawing her into his arms. She buries her face in his fleece, inhales the warmth of him and strains to hear his heart beating. They sway slightly in the wind and, with a sudden sinking of spirits, Marianne remembers what stands between them—literally now. She's about to say the speech she has prepared when Keir says, 'Marianne, there's something we need to discuss.'

'Oh? Well, as it happens, there's something I want to tell you too.'

'What?'

'No, you go first.'

'I'm going away again. To Kazakhstan.'

'*Kazakhstan?*' Her body stiffens. 'That's a very long way, isn't it?'

'Aye. Central Asia. It's one of the few places left with significant deposits of oil. I'm going to be looking for them. I'll be gone for three months.'

She wriggles out of his arms. 'Don't you think you might have mentioned this earlier? Perhaps before I came back to Skye?'

'Aye, maybe I should. But if I had, you'd have had to deal with what you felt about me. And then you wouldn't have come.'

'Dead right I wouldn't.' She shivers and folds her arms.

'I didn't pressure you to come, Marianne. And I didn't have to drag you into bed either. You asked if we could play it by ear and that's what we've done. I think that's how we should continue. I'll want to send you tapes while I'm away and I hope you'll let me ring you. But other than that . . . you're free. No strings. I hope when I get back we can pick up where we left off. If that's what you want,' he adds.

'Let me get this straight—are you asking permission to sleep around?'

'No. I'm giving *you* permission to sleep around.'

'Oh, thanks. I'm glad you brought that up. I was wondering how I'd cope. I'm so in demand, you know. The phone never stops ringing.'

'Marianne, I don't think I've handled this very well.'

'No, I don't think you have. But if you'd told me all this earlier, it would just have sounded like a sex-with-no-strings speech. Which is what it sounds like now, so there was really nothing to be gained by being frank. And this way we probably enjoyed the sex more.'

In the long silence that follows, Marianne realises that she too isn't handling the situation well and considers bursting into tears. Eventually she says, 'Oh, for God's sake, Keir, *say* something! You can't make a worse mess of things than I just did.'

When he finally speaks, his voice is even, the words measured, but Marianne hears the effort neutrality costs him. 'I haven't been dishonest. You knew about my lifestyle. I'll be gone three months. We've just spent two months apart, but we were able to pick up where we left off. In any case, I think this is my last trip. I've had enough. I want out.'

'Not because of me?'

'No. I've wanted out for a while. A long while. You knew that.'

'What will you do?'

'I don't know. But I thought three months in Kazakhstan might focus my mind.'

'So you expect me to wait for you?'

His composure breaks then. 'No, I *don't*! You're *free*.'

'And so are you.'

'Yes, I'm free too.' Keir looks out to sea, and narrows his eyes. 'I don't do the future, Marianne. You know why.'

'And I don't do the past. I had hoped we might be able to come to some arrangement about the present. But with a continent or two between us, I think that would be a tall order.'

'Are you not up for a challenge, then?'

'Oh, yes! Never let it be said that plucky little Marianne lacks courage! But I think I have enough on my plate at the moment. Coping with my condition.'

'Your condition?'

She hesitates for a moment, contemplates her future once again and comes to a final decision. 'Leber's congenital amaurosis. My blindness.'

'I see.'

'And I *don't*. Can we go back to the house, please? I'm getting cold.'

'Aye. Sorry, we should have kept moving. Will you take my arm?'

They turn their backs to the wind and set off along the beach. After a few moments Keir asks, 'What was it you wanted to tell me?'

'Oh, it doesn't matter now,' she replies, her voice leaden.

Louisa

I think Garth spoke for us all, summing up our feelings of utter dismay when he exclaimed, 'Where the 'ell is Kazakh-bleedin'-stan?' To make matters worse, I had the temerity to ask Marianne if she'd actually told Keir about the baby. My sister is incapable of a withering look but she more than compensated with the scourge of her tongue.

It seemed she regarded her relationship with Keir as over and said this made everything easier. I didn't really understand, but assumed she meant having the abortion. I offered to make another appointment at the clinic. She prevaricated and retired to her room, from which she barely emerged for three whole days.

You can usually judge Marianne's state of mind by the music she plays. She'd been through a Puccini phase recently, which I'd quite enjoyed, then she'd played Beethoven's *Hammerklavier* piano sonata, not exactly easy listening. Then she became obsessed with the Finnish bird concerto. The worrying thing was, after she got back from Skye the second time, she didn't play *anything*.

The only time I could remember Marianne entering a seriously silent period like this was after Harvey died. As the days went by, I began to wonder whether what she was processing (rehearsing in a way) was death and grief: the death of her husband, the death of two babies and the loss (which was after all a kind of death) of a man she'd realised, somewhat belatedly, she loved.

Then one morning, about a week after she got back from Skye, she emerged from her room and announced, 'I've come to a decision.'

I braced myself, but tried to sound casual. 'Oh? And what is that?'

'Don't get your hopes up, Lou. In a way I think what I've decided makes things harder for you. Probably for me too. But it feels like the right thing to do. And in a way the easiest. Certainly the most humane.'

'Darling, you know you can count on me. *Whatever*. Garth too.'

'Yes, I do know. I can't think what I've done to deserve such loyal support. But God knows, I think I *am* going to need you.' She took a deep breath. 'I've decided to go through with the pregnancy and put the baby up for adoption. I just cannot bring myself to abort that man's baby. It would be like killing *him*. I can't do it. I've had too much to do with death.

And so has Keir,' she added softly. 'So I'm going to let nature take its course. If the baby lives, it will bring happiness to another couple. That seems to me to make some sense of this appalling mess. But if I'm to see it through, I'm going to need your support.'

'Well, I'd be lying if I said I don't hope you'll change your mind about adoption, but I can promise you faithfully I'll never put any pressure on you. I think you know what would be my dearest wish.'

'Yes, I know. Which is why I think all this might be hardest for you.'

'Oh, that doesn't matter! Whatever you decide to do, it's you who have to live with the consequences for the rest of your life. I did think Keir had a right to know, but if he's going off to Kazakhstan . . . and God knows where next . . . Well, it's nobody's business but yours now.'

'Thank you.' Assuming the subject was closed, I turned away when she said abruptly, 'I do love you, you know. I'm such *rubbish* at telling people how much I care for them. But that doesn't mean I don't feel it.'

'Darling, I know!' I saw her lip tremble and threw my arms round her.

We stood in the kitchen, hugging each other, weeping and wailing for I don't know how long. When Garth let himself in, he stopped in his tracks, took one look at us and said, 'All right, then—'oo's died?'

Marianne

Keir and I didn't discuss what we felt for each other. Perhaps we *couldn't* have discussed it. I doubt we would have known how to describe what we felt, what to make of the sense that we hardly knew each other at all, and had always known each other.

Oh, we talked and talked, but not about *us*. Not until that last walk on the beach. Instead we made love. And that was overwhelming. Or rather, we were overwhelmed by our need for each other, the sense of urgency, our inexplicable but visceral connection that seemed to lead naturally and often to making love. And in some unlikely places.

We sheltered in the tree-house on the way back from a woodland walk. Rain was turning to sleet and inside the tree-house we stood in silence, listening to a fusillade of hailstones on the roof. Keir laughed; I've no idea why. He didn't laugh very often, but when he did it was somehow infectious. I laughed too; then he bent his head again and took my face in his hands and kissed me in a way that was so raw and needy I felt shocked. But shock didn't prevent me from responding.

We didn't even undress. I heard him drag something soft out of a box and throw it onto one of the makeshift beds, where it settled with a sigh. Then he lowered me onto the bed, cradled like a baby on his arm. I felt

both completely secure and as if annihilation might be imminent. I felt the weight and pressure of Keir above, then the breath was knocked out of me—not just by the violence with which he made love to me, but by the strength of my feeling for him.

Afterwards, Keir apologised for behaving 'like an adolescent'. I said there was no need for apology. I'd never felt so desired or so desirable.

Louisa

Marianne passed the thirteen-week stage at the beginning of May and we went back to see Dr Greig, to talk about adoption and preliminary wheels were set in motion. I was to be Marianne's official birth partner but I was spared antenatal classes. Marianne said she wasn't prepared to mix with happy couples half her age.

We had to go for the scan when Marianne was fifteen weeks. It was now mid-May and Edinburgh was fragrant with blossom. As we walked through the hospital grounds, she stopped suddenly, saying she wanted to smell the hawthorn. I felt pleased she was still able to take pleasure in simple things.

We both knew that when the baby was scanned, the radiologist might be able to determine the baby's gender and offer to tell us. Marianne had told me she didn't want to know. I tried not to look at the screen. (Marianne, of course, couldn't.) It must have been written into her notes about adoption because the radiologist didn't try to describe anything to her, she just informed us that everything appeared to be normal. And then came the moment I'd been dreading.

The girl said, 'Would you like to know the baby's gender?'

I launched into an explanation, but Marianne cut me off. 'It's all right, Lou.' The radiologist looked at Marianne expectantly and so did I. 'Yes,' she said. 'I would like to know.'

'It's a boy. And it looks like he's going to be a big one.'

'Ah,' said Marianne. 'That doesn't surprise me. Thank you.'

Stunned, I waited while Marianne got dressed. When she emerged from her cubicle, she took my arm. 'I'm sorry, Lou. I've felt all along that it was a boy and I suddenly wanted to know if I was right. Silly really.' I wasn't able to reply. She squeezed my arm and continued, 'It's all for the best, you know. Just imagine a boy being brought up by a couple of old spinsters. It wouldn't be right, would it?'

'No . . . I suppose not.'

For what must have been the first time in my life, I thanked God Marianne was blind and couldn't see my face.

Marianne

Hawthorn blossom. His smell. Life has a way of waiting till you're down, then giving you a good kicking. That May morning in the hospital grounds, the scent of hawthorn blossom stopped me dead. Keir was beside me. *Inside* me.

I didn't faint, but it was a close call.

Louisa

By the end of May I'd more or less come to terms with the results of the ultrasound scan. I'd abandoned my pretty-in-pink fantasies and was doing my best to quell the blue version. Marianne didn't relent. She still referred to the baby as 'it', which I found distressing.

One day I'd hit the gin long before the sun was over the yardarm (well, if you waited for the sun in Edinburgh, you'd die of thirst) when Garth put his head round the sitting-room door and said in a whisper, 'Is Marianne in?'

'No. She's gone for a walk. She should be back soon. Why?'

He crooked his finger and beckoned. 'Come an' take a look at this.'

I followed him into the study and he stood beside the PC. There were lots of windows open on the screen and Garth maximised one. It was a news website. I peered at the text. The item was headed BRITISH OIL WORKERS KIDNAPPED IN KAZAKHSTAN.

'Oh my God! It's not Keir, is it?'

'Dunno. It's just breakin' news, as they 'aven't released any names. Do we know 'oo Keir works for?'

'Well, I don't. I dare say Marianne does, but we can hardly ask her, can we? It probably isn't him . . . I mean, there must be hundreds of British oil workers in Kazakhstan—mustn't there?'

'Possibly. An' I suppose a lot of 'em would be Scots.'

My stomach turned over. 'Why do you say that?'

Garth maximised another window. 'Because this blogger describes the oil workers as an American an' two Scots. This guy thinks the oil workers 'ave been kidnapped by a group of Kazakh conservationists.'

'Conservationists?'

'Yeah. Militants. You know, like Greenpeace. He thinks they'll be 'oldin' the guys to ransom.'

'For money?'

'Doubt it. Political leverage, more like. This blogger says a lot of Kazakhs aren't very 'appy about what's goin' on in their country.' Garth clicked on another window. 'The scramble for oil an' gas is causin' a lot of damage to the environment.'

I stared blankly at the screen. 'How can we find out if one of these Scots is Keir?'

'If we knew 'oo 'e worked for, we could try an' contact them without Marianne knowin'.' Garth shrugged. 'Maybe we should just tell 'er. It'll turn up on the radio soon. TV an' all. She could get to 'ear about it.'

'Well, we'll just have to cross that bridge when we come to it.' I kissed Garth on the cheek. 'Thanks for researching all this. You are an absolute angel. At least we're prepared now. But it probably isn't Keir . . .'

But it was. They released the names the following day. Garth found them by Googling Keir's name and 'Kazakhstan'. 'So . . . do we tell 'er?'

I tried to think. 'Is it on British news websites yet?'

'Not yet. I've set up a Google Alert for 'is name, plus "kidnap" an' "Kazakhstan", so that should bring any news straight into your inbox.'

'Do we know *why* he's been kidnapped?'

'It's like I said, they're militant Greens. They want the oil companies to clean up their act. And the Caspian Sea while they're about it.'

'So it really isn't likely they'll harm him, is it? I mean, people who care about pollution aren't violent, are they?'

'Depends if they're fanatics. Animal activists can be a bit dodgy. But this crowd,' he said, tapping the screen, 'they sound like environmentalists. Probably young too—they're thinkin' about the future. If they speak any English—an' they probably do—they'll talk to Keir an' find out 'e's a diamond geezer. On the same wavelength.'

'So should we tell Marianne?'

Garth turned to face me. 'It's over between them, right?'

'Well, that's what she *says*, but I don't believe a word of it.'

'The only way she'll find out is on the radio or TV.' He picked up a pen and started to tap the desk with it. 'We can't risk Marianne findin' out by chance. The press are bound to make a meal of it.'

We looked at each other for a long moment; then I said, 'All right, I'll tell her. But when?'

'You could leave it till the BBC breaks the news. I think we can take whatever they say as gospel. An' for all Marianne will know, that'll be the first we've 'eard of it.'

'So we've probably got a day's grace?'

'Maybe,' he said, looking at the screen again. 'Uh-oh, what's this just dropped into your inbox? Don't tell me . . . Too late. The Beeb is quotin' Reuters now, namin' Keir as "one of three men kidnapped by the somethin'-unpronounceable environmental group of Kazakhstan".'

'Does it say where they're being held?'

He scrolled down. 'At sea. On a boat on the Caspian Sea. Oh *shit* . . .'

'What? Is it bad?' I peered at the PC.

'They say, if any attempt is made to rescue the men or scupper the boat, they'll kill one of the hostages.'

'Oh my God!'

'They're bluffin', take no notice. It's just big talk. They say they'll release two men when the oil companies agree to meet with representatives of their organisation an' they'll release the last man when they're 'appy with what's been agreed.'

'But that could take weeks!'

'Well, let's 'ope Keir is one of the first two to be released.'

'So now we really *do* have to tell her, but *not* about the death threat.'

'Nah, better leave that bit out.'

Marianne

I suppose I hadn't known until then quite how much I felt for Keir. I took the news calmly—more calmly, at any rate, than Louisa delivered it—then I went to my room and lay down on the bed.

It all came back to me . . . The waiting. The praying. I placed my hands on my swelling abdomen and prayed to a God I hadn't believed in since 1988 that I would lose this baby but that I wouldn't—dear God in Heaven, please, if you *do* exist—that I wouldn't lose Keir.

At least, not to death.

The days dragged by and life became surreal. I continued to walk in the Botanics and attend antenatal appointments. I listened to news bulletins on Radio Scotland. We contacted Keir's employers who referred us to his family without giving any contact details. Louisa suggested we should try to contact Keir's sister in Edinburgh, in case he'd been able to phone her, but I pointed out that we had neither her name nor her address. In any case, desperate as we were for information, I wasn't prepared to explain my connection with Keir, particularly in view of my now obvious condition. (Although, as Louisa cheerfully pointed out, given my age, people would assume I was overweight, not pregnant.)

Louisa bore up well to begin with and Garth was a tower of strength. He managed to maintain a sense of proportion and of humour amid mounting female hysteria, and keep us informed of any developments, putting tea, coffee or gin in front of us.

As the days wore on, the gins got stronger.

Marianne is on her way to the kitchen when she thinks she hears the sound of Louisa crying in her bedroom. She knocks tentatively. 'Lou? What's the matter? Can I come in?'

There is a muffled reply followed by a loud sniff. As Marianne opens the door, Louisa calls out, 'I'm on the bed, darling. Don't worry—there's no news. No *bad* news, anyway.'

Marianne makes her way towards the bed. 'So why are you crying?'

'Oh God, I don't know! Worrying about you and the baby . . . Worrying about Keir . . . These wretched negotiations dragging on.'

'It's only a week. We have to be patient. But is something else bothering you? You said there was no *bad* news. Do you have some *good* news?'

'Well, yes, I suppose so. The trouble is, I think it's precipitated a bit of a midlife crisis. I'm having to face up to things. My career. My future. Old age . . . All the big stuff.'

'Goodness, what's brought this on? Garth hasn't dumped you, has he?'

'No, he seems happy enough. Well, thrilled, actually.'

'Thrilled? What about?'

Louisa sighs and says wearily, 'They want to make a film of my books. Two films, actually. Possibly three. It all depends how the first one fares at the box office. Anyway, they've optioned half my books and the first film is going into production now.'

'Lou, how wonderful! Is this your agent's doing?'

'No, it's all thanks to Garth. His brother Rhodri is a film cameraman and they were talking about my books, apparently. Garth has a much higher opinion of them than *you* do, I'm happy to say. He was telling Rhodri what an ideal subject they'd be for a film—sort of *Buffy* for the big screen, set in Victorian Edinburgh. Anyway, Rhodri happened to be making a film with Johnny Depp and told him about my books. Johnny Depp apparently took a look at one of them and mentioned it to his agent and one thing led to another. One of the Hollywood studios picked it up and now the first film is in production.'

'With Johnny Depp as one of your vampires?'

'That's unconfirmed. They're undecided just how Scottish to make it. Anyway, *whoever* they cast,' she finishes gloomily, 'it's going to make me pots and pots of money.'

'So why are you crying, for heaven's sake?'

'Because,' Louisa wails, 'I've nobody to spend it on! What use is half a million dollars to *me*? You can only drink so much gin! I wanted to give some to Garth, but he won't take it. I offered to buy him a car. He said, thanks, but he wasn't interested because parking in Edinburgh's such a

nightmare. He says if I insist, I can take him away for a dirty weekend at Gleneagles and teach him to play golf. Oh, and he wouldn't mind having another new suit. I thought he meant Savile Row but he said, no, from Next. Honestly, as a gigolo he's just *hopeless*.'

Marianne sits for a moment, her arms encircling her growing bump. 'You know, you could use the money to buy yourself some time.'

'What do you mean?'

'Stop writing the vampire books. Get off the commercial treadmill and think about what you really want to write. You're a historian at heart, Lou, not a fiction writer. You've always said biography and social history were your first loves. Why don't you change direction? Write the book of your heart. Is there one?'

'Well, yes, actually, now you come to mention it, there is. I've always wanted to write a biography of Isobel Gowdie.'

'The witch?'

'Well, she was *said* to be a witch.'

'Seventeenth century, I seem to remember?'

'Yes. Not really my period, but an interesting one. They put Isobel on trial and got these amazing poetic confessions out of her—apparently without recourse to torture—all about being transformed into various animals and having sex with the devil. *Riveting* stuff. I thought about turning it into a historical novel years ago, but my publishers just wanted the next vampire book. I've kept my notes about Isobel, though.'

'So take a sabbatical. Tell your editor you're taking a year off to do some research. You don't have to tell them what you're researching.'

'No, I suppose not. But they'll give me a hard time if I don't come up with another vampire book.'

'Just say *no*, Lou. You're a grown woman. Act your age, not your shoe size, as Garth would say. What *does* Garth have to say about all this?'

'Much the same as you. That I should try something new. He says the film deal is a golden opportunity for me to spread my wings.'

'You should make that man your manager. You could certainly do with one, especially now Hollywood's come calling. You'll have to upgrade your website too.'

'I know. I thought I'd increase Garth's salary and let him take over all that side of things. It's quite beyond my capabilities. But I do worry that when we split up—which, of course, we inevitably *will*, when he comes to his senses and finds someone his own age—well, it could all be rather messy. I could be left dangling, professionally. I wonder if it would be better to keep business and pleasure separate?'

'Isn't it a bit late for that?'

Louisa's lip quivers and she reaches for the box of tissues. 'Oh, it's all such a muddle! And what with poor Keir and the baby, I just feel over-whelmed. I'm sorry, Marianne, I didn't mean to burden you.'

'Not at all. I'm glad of the distraction. It makes a change from dwelling on heartburn and varicose veins, and thinking about either of those is preferable to thinking about what Keir might be going through.'

Louisa puts an arm round her sister. 'You know, he struck me as very tough. Resourceful. He'd cope well in a tight spot, I'm sure. And the kidnappers are conservationists. They love nature. And their country. If they've managed to communicate with Keir, they'll have discovered he's just like them. I expect by now they've all bonded and are discussing the flora and fauna of Kazakhstan.'

'I suppose you might be right. Let's hope so.' Marianne stands and rubs her aching back. 'Is it too early for a gin, do you think?'

'Darling, it's *never* too early for a gin,' Louisa says, scrambling off the bed. 'Go and put your feet up and I'll bring you one.'

Marianne

It's always a mistake to assume things can't get any worse. They did, in a thorough-going sort of way. Two of the men were released—the ones with wives and children—and I started to bleed.

Louisa called the doctor and insisted I retire to bed, even though I pointed out it had always been my intention to let nature take its course. But she was so upset about Keir remaining in captivity that I took to my bed to spare her and perhaps to spare myself.

The bleeding stopped within twenty-four hours and I got up again. After the first two men were released, a meeting was scheduled for June 10, to take place on a yacht owned by a Kazakh government minister. The oil company demanded that Keir be produced as a gesture of good faith, so he too was to be transported to the yacht in the dilapidated cruiser that had housed the men during their captivity.

This much we learned afterwards. After the explosion.

Reports said that as soon as the cruiser's engine started up, there was an explosion and the craft burst into flames. Burning debris and fuel were scattered over a wide area. An eyewitness said, 'It looked like the sea was on fire.' Two of the kidnappers survived, although one wasn't expected to live. One of them died and his body was recovered. Keir's body wasn't.

As we listened to the news, Louisa and Garth had the sense not to say

anything. I left the sitting room and went to my room. I kicked off my slippers and climbed into bed, fully clothed.

I lay still for some time, listening to the hum of evening traffic, the swish of tyres on wet tarmac; then I reached out to my bedside table. My unerring fingers found the CD buttons and I pressed PLAY. A solo flute meandered, sounding like a bird, then a real bird began to sing, followed by another, then another. These were birds from the Arctic marshes of Finland; birds whose stark, cold song formed a bleak requiem for a man I had loved but never known. And now never would know. I'd always meant to ask Keir the names of these birds. He would have made it his business to know. He would have rejoiced in their names, their song, their habitat.

So much *life* . . .

There were so many things I'd wanted to ask Keir, but there hadn't been time. Now I couldn't remember what I'd wanted to know about him, apart from everything. But I remembered one question and I remembered his answer. He'd sat on the edge of the bed and I'd laid my hand on his broad, naked back as he'd told me of his vision . . . *'I never knew what it meant, just that it was bad. Very bad.'*

And I had asked, *'What did you see?'*

He said, *'I saw the sea . . . and it was on fire.'*

There was fire now behind my eyes as tears refused to come; ice in my heart as the blood seemed to slow to a standstill in my veins. Then, with ludicrously inappropriate timing, Keir's baby kicked.

And—as it always does—life went on.

Summer—2007

CHAPTER EIGHT

Louisa

Marianne's anger was terrible to behold. She seemed to solidify, to become a pillar of fury. I'd never seen anything like it, not even in the aftermath of Harvey's death. It was like having an unexploded bomb in the house. The poor girl was in a state of suspended grief: cold, calm, at times almost inanimate, except that one sensed a raging torrent of emotion, arrested temporarily, like a frozen waterfall.

She took to sitting on our little balcony, apparently listening to the birds. At her request Garth fixed up a bird table and I bought some seed and hanging feeders. She asked particularly for some dried mealworms. I thought she'd taken leave of her senses.

Marianne would sit on the balcony, perfectly still, her flat hand offering a small pile of mealworms, she waiting patiently for birds to come and feed. Eventually, after she'd sat like this for over an hour, one did. I happened to be looking out through the open French windows when I saw a robin descend and inspect the trail of worms she'd scattered on the table near her hand. I watched the bird eat up the scattered worms, then fly away. Marianne didn't move. The robin returned almost immediately, inspected the table for more worms and then her hand. He turned his head this way and that, then pecked briefly at the worms in her palm and flew away again.

Then I saw Marianne's shoulders start to shake. They were moving up and down, heaving, as she sobbed. She was saying his name, or trying to, over and over again, in between convulsive, almost silent sobs: 'K–Keir . . . K–K–Keir . . . ' I clapped my hand to my mouth and, making no noise, fled before my grief could intrude on hers.

Marianne

Keir had taken my arm and led me out into the garden. 'I thought we'd try to get the robin to eat from your hand. Would you like that?'

'Oh, yes! Do you think he will?'

'Aye, he might. But a certain amount of subterfuge will be necessary. The bench is behind you. Sit down by the armrest. Now, hold out your hand.' He took my hand and sprinkled something into my palm.

'Is that birdseed?'

'Och, I was hoping you wouldn't ask. I'm afraid it's dried mealworms. But they're very dead. And robins love them. Close your hand up now. I'm going to sit beside you and put my arm round you like this . . . I'm going to extend my arm along the bench and I'll put yours on top . . . We're trying to look like one person. Comfortable? Now, open your hand carefully. Keep it flat and sit very still. Here he comes. He's checking us out. He knows something's up. Wheesht, now . . .'

And Keir was silent. I sat quite still. After a minute or so he whispered, 'He's on my fingers . . . Looking at yours. Don't flinch when he lands.'

I felt a touch, no weight at all, just a pricking that jumped across my fingers; then my palm was tapped repeatedly by something sharp. The pecking wasn't painful, just unfamiliar. The robin fed from my hand for

perhaps half a minute; then he took off in a flurry of feathers. I felt a faint current of air move over my hand.

After the robin had gone, it was several moments before I could speak. Eventually I said, 'He weighed *nothing*!'

'About eighteen grams. The skeleton is very light. Has to be, to fly. Och, he's back! And giving you the eye. Sit still now.'

I sat still, so very still, and time congealed, solidified into a moment I will never forget. If I'd been turned to stone then, I wouldn't have minded— frozen for ever in that instant, with Keir's breath in my ear, his scent in my nostrils, his limbs lying along the length of mine, and a robin dancing in the palm of my hand.

When we'd said goodbye in Edinburgh, on the doorstep where we first met, he said, 'Do you know the Gaelic blessing?

'May the road rise up to meet you.
May the wind be always at your back.
May the sun shine warm upon your face, the rains fall soft
    upon your fields,
And until we meet again,
May God hold you in the palm of His hand.'

I felt the press of his lips on my palm; then he was gone.

The results of the amniocentesis test came through the day after Keir died. It appeared that I was going to give birth to a normal baby. My navel was fast disappearing, as was my waist. Bending had become difficult and I now felt most comfortable standing or walking. It was no longer possible for me to ignore my pregnancy, or the baby himself. He made his presence felt by prodding me whenever I was horizontal. I felt physically well and strong. Mentally and emotionally, I was in pieces.

At the end of a broken night, disturbed by vivid dreams of the Piper Alpha explosion and making love with Keir, I rose early, wrecked but resolved. In my hours of wakefulness I'd come to a decision.

'Lou, are you busy? Can I disturb you for a moment?'

'Please do. I'm just staring at the screen. Come in and sit down.'

'I've been thinking about my future. And the baby's. And I've come to a decision. One that entails a drastic change of plan.'

'Oh?' Her voice quailed with hope but she said nothing more.

'I've decided to keep the baby. If by any chance you've changed your mind about your generous offer of support, I'm perfectly happy to go it

alone. I'll manage. I'd have to move, of course, but you can buy me out of the flat and then I can rent or buy something small. But I just wanted you to know that nothing and no one is going to part me from this child. Not now.'

I heard the sound of tissues being snatched by the handful from a box on the desk. There were spluttering sounds; then Louisa finally managed to speak. 'Marianne, I don't know what to say! I'm . . . I'm overjoyed! And I won't hear of you going it alone! We're in this *together*. Let's get out of this poky old flat and . . . and spread our wings!'

She laughed and flung her arms round me. I let her hold me for a moment then, my voice surprisingly steady, I said, 'There's a gap in my life where Harvey should have been. And now there's a gap in my life where Keir should have been. I'm damned if there's going to be a gap in my life where a child should have been. So I'm keeping Keir's son. I'm going to call him James. James Stewart.'

'Wonderful! James Stuart . . . After the kings?'

'No, after the actor. James Stewart played the man who saw a six-foot rabbit called Harvey. Keir bought you the DVD—don't you remember?'

'Oh! *Jimmy* Stewart! Yes, of course! Even better! I'm so thrilled, you cannot *possibly* imagine! You know, I'd already been looking at larger properties, in a half-hearted sort of way. I thought it might be nice for us to have a big garden. After all, you get so much pleasure from trees and birds. Now we have the perfect excuse to go house-hunting! When you feel up to it,' she added hurriedly. 'Oh, I can't wait to tell Garth! You'll see—we'll be quite the happy family! It will be just like an episode of *The Waltons*. Nauseating.'

'Lou, you *are* a dear. I'm so grateful.' I rubbed my aching back. 'Being blind does have some advantages. I'll never have to see a resemblance between father and son.'

'No. You'll be spared that . . . I suppose you might *hear* it one day.'

'My son won't grow up on Skye, so he'll never have his father's accent.'

'Would you have liked him to grow up on Skye?'

'It's what Keir would have wanted, I think. He was always trying to work out a way he could go back there, for good. Perhaps that's where he is now. In spirit. On Skye. At least, I like to think so.'

'**I**'m taking you somewhere special. Well, special to me. Can you guess where you are?'

'We've moved out of the wind . . . and it's suddenly much warmer. The smells are different, too. It reminds me of something . . . Earthy . . . Oh, it's the glasshouses at the Botanics!'

There's a sudden gust of wind, followed by the flap and slap of plastic. Keir says, 'That was a big clue. And here's another.' He takes her hand and directs her fingertips.

'Oh! . . . Saplings, so this is your tree nursery . . . Inside a polythene tunnel . . . And the tunnel is open at both ends, I suspect. I didn't hear you open a door and I can feel a through-draught.'

'Och, you don't need seeing eyes, they'd be totally redundant! You have perfectly good eyes, they're just not in your sockets.'

'What are you growing here?'

'Native trees. Hazel. Birch. Holly. Oak. In here I've got seedlings and two-year-old saplings in pots, ready to go into the ground.'

'Whereabouts are you planting?'

'I'm filling in gaps and extending the woodland. Hazel's not long-lived—only about sixty years. And oak propagation is a chancy, wasteful business. For every ten thousand acorns, only one will make it to a mature oak. So I'm trying to give nature a leg-up.'

Marianne fingers the saplings. 'How long before these are tree-sized?'

'Those are hazel. They'll grow to about six metres in ten years.'

'So you'll be . . . fifty-two before they're mature.'

He places a flower pot in her hands. 'That's an oak. When that reaches maturity, I'll have been dead for about eighty years. At least.'

'It's strange to think of doing something like that. Planting a tree, knowing you won't ever see it fully grown. Knowing it will outlive you.'

'I'm planting it *because* it will outlive me. This wee feller is my bid for immortality. Well, five hundred years maybe. That'll do me . . .'

Marianne

To celebrate the results of the amniocentesis, Louisa suggested we go shopping for the baby. I warned her we wouldn't be buying much. At twenty weeks I was now unlikely to miscarry but I wasn't prepared to tempt fate. Instead we did what Louisa referred to as 'reconnaissance', in Mothercare, Marks & Spencer, Boots and Jenners, stroking, exclaiming, Louisa squealing with delight and anticipation. She would hand me baby-gros and sleep-suits to feel. 'Oh, this one is just adorable! It's got a dear little pixie hood—here, can you feel?—and mittens that fold back on themselves. How clever!'

'They feel like doll's clothes!'

'Of course they do. That's the size the baby will be. Only a lot heavier, of course. Come and smell the bath stuff.' She unscrewed the lid of something fragrant and held it under my nose. 'Isn't it delicious? That's baby

lotion. And this . . .' She offered me something else to smell. 'That's bubble bath. Now let me show you this very clever contraption. It fits inside a plastic baby bath. You put the baby in *here*—there, can you feel?—and it sits up, supported, so your hands are more or less free. The baby will be quite secure and once you get the hang of it, you'll be able to bath him on your own, quite confidently.'

'You really think so?'

'Oh, no question! You're by no means the first blind woman to give birth, darling. Garth and I have been researching online and there's all sorts of support groups now for visually impaired parents. We didn't tell you about them because you were so set on adoption, but I wanted to know the facts, know whether we'd be able to manage, if you *should* happen to change your mind.'

'You never gave up hoping, did you? You really think we'll manage?'

She put an arm round what remained of my waist. 'Darling, we will do more than *manage*. We are going to have the time of our lives!'

I put our few baby purchases away in a cupboard then, working on the principle that the task would never get any easier, I decided to put away the few things I had that were mementos of Keir. I filed the Rautavaara concerto away on my music shelf, in between Rachmaninov and Ravel, where it would languish unplayed for a very long time, perhaps for ever. There was the postcard Keir had sent Louisa from Skye. She'd found it weeks ago when tidying her desk and asked me if I wanted it. Then there was the tape of the Northern Lights, the only recording I had of Keir's voice. I couldn't imagine ever being able to listen to it again—it had reduced me to tears when he was alive—but it would be kept safe, in the wooden box where I stored Harvey's audio-letters.

Finally there was Keir's cashmere scarf that I'd stolen from Skye, then surreptitiously returned. I'd hoped he hadn't noticed its absence but, as Louisa once remarked, that man's eyes didn't miss much.

'**O**ch, it's back! Like the swallows.'

'What's back?'

'My scarf. You needn't have bothered. You're welcome to it. You've probably more need of it in Edinburgh than I have here.'

'You're teasing me. I know I deserve it.'

'Why did you take it?'

'You know why. Or you can work it out.'

He holds the scarf to his face. 'I can't smell anything.'

'That's because your sense of smell isn't very sensitive.'

'I'll have you know my sense of smell is *very* sensitive. They used to send me below on the platforms to smell out leaking gas.'

'Well, maybe you can't smell anything because you're surrounded by it all the time.'

'Is it a good smell?'

'I like it. When I missed you, I'd stroke it . . . inhale it. Smells are instant and total recall. It was as if you were in the room.'

He folds the scarf slowly, then hands it to her. 'Keep it.'

'No, really, I shouldn't have taken it, it was very silly of me—'

'I want you to keep it.'

'Why?'

'In case of emergencies.'

Marianne

I folded the scarf, put it in a plastic bag and placed it on a shelf in my wardrobe, at the back. As I sank onto the bed, exhausted, the phone rang. I got to my feet and slowly headed for the sitting room. I lifted the receiver. 'Hello?'

'Marianne?'

I slammed the phone down and stood shaking. Now I was hearing things, going mad. It was my hormones. Defective hearing. Just grief, bloody grief . . .

The phone rang again and I jumped. I let it ring for a long time, then picked it up but didn't speak. The voice said, 'Marianne? It's me. Keir.' I swallowed a sob. The voice continued, 'Sorry I startled you. I gather I've been reported as dead. I'm not. Well, *obviously* . . . So I wanted to let you know. I thought you might have seen the story. It was big news in Scotland, I gather . . . Marianne, are you there?'

'*Keir?* You're *alive?*'

'Aye.'

'Where *are* you?'

'Still in Kazakhstan. Flying home tomorrow.'

'Keir, we thought you were dead!'

'Aye, I know. So did I at times. It's a long story.'

'But—the explosion . . . how did you survive?'

'I saw it coming. Och, not like that! I mean I had some warning. I could smell leaking fuel. I tried to tell the guys we were in trouble but their English didn't run to leaking fuel tanks and since my hands were tied, my sign language wasn't exactly eloquent. So I threw myself overboard as they

switched on the engine. I kicked my way to the surface and came up underneath an upturned dinghy.'

'You hid under the dinghy?'

'Aye. There was air and I was protected from burning fuel and flying debris. The only problem was keeping afloat with my hands tied. But if I stayed under the dinghy, I could hold on to the seat. So I just drifted with the current. I reckon I must have drifted in and out of consciousness as well. But I came to every time I started drowning.'

'Did somebody find you?'

'Eventually. I heard a fishing boat so I ducked out from under the dinghy and started yelling. This old guy hauled me in with a boat-hook. We put in at some godforsaken village and I shared a fish supper with his family. It was all very convivial considering we didn't have a common language. But things went downhill from there.'

'What happened?'

'Well, I had no ID—the kidnappers took all that, along with our phones and our money—so I had to find the nearest policeman, throw myself on his mercy and hand over the statutory bribe.'

'You had to bribe a *policeman*?'

'Oh, aye, that's how the system works out here, which is why I never travel without US dollars in a waterproof bag in my shoe.'

'Did he take you to the British embassy?'

'Did he hell! He banged me up in a cell and that's where I stayed until I produced the rest of my dollars. *Then* I was allowed a phone call. And that was when I discovered I'd been dead for three days. Anyway, I'm thoroughly alive and coming home. Can I see you when I get back?'

The baby fluttered and I placed my hand instinctively on the bump. 'I'm not sure, Keir. I need time to think . . . I thought you were *dead*.'

'Aye, I'm sorry. You should have heard the row my sister gave me. She said she thought she was going to lose the baby.'

'Is she all right now?'

'Aye, she's fine right enough. The baby too. Can I give you her number? That's where I'll be when I get back. For a while, anyway. I'll head off to Skye when I can. I'm on indefinite leave for now. I'd really like to see you. I've thought about you a lot.' He paused again and the silence yawned between us.

'I need some time, Keir . . . It's so much to take in. I'm very relieved you're alive, but . . . a lot of water has passed under the bridge.'

'I know. And we said "no strings" . . . Och, well, goodbye, Marianne.'

'Keir! Don't hang up! I just wanted to say . . . You mean a very great

deal to me. I realise that now. But I think it's probably best we don't meet.'

'Is there someone new in your life?'

'No! . . . Well, yes. Yes, there is, actually . . . He's called James.'

There was a long silence. Then, sounding almost jaunty, Keir said, 'OK. Thanks for being straight with me. Take good care of yourself now. James is a lucky guy.' And he hung up before I could say goodbye.

Louisa

Now don't get me wrong. I adore my sister, respect and admire her more than anyone else I know. But there are times when I just want to slap her.

'You said *what*?'

'I said . . . I thought it best we didn't meet.'

Louisa regards her sister, lying on the bed, her face pale; registers the damp contents of the wastepaper bin. Suppressing apoplexy, she tries to sound calm. 'But I don't understand. *Why* did you say that?'

'Because I don't want him to know I'm pregnant. If I were still putting the baby up for adoption, then perhaps I could have seen him. But I'm not, so it's out of the question. The reason I didn't tell him before was because I didn't want him to feel he had to take responsibility—moral, emotional or financial responsibility for this child.'

'But supposing he *wanted* to?'

'He's not going to get the opportunity,' Marianne says firmly. 'There's no way I'm going to meet him in this state, like some deflowered virgin in a Victorian melodrama. I cannot and will not subject myself to anyone's pity, Lou. Nor am I prepared to exploit whatever scruples he might have about my coping on my own. You and I agreed we would manage. And we *will*. So can we please drop the subject?'

'But if you'd told him—'

Marianne sits up suddenly, her fists clenched. 'It's *my* life, *my* body and *my* baby! And he's *my* bloody lover! Don't tell me what I should have done!' Her voice breaks. 'I *know* what I should have done! And I should have done it a long time ago! But it's too late now.'

Louisa puts an arm round her. 'Darling, I'm only trying to help.'

'I know you are. I'm sorry. There was a time—before I decided to keep the baby—when I could have told Keir. I *meant* to. I might have found out then how he felt about being a father. About me. But he told me he was going to the other side of the world for three months. And *he* suggested we be free agents. I couldn't tell him then and I can't tell him now.'

'But why not? What's the worst thing that can happen?'

'The worst thing that can happen is he will realise I wanted him to be part of my future . . . and then walk away.'

'He might not.'

'Of course he would! He's forty-two. He's never married, never even been engaged, as far as I know. He said his relationships with women are always casual and that's the way he likes it. He's a drifter, one of life's bachelors. Attractive. Kind. Intelligent. And irredeemably single.'

'But the man you describe wouldn't have taken up with a blind woman in the first place! Far too much trouble. And a man as shallow as you describe wouldn't have sent a postcard from Skye, just to let me know you were enjoying yourself.'

'Being interested in me as some sort of curiosity doesn't mean he'd want to settle down and have a family. Don't you see? This isn't about Keir and me, it's about the *baby*.'

Louisa is silent for a moment then, taking a deep breath, she says, 'You could still have the baby adopted, you know.'

'Oh, Lou, what did it cost you to suggest that . . .? No, it's easier to give up Keir than the baby. Can you imagine how I'd feel if I gave up my only child for adoption, then Keir buggered off after six months?'

'So keep the baby but try to keep Keir as well! Talk to him. You can't possibly know what he wants now. The poor man almost *died*. God knows, that would change your outlook on life, surely?'

'No, Keir and death are old mates. He's spent all his working life dodging earthquakes, explosions, terrorists. Now he's just missed being blown up. *And* drowned.'

'Oh . . . I *see* why you won't tell him. Why you won't even give him a chance. You're afraid he'll die. *Really* die. You think if you allow yourself to love him, he'll go and die on you. Like Harvey.'

Marianne sits very still. She bows her head. 'Die. Or leave . . . I can't do it, Lou. I won't be that needy. That vulnerable. Never again. I've lost so much already. I can't cope with losing any more. And I can't cope with any more *uncertainty*. I don't know if my baby will be normal. I don't know if he'll survive. I don't even know if I'll love him! But I do know that I've got to be strong. I've got to feel certain I can cope. And I'm not certain of Keir. Just certain that I love him.'

'Oh, darling—are you?'

'Yes, I am now. Grief makes you honest. Keir being "dead" forced me to admit what I felt. Now he's alive again, I can't deny that, I can't just pretend. Not to myself anyway. Or to you.'

'But you'll deceive him?'

'Is it deceit? He didn't ask me if I loved him, just if I wanted to meet with him again. And I didn't. So I said no. And there's no going back. I told him there was someone else.'

'Oh, Marianne—you *didn't*!'

'And I don't have a number for him any more. His mobile was taken in Kazakhstan. I wouldn't let him give me his sister's number. And I still don't know her name or address. So you see, I've burned all my boats.'

'How could you *lie* to him? After all he's been through!'

'I didn't lie.'

'You told him you had a new man!'

'No, I didn't. I said there was somebody new in my life. And there is. My son. That's changed everything.'

'Oh, why do you have to be so bloody *heroic*?'

'This is cowardice, Lou, not courage! See me for what I am.'

'I do. And so does Keir. And *I* think he loves you.'

'Maybe . . . He'll get over it. And I'll get over him. But I don't think I'd get over him leaving. So it's just you and me now. And the baby. Honestly, it's better that way.'

Louisa strokes her sister's hair back from her face and kisses her on the cheek. 'You must do what feels right for you, darling. All I can say is, if Keir's so easily discouraged, he's not the man I take him for.'

'No, he'll be the man *I* take him for.'

'Well, we'll see, won't we?'

Louisa

I'm not one of life's pessimists and there was much to be thankful for. Keir was alive; Marianne was healthy and so, as far as we knew, was the baby; I was soon to become an aunt; I was Hollywood's darling; and I had the personal and professional support of Garth.

But I wanted more. For Marianne. I did understand her scruples. Her arguments were morally and intellectually unassailable, apart from one thing. Well, two things. She loved Keir. And—I was convinced of it—Keir loved her.

My heart bled for them both but I couldn't see any way round it, so I buried myself in glossy estate agents' brochures for country houses. I hadn't discussed the move with Garth but he must have known it was on the cards. The flat was overcrowded with the three of us and couldn't possibly accommodate a baby and all its paraphernalia. (He had never moved in and still maintained his tiny bedsit in a notorious part of

Edinburgh, made famous by the novels of Ian Rankin. An area nothing would induce me to visit after dark.)

Garth and I never discussed our relationship. I tried to once. He just laughed and said, 'If it ain't broke, don't fix it.' We enjoyed ourselves in bed and there was never a cross word between us, so I didn't ask myself Where All This Was Leading, until, that is, Marianne decided to keep the baby. As she said herself, that changed everything.

Garth must have thought so too. He asked me out to lunch and said he was buying. I knew this would mean Starbucks. As I felt in need of a quiet word with him, I suggested we go somewhere quieter, my treat. We'd ordered food and were settling into our gins when he announced, 'I'm chuckin' me PhD.'

'Oh, Garth! Why?'

'Lost interest. Seems pretty pointless, anyway. I don't want to become an academic an' what else could I 'ave done with it? Me supervisor's been on at me to come up with the goods an' I can't be arsed, frankly.'

'So do you have any alternative plans?'

'Well, I'm 'appy to continue workin' as your webmaster and researcher, if you want me to. But I've got meself a part-time job in Starbucks. As a barista. It'll pay me rent—well, nearly—an' give me lots of thinkin' time.'

The waiter brought our starters. I eyed the bread basket, decided to be strong and pushed it towards Garth, saying, 'Whatever you're paying for that dreadful room, it's daylight robbery.'

'Daylight robbery's the speciality of the neighbour'ood.'

'Seriously, Garth, I do wish you'd move. I dread opening the *Scotsman* one morning and reading about your violent demise.'

'Sweet of you to worry, but there's no need. Anyone can see I'm not worth muggin'.'

'But we *were* mugged! I still have nightmares about it. That's one of the reasons I want to move.'

'Another bein' the baby?'

'Yes. Marianne and I have to move to something bigger, obviously. And we want a garden. I'd like a *big* garden, in fact.'

'So you'd abandon Auld Reekie, then?'

'Yes. I'm not prepared to spend a million acquiring six bedrooms and a garden in Edinburgh, only to lie awake at night worrying about being burgled. I've always thought I needed the buzz of the city, but actually I think what I'd really like to do is become a *recluse*.'

Garth nodded sagely. 'You know, in terms of career development, that could be a smart move, especially if you're goin' to write a serious book.

There's a lot of distractions in the city. So where are you movin' to?'

'No idea. I'd thought of the west coast. It's mild and property is so much cheaper than Edinburgh. But now Keir's back on the scene—or rather, now he's *not*—I don't think that's an area Marianne will consider. Too close to Skye. But a milder climate does appeal. And somewhere safe to bring up a child. That's definitely a priority.'

'Well, I can still run your website from 'ere, obviously. You can go anywhere and still count on my services.'

I fixed him with a meaningful look. '*All* of them?'

He arched auburn brows and grinned again. 'Well, I dunno what me Starbucks shifts will be, but I must get some weekends off.'

'And would that be what you wanted?'

'Yeah, it would. If that suits you.'

'Yes, it does. Although,' I said, leaning forward, 'what I would actually *prefer* would be for you to move in with me and Marianne. I'd pay you a salary—a good one—for running my website, dealing with my correspondence and helping Marianne with the baby. She doesn't need a nanny really, she just needs another pair of hands. If she had you and me to help out, well, it would be more like a *family*.' Garth laid down his cutlery and went very silent. 'Don't misunderstand me, I'm not trying to set up anything permanent. You could leave whenever you wanted.'

'An' you'd want me to live in?'

'Yes. I'll still have to go away for work now and again and I'd feel happier if someone else was around for the baby. Preferably a car driver.' The waiter cleared away our plates and as soon as he was out of earshot, I continued, 'No hard feelings if you decide it's not for you, Garth. Or *I'm* not for you. I'm fifty-one, I've had a wonderful time with you and would love it to continue, but if I thought about the future—*your* future—I'd have to say, "Leave me, get a life, find a woman your own age."'

Garth took a sip of his mineral water, then looked me in the eye. 'You know, I don't 'ave a lot of time for the future. I mean, I could be dead next week. So could you. I'm 'appy just to take it one day at a time. So if it's all right with you—an' Marianne, of course—I think I'll tell Starbucks they need to find themselves another barista.'

I was so pleased I'd helped myself to a piece of bread and wolfed it down before I knew what I was doing.

As the waiter deposited our main courses, Garth said to him, 'Would you bring us a bottle of champagne, please? Your best.' He looked back at me and said, 'This is on me. I insist.' He sat back and beamed. 'I've always wanted to do that!'

The wine waiter brought champagne and filled our glasses. Garth raised his with a flourish and said, 'To Marianne and the baby!'

I raised mine. 'To pastures new! And a big house in the country. With an orchard. And a secret garden!'

'An' 'ere's to *us*.'

'Yes, here's to us. Thank you, Garth. For everything.'

CHAPTER NINE

Louisa

The summer wore on and wore Marianne out. She took fewer walks and slept more. She showed little animation except for matters concerning the baby. Her interest in house brochures was dutiful, though she seemed pleased Garth was to become part of the fixtures and fittings, and agreed it would be good to have a man about the house. She liked the idea of a garden but showed more interest in flowers and vegetables than trees. I couldn't engage her on the subject of planting orchards or woodland and it was Garth who guessed why. I hastily dropped the subject.

Marianne drifted around the flat in flowing cotton or linen gowns, silent, like a ghost. She was nearing the end of her middle trimester now and blooming. Her hair was thick and lustrous and her flawless skin now lightly tanned. In her straw hat and a pretty dress—full-length, gathered empire-line under her now opulent bust—she looked like something out of Jane Austen. I thought she looked quite, quite beautiful.

June became July, the month when Marianne paid her yearly visit to the Piper Alpha Memorial in Aberdeen. I thought she might give it a miss this year, what with the pregnancy, but no. So I booked bed and breakfast in the place we usually stayed and on the morning of July 6 I escorted her to Hazlehead Park, to the North Sea Rose Garden, where she would pay her respects to Harvey and his dead comrades.

Marianne and Louisa stop at the entrance to the Rose Garden and, as is their custom, Louisa reads aloud the words on the plaque that describe the memorial to be found in the centre of the garden.

Piper Alpha Memorial

This commemorates the 167 men killed in the prime of life, on July 6, 1988, at the occidental oil platform Piper Alpha, 120 miles offshore in the North Sea. Only 61 men were rescued from the platform.

On the south face of the memorial plinth above the Celtic Cross the names of the 30 men with no resting place onshore are inscribed. A casket of unknown ashes is interred behind the cross. On the east face of the plinth are inscribed the names of the 2 heroic crewmen of the Sandhaven who made the supreme sacrifice for their fellow men . . .

After a suitable pause Louisa says, 'Usual arrangements?'
'Yes. Come back in an hour and we'll go for coffee.'

Marianne

I have a set routine which I've followed since 1991, the year the Piper Alpha Memorial was unveiled. The North Sea Rose Garden is square and laid out in a grid pattern. It's quite straightforward to follow a broad brick path from the entrance up to the memorial in the centre. That is what I do, have always done and did that day. I approached the memorial with my hand extended and found the smooth granite face of the plinth on which 167 names are engraved. (The lettering is gold, apparently.) I know exactly where to find Harvey's name.

HARVEY FRASER, 33

I ran my fingertips over some of the other names, reading them. If I raise my arm above my head I can just reach the foot of one of the three figures representing oil workers. I wish, as I always do, that I could run my hands over the bronze figures to read them, to get a sense of what I'm told is a striking group. But I have to content myself with touching a booted toe. At that point, I think of Bill Barron, one of the survivors, who posed as a model for the sculptor and I wonder if, with the passing of the years, it gets easier or harder to live with the burden of having survived.

And at that moment I thought of Keir. I had tried to banish him from my mind but the baby chose that moment to do one of his slow cartwheels. I walked all the way round the four sides of the memorial and then headed back the way I'd come, pausing to smell some of the many roses in bloom. I ran my hand gently over the petals and felt some cascade through my fingers. Repeating the movement, I caught a handful, opened my handbag and withdrew an envelope, placing the petals inside, then putting it back in my bag. These would be dried and added to a new bowl of potpourri in my bedroom, a ritual I performed every year.

Moving onto the grass, I located a bench with my cane. To be certain I wasn't intruding, I said softly, 'Is this bench free?' There was no answer and so I sat down and collapsed my cane. I knew I was now facing the memorial. I hadn't heard anyone else enter the garden. I thought I was probably alone.

I laid my hand on my bump in a gesture that had become habitual. I used to think I did it to calm the baby. Now I realised I did it to calm myself. I never felt alone now. I was used to the baby's company, to the idea of a watcher within. So it was easy for me to distinguish that sensation from the one I was aware of now: being watched from *without*.

With sensory hindsight, I registered that I'd felt watched for some time but had dismissed it as Harvey's presence in the garden. Sentimental nonsense, as his body was never recovered. I sat still, straining every sense, but heard nothing. Telling myself I was being foolish and jumpy, I turned my face up to the sun and inhaled the scent of roses.

I must have been thinking about Keir. That's why I could smell hawthorn blossom. There can't have been any in the garden: hawthorn had finished flowering weeks ago. Dismissing this olfactory déjà vu, I tried also to dismiss thoughts of Keir. I'd come to this place to remember my dead husband, not a discarded lover. But when a robin started to sing, I was overwhelmed by a sense of loss so acute it was like a physical pain. I fought back tears and took a deep breath. Hawthorn blossom again . . . I stood up and snapped open my cane.

As I walked away from the bench, I knew with absolute certainty that the person who had been watching me was now at my back. I wheeled round, straining to hear any sound. There was none. Then a voice—*his* voice—said, 'Well, is it mine? Or Jimmy's?'

'Keir?'

'Aye.'

I thought if I didn't try to move, my legs would probably continue to support me. I said, with all the dignity I could muster, 'It's yours.'

'You're sure now?'

'Perfectly. You're the only man I've slept with in three years.'

'Poor old Jim. What's he doing wrong?'

'Why are you here?'

'I wanted to see you. And I knew you'd be here. Today of all days.'

'How long have you been here?'

'Since they opened the gates.'

'So you saw me arrive? You've been watching me all this time?'

'Not watching. Waiting. I wanted to give you time. I didn't want to

intrude. You came to pay your respects to Harvey . . . . Why didn't you tell me about the baby?'

'Because I was going to get rid of it. It was just a *mistake*. And I was convinced I would miscarry anyway. Or the tests would show it was abnormal and I'd have to terminate the pregnancy. So I didn't tell you.'

'You didn't think I had a right to know?'

'No, I didn't. Louisa did, but I didn't. I came to Skye the second time intending to tell you I was pregnant and that I was going to have a termination. But then you said you were off to Kazakhstan . . . And we agreed there were to be no strings . . . So I didn't mention it.'

'But you didn't terminate the pregnancy.'

'No. As you see . . . Would you mind if we sat down? This is proving to be rather a trying morning for me.'

I dreaded he would touch me, guide me back to the bench with his hand, but he didn't. I retraced my steps, found the bench with my cane and sat down at one end. Keir sat beside me, not touching, and I continued, 'I changed my mind. I couldn't bring myself to get rid of it. I decided, if I didn't miscarry, I would have the baby adopted.'

'And is that what you're going to do?'

'No. I'm keeping it now.'

'Why?'

'Because you died. You died, Keir, and I thought I was damned if I was going to lose you *and* your baby.'

'Is that why you didn't want to see me? Because of the baby?'

'Yes. And because we'd more or less agreed there was no future in our relationship. You said you didn't do the future.'

'I said that? *Shit* . . .'

'Oh, don't worry about it. I knew what you meant.'

'I'm sorry, Marianne.'

'Don't be. Louisa and Garth have been the most wonderful support. Lou is beside herself with excitement. Far more excited than me, in fact. I realise, now you know about the baby, you might want access of some kind. I'm sure we can come to some arrangement. But I don't expect—or *want*—any financial support from you. Do you think you might want access to the child?'

After a long moment's silence, Keir said, 'No, I don't want access.'

'That's fine. Much simpler all round.'

'I want to marry you. I want us to be a family.'

I felt as if I'd been struck. Gasping, I said, 'I *knew* you'd do that! That's why I didn't tell you!'

'What the hell are you talking about?'

'I knew you'd do the decent thing! Offer to marry me and give the baby a name—all that crappy romantic-hero stuff!'

'It's not crappy romantic-hero stuff, it's what I bloody *want*! Jesus, Marianne—I'm currently unemployed and my assets are negligible. D'you think I'd saddle myself with a blind wife—and for all I know a blind baby—if I wasn't heart and soul *in love* with you?'

'What?'

'You heard.'

The robin started to sing again, impossibly loud. Taking several deep breaths to calm myself, I said, 'The baby won't be blind.'

'How d'you know?'

'Well, I don't, not for certain. But it's extremely unlikely. You'd have to be a carrier for LCA and that's a one in two hundred chance. I assume there's no incidence of blindness in your family?'

'No. Rather the reverse.'

'Sorry. That was rather tactless of me.'

'Hell, I don't think we have too many behavioural precedents here.' I heard him get up off the bench and make some sort of movement I couldn't place. 'Marianne, will you please marry me?'

'Keir, are you kneeling down?'

'Aye.'

'Don't be ridiculous. Get up!'

'Will you marry me, Marianne, and let me be a father to our child?'

'No.'

'Why the hell not?'

'Because it would be a shotgun wedding! Because I'm blind and pregnant and you feel *obligated*.'

'I do not! I came here to ask you to marry me anyway. I didn't know you were pregnant. But I came to Hazlehead Park hoping you would be here. I wanted to ask you—beneath the memorial that commemorates your husband's death—if you would do me the honour of becoming my wife.'

'I don't believe you.'

'O ye of little faith! . . . Hold out your hand. Your left.' I extended my hand and felt him slide a ring onto my third finger. 'The stone's an opal. It matches your eyes. Cloudy blue with fiery depths. Sparks leap from it. It's beautiful. And it's yours to keep, whatever. But I was hoping you'd accept it as an engagement ring.'

I examined the ring with my fingers and exclaimed, 'It fits.'

'Aye. Louisa measured another ring of yours and told me the size.'

'So *Louisa* told you I was pregnant!'

'*No!* Christ! If Louisa had thought there was *any* chance I'd marry you, d'you think she'd have told me you were pregnant?' I heard him get up off the ground and the bench shuddered as he sat down again.

'But . . . you'll surely want to reconsider now. I mean, it's one thing taking on a blind wife—'

'Aye, and a crabbit one.'

'But to take on a baby as well—'

'This isn't just *any* baby. It's mine.'

'But where would we live? What would you *do?*'

'Details! Marry me.'

'You don't have to marry me. You can offer support without our being legally bound to each other.'

'Mrs Fraser, are you proposing we live in sin?'

'Yes, I suppose I was. Why, do you have a moral objection?'

I heard him whistle between his teeth. 'Och, I think my granny might have something to say about that. Especially if we did it on Skye. If word got round that Keir Harvey had a bidie-in, the shame of it would kill her. And that would be on my conscience.'

'You have a *granny?* On Skye?'

'Aye. She's a sprightly ninety-four. Sharp as a tack still.'

'You don't have to tell her you're living in sin.'

'She'd find out. She may be housebound but her spies are everywhere. There'd be hell to pay.'

'So we have to get married to appease your granny?'

'Aye, I think it best.'

There was a long silence during which I heard some people enter the garden. They spoke in hushed voices and walked along the brick path, towards the memorial. As their footsteps receded, I said to Keir, 'I'll marry you on one condition.'

'Which is?'

'That you get married in full Highland dress.'

'But you won't be able to see me!'

'No, but Louisa will. And she would just adore to see you in full Highland rig. So would Granny, I imagine.'

'So if I meet this *bizarre* condition, you'll marry me?'

'If you insist.'

'I do. I insist on kissing you too, if you think the ghost of Harvey wouldn't object.'

I raised my hand to his face and touched the bones I knew and loved.

'He might. But my priorities are the living now, not the dead.' I pulled his face down towards mine and kissed him. At length, resting my head on his chest, I said, 'I won't be able to do all the things that sighted mothers do. Once the baby's toddling about . . . well, there will be problems.'

'Aye, I know. That's why I reckon it has to be a team effort. May I lay a hand on the baby?'

'Of course.'

He rested his enormous hand on the bump and I felt the warmth of his skin. 'Has it moved yet?' he asked, sounding awestruck.

'Oh Lord, yes. It moves all the time . . . There! Did you feel that?' He didn't answer, but I heard him swallow and, as I leaned against him, felt his chest rise and fall once, in a great sigh. I laid my hand on top of his. 'There's one thing I *do* know about this baby.'

'Something bad?'

'No. Its gender. It's a boy, Keir. I'd decided to call him . . . James.'

He laughed then, loud and delighted, and I felt the baby kick again. I sat up and laid my fingers on Keir's lips. 'Are you *really* in love with me?'

'Aye.'

'You called me crabbit earlier.'

'Aye, and so you are! You could pick a fight in an empty room. You'll make the poor wee bairn's life a misery if I don't look out for it.'

'Him.'

'*Him* . . . James is a good name. My grandfather's name. Granny will approve.'

'Well, that's a load off my mind. Will she come to the wedding?'

'Not unless we have it on her doorstep.'

'Well, that would be quite appropriate. After all, we met on a doorstep. But even if we got married straight away, you'd still be for the high jump. She'd see I was six months gone.'

'We'll go and visit her seven months after the wedding and tell her you had an enormous premature baby.'

'Don't joke—with your genes, maybe I will.'

'Och, here comes my future sister-in-law. My, but *she* looks happy!'

'That makes two of us.'

'*Three* of us . . . No, make that four. Wee Jimmy. D'you not think he's pleased?'

'Oh, yes. He's turning cartwheels. *Feel* . . .'

Linda Gillard

Before reading *Star Gazing*, I'd never considered how to describe something to someone who has been blind since birth. Did you do a lot of research into blindness?
I must confess I didn't do a lot of research. I live on the Isle of Skye so my research options are a bit limited. I read a few books written by blind people and looked on the internet, but mostly I relied on my imagination. It was really just a question of removing the visual element from my thinking and allowing other senses to come to the fore.

And the idea of using music as a descriptive element?
I was led to music by my research. I'd read that some sighted people translate visual experiences for their blind relatives into things experienced by other senses. Marianne is blind but a music lover, and music gives her a 'window' onto the wider world. I think *Star Gazing* has changed the way I write, even the way I think. I've realised how limited we are by sight. Our culture is visually fixated, but we look without really seeing and we rarely bring our other senses fully into play.

If you had to describe yourself in music, how would you do it?

I have no hesitation in choosing the composer—Schubert. I see a lot of myself in the changing moods of Schubert's music.

Why did you decide to tell the story in two voices—Louisa's and Marianne's?

Marianne's voice is that of a blind woman, so there's no visual element at all. I realised that would be unusual and interesting for the reader, but it would also be a strain. A reader wants and needs visual description. If nothing else, they want to know what the hero looks like! So I split the narration between the two sisters—one sighted, one blind.

It's great to have heroines in their forties and fifties. Did you specifically want to write about this age group?

Oh, yes! This is a bit of a bee in my bonnet. I started writing fiction when chick-lit was in its heyday. I was in my forties and I just couldn't relate to it at all, all this obsessing about shoes, diets and getting a man. When I came to write my first novel, *Emotional Geology*, I made a point of making my heroine forty-seven—my age at the time—and I provided her with two drop-dead gorgeous heroes. Do you detect an element of wish-fulfilment fantasy here?

Garth the Goth? Where did he come from?

Yes, where *did* he come from? I think he owes a lot to my love of Charles Dickens. Garth was a joy. Sometimes you create a minor character, without thinking too much about it, then that character grabs hold of you and says, 'I want a bigger part in this book. I'm not a cameo, I'm a star.' And that was Garth.

Have you ever seen the Northern Lights?

No. They can be seen from Skye, but in seven years I've never caught them.

What prompted you to move to such an isolated location as Skye?

I had been very ill. Before I started writing fiction I was a primary-school teacher in Norfolk and I'd cracked up as a result of overwork, stress, and violent and abusive pupils—sadly, it's a common enough story in teaching nowadays. After I was punched by a pupil in a lesson, I went off sick and never returned to teaching. I became depressed and was eventually given a diagnosis of bipolar affective disorder—manic depression. I was put on medication and finally began to recover, although bipolar is for life. You can't ever cure it, but it can be managed. The diagnosis was a terrible shock and I had to reassess my entire life. I'd learned that what suited me best was a quiet, contemplative existence with a regular routine. I'd also found landscape to be soothing and restorative. So my husband and I decided to relocate to Skye, an island that is very beautiful, quiet and safe. There's little traffic and no crime to speak of—people don't even lock their doors! There's a downside though: it's very wet and we have terrible 80 to 100mph gales. It's quite unnerving to watch your windows bow or feel the house lean in the wind!

Jane Eastgate

After River

DONNA MILNER

I must have known.

In all these years no one has ever said it out loud. But I could see the unasked question in their eyes. How could I not have known?

Thirty-four years later, I still ask myself the same question . . . and it leads me back to the very beginning.

And to River.

CHAPTER ONE

HE CAME ON FOOT. Like a mirage, he rose in a shimmer of heat waves above the winding dirt road leading to our door. I watched him from the shadows of our enclosed porch.

I was fourteen on that hot July day in 1966, would be fifteen in less than a month. I leaned against the porch doorway and squinted into the sun. Outside, the week's laundry hung limp and motionless on the three clothes lines stretched across the yard. Mom stood out on the wooden laundry platform, her back to the road. She reached down and plucked a denim shirt from the wicker basket at her feet, snapped out the garment with a crack of wet fabric and pegged it to the line.

There was something different about my mother that day. On wash-days she usually wore a kerchief tied in a rolled knot in the middle of her forehead. That afternoon, bobby pins and combs held up her hair. Wayward blonde locks and wispy tendrils escaped around her face and at the nape of her neck. But it was more than that. I was certain she had applied a touch of Avon rouge to her cheeks.

Her attention was not on the road as she hung the last load, and I saw him before she did. I watched as he came round the bend by our bottom pasture. He carried a green duffle bag on one shoulder and a black object slung over the other. As he got closer I saw it was a guitar case bouncing against his back in the easy rhythm of his unhurried steps.

Hippie. It was a new word in my vocabulary. It meant oddly dressed young Americans marching beneath peace signs that urged, 'Make Love, Not War!' It meant Vietnam War protesters sticking flowers into the gun

barrels of riot police. And it meant draft-dodgers. Some of whom, it was rumoured, were entering Canada through the border crossing a mile and a half south of our farm. I'd never seen one in the flesh. Until now.

'What's wrong?' Mom's voice broke my trance. She stepped in from the laundry platform and handed me the empty basket. Before I could answer she turned to look down the road. As she did, our cow dog, Buddy, lifted his head, then bolted off the porch step where he had been sleeping. The border collie leapt over the picket fence and raced past the barn, a blur of black and white, barking a belated warning.

'Buddy!' Mom called after him. But by then the long-haired stranger was kneeling in the dust on the road, murmuring to the growling dog. After a moment he stood and, with Buddy at his side, continued up to the yard. He smiled at us from the other side of the fence as the border collie licked his hand. Mom smiled back, smoothed her damp apron and started down the porch steps. I hesitated for only a moment before I put down the laundry basket and followed. We met him at the gate.

She was expecting him.

She wasn't expecting the heartache that would follow like a cold wind.

I must have known. How could I not have known? Thirty-four years later, I still ask myself the same question.

Sometimes I catch myself falling back into memories. Back to the 'before' of my childhood. Before everything changed. Back to the time when my entire world was our family farm, four hundred acres carved out of a narrow valley deep in the Cascade Mountains of British Columbia. Everything else, the town of Atwood three miles north, and its 2,500 inhabitants, appeared to be only a backdrop to our perfect lives. Or so it seemed until I was almost fifteen years old.

That's when the 'after' memories begin.

Sometimes I can stop them, those 'after' memories. Sometimes I can go for weeks, months, even years, pretending none of it ever happened. Sometimes I even believe it.

Still, it's impossible to forget that summer day in 1966. The day that marks the time when my family was whole and good and right, to the time when nothing would ever be the same again.

The beginning of the sequence of events that would change all our lives wasn't catastrophic or earthshattering. Afterwards, Mom would blame everything that happened on the world encroaching upon our little farm. New highways were being built; one would connect our town to the Trans-Canada Highway. In the East Kootenays, valleys were

being flooded and dams constructed to carry electricity to a growing province.

'There's too many jobs available,' Mom had worried out loud during dinner the evening Jake, the hired hand who had been with us for as long as I could remember, left without warning. 'Who's going to be interested in working on a small dairy farm in the middle of nowhere?'

'We'll get along,' Dad said between mouthfuls. 'Morgan and Carl will take up the slack and Natalie can help in the dairy. We'll be fine.'

'No,' Mom said. 'You keep increasing the herd, and my boys keep quitting school. At least one of my sons is going to finish high school.' She didn't add, 'and go to college.' She never spoke this dream out loud any more. Carl was her last hope.

She hired the first and only person to call about her two-line ad in the *Atwood Weekly*. 'He has a nice voice,' she said after she announced it that July morning. She started to gather up the breakfast dishes. Then, as if it was an afterthought, she added, 'He's American.'

I glanced over at my father. His thick eyebrows lifted as he digested her words. I knew my parents held opposing views on the idea of young Americans fleeing the draft and seeking refuge in Canada. I wondered if, for the first time, I would see my parents have a real argument. Dad said nothing. Still, by the way he stood up and snatched his snap-brim fedora—his milk-delivering hat—from the peg by the door, then slammed it onto his head, I knew he was not pleased.

'Well,' Mom said after the kitchen door closed behind Dad and Carl, 'I think that went well, eh, Natalie?' Then her face turned serious as she said, 'I refuse to lose another son to this farm.'

From the moment they could carry a bucket, my three brothers were hostages to the milking schedule. Each morning they woke up in darkness and pulled on their overalls.

Boyer, the eldest, had a room—more of a cubbyhole—to himself in the attic. When he was twelve years old he got tired of sharing his bedroom with Morgan and Carl. So he made himself a nest among the rafters above the two upstairs bedrooms. The room was his sanctuary, and those of us privileged enough to be invited in, to share his company and the books that eventually filled every available space up there, envied the world he'd created under the eaves of the farmhouse built by my grandfather at the turn of the century.

I was the only girl and so had a bedroom to myself. It had been Boyer's room before I came along and threw out the sleeping arrangements. If he ever resented me for it, he never showed it.

Every morning Boyer was the first one to make his way down the stairs into the kitchen and onto the front porch where he pulled on knee-high rubber boots, winter or summer. And every morning, at exactly ten minutes before five, Boyer let the kitchen door slam behind him. His cue to let everyone know he was on his way to the barn. In the early darkness he and Jake, the hired man who lived above the dairy, herded the cows in from the pasture.

Morgan and Carl were never anxious to begin the day. Most mornings my father would holler up and threaten his youngest sons with ice water. Morgan was two years older than Carl, but from the time they were toddlers Carl towered over him. The two of them were best friends, inseparable. Once Morgan stumbled down the stairs wiping the sleep from his eyes, we knew Carl would not be far behind.

My brothers' morning parade was as regular and expected as my mother's prayers. Mom prayed at every occasion. When we were growing up she made sure we did too. At each meal we bowed our heads before a fork ever clicked against a plate. Every night after the milking, beads in hand, she gathered us all together in the parlour. 'Hail Mary, full of grace, the Lord is with thee.' She led the rosary while I knelt beside my brothers, trying not to fidget.

Mother grew up Protestant. When she and Dad married she converted. She embraced the Catholic faith with enthusiasm and promised her future children to the Church. But the truth is, except perhaps for Boyer at one time, none of us ever became as devout as she was. Even our father, who had been born Catholic, was not as pious. Every Sunday, before he started his deliveries, he dropped us off at St Anthony's. When his route was complete he picked us up. If the chores were finished at home, he headed back into town for a later Mass. Mom would return with him, attending twice on those Sundays.

She said nothing about his sporadic attendance. She knew the farm came first. Still, he joined us every evening for rosary in the parlour, and when my parents went to bed I often heard them murmur prayers in unison. I imagined them kneeling beside their four-poster bed like two picture-book children, hands folded in reverence, heads bowed.

Prayers were not all I heard. The open ceiling grates that allowed heat to rise to the second-storey hallway also allowed the noises of the night to drift up. Noises not meant for children's ears.

They must have realised to some extent that sounds carried upstairs, because my parents seldom had conversations in their bedroom. The only words I ever heard were the perfunctory, 'Good night, Gus,' and,

'Good night, Nettie,' after their prayers. Then I'd hear the slow groaning of springs as they climbed into bed. And sometimes the rhythmic creaks and muffled animal sounds, before the night filled with my father's throat-catching snores and my mother's quick sneezes.

It was not until years later, as I watched my mother hold herself together during the days following my father's death, that I realised my mother gave three stifled sneezes whenever she was holding back tears. I don't think my father ever realised it.

He seemed as oblivious to her nocturnal wanderings.

Often, deep in the night, I would wake to the protesting sound of bed-springs, then hear my mother's footsteps as she left their room. I never once heard my father get up to join her or ask her to come back to bed.

During the day it was a different story. My parents used any excuse to hold hands or put their arms round each other. At the kitchen table, my mother constantly touched Dad's shoulder or stroked his arm while they discussed the business of the farm. And whenever they were out-side together they walked hand in hand. Yet it seemed, when the day was done, as if all personal conversation was cut off at their bedroom door and they became intimate strangers. I cannot imagine the strange couplings, which must have taken place through layers of nightclothes, leading to my mother giving birth to four children by the time she was twenty-six years old.

Years later, after my father died, my mother told me—in an unusual late-night conversation brought on by grief and wine—that she'd never seen my father without his clothes on, and that he'd never seen her fully naked. From the way she said it I understood this was not her choice, but just the way things were with him. I imagined my mother, behind her wardrobe door, slipping out of her printed dress and pulling a floor-length cotton nightgown over her head. And in the other corner, I envisioned my father stripping down to his woollen under-wear. Long johns. He wore them like a second skin, winter and summer; the only time he was out of them was for his infrequent baths.

My father refused to take regular baths like the rest of us. He swore that every time he bathed he got a cold, or pneumonia. Every night after the evening milking we heard splashing behind the locked door as he sponge bathed at the bathroom sink. Once a month he risked death and disease and took his ritual bath. And sure enough, the next day he was coughing and swearing he would never climb back into the tub.

Dad said he didn't need baths; his long johns soaked up his sweat. He had three pairs, which he rotated throughout the week. Despite his

refusal to bathe, I never thought my father smelt any different from the rest of us. We all carried that same barn aroma of cow manure, sour milk, and hay. When other children held their noses in the schoolyard it never occurred to me that those odours were offensive to others.

But I couldn't help notice the odours on washday. Every Saturday morning my mother and I sorted the mountains of soiled clothes on the floor of the front porch. Every week two pairs of father's long johns ended up in a pile with my brothers' jockey shorts and T-shirts.

Mom once told me that it was interesting what you can tell about people's lives from their laundry. She knew my brothers' secrets from the state of their clothes and the contents of their pockets. Not that she ever used it against them. She adored her boys and was only surprised when she discovered some clue that betrayed they were human after all: the tobacco leaves in the lining of their pockets, broken matches and gopher tails. She read stains like a private diary.

I'm sure Mom read my laundry as easily as she read my brothers'.

She knew whenever I had been up in the hayloft in the summer. Our mother had a morbid fear of fire, so in the hot days of August, after all the hay was in, and the loft was full, we were forbidden to play up there. It was one of her few rules.

She knew it was me who had sneaked into the root cellar and polished off three jars of canned cherries when I was seven years old. And she knew when, at thirteen, I was about to start my monthly period. I paid no attention to the pink streaks in my cotton underpants. But she did. Before I knew I needed them, a large blue box and an elastic belt appeared on my bed one Saturday afternoon. When I realised what they were for, I thought she had read it in my tea leaves.

My mother read tea leaves for her women friends when they visited. Sometimes, when Dad and my brothers were off haying or cutting firewood, she would say, 'Come on, Nat, let's have a tea party.'

She would take out the good teacups, her mother's china, from the glass-fronted cabinet in the parlour. She'd set our teacups and cookies at the corner of the huge oak table and we 'girls' had our stolen afternoon while the 'men' worked. After I finished my cup of milked-down tea, she would have me flip the cup upside-down in the saucer and turn it three times. Then she'd read my future and my secrets in the leaves.

Years later, when I had a daughter of my own, I realised it was really the laundry she read. The laundry gave away all our secrets.

So, when I think of everything that happened after that summer day, I wonder, how could *she* not have known?

October 2003

My mother is dying. She's been threatening to die for the last five years. This time I think she means it. I hear it in Boyer's words: 'She's asking for you, Natalie.'

Still half asleep, I am unprepared for the quiet gentleness of my brother's voice. I can't remember the last time we spoke on the phone. An uncomfortable silence fills the line while I search for a reply.

That's how it is with Boyer and me. Our conversations are stilted. It's as if we fear any attempt to repair the damage; damage of wounds so old, scars so healed over, that to pick at them would be like taking a knife to new flesh. So, whenever Boyer and I find ourselves together during my visits to Atwood, we talk about the weather, the road conditions, my trip. Anything, except what stands between us.

'I think you'd better come,' he says now. It's the first time my brother has given me advice, or asked anything of me, in over thirty-four years.

'I'll be there tomorrow,' I say and we mumble our goodbyes.

After I hang up Vern rolls over and places his hand on my back.

'It's my mother,' I say into the darkness. 'I have to go to Atwood.'

'I'll drive you.' Vern turns on the lamp. That's my husband. No hesitation, no questions, just a direct route to fixing whatever needs fixing.

I turn to him and attempt a smile. 'No, that's OK,' I say, then throw back the covers. 'I can take the bus.'

The plane is not an option, and not only because of my irrational fear of flying. We live near the city of Prince George, in the centre of British Columbia. Atwood lies in the southernmost part of the province. There are no direct flights. With an overnight connection in Vancouver it takes two days to get there.

Vern sits back against the pillows as I get out of bed. I know what is coming. Although Vern and I have been together for almost ten years he has never been to Atwood. Never met my mother. Or Boyer.

'I want to go with you, Natalie,' he says. 'John or Ralph can take over the crew for a few days.' Vern has a tree-planting business. 'We can get there much quicker in the car,' he adds.

'No, really, it's better if I go alone.' I pull on my dressing gown. 'I don't know how long I'll stay. And I don't want to drive myself in case there's snow in the mountain passes. I don't mind the bus. It will give me time.'

Time? Time for what? For Mom to die?

With a sudden pang of guilt I wonder if I have deliberately waited too long. We each have our secrets and regrets, Mom and I. Is it too late for the confessions and questions that I have yearned to voice?

I pat Vern's shoulder. 'Go back to sleep,' I tell him. 'I'm going to go and check the Greyhound schedule.' As I reach up and turn out the lamp Vern's sigh is heavy with frustration, but he does not argue.

Moonlight spills through the windows in my home-office. I sit down at the computer without switching on the lights. The screen flicks on as soon as I touch the mouse and after years of making my living as a free-lance journalist, it moves like an extension of my body.

The Greyhound schedule flashes up. The next bus is at 6 a.m. With transfers the trip to Atwood takes fifteen hours. It seems all the roads of my life have led me further and further away from that remote West Kootenay town; as if distance alone is enough of an excuse not to visit, to stay away from my mother and brother. And now my daughter.

I glance down at my watch. Eleven-ten. Too late to call Jenny? No, like her grandmother, my daughter is a night owl. Her nocturnal wanderings are only one of the many inherited traits that bypassed me.

She looks nothing like me, this daughter of mine. She is her grandmother's child. The ash-streaked hair, the high, wide cheekbones, the robin's-egg blue eyes and the flawless skin that soaks up the sun so greedily, all have skipped a generation. At least with the women. Boyer inherited those same features: the eyes, the profile, the smile, all the same handsomeness that was—still is—so uniquely my mother.

I inherited my father's brown eyes and hair, his milk-white skin and blunt features. I look like what I have become, an outsider, a stranger.

I was named after my mother. Everyone calls her Nettie, but Mom's given name is Natalie Rose. Our first name is where the similarities end. I might have suspected I was adopted if I had not heard the story from Dad of how, while he was delivering milk on the day of my birth, my mother walked the three miles into town and up the hill to the hospital.

I was born on August 12, 1951. On the exact same day my grandmother, Amanda Margaret Ward, was born sixty-two years before. She had been the first baby delivered in St Helena's, the brick and stone hospital whose windows overlook the main street of Atwood. Her great-grandchild would be the last.

Tonight my mother lies in that same hospital, perhaps in the same room where I was born, and calls my name.

Nettie
She hears the baby crying. The insistent mewing of a newborn drifts through the darkness and calls her from her unquiet sleep. No, wait. That can't be right. The baby was stillborn. But he's crying. How can

that be? The child is dead. He has gone to Heaven. No. To Purgatory.

Now she knows where she is. With him. In limbo. For ever. She has condemned the unbaptised child to spend eternity in nothingness. She deserves to be here, but he doesn't. She must tell someone he's crying.

'Hush, Nettie,' a soft voice whispers, 'there are no babies on this ward any more.'

She feels a warm hand on her forehead, pushing back the strands of hair. She swims up, against the current of drugs flowing through her veins. She surfaces to meet familiar eyes looking down at her. Kind, caring eyes. They belong to Barbara Mann, the granddaughter of an old friend. Now she knows where she is. She's in the hospital.

Barbara is the night nurse. Nettie used to change her diapers.

The voice, the touch, pulls Nettie back, but the drugs are stronger. She fights to stay for a moment longer. She tries to clasp hold of the nurse's arm. She needs to tell her, to tell someone.

'It's all right, Nettie,' Barbara croons. 'Go back to sleep.'

And Nettie calls from a long spiralling tunnel, 'Natalie . . .' But it's too late. She slips through an invisible trap door.

Somewhere the baby cries again, but now Nettie is standing in her kitchen at the farm. This is real, she thinks, the rest was a dream.

Everything is so clear. She studies the green-speckled linoleum table-top. This table is solid, real, and as old as the farmhouse. She surveys the vegetables spread out on the tabletop. The aroma of rich, loamy soil still clings to the potatoes, carrots and beets. She must hurry to prepare them. There are mountains of meat to be chopped and ground, chickens to be plucked. She will never finish before everyone arrives.

Natalie's footsteps sound behind her. Her daughter is leaving. Nettie wants to turn and tell her not to go, but there's too much to be done. Her hands are busy. Chop, chop, chop. A pile of cubed meat rises in front of her. She hears the creak of the screen door. She grabs a handful of wet meat and tosses it into the grinder.

The kitchen door slams; still she does not turn. She wants to call out, but she needs to get this done. Footsteps sound, unhurried, hesitant, on the porch steps. Nettie counts each footfall, each step. On the fourth tread, her daughter stops and waits—waits to be called back. Nettie opens her mouth but no sound comes. She wants to call out. She wants to tell Natalie she heard the baby cry, but she cannot form the words. Too late. The last footstep echoes and disappears.

The tabletop swirls before her. She dives into the green linoleum sea. It swallows her up and she drowns in the darkness, the nothingness.

In the glow from the computer screen, I press the first speed dial on my phone: Jenny's home number.

'Hello?' Nick's voice answers after one ring.

'Hello, Nick. I hope it's not too late to call.'

'No, of course not,' he assures me, then asks, 'How are you?'

We chat for a few moments, the small talk that is expected. Nick Mumford, my son-in-law of three years, whose grandfather was our family doctor when I was growing up, is one of life's little twists that show up with an ironic sense of inevitability. Just like the fact that Jenny chose to do her medical internship at St Helena's Hospital in Atwood. The moment she told me she was dating old Dr Allen Mumford's grandson, I knew she would end up with him. And I knew she would end up staying in the town I have spent most of my adult life avoiding.

'Here's Jenny.'

'Hi, Mom. How are you doing?' At the sound of my daughter's voice I am overwhelmed by how much I miss her.

'I'm fine. I just talked to Boyer.'

'Yes, I know. I saw him at the hospital earlier. I asked him to call you.'

I'm not surprised. When it comes to her uncle and me, she uses every excuse to force us to talk to each other.

'Jen, how is she really? I mean, how long—?'

'It's hard to tell,' she says. 'She's weak, but she could still rally or, well, we just don't know. Don't wait too long, Mom.'

'I'm taking the six a.m. bus,' I tell her. 'It should arrive at the junction at nine tomorrow night. Can you pick me up?'

The turnoff from the Trans-Canada Highway is thirty miles north of Atwood. The bus will only stop on that lonely piece of highway if someone is waiting for connecting passengers.

'Of course I'll be there,' Jenny says. 'We can stop in at the hospital and see Gram on the way home.'

'Good,' I say, then hesitate. 'I'm going to stay at the Alpine Inn though.'

'Why?' she asks. 'We have lots of room in our new house, Mom. You haven't even seen it yet.'

'I know, and I will. I will. It's just that I can walk next door to the hospital from the bed-and-breakfast.'

'You can use one of our cars while you're here.' When I don't reply right away she adds with an impatient sigh, 'You can't even see the farm from where we've built our house.'

I know. I know exactly where her new house is.

'Please, Jenny. I want to stay in town. Just pick me up, OK?'

'All right,' she says with resignation. 'We can argue about it on the drive into town.' There's a moment's silence on the line before she adds, 'There's something else I need to talk to you about, Mom.'

My empty stomach lurches. I manage to keep my voice even as I ask, 'What is it?'

'Not on the phone.'

Back in bed I am unable to sleep. I am tempted to get up and read to pass the night away. *God, I'm finally turning into my mother.*

Beside me Vern's even breathing fills the quiet while I fight the images of my estranged family.

It wasn't always this way. There was a time when I couldn't imagine my family wouldn't always be together. There was a time when all I wanted was to be with my oldest brother, Boyer, whom I idolised during my childhood. Back then, my favourite part of the day was sitting in his room playing 'penny words'—a spelling game Boyer had taught me as soon as I was old enough to talk. And in the evening lying in bed listening to my mother playing my favourite song, 'Love Me Tender', on the piano downstairs in the parlour.

The alarm rings. As if he has been waiting for it, Vern sits up. He pulls back the covers and swings his legs over the side of the bed with slow, deliberate movements. I know he thinks I'm still asleep.

'There's a bus at six,' I say as I climb out of bed. I explain the schedule as I follow him into the bathroom. He offers once again to drive me.

'I want to be there for you, Natalie,' Vern says. 'I'd like to meet your mother before she—' He bites off the word before it escapes from his mouth. 'While I still have the chance.'

I stiffen. 'There's lots of time, I'm sure. I'll call you when I get there. When I know more.'

Vern raises his eyebrows. 'Promise?'

'Promise.'

'Stubborn,' he mutters. But his eyes smile back at me.

I study him in the mirror while I brush my teeth.

We've been together for almost ten years now, married for seven of those years. He was the one who pushed for marriage. I resisted. Given my track record, I warned him, I wasn't a very good bet. 'If you don't get married, you don't get divorced,' I told him.

After two failed marriages I wasn't anxious to try a third.

'You just hadn't met the right one until now,' Vern insisted. Eventually he wore me down.

We met while I was living in Vancouver. Early one rainy morning we ran into each other on the Stanley Park sea wall. Literally. We were both about to pass slower joggers from opposite directions when Vern's elbow clipped mine and sent me sprawling. After that we began greeting each other on our morning runs. Before long we fell into a routine of running together. That led to after-run coffees at Starbucks and then to dating. Besides running, we found we shared a passion for reading, sushi and oldies music. Before long he infected me with his passion for fly-fishing.

Vern was a widower. He had sold his logging company on Vancouver Island to move closer to the clinic where his wife eventually lost her battle with breast cancer. Afterwards he remained in Vancouver.

When we first met he was in the throes of starting his tree-planting, contracting and consulting company.

'It's karma,' he joked. 'From forest-destroyer to forest-restorer.'

Now as I watch him brush his teeth, I am still taken by how handsome he is. Vern is five foot ten, not much taller than I am, perhaps three inches at the most. At fifty-five he still wears jeans without embarrassment, although lately I have begun to notice a thickening around the waist. His olive skin, thick dark hair and black-brown eyes hint of First Nations ancestry somewhere back down the line.

He leans over the sink to spit. As he straightens up he catches me studying him in the mirror. 'What?'

I open my mouth, a word or two away from giving into the temptation to accept his offer. But I have never burdened him with my past. It's too late to start now.

I reach up and stroke his cheek. 'Nothing,' I say, then turn away to switch on the walk-in closet light.

As I rummage through my underwear drawer I am suddenly startled by the thought of what to wear to a funeral. My mother's funeral. Vern's unspoken thought is more reality than probability.

The idea of attending a ceremony in St Anthony's Church, of sitting in the front pew while a priest chants the ceremony and speaks of my mother's life, is almost too much. I stand in the middle of my closet and hold my breath to stifle the sneeze I feel building between my eyes.

At the downtown bus depot, Vern unloads my suitcase from the back of his pick-up truck while I go inside to the counter to buy my ticket. By the time I rejoin him outside he has placed my suitcase in front of the only occupied bus stall. A young couple stands nearby, huddled in the cold, saying their goodbyes.

'I want to be there for you,' Vern says again. He searches my eyes. 'At least promise me you will let me come down and get you.'

I slip the return ticket into my pocket as he takes me into his arms.

'I feel like I'm losing you,' he murmurs into my hair.

'I'm just anxious to get going,' I say and start to pull away.

'Not just this morning,' he says. 'Lately I feel like you're getting ready to bolt.' He releases me, then steps back with a smile. He holds his arms out in a gesture of surrender. He won't keep me against my will, I know, but he'll do his best to interrupt this dance of leaving.

That is Vern. His strength is what has kept me with him this long, his strength in being able to let go. But he's right. It's just a matter of time. This is what I do. I run. I leave. He's the first man to recognise this. And he's the first one who will not be surprised when I go.

The bus driver strides out from wherever it is bus drivers hide at these stops. He pushes the sliding luggage-compartment doors and begins to throw bags into the belly of the bus.

Behind me the bus doors fold open and I put my arms round Vern for a final hug. He hangs on for a moment after I let go.

A part of me wants to tell him I'll call for him when the time comes. That I will cry on his shoulder. But we both know it wouldn't be true. Besides, he only knows my mother from what I have told him. And she doesn't know him at all. My mother gave up on the men in my life after my second husband. And for the last five years she's been too busy dying.

I place my hand on the window in a silent wave to Vern as the bus backs away from the Greyhound station. He stands motionless beneath the neon sign, his shoulders hunched in his jacket, his hands thrust into his jeans pockets. As his figure recedes into the morning mist I think about long-ago summer mornings when I stood watching a bus pull away with my daughter on board. And I remember feeling that same sense of sadness and panic I now read on Vern's face.

When Jenny was ten years old I gave in to my mother's pleas to let her spend part of her summers at the farm. I couldn't deny my daughter the chance to know her family. They were all she had besides me. Jenny's father died when she was seven. He had no family to offer her. Her uncles, Morgan and Carl, both live on the Queen Charlotte Islands, off the West Coast. Jenny has seen them only sporadically over the years. For the most part, while Jenny was growing up, I was the only real family she had. I was not enough.

While I continued to find excuses not to return to Atwood, Jenny

became my surrogate. The buffer between me, and Mom and Boyer. And every summer, after I put her on the bus, I began to worry that while she was there she would hear the old gossip. When she returned at the end of each visit I listened carefully and watched for any hint of a change in how she saw me; any sign of disappointment at finding out I wasn't who she thought I was.

The Greyhound bus pulls onto the highway, and just like every time I return to Atwood, I fight the panic I feel rising in my chest. I've only been back twice since Jenny settled there. Both times I stole into town like a thief and stayed cooped up in her rented house by the hospital. Each afternoon Jenny brought Mom over to visit—as if I was the one who was the invalid. I ventured outside only for my daily runs.

I lean back in my seat and close my eyes. Jenny's words haunt me. What is it that she needs to talk to me about? If it isn't about Mom, then is this, finally, the conversation I've been avoiding?

I knew someday I would have to fill in the blanks for her—the circumstances that created this fractured family of ours. But the years passed and she has never asked. Maybe the time has come to tell her the truths, the secrets, as I know them, or have imagined them. All of it. The forgivable and the unforgivable.

The shattering of our family did not occur gradually. There was no drawn-out series of events that could be pointed to and blamed. It came suddenly. The irreversible tragedy of errors was accomplished in the course of a few long-ago summer days. It left everyone in our family with their own secret version of what happened. And gave them the rest of their lives to come to terms with it.

On that July afternoon I watched Mom unlatch the gate. For a moment I wondered if she knew when she hired him that the young man who stood on the other side of the fence was one of those 'long-haired freaks', as my father called them. I wasn't sure if I wanted to be around when Dad, and my brothers, came back with the next load of hay.

He was dressed like no one I knew. Instead of the denim or plaid snap-button shirts my father and brothers wore, a beige Indian cotton tunic hung loose over dark bell-bottom trousers. Instead of cowboy boots, he wore leather moccasins. A carved wood emblem, a peace sign, dangled from a leather cord round his neck. His hair, the sun-streaked yellow of a hayfield drying in the sun, hung loose around his shoulders.

But it was his eyes that held me. His eyes were the colour of a blue-green ocean, an ocean I had seen only in my imagination. When he

blinked, they closed and opened slowly, almost as if the thick, dark eye-lashes were too heavy for his lids. I later heard Mom describe those eyes, saying he had lashes that 'most women would kill for'.

The stranger smiled as Mom opened the gate. He set his guitar case and bag down, then held his hand out. 'Good afternoon, ma'am,' he said, the 'a' in ma'am stretching out with a hint of a drawl.

'Nettie.' Mom smiled and took his hand. 'You can call me Nettie.'

'Nettie,' he repeated. Her name slipped from his lips and into the air between us. It came as so much more than a word. It came soft and warm, a musical note.

'And you must be Richard Jordan,' Mom said, her hand still resting in his.

'River,' he said. 'My friends call me River.'

Listening to his voice, I knew. I knew right then why my mother had hired him sight unseen. His voice was his recommendation. His voice was hypnotic, mesmerising, as soothing as a familiar melody.

'River,' Mom repeated. 'I'm happy to meet you.' She let go of his hand then turned to me. 'And this is my daughter, Nat.'

'Natalie,' I corrected her. I wanted to hear him say my whole name. I wanted to hear it slide from his tongue and caress my ear the way my mother's name had. I wanted to take it in and keep it in my memory.

He held out his hand. 'Well, it's a pleasure to meet you, Natalie,' he said. And my name fell flat into the still air, thudded and was gone. No magic, no music, just three flat syllables. Nothing more.

He captured my hand in a firm grasp, where it went limp from the heat of this stranger's skin. I stood there frozen, tongue-tied, suddenly feeling conscious of my childish ponytail, my jeans and loose T-shirt, and my tomboyish looks, of which up until that moment I had been proud. I jerked my hand away and held it behind my back.

My mother hurried to fill the silence. 'Well, now,' she said. 'Well, River, come with me and I'll show you your room above the dairy. You can get settled, put your things away, then come back to the house for something to eat.' Mom's sure-fire solution to everything: fill their bellies and get to know them while they're off guard.

River picked up his bags and they headed to the dairy. Buddy followed at their heels, his tail wagging. As they passed the rose arbour I heard River say, 'That's a beautiful garden you have there, ma'am.'

'Thank you.'

'Did you know that Jacqueline Kennedy had a rose garden when she was in the White House?'

'I'll bet she never had to prune it,' my mother replied with a laugh.

Pruning that garden was always an ordeal for Mom. Once a week, from spring to fall, she put on Dad's oilskin jacket, leather gloves and rubber boots. Then she attacked those rosebushes with the vengeance of a warrior. Still, the angry thorns found their way through her armour, leaving tiny streaks of blood on her delicate skin.

That afternoon I watched as my mother and the stranger strolled past the rose garden. I stood by the gate feeling excluded.

As they made their way across the farmyard, something about these two together looked familiar. And then I realised that, from behind, River resembled Boyer. The hair colour, the carriage, seemed similar to my brother's. Boyer in hippie clothes. The thought made me smile.

Walking along beside River, Mom looked like a young girl, her hips swaying with a lilt I had never noticed before. For the first time in my life, I resented my inheritance of my father's frame and blunt features. For the first time I felt something for my mother other than adoration.

CHAPTER TWO

'WE WEREN'T POOR,' my mother often said about that time in our lives, 'we just didn't have any money.'

Whenever we seemed to get a little ahead, according to her, my father went out and bought more cows or equipment. Still, the only thing I remember her complaining about back then was the lack of a 'decent family photograph'.

I keep the results of my father's giving in to her lamentations in an old shoebox along with the stray snapshots that I keep promising myself I will someday put into an album.

The family portrait was taken back in the sixties, by a travelling photographer. Every September or October, a large blue van, a mobile studio, showed up in the empty lot next to the Texaco station on Main Street. It drove Jeffrey Mann, the local photographer, crazy, to see people line up outside that van.

One fall afternoon in 1965, the year before River arrived, my father

returned from town and handed Mom a flier. 'What d'ya think, Nettie?'

Mom took the glossy pamphlet and studied the prices. 'Not bad,' she mused. 'They even have Christmas cards in these packages,' she added wistfully. 'But I just don't feel right taking business away from Jeffrey.'

'It wouldn't be like we were taking business from him if we can't afford it in the first place,' my father said. I watched my mother struggle with the temptation of finally having a family portrait done.

Two days later, under the cover of darkness, we stood outside the parked van, waiting our turn to sit in front of the blue-sky and fluffy-cloud backdrop. Everyone was dressed in their Sunday best but anyone looking at the finished portrait would smile at the hodgepodge of bodies that made up our family. Mom and I sat on a bench, with Dad and the three boys standing behind us. Boyer was twenty-two when the picture was taken. With his blond hair and blue eyes he was the only one of us who truly resembled Mom. Except for his height. He was six foot tall—two inches taller than Dad, who stood on his right.

Dad was bluntly handsome. Like a rugged John Wayne, his looks only improved with age and the inevitable map of laugh lines marking time on his sun-scorched skin. Morgan and I inherited his dark eyes and brown hair—'mouse-turd brown', my father called it.

Morgan stood on the other side of Dad with the same laughing eyes, widow's peak and strong jaw. But, unlike Dad, he was short and stocky. At seventeen Morgan was only five foot six. He would grow no taller. Carl was fifteen years old, all hands and feet that he had not finished growing into. As usual, he stood beside Morgan, dwarfing his older brother. Carl was the anomaly, with his red hair and freckled skin, a throwback, Dad often teased him and Mom, to some married cousins on Mom's side.

How easily we all smiled for the camera. The smiles of a family who—though they knew no excess of money—were aware their lives were as rich and sweet as Mom's freshly churned butter. I wonder if any of us has ever smiled that openly since? Even Mom, who was camera-shy, smiled with a pride barely held in check.

At fourteen, I was already two inches taller and probably fifteen pounds heavier than she was. Mom was five foot two—tiny, but not delicate. It was as if her small-boned body was made of steel. Gracefully strong is the only way I can describe her. She looked like good music should sound. Back then I'm sure I looked and moved like the prover-bial ugly duckling, waddling under her mother's beautiful wing.

I wasn't very old when I became aware of the fact I would never be beautiful, never turn heads the way my mother did. It wasn't until

midway through my teenage years that I began to covet my mother's beauty. Not until after River. Up until that time I lived in the glow of her beauty. Even when others carelessly pointed out the difference.

The first time I overheard one of those thoughtless remarks I was seven years old. That winter I was chosen to recite a ballad at our school Christmas pageant. The poem about our town's founding father, Daniel Atwood, was written by none other than my hero, Boyer Angus Ward. He coached me every evening for weeks before the concert.

The first time I read the ballad I was sitting in Boyer's narrow attic room. 'Won't this make Mr Atwood angry?' I asked.

'Don't worry.' Boyer smiled at me from across his desk. 'This is about the first Mr Atwood, old Daniel. Stanley Senior is his son and he's nothing like his father. Stanley could be called a philanthropist.'

'Philanthropist?'

'There's your ten-penny word for the week,' Boyer said and handed me his *Webster's Dictionary*.

The next day I took the ballad to school as my project for the concert rehearsal. When the teacher asked who had written it, I kept my promise to Boyer. I was pretty proud of that word too. Anonymous.

Boyer and I rehearsed the verses so many times that I could repeat them in my sleep. I still can. I know that the composition penned by a fifteen-year-old boy was not literary genius, but it was to me then and I felt a responsibility to do my brother's words proud. The night of the concert I stood on the stage in Atwood Elementary and swallowed.

Mom sat in the front row beaming at me as I waited to start. Beside her, my father winked and flashed me his white-toothed grin. Morgan and Carl sat in the back row making monkey faces. I focused on Boyer's encouraging smile and began:

> 'Oh, there are tales they tell at the Atwood Hotel,
> Between the card games and the chewing of snoose.
> And the stories go 'round, how gold was first found,
> By Daniel Atwood, the Old Bull Moose.'

I threw the words out into the air, directly to Boyer, just the way he had taught me in his room. He nodded at each one as if he had caught it. When I was finished I couldn't tell if the laughter that rippled beneath the applause was at the words, or me, but Boyer's smile was enough.

After the concert I followed the flow to the back of the now brightly lit room where parents, teachers and performers milled among tables laden with cookies, cakes and cups of punch. As I grabbed a paper

plate I glanced up and saw Boyer at the back of the room by the exit doors talking to Mr Atwood and an auburn-haired boy about Boyer's age whom I had never seen before. As I wove my way through the crowd towards them I heard my name. I peered over the heads of my classmates and spotted Mrs Royce, the wife of the pharmacist, talking to our neighbours, Ma Cooper and Widow Beckett.

'Yes, that's right,' Ma Cooper said. 'That was Nettie Ward's daughter.' She was a huge woman, Ma was. The only dainty things about her were her tiny hands and feet. I always thought her feet looked too small to carry her enormous bulk, but every Monday she and Widow Beckett walked two miles out to our house.

They looked like female versions of Laurel and Hardy as they came up our road, Ma rolling along in her rocking gait while the willowy thin Widow hurried along beside her taking two steps to each single stride of Ma's. These two were fixtures in our kitchen each Monday. As members of the Catholic Ladies Auxiliary, every week they pressed and mended uniforms for the girls of Our Lady of Compassion.

Although the sign over the oak gates leading to the building next to St Helena's Hospital read SCHOOL FOR GIRLS, everyone knew it was really a home for unwed mothers, run by the Catholic Church.

There wasn't much going on in town that Ma didn't seem to know about. And she brought all the local news into our kitchen each week. My father called the Monday ladies the 'steam team' because, as he said, 'There's a lot more steamy gossip going on in that kitchen than ironing.'

Widow Beckett usually said very little, letting Ma Cooper keep her position as the authority on local goings-on. The Widow was never far from her friend though, and could be counted on to agree and encourage her. And sure enough, after the Christmas recital, there she was, standing next to Ma Cooper, nodding at her friend's words.

'Nettie Ward's daughter? Really?' Mrs Royce replied to Ma Cooper. 'My, she certainly doesn't look anything like her mother, does she?'

Widow Beckett responded with a silent tsk-tsk shake of her head. I moved closer to them as Ma Cooper leaned in, and in a voice that was meant to be a whisper, but was not anywhere near to it, said, 'Homely as a mud fence, that one.' Then she straightened up and added with a note of pride in her voice, 'But her teacher says she is brilliant.'

Thanks to Boyer, and his penny words, at seven I already had a large vocabulary. I knew the meaning of lots of words, but 'homely' was not one I had come across. I made my way to the back doors, but Boyer was gone. Suddenly Mom was beside me. 'What is it, Nat?' she asked.

'I'm just looking for Boyer,' I told her. Normally I would have asked Boyer about a new word, hoping it was a ten-penny one, but something told me that this wimpy-sounding word had little value. So I asked Mom. 'What does homely mean?'

'Where did you hear that?' she asked, frowning.

I told her what Ma Cooper had said. My mother's eyes narrowed for a brief moment, then she smiled and touched my face. 'Well, it could mean many things, honey. My guess is that it means you're good around the house. She knows what a help you are to me.'

I wondered for a moment what that had to do with a mud fence, then decided that this was probably one of those Santa Claus fibs. So I chose to believe her. Later I could look it up in Boyer's dictionary.

Before we left, Mom walked over to Ma Cooper and Widow Beckett. The smile never left Mom's face as she spoke, but Ma's smile melted down. I could not make out Mom's words, so I went and stood beside her in time to hear Widow Beckett say, 'But Nettie, we only meant it in the kindest of ways.'

'There is nothing kind about insinuating,' my mother started, enunciating each word in a voice so brittle, so unlike her, that I grabbed her hand. She stopped and looked down at me, clamped her mouth shut, and squeezed my hand. She then nodded to her friends, spun round and marched away straight-backed with me in tow.

For the next few weeks my mother did the Monday ironing by herself. 'Where's the steam team?' my father asked at lunch on the first Monday Ma Cooper and Widow Beckett were absent.

'I told them not to come,' Mom said. 'They needed a break.'

A few weeks later, on Christmas Eve, they showed up at our door just as all my parents' friends and neighbours did each year. They stood on the porch stamping snow from their boots and looking sheepish. As my mother ushered them in, hugged them, and wished them Merry Christmas, I swear that I saw stern old Ma Cooper blink back tears. Widow Beckett's voice caught as she said, 'We're so sorry, Nettie.'

Mom shushed her and said, 'That's forgotten.' And she meant it. 'Forgive and forget,' that was Mom's credo in life.

'It's OK if you bruise easy,' she told me. 'As long as you heal quick.'

Things went back to normal after that. Monday's ironing and gossip days continued and the incident was never spoken about again. But every time I ran into Ma Cooper, she found some reason to throw a compliment at me, while Widow Beckett nodded agreement. Most of

her compliments revolved around the other thing I heard her say about me that night, which was that I was brilliant. That was a word I knew. The only other person who ever called me brilliant back then was Boyer. From the time I could hold a book my brother was my mentor. But I was not brilliant. I had a good memory. That's all. I could memorise anything: facts, numbers, names, words and nursery rhymes.

Still, it was not brilliance. It was Boyer who was brilliant; Boyer who had the analytical mind that craved knowledge. Mom told me once that after Boyer's first day of school he raced into the house and announced he was going to be a teacher when he grew up.

'A teacher?' Dad had laughed. 'You don't need to be a teacher. We're farmers.'

'Boyer's face fell,' Mom said. '"Can't I be both?" he asked. When your father didn't answer I told him, '"Of course."'

So Boyer began to bring his books home from school every night to practice teaching on Morgan and Carl on the wooden apple crates he hauled up to their shared bedroom.

Not long after, when I was old enough to join Boyer's makeshift classroom, Morgan and Carl started school and lost interest. I never did.

Do all little girls think they will marry their older brothers when they grow up? I did. Up until I was six years old I assumed it was the natural order of things. It was not until a week before I started school that Morgan and Carl put an abrupt end to that childish notion.

Boyer was an altar boy for a number of years. When he was thirteen he began spending time in discussions with our parish priest, Father Mackenzie. They met each week, either at St Anthony's or at our house.

Everyone in our town knew and loved Father Mac: Catholics and Protestants alike. He could often be found sharing a shot or two of Captain Morgan's rum with the locals in the Atwood Hotel. Mom said sometimes she believed he heard as many confessions from his barstool—where he had patience for even the most inebriated souls— as he did in the confessional. But the most trying test of his patience he would joke was his friend and bridge partner, Dr Allen Mumford.

Dr Mumford, the town doctor and a self-proclaimed agnostic, was the polar opposite of the priest. He was a loud, outspoken and opinionated man who fought with his bridge partners. Finally, it was only Father Mac who had the patience to be his partner.

One evening a month, Mom and Dad went into town to play bridge with them. And on many Sundays Father Mac joined us for dinner.

He had no shortage of dinner invitations. Yet, it was our table the priest

chose most often to grace. 'It's my roast beef and Yorkshire pudding,' Mom told anyone who questioned his preference. Dad said it was really because they always watched the priest's favourite television show, *Bonanza*, after the milking on Sunday nights.

One Sunday evening, just before I turned six, I stood anxiously in the sunroom doorway, hoping to catch a glimpse of Boyer and Father Mac returning from a walk. Behind me Mom, Dad, Morgan and Carl settled themselves in front of the television. Suddenly I heard Morgan ask, 'Mom, is Boyer gonna become a priest?'

A priest? Boyer a priest? I knew very little about priests, but I did know they lived alone and had no family.

Before Mom could answer, I spun round and blurted, 'Boyer can't be a priest, he's going to marry me.'

Morgan threw himself against the back of the couch and screeched, 'Dummy, you can't marry your brother!' He jabbed Carl in the ribs. Carl rolled on the couch, holding his side. 'What a dummy!' he hooted.

Mom leaned forward in her recliner. 'Boys,' she said and shook her head at them. I couldn't read the expression on her face as she chastised Morgan and Carl. Beside her, Dad sat in his recliner, a stream of blue smoke rising from the cigarette hanging from his lips, staring straight ahead at the television, as if the conversation and all the commotion my brothers were making was not happening.

Panicked, I ran to my mother. 'Is it true?' I demanded.

'Well, Boyer is talking to Father Mackenzie about many things,' she said. 'But the decision about entering the priesthood is a long way off.' She smiled and pulled me onto her lap. 'And yes, it's true that brothers and sisters don't get married. But no matter what, Boyer will always be your brother. He'll always be family, and always love you.'

Except for that conversation, the subject of his becoming a priest was never openly discussed in our family. I said nothing to Boyer. I guess I was afraid he would tell me it was true.

Then one afternoon in the spring of my first school year, I sat on the steps to Boyer's room while I waited for Father Mac to leave. The murmur of their voices leaked down into the hall. I caught the odd word like 'commitment', and 'calling'. After a while I heard Father Mac ask Boyer a question. I could not make all of it out, but heard the last few words, '... as an excuse to avoid the real world?' Then Boyer's door opened. Before the priest came down the stairs he said, 'You will have to wrestle with those feelings yourself, my son. But not in the seminary.' His voice was kind, but I heard finality in his words.

At dinner a few weeks later Morgan asked where the priest was these days. Boyer quietly announced he would no longer be an altar boy.

My father could barely disguise the smile that came to his lips. It was harder to read my mother. I wasn't sure if it was sadness or relief I saw in her eyes as she nodded silently at Boyer, then rose and busied herself.

'Does that mean you're not gonna be a priest?' Morgan asked.

'No, Morgan,' Boyer said not unkindly, 'I am not "gonna" be a priest.'

'Guess that means you can marry Natalie now, eh?' Carl chimed in, then poked Morgan in the ribs.

'Good one,' Morgan laughed and pushed him back.

I didn't care about their teasing. I was just relieved to hear Boyer wasn't going away. That everything would stay the same. I stuck my tongue out at my brothers across the table as Boyer ruffled my hair and said, 'Natalie will always be my girl.'

Even after I entered grade one, I continued to go up to Boyer's new room in the attic, to read and play his penny word games. The game started out with spelling simple words for a penny. At some point, Boyer added ten-penny words, difficult and unusual words, words I not only had to spell but define as well. Over the years it remained a challenge for both of us to find words that the other did not know.

During my childhood I spent most evenings at his homemade desk. With dictionaries open beneath the glow of the lamp he taught me the power of words while the rest of the family sat two storeys below in front of the television.

Thanks to Boyer, I learned to read long before I received my first yellow copy of *Dick and Jane*. Unfortunately I thought everyone else should be able to as well. One of my earliest memories is of my grade one teacher, Mrs Hammet, asking Bonnie King to read.

Bonnie stood up beside her desk. She stared intently at her open book before she finally stuttered, 'S— s— see, S— Sa—Sally—'

Elizabeth-Ann Ryan sat at the desk in front of me. I admired her and I wanted to impress her. I leaned forward to whisper, 'Isn't she stupid!'

Mrs Hammet turned to me. 'Natalie Marie Ward, stand up!'

I thought she was going to ask me to read, to show Bonnie how words were supposed to sound. I picked up my book and stood.

'Now, Natalie, tell us what you just said to Elizabeth-Ann.'

In a shaking voice I repeated my three-word opinion of Bonnie's reading. The classroom filled with titters and giggles. I looked at Bonnie; her face reddened, but she held her chin out and glared at me.

'Come to the front of the class,' Mrs Hammet said, her voice harsh.

She picked up her wooden ruler. I hid my hands behind my back as I stood before her with my head down. 'Palms up!' she ordered. Moments later I watched the black blur of the inches marks on the ruler smack down three times on each of my trembling hands.

Word of my punishment never did reach my parents. But Boyer missed little. That evening, as I sat in his room he reached across and picked up my hands. His eyes softened as he turned them over. 'What happened, Nat?' he asked.

The fading evidence of the red marks on my palms stung far less than my confession about calling Bonnie stupid.

'The thing about words,' Boyer said when I finished, 'is once they're said, they're like spilt milk, impossible to retrieve. Words are too powerful to use carelessly. You had two chances not to let your words have the power to hurt. When you first said them and then when your teacher asked you to repeat them. Sometimes telling the exact truth is not as important as sparing someone's feelings.'

'A lie?' I gulped back the tears. 'I should have told Mrs Hammet a lie?'

'Not exactly a lie, but perhaps if you had used a little discretion, taken a moment to think, before you spoke in the first place,' he said, all the while holding my hands, 'well, that and a little white lie might have avoided some hurt. For you and for Bonnie.'

Then, as if to take away the sting, he said, 'Then you could have done a few Hail Marys as penance.' He winked. 'Remember, a little white lie, and a little discretion.'

Discretion. For a six-year-old that was a ten-penny word. And a lesson I would take far too long to learn.

CHAPTER THREE

THE BUS HUMS ALONG Highway 97 South. We pass rolling fields edged with orange and yellow, frost-touched trees. The clear autumn sky is blue, crisp and clean. I have always loved the open sky of the Cariboo and Chilcotin plateaus, where it takes an honest day for the sun to pass from east to west. Such a contrast with Atwood.

When I was growing up I paid little attention to the fact that the mountains dominated the landscape. I didn't notice the absence of sky. Now I have to brace myself for the suffocating claustrophobia that grips me once I am in the shadows of those alpine slopes.

When I lived there the mountains that loomed over our farm were as familiar to me as family. I knew their shapes, their locations, their size and elevations. I knew their names. Mostly thanks to Boyer.

From as early as I can remember I rode his shoulders whenever he went hiking through the surrounding woods.

'I'm the queen of the mountain!' I hollered from my perch one afternoon. A weak echo tried to reverberate across the slopes.

'Well, princess, maybe.' Boyer laughed.

He stopped to catch his breath on a mountain clearing. We sat side by side in the meadow grass as Boyer pointed out landmarks and taught me how to orientate myself by finding Robert's Peak. 'On the other side of that mountain is the United States of America,' he told me with a note of wonder in his voice.

'Are the people there different?' I asked.

'Well, there are certainly a lot more of them. But they're pretty much the same. We're fortunate to have them there,' he added. 'It's kind of like living next door to a big brother.'

'Like you.' I smiled.

'Something like that,' he said and hugged me.

As Boyer pointed out the boundaries of our land he told how our grandfather had arrived in the area after the first rush of gold fever. 'It didn't take him long to realise that prospecting wasn't for him,' he said. 'So he decided to make his living from the miners, instead of with them.'

Our grandfather bought two Holstein cows and a bull. Then he began his return to what he knew best, dairy farming. He homesteaded the only usable acreage in the narrow valley south of town. He also laid claim to a good deal of the surrounding hillsides and forests. Four hundred acres of hill and dale, rock and dirt.

Even when I grew too heavy to ride on Boyer's shoulders I tagged along with him whenever he went hiking. Morgan and Carl often joined us. As Boyer shared his love of the forest he constantly reminded us of the hidden dangers in the mountains that toed into our fields and meadows. Both he and our mother made sure we did not forget.

One summer day, when I was five or six, Morgan, Carl and I went with Mom to pick wild huckleberries that grew in the forest behind our farm. My mother's blue-flowered cotton dress swished against her black

rubber boots as she walked in front of me. Mom always wore a dress, even in the bush. My father hated to see her in trousers.

Sunlight seeped through the canopy of trees and danced through the branches as we hiked up the mountain that day. Mom jingled as she moved. Christmas bells, from the horse's halter, hung around her neck. 'We're in bear territory now,' she told us.

'Bears!' I shrieked.

'Yeah,' Morgan chimed in. 'We're gonna get eaten by bears.'

Mom ignored the boys' laughter. 'Bears don't eat people,' she said to me. 'They eat berries. Still, we don't want to surprise them.' She lifted the bells and gave them a shake. 'We've got to give them fair warning.'

She promised the noise would be enough to keep the bears away. I believed her. But then I believed every word she said.

I followed close behind her, my red bucket swinging. My brothers and I ate more of the fat blue huckleberries than we put into our buckets.

Neither of my brothers wanted to be there. They wanted to be with Boyer and Dad who were cutting trees for our winter's firewood. They were bored with searching for berries. They laughed and poked at each other as we entered a clearing in the sweltering afternoon sunshine. Clicking grasshoppers leapt from the dry, overgrown alpine grass as we passed through. Back in the cool shadows on the other side, the musty odour of dried lichen and crushed pine needles filled the forest air. In the shade of the overhanging trees we came upon a dense stand of bushes, their branches heavy with the purple-blue huckleberries.

The four of us slowly worked our way through the patch. Even I managed to cover the bottom of my pail. The bushes thinned out as we moved further into the trees. I followed Mom as she meandered back along the edge of the clearing.

Suddenly, Morgan and Carl started to holler. I glanced up to see them scrambling over a mound of rubble, an enormous pile of weathered tree stumps and boulders, overgrown with weeds and vines.

My mother stopped picking and called out, 'Come down from there.' She beckoned me to follow her to the bottom of the pile where she stood and waited for them to descend.

My brothers groaned, then reluctantly backed down. When they reached the bottom Morgan stood back and looked at the heap of tangled debris. 'What is it, Mom?' he asked.

'It's a long story,' she said as she ushered us away.

We had walked a short way when Mom stopped and set her pail on the ground. She sat down on a moss-crusted log and stared back at the

mountain of rubble. 'It's really your father's story,' she said. She removed the bells from her neck. In the blinking light of the forest she began to speak matter-of-factly, without emotion. I still remember her words.

'It happened in 1927,' she began. 'One fall morning, your father, and his older brother, Emile, headed out with their dog to hunt grouse. Your dad was twelve; Emile was fifteen. It wasn't unusual for the boys to hunt alone. Your grandfather, Angus Ward, taught them early how to handle guns. Things were different back then. Necessity and competency were the only licence they needed.'

The background drone of insects accompanied my mother's voice. 'The boys usually returned home with an abundance of birds hanging at their sides. Their mother, your grandmother Manny, was always pleased to receive their bounty. But as the sun rose above the tree tops that morning, their dog, a blue heeler, had little success flushing out their prey. He zigzagged through the undergrowth. The brothers followed him further up the slopes. The sun grew warmer. They still had no birds tied to their belts.

'When the boys came to an old clear-cut—that clearing we just walked through—the dog ran ahead. Your father turned for only a moment to look down at the farm.

'Behind him the dog gave a bark of discovery and bolted across the clearing. Your father spun round and saw the startled eyes of a young doe standing motionless against the backdrop of tree trunks. Then with a flash of white tail she leapt into the underbrush, flushing a covey of grouse as she disappeared. The birds rose in a whirr of flapping wings. Emile lifted his rifle and fired. A wounded bird hung in the air, and then fought against the descent into the thicket. The blue heeler bounded into the bush, with Emile close behind. Your dad took up the chase and followed them into the forest. In the shadows of the trees he spotted their dog as it leapt through the air above a fungus-covered snag. Emile ran ten feet behind, changing his shells on the fly as he ran towards the deadfall. In the next blink Emile was gone. Gus thought the flickering light was playing tricks with his eyes. He raced towards the log. He saw the gaping hole at his feet just in time. He threw himself to one side, his fingers clawing at brambles and roots as his feet slid on wet grass.'

Mom took a deep breath. 'Oh, what sounds for a young boy to carry with him into the rest of his life,' she sighed. She was no longer speaking to us. 'Those sounds, the commotion, all melded into a single moment: the muffled thuds of flesh against unyielding rock, the receding scream, the dog's furious barking, the clatter of the falling gun, and finally the

gun shot, the thunderous shot ricocheting, echoing, in the depths of the air shaft at your father's feet. Then the ringing silence. A silence broken only when the dog raised his head to howl to the heavens.'

She told us how, half blind with tears and shock, Dad raced, stumbled and fell his way down the mountainside. Covered in blood and dirt he made his way home. Deafened by the pounding in his ears, gulping each breath as if it were his last, he could not hear his own voice as he told his parents the unbearable news.

Mom said it took the rescue party, led by my shell-shocked father, until nightfall to retrieve his brother's twisted, lifeless body. My grandfather himself rappelled down the shaft to carry his son to the surface.

Manny Ward stood in the clearing, apart from the rescue party, her thin mouth an expressionless line on her tearless face. She stared straight ahead as the afternoon sunlight passed over the scene and she waited for her son's body.

'For months after, your grandfather spent every free moment of his time carting boulders and felled trees to throw down that mine shaft. He didn't stop when it was full. He piled more on the top, creating this rock and wood memorial for his first-born son,' my mother mused.

My grandfather continued to search for and fill, or board over, every mine shaft he could find on his land. Neither my grandfather nor my father, ever picked up a shotgun again.

I never heard my father speak of his brother, or say anything to us about mine shafts. Perhaps he felt that his father had taken care of them and there was no longer any danger. Still, our mother warned us that day, 'Even your grandfather couldn't be sure he'd found them all.'

It's hard to be certain now how much of the story was actually told by my mother, and how much is my memory filling in the blanks. I only know her words painted a picture of the tragedy so clear it was as if I were watching it play out before me. But I was only a child then; the sadness lasted as long as the telling. Suffering and grief were not part of that sunshine time of our lives. They were something that happened to others, not to our perfect family.

On a September afternoon, when I was eight, I came into the kitchen after digging potatoes to find my mother and father at the table with a young man I'd never seen before.

I rinsed my hands, then dried them while I stood behind my mother, peering over her shoulder. An array of black-and-white photographs was spread out on the table in front of her. They were overhead shots of

our farm, and one of the town of Atwood, taken from an aeroplane.

I sat down beside Mom and studied the photographs. I could make out the landmark stone and brick buildings: the post office, the court-house, even Our Lady of Compassion, next door to the hospital. The town looked neat and orderly from this bird's eye view.

The young salesman watched as we scrutinised the pictures. 'The finished portrait will be hand-painted by a watercolourist,' he said as he reached for a huckleberry tart on the full plate in front of him.

Mom leaned over the pictures. She ran her fingers slowly, lightly, down the roads, over the fields, without touching the paper.

'It looks so beautiful,' she crooned. 'So beautiful.' Her fingers found the house, the barn and the dairy. 'Everything seems so close. Oh, look, Natalie, you can see the lake, the old miners' cabin.'

My father leaned forward for a quick glance, trying hard to put on his stern, in-control face. Even to my young, scrutinising eyes, he failed.

'So. How much?' he asked.

'Well,' said the salesman, with the confidence of someone who knew that a sale was in the bag. 'That all depends on size and framing—'

'How long will it take to paint, frame and deliver the large portrait size?' my mother asked.

My father coughed. 'Now wait a minute, Nettie,' he said. 'We haven't decided anything yet. Let's just hear the prices first.'

Mom was the most patient person I know, but when she made up her mind on something she expected action. Still, she seldom went against Dad, and certainly never in front of a stranger. But she had made up her mind to have this portrait.

The salesman looked helplessly from Dad to Mom.

Then I saw it in her eyes. The briefest flicker, a movement, a flash, there, then gone. In that fraction of a second she told him, without saying a word, where the sale rested.

'Well, Mr Ward sir, let's see,' the salesman said as he pulled out a letter-size sheet of paper from a flat leather folder. 'Here we are.' He passed it down to my father. 'The price list. The sizes, descriptions, all the prices are there.'

My father crushed out his cigarette and put on his reading glasses. He picked up the paper and leaned back in his chair. The clock over the stove ticked into the silence as my father pondered. After a few moments he laid the paper flat on the table and smoothed it with his hands. Mom's eyes followed his fingers down the list. As he touched each description, I saw her shrug her shoulders as if indifferent to the

selection. When he reached the last line, she gave the briefest of nods.

'Well, Nettie,' my father finally said. 'I think this one might do.'

My mother smiled. 'Yes, I think you're right,' she said. 'And the mahogany frame will go nicely above the piano.'

Father handed the sheet back to the salesman. 'All right then, that's the one we'll have.' He flashed a smile and a wink at Mom. 'Now, how long before you deliver it?'

The salesman began writing the order. 'Let's see, large portrait size, thirty inches by forty-two inches, hand-painted watercolour, mahogany frame. Hmmm. That should not take more than a few months,' he said, directing his words to Mom. 'You should surely have it by Christmas.'

My mother's mouth opened, her shoulders sagged. 'Christmas?'

'Let's just put a rush on that,' the salesman said quickly and wrote a note on the invoice. Even strangers could not stand to disappoint my mother. Sometimes I believe she relied on that.

He tore the sheet from his order book. He gave the carbon copy to my father, who glanced at it, then folded it and tucked it into his shirt pocket.

'That will be half now and half when it is delivered,' the salesman said. 'Will that be a cheque or cash?' He pulled out a receipt book. 'That's an even eighty-five dollars for the first payment.'

My father's mouth opened briefly and then clamped shut. I could see his jaw muscles working as he started to rise. 'I'll get my wallet,' he said.

'No,' Mom said. 'The egg money is going to pay for this.' She rose and walked out of the kitchen. I heard her go into her bedroom and open the doors to her wardrobe. She returned carrying a folded white envelope. She counted out a stack of one- and two-dollar bills.

I'd never seen Mom dip into her egg money before. I knew how much she wanted this portrait when I saw those wrinkled bills hit the table. She'd earned them selling chicken eggs at fifty cents a dozen. It was her dream money. Her dream that one of her sons would go to college. It was not a dream she shared with Dad. His dream was that his boys would take over the farm. I knew he had quit school before he finished grade eight to work alongside his father. So, although the egg money was my mother's, he had no sympathy for its final destination.

I expect she had her own reasons for paying. I watched the silent messages pass between my parents and realised that somehow Mom had tricked him into buying the most expensive portrait. As my father tried to hide his shock at the price it dawned on me how she had manipulated him. I was stunned to realise their shared secret. My father could not read.

When I was nine, Boyer left school. Quit. And just like that, on a snowy November day in the middle of his final year, Mom's vision of one of her sons going to college began to fade round the edges.

I never heard my father directly ask any of my brothers to quit school. But it was always there, unspoken. The first time I sensed it was during the days following Boyer's sixteenth birthday.

After the milking each morning Boyer changed into his school clothes as usual and squeezed into the cab of the truck with the rest of us. Every day Dad raised his eyebrows and heaved an exaggerated sigh, but said nothing as we drove into town. He didn't need to speak. The words hung there in the air. *The farm needs you.*

Then there was Jake, the hired hand. Whatever Dad wasn't saying, Jake was. I don't know how Jake ended up at our farm, but he had lived in the room above the dairy for as long as I could remember. His bristled face carried a perpetual scowl. What little he had to say was blunt, sarcastic or teasing. But unlike Morgan and Carl's good-natured, elbow-in-the-ribs, wink-wink kind of teasing, Jake's was sharp, cutting. Behind his back Morgan and Carl called him the Anti-Dad. He was so much the opposite of our father.

Jake was fiercely loyal to Dad. His devotion did not extend to the Ward family. He tolerated us. I stayed out of his way. Mom said his bark was worse than his bite, but I didn't want to test it.

Between Jake and Boyer there was a civil respect. Boyer treated him with the courteous regard of a youth for his elder. And Jake seemed to hold a grudging admiration for Boyer's devotion to his family and the farm. At least until after Boyer turned sixteen.

When Boyer seemed in no hurry to leave school, Jake saw it as his duty to start prodding him. He made grumbling remarks at the supper table each night. 'Sure could use an extra hand around here,' he muttered to no one in particular; or, 'I won't be around for ever, yer know.'

'The mine is hiring,' I heard him remark one afternoon when Boyer was seventeen. 'With this year's price of hay going crazy your folks could use the extra income.'

The mine? Boyer working at the mine? I looked at Boyer as he opened the door to the stairway, holding an armload of books.

Jake called after him, 'Hey, book-boy, got any girlie magazines up there?'

Boyer stopped on the first step, turned and held up the books. 'Would you like them, Jake?' he asked. 'They're my school books. I won't be needing them any more.'

For the first time I could remember, dinner was eaten in silence that

night. After the milking, Mom went straight to her bedroom and closed the door behind her. Morgan and Carl washed up without their usual jousting and then, without a word, went into the living room. As I finished the dishes I heard the familiar whip-crack of the *Rawhide* theme coming from the television. I made my way up to the attic where Boyer sat on his bed reading. He looked up as I entered.

'Did you really quit school?' I asked.

'Yes, I did,' he said.

'Why?' I fought back the tears. 'Are you going away?'

'No, nothing's going to change,' he said and turned to face me. 'I'll still be here every night.' I could hear the false cheerfulness in his voice.

'It's Dad, isn't it?' I blurted. 'Just because he hated school he expects everyone to.' An anger that surprised me surfaced with my words.

'No, this was my decision, Natalie. It's just the right thing to do.'

'He can't read! Do you know he can't read? That's why. He doesn't want you to be smart either!' The words rushed out of my mouth as if they could argue him into staying in school.

'What makes you say he can't read?' Boyer asked, handing me a tissue.

As I blew my nose I told him what had happened in the kitchen between Mom and Dad the day they bought the portrait of the farm.

Boyer sighed. 'Look, first of all, not being able to read doesn't mean a person isn't smart. Dad just never experienced school in the same way as you and I. Things were different then. Farming was all Dad ever wanted to do. Secondly,' he said, 'he's a proud man. Promise me, Natalie, that you won't say anything to him about the reading. Try to understand how it is for him. Try to imagine not being able to read.'

Of course, I promised.

The next morning, Boyer's English teacher showed up at our door. I heard the insistent knock as Mom and I pushed the wringer washer back into the corner of the enclosed porch.

Mrs Gooding wasn't much taller than I was. Grey hair poked out from beneath her brown felt hat. Her slight frame made her appear frail at first glance, but I shrunk back from the steely determination in her eyes. Mom ushered her into the porch.

'Let me take your coat,' Mom said once we were inside the kitchen.

'No, I won't be staying long,' Mrs Gooding replied as she placed a package on the counter. 'I promised Boyer I would not speak to his father. So I want to be gone before Mr Ward returns from his milk deliveries.' She sat down on the chair my mother pulled out from the table and held her gloves on her lap. 'I doubt that Boyer has told you

how I reacted to his announcement yesterday,' she said. 'But I don't mind telling you that I am ashamed by this waste of a brilliant intellect.' Mom's mouth opened but before she could form a response Mrs Gooding continued. 'After I got over the initial shock, I made a few phone calls. First I called Stanley Atwood. I swore that if he let that boy go underground I would report him to the Child Welfare. Apparently my threat was not necessary.' She sniffed. 'Mr Atwood is chairman of the School Board and if Boyer wants it, there's a job for him in the bus maintenance yard starting Monday.' A small smile of triumph lifted the corners of her mouth.

'Then I talked to Boyer's other teachers.' She patted the package on the table. 'These are the textbooks for the final semester. If Boyer picks up the lessons once a week, we see no reason why he cannot write the exams at the end of the year like everyone else.' She added, 'There's no reason for his name to come off the school register.'

I heard my mother's intake of breath and knew her dream had been rekindled.

Mrs Gooding stood. 'Although I gave my word not to confront his father,' she said, 'unlike Mr Ward, I refuse to give up on Boyer.'

Mom finally found her voice. 'I'm grateful for what you've done, Mrs Gooding,' she said. 'But I want you to understand that, while it's no secret that we can use the extra income, my husband did not make Boyer quit school. That decision was Boyer's.'

The teacher's raised eyebrows betrayed her disbelief.

'My husband's a good man,' Mom insisted. 'But he's first and foremost a farmer. Dairy farming is all he knows. It's who he is.'

'Yes,' Mrs Gooding replied, 'but it's not who Boyer is.'

My father was not a complex man. Everything he was could be read on his face. The essence of his personality was etched into those permanent laugh lines at the sides of his mouth, into the V furrow between his eyes. When my father smiled, his right brow lifted higher than the left. That, along with the widow's peak on his forehead, gave him a devilish or rakish look, depending on who he was looking at.

I can picture him, wearing coveralls and gumboots, walking to the barn in the evening twilight, or waving from the cab of his milk truck, his handsome face a flash of teeth and tan beneath his hat. I can see him steering the tractor through a field of freshly mown hay, or tinkering with equipment in the machine shed. He seemed to spend half his waking hours with his feet protruding from beneath a tractor or mower.

Mostly, I can visualise him at our kitchen table. Even there he was animated. His arms and hands waved and poked at the air while he ate, or directed the constant table talk. And I see him smoking. My father always seemed to have a roll-up in his mouth, the thin cigarette moving across his lips as if on its own.

As I grew older, I noticed that his female customers found him handsome as well. I could tell by the way they looked at him.

On weekends and holidays Morgan, Carl and I took turns delivering milk with Dad. At many of the houses, women suddenly appeared on their front porches when he arrived, as if they had been waiting behind their doors. My father would wave, flashing his famous smile, calling out, 'Good morning, darlin'.' Then he would wink at me as he climbed back into the truck and lit another cigarette.

Everyone knew my father. And they knew I was his daughter. 'Nat, Nat, milkman's brat, butter and cream make her fat, fat, fat.' The silly rhyme followed me through the playgrounds of elementary school.

There are worse things than being teased. There are worse things than wearing homemade dresses instead of reversible pleated skirts and pastel sweater sets. There are worse things than being called 'heifer' and 'fatty, fatty two by four'. But when you are a young girl it's hard to imagine what that would be.

The only thing that got me through those early school days was knowing that when the final bell rang I would spend the rest of my day with my father, my mother, Morgan, Carl and Boyer. Especially Boyer.

Still, I wasn't above revenge. When I was in grade school I took my revenge in the only way I knew how. I took everything I learned from Boyer and used it to compete with them. And I beat them. I beat them at every spelling bee, pop-quiz or book report. Of course, my abilities did nothing to improve my popularity.

Looking back, I realise that my alienation in elementary school was, in large part, my own doing. I did nothing to encourage friendships. I either competed with the other girls or I ignored them. The games that drew them together, the skipping, hopscotch and Barbie doll fantasies held no interest for me. I had Boyer, our word games, and books. And when Boyer was eighteen and became the school bus driver, I got to sit right behind him while the other girls watched with envy as my handsome brother, his eyes smiling in the rearview mirror, talked to me about my day.

Because of Boyer, school for me was only about learning, about soaking up knowledge so I could go home and impress him. By the time I

reached grade six I was a serious 'teacher's pet', shunned by the rest of the class. I had no friends, did not know how to make friends, and I didn't care. At least I'd pretended I didn't care for so long that I believed it.

So when Elizabeth-Ann Ryan—who was easily the prettiest and most popular girl in school—came to me a few weeks after we entered high school and said, 'Want to come to a sleepover at my house on Saturday night?' I had no idea how to respond.

Something had shifted over that summer. The girls who entered grade seven that September looked and behaved far differently from the girls who had left elementary school a few months before. Barbie dolls and skipping-ropes were forgotten. Frizzy hair and nylon stockings had replaced bobby socks and braids. They had discovered boys. More exactly, they had discovered my brothers. Morgan and Carl were both in grade eight now and as inseparable as ever. Mom swore that Morgan failed grade six on purpose so that he wouldn't have to move on to high school two years before Carl. It wasn't hard to figure out that they were the reason for my sudden popularity.

'Everyone's coming at eight,' Elizabeth-Ann said, smiling at me with a look that said how grateful I should be for this invitation.

'Why?' I asked, not sure what kind of joke this would turn into.

'Why what?'

'Why would I want to sleep at your house?'

'It's a pyjama party,' she said sweetly. 'Come on, it'll be fun.'

'I'll think about it,' I told her.

I had never been away from home overnight. It was hard to imagine sleeping in the same room as a group of girls.

'Why, Natalie, that's nice,' Mom said when I told her about the invitation. 'Pyjama parties can be fun.'

'What do they do?' I asked, trying to sound uninterested. 'Play games?'

'Maybe,' Mom smiled. 'Though they probably spend more time talking about boys if sleepovers are anything like the ones I went to when I was a teenager.'

So I went. If it was good enough for my mother, it was good enough for me. I was nervous, but secretly I was curious.

Boyer drove me in on Saturday evening. He parked in front of the Ryans' house on Colbur Street. 'Smile,' he said as I opened the truck door. 'You look like you're going to a wake instead of a party.'

I shrugged. 'It'll probably be just as boring.' I grabbed my pillow and a cloth bag that held my flannel nightgown and toothbrush.

'Then I hope you have a book in your sack.'

I groaned. I had forgotten to pack one. Boyer reached inside his jacket and pulled out a small paperback. 'Here, take this one,' he said, handing me *The Catcher in the Rye*.

I tucked the book into my bag and kissed Boyer goodbye.

Mrs Ryan answered my knock. Every time I saw her, Elizabeth-Ann's mother looked as if she were on her way to a party. Her angora sweater, tweed skirt, and high heels were in such contrast to my mother's bibbed apron tied over a printed cotton dress.

'Hello,' she said. 'Natalie, isn't it?' she asked as she waved me inside. I nodded.

'The girls are upstairs.' She smiled and gestured to the stairway.

'Thank you, Mrs Ryan,' I said. As I headed towards the stairs I heard the clinking of ice against glass. 'Well, if it isn't the pretty little milk-maid,' Elizabeth-Ann's father called out from the living room.

Gerald Ryan, the owner of Handy Hardware, was the mayor of Atwood. Somehow being called the milkmaid by him did not sound the same as when my father said it.

Unbidden, a forgotten image welled up from when I started helping Dad deliver milk years ago. As I placed milk bottles on his porch early one morning I glanced down and saw Mr Ryan standing at the basement window. At first I felt embarrassed that I'd caught him scratching himself and I hurried away. The following weekend he stood in the basement again, his hand rubbing the front of his trousers as he stared out of the window. I plunked the full milk bottles down, almost dropping them in my haste. I spun away, but not before his narrow, red-rimmed eyes met mine. His lips opened in a leering smile. I didn't tell my father. I still can't say why. Perhaps it was because I didn't understand why it frightened me. But I did ask Dad to change sides of the street with me when we delivered to houses on Colbur Street. Without questioning, he said, 'OK, Sunshine.' As Mr Ryan winked at me over his raised glass, I felt the same revulsion I had back then.

'Hello, Mr Ryan,' I mumbled. I kept my head down, but I felt those red, rodent eyes follow me as I hurried up the stairs.

It looked like half of the grade seven girls' class was in Elizabeth-Ann's bedroom. They were sprawled about, lying or sitting on the twin beds, and on the jumble of sleeping-bags covering the floor. *Movie Star*, *True Story* and *Mad* magazines were scattered everywhere.

I noticed eyebrows rise as I walked in. *Who invited you? What's she doing here?* Elizabeth-Ann called from her bed. 'Hi, Nat, come on in.'

A few of the other girls smiled and said, 'Hey, Natalie.'

'Come and put your stuff over here.' Elizabeth-Ann indicated a sleeping-bag next to the bed she sat on.

I stepped round the air mattresses on the floor, feeling self-conscious and clumsy.

'Listen to this,' Sherry Campbell shrieked. Sitting cross-legged on the other twin bed, she was wearing pink baby-doll pyjamas and had matching giant pink rollers in her hair. She held a copy of *True Confessions* magazine. '"I was a teenage love slave",' Sherry read. The other girls leaned closer and listened, sometimes giggling behind their hands. I sat on the sleeping-bag, feeling awkward, fat and separate.

'"I felt his hands on my tender breasts, harsh and demanding, as he forced his tongue in my mouth",' she read. There was something deliciously wicked about hearing the forbidden words. When she finished, Sherry held the magazine to her chest and breathed, 'Oh, that poor girl!'

'Oh, that lucky girl!' someone else laughed.

'I want to be someone's love slave,' Bonnie King sighed.

'I want to be Morgan Ward's love slave,' someone cried. I whirled round to see who it was, when another voice said, 'No, Carl's!'

'Yes, yes, Carl's!'

'Is Carl going with anyone?' someone asked.

'What about Morgan? Does he have a girlfriend?'

Everyone's eyes were on me. I was the centre of attention. So it was true. My brothers were the reason I had been invited. I was not surprised. I was surprised, though, at how I felt about all the eager faces waiting for my words. I found I liked the feeling.

I straightened up. 'Morgan and Carl have lots of friends,' I said. It was true. Lately it seemed our sunroom was always full of kids from town who came over to listen to records and dance.

The questions kept coming. Some of the girls began changing into their pyjamas as the chatter continued. I pulled out my flannel nightgown, trying not to look at the half-naked bodies. The room became a blur of baby-doll pyjamas, bikini panties and bras. Bras! The only one in the room who needed a bra was me. I had not even considered one until that moment. I turned my back and stripped down to my cotton briefs and vest, then yanked my nightgown over my head.

The giggling and chatter continued into the night. Once Mrs Ryan called out, 'That's it, girls. Lights out.'

Later Mr Ryan's slurred, singsong voice called up from the bottom of the stairs. 'If I hear any more giggling up there, I'll have to come and paddle some pretty little bottoms!'

My stomach lurched. Elizabeth-Ann groaned. She leaned over and switched off the lamp. Much later, when I thought everyone was asleep, I heard her whisper in the dark, 'Natalie, does Boyer have a girlfriend?'

Boyer? Every muscle in my body stiffened. Why would she ask about Boyer? Until that moment I had never imagined him with a girlfriend.

'No, my brother's too busy with his job and the farm.' My voice was tight, protective, possessive and jealous. 'He doesn't have time for girls.'

'Oh,' she sighed.

The next morning I dressed before anyone was awake. I crept down in the silence and slipped out of the house. I walked to the corner of the street and sat down on the kerb to wait for my father. When he pulled up I breathed a sigh of relief and jumped into the milk truck.

'Well, how was the party, Sunshine?' my father asked.

'It was OK,' I mumbled.

I didn't tell him about how I had cringed inside my sleeping-bag, pretending to be asleep, when in the middle of the night the bedroom door opened. I peered out from the opening in my bag as Mr Ryan slipped into the room. I thought Elizabeth-Ann was asleep until I heard her hiss, 'Go away, Daddy,' as he leaned over her bed.

I didn't tell him about the fear I felt as Mr Ryan backed out of the room, the moonlight exposing the gaping front of his pyjama bottoms.

As my father and I finished delivering milk that morning it dawned on me how silly I had been to feel ashamed of him because he couldn't read. I had just found out that some fathers have far worse secrets.

CHAPTER FOUR

DURING THOSE TEENAGE YEARS, extra bodies often crowded in at our table at mealtimes. Town kids. Morgan and Carl's friends. They were all willing to carry milk buckets, chase cows or throw hay bales in exchange for the privilege of spending time 'out at the ranch'. They showed up regularly on weekends and summer holidays. It seemed everyone wanted to be at our place during those blameless years.

After I started high school our home was suddenly filled with the

twittering noises of young female voices. My new-found friends. They never seemed to know when to go home.

Elizabeth-Ann was the most frequent visitor. The first time she phoned and whispered, 'Natalie, my dad's drunk. Can I come out?' I was unable to turn her down. Before long she stopped asking and just showed up, sometimes even on school nights.

Since the slumber party, I hadn't returned to the Ryan house. Besides not wanting to run into Mr Ryan, I had no interest in town life. I believed that my family, my home, was far better than anything those neat houses stacked on the hillsides of Atwood had to offer.

Elizabeth-Ann and I became close, I suppose, in the way friends do who need something from each other. Even though I knew Boyer had been the attraction at first, my friendship with Elizabeth-Ann grew, and I began to look forward to her company.

I'm certain that she, like the other girls, thought it was a fair exchange. They got to spend time at the same table as the Ward boys. In exchange they gave me their friendship. They tried to teach me the latest beauty tricks; they loaned or gave me the latest-style short skirts and sweater sets.

Our hayloft became a favourite hangout once we convinced Mom that no one smoked. I followed as they climbed the ladder on the side of the barn and scrambled over the loose hay to the open overhead doors. From this vantage point they spied on my brothers working below, then fell into fits of giggling at the slightest glance their way. Of course, my brothers were aware of all this. Morgan and Carl strutted around during those days, posturing like bantam roosters. I watched closely as Elizabeth-Ann tried her wiles on Boyer. At mealtimes she jockeyed her position at the table to sit close to him, shamelessly batting her eyes every time she spoke to him.

Boyer was immune to her obvious flirting, treating her with the polite indulgence he showed anyone but family. Every time he winked or smiled at me I felt a smug superiority, knowing I was still 'his girl'.

Everything changed after River arrived. River Jordan. He flowed into our lives as easily as water finding its course. And like water, in time, he would erode the jagged edges of resistance.

Morgan and Carl were the first to yield. They didn't crumble right away. It took them at least a day.

Before supper, River came back to the house. He rapped lightly on the side of the screen door as he peered in.

'No need to knock here,' Mom called out from the sideboard, where she was cutting bread.

'Just like home,' River answered and stepped into the kitchen.

Mom looked up, her face still flushed from the day's heat. 'Good,' she said with a smile. 'I hope you will come to feel as comfortable here.'

'I'm certain I will,' he said, then hurried over and took the stack of plates I was reaching for in the cupboard. 'Here, let me get that, Natalie.'

'Thanks,' I mumbled, sure my face was as flushed as Mom's.

'My pleasure,' he said, his blue-green eyes crinkling with a smile. He helped me set the table for supper while he and Mom chatted as easily as two old friends. As we pulled the table away from the wall I heard Morgan and Carl out on the porch with Dad.

'Come and meet River before you wash up,' Mom called out. She smoothed down her apron. 'Everyone, this is River Jordan,' she said.

I thought I heard a hint of anxiety in her voice as she introduced him to Dad. Maybe it was me. Maybe I was the one who was apprehensive about how my father would react to this stranger. But I don't think so.

Dad's right eyebrow lifted, either in response to the unusual name, or to the sight of the shoulder-length hair and flowing Indian cotton shirt.

'How do you do, sir?' he said, stepping forward and offering his hand.

My father took his hand and gave it a single, firm shake. I thought I saw a quick wince behind River's smile.

'River?' Dad said. 'Can't say I've heard of anyone called River before.'

'It's not my real name,' River answered. 'Just a nickname. My given name is Richard.'

'Well, Richard,' Dad said, 'these guys here'—he nodded at Morgan and Carl—'are big on nicknames. This'll save 'em from figuring one out for you.'

'Oh, I'm sure we'll think of something,' Carl said as he took River's outstretched hand. I caught the smirk that passed between him and Morgan and knew that River would not escape the razzing that every new person at our table endured.

Just then the screen door opened once more and Boyer came into the kitchen. While Mom introduced River, I was struck again with the thought I'd had earlier when I'd watched him walk across the farmyard. Even though River was shorter, his features finer than Boyer's, and his eyes bluer, as their hands came together in a handshake I couldn't help thinking again that they were somehow similar. The resemblance was more than just the colour of their hair. Perhaps it was the reserved nods they exchanged as they acknowledged each other. I knew Boyer was

never quick to judge anyone, and something told me River was the same. Yet as he released River's hand I saw a brief smile cross Boyer's face. A smile mirrored in the aquamarine eyes looking back at him.

River slid onto the bench at the back of the table beside Morgan and Carl. With the final Amen of the mealtime prayer, Mom reached over to the middle of the table and lifted the lid from the cast-iron pot. She picked up the ladle and began spooning out the soupy mixture.

'Thank you, ma'am,' River said to Mom as she placed the first steaming serving in front of him.

'Ma'am?' Carl and Morgan parroted River's accent. Mom frowned.

'Nettie,' she reminded River as she continued serving.

'Yes, ma'am,' River said. 'Nettie.' And he nodded to Mom with a smile so genuine that even Carl and Morgan could not have doubted his sincerity.

Mom set a plate of stew down in front of Morgan. 'Mmmmm,' he said as he breathed in the aroma. 'Stewed brains, my favourite.'

Mom's hamburger stew was hearty and tasty, if not colourful. Other victims of this worn-out joke usually turned pale as they were handed a plateful of the pinkish-grey concoction.

'You like brains, River?' Carl asked.

River didn't miss a beat. He picked up his fork and dug in. 'Sure do,' he said after swallowing the first mouthful. 'I especially like them for breakfast, fried up with onions and hot sauce.' He retrieved a thick slice of bread from the platter Mom offered. 'I'll cook up a batch for you guys sometime.' He flashed a conspirator's smile across the table at me.

Morgan and Carl's smirks began to fade. A hint of a grin played at the corners of my father's lips. Dad was the only one in our family who liked brains. He ate every organ Mom would cook: the heart, liver, kidneys and even the tongue. My brothers would never touch 'innards'. Whenever Mom served these delicacies, they ate leftovers or sandwiches.

'I have to say, Nettie,' River said, 'this tastes exactly the same as my momma's stew. She mixes the cow brains with hamburger just like this. If you didn't know, you could never tell they were in there.'

Morgan and Carl looked down at their plates, then back up at Mom. She raised her shoulders in an innocent shrug. The corners of Boyer's mouth twitched. Morgan and Carl poked suspiciously at their stew.

Then Dad began his interrogation. There was no other word for it: he began to fire questions like accusations. 'So, how come ya left the States?' he asked.

River wiped his mouth with his napkin. He looked directly at my

father. 'Well, sir, I left because I don't believe in the war in Vietnam.'

'A draft-dodger,' my father said, and took a mouthful of stew.

'Gus!' Mom cried.

'I prefer war-resister,' River said. 'But I guess you're right, draft-dodger is probably the label I'll have to live with.'

'I'll say one thing right now,' my father said. 'I believe a man should fight for his country when he is called to.'

'And I respect that, sir,' River answered quietly, 'but I don't see where this war in Asia is my country's war.'

I watched River's face as he contemplated my father's questions. He thought each through with patience and respect before he replied without apology. He told Dad he was neither a crusader nor an anarchist. To him it was simple: he could not take part in an immoral war.

'Those are just words,' Dad said. 'Excuses you young people make to avoid your duty.'

'What if it were our sons?' Mom asked Dad.

'All I'm saying is a man has a responsibility to his country,' my father muttered without looking up from his plate. 'Freedom comes at a cost.'

Boyer spoke up. 'I doubt if America's freedom is at stake in Vietnam,' he said, looking straight at Dad. 'Any more than ours is.'

'A man has a duty to his country,' my father responded.

'To his country, yes,' River said. 'But I don't believe that blindly following the orders of corrupt politicians is my duty to my country. I would die for my country, sir. That would be easy. Living with killing people who have done us no harm would not be.'

Dad grunted and continued eating. After a moment he asked, 'And what do your parents think of all this, of you leaving your home, maybe never being allowed to go back again?'

'My father's dead,' River answered. 'My mother doesn't believe in this war either. And my grandfather, well, he doesn't agree with my decision to defy the draft. And he never understood my choice to leave college in the first place.'

'College?' Boyer's voice betrayed his surprise. 'If you were in college, weren't you safe from the draft?'

River directed his attention to Boyer at the other end of the table. 'Yes,' he said, 'that's true, if I had stayed. But I couldn't sit back while the war was escalating and not stand up against it. I joined the peace movement. When I received my draft card, burning it, leaving, was my only way to protest the actions of a government I no longer believe in.'

'Well, I guess Canada's not as bad as prison,' Dad snorted.

'Being in exile is its own prison,' River said.

There was a silence at the table. I wondered what Morgan, Carl and Boyer would do if they had to face the same decisions. I wondered if they too were thinking that it was only an accident of birth, of being a few thousand feet from an invisible line, that made their choices so simple compared to this young American.

'Have ya ever worked on a dairy farm?' Dad asked.

'I grew up on my grandfather's farm in Montana,' River told him. He didn't tell him the size of that farm, or that it was a modern automated operation that shipped milk out each day in gleaming stainless steel tanker trucks. We would learn that much later.

Dad's chair scraped on the kitchen floor. 'Better grab a pair of rubber boots from the porch,' he said as he headed to the door. 'Those moccasins are about as useless in the barn as socks in a bathtub.'

River smiled. 'Yes, I expect so.' He slid out from behind the table.

After I finished clearing up and washing the supper dishes, I went upstairs. My bedroom window looked out over the enclosed porch. Sometimes, when I was alone, I took a book and climbed out of the window to sit on the sloped porch roof. From there I could see the entire farmyard, the dairy and the barn.

That evening I sat with my back against the faded, whitewashed siding and gazed down the dirt road that had brought River to us. I listened to the familiar sounds of the evening milking carrying up from the barn. Before long, Morgan and Carl began carrying the full stainless-steel milking machines from the barn to the dairy. Inside the dairy, Mom and Boyer would run the warm milk through the cooler and the cream separator. Then they filled the sterilised milk bottles to be stored in the walk-in cooler for the next day's delivery.

From the way Morgan and Carl were hustling it was easy to see that Dad and River were supplying milk much faster than Dad and Jake ever had. When the milking was complete River came out from behind the barn. His hair was tied back in a ponytail and tucked into the collar of the green coveralls he now wore. With his arm draped across the shoulder of the lead cow he leaned down and whispered something in her ear. She followed him to the pasture across the road as if she had been doing it every day of her life. He held the gate open and patted each of the cows on the rump as they filed through.

He closed the gate, turned and caught sight of me on the roof. He lifted his arm in a wave. And even from that distance I believed I could see the sparkle of those aquamarine eyes.

For as long as I remember visitors were always showing up at our farm on one pretext or another. They came to pick huckleberries or mushrooms on the mountain slopes behind our house. They came for Mom's eggs or cream, or simply for a Sunday drive. And they always found an excuse to enter our kitchen.

Everyone wanted to spend time around our family back then. I took pride in the fact that others seemed to envy our lives. I had yet to hear the saying, 'Those the gods would destroy they first make proud.'

After River arrived the visitors increased. As word spread, a steady stream of the curious, young and old alike, dropped by to check out our new hired hand. And without even trying, in his quiet gentle way, River charmed them all. He seemed unaware of his effect on people. He treated everyone with an old-fashioned respect. All men were 'sir', and all women 'ma'am'.

Whenever River spoke to anyone his eyes held theirs with a soft intensity. It was so easy for me to believe I was the most important thing in the world when he looked at me. By August I was completely infatuated with River. I am certain everyone was. Except Dad.

He was not rude but he held something back. Mom treated River with the same hospitality she shared with anyone who showed up at our door. Maybe more. Did she really laugh more when he was around? Did she really seem younger, prettier? If I thought she did, surely my father must have noticed. Was it possible he was jealous? I know I was.

After the first night's initiation, it was obvious Morgan and Carl were, according to Dad, smitten. The increasing length of their hair during the following months did nothing to help our father warm to River.

'You both need to get your ears lowered,' he told the two of them one morning. 'You're starting to look like a couple of wacko beatniks.'

'That's hippies, Dad!' Carl laughed. 'Hippies!'

Confused by my feelings, I kept my distance and watched. At first, anyway. One afternoon, a few weeks after River arrived, I climbed out of my bedroom window to sit on the roof above the porch. Morgan and Carl had gone off riding with their friends. Mom and Boyer were in town.

I sat down in the shade to read. A few minutes later I heard the clanging of a wrench against concrete followed by my father's groan.

'Every time the sun shines upside-down!' Dad's voice bellowed out from the machine shop.

I smiled to myself. This expression of my father's was the closest I ever heard him come to cursing.

'The tractor must be fighting back,' River called out from the yard.

I gave a startled laugh, surprised to see him there. 'You've heard Dad's idea of swearing?'

'A time or two.' River stopped at the gate and smiled up at me. It was impossible not to smile back. 'What're you reading?' he asked.

I held the book up. '*Sometimes a Great Notion.*'

'Seems you've always got your nose in a book,' he said. 'You must haunt the library.'

'Yeah, Boyer's library,' I laughed.

'Boyer's?'

'Come on up, I'll show you,' I offered.

We met in the upstairs hallway and I led him up to the attic room, thrilled at being alone with him. River stood in the doorway and whistled. 'Man, I see what you mean.'

Books filled every available space in Boyer's room. They lined shelves, covered his desk and the window seat.

'Do you think he will mind if I look through them?' River asked.

'He won't mind at all,' Boyer's voice answered from behind us.

Up until then Boyer had treated River with the same polite indifference with which he treated anyone but family. But that afternoon I saw a look of acceptance as he ushered River into his sanctuary.

'Cool.' River pushed back his hair as he surveyed Boyer's collection. 'Did you raid a secondhand bookstore or something?'

'Something.' Boyer sat down at his desk, leaned back and folded his arms. 'Most of these are from an old high-school teacher of mine. Thanks to her, I get the rejects from the town's library.'

'Some teacher,' River murmured. 'You mind if I borrow a few?'

'Any time.'

I leaned against the doorway and watched them discuss different books. Up until then I never knew Boyer to have any outside friends. I mentally patted myself on the back for bringing them together, and I tried to ignore the sudden pinch of envy I felt.

The long hot summer of 1966 produced a bumper hay crop. My favourite memory is of my father, brothers and River working in the fields. I carry a mental picture of them drenched in the golden glow of the late-summer sun. I keep this precious gem hidden deep in the dark closet of my mind, behind all of life's stored clutter.

One day in the middle of August, in the thickness of the afternoon heat, I carried ice-cold lemonade out to the back hayfield. With Elizabeth-Ann tagging along at my side, I made my way down the dirt road.

I heard my brothers before I spotted them. Morgan and Carl's voices carried over the mechanical drone of the tractor. They called out to each other, teasing and laughing, mocking the backbreaking work. River's voice joined in, floating like a song on the summer breeze.

Elizabeth-Ann and I paused at the edge of the hay meadow in waist-high grass. The sweet aroma of drying alfalfa filled my nostrils. Out in the field my father drove the tractor, pulling the haywagon along neat rows of baled hay. With his right hand on the steering wheel, he peered over his left shoulder at Morgan and Carl pitching bales.

Boyer and River, both stripped to the waist, stacked the heavy bales on the deck of the wagon. Rivulets of sweat streaked through the fine hay dust covering their naked torsos. Their heads turned as first one, then the other, caught sight of us. I smiled at the relief in their eyes. The noise of the tractor engine wound down as I hurried across the dried stubble of the mown field.

Delivering Mom's thirst-quenching lemonade on these hot summer afternoons was a chore I never tired of. I enjoyed it even more when any of my friends—in particular Elizabeth-Ann—came with me. I secretly relished the envy I saw in her eyes as I passed out the cold drinks.

'Thank you, Sunshine,' Dad said, reaching for his tin cup.

'Ah, sweet Natalie, the lifesaver,' River said. He sat down on the back of the haywagon and wiped the sweat from his brow. Then he held up his arms to strum an invisible guitar and began singing 'Aura Lee', an old American Civil War song with the same melody as 'Love Me Tender'. And as he crooned, he substituted my name for Aura Lee. And the magic of my name filled the meadow and warmed me beyond anything the afternoon sun could ever do.

Feigning annoyance, but secretly thrilled, I passed him a drink. He gave a mock bow of his head then raised his tin cup in a toast to me.

I dipped another cup into the jug and Boyer jumped down from the wagon to get his drink.

'This deserves a hug,' he said and pulled me into his arms in a bear hug, deliberately smearing my T-shirt with his muddy sweat.

I giggled and shrieked as I tried to wriggle away, fully aware of the frown that crossed Elizabeth-Ann's face.

Afterwards, as we walked side by side back to the house, she said casually, 'Wow, that River sure is mint.'

I stopped abruptly and scowled at her.

Elizabeth-Ann was beautiful. I was not. If she set her sights on River, how could he resist? 'I like him,' I said.

'Oh,' she answered, then shrugged. 'OK. You get River. I get Boyer.'

She had made no secret of her attraction to Boyer. In the beginning of our friendship I fought the stay-away-from-my-brother thoughts that welled up each time she spoke about him. Still, I felt a relief as she put her arm round my shoulder and marched back to the house with me, our childish bargain sealed. Besides, somehow I knew that her affection for my brother would not be reciprocated.

My relief turned out to be short-lived that summer afternoon. Just as we arrived at the gate, a black Lincoln Continental pulled into the yard.

'What's he doing here?' Elizabeth-Ann moaned as she saw her father's car.

Mom stood at the open screen door wiping her flour-dredged hands on her apron. 'Well, Gerald, to what do we owe this honour?' she called out as I brushed by her. 'We can't vote in a town election, you know.'

I stood behind Mom for a moment and looked over her shoulder.

'Oh, no, I'm not campaigning, Nettie.' Mr Ryan puffed up the porch steps. 'Just thought I'd drop by and see what the big attraction is. Seems my daughter here'—he smiled up at Elizabeth-Ann—'spends more time at your place than at home these days.'

Elizabeth-Ann rolled her eyes and stepped past Mom, following me as I fled up the stairs. In the upstairs hallway I slid down the wall and sat by the open floor grate. Downstairs, I heard Mr Ryan settle in a chair and accept the lemonade Mom offered.

'Thought I'd take the opportunity to come out and meet this new fellow I've heard so much about,' he said between slow gulps.

Mom's rolling pin slammed down on the table as she worked the pie dough. 'Well, then I guess you'll have to wait until dinner time later tonight,' she said. 'They'll be haying until the last minute.'

'I hear this young fellow's American. A hippie. Maybe a draft-dodger. What did you say his name was?'

'I didn't,' Mom replied. 'Why?'

'Well, I'm just thinking, as mayor, that it's my duty to run a check on him. Make sure he's here legally. Maybe make some enquiries with the FBI. We should be certain he's legit, not running from the law or anything like that. For your family's own protection and the town's.'

'Oh, there's no need to bother yourself with that,' Mom said sweetly. 'I can vouch for him. He's family. Richard's my cousin's boy from Montana. Now, you wouldn't want to interfere with family, would you?'

Family? Her cousin's boy? I put my hand to my mouth and choked back the giggle I felt bubbling up.

Elizabeth-Ann mouthed, 'Is that true?'

I shrugged my shoulders and she clasped her hand over her mouth to stifle her own giggles.

We stayed upstairs while the overly polite conversation droned on in the kitchen. Finally Mr Ryan called up for Elizabeth-Ann. She rolled her eyes again. Before she left she whispered, 'Don't worry, I won't tell.'

Mom and I spent the next morning pulling weeds in the garden.

Working out in the vegetable garden with my mother was another of my favourite chores. I loved the feel of the soil on my hands, the smell of the earth and the sun-warmed plants. I loved listening to the sound of my mother's soft voice as we chatted across the rows.

We worked side by side hilling potato plants. The midday sun warmed my back. My nostrils filled with the heavy perfume wafting over from the rose garden.

The rose garden was Mom's domain. I used to think Mom insisted on tending it alone because it was my father's wedding gift to her. Lately I noticed her weekly excursions looked more like a contest of wills than a labour of love. She attacked the rosebushes with pruning shears, clippers and even a handsaw. She could never keep ahead of the prolific runners and suckers. Each spring new shoots sprouted and filled the garden with thick, thorn-laden branches and rosebuds once again.

'How come you never pick the roses, Mom?' I asked. Just then I heard the milk truck pull up to the dairy.

Mom leaned her hoe against the fence. 'Roses die too quickly,' she said. 'Besides, flowers in the house only make me think of funerals.'

The only person I ever knew who died was my grandmother. I was twelve years old when Grandma Locke passed away. She visited us only a few times, but I never forgot the way she looked at my brothers and me, as if we were to blame for her daughter's lot in life. As if, by merely existing, we held our mother, who was meant for much finer things, captive against her will. And I remember the only words of advice my grandmother ever shared with me. 'Never marry a farmer, Natalie,' she told me. 'Remember it's just as easy to love a rich man as a poor one.'

I followed Mom out of the garden. 'Why didn't Grandma Locke like Dad?' I asked her, but my eyes were watching River climb out of the truck. He started unloading the empty crates.

Mom closed the latch on the gate behind us. 'Oh, it wasn't so much him she didn't like,' she said, 'as what he did for a living.'

'Ah, yes, the late, great Leslie and Christine Locke,' Dad's voice called

from inside the back of the milk truck. 'The king and queen of Victoria.'

'Oh, Gus,' Mom answered. I'd heard her use this expression so many times that, when I was little, I thought it was one word.

'I don't think your folks ever forgave you for marrying a milkman,' Dad replied, passing an empty crate to River. 'And according to them an ill-bred one at that.' Then he added, 'Maybe that was the attraction.'

I hurried to the back of the truck and reached up to take the next milk crate, then followed River into the dairy. He stacked his crate, then smiled at me as he reached to take mine.

'Got a little sunburn there, Natalie,' he said, and tapped me on the end of my nose..

I wondered just how much was sunburn and how much was from being around him. Although he had been there for a month I was still finding myself tongue-tied.

Outside, he gave me a conspiratorial glance as my parents continued to banter. After the last of the empty milk bottles were stored in the dairy, we followed Mom and Dad up to the house for lunch.

Dad threw his arm round Mom. 'So, Nettie,' he said, 'I hear congratulations are in order.'

'Congratulations?'

'On finding your long-lost relatives,' Dad said slyly. 'We ran into Gerald Ryan this morning.'

Mom stopped abruptly. She turned and looked at River, who was fighting to keep a straight face, then back to Dad. 'Oh, I—' she stammered, a flush rising in her cheeks. 'I didn't— I thought—'

'Yes, thanks for vouching for me, Cousin Nettie,' River drawled.

'I always knew you wanted a large family,' my father said. 'I just didn't realise what lengths you'd go to get it.' He laughed and hugged Mom closer.

I let go of the breath I had unconsciously been holding.

'And that's the only reason I married you.' Mom sniffed and shrugged off his arm in feigned anger. But I could tell she was relieved too.

'Don't ya believe it,' Dad said. 'It was love at first sight when your mother saw me.'

'Ha! For you, maybe.' Mom made her way up the porch steps.

Dad hurried after her and pulled open the screen door. He held it as Mom and I went into the kitchen. Then he followed, letting the door close behind him. River caught it just before it slammed. Inside, Mom and I stood together at the kitchen sink, rinsing the dirt from our hands.

'If you could have seen the goofy look on your father's face when he

saw me, instead of Aunt Elsie, at her door on my first morning in town,' she said, ignoring my father.

'So what brought a city girl to Atwood in the first place?' River asked.

Mom thought for a moment then said, 'Well, my father joined the navy in 1939, as soon as war broke out.' She fetched the kettle from the stove, took it over to the sink and filled it as she spoke. 'He left my mother and me in Victoria on Vancouver Island and shipped out. After Pearl Harbor, when the Americans joined the war, Mother suddenly realised that Japan was "just across the water". A week later she sent me to live with her aunt Elsie here in Atwood.'

'And then she saw me and was a goner,' Dad said. He winked at me before he headed into the bathroom.

'Not exactly,' Mom said over her shoulder.

'Tell River about the dance,' I prompted. I thought the story of how my parents met was so romantic that I wanted River to hear it too.

Mom continued. 'Your father couldn't even stammer a hello that first morning. I'd completely forgotten him by the time he showed up at the Christmas social at the Miners' Hall the next weekend.'

Dad emerged from the bathroom drying his face with a towel. 'I headed straight across the dance floor to where your mother stood and said, "I believe this is my dance." She glanced down at her dance card, back up at me, put the card in her pocket and said, "Yes, I believe it is."'

As River slid into his seat on the bench behind the table, he mouthed silently, *Dance card?* and we exchanged a secret smile.

'I was never one to make a scene,' Mom sniffed. She was slicing bread at the sideboard. 'It wasn't as if I had many partners to choose from. There was a war on after all. There was a shortage of eligible men and I was new to town. When the song was over—'

'And what was the name of the song?' my father crowed.

'"It Had to be You".' Mom rolled her eyes at me as we set the table. 'Anyway, when the dance ended I thanked your father cordially, but firmly. Then I returned to Allen Mumford. He was the town's new doctor then. It was his name that was really on my card. As Allen led me out onto the floor, I saw your father leave.'

'I was never one to overplay my hand,' Dad retorted. 'The next morning, when I delivered the milk to Aunt Elsie's, her front door opened and out comes your mom. She bounces down the stairs, opens the passenger door of the milk truck, jumps in, slams the door and says, "I believe this is my seat," without even cracking a smile.'

Contrary to my grandmother's belief, my mother never regretted

becoming a farmer's wife. From the moment she first stepped out of the milk truck at the Ward Dairy Farm, she said her heart was captured.

'It was really the farm I fell in love with first,' she said wistfully. 'It was like a Christmas card. The snow hung heavy on the branches of trees, it rolled off the barn roof like thick icing. Fat, silent flakes fell, dusting the backs of the cows and horses. A stream of smoke curled up from the brick chimney of the farmhouse. It was beautiful . . .' she mused. 'In the dairy, the smell of cream, wet cement and bleach was as familiar to me then as it is now.'

'You sure it wasn't the kiss I stole as soon as the door closed behind us?' my father teased.

Mom ignored him as she poured boiling water into the teapot. She knew with certainty, she went on, that as she followed Dad to the farm-house that it was her future in-laws she was about to meet.

As she placed the teapot on the table, Dad came up behind Mom and wrapped his arms round her waist. 'And that was our lucky day,' he said as he spun her round. 'Underneath those snow clouds, the sun was shining right side up. Eh, Nettie?'

I saw a brief flash of something akin to sorrow filling Mom's eyes as Dad took her into his arms. It was there, then disappeared so quickly I thought I imagined it. I couldn't tell if River had noticed because when I glanced over at him he was studying his fingernails.

While Dad sang an off-key version of 'It Had to be You', Mom frowned in mock exasperation.

'Oh, Gus,' she sighed, letting him lead her round the kitchen in an exaggerated, swaying, slow dance, 'of course it was.'

'It's an ill wind that blows no good,' Mom was fond of saying. But I wonder what she would have called the winds that blew River Jordan into our lives.

'The winds of discontent' River called them one night when the con-versation turned to the protests sweeping through America. He told us that for him, those winds began in Washington, DC the year before.

'On November the 2nd, 1965,' he said, 'beneath Defense Secretary Robert McNamara's Pentagon window, a young Quaker pacifist, Norman Morrison, doused himself in gasoline. Then he lit a match.

'A split second before he exploded into flames,' River went on, his voice quiet, 'he handed his one-year-old daughter to a bystander.'

I shuddered as the image of a human fireball flashed through my mind.

River looked up and his eyes met mine. 'When I heard the news in

my dorm room at Montana State University,' he said, 'I felt that same shudder in my soul.' He reached into his jeans pocket. 'The next day I found this article on the front page of the *New York Times*.' He pulled a folded newspaper clipping from his wallet. As he passed it to Boyer I caught the headline: VIETNAM FOE BURNS TO DEATH.

'It was the word "foe" that caught me,' River said. 'How easily they used that word. I knew it wasn't meant that way, but to me it felt as if to be in opposition to the war made him the enemy.'

While Boyer read, my father cleared his throat and pushed his chair back. He slipped out of the door as the article was passed around.

'Norman Morrison woke me up,' River said. 'I couldn't ignore what was happening any longer. I wasn't willing to make his sacrifice but I could stand up and be counted.'

He told us that after he left college he began marching in protests, attending rallies and sit-ins across the country. 'When my draft card came it was an easy decision to burn it.'

The table was silent. Neither Morgan nor Carl, or any of their friends, had a witty comeback for River's quiet words that day.

It was obvious from the first that he was different from the usual strays who found their way out to our farm. Like Boyer, River had no need to fill the empty spaces in conversation with words. His quiet maturity made the constant bantering between all the town kids who crowded round our table seem like mindless chatter.

Indirectly, I guess, all those young people could be held responsible for everything that happened after River. If they hadn't crowded Jake out, River would never have come to us.

Like each person in our family, while Jake lived with us he had his customary place at mealtime. He sat opposite Dad, beside Boyer. Guests either squeezed in on the bench with Morgan and Carl or pulled extra chairs up beside Mom and me. If anyone dared sit in Jake's chair, he grabbed his plate and filled it up before slamming out of the door.

Mom blamed our expanding circle of friends for his leaving. 'Poor Jake,' she said after, 'he just couldn't tolerate all those young people.'

Whatever the reason, out of the blue one day, Jake packed up and said, 'Well, guess it's time for me to move on,' as if he had been there for a few weeks instead of over twenty years. Then he surprised all of us by moving in with Widow Beckett. On the day he left, he and the Widow, who had never been known to even talk to each other, much less have a relationship, were married at the town's courthouse. We saw little of them after that.

During the time he was with us River never sought anyone's company; neither did he avoid it. He seemed as comfortable left alone or spending time with whoever showed up in his room above the dairy.

Once Boyer started spending his evenings there I tagged along. I sat at the chrome table in the corner and listened as Boyer read the poetry of Dylan Thomas, or River played the guitar and sang Bob Dylan songs. The more I saw them together the more I saw how similar they were in their quiet accepting ways. I watched from the sidelines with a growing envy over the time they spent together. I wasn't quite sure if the twinge of resentment I felt was directed at Boyer or River.

By default, Elizabeth-Ann, instead of Boyer, was now my best friend. We became co-conspirators, plotting ways for the four of us to be together. And like everyone else we were always welcomed when we showed up in River or Boyer's rooms.

Folk songs, poetry, and talk of world events would only hold Morgan and Carl's attention for so long though, before they headed back to the house to dance to rock-and-roll 45s out in the sunroom. On many evenings Elizabeth-Ann and I had to choose between following the gang to the sunroom, or out to the lake, or staying to listen to poetry and songs of protest. For me there was no contest.

Every summer my parents held a barbecue at the farm on the Labour Day weekend. Half the town came. Mom loved those get-togethers. I'm sure it was the highlight of her year. She worked for days preparing. Everyone who helped with the haying was rewarded with thick steaks, endless potato salad, Mom's fresh baked bread and platters of steaming hot corn-on-the-cob drenched in her fresh-churned butter. Mom kept plates full, and drinks refilled, while my father and the men played horseshoes and the women sat in gossip circles on the lawn. I noticed she danced expertly around, or ignored, any questions and references to River being family.

With all the extra hands, the evening milking was done early, leaving my brothers and their friends free to head out to the small lake by the old miners' cabin. It was not much of a lake, more of a pond, but large enough for swimming. Lily pads and weeds floated around the muddy edges. Years before, Morgan and Carl had built a wooden raft. That summer someone anchored it in the middle.

Everyone took turns changing in the abandoned log cabin by the lake. I think most teenagers from town must have been at the lake that day. They splashed in the water, lounged out on the raft or on towels

spread in the meadow grass. Every once in a while Elizabeth-Ann snapped a picture with her new Instamatic—another one of the many gifts her father was forever buying her.

She caught Carl and Morgan wearing girls' petal bathing caps on their heads and towels wrapped around their waists like skirts. They hold their arms up in a clowning hula dance. Behind them Boyer leans against the doorway of the cabin. When Elizabeth-Ann showed me her pictures the following week, I noticed Boyer was in the background of each photograph. Even in the one of River.

I kept that picture, folded down the middle, tucked inside my wallet, or whatever book I happened to be reading. Boyer's image showed on the front, with River's hidden away on the other side. I took the photograph out whenever no one was around and turned it over. I studied River's face secretly, memorised it, and, just as any adolescent might do I supposed, I sometimes even kissed it.

Elizabeth-Ann's camera caught River sitting backwards at the picnic table, his guitar in his arms. He is aware of the camera's eye on him as he strums. His smile flashes carelessly into the future. A smile I pretended was for me.

Boyer sits on the ground leaning against the trunk of an old apple tree. His elbows rest on his knees; a book is in his hands. He's not reading though. He's gazing over the top of the pages at River, unaware of the camera catching this moment. The usual detached indifference is gone from his face, replaced by an expression I could not read.

When I first saw the photograph, I was struck by the contrast between River's open smile and Boyer's intense focus. I was blind to the similarities in those unguarded expressions.

That day, I watched from the shore as everyone swam in the lake. The girls resembled huge flowers bobbing in the water in their brightly coloured petal bathing caps. Some soaked up the dying rays of the sun out on the raft. They leaned back in their two-piece bathing suits, trying too hard to look like the swimsuit models of teenage magazines.

The boys did posturing of their own, diving and racing, competing for the admiration of female eyes. Morgan and Carl seemed unaware of the contrast between their tanned torsos and their pasty white legs as they performed cannonballs off the raft. Boyer and River swam in a leisurely way out to the raft and back—enough to cool off—then retreated, Boyer to his book, River to his music.

'Hey, Nat,' Carl hollered from the raft. 'C'mon in.'

I ignored the calls as I set out desserts and drinks on the table where

River sat picking at the guitar strings and singing softly. I still can't hear Dylan's 'Love Minus Zero/No Limit', without thinking of River and that summer day.

I discovered that summer that being in love changes you. It makes you want. I wanted to be pretty. I allowed Elizabeth-Ann, who wanted to be a hairdresser, to cut my hair into a pixie. I still was not ready for the teased bouffant hairstyles all the other girls were wearing. And I wanted to be thin. I began to eat nothing unless it was first drowned in vinegar, another trick taught to me by Elizabeth-Ann. By September I was no longer the pudgy milkmaid. No longer 'Nat the Fat'.

Still, I was reluctant to change into my bathing suit. I knew my new lean body looked more like a boy's than like the bronzed bodies of the girls in the water. I still wore my pedal-pushers and a T-shirt. My bathing suit, wrapped in a towel, lay on the counter in the cabin. The basket of desserts and drinks was my excuse to avoid putting it on.

River looked up from the guitar. 'Just like your mom.' He grinned at me. 'Always feeding the masses.'

I didn't mind being compared to my mother. In any way. Especially by River. I felt my heart swelling at the softness of his voice.

'C'mon, Natalie,' Morgan's voice taunted across the water. 'If you don't come in, we'll come and get you.'

'Better to go in on your own than be thrown in,' River warned me while he continued to strum his guitar.

'Right,' I said and headed to the cabin. I knew I had some time before Carl and Morgan would reach the shore.

Inside the cabin I changed in the dark. Back outside I hurried to the lake, anxious to be hidden by the water. By the time my feet sank into the muddy bottom, everyone was arriving at the shore. They splashed and teased as I waded in. Suddenly I stood frozen, the hidden muck oozing between my toes.

'Grab her feet,' Morgan called to Carl. 'I'll get her arms.'

I was surrounded, trapped, more afraid of making a scene, having the attention on me, than of the water. It felt as if the mud was quicksand, as if my lungs were drowning in the air. I began to hyperventilate.

'Wait,' River called out. 'Let her go in on her own.' He joined me in the water, moving backwards in front of me. I lifted my feet out of the mud and followed. When he was waist-high in water, he said, 'Lean forward.' His voice was gentle. 'Just lay on top of the water and let it take you.'

I followed him as he moved backwards. 'Keep breathing,' he said.

I lowered my torso into the water and paddled towards him. River

laughed and lay back. He backstroked to the raft, rolled under and came up beside me. His arms made clean, sure strokes through the water as we swam side by side. He lifted himself up onto the raft and held his hand out to me, then pulled me up onto the wooden boards.

I don't know why I felt such triumph in that moment. I only know I felt safe being there, on that raft, alone with River. It was enough. It was everything. On shore we were forgotten. Everyone was caught up in another bout of splashing and screaming.

Then I noticed Boyer still sitting under the apple tree. Watching us. He peered over his book with an expression I did not recognise. I lifted my arm and waved. Either Boyer did not see my wave or he ignored it. Bending his head down, he went back to reading his book.

CHAPTER FIVE

GHOSTS DANCE ON the edge of my vision. They follow me, stalk me, then vanish when I take notice. I turn quickly when I see them flirting with daylight in the corner of my eyes, but I am too slow. Or they are too quick. The teasing shadows evaporate before I can catch up to the blurred movements. But I know they are there.

Even here, sitting on this bus that is speeding into the past, I catch a sudden dark movement in my peripheral vision. I turn and see him sitting in the seat across the aisle. My father. He is wearing his dark blue Sunday suit, a red poppy pinned to his lapel. He turns his head.

An unfamiliar face stares back at me. A questioning smile forms on his lips. 'Do I know you?' the look asks. The face is that of a stranger. There is no Sunday suit. But the poppy on the tattered black windbreaker is real. I have been caught again, played with by the shadows.

It was the poppy that did it. It's only mid-October. My father was the only person I knew to wear one this early. Every year in the middle of October he took last year's poppy down from the visor in the cab of his truck. He pinned it to his lapel and wore it until the Legionnaires appeared on the streets with boxes of new ones strapped round their necks. My father was always one of their first customers. Only then

would he discard last year's dusty felt flower, replacing it with the new one. After the Remembrance Day ceremony, he removed the poppy from his lapel and stuck it on the visor, where it stayed, ready for the same ritual the following year.

My father never went to war. Like Dr Mumford he was denied enlistment. I once heard him joke that delivering babies and delivering milk were equally essential to the home war effort. Knowing how he felt about guns, I often wondered if his regret over not being allowed to fight for his country was feigned. Still, every November 11, my father would attend the annual Armistice Day parade.

The last time we went as a family was during the years River was with us. My father still had not warmed to River by that first November. Yet, one afternoon I came into the kitchen to find the two of them huddled together at the table.

'It wouldn't cost much,' River was saying as he scribbled notes on a series of diagrams. 'We can use a lot of equipment you already have.'

I peered over Dad's shoulder at the intricate plans spread out on the table. He said nothing. I watched as River went over the diagrams and written instructions. Then I noticed that, as he explained the automated system for removing manure from the milking stalls, he had stopped using written notations and was drawing more detailed sketches.

The following week, the system was built and installed in the barn. 'Shoulda' thought of this years ago,' Dad said. Not long after that River began to go with Dad on the milk route, even on weekends.

At breakfast on Remembrance Day, however, Dad asked me to come along on the milk route. Mom, Morgan and Carl would come in with Boyer to meet us for the services. I grabbed my coat and followed Dad outside, excited at the thought of sitting so close to River.

River was waiting for us by the dairy. Even though he had told us that wearing poppies was no longer a tradition in the States, a red felt flower was pinned to his jacket. When we reached the truck, Dad said, 'No need for you to come, Richard. Natalie's helping me today.' Dad opened his door. 'We're all headed to the Remembrance Day ceremony afterwards,' he said. 'I'm sure you're not interested in that.'

River opened the passenger door and motioned me in ahead of him. 'Well, if it's all the same to you, sir,' he said, 'I'll come along on the milk run. Then I'd like to attend the ceremony with you all.'

My father muttered, 'A pretty strange place for a pacifist, isn't it?'

'Well, I don't know about that, sir,' River replied, climbing into the truck. 'But isn't Remembrance Day here much the same as Veterans Day

at home? Isn't the purpose the same? To remember the horrors of war and to honour those who died? I've attended both Veterans Day and Memorial Day services with my mother and grandfather every year for as long as I can remember.'

'What for?' Dad grumbled. 'I thought you were against war.'

River banged the truck door shut. I felt the heat of his body as he settled in the seat beside me. 'Yes, sir,' he replied, 'I am. But, for me, today isn't about protest.' Then his voice became even quieter. 'It's about my father and my uncle,' he said slowly. 'To remember them. They both died in the Battle of Okinawa, three months before I was born.'

There was silence for a moment. Then my father reached down and threw the truck into gear.

It doesn't take long for the small procession to march down Main Street in Atwood each November 11. That morning, with the promise of snow in the crisp autumn air, we stood on the sidewalk and watched the silent parade make its way to the cenotaph.

A handful of ageing veterans, wearing tight-fitting uniforms, came first. They marched in stoic and proud rhythm, staring ahead to some place those of us on the side of the road could not see. The young cadets, with their serious faces brought up the rear. They marched by, slow, solemn, reverent, to the granite war memorial at the end of Main Street.

I looked over at River standing erect as the procession moved down the street. I thought about his father and uncle. For the first time, I felt the reality, the sadness of this memorial to fallen soldiers.

After the small troupe filed by, those of us watching began to fall in behind. The wives and mothers of soldiers, present and gone, joined in. Then, as they did every year, my father followed behind with his three sons. Before Dad started marching, I saw him turn and wave at River to join them. Mom and I brought up the rear.

At the end of Main Street, the crowd gathered round the cenotaph, a looming monument honouring Atwood's fallen sons. During the ceremony, a number of women, including Widow Beckett, stepped forward to place poppy wreaths below the brass plaque, which bore the names of those lost in both world wars. Following two minutes of silence, gunshots broke through the air. As each shot rang out, I saw my father's body flinch violently. And, on either side of him, I noticed both Boyer and River's shoulders jerk with the identical involuntary spasm.

After the service, as we did every year, our family headed to the Atwood branch of the Royal Canadian Legion to join the local veterans

for lunch. As we strode down the street I spotted Jake up ahead with Widow Beckett at his side. My father called out and they turned to wait. It was the first time I had seen Jake since he left the farm. I did a double take, surprised to see that he could actually smile.

While Mom and Widow Beckett greeted each other with hugs, my father shook Jake's hand. 'So, looks like married life agrees with ya,' Dad said. Each of my brothers greeted Jake and shook his hand. Then Dad gestured to River and said, 'Jake, I'd like ya to meet our new man, Rich . . . er, I mean, River. River Jordan.'

After lunch, I climbed into the cab of the milk truck with Dad and River. Once again I felt the electric thrill of sitting so close to River. As we drove home I noticed two poppies pinned to the overhead visors.

Snow was a constant in our lives for four to five months of the year while I was growing up. Every winter our farm became a labyrinth of trenches between the house and the outbuildings. Most mornings Dad had to clear the yard between the barn and the dairy with the tractor.

The snowfall was unusually heavy the year River came.

'Man, I've never seen so much white!' River called out to me as he trudged through the fresh powder after the first overnight storm.

'Ha! Just wait,' I puffed. I lifted my shovel and tossed a load of snow from the walkway over my shoulder.

'Here, let me do that for you,' he said and reached for my shovel.

'No, I like this job.' I nodded at the porch. 'Get your own,' I laughed.

'Ah, a women's libber,' he grinned. 'Good for you.'

Fat flakes fell silently onto his wool cap and shoulders. They landed on his cheeks and thick lashes where they melted from the heat. And I felt myself melt as he reached over and brushed off my face with his mitten. Even in the cold I could feel the blush rise. I lowered my head and dug my shovel in while River turned and ran up the porch steps. Then just as quickly he was back. We worked side by side on the path.

Over the months I had become used to River's presence. More than used to it. I couldn't imagine my life or my family without him.

After we reached the gate River looked down the road. 'Good thing the milk truck's a four-wheel drive,' he mused, 'or we'd have to hook up the horses to pull us into town.'

'It wasn't so long ago that we did just that,' Dad answered him from the porch. 'And sometimes we still do. Eh, Nat?'

Before I had a chance to respond, Dad called out to River, 'Looks like ya missed breakfast.'

'That's OK,' River answered as Dad came down the steps. 'Natalie and I like this job.' He grinned at me, then handed me his shovel so that he could take the Thermos and a brown paper bag from Dad.

'Toast.' Dad nodded at the bag. 'Can't have my copilot starving.'

I watched as they walked together over to the truck. River peered into the bag and said something I couldn't hear. Dad threw his head back and laughed out loud. They looked so at ease with each other that it made me smile.

Lately I had noticed that River and Dad took longer and longer to deliver the milk each morning. Dad said that when he stopped to pick up his newspaper at Gentry's they stayed for coffee so River could get to know the locals. River never disputed this explanation, but I had a hard time imagining Dad leaning over his paper at the counter, pretending to read, while River chatted with Mrs Gentry or the other patrons.

Yet, even though Dad told River he could take the weekends off, each day the two of them went together on the milk route.

Except at Christmas. Early Christmas morning Mom and I carried quilts and blankets down to the front of the barn as my brothers harnessed up the horses. Like every other year Mom would ride along in the milk truck with Dad for the Christmas Day deliveries, while my brothers and I followed behind in the flat-bed sleigh.

I threw the blankets onto the loose hay on the sleigh as the door above the dairy opened.

'What's this?' River stood at the top of the stairs, looking from one of us to the other while our entire family stood waiting with smirks on our faces. We had deliberately kept this part of Christmas a secret to surprise him. We all knew he was missing his mother and grandfather and hoped our Christmas morning tradition would take away some of the sadness of not being with them for the holidays.

'Merry Christmas!' I sang, excited at sharing this day with him.

River looked up at Boyer, who stood up on the sleigh, holding the leather reins. 'So what's happening?' River asked.

'Hop on and you'll find out,' Boyer called down.

River's blue-green eyes crinkled in a smile as he glanced over at Mom standing beside the milk truck. 'What about the milk route?' he asked.

She smiled at him. 'This is my seat today, River. You go with the kids.' She took a deep breath of the crisp air. 'It's going to be a perfect day,' she said and climbed into the cab. As the truck pulled away she leaned out of the window and called, 'Don't fall off now.' She said that every year.

Boyer clicked his tongue. The horses leaned into their harnesses and

strained forward. River reached under my shoulders and boosted me up, then threw himself onto the sleigh as it began to move.

He crawled up beside me and rested against the empty wooden boxes stacked at the front of the sleigh. 'And what are these for?' he asked.

'You'll see,' I said.

The horses tossed their heads, fighting the first taste of the bits. Clouds of white vapour puffed up from flared nostrils. Rows of silver bells attached to their manes jangled when they surged forward. The sleigh runners glided along soundlessly on the hard-packed snow.

'This is my favourite part of Christmas,' I shouted above the bells.

'And now it's mine too,' River shouted back. He put his arm round my shoulder and hugged me to him. And despite being bundled up I imagined I felt the warmth of his body through my heavy woollen coat.

When the sleigh slowed down on the first hill, I felt a sudden shove from behind. The next thing I knew I was tumbling into a sea of snow, Morgan and Carl's laughter following me. I surfaced and blew out a mouthful of powder as River landed next to me. He rolled over and laughed. He lay back and stared up at the clear sky for a few moments. 'Wow,' he breathed. 'Neat.'

As the sleigh crested the hill he sat up and offered me his hand and we pulled each other up. Like snow-crusted penguins, with arms straight out at our sides, we tottered back to the sleigh. Before we jumped on, River nodded to me, and by unspoken agreement we pelted Morgan and Carl with the snowballs we had hidden in our mitts.

In town, the horses trotted behind the milk truck as Dad and Mom made deliveries. The whole town appeared to be sleeping, yet at every house we stopped, doors flew open. Dad's customers, many in dressing gowns and pyjamas, greeted us with choruses of Christmas wishes. Hot toddies, Christmas cookies and presents were pressed into our hands. By the time we'd finished the bottom half of town the wooden boxes on the sleigh were brimming with gifts and Christmas baking.

Hand-knitted mittens, caps and scarves filled an entire box. Fruit-cakes, cookies, homemade jams and preserves filled the others.

River laughed out loud as Morgan and Carl sorted through the bounty and offered up treats. 'Man, all this on top of your mom's mountains of Christmas baking? Whatever will you do with it all?' he asked as he popped a butter tart into his mouth.

'You'll see,' I answered.

When we reached the end of Main Street, Boyer took off his gloves, cupped his hands together and blew into them. Then he turned the

reins over to Carl. I rode between River and Boyer as the horses started the climb to the top part of town. We sat with our legs dangling over the side while River talked about Christmases growing up in Montana.

'You're so lucky to have a large family,' he told us. 'Pretty hard for an only child to go on a hayride. But what I did love about Christmas was going carolling. Every year on Christmas Eve, Mom and Granddad and I went from farm to farm, visiting and singing Christmas carols.'

'We can do that,' Morgan called and started singing, 'We Wish You a Merry Christmas.' Everyone joined in, even Boyer, our voices ringing out in song as we glided along the snow-covered streets of town. I wanted the moment never to end.

But it did. As soon as we turned onto Colbur Street.

We stopped in front of the Ryan house. Elizabeth-Ann came hurrying out, carrying a tray of mugs and calling, 'Merry Christmas, everyone!' Her mother followed with a steaming jug. Mrs Ryan poured hot chocolate into the mugs her daughter held up.

'Well, if it isn't the famous Wards,' Mr Ryan called out from the open door where he stood in his dressing gown. 'Atwood's favourite family. And their long-lost American . . . uh . . . nephew, isn't it?'

'Cousin!' Morgan and Carl cried at the same time, then laughed.

'So,' Mr Ryan asked, coming out onto the porch, 'does that make you kissing cousins then?'

I shivered and shrank back between River and Boyer.

River looked from me to Mr Ryan. 'Well, by gosh, sir. I guess it does,' he said in an exaggerated drawl. He turned and smiled down at me. I saw his eyes flicker for an instant over to Boyer, before he took my face between his hands and planted a loud smacking kiss on my cheek.

Morgan and Carl hooted while I sat there momentarily stunned.

'Well, although I'm sure the ladies like the new milkman here,' Mr Ryan's slurred voice continued, 'I must say I miss the pretty little milkmaid coming to my door.'

Mrs Ryan finished pouring the last mug and glared up at her husband as he stood on the edge of the porch steps, a drink in his hand. She shook her head. 'Go back inside, Gerald, before you catch a cold,' she sighed. 'Or fall down,' she added under her breath.

At the same time both River and Boyer placed their arms protectively round my shoulders. Before the sleigh jerked forward Elizabeth-Ann passed me a mug and said, 'You're such a lucky duck, Natalie Ward.'

When the milk route was completed, when the wooden boxes on the sleigh were full-to-bursting, we came to a stop before the building next

to the hospital. Mom and Dad climbed out of the truck. They came back to the sleigh where Morgan and Boyer handed each of them one of the full boxes. I jumped down and reached for one too.

River passed the box to me, his eyes watching Mom unlatch the heavy wooden gate between the hedges. OUR LADY OF COMPASSION, SCHOOL FOR GIRLS, the sign above the gate read. But by then, even River knew what the stone building next to the hospital really was.

'Is this all going here?' he wondered out loud.

'Yes,' Boyer said, as he pushed more boxes to the edge. 'Every year we take most of our Christmas haul from Dad's customers to the home.'

Morgan sniggered and said out of the side of his mouth, 'Yeah, kind of ironic given how everyone in the town gossips about this place.'

River jumped down and grabbed a box. Boyer did the same. When they started to follow us Dad glanced at Mom with a cocked eyebrow. Mom hesitated for a moment, then said, 'All right, but just to the front doorstep. Even that will probably throw the nuns into a tizzy. But I'm sure the sight of a few handsome young men will give the young ladies peeking out of the windows some Christmas cheer.'

Carl stayed at the reins. When Morgan made no move to leave the sleigh, River called back, 'Aren't you going to come along to add to the young ladies' Christmas thrill?'

Morgan jumped down and grabbed a box from the sleigh. He hurried after us, his out-of-tune voice rising in another round of 'We Wish You a Merry Christmas'.

We all joined in the singing while we deposited box after box on the front steps of the school.

CHAPTER SIX

ONE NIGHT IN JANUARY, Boyer announced his intention to fix up the old miners' cabin by the lake. I looked up from my plate.

'What for?' I asked.

'To live in,' he said. 'I'm going to move out there.'

'No!' I blurted without thinking.

Boyer ignored my outburst. 'I'm almost twenty-four,' he stated. 'It's time I had my own place. It's less than a ten-minute walk, Natalie. Besides, it's not as if you won't still see me every day.'

The thought of Boyer not being upstairs in the attic room left me with an empty feeling. Yet, for the rest of the winter I became caught up in the plans formulated at our kitchen table. In the spring I joined the work bees along with my brothers, Dad and River. After school and on weekends there were more than enough spare hands busy with hammers and saws. Before long a framed addition with a small bedroom and bathroom was added onto the side of the log cabin.

In April, Boyer moved in. I sat in the cab of the pick-up truck between him and River on the day we drove out with the final load. As we crossed the meadow in the afternoon shadows I thought that the ancient apple tree, which stood so close to the cabin, looked like a sentry keeping guard over Boyer's home.

As we pulled up to the door, ebony wings rose from the branches above the roof. Harsh voices barked with annoyance at the interruption as the flock of crows took to the sky.

Boyer looked up. 'Corvine?' he challenged me.

'That's easy,' I scoffed. I spelt the word out, then said, 'An adjective, pertaining to the crow.'

Boyer opened his door and climbed out of the truck. He shoved his hand into his jeans pocket and came out with a dime.

'I'm too old for that,' I said, feeling embarrassed in front of River.

Boyer tossed the silver coin to me. 'Too good, maybe,' he said, 'but not too old. Never too old.'

Boyer pulled down the tailgate and started to unload the truck.

Inside, he lit the gas lamps. 'Propane will do until I can afford to bring out hydro lines,' he said.

As I unpacked and organised the array of novels, which filled most of the boxes, it occurred to me that Boyer had created this space as much as a home for his book collection as for himself.

The heavy wooden door closed and River came in. Over the winter I had watched with envy as Boyer and River's relationship developed into a quiet friendship. Up until that time I'd never seen him spend so much time with anyone except our family and Father Mac.

'That's the last one,' River said, placing the box on the table. He breathed an exaggerated sigh and picked up a hardcover book from the top of the box. He looked at the front cover then turned it over to study a photograph of President Kennedy on the back.

'It's hard to believe that in November it will be four years since he was killed,' he mused. 'What was it like up here—for Canadians—then? How did the news affect you when he was assassinated?'

'I was only twelve,' I said, conscious of River's eyes on me as I spoke. 'I don't think I really understood it then.'

Boyer pulled a chair up to the table and sat down. 'I was stunned,' he said quietly. 'Like most Canadians, I think, I knew we had lost a friend. When he died, we mourned him as if he was one of our own.'

The hiss of the propane lights filled the silence. After a moment River spoke. 'I was in my twelfth-grade history class when the announcement came over the PA system. Our teacher laid his head on his desk and waved us from the classroom. The halls were eerily silent as we filed out. No one spoke. That night I met with three of my buddies, Ray, Frankie and Art. The four of us sat in front of the TV trying to make sense of it all. None of us wanted to accept that he had been murdered so easily. We were convinced it was the Russians. We all wanted something bigger to blame than the skinny little man they arrested. As the night wore on, talk turned to the possibility of war. And to enlisting. Ray and Art already planned to join up as soon as they graduated. They saw it as a career choice. But neither Frankie nor I had any intention of becoming universal soldiers. Yet, the strange thing was, there was a moment, a moment when I thought the Russians were behind it—that it could have really meant war—when I imagined myself in a uniform, with a gun in my hands.' He shook his head slowly at his admission.

'Half of us ended up wearing that uniform,' he said. 'Ray was no surprise. But Frankie was such a gentle soul. He talked to his priest about refusing the draft on religious grounds. The priest convinced him to serve. As a conscientious objector, in a noncombatant role. Sure, noncombative, but you still go through boot camp—learn to carry a gun.' River leaned forward, his hair hanging loose round his face.

'I got a letter from Ray last spring,' he said without looking up. 'Three days after Frankie arrived in Nam, he and Ray ended up together on a medical supply boat on the Mekong River. They were caught in a sniper attack and ordered to take arms. As Frankie shouldered his gun he begged, "Please, God, don't let me kill anyone." As the last word came out of his mouth, a bullet hole appeared in the middle of his forehead. Ray wrote that as Frankie slumped to the deck he was smiling.' River sighed then said, 'I guess his God answered his prayer.'

He looked up. 'Ray's still over there,' he said. 'He'll probably come through this unscathed—come home a hero. I hope he does anyway.

He deserves it. Anyone willing to risk everything, to die for what they believe in, is a hero. Frankie was a hero. The boys—men—over there are all heroes. It's the politicians, the leaders willing to sacrifice young men for their own political games, who are the cowards. Thank God we still have Robert Kennedy to stand up to Johnson and his lies. When Bobby's president, he'll put an end to this war.'

The room grew silent once again. After a few moments Boyer asked, 'And your other friend?'

'Art?' River smiled. 'He tried to volunteer. He failed his medical. An inner-ear problem. He cried like a baby when he was denied enlistment,' he said. 'And then there's me. I hid away at college. Nice and safe in classes. Until Norman Morrison lit that match.'

'Have you ever regretted your decision?' Boyer asked.

'I don't regret protesting against the war,' he said, then looked up and met Boyer's eyes. 'But, of course, I'm sorry I had to leave my home and that I had to give up my education.'

'So what are your plans now?' Boyer asked. 'Do you think you'll ever go back? To college, that is.'

I was startled by the question. Up until that moment I hadn't thought about River leaving, but suddenly it made sense. Of course he would not stay for ever. I waited nervously for his answer.

'I have a trust fund from my grandmother that matures when I am twenty-four,' River said. 'When I first came up here I thought I would get to know Canada by travelling around doing odd jobs. But I'm content to stay here if your family will put up with me until then. When I come into my trust I guess I'll apply to college in Vancouver or Calgary.' He smiled at Boyer. 'Which one do you think is best?'

Boyer shrugged. 'I haven't given it much thought.'

As they spoke I did a quick mental calculation. River was twenty-one. In three years I would be finished high school. For the first time I considered going to college.

But it was to Boyer that River directed his question. 'Well, why don't you? Why don't you think about coming with me?'

'That's not an option.' Boyer attempted a laugh.

River stared intently at Boyer as if he were weighing his thoughts. After a moment he said quietly, 'You once asked me how I could deliberately give up a college education. But isn't that exactly what you're doing?'

'It's not the same thing,' Boyer said, taken aback by River's remark.

'Isn't it?'

Boyer avoided his eyes. 'All the education I need is right here,' he said and waved at the books surrounding us.

'And the real world is out there.' River nodded towards the window. 'Just be certain you're being honest with yourself, man. That you're not using the farm—or your father—as an excuse to avoid that world.'

I smell it in the air.

In Kelowna, I waited inside the bus depot for my connection and still I could not escape the clinging odour of smouldering forests. Now, as the bus pulls away from the Okanagan town heading east, I can still smell it. I avoid looking out of my window. I don't want to see the destruction caused by the recent wildfires. I don't want to deal with my own memories of charred and blackened buildings.

It's a strange feeling to travel on a bus, like being in a separate world, a time machine, carrying me—in slow motion it now seems—back to my past. The first time I travelled by bus was when I left home in 1969. The next time was after my father's funeral.

I'm startled by the sudden thought that when my father died he was only four years older than I am now. In the end it was not the cancer that killed him. It was the farm. My father died on the cold concrete floor of the machine shed, underneath his Massey-Ferguson tractor.

Morgan called to tell me. I took the first flight home.

Jenny and Vern tease me about my fear of flying, but they wouldn't if they'd seen me on that flight. They have no idea of the extent of my phobia. I hadn't either until I strapped myself into an aeroplane seat for the first, and last, time. As soon as the stewardess pulled the cabin door closed I nearly bolted from my seat. My hands gripped the armrests. I felt the perspiration run in rivulets under my sweater as the plane began to taxi down the runway. I forgot how to breathe. Then, as we lifted into the air, it was all I could do not to scream to be let off. I kept my eyes squeezed shut until someone tapped my shoulder. I looked over to see the woman in the seat beside me hand me a paper bag. Just in time.

The airport shuttle-bus delivered me, shaken and weak, into Atwood. As we arrived on Main Street I saw the old milk truck angle-parked in front of the bus depot. The cab door opened and Morgan climbed out of the driver's seat. The awkwardness of returning home for the first time was lost in the need to bury our father. My brother took me into his arms without a word. Behind his welcoming smile was a steely determination not to shed tears. I was grateful for that.

On the drive home, he filled me in on the details of Dad's accident.

'The jacks slipped,' he told me. 'The tractor engine landed in the middle of his chest. His silver cigarette case was actually embedded in his chest. Her gift broke his heart, Mom says.' He shook his head and continued. 'He must have been pinned there for quite a while. Carl and I were out working in the wood lot. Mom and Boyer were in town, so there was no one there.'

'Oh.'

'Yeah, I can just hear his final words.'

'Every time the sun shines upside-down!' We murmured the words together. Morgan smiled, his Adam's apple going up and down in a swallow. I turned and stared straight ahead while I held back my own tears. And the sneezes.

'How have you been?' he asked.

'I'm OK.'

'You're working at a newspaper I hear. Gonna be a famous reporter, eh?'

'No.' I tried a laugh. 'I'm just selling advertising. But it's a start.'

The truck slowed down as we turned into South Valley Road. 'How's Mom?' I asked.

'Oh, she's, ah, well, she's Mom. You know. Busy feeding and comforting everyone who shows up to offer sympathy.'

While Morgan parked the truck in the carport beside the dairy, I walked up to the house. I stood in the shadows of the porch. And I smelt him there. My father. The musky scent of Old Spice and tobacco wafted from his jacket which still hung by the screen door. Then, through the mesh screen, I saw my mother. She stood at the kitchen table, her back to me. Exactly where she was standing the last time I saw her.

She turned at the first creaking of the screen door. Over two years had passed since I last saw my mother's face. Her eyes took me in as if it was only yesterday. Her smile was open, warm, vulnerable, and naked with love.

'Natalie.' She rushed over and threw her arms round me. And just like every hug that Nettie Ward has ever given any of her children, she hung on a little too long, a little past the point of comfort, and then she kept hanging on, until you gave in to it.

I stood there, stiff and remote. My unyielding arms hung at my sides, still holding my suitcase and an oversized book-bag. A part of me wanted to melt into the hug—as I always had as a child—to melt into the love, the acceptance, the arms of home. But I could not. I could not, even in that moment of shared sorrow, let go of my resentment. The unnamed resentment I'd carried with me out of the door the day I left.

'I'm so sorry, Mom,' I heard myself say.

'Hush, darling. There's nothing to be sorry about.' She said it as if she thought I was apologising.

I'm sorry. It's what you say, a greeting, when someone dies. What did she think I was apologising for? Sorry for? What did she mean, 'There's nothing to be sorry about.'? Of course there was. I was sorry my father was dead. I was sorry her husband of twenty-nine years was dead. For the way he died. I was sorry I wasn't there, that I hadn't seen him for over two years. Sorry I would never, ever have the chance to be with him again, to talk to him again. And I was sorry I did not have another chance to tell him I loved him. To tell him I was sorry. And I was sorry our family was even more broken.

Mom reached up and brushed the hair from my face. Her eyes filled. She pulled a tissue from her pocket and pressed it to her nose. After three quick sneezes, she squared her shoulders. 'Just look at all this food.' Every available space was covered with casseroles, cakes and pies. 'Whatever will I do with all this food?'

'I'm sure you'll see that it all gets eaten.' Boyer's voice came from the doorway to the parlour. I had not seen him through the film of tears I was blinking back. Cowardice stifled them. I avoided looking at him, just as I have avoided thinking about what I would do when this moment eventually arrived.

'Hello, Boyer,' I said. 'Good to see you.' But it was a lie. I looked any-where but his face.

'I'm really tired, Mom,' I said. 'I'd like to lie down for an hour.'

'Of course, dear,' she said. 'Go on up to your room. It's exactly as you left it.'

'The wake is at seven o'clock tonight,' Boyer said, a tired resignation in his voice. 'We should head into town at six thirty.'

He withdrew back into the parlour. I heard the murmur of hushed voices coming from the living room and wondered which neighbours, which of the few friends we Wards had left, were gathered there. There was no more family to come. We were it: Mom, Boyer, Morgan and Carl. And me. Our entire family—such as it was.

I slept. I slept in a bedroom that was, as Mom said, exactly as I had left it. My books still lined the shelf above my bed. The patchwork quilt she made for my tenth birthday lay on my bed, fresh, clean, and invit-ing. Everything right where I left it. A jar of pennies, silver dimes scat-tered amongst the copper, still sat on my desk. The room had the appearance of a dead child's bedroom. It was.

The drive into town is not long, but it stretched out in the silence that day, each of us lost in our own private memories of our father. I sat on the red leather seat, between Morgan and Carl, in the back of Boyer's Ford Edsel. He sat stiff and formal behind the wheel of the car.

Before we reached the highway, Mom shifted round and said to me, 'This accident may have been a blessing for your father.'

I was stunned by her words. I couldn't imagine any blessing in dying pinned under a tractor, with the motor crushing your chest.

'When they did the autopsy, they found he was full of cancer. Allen Mumford told me it was a wonder he was still walking around at all. He said your dad couldn't have lasted much longer without feeling it. God spared your father from suffering a long and painful illness,' she said as she turned back round in her seat. Then, as if it gave reason to his bizarre death, she added, 'It would have killed him to be in the hospital.'

I put my fist to my mouth to choke back the sudden unexpected urge to laugh.

'You know,' she added wistfully, 'he took his monthly bath the night before.'

That did it. I lost control. The repressed giggle burst through my fist. On either side of me I felt Morgan and Carl's bodies shake. Suddenly the car filled with choking laughter. Even Boyer and Mom's shoulders started to shake.

Boyer stopped on the side of the highway before we reached town so we could compose ourselves. It took more than a few moments for the fits of hysterical laughter to quiet down. As the car started again I shrank back in the seat and avoided Morgan and Carl's eyes in fear that the inappropriate giggles, or sobs, would start up again. I pressed my tissue to my nose. My muffled sneezes were echoed by my mother.

We parked in front of St Anthony's. Reluctantly I climbed out after Morgan. I steeled myself to get through this, unemotional and detached.

Boyer took Mom's arm. She was only forty-six, but for the first time I had a glimpse of what she would look like as an old woman. Shrunken, smaller, worn down by time, yet still strong.

I followed behind with Morgan and Carl. Inside the chapel solemn faces turned to greet us. Some I recognised and some I knew I should. Ma Cooper hugged Mom and murmured something to her as Widow Beckett and Jake, red-eyed and grim-faced, stood waiting to offer comfort. Boyer, too, waited at Mom's side as she accepted hushed condolences. Then they continued making their way towards the wooden casket at the front of the room. The small crowd parted and let them pass.

Morgan and Carl followed. I held back. The coffin, surrounded by flowers, seemed surreal. The heavy fragrance from the blossoms repulsed me. No wonder Mom never liked cut flowers in the house.

Somehow my legs carried me forwards towards the mahogany casket. The open casket. I stood behind Mom. She whispered something to Boyer. Then she leaned down to kiss my father.

But the waxy face enfolded in cream satin resembled no one I knew, least of all my father. There had been a mistake. This was not my father! Why was my mother kissing this apparition? Tears slid down her cheeks and dripped from her chin as she caressed the sunken face. Then she patted the folded hands, just as she had patted my father's hands every time she poured his coffee at the kitchen table. But she was patting the wrong hands. Couldn't she see that?

She reached over and put her arm round my shoulders, urging me closer. 'Kiss your father goodbye, Natalie,' she said.

I recoiled, almost fell, as I tried to step back. She took my hand and placed it on the chest of the impostor. I felt the scratchy wool of my father's Sunday suit. But underneath was a hollow hard nothingness. *This is not my father! This is not my father!*

'It's OK, Nat.' Morgan took my arm. Had I said it out loud?

Behind me I heard whispers. 'What's Natalie Ward doing now?'

Even here, even now, they would talk. Talk about me. Talk about Boyer, our family. I bristled. I would not make a spectacle of myself, my family. I leaned over and kissed the cold, grey cheek of the stranger who at one time must have been my father.

That evening, the next day, the funeral, all passed in a blur. I was there in body, but like a swimmer caught too far out I was treading water, watching my breathing, trying not to panic. I slept so deeply that Carl had to come in the next morning to wake me.

'Natalie, come and look at this,' he said. He hurried across the room and threw open the window.

I climbed out of bed and joined him. I followed his gaze down to the rose garden. It was Mom. She had on our father's jacket and woollen pants. My mother was wearing trousers! The shock of seeing her in them was almost as startling as the state of the garden. All around her lay pieces of thorny branches and chunks of rosebushes. Mom stood swinging an axe over a half-felled yellow rosebush. Chips of barbed branches, thorns and petals flew in the air with each swing. I glanced at Carl, then both open-mouthed, we watched as Boyer and Morgan approached the garden. They moved towards Mom cautiously, as if

afraid they might be next to be attacked. 'Mom?' Boyer called tentatively.

It looked as if she had not heard him. She gave no reply. She dropped the axe, then leaned over, picked up a handsaw, and began working at the gnarled branches at the base of the bush.

'Mom?' Boyer called again.

'What?' She kept on sawing.

'What— What are you doing?'

'What does it look like I am doing?' she answered with a quick glance up. 'I'm getting rid of these old bushes.'

Boyer surveyed the destruction. 'But, your rose garden—'

'It was never my rose garden,' Mom said, punctuating each word with a saw stroke. Then she dropped the saw and kicked at the severed plant with her boots. 'This garden was always your father's.' She grabbed a shovel and jammed it into the roots. 'He doesn't need it any more.'

Boyer and Morgan remained motionless, unsure what to do next.

'Don't just stand there gawking.' She stood on the shovel blade and wiggled it into the earth. 'Grab a shovel and help,' she puffed.

I felt, rather than saw, Carl step away from the window and leave the room. I remained there, riveted, unable to pull myself away.

For the rest of the day I sat on the window seat and watched the four of them dig up the garden. The twisted and snarled roots, tangled branches, sharp hooked barbs and thorns, all lay in an angry-looking pile in the fading afternoon sun. After Mom raked up the last remnants of pastel and blood-red petals, she took Dad's silver Zippo lighter from his jacket pocket and held it to the dried branches. The air filled with the smell of pungent smoke, mingled with the aroma of freshly turned earth and the sweetness of crushed petals.

Mom stood and leaned against her rake watching the smouldering fire. 'Peonies, now there's a nice soft plant,' I heard her say. 'In the spring we'll plant peonies. They don't bite back.'

I smiled at her words. I knew she was not speaking to anyone standing there.

Nettie

Gus's face floats before her. She reaches out to touch him. Her eyes open. She tries to focus, to search the room for him. But the room is bare.

'I'm coming, Gus,' she whispers.

But death is taking its merry time. She fights the dark spectre, not willing to surrender at the first assault. First—first, there is something she needs to do. What is it?

Natalie's name comes to her lips. Where is she? There is something she must tell her. It's more than goodbye. But what?

She hears the nurses' voices in the hallway. The morphine is wearing off. The afternoon light is fading. Night is coming. It's not the pain she wants to avoid; it's the night. The night is not her friend; it never was.

The pain begins to seep in. She does not resist it; with the pain comes a lifting of the fog. She wants to clear her mind, to be able to think, to find her way back to memories.

She sees the darkening sky through the window. And she suddenly remembers long-ago nights and shudders. It was only during the night-times that she had lost her way. Only as she lay in the dark beside Gus that she wondered. She would try to drown her thoughts in lists of chores, meal plans and prayers. Yet too often, like the nauseating perfume of the roses, the voices bullied their way back in. Until she reached for the book always waiting on her night table, and left her bed.

Sometimes she believed her reading was a curse. Sometimes she thought it would be a blessing to be like Gus, to never have read a novel in her life, to be unaware of what she was missing, to be ignorant of the possibilities. She was certain that all of Gus's carnal knowledge came from observing the farm animals. His lovemaking was as businesslike, and over as quickly, as any barnyard mating.

Only once did she shed her shyness and try to put into words what she was feeling. But she quickly learned that for all his public displays of affection, her husband could not, would not, discuss the intimacies of their bedroom. So she pushed back the unspoken yearnings on those nights when the only relief was the weight of her husband's body falling away from hers. And then, in the mornings, as her family surrounded her at the breakfast table, the family she had longed for all the years of her only-child youth, she wondered how she could question her life. Until River.

River? Now she remembers what she needs to tell Natalie.

We're getting closer, almost there. I see nothing except my blurred reflection as I try to peer out of the side window. But I don't need to see to know we are nearing the turnoff to Atwood.

The bus driver glances at me in the rearview mirror. 'Going home?' he asks as he catches my eye.

'Yes,' I answer automatically, and then wonder why. Atwood has not been my home for over thirty-four years.

Home. Such a simple word. What does it really mean? Where is it

exactly? I think of the line from the Robert Frost poem, 'The Death of the Hired Hand', once one of Boyer's favourites:

> Home is the place where, when you have to go there,
> they have to take you in.

And they would take me in. No one sent me away or shut me out. My exile was self-imposed.

But there's really no 'they' left there any more. Only Boyer. Now that Mom is in St Helena's, Boyer is the only member of our family who still lives out at the old farmstead.

Even the farm is not the same any more. The year after I moved away, shortly before my father died, the barn was automated and the milk sold in bulk to the large pasteurising dairies. And not long after that Morgan and Carl moved to the Queen Charlotte Islands.

The bus begins to slow and a flurry of conflicting emotions grips me. I push the anxiety back down and begin to gather my belongings.

We pull to a stop at the side of the junction. Parked beneath the highway sign is the old Ford Edsel. *Boyer?* Boyer has come to pick me up? My body goes rigid with sudden panic. Oh God, alone with Boyer for the forty-minute drive into Atwood? Where's Jenny? Then I feel the heat rise to my face. *Mom?* Maybe I'm too late.

But it's not Boyer who climbs out of the driver's seat as I stand waiting for the bus door to open. An involuntary sigh of relief escapes from my throat as I step off the bus and into my daughter's arms.

Through our tearful hug, Jenny assures me that Mom is all right. 'She was sleeping a bit fitfully when I saw her earlier tonight,' she says, 'but she has some fight in her yet.'

The sharp mountain air bites my face as we load my suitcase into the trunk. The bus taillights recede. Darkness enfolds us.

'I was surprised to see you with Boyer's old car,' I tell her once we are settled inside.

'My car,' she says. 'Uncle Boyer gave it to me. I'm just taking it out for the last spin before the snow flies.'

We drive in silence for a few miles, then without taking her eyes off the road Jenny says quietly, 'Tell me about River.'

I am momentarily stunned at hearing his name. A name from another lifetime. A name I haven't given voice to for years.

'Mom?' Jenny glances at me. 'Who was he? Tell me what happened to him—what happened between you and Uncle Boyer.'

So there it is. This is what she wanted to talk to me about. I've always

known this day would come. Still, I am startled at her request, not ready to speak it all out loud, and I tell Jenny so.

'But now is the time,' she says, her voice firm, but kind. 'Now, while Grammie is still with us.'

'How do you know about River?' I finally ask.

'Gram,' she says. 'She's said some pretty strange things in her delirium. And I've talked with Uncle Boyer. He said if I wanted to know more, I had to ask you.'

Jenny's questions create mixed emotions. Would it be a relief to finally unburden those secrets? Can I tell them all to this person whom I love more than I fear the past? The only other person I have ever felt that temptation to tell is Vern.

From the start, Vern and I resisted the urge to play the 'tell-me-something-you-have-never-told-anyone' game all new lovers seem to play. I realise with a start that the real reason I don't share my past with him, why I avoid bringing him to my childhood home, is I do not want him to see how much devastation I am capable of.

I wonder how much Jenny already knows? What have Mom and Boyer told her? Have they told her about that long-ago summer night? The night it all started to go wrong?

They couldn't have. They weren't there.

CHAPTER SEVEN

NO ONE WAS HOME that night except me. And in the room above the dairy, River.

June 8, 1968. The date is easy to remember because two days earlier Robert Kennedy had died. It was the only time I ever saw River cry. On Thursday night, he sat with Dad and Boyer in front of the television set in the living room. Silent tears spilled from his eyes and rolled down his cheeks while the image of the senator lying on the pantry floor of a Los Angeles hotel played out in the news.

'He was our hope to end this war,' River said, his voice almost inaudible, as he left the room.

On Saturday afternoon Boyer drove to Kelowna for the School Board to take delivery of a new school bus. He would stay in Kelowna overnight and drive the bus back to Atwood on Sunday morning. Morgan went along to drive his car home. Of course Carl wasn't about to let Morgan go on an excursion to the 'big smoke' without him. The three of them would be back the next day.

That Saturday evening, after supper, I worked with Mom in the dairy and River took over Morgan and Carl's job. River had been with us almost two years that June. He was like a part of our family.

Without my brothers the milking took much longer that evening. After Mom and I finished hosing down the dairy, we strolled together across the yard. The evening air felt still and heavy. Billowing white clouds boiled up over the mountains behind the house. Distant rumbling in the skies warned of thunderheads that could not be far behind.

After Mom and Dad took turns washing up, I filled the claw-foot tub in the bathroom. As I lay soaking, I heard them leaving for their monthly bridge game with Father Mac and Dr Mumford.

'Don't forget to bring in the rest of the wash, honey,' Mom called out before the screen door slammed.

I finished my bath and pulled on a cotton nightgown. As the sky outside darkened, I sat at the kitchen table studying for my grade eleven final exams. The soft aroma of sweet peas wafted in through the window screen. I felt restless. My mind was not on the books spread out on the table. My mind was in the room above the dairy.

I stared out of the window. The last colours of the day darkened as heavy black clouds rolled in. I suddenly remembered the wash. Outside the clothes snapped in the heightened wind. I stepped out onto the laundry platform and began to pull shirts, socks, trousers, and underwear, wooden pegs and all, from the line. I tossed everything into a wicker basket while wind and dust swirled around my bare legs.

Then I glanced up and saw him in the window above the dairy. River. He stood there, backlit by the soft glow from his room. He raised his hand and waved. But I saw what I wanted to see. I do not even see the truth in memory. I have replayed that gesture many times over the years. My memory will not let it play any different. I saw him beckon for me to come to him.

I finished yanking the laundry from the clothes line and carried the last basket into the porch. I grabbed a shirt from the top of the pile and pulled it on over my nightgown. I wrapped it around me and skipped down the porch steps. The night sky was now black with the fury of

roiling clouds. The only light in the yard was a circle of yellow from the bulb over the dairy door, and the glow in the empty window above.

When I was halfway to the dairy, a lightning flash lit up the night. Seconds later thunder ripped through the air. At the same moment the sky opened up and a deluge of rain spilled over me. By the time I reached the bottom of the stairway at the side of the dairy I was as drenched as if I had swum there.

The faint sounds of guitar music came from River's room. I had to knock twice before the quiet strumming ceased and the door opened. River stood in the dim light dressed only in a pair of cut-off jeans. Startled, he exclaimed, 'Natalie, man, you're soaked.' He ushered me inside and sat me down on the bed. He disappeared into the bathroom and returned with a towel and began to rub my head.

Three fat candles burned on the table next to the bed, filling the room with a soft orange light. The thrill of being alone with River, the pressure of his fingers through the towel, the tingle on my scalp, felt invigorating. I became bold. 'Can I try some?' I asked, nodding at the thin cigarette resting in an ashtray on his guitar case.

'Oh, no,' River laughed. 'I promised your father. None of my wacky-tabacky, as he calls it, for any of his family.' He reached over and pinched the tip of the marijuana butt, extinguishing the tiny glow.

We sat together on the iron bed with pillows propped up at our backs and watched the storm play out in the picture window across the room. Outside, the wind was working itself into a frenzy. The storm wrapped itself around the dairy, isolating us, cocooning us.

It felt somehow magical, otherworldly, being caught in a storm with River. It was easy to believe the world was distant, as if only the two of us existed, while nature swirled around us. It felt as if that moment in time was separate, unconnected.

I picked at the threads on my grandmother's quilt while I pretended there was nothing unusual about sitting beside River in my nightgown, while his naked torso reflected the golden glow of candlelight.

But inside I was weak with the thrill of it. My whole being felt his nearness. I wondered if he could hear my heart pounding.

After a while he reached down to retrieve his guitar from the foot of the bed. Melancholy strumming filled the air, while guttering candles created dancing shadows in the corners of the room.

I don't have the luxury of being able to say I was seduced to excuse what followed. It's difficult to explain how a young girl as naive about sex as I was could be the seducer, but that is what happened. Until that

night, other than what I read in books, my only experience with the opposite sex was a few awkward kisses during spin-the-bottle games held in the glow of campfires out at the lake. And yet there I was, alone with River, sitting on his bed knowing there was nothing I wanted more than to have his naked body pressed to mine.

I pulled my legs up and wrapped my arms around them. I rested my head on my knees and watched him as he played. His eyes were closed as if he were asleep, but his hands caressed the guitar strings with the knowledge of a lover. As he strummed, his heavy lids raised, and his blue-green eyes crinkled in a smile. A smile so tender I ached to reach over and stroke his face. Instead, I touched his shoulder, feeling the heat from his skin run up my arm. 'Teach me,' I said. 'Teach me to play.'

He passed his guitar to me and slid over to my side of the bed. 'I'll show you three easy chords you can use to play almost any song,' he said. 'Even,' he added with a warm smile, '"Love Me Tender".'

To say I was paying attention to anything other than River's closeness as he placed my fingers on the frets would be a lie. I don't know how much time passed as the storm played itself out in the night while I pretended to be interested in his patient instructions.

In the end it was me who put the guitar aside. I bent down and placed it on the floor. Then I tentatively placed my lips on River's. I took his lack of response as surprise. And suddenly I was pressing harder. But the hunger, the heat in that first kiss was all mine. I was the one who lay back, pulling him to me. I felt the rigidity of his body, but I did not stop. I caressed his face, his neck, his naked chest. My fingers undid the zipper of his jeans. My hands reached down and pushed up my nightie to expose my naked body. My hips lifted to his, guided him to me, while he lay with his face buried in the shirt on my shoulder, barely there. I ignored the robot-like response of his body, wanting to believe that he was holding back because he didn't want to hurt me. In the end, the coupling that took place was all my doing.

I knew—even then I knew—the part of River I wanted was not there. The whimpering coming from his throat was not that of passion, but of sorrow. He was still in mourning I told myself; his grief was for Robert Kennedy, for his country. Still I held on to him, unwilling to let go, to believe what my heart knew.

Even though I've played that scene over endlessly in my mind, reliving our hurried encounter, it could not have lasted more than a few minutes before River pushed himself away, as if he had suddenly woken up. 'Oh God,' he moaned as he rolled off me. 'This is wrong.'

'It's all right,' I murmured and tried to pull him back.

'No, no, it's not,' he cried. 'This is so wrong, so wrong.' He threw his legs over the end of the bed and leaned over, his face in his hands. 'God! I'm so sorry, Natalie.'

'I'm not.' I pulled my nightie back down. 'I love you,' I whispered.

He looked up at me. 'And I love you too, Natalie, but not like this.'

Outside the wind was winding down. The rain had stopped. Then I heard the crunch of tyres on gravel as Dad's truck pulled into the yard.

Suddenly there was nothing to say. The world turned back on. River grabbed his jeans and retreated into the bathroom. I couldn't leave. I knew I was stuck there until my parents settled in for the night. I curled up on the bed while I waited. I closed my eyes and tried to ignore the muffled sounds of retching coming from behind the bathroom door.

I glance at Jenny as she drives and I sort through memories. Then I lean back and in a detached voice I tell her about how River came to us, became part of us, how we all fell in love with him. And I tell her briefly about the night I went to his room.

It all sounds so banal, so commonplace—a young girl, who was so blinded with what she believed was love that she lost sight of reality. A child lost in the moment, believing that her desire made her an adult.

I don't bother telling Jenny that 'nice' girls didn't do 'it' in those days. I don't say that what happened in that room all those years ago filled me with guilt and remorse. It did not. Not then. That came later.

That night I lay curled up in River's bed, hugging myself and hanging on to his words. *He said he loved me!*

He thought I was too young for him, that was all, I told myself. I was sixteen. River was twenty-two. My father was ten years older than my mother, I would remind him. She was seventeen when they married, and look at them. In less than two months I would be seventeen; six years wouldn't seem so much of an age difference then. I could wait. We could wait. I drifted off to sleep convinced he would see that too. He would wait for me, everything would work out, would be all right.

Except, of course, it would not.

I don't know how long I slept. I woke to a gentle hand on my shoulder. 'Natalie, wake up.' I opened my eyes to find River standing over me. 'You should go back to the house,' he said, not unkindly.

He was fully dressed in jeans and a shirt as if it were morning. The fragrance of Ivory soap radiated from his body. His hair, still wet from a shower, dripped onto the shoulders of his cotton shirt.

River picked up his journal from the nightstand and went over to the chrome table beneath the window. Bright light from the open bathroom door spilled into the room. He sat hunched over the table, his back to me. Through the window, I saw the storm had passed. I climbed off the bed and took a step towards him. 'Go home, Natalie,' he said without turning round. It was more of a plea than a statement.

'Everything will be OK,' I said. I wanted him to feel the same joy I did. I knew he did not.

'We'll talk tomorrow,' he said with a sigh.

I didn't want to leave, but the promise in those words moved me. I leaned over and retrieved my wet shoes from beside the bed. At the door I turned back and whispered, 'Good night.'

There was no response. River sat bent over his journal, a pen in his unmoving hand. He stared out into the night. Then his shoulders sagged and his head dropped as if in defeat. I wanted to run to him, to beg him not to be upset, but instinct held me back.

I hesitated only a moment before I quietly closed the door behind me. I shook off the feeling of sorrow as I climbed down the stairs.

I did not hurry. I stepped carefully through the gravel- and mud-puddle-strewn yard. As I made my way past my mother's rose garden, the air was heavy with barnyard aromas and the perfume of rose petals bruised by the heavy rain.

When I reached the porch, I opened the screen door slowly, stopping when it squeaked, then held my breath until the silence returned. I closed the kitchen door behind me and stood in the darkness for a moment. Grateful for the childish games of blind walking, I tiptoed up the unlit stairway, counting each of the eighteen linoleum-topped steps. In the narrow upstairs hallway, I turned left and counted six steps to my door, then felt my way across my room to my bed.

Even as a child, the dark had held no fear for me. Perhaps if I was not so at ease with the night I would have paid more attention. Maybe I would even have felt the eyes watching me as I crossed the yard. Then I may have glanced back over my shoulder, or turned round and looked behind me. And perhaps I might have seen her there—my mother standing in the shadows beneath the dairy stairs.

Nettie
Even in her dreams the perfume haunts her; the heavy fragrance drifts into her sleep. Nettie's eyes open and search the darkened hospital room for the offending blossoms. Have they forgotten she does not

want flowers in her room? Especially roses. And there are none now. Yet the pungent aroma that stole its way into her dreams was so real.

She cannot escape it. She cannot get up and leave her bed like she did on long-ago nights at home. Nights when she lay in the dark feeling empty and used. All those nights blend together in her memory. Except one. The memory of one June night remains clear.

Gus insisted they come home early. He feared the lightning might knock out the hydro as it often did in the heat of a summer storm. He needed to be there to start the gas generator for the cooler. So after their bridge game they left Dr Mumford's before the usual midnight snack.

The storm's fury was spent by the time they pulled into the yard, and the yard light and kitchen lights in the farmhouse were on.

'No power outage here,' Gus said, relieved, as they made their way up to the house.

Nettie picked up a laundry basket beside the screen door. She smiled. She could always count on her daughter.

Gus switched off lights as he followed her through the kitchen. 'I don't remember the last time the house was this empty on a Saturday night,' he said. He took her hand before they reached the bedroom door. 'While the mice are away, the cats can play,' he whispered.

In the silence of their room, before their nightly prayers, he lifted the bedroom window. 'Leave it closed,' Nettie said.

'It's so stuffy in here,' Gus told her, then slid the window halfway up in concession. But no breeze lifted the curtains to enter the room.

In their bed, in the darkness, his hands reached over and lifted Nettie's cotton nightgown. In all the years of her marriage, she never refused her husband. She lay there and waited for it to be over.

Later, a satisfied Gus patted her on the hip then rolled over. Nettie turned her face into her pillow. She tried to sleep. As the demons of the night overcame her, she rose. She pulled on her dressing gown then left the room, quietly closing the door on her husband's snores.

She slipped through the shadows of the silent house. Out on the porch the battered wicker chair creaked in protest as she sat down. Even on the porch Nettie's sensitive nose detected the roses. The warm scent always brought the memory of lying in a sea of loose hay, watching her young children bouncing in the spongy fullness of the loft. But it was not the aroma of the hay, or memories of lost summers that tugged at Nettie's mind as she sat looking out across the farmyard. It was River.

It was the image of River climbing up to the loft earlier that day to

throw bales down to the calving pen. He was halfway up the rungs on the side of the barn when she looked up from where she stood hanging the wash on the clothes line. Her hands stopped in midair as she spotted him. Except for leather gloves, he wore nothing from the waist up. His blond ponytail bounced on his tanned shoulders. When he reached the top, he swung round and glanced back. She felt the heat on her face rise as his eyes met hers. He waved and called, 'Hey, Nettie,' as if it was perfectly natural for her to be standing there, frozen, with a pair of long johns dangling in front of her.

She willed herself out of the trance and finished pegging her husband's wet underwear to the line. She half raised her hand to wave back then glanced around to see if anyone had caught her staring so brazenly.

As she finished hanging the wash she tried not to compare River's tanned body with her husband's red farmer's tan, which ended at his elbows and at the V of his neck. But in the loneliness of night Nettie allowed herself to wonder what it would feel like to touch River's bare skin, what it would feel like to have his touching hers.

Nettie stared up at the window above the dairy. Yellow light from the bathroom clicked on and River's silhouette moved across the room. She felt less alone in the night knowing he, too, was awake.

Nettie pushed herself up. She moved across to the porch doorway, down the steps, and across to the yard gate as if sleepwalking. Her slippered feet carried her over the gravel path, past the rose garden, and across the farmyard to the bottom of the stairway at the side of the dairy. As she placed her foot on the bottom step, the door above opened. With her right foot in the air above the second tread, Nettie froze.

The sound of Natalie's voice whispering, 'Good night' stunned her into movement. Nettie quickly backed away, then ducked into the shadows underneath the stairs.

Moments later she watched as her daughter, dressed only in her nightgown and what looked like one of Boyer's shirts, came down the stairs. She passed so close that Nettie could have reached out and touched her through the wooden steps.

And as she passed, Nettie smelt it. Above the odours of the barn, the night storm and the roses wafted the unmistakable musk of sex.

The next day, I woke to sunshine streaming in through my bedroom window. It was not morning light. I had slept in.

The house was silent, empty. The alarm clock on my nightstand read ten o'clock. Except during a few childhood illnesses, I never stayed in

bed that late. It felt strange to be getting up at that hour. Stranger yet was the fact that my mother allowed it. I should have recognised this as the first warning sign that things had changed. But I didn't see it then.

Downstairs, the breakfast dishes still sat on the kitchen table, along with my schoolbooks pushed to the side. I found a note on the counter from my mother telling me—as if I wouldn't know where she would be on a Sunday morning—that she'd gone with Dad.

Natalie, please start lunch, she wrote. *Your brothers should be back from Kelowna some time this morning.*

After I washed up my parents' breakfast dishes, I spent the rest of the morning pretending to focus on the war of 1812.

If my mother behaved differently, if she was quieter, more subdued when she and my father returned from town that day, I barely noticed. If she seemed distant while we set the table for the noon meal, like my father, I put it down to her worrying about my brothers on the road.

Right on time, as if they'd heard a dinner bell ring, Morgan and Carl blew in the door in a whirlwind of excitement and travel fatigue.

'You can relax now, Nettie, your boys are home,' Dad teased. But I was too lost in my own thoughts to wonder why she still seemed distracted. I was too wrapped up in reliving the images of the previous night, too certain that my delicious secret must be obvious to everyone, to be able to see a change in her.

As I watched the door, anxiously waiting for River to come through, I let the imagined promised conversation run through my mind. But lunch passed and no River.

Later, at Mom's insistence, I reluctantly went with her to afternoon Mass. I assumed she had gone to Mass earlier. It never occurred to me that my mother had delivered the milk with Dad that morning.

In St Anthony's I went through the service by rote. I knelt when Mom knelt, crossed myself when she did, but my mind was elsewhere.

Following Mass my mother went to confession. I sat out on the cold marble steps in front of the church and waited for her.

After my mother emerged from the church doors she said to me, 'Natalie, aren't you going to confess?'

I was momentarily surprised by her words. I refused to meet her eyes. I stood and hurried down the steps saying, 'Not today.'

We ate at the dining-room table that night. We always did when Father Mackenzie joined us for dinner. The best china and silverware came out. It was the only time, except at Christmas, that we had wine, supplied by the priest, with our meal.

Neither River nor Boyer showed up for supper. Boyer had arrived home from Kelowna late in the afternoon and went straight to his cabin. I was not surprised by River's absence. He never joined us when Father Mac visited. Perhaps it was simply because River was not Catholic, but I believed it was because he could not forget the priest who advised his friend to enlist.

I was anxious to see River, but a part of me was relieved he was not there. I was certain that even if no one else noticed the change in me, Father Mac would see the lust in my heart just by looking at my face.

After supper Father Mac took off his jacket and rolled up his shirt-sleeves. My father protested, as he always did, that there was no need for the priest to help with the milking. And as always he followed my father out of the door saying, 'I can always carry a few buckets. A little physical work is good for the soul.'

I knew there would be no opportunity to see River that night.

Monday passed in a blur of exams and studying. Again River did not show up for meals. No one questioned his absence. Perhaps they thought he was on one of his periodic cleansing fasts. I knew this was not one of those times. By that evening I was in a state of panic.

After supper, after everyone had gone to the barn and Mom to the dairy, I hurried through the dishes and went upstairs to my bedroom. Instead of climbing out on the roof I stood at my window and watched. I watched as Morgan and Carl finished carrying the last milk containers to the dairy. I heard the blasting spray of hoses washing down the stalls. I watched as first the lights of the barn went out and then the dairy. From behind my window I saw Boyer get into his car and drive up the road to his cabin. Morgan and Carl made their way to the house, their steps subdued, displaying none of their usual jostling or rushing to get into town. Mom and Dad followed behind. But still no sign of River.

I waited until the only sound in the house was the staccato canned laughter coming from the television set in the parlour. Then I crept downstairs and out the kitchen door.

I hurried across the yard and ran up the dairy stairs. The rap of my knuckles on the wooden door sounded hollow. I opened the door and looked inside. My grandmother's quilt still covered the bed but there were no books on the nightstand or the chrome tabletop. No guitar leaned in the corner. His absence filled the room.

I ran over and pulled open the closet door. No green duffle bag waited inside, no clothes hung there smelling of him. There was no trace of life in this room, no trace of his presence. I fled from the empty

room and ran down the steps and across the yard. I stopped at the gate. Up on the porch Mom stood in the shadowed doorway as if she was waiting for me. She *was* waiting for me. *She knew!*

Somehow she knew, and she had sent him away!

I rushed up the path and stood at the bottom of the steps. 'Where is he?' I demanded, the panic in my voice leaking out, accusing, begging.

'He's gone,' she answered, her voice flat.

'Why?' I yelled. 'Why?' I felt my foot stamp with each 'why'. I was outside myself, watching myself having a childish temper tantrum. And I could not stop.

'It's for the best,' my mother said, her eyes focused beyond me. Then, for the first time in my life, my mother turned her back on my tears.

As I watched my mother disappear into the house I felt the searing heat of rage seep through every part of my body. *She sent River away! Somehow she knew, and she sent him away!*

I spun round and ran out of the yard. *Boyer! I need to tell Boyer!*

I fled up the dirt road, past the alfalfa field behind our house, wiping the tears and mucus from my face with the back of my sleeve.

Boyer will fix it! Boyer will fix it! I kept telling myself. Exactly how he would do that was not part of my hysterical mantra.

In the grey light, Boyer's cabin looked empty, abandoned. From the outside the only hint that anyone lived there at all was Boyer's Edsel parked at the side.

Oh, how I wished I had sensed the danger, the harsh unwanted knowledge that lay behind that heavy wooden door, before I rushed up and, without knocking, pushed it open.

I stood in the doorway, catching my breath and squinting into the dim interior. I heard a muffled sound and turned towards the bedroom. There was a sudden blur of movement on Boyer's bed. As my eyes adjusted, my mind could not keep up with what I was seeing, could not comprehend what was happening. A flash of bare buttocks, a mus-cled back, naked arms and legs tangled. At first I thought I had caught Boyer sleeping. I was about to turn away from his nakedness when I saw the surprised face staring back at me was River's. And beneath him, raising his head off the pillow, was Boyer.

I stood frozen. The scene in front of me, the rumpled bed, the clothes strewn on the floor, I took it all in. But it made no sense. The relief of finding River there conflicted with the truth of what I was seeing. I heard Boyer's voice groan, 'Oh God, Natalie.'

On the floor, at the end of the bed, two pairs of jeans lay crumpled.

Both Boyer and River scrambled for them. They hurried to pull them up over their bare legs. Still, I did not turn away. Even in my shock, in some place deep in the back of my consciousness, I noticed how beautiful they both were. Then, as suddenly as light snapping into a room, it hit me what I had just witnessed.

I felt my stomach sour and rise to the back of my throat. I cupped my hands to my mouth to stifle the moans that rose with the bile.

'Oh, no! No!' I could not stop the rush of confused words that spilled through my fingers and out into the room. 'Shit! What . . . why . . . you can't . . . what are you doing?'

River slumped onto the edge of the bed, his shoulders rounded, his elbows on his knees, his head down, as if he were faint.

Boyer came through the bedroom doorway. He lifted his arm and reached out to me. His eyes did not avoid mine. They were weary, sad, but I saw no shame hidden there, just hope, hope that I would understand, that I would accept this unimaginable truth.

I twisted away from his touch. 'No, this is wrong, wrong. You can't do this,' I cried. I looked past him. 'River . . . River . . . I thought . . . you said you loved me!'

River raised his head. In his eyes was the same plea for understanding. 'I do love you, Natalie,' he said. 'But not that way.' His face softened. He looked up at my brother. 'I love Boyer that way,' he said.

'But . . . but . . . what about us . . .?' I stammered as if this were an argument I could win. 'We . . . we made love.'

At my words, they both seemed to stop breathing. Boyer turned to River. 'What? You what?' His voice was a hoarse whisper. Suddenly it was as if I was not in the room. The looks that passed between them needed no words. Boyer waited for the denial he knew was not coming; while River's eyes confirmed the horror of the truth.

'It was a mistake.' His voice was barely a whisper. 'A terrible, terrible mistake. I'm so . . . so sorry.'

'A mistake!' I cried. 'I'm a mistake!' But no one was listening to me.

Boyer leaned down and grabbed River's boots and socks. He flung them through the bedroom doorway where they landed at River's feet. 'Get out,' he said, his voice barely audible. 'Take your things and leave.'

'Please, Boyer,' River pleaded. 'I was going to tell you. Should have told you.' He looked to me. 'Natalie?'

I knew what he wanted, what he was asking of me. Even in the half-light of the bedroom I could see the panic in his eyes, the silent plea for me to explain, to say the words that would make Boyer understand. I

would not give them to him. 'Yes, go . . . go . . .!' I spat, 'both of you go! I hate you! I hate you both!'

I backed out of the cabin. 'Oh God,' I moaned. 'I wish I was dead.' I turned and ran out, screaming back ugly words of hate. Words that came out of a frightened hysterical place, a cruel place that I did not even know existed inside me.

I heard Boyer call, 'Wait, Natalie. Don't go.' Concern for me filled his voice, as if he hadn't heard my condemnations.

I fled across the meadow grass in the fading light. I hurried, not down the dirt road that led home, but up. Up to the ragged edge of the woods. I looked over my shoulder and saw my brother rushing out of the cabin, hopping on one foot, while trying to pull on his other boot.

Shadows wrapped around me as I entered the trees. Dried pine needles and twigs crunched under my feet as I scrambled up the slope. Branches scratched at my bare legs. I wished I wasn't wearing a miniskirt—a new outfit that I had put on earlier that day hoping to impress River. Below, I heard arguing as they struggled to get dressed.

'Just leave,' Boyer shouted, as he ran out of the door. 'I'll go find her.'

I glanced back over my shoulder. Through the trees I saw River rush out of the cabin after Boyer. 'I'm coming with you,' he shouted back as he followed Boyer up the hillside. The fury of their frustration rose with their voices in the night air and carried up the mountain.

Halfway up the slope, I turned north and began traversing the mountainside, stopping only a moment to catch my breath and get my bearings. A full moon rose in the starlit sky, casting lacy shadows through the trees. I heard the scurry of small feet in the undergrowth.

Our mother instilled in us a healthy respect for the wildlife of the forest. The more noise I made, the safer I would be. Below, Boyer and River's voices created enough noise to keep any nocturnal animals far away. I heard Boyer once again yell at River to leave, then both of them calling my name repeatedly in the darkness.

As they came closer, I pulled myself up into the crotch of a giant cedar tree. Bark scratched my bare thighs; mosquitoes attacked exposed skin. I concentrated on being still as their shouts came closer. Just before they reached the tree where I sat crouched, they veered in the opposite direction. I waited and listened as their voices receded. Then I climbed out of the tree. In the glow of the rising moon I fought my way through the thick underbrush. I continued along the slope until I came to the edge of the gravel pit and scurried across to the dirt road leading to the highway. To Atwood.

CHAPTER EIGHT

ALL MY LIFE I have wrestled with the question of why I did what I did. What ridiculous, needy part of me led to such a foolish decision? There's no explanation that makes sense.

Even as I ran through the streets of Atwood, I knew I could have—should have—gone home. I should have climbed into my bed, pulled the covers over my head and sobbed out the confusion, hurt and anger until I had come to my senses, to the truth, to acceptance.

Instead, I ended up standing, panting and out of breath, on the porch of the only friend I could think to run to. Elizabeth-Ann opened the door to my pounding.

'Natalie! What is it?' she cried. I opened my mouth, but no words came. And in that instant, that millisecond of time, and for ever after, I asked myself why I was there. Although Elizabeth-Ann had become my closest friend, I had not been on this porch since her pyjama party years ago. I started to back away as my eyes frantically searched for signs of Mr Ryan. But when Elizabeth-Ann reached out and pulled me into the entry foyer and up the stairs to her room, I let her.

She closed her bedroom door behind us and led me to the canopied bed. She sat down beside me. Concern shone in her eyes. My friend, my best friend, held both my hands in hers and asked in a hushed voice, 'What is it, Natalie?'

'Boyer,' I sobbed, gasping to catch my breath. 'Boyer and River!'

'Boyer?' Panic flooded her face. 'Did something happen to Boyer?'

And without a thought I told Elizabeth-Ann how I had found Boyer and River together, in each other's arms. *Lovers! God! They were lovers.*

Elizabeth-Ann remained silent, her full-lipped mouth half open, as my stream of words, barely connected, but for ever betraying, told all. I hardly noticed the change of expression on her face as I went on. Then I saw it, the slight lift of the corners of her mouth as she fought to control a smile. *A smile!* She looked beyond me, through me.

'Ohhh,' she said, the word stretching out as understanding took hold. 'Oh! So that's it. That's why.'

'What? Why what?' I stammered, already realising that I had released something that could never be retrieved.

'No wonder he wasn't interested in me. He's a *queer*!' She spat the word out—the word I had not even allowed myself to think.

Her eyes narrowed and once again focused on me, the smirk on her face complete now. I knew that look.

'Oh, poor Natalie,' she said, her voice a little too sweet. She pulled her hands from mine and wiped them on her skirt.

And just like that I was once again 'poor Natalie', farmer's daughter, 'Nat the Fat'.

'A queer!' Elizabeth-Ann giggled, then pressed her hand over her mouth. The giggle turned into a laugh, a laugh that I imagined following me as I fled down the stairs, out of the front door and into the street.

What have I done?

I fled through the streets of town. There was nowhere else to run, nowhere else to go. Except home. I retraced my steps out of Atwood. At the end of Main Street I turned south and hurried down the empty highway. Suddenly the glare of headlights cast long shadows on the road before me. I increased my pace as the black Lincoln pulled up beside me and the passenger window whirred down.

'Let me give you a ride home, Natalie,' the familiar voice called. Mr Ryan leaned over from the driver's seat to open the passenger door with one hand as he held the steering wheel with the other.

'It's OK. I want to walk,' I said, moving faster.

'Don't be silly,' he said. 'Get in the car. I can't let you walk home in the dark. Especially not while you're so upset.' When I didn't respond, he said, 'Natalie, I heard what you told Elizabeth-Ann. Imagine what will happen if the wrong people find out. Think of Boyer's job, your father's business?'

Suddenly it was hard to breathe, as it struck me how much pain my careless words could bring. My lack of discretion.

'Now if you don't want the whole town knowing about your brother, I suggest you get into the car,' Mr Ryan demanded.

I can't explain why I thought I could undo the damage, somehow protect Boyer, by getting into that car. I can't say why, when every instinct within me warned me not to. I stopped walking and let Mr Ryan push open the passenger door for me.

I felt his pink-rimmed eyes watching as I climbed in and pulled the heavy door closed.

'Thanks,' I said, but I kept my hand on the door handle.

'Well, that was quite the story you told Elizabeth-Ann,' Mr Ryan said as the car gathered speed along the highway. 'No wonder you're upset.'

I remained silent, wondering how much he had heard.

'Seeing those two boys—men—like that,' he sneered, 'well, that's pretty disgusting.'

My betrayal was complete.

'Please, don't tell anyone, Mr Ryan,' I begged. 'I was lying. I didn't really see anything. I was mad at my brother. I just wanted to hurt him. None of it's true,' I ranted. 'I was lying to Elizabeth-Ann. It's not true.'

'We both know it is true, don't we?' he said, ignoring my outburst. 'We're going to have to be very careful about who else finds out,' he said, his voice now that of the mayor of our town, concerned about the morality of his citizens. The Lincoln slowed and turned off the highway.

'No, wait, this isn't my road,' I said. 'South Valley is the next one.'

'We'll just turn around up here,' he said, pulling into the gravel pit, the same abandoned pit I had walked through less than an hour before.

The crunch of tyres on gravel sounded hollow in the interior of the car as we swung a slow wide arc. But instead of driving back to the road, back to the highway, back to safety, the car rolled to a stop. Mr Ryan leaned down and reached under the seat with one hand.

'I have to go home,' I said, clutching at the door handle. The lock snapped down.

'Oh, what's your hurry?' A silver flask appeared in his hand. 'You shouldn't go home like this.' He unscrewed the cap and held the flask up to me. 'Here, have a sip of this. It'll calm you down.'

'No. No, thanks.' Even in my growing panic, the need to be polite to an adult remained. 'I can walk from here,' I said, keeping my eyes on him as my fingers searched for the lock on the door.

'We have to talk,' he said. 'We have to think about how we can keep your brother and his boyfriend's dirty little secret.' He put the flask to his lips and took a long drink, then held it up to me again. 'Come on.'

I shook my head and pulled back, trapped. I shrank against the door, pulling on the handle, which snapped back, useless.

'You know what I think you need, Natalie?' Mr Ryan said as he pulled the keys out of the ignition and slipped them into the pocket of his sweatpants. 'I think you need a real man.' He lunged across the padded leather seat, reaching for me.

He shoved his face against mine. Stale alcohol breath assaulting my nostrils. Wet lips sought mine. His hands were everywhere, reaching, groping, finding their way inside my shirt, while mine blindly searched

the passenger door for the lock and frantically yanked at the handle.

'Please, no,' I sobbed.

Somehow my shaking fingers found the silver knob on top of the door and pulled it up. At the same time my other hand yanked on the handle. The door flew open. I tumbled out backwards. My head landed heavily, momentarily stunning me. As I tried to push myself up, Mr Ryan's hand gripped my ankle.

'Oh no you don't.' His voice was harsh. 'You're not going anywhere.'

Twisting and kicking, I pulled my foot from his grasp and managed to get to my feet. I bolted away. After a few steps my head snapped back. In a blur I felt myself flung round and slammed face first onto the hood of the car. Hard fingers tangled in my hair. I was held pinned by his body, my right arm caught under my stomach. My left flailed in the air.

'Like it rough do you?' His free hand grabbed my arm and bent it across my back. He yanked my head back from the hood. 'We'll just call this payment for keeping your brother's secret, won't we, Natalie?' he whispered.

When I continued to struggle he pulled harder on my hair while he pushed my twisted arm further up my back. Pain burned though my skull. I wasn't sure which would snap first, my neck or my arm.

'Won't we?' his harsh voice insisted.

'Yes,' I choked. And I let my body go limp.

'That's better,' he said, breathing heavily. 'We'll just have our own little secret.' And still hanging on to my hair, he released my arm. I could feel him fumbling with his sweatpants. A knee pushed between my thighs and forced my legs apart. A hand tore at my underpants.

I focused on the burning pain of hair being torn from my scalp and tried to ignore the assault to my body. I pretended I wasn't there.

When it was over, when he was finally finished, he slumped against my back with a groan and his hand relaxed its grip on my hair.

I moved quickly. I spun my body round and, with every ounce of energy I had left, I lifted my knee and slammed it into his exposed crotch. With a grunt he slipped down while, too late, he tried to protect himself with his hands. I lifted my knee again.

His folded body crumpled to the gravel as I stepped away. I started to run, but first I reached down and grabbed at his sweatpants gathered at the bottom of his bare legs. As I yanked them from his writhing body, one of his moccasins caught in the leg. I clutched pants and slipper to my chest and carried them away with me as I fled.

Behind me I heard his groans turn into curses as he struggled to get

up. I ran out of the gravel pit, through the trees, not daring to look back, expecting at any moment to feel a hand grab my hair.

Screaming words of rage followed me as I stumbled through the undergrowth. When his roar became a fading noise, when I was sure he was not behind me, I slowed down. I skirted a moss-covered deadfall. In the moonlight I leaned over to stuff his pants and slipper in the hollow end of the log. The car keys fell from his pocket. I picked them up, lifted my aching arm, and flung the keys into the darkness.

I hurried through the trees along the edge of the highway. The headlights of passing cars splashed on the road then disappeared. After a while I came to South Valley Road. I stayed in the brush and followed the road home, unafraid of the dark. The worst that could happen in the blackness of the night had happened.

Somewhere in the distance the lonesome cry of a train whistle sounded. It relayed through the mountains and dissipated down the valley, reminding me that other people moved carelessly through the night, their lives unchanged, while mine had just come apart at the seams.

I knew before I reached home, before I stumbled through the bottom field. Before my bruised and battered body climbed over the snake fence onto the road, before I saw our porch light burning. And I knew before I crept into our dark, empty house and locked myself in the bathroom. Mr Ryan was right. I would never tell.

I was for ever bound to him by our shared secret. I would tell no one, not my mother, my father, my brothers or the police. I would never feel the relief of revenge. I would never whisper words into the darkness of a confessional to the waiting ears of a priest who would grant absolution. My penance would be to carry this ugly secret alone.

And even after all these years I still cannot tell my daughter.

'Mom?' Jenny's voice calls me back. 'Mom. We're here.'

I look around. While I was lost in my dark memories we had entered town, driven through Main Street and up the hospital hill. We are parked in the wide circular driveway in front of the Alpine Inn.

The Alpine Inn. Such a ridiculous name. Surely they could have come up with something more fitting for this place that at one time was Our Lady of Compassion School for Girls.

Next door is the hospital. I look up to the second-floor windows to where my mother sleeps. My heart lurches. Suddenly all I want is to see her. Until now I have managed to ignore the nagging thoughts that I might be too late. Now I need to see her, to touch her, to be certain.

'I want to go up and see Mom before I check in,' I say. 'Do you think we can go in this late?'

'I've already warned the nurse that we're coming,' Jenny answers.

We leave the car and cross the lawn that separates the two buildings.

'So, when are Morgan and Carl getting here?' I ask.

'Sometime tomorrow. They're all staying out at the farm with Boyer and Stanley.'

Boyer and Stanley. She says those names as easily as if she were talking about an old married couple. And, in fact, of course she is. Jenny has always accepted her uncle, his partner, his homosexuality, as naturally as her love for him. And why shouldn't she?

But I wonder if she can possibly imagine how different it was for our generation. Does she realise homosexuality was a criminal offence in Canada up until 1969? Would she be surprised to learn that it was not until June of this very year, 2003, that a United States Supreme Court decision finally and fully decriminalised homosexuality across America.

Unlike Jenny, I did not grow up in an era of acceptance. I had to learn it.

In the harsh bathroom light I filled the deep claw-foot bath with steaming water. I pulled off my torn clothes, clothes that must never be allowed to find their way into the laundry for my mother's eyes to read. I would hide them in the crawl space under the eaves in my bedroom until I found a chance to burn them in the basement furnace.

I lowered myself into the hot water and scrubbed my body until it was numb in a frantic attempt to wash away the evil, the memory, and let it swirl down the drain with the dirt and the blood. I sat hugging my knees as the bath emptied. Then I turned the water on again and lay against the sloped porcelain back. I let the water fill to the overflow, let it slowly crawl up and cover my entire body until only my nose and closed eyes were above water. I lay immersed, allowing my body to float suspended, in a world without sound, without light, without hurt. I wanted to stay there for ever. I wanted to sink down and let it claim me.

I pushed away the visions and the cries of outrage that wanted to bubble up. I could not, would not, give them voice. It was all I could do, all I must do, to live with the torture of this secret eating at the lining of my stomach, trying to find a way out, to scream to the world, *Look! Look what has happened to me, what was 'done' to me!* I refused to give the beastly act a name. I would keep it locked up in darkness, give it no voice to whimper in self-pity. And I would give no one the right to

look at me with eyes filled with sympathy while they hid their revulsion and their curiosity.

No, I would not be a victim—his victim.

I even allowed myself to fantasise for a moment, to indulge in the bittersweet thought of making him a victim. Before I locked myself in the bathroom, when I was certain that the house was empty, I had picked up the wall phone by the fridge. The clicking of the rotary dial seemed to take for ever for each of the four numbers of the local Royal Canadian Mounted Police detachment.

At the sound of a voice on the other end of the line, I whispered, 'Check the gravel pit,' and then put the phone back on the hook. Yes, I would keep the secret, but as I lay in the bath I imagined Mr Ryan trying to explain his half-naked condition to the police. But even these thoughts brought no comfort. I sank lower, totally submerging myself, and concentrated on the ringing silence in my water-filled ears.

The bath water had cooled when I felt vibrations ripple through my watery cocoon. I lifted my head. Footsteps pounded up the porch steps, the kitchen door opened. 'Natalie?' my mother's voice called out. Her knuckles rapped on the bathroom door. 'Natalie, are you in there?'

I tried to find my voice and was surprised by the flat normality of the 'yes' that finally came.

'She's home.' I heard the relief in her voice.

Behind her my father asked, 'Where's she been? Doesn't she know everyone's been out looking for her?' Worry hardened his words.

'It's OK, Gus,' my mother said. 'You go with Boyer. I'll talk to her.'

'What was she thinking, running off in the dark like that? Letting everyone chase after her.' A mumbled trail of his words disappeared behind the slamming of the screen door.

'Are you OK?' Mom asked from the other side of the bathroom door.

'I'm fine,' I answered. 'I'm—I'm just taking a bath.'

I wanted her to go away—I wanted her to come in and sit on the edge of the bath and talk to me like she did when I was young. I wanted her to leave me alone—I wanted her to take me upstairs to bed and tuck me in like a child, tell me everything was going to be all right, then lay beside me until I fell asleep, keeping me safe and warm.

'Do you want a cup of tea?' she asked.

Tea. My mother's solution to every crisis. Oh, how I wanted that to be enough.

'No, thanks. I just want to go to bed,' I called out.

I waited a while, then pulled the plug and climbed out of the bath. I

took my time, rubbing myself dry while the water drained. I cleaned the bath, making sure there were no traces left there to cause wonder. Then, wrapped in a bath towel and clutching the bundle of clothes close to my chest, I opened the bathroom door. My mother sat at the table waiting, a teacup lifted to her lips.

I could not bring myself to look into her eyes. I reached for the handle of the stairway door. 'Good night,' I murmured.

The china teacup clinked into the saucer. I expected her to ask where I'd been, or why I had run off. The questions never came. Perhaps Boyer had told her everything, or perhaps, as she always seemed to, she just knew. Or perhaps she was too relieved to care. Or too worried, because the words she did say were, 'River's lost.'

Lost, how could he be lost?

'From what I understand they got separated when they were searching for you,' Mom said. 'When Boyer finally returned to the cabin, River wasn't there. But his things still are.'

I watched Mom's face as she spoke, looking for signs of anger, or even surprise, that instead of being gone, as she told me he was, River had been at Boyer's cabin. But I only saw worry in her eyes.

'Boyer was certain that eventually you would come home,' Mom said, 'but River isn't as familiar with these mountains—doesn't know every ridge and gully the way we do.'

I didn't know what to say. There was no accusation in her voice, but I knew, as I was certain she did, that if anything happened to River, it would be my fault. I was the reason he was lost. 'Boyer and your father are going back out on the horses to search for him,' she told me.

A few minutes later, I watched from my bedroom window as Dad and Boyer led the horses from the barn. Mom hurried out with a Thermos and a first-aid kit. Dad stuffed them in his saddlebags, and then he and Boyer rode up the road towards the back field and out of sight.

I crawled into my bed. Curled up in a ball under blankets and quilts, I lay shivering while Mom sat alone downstairs.

I prayed. I prayed for River to come back safe. Somewhere in my prayers was the beginning of acceptance. I realised I could not stop loving River, any more than I could have stopped loving Boyer when I was six years old and learned that you can't marry your brother. I would just have to learn to love River in the same way.

Before long I heard Morgan and Carl arrive home from town. 'We'll go help search,' they said, after Mom had told them about River.

'No,' she insisted. 'No, you won't. We don't need anybody else wandering through the bush tonight.' Her voice was firm. 'Someone has to be here to do the milking in the morning.'

'Oh, he'll show up by then,' Morgan assured her.

But he didn't. There were no answers to my prayers that night. Before dawn, Dad came home. Alone. He joined Morgan and Carl in the barn. Full udders will not wait while emergencies are resolved.

Downstairs my mother took refuge in routine. I dressed in a flannel shirt and shapeless trousers and joined her. We cooked breakfast in silence. Breakfasts that would grow cold on platters while my brothers rushed off to join Boyer in the search. I went with Dad to deliver the milk.

We rode into town without speaking, both of us lost in our own thoughts. It had been so long since I had gone with him on the milk run. Would my father remember our routine on Colbur Street? How could I ask him to deliver to the Ryan house? How would I find the strength to walk up onto that porch?

I didn't have to worry. When we pulled up in front of the Ryans' house it was dark, all the curtains closed. A piece of white paper was stuffed into one of the empty milk bottles on the step. I knew what the note would say before I dashed up onto the porch and grabbed the bottle and hurried back to the truck. *No more milk!*

Two members of the Royal Canadian Mounted Police stood in our kitchen talking with Boyer after we returned from the milk run.

These fresh-faced policemen had often found their way out to our farm for afternoon or midnight snacks with our mother. They stood now with their hats in their hands, their faces serious beneath identical white-scalp crew cuts.

'It's too early,' the taller RCMP officer was saying.

'Too early?' Boyer said. 'He's been missing since last night.' He sat on a kitchen chair lacing up his hiking boots. Mom stood beside him staring at the officers, her arms folded.

'Well, he's a grown man,' the officer answered. 'Now if it was a child that would be different. But an adult has to be missing forty-eight hours before we can organise a search. Who knows why he took off? Maybe—'

'He's lost,' Boyer interrupted without looking up. 'He's in trouble.'

'Isn't he a draft-dodger?' the other officer asked.

'Conscientious objector,' Boyer sighed, as he tugged at his laces.

'Well, maybe he went back to the States. Maybe he decided to slip across the border and go home.'

'His things are still here.'

'OK,' the taller officer said. 'If he doesn't show up by tomorrow, we'll bring in a tracking dog—'

'It could be too late by then,' Boyer said. He stood up and stalked out of the kitchen, the screen door slamming behind him.

Dad caught him on the porch. Through the screen, I saw him put his hand on Boyer's shoulder. 'Go get some sleep, son,' he said. 'I'll go out with Carl and Morgan after we grab some lunch.'

While Dad and Boyer spoke out on the porch the two officers stood, caps twisting in their hands, looking out of place and uncomfortable in the heat of our kitchen. Mom walked over to the sideboard in the corner and turned her back on them as if they weren't there.

'Must have been quite a full moon last night,' the shorter one said, searching for words that would return our kitchen to a place where they had often found respite from the tensions of their job. 'People traipsing through the bush. You wouldn't believe who we picked up skulking around last night with his pants down—literally.'

My stomach lurched. I glanced over at Mom. She stood at the sideboard slicing bread with a determination born of withheld anger. She was in no mood for local gossip. She spun round, pushed her way past them, and slammed the plate of bread on the table.

'Look, Mrs Ward,' the taller officer said. 'As soon as we call a search, as soon as we put out a missing person's report, we have to notify Customs, the authorities in the States, the FBI, and, well, do you really want to alert them if this fellow is trying to sneak home for a visit?'

'He's not,' she said. She moved to the stove, her back once again to them, dismissing them.

It was the first time I witnessed my mother not invite someone who was in our kitchen at mealtime to join us.

The grapevine of a small town has its advantages. When the word spread that River was missing, a few people came out to help search. Very few. Mom always said you can tell your friends by those who show up in a crisis. Even more telling is the number who don't. She wondered aloud about all the young people, all our friends who had practically lived at the farm on weekends and holidays. Where were they all now?

Jake came, though not to search. 'I'm too old to be climbing these hills,' he grumbled, but he quietly helped with chores and milking.

Even while the search continued, the routine of the farm had to be kept. Cows had to be milked and the bottled milk had to be delivered

daily. The following morning more empty milk bottles waited on porches with notes instead of quarters inside. By the end of the week we would lose ten more customers.

On Thursday afternoon, Morgan went into town to pick up the grocery order. When he came out of the Super Value, he found written in the dust on the side of the truck the words HOMO MILK! and FAIRYLAND!

The next night someone climbed up on our gate and spray-painted the words FAG FARM! onto the Ward's Dairy Farm sign. In the morning, Dad took the sign down and burned it. It was never replaced.

The anonymous phone calls started that evening. I cringed the first time I heard a muffled voice promising us 'hell and damnation'. Each time Mom answered the phone only to slam it back down, I knew she was hearing similar threats. And still there was not one word spoken in our house about the root of those rumours. As we rushed past each other, frantically doing what we could during those days, no one questioned the accusations about Boyer's sexuality. No one asked how and why the rumours started. No one questioned my part in all of it.

As the rumours spread, rumours that I knew could only have begun their ugly web of gossip from one house in town, there were those who ignored them. Before the RCMP finally began an organised search, Mr Atwood and his son, Stanley Junior, showed up. They arrived with two three-wheeled ATVs on the back of a flat-bed. I heard Jake tell Dad there had been an announcement at the Bull Moose Mine that any man who joined the search would be paid overtime wages.

Ma Cooper, strangely silent for once, and Widow Beckett, came and worked with Mom to feed the small group of searchers. I begged to join the search, but Mom kept me busy in the kitchen at home.

The police notified River's family. His anxious mother confirmed that neither she, nor his grandfather, had heard from River and had no reason to expect him. Mom spoke on the phone with her every day while the search went on.

By the following Sunday they had turned up nothing. There was no sign, no clue, to lead them to River. Convinced that he had found his way across the border, the RCMP called off the search.

In the next few days almost everyone else gave up as well, believing that the police were right and River was back in the States. Even Dad, Morgan and Carl began to question if that might not be the case. Only Boyer and I were certain it wasn't true, and perhaps Mom.

Boyer kept searching. He went further and further into the mountains each day. He was exhausted. I could see the hope had drained

from his eyes. Still, he would not let me search with him. He'd hardly spoken a word to me since Tuesday night. I knew he saw the ugly words splashed onto our sign before Dad burned it. He must have known that only my thoughtless tongue, my lack of discretion, could have started the rumours. The morning Dad removed the sign I had caught Boyer on the porch. 'I'm sorry—' I started.

He held up his hand to halt my mumbled apology. But I couldn't stop the rushed words. 'Please, please let me come with you,' I rambled on nervously. 'I know these mountains, I can help in the search.'

'Just stay and help Mom,' he said, dismissing me.

The next day I was standing peeling potatoes at the sink, when the screen door screeched open. Boyer stood silent and darkened by the backlight in the doorway. 'I found him,' he said.

At the stove my mother's hand rose to her mouth. She stood frozen, the unasked question not making it past her eyes. I stopped breathing.

Boyer shook his head, his silent answer filling the room. He made his way across the kitchen and picked up the wall phone beside the fridge.

The crows led Boyer to River, Morgan told me later. He followed the crows as they circled above the trees and blackened the branches of an aspen grove, a choir of hoarse-throated mourners keeping vigil.

Boyer untied the rolled tarp from the back of his saddle. He swatted away the black-winged scavengers and the haze of iridescent bluebottle flies. Then, he gently covered what was left of the body he had found lying on the edge of a shallow mine hole. He needed to call the police. And River's mother. It was the last thing he could do for him.

While Boyer waited in the kitchen for the RCMP to arrive he gave in to his exhaustion. He sat down and laid his head in his arms on the table. His shoulders heaved with muffled sobs. Mom stood behind him with her arms wrapped round him as if she could curb the shaking. She leaned over and kissed the top of his head. Silent tears ran down her cheeks into his hair as she mumbled something I could not hear.

'God!' Boyer moaned. 'I sent him away.'

But I was the one responsible. I had sent him to his death. *I killed River.*

'A freak accident,' the police would say when they concluded their investigation. River had stumbled over the mine shaft in the dark. The hole was so shallow it shouldn't have killed him. But his head snapped back and struck bedrock when he landed. The officer who brought the report out shook his head with sympathy before he left and said, 'He would have been able to crawl out if he'd survived the fall.'

As it was, a wild animal, a bear or cougar, dragged his body out.

CHAPTER NINE

WHILE BOYER LED the police to River and Mom murmured mournful words of comfort to his grieving mother on the telephone, I went out to Boyer's cabin to do the last thing I could do for River.

I peered over my shoulders into the bush as I hurried out alone. Every movement in the shadows held terror for me now. And every time I closed my eyes during the long sleepless nights since the assault, the horrors played out again.

Still, I forced myself on. I knew the police wanted River's personal belongings. I would make sure no prying eyes read his private journals. I would get rid of any marijuana hidden in his duffle bag. The gossip-mongers had had enough of him. I would let them have no more.

In the cabin I sorted through his things. Tears rolled down my cheeks as I undid the zipper of the duffle bag and lifted out the clothes that smelt of him. At the bottom of the bag I found his journals and a small plastic bag of rolled smokes and matches. I wiped my eyes on the sleeve of my sweatshirt as I placed the journals on the table. Then I opened the small plastic bag and removed a thin cigarette.

I placed the cigarette between my lips and struck a match. I'd never even tried to smoke before, but I wondered if this sweet-smelling drug would make me not care for a while. I wondered if that was what he had felt when he inhaled this fragrant weed; what he had felt on the night we were together. I wanted to understand why he had allowed himself to be with me for those few brief moments that night. I thought I might find some understanding in the smoke and in the journals.

But I found no answers in either. I felt nothing from the marijuana except nausea. I found it difficult to keep the thin cigarette lit. When it went out, I lit another. Three cigarettes burned down in a saucer between my short puffs and coughing fits, while I sorted through River's journals. Still, I felt only slightly light-headed. Finally, with my throat burning, I gave up and concentrated on the journals.

The entries were dated from before he left the States. I started reading about his difficult decision to leave his country, his family. I skimmed

through the pages trying to find any reference to our family, to me. But as I read his daily entries I found it impossible to hang on to the meaning of his words for anything more than a few seconds. Through the haze of my sleep-deprived mind I wondered if this was what if felt like to be high. I closed my eyes for a moment.

The night had crept up and dimmed the light in the cabin when I reopened my eyes. I flipped through the pages of the last journal. Half-asleep I recognised the angst of a gentle soul trying to find meaning for his feelings, his sexuality, his attraction to Boyer. Then I came to the final date. *June 8.* The night I was in his room. I felt the pain in his words as he chastised himself for his lack of judgment.

What have I done? By trying to deny the truth of who I am I have destroyed everything. I have betrayed her, betrayed everyone. And myself. For what? A thoughtless moment of curiosity? How inadequate the word regret is.

Scribbled on the very bottom of the page was his last entry. Stunned, I read the words telling how, as he looked out of the window as I was leaving his room, he saw my mother duck under the dairy stairs.

My mother? My mother was there?

So it was true, she knew I was in his room that night. But why was she there? Was it possible that she too . . .? No, that couldn't be. But what was she doing there? My mind raced with unthinkable thoughts.

Suddenly headlights flashed in the window. Boyer was home. I jumped up and dumped the ashes, spent matches and butts, along with the rest of the marijuana, in the rubbish under the sink, then quickly rinsed the saucer. I rushed to gather the journals.

Boyer came through the door, defeated, tired, somehow looking smaller, as if a part of him had been cut away. He sniffed at the air and shook his head wearily. Then he spotted the journals.

'These belong to River's family,' he said, reaching for them. As he picked them up he said, 'Come on, I'll drive you back to the house.'

In the past I would have argued that I could walk that far, that I was not afraid of the dark, and he would have let me. But not that night. We drove the short distance in silence.

'Are you sure we should give those journals to River's mother?' I said before I climbed out of his car. My tongue felt thick as I rambled on. 'I mean, do you think he would want her to read them? To know . . . to know all this?'

'His mother knows,' Boyer sighed. 'A mother always knows.'

Mom's nocturnal wanderings saved Boyer's life that night. She smelt it first. The hint of smoke drifted across the alfalfa field behind the house and in through an open window in the sunroom. Her sensitive nose turned to the scent carried on the night breeze. She peered past her reflection in the darkened window. Above the trees behind the field, she saw her fear of fire manifested in an ominous pink glow in the sky.

At the sound of her screams ripping through the house, I pulled myself up from my drugged sleep. 'Gus! Gus! Get up! There's a fire! Oh God! Hurry! Hurry! It's Boyer's cabin!'

As I jumped out of bed, I heard Morgan and Carl rush out into the hallway and down the stairs to the kitchen. I ran behind them in my nightgown. Through the kitchen window, I saw my father, still wearing his long johns, run across the farmyard and into the machine shed.

I flew out of the kitchen and leapt down the porch steps. My shaking fingers fumbled with the gate latch. I forced it open and bolted up the road towards Boyer's cabin. Up ahead Mom ran along the back field, Morgan and Carl close behind. I raced after them in my bare feet. The roar of the tractor sounded behind me. I threw myself back against the fence as the steel fork-lift prongs on the Massey Ferguson passed. My father stood over the steering wheel, urging more speed from the old machine, the screaming protest of the engine matching the hysteria I felt shrieking in my head.

I caught up with, then passed, the red taillights. I ran ahead of the tractor, down the seemingly endless road and into the meadow. I rushed into the clearing and stumbled towards my brother's cabin.

At first I thought the lake was on fire. The shining reflection of flames leaping from the log cabin created a mirrored blaze in the dark waters of the lake. Hungry flames escaped from the open kitchen windows. Greedily they reached out and fed on the branches of the apple tree. I stifled the screams rising in my throat as the ancient tree burned like a giant torch in the night sky.

Blistering heat radiating in waves distorted the strange dance being performed in the flickering shadows. In front of the cabin, Morgan and Carl, on either side of Mom, struggled to hang on to her arms, to hold her back. She fought viciously to get away. A voice I barely recognised screamed at them, demanded, threatened and begged them to let her go, to let her go to her son.

I whirled round and ran to the side of the cabin, to Boyer's bedroom window. I threw myself up, clawing at the wood, as I too screamed my brother's name. Strong hands grabbed me and pulled me back. I

scratched and bit at Morgan's arms as I fought to escape. The tractor roared behind us. Morgan dragged me away as our father rammed the front of the Massey Ferguson into the side of the cabin. I slowed my struggles as I saw my father's determined face. He backed up the tractor to take another run at the frame walls. As he willed the tractor forward again and again, the fork-lift prongs tore into the siding and plywood wall until it ripped apart, leaving a gaping hole into Boyer's bedroom. The fire inside, fed by the fresh oxygen, exploded through the opening.

It took a moment before I recognised that the fireball that shot out and landed at our feet was human. It was Boyer.

I bargained with God. As my parents rushed Boyer to the hospital, I knelt on the linoleum floor in the parlour. I promised untold penitence in return for my brother's life. As the hours passed, I pleaded with, and then, in anger, threatened, a nonchalant God, a God who allowed so much tragedy to strike our family. Still, I held little hope that the body that Mom and Dad wrapped in wet towels and laid on quilts in the back of the pick-up truck would return to us as Boyer.

Morgan and Carl returned home from Boyer's cabin before dawn. The three of us sat at the kitchen table. Coffee grew cold in mugs. My brothers spoke in hushed voices about how everything was lost in the fire. Boyer's books, River's journals, all ashes. I listened, mute with guilt, while they speculated over what caused the fire. 'Must have been the propane gas,' Carl concluded and Morgan nodded.

Just before five o'clock, my mind numb, I followed them outside. As we headed across the farmyard to let the cows into the barn, Dad drove up. He climbed out of the truck. He looked hollow, older. He stumbled by us as we stood waiting for news.

'Dad?' Morgan called after him, his voice gentle but insistent.

Our father stopped and turned slowly, looked at us with vacant eyes.

'They're taking him to the airport by ambulance, then airlifting him to Vancouver,' he said. 'They've done everything they can for him here. Your mother's going with him,' he added, then headed into the barn.

The police investigation lasted all of two days. At first, the police, like my father, suspected the fire was deliberately set, but there was no proof. The same two RCMP officers, who had spoken to Mom and Boyer about River, showed up a week later with the final report. I stood slumped behind the bathroom door with a molten lump of guilt lodged in my throat and listened to them report to my silent father that the fire had started somewhere at the front of the cabin from 'unknown causes'.

Mom was gone for two weeks. It would be another five months before Boyer came home. River's mother and grandfather came and went. They took away what was left of him in a pine box. There was nothing else to take. I knew if my mother had been there, if Boyer had been there, they would have found the right words of comfort to share. I tried. I took his mother over to the dairy and showed her where River had lived. I told her about his time here with us, about his words of love for them in the burnt journals; they deserved at least that, as Boyer said. But in the end they went away with only their sorrow.

While Boyer fought to recover, enduring the endless skin grafts and surgeries in the Vancouver Burn Unit, we went through our days like shell-shocked survivors. And the gossip went on. Rumours about River and Boyer turned into outright lies. We received a poorly written letter, condemning Boyer for trying to commit suicide over the death of his lover by setting himself on fire.

Lewd suggestions about Morgan and Carl's relationship were uttered on the phone too. They stopped going out in the evenings and the few friends who tried to come back were sent away. My brothers wanted nothing to do with town now, only going into Atwood when necessary to pick up the mail or groceries.

I went to the high school and cleaned out both Carl's and my locker. I was finished with school for the year. Carl was finished with it for ever. It was just as well he refused to go back. At least he did not have to see the ugly words scratched into the metal doors of both our lockers.

By the end of the month almost one-half of Dad's customers had cancelled deliveries.

That summer, a summer I had looked forward to with such foolish romantic anticipation, dragged on. Something more than Boyer was missing from our family. We each moved through our days in solitary worlds. Our connectedness, the glue that had held us together, had vanished. Stilted conversations, either about the business of the farm, or of Boyer's progress, became our method of communication.

While Mom was in Vancouver, we fell into the habit of eating only when we were hungry, each of us grabbing leftovers from the picked-at meals I prepared each day. Grazing, Mom called it when she came home and put a stop to it. She insisted we all sit down at mealtimes. 'We need to get back to normal,' she said. But we never would.

Our family became isolated. Except for a few old friends, we were shunned. The only guest who ever joined our table during those days was Father Mackenzie. And starting in October, *Ruth*.

Ruth was one of the girls from Our Lady of Compassion. She would become the last resident there before the home closed down. Morgan and Carl began keeping company with her after Morgan bumped into her in front of the post office as he rushed out one afternoon.

Tall and willowy, it was hard to tell that she was an expectant mother, except for a small bulge under her blue smock. Morgan walked her back up the hospital hill that day and their friendship began. Both he and Carl escorted her to the Roxy Theater every week. Then they began to bring her home for dinner. It wasn't long before everyone in our family was drawn to the dark-haired girl from the Queen Charlotte Islands. I suppose she gave us something to focus on outside our own miseries. We were all aware of her sadness at carrying a child she would not be allowed to keep. Still, she charmed us all with her quiet acceptance of life. Even I began to look forward to her visits.

Back at school after the summer vacation, I ignored the huddled groups watching as I walked the hallways. The looks of pity cast my way were as hard to take as the whispered gossip that reached my ears. I pretended not to see, not to hear. I pretended I wasn't there and hid behind shapeless sweatshirts and baggy trousers.

When I wasn't in school, or with Dad on his dwindling milkround, my existence was limited to the house and the dairy. In the hours in between, I slept. I slept and I ate. While the rest of my family lost their appetites, I took comfort in food.

Some weekend mornings Dad insisted I come along with him on the milk run. He certainly didn't need me, and I suspected it was just to get me out, but I couldn't refuse him. Each time we approached Colbur Street I felt myself start to hyperventilate.

I knew that sometime during the summer Elizabeth-Ann and her mother had left town. Ma Cooper regaled us with the latest gossip.

'Seems the mayor's wife and daughter ran off on him,' she told Mom. 'He came home from work one night and found the house emptied.'

And even though Ma Cooper reported that Mr Ryan had disappeared shortly after, I couldn't shake the panic that rose up every time we drove by the empty house. She stood by us, Ma did, and so did the Widow and Jake.

But in October, after Morgan started keeping company with Ruth, Ma Cooper could not keep her mouth shut.

'It's none of my business, Nettie,' she said, 'but you have enough troubles in this family without Morgan parading around town with a pregnant girl, and an Indian at that.'

'She's Haida,' Mom corrected her.

Ruth's mother was part Haida from the Haida Nations Indian Band on the Queen Charlotte Islands. Her father was a commercial fisherman there. It was her strict Irish Catholic father, Ruth told Mom, who had sent her away to have her baby when she got into trouble.

'You're right, Ma,' Mom said in her no-nonsense voice. 'It is none of your business. And if Morgan and this young lady,' she continued, 'find comfort in each other's company, I'm happy for them. And I'm not interested in the foolishness of wagging tongues.'

I will say for Ma Cooper though, that when she saw how strongly Mom felt, she held her counsel and stood by us once again. And even Ma, after she came to know her, fell in love with Ruth.

Beautiful Ruth with the sparkling dark eyes and shy smile. She became the lifeline to our floundering family. And on the day when Boyer finally returned, it was only Ruth who could look into his face without flinching, without shock, without fighting back tears.

Snowflakes drifted down from the grey sky on the November day Boyer came home. We had all been warned about the scars that were still healing but, except for Mom, I don't think any of us was truly prepared.

I stood trembling behind the porch window and watched as Mom and Dad climbed out of the car. Mom opened the back door and leaned down to help Boyer. As he carefully stepped out then straightened up, I saw the patches of pinto-like skin creeping up the side of his neck. I breathed a sigh of relief. Then he turned.

I gripped the window ledge as the devastation on the other side of his face was revealed. His face! It was as if the whole left side had melted. Somewhere under the angry red scar tissue was where his ear, his cheek and the left side of his mouth had once been.

As Mom slowly led him up the path to the porch, I fled into the kitchen. When he finally came through the door, I tried to look past the scars, tried to find Boyer in the eyes. There was nothing there. He looked back at me for less than a heartbeat and then through me, beyond me. It was as if I had disintegrated, as if I didn't exist.

I don't know how long it would have taken my brothers to speak if Ruth hadn't stepped up and held her hand out to Boyer. 'I'm so happy to meet you,' she said in her gentle voice. 'I'm Ruth.'

We had all been warned that Boyer was still having trouble speaking because of the tracheotomy performed on his smoke-damaged throat. Mom said it was still painful for him to talk. He slowly raised his hand. Ruth took it and held it cupped gently in both of hers.

Morgan and Carl, usually so quick with words, stood there gaping, as if they'd lost their voices. Finally Morgan found his. 'Hey. Welcome home. Have we missed you!'

Boyer nodded to them and then walked through the parlour into the sunroom.

Mom said he was still in shock, still needed time to heal, that it was normal for burn victims to retreat inwards, to feel anger.

For the next few months, Boyer slept out in the sunroom. The stairs were too difficult for his stiff, recovering body. He healed in private, keeping his scars and his pain to himself.

I confined myself to the kitchen, the bathroom and my room while I tried to be invisible. Late at night when the rest of the house was asleep, when I was sure Mom was not up, I began to sneak downstairs and carry food back to my room. I stayed awake as long as I could, reading and eating, stuffing myself with words and food, hoping to ward off the images that came with sleep. Still, every night the visions came— dreams of tendrils of smoke rising from under the kitchen sink in Boyer's cabin. Because no matter how many times I heard Mom tell someone that the police suspected that the fire was arson, I knew who the arsonist was. And every time I closed my eyes I could see the embers, from marijuana butts that I had so carelessly emptied into the trash, smoulder—smoulder and ignite while Boyer slept.

I don't know how Boyer and I lived together in the same house that winter. Yet during the months after he returned from the burn unit, we somehow managed to avoid each other.

When I wasn't at school or doing chores, I hid out in my room. Boyer lived between the sunroom and the kitchen. An entire world away. Sometimes I caught glimpses of him passing through the kitchen on his way to the bathroom. It was as if a stranger had taken over his body. I couldn't see Boyer even in the relatively normal right side of his face. Certainly it could not be my brother who sat for hours on end in Dad's recliner in front of the television set.

Mom became his keeper. She protected him from the curious eyes of visitors and even from us. She took meals out to him in the sunroom. Each morning she ran his bath, tested the water, and then led him like a reluctant child into the bathroom. She rubbed his thickening scars with oils and insisted he keep mobile. Every few hours, she took him by the arm and led him on short walks, first around the house, then outside, his temperature-sensitive skin bundled up against the cold.

The snow arrived early that winter. I watched from my window as the snow plough came up our road in the early morning. Like the mail, the milk must go through. South Valley Road was the first road to be cleared each day. But except for the milk deliveries and necessities, we rarely went to town. Mom still attended church each Sunday morning, the only one of us who went on a regular basis now. I refused to go at all. No one challenged me.

Before Christmas a few of Dad's old customers tried to renew. He ignored their requests while Mom argued we couldn't afford to be proud. 'I'll sell some cows in the spring,' he argued. 'Well it's either that,' Mom threatened, 'or sell the milk in bulk to the commercial dairies.' That was a solution my father said he'd rather die than see happen. He almost got his wish.

Our dairy was one of the last in the province to bottle and sell raw milk. 'Those suits from the city want to sterilise everything,' he used to say. 'If they have their way, pretty soon there won't be any goodness, anything natural, left in anything.' That winter the inspector from the Milk Board began to show up on a regular basis to do quality checks.

'Someone's looking for an excuse to shut us down,' Dad complained each time they showed up. The tests always came out clean.

During the Christmas break it was harder to avoid Boyer. Whenever I wasn't doing chores I retreated to my room. One afternoon, my mother called after me as I plodded upstairs. 'Go to Boyer's old room and bring down some of his books,' she told me.

The attic bedroom had been empty ever since Boyer moved out to the cabin the year before. Neither Morgan nor Carl had any inclination to move up there, both of them content to remain room-mates.

Most of Boyer's books were lost in the fire, but some still remained stacked in his old room. I trudged reluctantly up to the attic and hesitated for a moment before I entered. Once inside I began to search hastily through the piles of books. I carried an armload to the kitchen and placed them on the table for my mother's inspection. They were familiar novels, classics, which I was sure both she and Boyer had read a number of times. Finally she chose *A Tale of Two Cities* and shoved it at me.

'I want you to read this to Boyer,' she said.

I stepped back, recoiling from the book. 'But—but, I can't,' I stammered. She had no idea what she was asking of me.

'Yes, you certainly can,' she insisted. 'It's too difficult for him to hold a book for any length of time.' She nodded towards the parlour. 'Now go in and sit down beside him and just read. It will do you both good.'

In the parlour Boyer lay in Dad's recliner, his eyes closed. On the television screen the Galloping Gourmet chopped onions. I walked over and switched off the set. When I turned back Boyer was sitting up. I could feel his eyes following me.

'Mom said, she said I should read to you.'

Boyer said nothing. I stared at the book in my hand, at the oval rag rug at my feet, anywhere but into that face.

I sat down in Mom's chair on his right side and began to read. 'It was the best of times, it was the worst of times . . .'

I read the words, but I heard, felt, none of them. I kept my eyes on the pages while my monotone voice droned on. We must have appeared a strange pair, the two of us sitting straight and rigid in our parents' chairs, ignoring each other's presence. Boyer, who taught me to read, who taught me to pay attention to the rhythm, the music of the words, stared straight ahead.

When I finished the last sentence of the first chapter, he stood up. The voice of a stranger said, 'Thank you,' a harsh gurgle sounding in his throat. He retreated to the sunroom.

I held the sleeve of my sweatshirt against my nose to stifle the sneezes and the tears I felt building. Those two words were the first my brother had spoken directly to me since the night of the accident.

The accident. That's what my family had come to call it whenever they spoke of the night of the fire, which was seldom. I never spoke of it at all. But I ached to blurt out the truth. The next afternoon I sat down beside him to read again. But before I started, I decided I would tell him. I must tell him. I set the book unopened on my lap and took a deep breath as I searched for the words. 'The fire, Boyer, I . . .'

I felt him wince as he leaned back. 'Not now, Natalie, I'm tired.' The raspy voice of a stranger dismissed me. I fled to my room.

When I came downstairs later to help with dinner, I heard Dad's voice coming from the parlour. I peeked in to see him sitting in Mom's chair beside Boyer. My father held a Dr Seuss book in his hands and was reading out loud from it. I backed into the kitchen and turned to my mother. 'When did Dad learn?' I whispered.

For the first time since summer, his name passed between us. 'River,' she said. 'He was teaching him. That's why he went on the milk round. They stopped for lessons at a booth in the back of Gentry's every day.'

I went and stood in the doorway. My father was concentrating on the words while Boyer listened with his eyes closed. A smile lifted the right side of his lips. I turned away but not before seeing the trickle of

moisture move down the smooth skin below his right eye. I listened to my father read those simple words about green eggs and ham as if they were the most important in the world. At that moment they were.

Something changed for Boyer after that. Every afternoon he and Dad sat together in the parlour while Dad read to him. Before long they moved to the kitchen table with books spread out in front of them. By the end of January, my father was reading the newspaper for real.

Boyer moved back up to the attic room. He took his place at the table for meals again and started working with Mom in the dairy. And the more he joined the world, the more I retreated.

Once again, most nights I refused dinner and would later sneak down to raid the kitchen while everyone slept. One night in mid-February, I loaded my plate by the light of the refrigerator.

'How long can this go on, Natalie?' My mother's voice startled me. She stood in the parlour doorway in her nightgown.

'What?' I asked and shut the fridge door.

Mom switched on the kitchen light. She came to me, put her hands on my shoulders, and spun me round to face the mirror on the kitchen wall. I didn't need to see the image; the tangled hair and swollen face. I knew what I looked like standing there in a baggy, food-stained shirt and sweatpants, clothes I had been living in night and day. I didn't care. I twisted away from her and headed towards the door hunched over a plate piled high with bread, hunks of cheese and a wedge of apple pie.

'Boyer is learning to live with his scars,' she said wearily. 'Why can't you?'

Because those scars are my fault, I wanted to scream. I wanted to tell her then, all of it, but I remained silent, sullen. How could I tell her? How could she still love me if she knew the truth?

Later that same night I woke to the sound of my own muffled moans. A few minutes later, I heard Boyer's voice. He pushed open the door. 'Are you all right?' he asked from the doorway.

I could feel him standing there, just as he used to when I was a child and had woken from a nightmare. For a moment it was as if everything was the same again.

'Yeah, I'm OK,' I said. 'I must have been dreaming.'

'I could hear you from my room,' he said. 'Are you sure you're all right?'

'Just a stomachache,' I said. After he left, I pulled a pillow to my stomach as another cramp twisted my abdomen.

I drifted in and out of sleep on waves of pain. Some time later, I

woke to Mom leaning over me, her hand on my forehead. Boyer stood in the doorway behind her.

'It must be her appendix,' Mom said. 'Does your side hurt?' Before I could answer, she lifted my shirt to feel my right side.

'Dear God!' she said as her hands touched me.

I pushed her away. She turned to Boyer. 'Can you drive us to the hospital?' she asked.

Growing up on a farm means knowing where things come from. Living close to raw nature means nothing is secret. You know birth and death, the realities of life. And yet, I still cannot explain how unprepared I was for Dr Mumford's words in the emergency room. 'We'll take her up to the delivery room,' he said as he removed his hands from my stomach.

Delivery room? What was he talking about? Delivery room? I tried to sit up on the examining table but another pain gripped me. I felt the firm touch of a nun's hands insisting that I lie back down. As the grim-faced sister wheeled me away, I heard Mom's voice repeating the questions that had formed in my head.

'Delivery room? What?'

'She's about to give birth, Nettie,' Dr Mumford told her. 'Surely you knew that.'

For the rest of my life, I would wonder how I could not have known. How I could have carried life inside my body for almost eight months and not know of its existence. But until that moment I had no idea. And yet, when I heard Dr Mumford say those words to my mother, my heart recognised the truth in them.

I gripped the icy stainless-steel side of the gurney as another pain ripped though me. And suddenly I was back in the gravel pit pressed against the black metal hood. The same searing heat assaulted my body, promising to rip me apart.

Since that June night, I'd managed to stay detached, numb. It was as if the horrors of that night, and the tragedies that followed, had shut me off. In the months since, I had walked around in a world removed. I acted on direction, doing what was asked of me, but unconnected from the life around me. With each wrenching pain, it was as if my body was waking up, being reborn against its will.

I fought to stay numb. I didn't want to return. I wanted to stay in the empty vacuum that had become my existence.

As the elevator doors closed, I heard the nun's firm voice. She was the first to say it. 'You must have known,' she said.

CHAPTER TEN

OUTSIDE ST HELENA'S HOSPITAL, Jenny leans into the intercom. 'Jennifer Mumford here,' she says.

A buzzer signals the unlocking of the door. Inside, Jenny ushers me to the stairway. 'It's faster to take the stairs than that old elevator,' she says.

I am visiting my mother here for the first time. The last time I was in this hospital, I left behind the lifeless body of a baby born too early. I've been running from that memory ever since. Tonight my need to see my mother is stronger than fright. I follow my daughter up the steps.

Every time I visit Mom I wonder if it will be the last time I see her. Yet each time I leave knowing there are things left unsaid.

Keeping secrets is a lonely business. The longer you hold them, the harder it is to let them go. I knew that my refusal to tell anyone, especially my mother, what Mr Ryan did to me that night in the gravel pit was a useless sacrifice. He never kept his end of the bargain and I protected no one by remaining silent. Yet once the events that followed began—River's death, Boyer's accident—how could I add the horror of rape to my family's sorrow? I let my mother, my family, everyone, believe that the stillborn child was the result of my night with River.

Between Mom and me, there had been some kind of unspoken agreement to avoid discussions about that time in our lives. What good would it do to drag up the past? It happened. Shared memories would change nothing. But sometimes I long to unburden myself, to confess my part in all of it, to say out loud how it all came about.

Sometimes I want to discuss the 'what ifs' with her just once. What if I hadn't gone to River's room that night? What if she hadn't seen me? What if I hadn't run to Boyer's cabin, not seen him and River together? And mostly, what if, instead of running off into the forest that night, I had simply gone home? How different would our lives have played out then?

But I can never say these things out loud to her. I can't tell her of the many moments when I could have made other choices, choices that would have left our lives intact. What would be the point? Because I'm certain that she already knows most of it, that she has always known.

What she doesn't know is the real cause of the fire in Boyer's cabin. And I wonder if my guilt would be any less if I tell her? Guilt is a stern taskmaster. It requires you to always be on guard, always watch what you say. So I resisted the temptation to unburden myself, the temptation that crept up every time I looked into my brother's face. And I avoided him. The last time I stayed out at the farm was at my father's funeral.

The hospital corridors are dim on the second floor. The nurse at the night station looks up. 'Doctor,' she nods at Jenny as we walk by.

The door to Mom's room is open. A nightlight glows on the wall behind her bed. She looks so tiny, so lost in the white sheets.

It started in her lungs. My mother, who never smoked a cigarette in her life, would pay the dues my father escaped. Yet even now, with this disease eating her from the inside out, her skin is that of a much younger woman. At seventy-eight, my mother is still beautiful.

At first she appears to be sleeping. Then I see the rapid movement of her eyes beneath translucent lids, as if she is fighting her dreams. I take her hand in mine and feel the warmth as it wraps round my fingers.

On the other side of the bed, Jenny flicks at the IV tube with her finger. 'She's out of morphine,' she whispers. 'I'll go get the nurse.'

My mother's eyes snap open. She reaches up and clutches Jenny's hand. 'No.' Her voice is weak, but she holds on to both Jenny's hand and mine. I'm surprised by the strength of her grip.

Her eyes focus on me. 'Natalie, I've been waiting for you.'

As if summoned, the nurse appears at the door, a syringe in her hand. 'She didn't want any more morphine until you came,' she whispers. She approaches the bed and smiles down at Mom. 'Oh, you're awake, Nettie,' she says. 'This will start working in a few minutes.' She deftly inserts the syringe into the stopper of the IV tube.

'Wait,' Mom says. She takes a laboured breath. 'I heard—' A mucus-filled cough breaks the words in her throat. She murmurs something unintelligible. Jenny motions for me to lean forward and listen.

'I heard the baby cry,' Mom whispers into my ear.

'The baby?' I am not sure I understood her.

'Oh,' the nurse muses, 'there are strange noises in this old building all the time. Your mother hears babies crying.'

'It's OK, Mom,' I say as I stroke her forehead. 'It's OK, there are no babies here any more.' But she becomes agitated and pulls me closer.

'No,' she breathes into my ear. It seems to take every ounce of energy she has left. 'No, Natalie,' she says. 'I heard *your* baby cry.'

Nettie

She felt it. Nettie felt it the moment she put her hand on Natalie's stomach. Instead of the yielding flesh, the layers of fat she expected, her fingers felt the taut skin, the hardened muscles of a swollen abdomen.

Still she told herself, just as she told Boyer and her husband, 'It's her appendix.' By the time they reached St Helena's Hospital she believed it.

In the glare of the empty emergency room she breathed a sigh of relief as Dr Mumford, wearing operating-room scrubs, rushed in. A surgical mask hung at his neck. He looked as if he had been up all night.

Wordlessly, his expert fingers probed Natalie's right side, then he held both of his hands cupped to her extended abdomen.

Even as Dr Mumford glanced up at her, the surprise obvious in his arched eyebrows, Nettie was not prepared for his words. Delivery room? Birth? Those words brought images of her own pregnancies; they had nothing to do with her daughter, her baby girl, who was being wheeled away by the stern-faced nun.

Dr Mumford put his arm round Nettie's shoulders and led her back to the reception area. Boyer stood as they came into the waiting room. 'Go home, Nettie,' Dr Mumford said. 'I'll take care of this.'

But she refused. She wanted to be with Natalie. The doctor appealed to Boyer. He, too, refused to leave.

'Then wait here,' Dr Mumford said and rushed out of the room.

Boyer took Nettie's arm and led her across the foyer to the hospital chapel. Inside they knelt together in the candlelight and prayed. They prayed for Natalie, for the child. For River's child, though neither of them would say it out loud.

They waited. When she could bear it no longer, Nettie left Boyer in the waiting room and made her way through the sleeping hospital and took the elevator to the second floor.

At the end of the darkened hallway, the delivery room doors pushed open. Dr Mumford hurried towards her pulling his mask aside. He put his arm around her, and gently turned her back to the elevator.

'The baby came too soon,' he told her. 'He was stillborn.'

And with his words, an unexpected flood of sorrow for the lost child—her grandchild—overwhelmed her. She stopped walking and tried to pull away. 'Natalie,' she said. 'I want to see Natalie.'

'I had to put her under anaesthetic,' Dr Mumford said. 'She won't be awake for hours. Go home now. Get some sleep. Come back and see her in the morning.'

'The baby. He needs a priest; we need Father Mac.'

'I'll take care of that,' he said. 'Look, Nettie, there's no need for anyone else to know about this. No one has to find out.'

'But, the priest?'

'Your family has been through enough. We can keep this confidential. Let me look after this for you.'

And she let him. She let him lead her back to the elevator. She allowed him to gently push her through the open doors. And she convinced herself that the sound, the tiny cry she heard as the elevator doors closed, was only her imagination.

Gossip spreads in a small town like germs on a warm wind. It doesn't matter if it's true or untrue; it infects and contaminates just as quickly. Within a few days everyone in our town would hear about how the milkman's seventeen-year-old daughter had gone into the hospital for an appendectomy and delivered a baby. So now our family had one more thing to not talk about. And the town had another juicy story to feed on.

The next morning I lay in the hospital bed and tried not to think about the baby boy who the nuns said was born too soon. I pressed down on my tender abdomen and felt the wobble of loose stomach muscles. Was life really growing there all those months? How could I not have known? I tried to think back on missed monthly periods. How could I have not paid attention?

I refused to give the baby form in my mind. I would not allow it a place in my heart. I felt nothing, I told myself, except relief. And yet an unexplained yearning tugged at the core of my now empty abdomen as if connected to some invisible cord.

A nun appeared soundlessly with a breakfast tray. She glided in and out of my room as if on cushions of air. My mother came on the soles of determination. I recognised her footsteps, winter boots on tiled floor sounded in the empty hall. She paused for a moment before she pushed open my door and breezed in, a smile set on her face. She was carrying a container filled with cookies. She leaned over the bed to kiss my cheek. 'Morgan and Carl send their love,' she said. 'Dad too, of course.'

'Do they know?' I asked. 'Does the whole town know?'

'No one but our family needs to know anything other than you had your appendix out,' she said. 'Dr Mumford will take care of that. All you need to do is just get better.' She chatted on as if it really was an appendectomy. She sat on the end of the bed and lifted the lid on my breakfast tray. 'You've got to eat, darling,' she said when she saw the untouched porridge and toast. I pushed the tray away.

'Ruth had her baby last night,' Mom announced. I noticed she didn't say too.

I recalled an image of someone being wheeled past me as I was pushed into the delivery room. Ruth.

'I guess she will be going back to her home in the Queen Charlottes soon,' Mom sighed. 'The boys will certainly miss her. Especially Morgan. I'll just pop over and visit her before I go home,' she said.

And not talk about her baby too, I thought.

It struck me, then, that it was always that way with my mother. She knew everything; she talked about nothing. This event in my life, our lives, was just another thing to be swept under the carpet. We would all know it was there, but we would carefully step round it. That was fine with me. I had no desire to talk about it, to give it life.

Mom never asked who the father was. I would let her go on believing that the birth we were pretending didn't happen was a result of the night she watched me leave River's room. She could mourn that child, I could not. For I felt certain that the baby was Mr Ryan's child.

The door to my hospital room opened. Boyer stuck his head in. He must have driven Mom in to see me. I was surprised. Except for last night, he had not left home since he returned from the burn unit. For a moment I wondered what it must have cost him to appear in town in broad daylight, to endure the stares of the curious. Yet, when he asked, 'Can I come in?' I pulled my blanket around me and turned away.

Back at home my isolation became complete. Through the grates I heard Mom tell Dad and my brothers that I would come around eventually, but I wondered how I would ever be able to look any of them in the eye again knowing the destruction and shame I had caused.

From my upstairs bedroom, I watched as the last days of February vented their fury on the countryside. The days lengthened and grew milder. The snow and ice on the roads began to recede, turning our farmyard into a spring sea of mud and manure.

All the while my mother brought trays upstairs and left them outside my door. She stopped trying to talk me out of my room, stopped pressing me to return to school. I didn't know if I was relieved or saddened by her silent acceptance. But often, in the evening, I heard her at the piano. I buried my head in my pillow as the music floated up through the hallway grate and seeped under my bedroom door.

'She can't stay up there for ever,' my father said one night in March, his voice rising up through the hall grates to find me.

A week later I sat in the cab of the milk truck as we drove away from the farmhouse. I resisted the temptation to turn and take one last look at my home. I was already gone.

Widow Beckett came up with the solution. I said nothing when Mom told me about the offer. I'd heard it all from my room.

'For Natalie's sake, for your whole family,' the Widow told Mom, 'you have to get her away from here.'

I'd heard the telephone calls to Widow Beckett's brother and his wife in Vancouver.

'They have a huge home,' Widow Beckett explained. 'They take in foster children all the time; one more won't even be noticed.'

Mom's carefully hoarded egg money would pay my room and board. 'It's only for the rest of the school year,' she told me. 'You have to catch up or you won't graduate.' I shrugged my acceptance.

On the day I left, she stood at the kitchen table, her back to me, when I came downstairs with my suitcases. On the table, pie plates lined with dough waited to be filled. A bowl of frozen huckleberries, Boyer's favourite, thawed in the sink. Mom slammed the rolling pin on the dough round as if her life depended on it.

I hesitated for only a moment before I pushed open the screen door with my suitcase and walked out. She did not come after me. I did not turn back. Neither of us was willing to give in to that awkward moment of goodbye.

'It won't be for long,' she'd said the night before as she left my bedroom. I think we both knew it wasn't true.

Dad and I rode in silence to the highway turnoff where we waited for the Greyhound bus.

'Well, this will be an adventure, hey, Sunshine?' my father finally said. 'Off to the big city, eh?' He reached inside his jacket pocket, then glanced up at me as he opened the silver cigarette case. I tried to return his crooked smile. He leaned into his cupped hands to light his cigarette, but not before I read in his eyes the toll the fight to keep the farm was having on my father's spirit.

He rolled the window down and blew out a cloud of smoke. 'Your mother and I want you to know that when you want to come home— that is, whenever you are ready—well, the minute you think you can come back, you just phone us and we'll have you on the next bus.'

I wondered if he really believed I would ever be ready to come back and face the gossip, the town, Boyer's broken life, the ghosts. Or even if he really wanted me to.

I wanted to go. I wanted to spare my family the constant reminder of the havoc I had created. Yet as the bus pulled away, as I watched my father's truck grow smaller, I could not stop the overwhelming grief that washed over me. For at that moment I believed I would never see my father, or hear him call me Sunshine, ever again.

I was right.

The city swallowed me whole. It was easy to disappear, to become invisible, swept away in the throng of students who streamed through the hallways of the high school whose population was as big as the entire town of Atwood. It was not so easy in the Beckett home.

The Beckett family lived in a two-storey house in East Vancouver. Her brother's home was not quite as large as Widow Beckett believed it to be, but it did have four bedrooms. Four bedrooms and one tiny bathroom, hardly big enough to turn round in, for six children and two adults. And then me. I slept on a campbed in the girls' room upstairs.

The two sisters, Judy and Jane, bickered every waking moment. Their bedroom was divided into territories by an invisible line, which ran down the middle of my campbed. The four boys ran amok. Unlike my brothers, they had no chores, no routine to guide them. Like frenzied ferrets, night and day they chased each other up and down stairs.

The house was a constant riot of noise. Whenever both Mr and Mrs Beckett were home at the same time, swirling cigarette smoke and angry-sounding words filled the air. The normal mode of conversation was top-of-the-lungs yelling, the hurried words lost in the rush to be heard. Meals were an eat-where-you-are affair, most often gobbled down in front of the constantly blaring black-and-white television set.

I tried not to compare their lives with those of my own family. Because I knew, for me, that way of life no longer existed. At night I would lie in my small campbed and try to choke back the homesickness that threatened to overwhelm me.

Every week a letter from my mother slid through the mail slot in the front door with chatty news of people and a town I would rather forget. I smiled when she told me Morgan was corresponding with Ruth, who had returned to the Queen Charlotte Islands.

I cringed when I read:

The local gossip never ends. Yesterday Ma Cooper said she heard your friend Elizabeth-Ann Ryan and her mother are living in Calgary. Her father returned to Atwood alone, but no one sees him. He's become a complete recluse, cooped up in his house, night and day. Drinking

himself into oblivion, the grapevine reports. Imagine that, from town mayor to town drunk. I have to say I'm not surprised. I've always thought there was something not quite right about that man.

He's no longer mayor, but he's still causing trouble. Apparently his last act before he left was to start an order in council to revoke our business licence. Mr Atwood and his son, Stanley Junior, along with Dr Mumford, held a protest at City Hall when they got wind of it.

Dad won the fight to keep his licence to deliver unpasteurised milk, but eventually he gave in and sold to the large dairies.

Perhaps it's for the best, Mom wrote. *I think the boys might even be relieved. With the automated barn and direct bulk sales now, there certainly won't be enough work to tie them all down here. Maybe Boyer can go to college after all*, she added cheerily. But I knew she saw it as just another event in the chain of tragedies that was tearing her family apart.

It wasn't Boyer who left in the end. Not long after Dad died, Morgan went on a fishing trip to the Queen Charlotte Islands. And to visit Ruth. When he returned, he announced he was moving there.

'Morgan's going to work on a fishing boat for Ruth's father. Morgan has fallen in love with the West Coast, the ocean, and most of all with Ruth. I'm happy for them. I adore Ruth. But it's such a long way away.' Mom added that she was sure it would be just a matter of time before Carl moved there too.

And, sure enough, shortly after Morgan left, Carl followed. They've all lived there since. Morgan and Ruth are married but, ironically, considering how they met, childless.

'Ruth got two husbands for the price of one,' Mom wrote. 'Although Carl doesn't live with them, his home is a pebble's throw away. Close enough to share most meals with his brother and his wife.'

Ruth doesn't seem to mind though. The few times I've seen them over the years, her shy, oval face portrays only love and acceptance; although I once caught a look of longing cross her eyes as she watched Morgan and Carl playing with Jenny, when they visited us.

I often wondered whether Ruth ever tried to find the child she had given up at birth. I once asked Morgan if they had ever searched for her baby. He told me that he'd wanted to but she had refused. Maybe, as Mom always says, it's for the best. You can't go back and repair the shattered parts of your life.

In Vancouver, I threw myself into school. And every afternoon I rode

the bus to the public library. I did my homework there, appreciating every moment of the hushed silence. Then I would sit and read until closing time. After a few months I was offered an after-school job there. I accepted. For the rest of the school year, I slept at the Beckett house, but the library was home. When summer came I told myself, and my parents, that I would rather be cataloguing books than delivering milk.

After I graduated from high school I went to work for a small community newspaper, then moved on to the *Vancouver Sun*.

I married the first man who asked me, before I realised I didn't need to be rescued.

In my room at the Alpine Inn I sit down and take a sip from the glass of sherry in my hand. In the matching blue paisley wingback chair across from me, Jenny waits while I settle. I lean back and close my eyes.

'Do you remember much about your father?' I ask. Jenny's father, my first husband, died before she was eight.

She considers the question. 'Yes and no,' she finally answers. 'Sometimes I think everything I remember about him is what you've told me over the years, and from our old pictures. I do remember his hands were always ink-stained when he came home from work. And I remember him reading to me at night. But I have trouble picturing his face.' She is quiet for a moment, then asks, 'Did you love him?'

I open my eyes and smile at her. 'Yes, I think I did, as much as I was able to at the time. I was so young, looking for a saviour. I probably half fell in love with the illusion of who he was. He was older, the editor of a newspaper. And very handsome.'

'He looked like Uncle Boyer,' Jenny says.

He did? Yes, I suppose he did. I never thought about that before.

'So did Ken,' she says, 'and Bert.'

I am startled by her words. With a jolt that is physical I realise the truth of the observation. All of them, all the men in my life, except Vern, have had some resemblance to Boyer. And to River. The implication of what she is saying is not lost on me. Is that what I do? Leave them, run away, when I realise they're not Boyer—or River?

And Vern? What does this say of him? Vern with his brown eyes and thick dark hair. He is nothing like the others, in any way. He's not a teacher, an editor or a writer. Like my father, Vern wears the dirt of the earth under his fingernails. And I have been with him the longest. I'm too weary to think about this now.

'I know about the baby,' Jenny says quietly.

So this is it. This is what she couldn't talk about on the phone. 'How long have you known?'

'I heard the rumours years ago,' she says. 'It's a small town, Mom.'

'Why didn't you say anything?'

'I thought that if you'd wanted me to know, you would have told me.'

'There was no reason to; the baby didn't live.' No reason not to either. Why hadn't I? As a doctor I'm sure Jenny has heard far more shocking confessions. But not from her mother.

'I didn't even know I was pregnant,' I tell her now. 'And when the baby was stillborn it was as if it was nothing more than a miscarriage.'

'Really?'

I open my mouth, close it, then say, 'No.'

'It was that baby Gram was talking about tonight, wasn't it?'

'I don't know what she was talking about.' I sigh.

Mom had become incoherent while I tried to soothe her. She mumbled something about Father Mac and Dr Mumford before the morphine took hold. 'Your grandmother couldn't have heard him cry. The baby was born too early, never took a single breath. He was stillborn.'

'No.' Jenny's voice is soft, almost a whisper. 'No, he wasn't.'

I feel as if a hot boulder has thudded into my chest.

'What are you saying? Of course the child was stillborn. Dr Mumford, the nuns, they said—' I shake my head. 'No, the baby didn't live.'

Jenny leans over, takes both my hands in hers, forcing me to look into her eyes. 'Mom, listen. You know there were two babies born that night. The other baby, Ruth's baby, was the one that didn't live.' Even though her voice is gentle, I can hear the urgency, the plea for understanding. 'I don't know how else to tell you, but it's true,' she says.

Confused, my mind races to make sense of her words as I pull my hands away. 'No! That's not right.' I stand up quickly, then sit down again. 'That's impossible—how can—after all these years? How?'

'There was a request for the medical records of the mother of a baby boy born on February 12th, 1969,' she says. 'But when the records were searched, something wasn't right. There were two births recorded for the date, both to the same mother. Both to Ruth, hours apart. The clerk brought the records to Nick and me. Nick confronted his grandfather. At first old Dr Mumford said it was a mistake. He insisted there was only one baby born that night. But he finally broke down and confessed. The baby who lived, your baby, was given to the adoptive parents who were waiting for Ruth's child.'

There's not enough air in the room. I cannot fill my lungs. I don't

want to hear any more. I stand again and turn to push open the window and gulp the cool air. 'No,' I insist with my back to her, 'that can't be right. The nuns! The nuns told me! They wouldn't lie.'

'Did the nuns actually tell you your baby had died?' she asks gently.

Born too soon. I have never forgotten the nun's no-nonsense tone as she said those words the next morning. *A baby boy, born too soon.* And suddenly I relate them to Boyer's childhood lesson about discretion, about using carefully chosen words to avoid the truth, the hurt.

I spin round and face her. 'That's enough!' I say, fighting the hysteria. 'I don't want to know any more. This conversation is over.'

'But you need—'

'No! No, I don't. That child was dead to me thirty-four years ago and he's dead to me now. Why drag up the past? Why tell me this now?'

But I know the answer before the words are out of her mouth.

'Because he's coming,' she says. 'He'll be here tomorrow afternoon.'

Nettie

They came together.

Nettie heard the hesitancy in their steps. Their shoes shuffled, barely lifted from the tiled hospital floor. They came into her room so close together they could have been one dark messenger with two heads.

Boyer stood at the head of her bed, which he had just adjusted for her comfort. Nettie lay with her head cushioned in pillows, watching as the two visitors approached the end of the bed.

Age had not cowed Dr Mumford. At eighty-five, his posture was still determinedly straight, but she noticed the slight tremor of his hands before he wrapped them around the metal bars.

She looked from him to Father Mac. The years had not been so kind to the priest. His shrunken frame was lost in the bulk of his great wool overcoat. His neck disappeared into his clerical collar.

The greetings were brief. Nettie was relieved her visitors did not ask how she was doing. They knew. Neither of her two old friends was about to waste time on polite lies and reassuring words. The priest spoke first. 'Allen has something to say to you, Nettie.'

The doctor made his way to the side of the bed, next to Boyer.

He took Nettie's hand. 'Nettie,' Dr Mumford began, but his voice cracked. Something inside him seemed to crumble. His shoulders sagged. Boyer pulled up a chair and the doctor slumped into it. 'I don't know how to tell you,' he said. 'Years ago . . . Natalie's baby . . .'

Nettie's heartbeat quickened as he confessed how he had played God

the night she brought Natalie to him. How he had lied about the child not surviving.

'There was a family waiting for the baby—Ruth's baby—it was so easy,' he said. 'So easy. I thought it was the right thing.' He lowered his head and wept onto Nettie's hand. 'I'm so sorry, so sorry.'

'I heard the baby,' she whispered.

And she recalled the sound coming from behind the delivery room doors. The tiny cry she convinced herself later was Ruth's child. But as the doctor sobbed his remorse at her side, she remembered. She remembered feeling the strong pull at the core of her being at that cry. It was the same overwhelming tug she had experienced at the birth of each of her own children. The memory rose to the surface, a memory buried so deep she'd never had to face the truth.

She searched the priest's eyes. Although she'd never confessed this one sin, she had lived her life doing penance for her part in Natalie's baby being condemned to purgatory. 'The baby,' she asked between strained breaths. 'Did Ruth's baby receive Last Rites?'

As the priest nodded, Nettie closed her eyes and felt relief wash through her.

She opened her eyes as Boyer asked, 'And Natalie's child? Where did Natalie's baby go?'

'The hospital didn't keep the adoption records,' Dr Mumford said. 'Our Lady of Compassion and the church handled that.'

Nettie's eyes shifted to Father Mac.

'I'm sorry,' the priest said, 'I can't give you that information. Adoption records are confidential. But,' he went on, 'we had a written request from an agency searching on his behalf. I've spoken with a representative from the agency. The young man, she told me, is not looking for his birth mother. But because he has a family of his own now he would like access to family medical history.'

His frail hand reached into the deep pocket of his overcoat. 'What I can give you,' he said, 'is this.' He held up a folded paper. 'It's the contact number of the agency that was enquiring on his behalf.'

Nettie watched as Boyer reached out and took the paper from the priest's hand.

The amber glow from the bedside lamp reflects on Jenny's face. A moth is trapped between the bulb and the shade. I hear the thuds as it throws its body back and forth in frantic attempts to escape. I know the feeling.

'And me?' I ask, my voice shaking, my arms folded. 'Why didn't

someone tell me? You had no right! No right to search for him, to find him.'

'He found us,' Jenny says. I can see the excitement growing in her face as she rushes to explain. 'Uncle Boyer sent him a message through the agency that was searching for his birth records. He called back right away. Uncle Boyer explained the circumstances of his birth. Told him how sick his grandmother—'

'Didn't anyone, anyone, stop to think to ask me if this is what I wanted?' I demand. The heat of fear turns into shivers of anger. I whirl round and slam the window shut. 'You had no right to decide for me.'

'I know. But it all happened so fast. There really wasn't time. He called yesterday to say he was flying up from Vancouver tomorrow. None of us wanted to tell you on the telephone,' she says. 'Gram wanted to tell you herself. That's what she was trying to say tonight.'

I face Jenny and feel my eyes narrow. 'Well, I won't meet him. I won't! I don't want to know his name. I don't care . . .' I'm rambling, but unable to stop myself. 'You have no idea what you're asking of me!'

Disappointment floods her face. Of course she would have expected my shock, but this—this aversion to meeting my own son—she cannot understand. How could she? She believes, they all believe, that this is the child of my teenage crush. They are each ready, eager, to accept him as family. If only it were that simple. If only he were River's son.

Suddenly I am very tired. 'I don't want to talk about this any more. It's been a long day. I'm going to bed.' I know my voice has gone flat, devoid of the conflict of emotions that wage a silent war within me.

Behind me, I hear Jenny stand. 'His name is Gavin,' she says wearily. 'He's an airline pilot.'

When I don't respond, she goes to the door. 'He's your son, Mom,' she says. 'But before you decide, for whatever reason you aren't saying, that he means nothing to you, remember he means something to us. He's the brother I never had. The grandson Gram never had. And the nephew your brothers and Aunt Ruth never had. And he's the son of the man who, from what I understand, is someone you all once loved. Is whatever is stopping you bigger than that?'

Now. Now is the time to tell her.

Before the door opens, Jenny adds, 'Uncle Boyer's picking them up at the Castlegar Airport tomorrow afternoon.'

'Them?' My voice is shaking.

'Yes. He has a family. A wife and three-year-old daughter.'

The door closes. As I listen to Jenny's footsteps I realise with a deep sadness that I'm letting history repeat itself. I'm doing exactly the same

thing my mother and I did. I am allowing the unspoken, the things I'm not saying, to create a wedge between my daughter and me.

A sudden flurry of delicate moth wings hammers against the light bulb and they turn to dust behind the lampshade. Like the moth, I am trapped, trapped between the heart-swelling excitement of my daughter's revelation and the frantic need to flee. And, like the moth, this time for me there is no escape.

Sleep eludes me. I toss and turn in the strange bed while I fight back the faceless image of a son I can't help wondering about. Jenny said he was flying in from Vancouver. Did he grow up there? Had I ever walked by him on some unremembered street? Who adopted him? Was he happy? What—who—did he look like? And did he ever wonder about me?

Finally, I sleep. When I awake it is still dark. Unable to find my way back to sleep I lie awake wrestling with the past, and with the present. I get out of bed and pull on my running clothes.

In the darkness of early morning I make my way through the empty streets of Atwood. Pink glow from the streetlights sifts down through the thick mountain mist. The rhythmic pounding of my running shoes rises from the pavement.

When I was seventeen, after I moved to Vancouver, I started running every day. At first it was an excuse to escape from the house, to have a few hours of solitude. It started as a way to numb my mind. It became a way of life. I've been running ever since—running from guilt and shame, from memories and secrets, from relationships. And from myself. But this morning I'm running towards something. I know exactly where my feet are taking me. I know what I must face.

I hasten down the deserted street, past the familiar old buildings that now house unfamiliar businesses. As I approach the edge of town, headlights cut through the lifting fog. I continue running, my shoulders squared. At the highway intersection I resist the instinct to turn north, away from Atwood, as I usually do. I take a breath and turn south, towards the border.

It's called Eaglewood now. The name, carved into a massive cedar log at the entrance, heralds its existence. The old gravel road has been paved. Overhead streetlamps light up sidewalks and driveways. I turn off the highway and run into the empty streets of the subdivision. Through the trees I see shadowed outlines of timber-frame houses. This development, of one- and two-acre lots, was carved out of the farm by Boyer and his partner Stanley Atwood. According to Jenny, the seasonal

owners of most of these homesites are Americans who have discovered our little piece of heaven here in the Cascade Mountains. I wonder briefly if any of the homes belong to young men who, after being pardoned at the end of the Vietnam War, returned to the United States.

My heart pounds in my ears. I push forward, past driveways, courtyards, decorative ponds and the dark houses set back in the trees. I turn a corner and suddenly I am there.

Even though everything is changed now, I know this place. I slow to a walk at the entry to a wide cul-de-sac. Across the way, a tree-lined driveway leads to a new post-and-beam home. I stop and stand panting while I stare across the invisible barrier.

A sudden gust of wind carries a flurry of dry autumn leaves through the trees. They flutter to the ground and skitter across the cobblestones and into the driveway of what was once the old gravel pit.

I take a deep breath and start walking. I resist the urge to look back over my shoulder, to flee. I am determined to erase this fear, to face it head-on. I focus on the glowing porch light on the house at the end of the driveway and let it pull me forward. I am no longer running but my heart races as I make my way across the vast expanse of the cul-de-sac and up the driveway. And then I am there. I have made it through. I stand at the bottom of the steps and look up at the house.

I don't know what I expected to find after all these years, what demons I thought I would confront. There is nothing here, no evil lurking in the shadows. No phantoms of the past wait for me. This is just a place. The gravel pit, which has haunted me all these years, no longer exists. It has been replaced by this beautiful home.

The cedar and stone house appears warm and inviting. It looks like a home in the country should look, as if it had grown there. Light spills from the kitchen bay window as I climb the granite porch steps.

As my hand reaches up to knock, I have to force back the thoughts that still try to push through. The gravel pit may be gone, but not the memory, and the dark secret buried with that memory. Now all the years of protecting that ugly secret are wasted. In a few hours I will be forced to face the results of the horrors of that night. And eventually the young man, too, will have to know the truth of his existence. *How can I tell them? How can I tell him, that he—'my son'—is the child of rape?*

I let my gloved hand rap on the wooden door. I hear footsteps inside. The door flies open. And Jenny reaches out for me.

'What time did you say they were coming?' I ask.

It's time to start filling in the blanks.

CHAPTER ELEVEN

THE HOSPITAL CORRIDORS are decorated in the colours of autumn. Picture cut-outs of turkeys, pumpkins, and scarecrows cover the walls of the second floor of St Helena's.

Still in my running clothes, I make my way to my mother's room. An unexpected calmness has overcome me since my uncensored disclosures to Jenny earlier. I am still surprised at the relief I felt at letting go of the secrets I had guarded for so long.

Mom lies back in her raised bed, her eyes closed. Even though Jenny told me that Mom is now down to seventy-nine pounds, I am surprised by the frailty of her body evident under the white sheet. Her thin arms are nothing more than skin over bone. 'There isn't much left, but spirit,' Jenny had told me. 'But that counts for a lot.'

Her eyes snap open and dart around the room the moment I enter. 'Is he here?' she asks as soon as she sees me.

I thought she had been waiting for me, but it is him that she has put off dying for. I can hear the urgency in her voice.

'Soon, Mom,' I tell her as I lean in to kiss her. 'He'll be here soon.'

My lips touch the delicate skin on my mother's cheek and she lifts her hand to my face. 'I heard him cry,' she whispers. 'I heard—'

'It's OK, Mom,' I say and take her hand in mine and press it to my lips. 'It's OK.'

Her eyes focus on me. 'I'm sorry, Natalie.' Her voice gurgles and she clears her throat. 'I heard him . . .' she continues, her voice somehow gaining strength. 'I should have . . . should have insisted that I see him. I walked away . . . I should have known.' Her eyes fight to hold mine, pleading as she struggles to get it all out. 'Forgive me.'

'There's nothing to forgive. We all believed—wanted to believe— what Dr Mumford told us.' The steady pump of the oxygen tank fills the empty space between our words. I feel the feather touch of her fingers on my cheek before her hand falls away and her translucent lids close. I sit beside the bed and stroke her forehead.

As I gently push a strand of hair behind her ear, her lids flutter open

again. Her thin lips part, then lift, in a weak smile. 'He'll come back to us,' she manages to whisper. 'Everything will be all right now.'

A saviour. That's how she sees her grandson. She sees him as someone who will bring this family back together, as the proverbial good that comes after an ill wind: River reincarnated.

And I can't—I won't—take that away from her. The speech I rehearsed on the way back from Jenny's disappears. The imagined conversations and confessions will not take place. I search her milky eyes, so full of hope, so close to death, and realise it's too late to burden her with my dark memories and secrets. I will let my mother leave this world believing her grandson is River's child.

'I should never—sent—away,' she murmurs.

'We all sent River away, Mom,' I say, believing she has once again read my mind.

'No, not River.' Her breathing is laboured. Every word has its cost. 'You. I should never have let you go away.'

'It's all right, Mom,' I say, trying to soothe her. 'I couldn't have stayed in Atwood.' It's not just words. It's true. Still, I remember the depth of the sadness I felt on that windy March day when I drove away with my father for the last time.

'I didn't know what to do with your grief,' she says. 'It was too deep.'

I had come to her, prepared to unburden myself, but it is she who gives voice to her regrets. Her hand closes around mine. 'You and Boyer were both suffering so deeply. His pain was more obvious. But yours,' she sighs. 'I just didn't know how else to help you heal.'

A feeling harboured in some deep part of me suddenly surfaces. As it rises I momentarily remember the resentment I felt the morning I walked out of the door while my mother stood with her back to me at the kitchen table. I thought she knew! I expected her to know. She knew everything else. Why didn't she know about my pain? I had done such a good job at keeping my silence, of hiding the horror and the guilt. I had made it look like anger but it had turned into resentment. Now that resentment surfaces, it surfaces and dissipates with her words.

I reach up and brush away the tear making its way down the side of her face into her hair. 'It was the right thing, Mom. The right choice. I would never have survived here.'

'I'm sorry I wasn't a better mother,' she says now.

And my heart aches.

'You were always a good mother. The best. To all of us.'

Her hand relaxes in mine. Her eyes close. I think she has fallen into

sleep until, without opening her eyes, she asks, 'Have you seen Boyer?'

'No, not yet.'

Her breathing quiets as sleep claims her, but suddenly she whispers, 'Are you ever going to forgive your brother, Natalie?'

Boyer? Forgive Boyer? I am startled by her question. 'Forgive him for what?' I say, but she cannot hear. My mother is asleep.

I sit by her bed and wonder at the sense of relief that flooded through me at the thought of blurting out the answer to her question. Was I really about to tell her that it is me, Natalie, who needs to be forgiven? That I cannot look into my brother's face without remembering that I'm responsible for his scars?

While she sleeps I lay my head on the bed beside my mother's hand. Her fingers instinctively stroke my hair.

The sounds of hospital life grow familiar. I begin to recognise the distinctive footsteps of different residents who pass the door on their slow relays up and down the hall. I don't know how much time has passed when I look up to see Jenny sitting on the other side of Mom's bed. She smiles across at me. A smile full of understanding.

Our conversation earlier this morning has gone a long way to bridge that gap of understanding.

'Uncle Boyer was just here,' she whispers to me. 'He didn't want to disturb you. He's on his way to the airport now. They should be back in about two hours. While Grammie sleeps do you want to go to your room to shower and change before everyone gets here?'

I nod, then sit for a few more moments studying Mom's face while she sleeps. This is the face of death, I admit to myself. Still there is a calmness in her breathing and a flush on her cheeks. Something is holding her back, giving her strength. She has something left to do. And so do I.

'**A**re you sure about this?' Jenny asks as the Edsel turns onto Colbur Street.

'No,' I answer, my voice unsteady. 'But everything I've read about victims of rape says healing starts when you confront your abuser.'

Victim?

'You know,' I tell her as she pulls up in front of Gerald Ryan's house, 'I spent so many years denying, refusing to be his victim, that I've become just that—by not allowing myself to talk about it. Today was the first time I've ever spoken it out loud.'

In her kitchen, early this morning, I told Jenny everything about that night in the gravel pit. Our tears flowed unchecked as I cleared

the cobwebs from the memories and exposed them to the light of day. Jenny listened without comment, but obviously feeling my anguish, as I relived the nightmare. Afterwards we held on to each other until our tears were exhausted.

When we had gained control, Jenny asked quietly, 'Mom, why are you so certain that the baby was Gerald Ryan's? If you were with River a few nights before, isn't it just as likely that he could be the father?'

And there it was, the crack in the rock-solid belief I had clung to all these years. Could I allow it to open and let hope seep in?

'I've always been so certain,' I sighed. 'Perhaps that was my way of coping. Maybe it was just less painful to accept that a stillborn baby was a result of rape, than to consider he may have been River's son.' I blew my nose. 'No,' I said as I shook my head. 'No matter how many times I imagine that night with River, I can't believe he could be the father. It only lasted minutes.'

'Still,' Jenny insisted, 'it's not impossible.'

'Perhaps. But not likely.'

Jenny turns off the motor and I force myself to look up at the old Ryan house. The once-immaculate yard is overgrown with weeds. Railings are missing on the sagging porch; the paint is cracked and peeling. This morning Jenny confirmed that as far as she knew an ailing Gerald Ryan still lived in this neglected house.

Jenny touches my shoulder. 'Do you want me to come with you?'

'No, I have to do this myself.'

'All right. But remember he suffers from alcohol-induced dementia. He may not know you.'

'It doesn't matter; I will know him.'

I push the car door open and get out in one quick movement.

I square my shoulders and as I walk towards the porch I refuse to let my eyes stray to the darkened basement window. Yet I can't help imagining him standing there in the shadows. My feet feel heavy as I trudge up the creaking steps. It takes everything I have to make my way over to the door and lift my shaking hand. I hammer on the door before I can change my mind.

The house is dark, silent. I hear no movement inside. I knock again, this time more insistently. Minutes pass before I hear a faint shuffle. The door begins to open and an eye appears in the narrow crack. It looks me up and down and then the door opens fully, revealing a bloated, heavy-set woman. A pink velours tracksuit stretches across sagging breasts and

stomach rolls. Stringy grey hair hangs, limp and unkempt, around a swollen face. Suddenly I recognise something behind the blank stare.

'Elizabeth-Ann?'

Her eyes narrow. 'Natalie Ward,' she says finally.

'I didn't expect . . .' I stammer.

From inside, a man's feeble voice calls out, 'Elizabeth-Ann?'

Unable to stop myself, I head into the house. Elizabeth-Ann steps back into the hall as I move towards the sickeningly familiar voice.

'Elizabeth-Ann?' The voice's repeated query has a whining urgency to it. And then I see the hunched form sitting in front of the silent television set in the living room. Like a frightened animal I stop, frozen, trapped, unable to move, hypnotised by the red-rimmed eyes—rodent eyes—that are looking, not at his daughter, but at me.

Beside me, Elizabeth-Ann slouches against the door. 'He thinks everyone is Elizabeth-Ann,' she says. 'Everyone, except me.'

I can't pull my eyes from the withered remains of what was once my tormentor. A plaid, food-stained dressing gown does not hide the cloth restraints that lash him to a pink vinyl chair. Yellow, parchment-like skin and tufts of transparent hair cover a splotched skull. Catheter tubing coils down from beneath his dressing gown to a full bag of urine hanging off the side of the chair.

'Elizabeth-Ann?' he pleads. Bulging eyes stare back at me. They look at me, through me, but do not see. There is no one behind those eyes, no one to connect with; no one left to hate. He is reduced to DNA.

How do I tell the son that I will meet in a few short hours that this is his legacy? I turn away. The plaintive call follows me as I retreat. At the front door, I stop abruptly. I whirl round and cross the foyer to the living room once again.

'I am not Elizabeth-Ann,' I say in a voice that is surprisingly calm. 'I am Natalie Ward. Remember me, Mr Ryan? Mr Mayor? I am the milkman's daughter. I am the girl you raped in the gravel pit thirty-five years ago.'

Behind me I hear Elizabeth-Ann's sudden intake of breath, but I can't stop now. All the black poison I have kept inside boils to the surface. It spills out like vomit with my words. There is not a flicker of understanding in the milky eyes below me, but I don't care. These are words I need to say. 'You think you took something from me? You think you got away with it? Well, you took nothing.'

I don't tell him what I thought I had come to tell him. That I have something to show for that night of terror. That I am about to meet the son who he will never, ever, know. A son he will never see, never even

understand exists. Because he no longer exists himself. I lean down and whisper directly into his ear, 'You're nothing.'

I turn away, shaken, weak, but somehow purged. Like the old gravel pit, the fear I have lived with, run from for so long, begins to disappear.

Elizabeth-Ann follows me to the front door. 'You too?' she says, her voice flat. 'I should have known. I'm sorry.'

'Yeah, we're all sorry,' I say, walking out.

Out on the porch I turn back to her and search her face. 'After all he did to you,' I ask, 'why are you here? Why are you looking after him?'

Her face is blank. She shrugs. 'He's my father.'

Jenny and I rush down the narrow hallway of the Alpine Inn. 'I can't believe I fell asleep,' I say as we hurry down the stairs.

'You needed it.' Jenny pushes through the front door and out into the autumn sunshine.

I feel like the world is spinning again. Everything is happening so fast. I was completely drained when I returned to my room after confronting Mr Ryan. Drained, but beginning to feel the healing balm of letting go. I showered and changed, then lay down on the bed for just a moment. It was three o'clock when I woke to Jenny's knocking.

'They're here,' she said breathlessly when I answered the door. 'Boyer called from the Gold Mountain Motel. He's bringing Gavin over to the hospital now while his daughter has a nap.'

As the hospital doors close behind us, Jenny asks, 'Do you want to wait in my office or up in Gram's room?'

I follow her across the foyer towards the stairs. The main floor of St Helena's is quiet, mostly reception and offices now. It still has the chapel. I stop before the wide oak doors. 'I want to wait in here.'

Jenny turns with a questioning look. 'Oh, OK,' she says, realising I mean the chapel. 'Do you want me to wait with you?'

'No, I need a few moments to myself. Will you bring him here? I'd like to meet him alone first.'

'Of course.' She smiles. 'I understand.'

She reaches out to take me in her arms. 'Are you all right?' she asks.

'Yes,' I reply as she hugs me. And just like her grandmother, Jenny hangs on to the hug far longer than expected. And I melt into it.

The inside of the hospital chapel is narrow and dark. The heavy door closes slowly behind me. I stand for a moment and let my eyes adjust to the light. At the front of the room votive candles illuminate a crucifix above the altar. I sit down in one of the two wooden pews. Once again I

feel a surge of envy for my mother's faith; for the strength she has found in her Church. The Church I turned my back on years ago. Still, I pray to whatever no-name God, whatever power in the universe, will listen.

Please, please, don't let him look like Gerald Ryan.

I feel, rather than hear, the sound of the oak door moving behind me. My heart begins to race. I turn round, in slow motion it seems, as light spills into the room.

And he is there. His darkened form silhouetted in the doorway.

I stand up on trembling legs as he begins to move towards me. Neither of us speaks as he approaches. I don't know what to say—hello seems so inadequate. The door silently closes behind him, and he is lost in darkness for a moment. Then suddenly he stands before me. I search his face as the candlelight exposes his features.

And my prayers are answered.

The dark eyes reflecting back at me, Ward eyes, smile with familiarity. In those eyes I see my father and Morgan. The fair skin, the brown hair, widow's peak, even the flash of perfect teeth as he attempts a nervous smile, all have passed down from his grandfather.

An ember of radiant warmth begins to grow in my chest. It spills through my body, filling an empty space, a space I did not know existed until now. And nothing else matters. Nothing except that this is my child, my son, and the longing for him that I had denied is now filled with love. Where, or who, he came from means nothing compared to this.

He lifts his right hand and offers it to me. 'Hello,' he says. 'I'm Gavin.'

And I hear that voice!

My legs turn to liquid and my knees buckle. He reaches out to catch me. With his arm under my elbow he helps guide me back to the pew.

'Are you OK?' he asks as I slump down.

The voice! There's no mistaking the voice. The memory of a sun-filled summer day floods through me. The familiar voice fills the musty air of the room with the same music, the same magic that River's voice had on that long-ago day.

I nod, not trusting my own voice for the moment. He takes my shaking hands in his while he waits patiently for me to recover. I search his face for any signs of resentment directed at a mother who would give him up at birth. There is nothing but a gentle concern there. With a bitter-sweet acceptance, I feel the full impact of sadness for the circumstances that kept us apart all this time. 'They told me you were dead, stillborn,' I finally say.

'Yes, I know.'

I can't drink in enough of him as he quietly answers my flood of queries about his life and talks about growing up in West Vancouver. I am relieved to hear about his childhood, about the parents who raised him, who were responsible for this beautiful young man in front of me.

'I'm not looking to replace them,' he says with candid sincerity. 'They've been wonderful to me and I love them both very much. They always encouraged me to find my birth family. But I never really felt the need to. And I always believed that my birth mother must have given me up for a good reason. I didn't want to impose on her—on your—life. But when Molly was born, my wife, Cathy, and I began to wonder about my genetic background. Cathy encouraged me to search for my birth parents. That led to my conversation with Boyer a few days ago. He explained the circumstances of my birth. When he told me about your mother, my grandmother, being so ill, I began to feel a real need to come. Fortunately, I have access to a small plane. And the weather forecast was good for the next few days. So, well, here I am.'

'Yes,' I say in wonder. 'Here you are.'

The guttering candles burn down as we talk on. I hear the pride in his voice when he talks about his daughter, Molly. Then my heart fills with warmth as he refers to her as 'your granddaughter'.

Before we get up to leave he says, 'I don't know what to call you.'

'Natalie would do just fine for now,' I tell him. 'Can you do that?'

His right eyebrow lifts with the same lopsided grin as his grandfather, a grin that once entranced so many Atwood housewives.

'All right,' he says. 'Natalie.'

And it comes off his lips like a forgotten melody.

Nettie

Gus stands beside her bed. She strains to see his handsome face. It's the face of the young Gus Ward she had fallen in love with on a snowy winter day of her youth. The one in whose eyes she had seen her future, her family.

'Have you come to take me home?' she asks.

But her daughter's voice answers, 'Mom, are you awake?'

Nettie remembers that Natalie was sitting at her bedside before she fell asleep. Now her daughter stands next to this apparition.

'This is Gavin, Mom,' Natalie is saying. 'My son. Your grandson.'

'Gavin,' Nettie repeats. She smiles. She wants to touch him, to make sure he is real. She reaches towards him. He takes her hand in his. She pulls him closer to search his face. Such a beautiful face. The face of his

grandfather. And yet, and yet, behind those dark eyes she sees the gentleness of his father, and the determination of his mother. This is Natalie's son. His familiar voice erases the sound she denied the night of his birth. The tiny haunting cry fades and dies.

She caresses his cheek. 'I've been waiting for you,' she says.

Boyer and Stanley appear on the other side of her bed. Jenny and Nick stand nearby. Behind them, Carl and Morgan and Ruth enter the room. Nettie's prayers have been answered. Her family, everyone, is here. She holds tight to her grandson's hand. She will not let go. She has missed his entire life and now will only have time for goodbye.

'I want to go home now,' she tells Boyer as he leans to kiss her. 'It's time for my family to all come home.'

Boyer looks across the bed to Natalie.

Nettie sees the question in his eyes. She turns to her daughter.

'Yes.' Natalie smiles back at her brother. 'Let's go home.'

The telephone on the other end of the line rings four times. I prepare to leave a message on the answering machine when I hear Vern's voice.

'Natalie?' he says out of breath, as if he has run to grab the phone.

'Yes, it's me.' I sink down in the paisley chair by the bed.

Next door at the hospital, Boyer, along with Jenny and Nick, are making arrangements to bring Mom home in the ambulance. Boyer's partner, Stanley, has taken Gavin back to the motel and is now waiting downstairs to drive me out to the farm. Later this afternoon, after Molly finishes her nap, Boyer will bring Gavin and his family out for dinner.

Gavin's daughter! My granddaughter!

I am still reeling from the emotional reunion in my mother's hospital room. The awkwardness of the hushed introductions was overshadowed by Mom's request to be taken home. We all knew what that meant.

'How's your mother?' Vern asks.

So much has happened since I last heard my husband's voice. So much has changed. There are so many things to tell him, so many things I want to say. It's hard to know where to start.

'Can you come?' I ask. 'I want you to meet her, to meet my family.'

'Of course,' he says, relief in his voice. 'Are you all right?' he asks.

'Yes, yes, I am,' I tell him. 'I just need you.'

'I'll wrap things up here and leave tonight.'

I give him directions to the farm.

'I'll be there,' he says.

'Hurry.'

We pull into the farmyard and park in front of the house. 'I thought you and Boyer might build yourselves a new home like the ones in your subdivision,' I say to Stanley, perhaps a little too heartily.

He smiles. 'No. None of those new houses have the charm of this old place.'

We stroll together up the path to the front porch and I notice the changes have kept that charm. The siding, windows and trim are all new. The house looks straighter, stronger.

Before I go upstairs Stanley proudly shows me the rest of the renovations. An addition—a new master bedroom with bathroom—now stands where the rose garden once grew. The sunroom at the back of the house has been turned into a suite for Mom. A hospital bed, placed to overlook the back field, is ready and waiting for her.

Upstairs my bedroom looks the same, only smaller. In my memory, the room I grew up in was much larger. The linoleum floor and the floral wallpaper are unchanged. But even though I have grown no taller since the last time I was here, I feel like a giant invading a child's space.

I set my suitcase down by the dresser and stand gazing out the window. The barn has been updated too and painted, but otherwise the view is unchanged. I have a sudden urge to lift the window and climb out onto the roof. Only time stops me. Time and a few stiff joints.

Downstairs everything is quiet. Stanley is the only other person in the house for the moment. And even though this is the first time I have spent any time with Boyer's life partner, I know that he is as much a part of our family as Ruth is. During the drive to the farm in his pick-up truck, I wondered aloud why I had never met him when we were kids.

'Well,' he said, his green eyes crinkling into a smile, 'I was in college by the time you recited your poem about my father and grandfather.'

'Boyer's poem,' I laughed. 'You heard about that?'

'I was there.'

I remember the auburn-haired boy talking to Boyer in the gymnasium that night. That hair has faded to a strawberry blond but there is still a boyish look to the rounded face.

'I was home for Christmas and went to the school that night with Dad. He loved Christmas concerts.'

I like this man, I thought as we shared a memory.

'I did come out here a few years later,' he added tentatively, 'during the search for River.'

'Yes, I heard that you and your father came to help. I didn't see you. I didn't see much during that time.'

I turn from my bedroom window at the sound of footsteps in the hall. Stanley pokes his head in at my door.

'Can I show you something?' he asks as he beckons me to follow him. We make our way up the new hardwood stairs to the attic.

As unchanged as my room is, this one, Boyer's old nest, is unrecognisable. The narrow space has been converted into a study. The bottom half of the sloped walls is still lined with books, but now they are all neatly organised on maple bookshelves. The framed arrangement hanging above the desk gets my attention. I look closer. Each picture frame holds a magazine or newspaper clipping. The entire wall is covered with clippings of my articles, stories and book reviews.

Someone—Boyer—has carefully mounted and displayed a history of my career. Even my very first article, published by the *Vancouver Sun* where I worked selling advertising, is there.

Stanley sits himself down on the chair in front of the desk. He watches while I study the display. After a few moments he slides open a drawer and pulls out a folder thick with papers. Without a word he hands it to me. Inside, I find reams of handwritten poetry. Boyer's poetry. I sit down on the day bed and read through some of them while he waits.

'These are beautiful,' I say as I take them in. 'Beautiful. I'm so glad he kept writing.'

'He misses you, Natalie,' Stanley says quietly.

I look up at him. 'And I miss him too.' I force a reply, trying to keep my voice from breaking. Oh, if he only knew how much I miss my brother. I feel his absence from my life every day, as if a part of me is missing. I carry on constant imaginary conversations with him, but each time I see his face the words I want to say die on my lips. I swallow. 'I can't believe he saved all these old pieces.' I wave at the wall display.

'He's so proud of you,' Stanley says.

I search his face with my eyes. It's the face of a kind man.

'It was because of Boyer that I became a journalist,' I tell him. 'He was the first one to pay me by the word.' I picture the jar of pennies on the windowsill in my bedroom. 'I get a bit more than a penny a word now.' I laugh. 'Not much though!' My laugh sounds forced.

'Are you ever going to forgive him?' Stanley asks. His words startle me. This is the same question that Mom asked me only a few hours ago. *Boyer? Me forgive Boyer?*

'Forgive him for what?' I ask.

Stanley's gentle eyes hold mine, but he says nothing.

Then I tell him what I have always wanted to tell Boyer. What I wanted to tell Mom earlier today. 'I'm the one who should beg his forgiveness.' Stanley shifts over from his chair and sits down beside me. 'I stay away because I can't face him. I don't deserve him. I don't deserve to be around him. It was my carelessness that ruined his life,' I tell him, and as simply as that it all comes out. My guilt, my shame, my betrayal—all are given voice in the quiet of Boyer's old bedroom. I tell him how my thoughtless words started the evil avalanche of gossip, which would shatter Boyer's, and our family's, image in the community.

'And River,' I whisper. 'If I hadn't run away that night, River would never have become lost, never have been killed.'

Finally, as unchecked tears slide down my cheeks, I tell him about the marijuana butts thrown carelessly under the sink in Boyer's cabin. 'I can't look at him without knowing I caused the fire, his scars.'

Stanley gently puts both of his arms around me. Nothing about having this man, who I have just met today, hold me feels strange.

'You were sixteen years old,' he says as I wipe my eyes. 'A child. Such a burden to carry alone all these years, Natalie. It's you who needs to find a way to forgive that sixteen-year-old girl.'

'The fire—' I start.

He takes my face in his hands and forces me to look into his eyes. 'The fire was arson.'

'I know the police suspected that, but—'

'No, they knew it, but couldn't—or didn't want to—prove it. There were anonymous calls claiming a group of boys had doused the logs at the front door with gasoline and set the fire. Your father found a gas can washed up at the lake shore the following spring.'

'Who—?'

'We'll never know. Kids playing a stupid prank or someone with an ignorant vendetta.'

'All because of my foolish words.'

'No, all because of prejudice,' Stanley says quietly, and I wonder what he and Boyer have had to endure over the years just to be who they are. 'But does it really matter now?' he asks. 'After all these years, does it matter how, or why, any of it happened? Is it worth not having your brother in your life to hang on to your guilt?'

When I don't answer he continues. 'What a waste.' He slowly shakes his head. 'This family never fights, never uses words as weapons. They use silence. And it hurts just as much. All of you let what is haunting you, what you are not saying to each other, come between you. Both

you and Boyer harbour guilt over River's death. But you never speak to each other about it.'

Momentarily numbed by the enormity of what he is saying I nod silently, then stand up.

'Talk to him, Natalie,' he says before I leave. 'Don't underestimate his capacity to love. And to forgive.'

Later, alone in my room, I think about Stanley's words as I search for something to give my granddaughter when she arrives.

I look at the jar of pennies by the window. It won't be long before she's old enough to start playing the penny game. A penny isn't much these days, I know, but then it's not about the pennies. It was never about the pennies.

I lean down and push open the door to the crawl space under the eaves. Perhaps there are some old toys in here. I was never much for dolls, but maybe Jenny has left something.

Cobwebs brush my fingers as I feel a box full of books. I drag it out and pick up the small book on the top. I flip through the pages of A. A. Milne's *When We Were Very Young*. Perfect.

I close the book at the sound of cars coming up the road.

I push myself up and hurry over to the window. My fingers grip the windowsill as I watch Boyer's Jeep pull up in front of the house. A parade of vehicles, Morgan's pick-up truck, the ambulance and Jenny's Edsel, follow slowly behind.

Gavin climbs out of the passenger side of the Jeep. A smile forms on his lips as he takes in his surroundings. The back door opens and a young woman climbs out. She leans back in and lifts a small blonde child into her arms. A black-and-white border collie, astonishingly similar to our old cow dog, Buddy, bolts out from under the porch. He clears the fence and joins the group. The girl tries to reach down to pet the dog, who, with tail wagging, leads them up the path to the porch.

It's hard to imagine River, frozen in time and in my mind still aged twenty-two, as a grandfather. But the three-year-old girl, whose blue-green eyes I recognise all the way from the window, the child who looks up and shyly returns my wave, can only be his granddaughter.

In the sunroom Jenny hooks up the intravenous line while Nick takes care of the oxygen. I can see the trip has taken its toll on Mom. After she is comfortable I adjust her blanket as I stroke her forehead.

'It's good to be home.' Mom sighs and attempts a smile.

I sit down by her bed and take her hand in mine.

'Go visit with everyone, Natalie,' she says. 'I'm going to sleep for a bit.'

On the other side of the bed Jenny nods at me and adjusts the morphine feed. I can feel Mom relax as the morphine begins to work.

Before dinner Ruth and I go over to the dairy to get the room upstairs ready for Carl. I switch the gas heat on in the chilled room and we turn the mattress on the iron bed. I reach up and pull linen from the closet shelf then stare down at the quilt in my hands. My grandmother's quilt. And it strikes me that this is where Gavin was conceived.

I turn to look at Ruth. As she takes a load of towels into the bathroom I wonder how all this was affecting her, how she felt to find out it was her baby who had not lived.

Determined not to let silence be part of this family's communication any longer, I turn to her. 'Ruth, your baby—I'm sorry,' I say quietly as she brings extra hand towels and flannels to put in the nightstand.

'It's all right. I grieved for him a long time ago. He stopped moving inside me days before he was born,' she tells me. 'When I woke up after the birth I couldn't feel anything. I signed the papers Dr Mumford gave me, but I knew my son's spirit was not in this world.'

I cross the room and wrap my arms around her.

'But Gavin is,' she says warmly. 'And he, and his family, have come back to us.' She turns to place the towels inside the nightstand. She bends down, looks inside, then tugs at something wedged at the back of the cabinet. 'Natalie, look at this,' she says as she straightens up.

An involuntary gasp escapes my lips as I realise what she is holding. She lets the black, hard-cover notebook fall open, then hands it to me. I sit down on the bed, unable to believe what I hold in my hands: one of River's journals. I thought all of them had burned in the fire.

I read the date at the top of the first page. *Monday June 10, 1968*. The day he left. I feel as if I have re-entered the past. Once again I read the remorse in his words for his failure of judgment in allowing himself to be carried away by curiosity and grief, and in denying the truth of who he was the night I came to him.

Nothing excuses what I've done, I thought I knew who I was, what I stood for, and now I see I don't know anything.

I'm leaving this morning, before Gus gets back from the milk route. Before Natalie comes home from school. Before Nettie comes to the dairy. And before Boyer returns from work. Can I leave without seeing him? Without facing the truth? Without finding out if my truth is also his?

And then I see my mother's name.

Nettie came in without knocking and closed the door. She held her hand up to silence me before I spoke. She sat at the table across from me. 'I don't want to know what happened here tonight,' she said after a few moments. 'I just want to remind you she's only sixteen years old.' Once again she held up her palm to silence any reply from me.

'You young people have it all wrong,' she said, more to herself than to me. 'There's no such thing as free love. There's always a cost.' We sat for what felt like hours in the silence after that. At the sound of morning birds outside the window, she looked up and said, 'You know you have to leave, don't you?'

I nodded.

She walked over to the door. With her hand on the knob she stopped, waited, then turned to look back at me. In a voice so low that I almost didn't hear her, she said, 'Take Boyer with you.'

I let the journal fall open in my lap. And there, lodged in the centre pages, is another part of the past. I pick up the old photograph. One I thought was lost. River must have found it. I study the folded black-and-white snapshot. River's face smiles out through time. I unfold the photograph to search for the face I know is on the other side. And there he is: a young Boyer, sitting leaning up against the trunk of the old apple tree, gazing over the top of his book. He is looking at River. And in that look I see so clearly now the love I had failed to recognise then.

CHAPTER TWELVE

FOR THE FIRST TIME in over thirty-four years our family eats dinner together in the parlour. Before we all sat down we went into the sun-room and stood around Mom's bed and prayed with her. I held her hand as, with her eyes closed, she began to repeat the rosary.

When we were finished Mom opened her eyes and pulled Boyer closer. 'Now don't let them get all maudlin and morbid,' I heard her whisper. 'I want to hear my family's laughter fill this house.'

At Mom's request the sunroom door is left open. I hope that even in her drug-induced sleep she will feel comfort in hearing the noisy chatter of her children at the dining-room table once again.

My brothers hold nothing back. They all sit in their same old places. Gavin's wife, Cathy, sits next to me. It was so easy to like this self-assured young woman. When Gavin introduced us earlier, she held out her arms with no hesitation and hugged me. I hugged her back and told her how grateful I was that she had encouraged Gavin to search for his birth parents. And that she had brought Molly to us.

'More people to love Molly can only be good,' she replied, smiling.

As I sit and watch this family, old and new, interact, I notice a new glow on Jenny's face as she chatters to Gavin. There is an obviously eager, almost childlike, acceptance of this older brother. For a brief moment I feel a pang of regret that she was denied this gift for so long.

Molly sits between her father and Boyer. Earlier Carl watched as Boyer set up a makeshift highchair for her. He eyed the thick encyclopedia under the cushion. 'Uh-oh, better watch out,' he warned Gavin. 'Boyer can get a little ambitious when it comes to words.'

Over the dinner conversation I hear the hum of the oxygen tank in the sunroom. My eyes stray every now and then to the open sunroom door. Even though she sleeps, our mother's presence fills the room.

As if no time has passed, Morgan and Carl hassle Boyer about the automated barn and the contractors who now run the farm. 'Hands-off milking for gentlemen farmers,' Morgan teases.

'Wish there was automated fishing,' Carl snorts.

The good-natured bantering goes back and forth throughout dinner, but it's obvious that Morgan and Carl are glad that the farm, although a scaled-down version now, is still intact.

I know they have accepted Gavin when they begin to tease him.

'Must be pretty nice, flying all over the world. Tough job, eh?' Carl grins as Ruth passes him another helping of chicken.

'Yeah, but someone's got to do it.' Gavin accepts their teasing as easily as they deliver it.

'Must pay pretty well too, owning your own plane,' Morgan adds.

'Well, I don't exactly own the Cessna we flew up on,' Gavin replies. 'I own a one-tenth share. So we get to use it a few times a month.'

'A busman's holiday,' Cathy interjects playfully.

'You love it, too,' Gavin says and Cathy smirks back at him.

I see satisfied smiles pass between Boyer and Stanley as they watch the exchange.

Suddenly, Molly tilts her head and studies Boyer's profile. I hold my breath as her fingers reach towards his face. 'That an *owie*?' she asks.

Gavin opens his mouth to speak, then decides against it, as Boyer leans closer to Molly.

When he is at eye level, Molly reaches up and strokes the mottled skin on the left side of his face.

'What's zat?' she asks with a frown.

'It's a scar,' Boyer tells her. 'A long time ago someone wasn't careful with fire and my skin got burned.'

'Oh.' Molly thinks for a moment then asks, 'Hurt?'

'Not any more.'

'Good.' Molly smiles and, satisfied, turns her attention to the bowl of ice cream Ruth has placed in front of her.

'Hey, where's mine?' Morgan asks, and once again Carl and Morgan fill the empty space with their kibitzing.

As I look around the table, I'm suddenly anxious for Vern to get here and be part of this. If he leaves tonight, he should be here before tomorrow afternoon. Gavin and his family are planning to fly out at two o'clock. They will have to leave for the airport with Stanley before one. I am hoping Vern will arrive in time to meet them before they go.

Boyer pushes his chair back and gets up from the table. He goes into the kitchen and returns with the coffeepot. As he leans over to fill mugs he asks, 'How long can you stay?'

I'm not sure who he's asking, but I answer without hesitating. 'As long as she needs me.'

Across the table, my brothers and Ruth nod in agreement.

'Good,' Boyer says.

Someone is playing the piano. The familiar melody floats up through the hallway grates. It seeps under the door and into my slumber. I lie in darkness and wonder if I am still sleeping, if this music is part of a dream I've forgotten. My eyes focus on the illuminated hands of the alarm clock on the nightstand: fifteen minutes before five in the morning.

I got little sleep the first night Mom was home. I didn't care. Since she came back to the farm Mom has slipped deeper and deeper into that in-between place between living and dying. I wanted to be near her, and so spent most of the first night in her room. Even with Vern here last night I was reluctant to go to bed.

So much has happened in the last seventy-two hours. A lifetime caught up to us all. It will take time to sort it out.

Although Gavin appears to be taking it all with a quiet acceptance, I am sure it is a bit overwhelming. Boyer has given him the information about his paternal grandmother who is still alive. 'Guess we'll be flying to Montana,' was Gavin's simple response to the news.

I am not surprised to learn that Boyer has kept in contact with River's mother all these years. I can only imagine how her life too will change with this unexpected gift.

Yesterday morning Gavin and I sat with Mom until Morgan came to be with her. Then we went for a walk together before Vern arrived. Aspen leaves fluttered around us as we stopped at the end of the log snake fence behind the back field.

'It's so beautiful here,' Gavin said as we strolled towards the lake.

I smiled as his gaze took in the mountains and the forests. I looked around, trying to see through his eyes. A thin sheet of ice covers the surface of the lake. The forest has crept closer to the grassy place where Boyer's home once was. There's no trace of the old cabin now. A new apple tree stands in the same spot where the tree that had burned like a torch, signalling to my mother on that long-ago night, once stood.

In the morning sunshine, I pulled River's journal from my jacket.

Earlier I had taken it, along with the folder of poems, and gone to search for Boyer. I found him at his desk in the attic room. I knocked on the open door. When he turned to me, I held up the folder.

'Stanley let me read these,' I said. 'They're incredible. They really should be published. Can I show them to my editor?'

Boyer smiled and took the folder from my outstretched hand. 'Oh, I think one writer in the family might be enough.'

'I'm just a glorified reporter,' I said. I pointed to his folder. 'Those are the words of a writer.'

Before Boyer could answer, I held up the journal. 'And so is this,' I told him. 'I found it in the room above the dairy. It's River's last journal. I think you should read it. His words explain what I should have told you about the night he and I were together.'

'Natalie.' Boyer's voice was gentle as he opened the drawer to file the folder. 'I don't need to read it. I came to terms with all that a long time ago.' Then he turned to me. 'The problem was we all thought River was perfect,' he added. 'But, like the rest of us, he was human. With flaws and frailties. I forgave him, and myself, a lifetime ago. Give the journal to Gavin. It will help him understand who his father was.'

'Yes, I intend to, but I just wonder if he really needs to know all this.'

'If I've learned one thing,' Boyer said, 'it's that secrets cause more

damage than truth. Give it to him. He'll understand. He can handle it.'

'Yes,' I said. 'You're right.' I turned to leave.

'He's a beautiful young man,' Boyer called after me.

I stood in the doorway and smiled. 'Yes, he is, isn't he? He looks so much like Dad and Morgan, doesn't he?'

'No, Natalie,' Boyer said. 'He looks just like you.'

'This is for you,' I said when I handed the journal to Gavin at the lake. 'It was your father's.'

The few short pages would tell him more about who his father was than any of us ever could. It's all there, in River's own words: his beliefs, his dreams and his loves. All of it told with the honesty that was River.

As Gavin took the journal it fell open in his hands. 'That's your father,' I said when he pulled out the photograph.

He carefully unfolded the old black-and-white picture. 'Which one?'

I looked down at the two beautiful young faces. I had forgotten how much alike they were.

It was easier to fall asleep with Vern by my side last night. He pulled into the farmyard before noon yesterday, had driven straight through. He made it in time to meet Gavin and his family before they left.

Beside me Vern stirs in his sleep. His body presses closer to mine. Yesterday afternoon, after he arrived, after he met Gavin, I led him to my mother's room. I thought she was asleep but her eyelids lifted when I made a hushed introduction to Carl, who was sitting at her bedside.

'Mom, this is Vern,' I whispered and pulled him closer to her.

She looked up into his face and smiled. 'Oh, yes,' she said, her voice barely audible. 'You're the one.'

Her lids closed and her face softened as she drifted off. It was easy to see that my mother was now at peace. She did not struggle against the inevitable. 'I'm ready,' she had told me last night.

Father Mac had come and gone. Mom would leave this world with the grace that had carried her through her life. In the end, she told me, she had what she prayed for, all her children and their families, finally together, in this house filled with memories.

Last night and yesterday we all took turns sitting with her, each of us cherishing the moments we knew could be our last with her.

As Vern and I sat together beside Mom's bed, I began to tell him my family's story. I watched my mother's face as I talked, convinced that even in her morphine-induced sleep she could hear each word.

After Vern and I went upstairs, he held me in his arms in the dark of my room and listened patiently while I told him more. Tomorrow I will begin to tell him the rest. All of it.

All day yesterday I watched him talking and joking with my brothers as if he had known them for years. How easily he fits in, I thought, and felt a tug of remorse at having waited so long for him to know them.

Yesterday afternoon, while Ruth sat with Mom, the rest of us gathered around Boyer's Jeep before Stanley drove Gavin and his family to the airport.

Before he got into the Jeep, Gavin turned and asked me, 'Do you ever get down to Vancouver?'

'Vern and I drive down for a few days once or twice a year.'

'Well, maybe you'll visit us sometime in West Vancouver when you're down,' he offered.

Vern squeezed my shoulder.

'Yes, I'd like that,' I said. 'And perhaps someday you'll come up to Prince George.'

'I'm sure we will,' he smiled. 'And when we're there, maybe you'll let me take you and Vern flying.'

I saw the quick sideways glance pass between Jenny and Nick. Morgan and Carl each gave a choked laugh. I felt Vern hold his breath before I returned his squeeze. 'Yes,' I said. 'Maybe I'll do just that.'

Downstairs the piano music continues. Like a lullaby the notes carry me to the edges of sleep. But the familiar song tugs at chords of memory and pulls me back. I know that song. It's the same one my mother used to play for me when I was a child. Who could possibly be downstairs playing that old melody? But whoever is playing the piano now plays exactly as she had, as if the song was once again being played for me alone. I wonder if I am imagining the music.

I ease myself out from under Vern's arm. Enveloped in darkness, I find my way into the hallway, and then down the eighteen steps that I still know by heart. I feel for the doorknob at the bottom of the stairway and open the door. Like a sleepwalker, I follow the music. The familiar melody lures me through the kitchen and into the parlour.

The piano lamp shines down on the ivory keys below. Scarred hands move fluently across them. I lean against the doorway and watch my brother at the piano. I had no idea that Boyer could play, but then he's had plenty of years to learn, and she's had plenty of time to teach him.

The door to the sunroom is closed. Through the glass I see that the

nightlight is turned off. The room is dark, quiet. No hiss from the oxygen tank rises over the gentle strains of the music that plays my mother home. I don't have to be told. And I don't try to hold back the tears that well up.

I wish I could say that the last words my mother spoke to me had been enlightening, or a profound revelation. But I can't. I thought she was talking in her sleep as I leaned close to kiss her good night when Boyer came in to sit with her a few hours ago. I barely heard her. Her final words to me, the words I will take with me into the rest of my life, were simple—and they were enough.

'Life is messy, Natalie,' she whispered from the fading fringe of consciousness, 'but it all comes out in the wash.'

The last notes of 'Love Me Tender' hang in the air now as Boyer finishes playing. From upstairs comes the sound of stirring. Soon the rest of the family will join us. And we will begin the process of sharing our grief. This time we will do it together.

At the piano, Boyer slowly turns round on the bench and his eyes find mine. For the first time I see, not the scars, but my brother's beautiful face. And I do not look away. I will never look away again.

A half-smile forms on his lips, but reaches beyond. It reaches up to his liquid blue eyes. Those eyes are the soul of my mother, in the face of my brother. There is so much I want to say, to tell him. And I will. But not now.

Now I smile back at him and say, 'I've always loved that song.'

'I know,' he says.

Donna Milner

Have you always dreamt of becoming a writer?

Yes and no. I worked in real estate for twenty-five years and I was one of those people who always said they were going to write once they retired. Originally, I was very secretive about anything that I wrote. I never thought it was good enough and would get rid of it, in case I died and someone read it. It was my husband who encouraged me to follow my dream.

Had you lived with this particular story for a while before you began writing it?

Do you know, my son asked me the same question. How long had you lived with this story? But I never 'lived' with it. *After River* began with four words. 'I must have known.' I was watering my plants when that just popped into my head. From there, the characters led the way and took over my life completely. And I loved every minute of it!

I did not realise that so many American men had fled to Canada to avoid the Vietnam War draft in the Sixties . . .

There is a discrepancy over the numbers, but over 120,000 Americans crossed into Canada at that time. They were not pardoned until the 1970s, by which time many had made their lives in Canada and stayed on.

Did you grow up on the west coast of Canada?

No, I grew up in Vancouver, but I spent many summers staying with an aunt who lived in a small town in central British Columbia. I ended up marrying a young man from there—my first husband. His family had a dairy farm—that's how I knew the sounds and smells.

Who were your favourite characters in the novel?

Nettie and Boyer. They never ceased to surprise me. Nettie is very much a complex woman of her times and Boyer is fiercely loyal to his family. Plus Boyer was homosexual. What surprised me most in my research, was that I discovered the case of a Canadian man who, in the 1970s, was sent to prison for life simply because he admitted he was a homosexual. Even after the law was taken off our statute books as a crime, he still languished in jail for years.

Did you always know who was going to be the baby's father?

No, the characters led me there. My first thought was: what if Natalie had this baby, gave it up for adoption, and then her daughter fell in love with her half-brother, and the priest and the doctor are the only ones who know. But when I started to write, the story changed. The characters led the way.

Are you working on a second novel?

Yes, I am. I was very worried about writing a second novel and thought: what if I don't have another book in me? I had signed a large publishing contract but I opted out of it when I discovered that it blocked my writing. I find that being bound by a contract takes away the discovery between me and the page. I write better when I know I can start off by doing it badly—free writing. I then like to search for the golden nuggets. I've learned to trust in myself.

What do you do in your spare time?

We own a one-sixth share in a thirty-eight-foot sailing boat and we took sailing lessons last year. We also own a cabin out on a lake where we try to live a 'green life' as much as possible. My husband built a writing room onto it and so now it is no longer a cabin but a house. We are talking about moving up there because we love to walk and go canoeing. And I like to read and play bridge, and I enjoy playing poker online. I'm also on the board of directors of the local Canadian Association for Community Living, working with adults who have intellectual disabilities. Three years ago we started a chime choir with the folks and I practise with them every Thursday—that is the favourite part of my week.

Jane Eastgate

ISBN 978-0-276-44279-7

www.readersdigest.co.uk

The Reader's Digest Association Limited, 11 Westferry Circus, Canary Wharf, London E14 4HE

of love & life